'The book works both ~~~~~~~~~~~~~~~~~~~~~~~~~~~~~ ror stories and as a cohesive nov ~~~~~~~~~~~~~~~~~~~~~~~~~ finale that reveals the shocking ev~~~~~~~~~~~~~~~~~~~~~~~~~~ *Guardian*

'A modern horror classic from one of the most exciting writers in the field today' *Starburst*

'*Thirteen Storeys* is an excellent horror . . . everyone will find something creepy in Banyan Court' *Grimdark Magazine*

'This is an astonishing debut from Jonathan Sims. A wonderful new twist on an age-old genre. 5 out of 5' *SFX*

'An excellent portmanteau novel. It's an ultra-modern take on the haunted house story, while each tale mixes in different subgenre flavours, from techno-fear and shifting architecture to creepy kids and beyond, all building to a joined-up climax that's pleasingly violent and gross' *Den of Geek*

'Sims really has created an innovative novel where everything falls into place within its thrilling climax' *Fantasy Hive*

'Thrilling, chilling and thoroughly entertaining'
Tattooed Book Geek

'A beautifully written contemporary horror novel that I know for sure will leave its mark on me. I don't remember reading anything like this before and it was an absolute delight'
Damp Pebbles Blog

'A book that takes old traditions and gives them a contemporary spin. Happy Halloween, all' *SFF World*

THIRTEEN
STOREYS

Jonathan Sims

This paperback first published in 2021 in Great Britain by Gollancz

First published in Great Britain in 2020 by Gollancz
an imprint of The Orion Publishing Group Ltd
Carmelite House, 50 Victoria Embankment
London EC4Y 0DZ

An Hachette UK Company

1 3 5 7 9 10 8 6 4 2

Copyright © Jonathan Sims 2020

The moral right of Jonathan Sims to be identified as
the author of this work has been asserted in accordance with
the Copyright, Designs and Patents Act of 1988.

All rights reserved. No part of this publication may be
reproduced, stored in a retrieval system, or transmitted
in any form or by any means, electronic, mechanical,
photocopying, recording, or otherwise, without the prior
permission of both the copyright owner and the above
publisher of this book.

All the characters in this book are fictitious,
and any resemblance to actual persons, living
or dead, is purely coincidental.

A CIP catalogue record for this book
is available from the British Library.

ISBN (Mass Market Paperback) 978 1 473 22874 0

Typeset by Deltatype Ltd, Birkenhead, Merseyside

Printed in Great Britain by Clays Ltd, Elcograf S.p.A.

www.gollancz.co.uk

To Sasha
You are the best of me

Prologue

LEGACY OF A BUTCHERED BILLIONAIRE: THE LIFE AND DISMEMBERMENT OF TOBIAS FELL

David Erikson,
Crime Editor

Five years on, it's an all-to-familiar cliché that the only thing more interesting than the life of Tobias Fell was his death. For most of his eventful career, he was lauded by the public as an entrepreneurial titan; it's no secret he remains *The Sunday* ▮▮▮▮▮▮s most interviewed non-political figure, and we certainly weren't alone in that regard, with his picture gracing the front of *The* ▮▮▮▮▮▮ *Business Post* no less than fourteen times since 1992. After his death this fascination has only increased, though it has now taken on a wholly different character. Even for those who don't follow such things it's been hard to escape a relentless tide of true crime investigations, conspiracy theories, even discussions on paranormal forums. The brutal slaying has found its way to the top of more than one online list of 'creepiest unsolved murders'. Alive or dead, nobody ever seems to tire of talking about Tobias Fell.

But there are those who never stopped digging, who never accepted the impossible facts of this baffling case. But with so tantalising a mystery surrounding his death, are we perhaps overlooking the darker corners of his life?

His origins were similar to any other billionaire: he was provided with a small fortune by his father's family and proceeded, through luck, skill and, many say, ruthlessness to turn it into a large fortune. But it has been noted by many that, even by the standards of his peers, young Tobias seemed utterly unconcerned with the ethical implications of his business practices. While many of his more public and well-profiled enterprises (including those covered in this very publication) were PR-friendly tech companies or well-beloved brands, it takes very little digging to notice his most profitable investments came from less cuddly sources: pharmaceutical companies; gemstone mining; environmentally devastating oil extraction and arms manufacture. There were accusations his companies were involved in sweatshops, land seizure and slave labour, with many progressives coming forward with their condemnations of him even when he was still alive.

None of these accusations, however, ever truly seemed to touch Tobias Fell. A ready wit and an instinct for keeping his distance from the less-savoury aspects of his businesses served to keep his image clean, and well-publicised charitable initiatives ensured nobody raised too much interest in his tax affairs (even if many of these philanthropic projects seemed to quietly disappear when the spotlight faded). Every eager would-be tycoon named him their inspiration as he topped rich list after rich list.

There were plenty of reports, of course. Human rights organisations condemned his companies' ethics, but his books on business advice, reputedly ghost-written, made for far easier reading. Indeed, looking through the archives of *The Sunday* ███████, it's hard not to see our own complicity in burying many of these stories in the back pages.

When Tobias began to retreat from the public eye in the years leading up to his death, this seemed only to cement his reputation. For every concerned activist railing against his businesses, there were a dozen admirers intrigued by this new mystique and the occasional long-lens paparazzi photograph of the now-reclusive billionaire. He gradually stepped back from running his companies, and his much-lauded philanthropy entirely dried up. It seemed the business world's golden boy wished to simply spend his time hiding away in the penthouse suite of Banyan Court, a building he commissioned.

It was often said that Banyan Court stood as a monument to everything Tobias Fell was; both to those who held him as their idol, and to those who hated him. A towering, thirteen-storey residential development in the heart of Tower Hamlets, one of the poorest areas of central London. The building burst from the old brick shell of a Victorian factory-turned-tenement and blossomed into a grand edifice of glass and steel, a love letter to tasteful opulence. Our own coverage of the construction ('Billionaire makeover for London's poorest', 3rd July 2004) talked of regeneration and of the project enriching the area. But critics saw only gentrification and the displacement of families, predictions which have largely been proven accurate.

One particular point of contention was the part of Banyan Court given over to 'affordable housing'. Local planning guidelines require new residential developments to set aside a portion of their space as available to low-income occupants, but alleged indifference by the government and enforcement agencies led to persistent rumours about the construction quality of some areas of the building. New residents of these affordable homes reported cut corners, shoddy materials and fire hazards. The flats at the back were apparently almost completely segregated from the glistening modern facilities of the main building, and within a year left-wing blogs began talking about the 'hidden slum' lurking behind the shining facade of Banyan Court. And sitting in his pristine penthouse at the top of it all: Tobias Fell.

But however fascinating his life may have been, his death is what most people remember him for. It has gone down as one of the most high-profile unsolved murders in history. The details that were released to the public (and many details that weren't) have been relentlessly dissected by the media and amateur detectives, and almost no aspect of it makes sense. The sheer brutality of the killing was breathtaking, and yet despite the fact that the murder must have taken place inside his penthouse, none of the blood found at the scene belonged to Tobias Fell. In fact, according to certain leaked case files, no positive identification was ever made. The billionaire was listed as the only victim, so why were there multiple reports from people who saw multiple body bags being removed by the emergency services?

Further igniting the imagination of conspiracy theorists was the matter of the witnesses. Tobias Fell wasn't alone when he was killed. There were thirteen other people with him, all of whom claimed to have been attending a dinner party at his unexpected invitation. Though not all lived in the building, all these 'guests' each had some connection to Banyan Court. Aside from a postcode, however, it seems they had nothing whatsoever in common. An avant-garde art dealer, a local plumber, a six-year-old child attending with her mother ... Few, if any, of the guests would be those expected at a billionaire's banquet. Even beyond that, each guest said the same three things: they had never met Tobias Fell before that night; they had received an invitation without any sort of warning; and that, despite the forensic evidence conclusively showing he must have been killed while they were there, none of them had any idea when or how their host had been murdered.

Despite this seemingly obvious pool of suspects, no arrests were ever made by the Metropolitan Police and no official explanation of the killing was ever given. In the five years since the crime, none of the police or medical professionals who were part of the initial call or subsequent investigation have made any comment on the record. Further fuelling speculation of conspiracy were the strange events that occurred in and around Banyan Court in the week leading up to Tobias Fell's murder: the deaths of Edith Kinney and James Andre, officially labelled natural causes and suicide respectively, as well as the disappearance of noted activist Diego Santi, who was last seen entering the building. Theorists have never found a satisfying explanation for any of them.

Now, after half a decade, Banyan Court is all but abandoned. As leases end, estate agents have been unable to find replacements, with other residents and landlords abruptly selling or, in some cases, simply disappearing. The once impressive building now stands silent, casting a lonely eye over the dilapidated buildings below. A thirteen-storey tombstone to a man whose shadow still falls as darkly as that of his creation.

The murder of Tobias Fell remains unsolved, and it is unlikely it will ever be known what actually happened that night, or what those thirteen ill-fated guests truly saw.

1st

Night Work

Violet Ng
114 Banyan Court

'I'm sorry to hear that, it must be awful.'

Violet's mother had always warned her against talking to strangers, of course, but unfortunately it seemed nobody had warned *them* against talking to her. She bit back her response as the old man gave a sympathetic little tilt of the head, his lips pursed as though sharing her pain.

'My son used to work nights as well,' he continued, ignoring her silence. 'He hated it. Used to say he could never get the sleep right. It's not humane, I reckon.'

Violet had grown up buried beneath her mother's paranoid fear for her safety, weighed down by a hundred cautionary tales, thinly veiled urban legends that supposedly happened to some distant friend of the family. She'd never even mentioned the greatest threat that apparently seemed to plague only her: sympathetic strangers. The elderly man sat opposite was leaning forward, clearly waiting for an answer.

'Must have been hard,' Violet said at last, doing her best to look anywhere else, but the windows of the underground carriage showed only darkness. Her mother's tales had always started the same way, with looking a stranger in the eye. It was her version of 'Once upon a time', but for ending with someone dead in an unmarked lorry. To Violet, the greatest danger of eye contact was that people thought you were interested in their opinions.

'I read somewhere working a night shift can take almost a decade of your life!' her new friend said, relentless in his concern for her wellbeing.

'It's not for everyone,' Violet replied, falling back into the rote half-answers she always ended up using on family who decided they needed to tell her how much she must hate working nights. It happened a lot.

'What exactly do you do?' the old man continued, undeterred.

Violet considered for a moment. She could try to explain it to him, how much she loved it. She could try to vocalise that sense of being adjacent to the world, walking through and beside it, but never quite letting it touch her. She could tell him about her 'lunch' breaks, walking the streets around her office, drinking in the 2 a.m. silence, that wonderful emptiness. Describe watching cars and lorries slowly streaking a down the motorway towards Reading or Basingstoke, like a slow-moving river of lights. She could try to vocalise the almost spiritual connection she felt to the slumbering city. A city her mother had always claimed would kill her.

'I work on the ingestion and editorial management of syndicated media for a large scale B2B-focused press-aggregator, ensuring licensing and copyright compliance for future consumption in data and analytics.'

That shut him up.

Violet emerged from Whitechapel station just as the sky began to fully turn to dawn. The early morning air was cool and refreshing, before the summer heat really started, and she felt the first tinges of a satisfied exhaustion at the edges of her limbs. Her eyelids were pleasantly heavy as she slowly walked home. It wasn't long before it loomed before her, blotting out the sunrise.

Banyan Court rose above the streets of Tower Hamlets, gazing down with a paternalistic pity for the homeless and the struggling who simply hadn't had the good sense to be born rich. Violet smirked quietly to herself and walked quickly past the shining glass front doors. They didn't like it if you loitered. She passed the small patches of immaculately maintained greenery and turned down the small alleyway that ran along the side of Banyan Court. Between the rows of huge bins far too unsightly to be left visible from the street (and easily large enough for a dismembered body, her mother would have said), and past the line where glass gave way to concrete and old brick. Violet made her way to Resident Entrance B.

The small concrete courtyard was swept about once a month by the council, but the bars over the ground floor windows prevented any attempt to keep the glass clean. Those bars, heavy and painted a bright warning yellow, had been added when the building was first renovated, and they had always struck Violet as being a message, rather than a response to any actual crime. Like the CCTV signs that became more numerous as you approached the door to the rear apartments, no longer warning passers-by that residents were protected by surveillance, but instead reminding the less-trusted occupants that they were being watched.

She took a moment to breathe it all in, taking a seat on the raised section of concrete where teenagers sometimes gathered to smoke and laugh. She placed her hand on the cold, rough surface and closed her eyes. Her family had never understood Violet's decision to move to the city. The youngest of two brothers and four sisters, raised in a warm home near the

Scottish border that had somehow always been kept immaculate, her choice of lifestyle baffled her siblings. They had made their lives near home, with children and dogs and wide-open sky. Violet's existence, by comparison, was grimy and cramped: living in a tiny, squalid flat to grind away at a pointless desk job in a lightless office. They never understood that that was the point. Violet secretly loved that hardscrabble urban life, skirting poverty and wearing her fingers to the bone. It was something that her parents had once dismissed as 'the resilience of youth', but here she was aged thirty-one and this was still the life she wanted. It was a part of her so deeply ingrained that no amount of what her mother called 'harsh reality' could dislodge it.

She looked over the rusty basketball hoop on the nearby wall, just above the defaced sign that had once read 'No Ball Games' and smiled as she remembered one of her mother's classic pieces of 'reality': the gruesome tale of a young man who moved to London and caught the eye of a violent gang. They killed him, of course, and played a rousing game of basketball with his head. Her mother had read it in the paper, she claimed, but couldn't quite remember which one, and got quite upset when Violet gently questioned how exactly one could dribble with a human head, which traditionally was one of the less-bouncy pieces of sports equipment.

Violet turned away and got out her key, but Resident Entrance B apparently hadn't latched, and she didn't need it. Still smiling quietly to herself as she entered the cool of the dark hallway, she ignored the vandalised letterboxes. Though her mother's dire predictions of robbery, murder or kidnapping had never come true (yet another way Violet had disappointed her), she had been right about how harsh and ugly London was. If you couldn't find the quiet joy in that ugliness, it might be a bit much for some people.

9

The lift was working for once. She leaned heavily against the smudged mirror, appreciating the slow journey towards her flat and ignoring the small voice that called her lazy for not taking the stairs. Home was two cramped and dingy bedrooms at the back of the eighth floor with a laundry list of problems that appealed to her stubborn pride. She loved it. She and her flatmate Marie were the last of their university friends still renting in central London. When they'd first seen the listing, a few years ago now, Violet had assumed the low rent must have been a mistake. The pictures had showed the luxuriant glass frontage, with only a couple of clearly recycled stock photos of the interior. Once they'd actually viewed the place the reality of 'Resident Entrance B' became clear. It might have been the closest Violet ever got to being in one of her mother's stories, as they were led to the crumbling, bare apartment by a shifty looking estate agent. But the doors never slammed shut behind them, the bedroom wasn't a secret kill-room, and by then Marie's housing situation had deteriorated to the point where being fussy simply wasn't an option. So, they'd had to take it. Violet would never tell her friend how glad she was that decision was forced on them, but sometimes she thought Marie knew.

As she quietly opened the front door, she took a moment to listen out for the tell-tale sounds of Marie's morning routine. Nothing. Nodding to herself, Violet made her way towards her bedroom. Fatigue fully caught up with her as she checked the blackout curtains and went through her bedtime routine. She loved this flat. She loved it in that hard, proud part of her that rejected the soft comforts of an easy life; that fragment of her soul that heard her friends complain of city life and secretly judged them weak. Nothing worth doing should be easy, she had always felt, and that included living.

*

'He was there again yesterday.'

'Who?' Violet didn't look up from her laptop.

'That guy hanging around next door,' Marie's tone was low, conspiratorial, like it always was when she was gossiping.

'I thought he lived there.'

'No.' Marie shook her head. 'The woman who lives there, she must be in her eighties or something. This guy's young.'

'You do know grandchildren are a thing, right?'

'Sure, but he's been there three times over the last week. And I haven't seen her at all.'

'Well A, she was closer to fifty, and B, I'm pretty sure she moved out. I saw a bunch of boxes last month.'

'Yeah, well I didn't see any boxes. And I definitely didn't see him move in.'

Violet put her laptop down and offered her a cup of coffee. Marie shook her head again, gesturing to her pyjamas.

'So, you think he killed her.' Violet smiled at her flatmate.

'No, that's not—'

'You know what that sounds like to me?'

'Don't start.'

'Hey.' Violet's grin widened. 'You're the one proposing our new neighbour murdered a harmless old lady and now lives there with her body, watching you, the sweet stench of decay still clinging to his clothes.'

Marie was unimpressed

'It's just he keeps hanging around outside the door. I don't like it.'

'Why don't you just go over and knock? Ask him if he murdered her.'

'I don't even know her name!' Marie's feigned indignation didn't quite cover up her genuine discomfort at the idea of actually speaking to a neighbour.

'Well, that's a perfect follow-up question, isn't it?' Violet said, eyes locked on their cheap Argos kettle as it gradually convinced itself to boil.

'I just don't like it,' Marie repeated. 'The hallway reeks of smoke every time he's been there.'

'Well, that's it then, isn't it?'

'What?'

'If she hasn't moved out, then maybe he's staying with his grandmother, or whatever, and she doesn't like him smoking in the flat.' The smell of the instant coffee hit Violet's nostrils and she sighed happily, looking out the window at the evening lights below.

'So, he does it in the corridor? Isn't there, like, a fine for that? And what about the smoke alarms?'

'What about them?'

'What, you don't think they work?'

'About as well as anything else in this place.' Violet tried a sip of coffee. Still too hot. There was silence for a moment.

'We're going to die in a fire, aren't we?' Marie said, the resignation in her voice only half-pretend.

'What's this "we" you're talking about? I'm going to work.'

Marie gave Violet a withering look, but her flatmate didn't notice.

The front door shut behind Violet with a weighty metal click. Marie had insisted they replace the flimsy lock with something a little more solid, and Violet couldn't deny that there was a certain reassurance to the sound. Their door stood halfway down the blank and utilitarian corridor. To their right a few flats lay between them and the intersection that led to the staircase. To their left, three more led up to a window looking out over the urban patchwork below, with the lift opposite the furthest one.

There were technically two lifts beyond Resident Entrance B. One of them, the one she'd occasionally use, was a cramped and foul-smelling thing that seemed out of order as often as it was working. It listed the floors from G to eleven, missing out floor six as the button had fallen off some time ago and had never been replaced, no matter how often the lift was repaired. Violet had got used to using the stairs, something Marie begrudgingly referred to as her 'cardio', while Violet simply smiled a sweet, bitter grin and told her to think about how much worse that poor billionaire in the penthouse must have it.

It was the other lift that really captured Violet's imagination. Through that dingy courtyard, past the rows of iron mailboxes, empty bike rails, and just enough snaking corridor to make a visitor doubt their way, there was a spiralling stairwell that stretched up through the back of Banyan Court. It was old, part of the original structure, with uneven tile steps that had clearly been resurfaced, but not repaired. At the centre of the curving steps was an ancient wrought-iron goods lift. Violet had no idea how old it was (turn of the century, maybe?) or why it had been left in place when the building was redeveloped. It should go all to the way to the penthouse. At least, it would if it worked, something she thought unlikely given the hazard tape, the warning signs, and the sturdy yellow padlock bigger than her hand. Marie swore that she'd seen the thing moving once or twice, but Marie swore a lot of things, and as far as Violet was concerned, it was nothing but a towering metal spine, a strange relic of iron vertebrae gradually falling to rust. One of the city's hidden bones that she had lucked into living beside.

Violet checked down the corridor, over towards flat 116. There was nobody there. No mysterious smoking stranger hovering menacingly between her and the lift, waiting to catch her eye as prelude to murder. She stopped for just a moment as she passed the door, straining her ears for any sound from inside, but all was quiet. She wrinkled her nose as the lift arrived and headed down towards her commute.

Work passed slowly. She had managed to leave her headphones next to her bed and having to give her full attention to what actually amounted to eight hours of copying and pasting text left her feeling almost comatose. She always forgot how silent the office was. There must have been almost forty people there, just as bored and unchallenged as she was, but the quiet of the night shift was almost never broken, an unspoken rule that Violet had always been in favour of, at least when she had been able to listen to her music or the occasional podcast. But tonight it felt heavier than usual, and there were moments it seemed almost like a physical weight, pressing down on her. She kept realising that she was holding her breath.

It wasn't just the dangers of the nocturnal streets her mother had warned her about. Working nights was top of the list of things to be dreaded, according to her. Burnout and suicide were the recurring conclusions of that strand of story, with one memorable tale of a man who had 'gone mad from the quiet', whatever that meant, and had burned down the office block with all his co-workers inside. The thought was enough to get her through the first few hours, as there was nothing more likely to inspire her to work harder than proving her mother wrong.

Violet watched as the smokers got up for what must have been their third break in as many hours, and tried to choke down the quiet anger she always felt watching them. She couldn't stand laziness. She knew, of course, that the job she worked was largely pointless, just busywork to keep money circulating between a handful of dying businesses, but that didn't matter. That was the work. And these people had no right to slack off, just standing around chatting among themselves. Violet didn't like this part of herself. She knew her personal standards were extreme, and she shouldn't judge other people for not meeting them, but she couldn't help it sometimes. She couldn't imagine being fulfilled as some housewife, placid and content in gentle domesticity, terrified of the world beyond your own four walls. Work was freedom, it was how you made your own life, and all too often she found herself hating people who didn't seem to appreciate that.

When the clock ticked over to half past one, Violet almost leapt up, quietly letting her manager, a solid, unremarkable man named Bob, know that she was taking her break. It took her less than six minutes to eat the salad pot she had bought for lunch, and then she was out the door and into the dusty night air of the city. She walked quickly, as if she could hurry along the relaxation, and tried to figure out why exactly she was so on edge. There were no special stresses at work (Bob was foretelling imminent layoffs, but he was always going on about that), everything was fine at home (Marie had brought up maybe wanting to move out next year, but that was a while away) and there weren't any money problems (the agency said rent was going up soon, but she could afford it, just about). So why did it feel like every nerve in her body was twisted up tight? It was as if she were about to break into a run at any moment.

Violet was so caught up in trying to examine her mood, she didn't notice them standing there until she was halfway down Augustine Road. Three figures, just at the edge of the street, no details clearly visible, all obscured by hoods and caps and thick jackets. They could have been talking to each other, probably were, but from where she was walking it wasn't clear. They seemed to just be standing there, motionless, the light of the streetlamp shining down on them.

People were exactly what Violet wished to avoid on her late-night walks, their messy presence always breaking through her quiet communion with the city. Instinctively, she started to turn, to retrace her steps and find another, more secluded route. But as she did one of the figures looked up, and his eyes beneath the bright blue baseball cap met hers. They were young, cocky, and even from the other end of the road she felt them judging her. He thought she was scared of him. A tiny surge of defiance rose up inside her. This was her city, her time, and she would not let the second-hand fears of her mother rule her. So what if she had looked him in the eye? If they wanted to hang out late at night in public, that was their business. There was nothing sinister to it, nothing obvious, at least, and she was certainly in no position to criticise them for being out late. So, she continued down Augustine Road, her footsteps a lot louder than she remembered them. In the back of her mind came that insistent pressure to cross the road, that urge to keep her distance, but she fought it down, determined not to let this fear win. The man exchanged some short words with his companions, watching her as she walked in their direction with all the confidence she could hold on to.

Violet was now within a few feet of them and could smell the waves of body spray covering up old joints and unwashed jeans. She ignored it, just a few more steps and she'd be past them, she'd be at the end of the road, turning a corner and breathing normally again. But as her eyes once again made that briefest moment of contact with his, she saw a sudden change in them, and her whole body spasmed in terror as he lunged at her.

'Boo!'

It took her a second to process what he had said. The young man had already turned back to his friends, who burst into mocking laughter, then just as quickly returned to whatever conversation they'd been having.

Violet tried to regain her feet, but her every nerve was on fire and her legs wouldn't stop shaking from adrenaline. She wanted to say something, to scream, to hit them, but it seemed like they'd already forgotten her, so instead she just started walking again. She turned right at the end of the street and headed immediately back to her office.

It took hours for the shaking to subside, and the work she was supposed to be doing sat forgotten on her screen. She was so angry she could barely think, and not at the arsehole that made her jump, but at herself for letting it get to her. It was harmless, a joke. She was overreacting. But that didn't do anything to soften what she felt.

Violet left the office that morning exhausted, utterly drained, and travelled back to Banyan Court in a daze. She felt disconnected from the space around her, and with every step she found herself surprised that her foot landed on solid ground. She didn't remember the train home, and moved off the tube like a ghost, drifting into the building and up the stairs without really taking anything in. She only stopped for a second as she got out her keys, dimly registering the faint scent of old tobacco. She looked listlessly to the next door over, but it was closed. The corridor was empty as always.

She had no appetite and Marie was still asleep, so Violet quietly moved through the darkness to her room and crawled into bed, barely remembering to kick off her shoes. Sleep hit her like a fist, and she spent that day dreaming of three figures whispering to each other under a street light. But no matter how close she got, the words remained muffled and secret.

*

Her eyes opened slowly, groggily. How long had it been? She looked at her clock. 8 a.m. She'd barely slept an hour and her head was pounding. No, it was the door, Someone was knocking and—

'Violet?'

Marie's voice. She pulled herself slowly out of bed and opened the door a crack. The light from the hall stung her eyes and she blinked several times before the lights resolved themselves into the figure of her flatmate, still wearing her pyjamas.

'Aren't you going to be late?'

Marie shook her head. 'I need a favour.'

'What?' Violet's stomach dropped slightly.

'I've got a thing I need to be at today, but I kind of double-booked myself.'

'I thought you had work?'

'Yeah, like I said, double-booked. So I need to call in sick.'

Violet tried her best to suppress the little flame of rage that rose up at Marie's blasé tone. This certainly wasn't the first time Marie had done this, her approach to work was no different than it had been at university, but right now Violet had to bite her tongue. Had Marie got her out of bed literally to just rub her laziness in Violet's face?

'Say you have a migraine. That usually works.' It took all her self-control to keep her voice level. She just needed to sleep. She had work to do in the evening.

'Sure, for a day, but this might end up needing to stretch out a bit, you know? I figure if I'm "too sick" to call in for myself, like a fever or something, and need you to do it for me … I mean, that's got to be most of the week taken care of. Look, I know it bugs you, but I'd massively owe you one.'

There was a very long moment where Violet could feel herself about to reach for the phone in Marie's hand. To call the office and tell them exactly what Marie was doing. To let her feel all the consequences of her useless shirking. But instead she just closed the door. It took all her restraint, but she did not slam it, and she did not vocalise any of the thoughts that flooded uninvited into her mind.

Marie knew better than to push her any further, and sleep found Violet quickly.

The next time she woke up was to an empty flat. Marie must have been out at whatever was so much more important than work, but Violet gave her door a gentle knock anyway. She had no intention of apologising for earlier, she'd been totally in the right, but given their housing situation, Violet was wary of creating any rifts with her old friend. And today their tiny flat felt like an oddly lonely place to wake up to silence, so she would have welcomed the company. But there was no response, so Violet made her way to the kitchen. The roar of the kettle grated on her in the quiet, and she noticed her right hand shaking ever so slightly as she spooned out the coffee granules.

She was fine. There was no reason for her not to be, so she was fine. It was times like this she'd welcome the reassuring *scratch scratch scratch* of a murderer living in the walls. At least it would be some company. She couldn't quite bring herself to laugh at her own joke as she drank her coffee and told herself she felt better.

There were people in the lift when it finally arrived. She'd been standing so long in the cigarette-scented hall she'd almost written it off as broken again, but just as she turned towards the stairway the doors started to open. Two figures stood inside, huddled close together, facing towards the back corner as though in close conversation, though Violet couldn't make out what they were saying. She tried to get a look at their faces, see if she recognised them from around the building, but one had a thick hood pulled up over their head and the other was turned too much away from her. Their clothes were muted, denim and canvas, and neither seemed to be paying her any attention at all.

For some reason, the idea of stepping into that lift, slowly riding down those eight floors next to them, filled Violet with horror. Was it because of that arsehole from yesterday? Had one 'boo' left her feeling like this forever? No, this was something else. It must be.

Perhaps she was worried it would break, trapping them all inside for four days until they had to eat her. Again, the memory of her mother's stories failed to raise the usual smile. She'd just take the damn lift, she decided, but by that time the doors were already closing again. Violet took the stairs.

Work went slowly, as it so often did. She was tired, and the machine-dispensed coffee didn't seem to be helping. She cycled through the strange, synthetic menu, trying to find the one that would finally break through her haze. Instant coffee, 'freshbrew' coffee, latte, they all tasted of the same chemicals her tongue has adapted to years ago, but none of them could shift this weariness. She found herself measuring out the work day by the smokers' cigarette breaks, the rise and fall of that familiar irritation as regular as any clock. When she finally left to take her walk and passed them huddled in the chill outside the front door, she found herself mumbling about their laziness, but they kept their backs to her and didn't appear to have heard.

She avoided Augustine Road, and turned once or twice when she almost crossed paths with another late-night wanderer. She hated herself for it but decided that having a peaceful walk was more important than proving some sort of point. Even so, relaxation was elusive tonight, and she ended up staying out ten minutes longer than she technically had for her break. Nobody seemed to notice, but it bothered her.

Back at home, Marie was sullenly getting ready for work.

'I just called in a migraine yesterday, so have to go in today.'

'Sorry,' Violet said. She wasn't.

'Oh, and your mother called, something about your uncle's sixtieth?'

'Thanks. I'll call her back,' Violet said. She wouldn't.

In the cold, cultivated darkness of her room, Violet lay down on the bed, trying to figure out what was wrong. Everything was fine. Everything was normal. So why did her jaw ache from clenching her teeth? Why was she so tired? She lay there and surrendered to sleep.

The next night was strange. Violet woke up. She must have. But there was still that disconnection, as though she had been somehow severed from the world. Everything was muted, and when she tried to focus on any one thing too closely her head started to ache. Marie had clearly had a difficult day and she did not seem inclined to chat as she ate her dinner, leaving Violet to her breakfast: toast that didn't want to cook right and coffee that got cold almost as soon as it was put down. She still drank it, though, desperately trying to grasp just a splinter more wakefulness. It was half an hour later than usual when she finally got out of the door, and she had no idea what she might have been doing for all that time.

She stepped out into a cloud of cigarette smoke and stopped, coughing, at the unexpected sensation. Thrust into the real world again, if only for that moment of physical discomfort. She looked around and, sure enough, standing in front of the door to 116 was a young man in an old grey suit. His shirt should have been white, but time had rendered it the same dull colour as his jacket, and he wore it unbuttoned over the sun-darkened skin of his chest. His curling black hair was just long enough to be dishevelled. He did not seem to have noticed Violet leaving her flat, or her reaction to the waves of smoke that rolled from his cigarette and curled around a peeling 'No Smoking' sign. All of his attention seemed focused towards the end of the hallway, past the lift, to where a window looked down over the night-covered city below.

The fluorescent bulb above that window had burned out weeks before and had not been replaced, leaving that part of the corridor shadowed and dark, but as Violet followed the stranger's gaze she could just about make out a silhouette. She blinked, trying to focus on it. Somebody was there. They seemed to be standing very still, and it wasn't immediately clear if they were facing away and looking out through the glass, or staring back down the corridor.

Violet wanted to ignore them, to just cross over to the lift and go to work (she needed to get to work). Her nerves were still alight from her encounter two nights before. Yet there was something about the figure by the window that made her certain that they were looking at her. Not the man with the cigarette, her. She felt compelled to call out, greet them, assure them that she was going to work, she was, when a hand grasped her firmly by the arm. She spun around to see her strange neighbour shaking his head insistently.

'Do you see them?' he asked her, his voice thick with concern and an accent she couldn't quite place.

She nodded, her mind racing. Which of her mother's stories was this?

He seemed visibly relieved. His grip relaxed and she pulled her arm away, instinctively stepping back. His face softened for a moment, and he stammered out an apology. As if sensing her next question, he gestured to the door behind him and, Violet assumed, to the old woman who lived behind it.

'Old friend,' he said, as though expecting this to answer all her questions, but her head was starting to swim again, and the blood pounded through her ears, drowning out the choking silence of that hall. She turned to leave, not wanting to ask this stranger any more questions when her eyes flicked instinctively back to the window and she froze. There were now two people standing there. The second was just as much a silhouette as the first, and just as still. Their heads leaned towards each other, as though passing some quiet conversation, and if she strained, Violet thought could just about hear the faintest whisper of what they were saying …

When her neighbour looked back, it took a second for him to notice the second figure, but as he did his face contorted into a look of suspicion and unease. He turned slowly to her, a bead of sweat rolling across his face.

'I, uh—' He struggled to find the words. 'Be safe.'

Violet turned right and hurried down the stairs. Two floors down she could still hear the figures whispering.

Violet was late to the office that night. She tried her best to collect herself, to sit down and focus her mind on her task, but the words seemed very far away, and the silence of the office left her floating and unsettled. Her fingers ached before she even started typing, and the central heating felt like it was going to smother her. Every few minutes she would catch herself listening intently, as though straining to hear some quiet conversation, and the coffees she was sure she had just made would be long cold. She kept drinking them, trying to fight off a fatigue that had been building in her all night, terrified that if she closed her eyes she would sleep. How many cups was it in her mother's story before the stressed office worker had a heart attack? Or was that the same one who ended up burning down the building? They'd all started to blend together.

She was terrified her exhaustion would show, that they would know she wasn't doing her work. They would all know. Every clack of the keyboard was like a finger being drummed right onto her skull.

In spite of everything, she still tried to take her walk. Bob had leaned over and asked her if she was planning to take her break and it was like a rope had been cut. She almost leapt from her seat. Her steps were unsteady, and the silent streets offered her no comfort, but the idea of staying in that office for another second made her feel faint. At least the night air was unchanged. It still offered that crisp reassurance that the world still lived, but she did not walk as far as normal, nor as fast.

Augustine Road was empty. No figures standing at the other end, no whispering strangers waiting for her. There was nothing there. So why was she so reluctant to walk any further? Why did she already feel like she needed to head back to work? She carried on, trying to ignore it, pushing the possibilities from her mind, but she ended her walk soon afterwards. There was no peace to be found in the city that night.

As she returned to the office, she saw a small crowd outside the door. The smokers, six of them, huddled together, talking quietly. She knew they emailed each other to orchestrate their breaks, and now they were lurking outside, as if waiting for her, whispering to each other. Shirking. They didn't look up as she passed, and she had to stop herself barking at them to get back to work. She rubbed her exhausted eyes, fingers stained with coffee and dirt, and pushed herself back into the office.

*

By the time she got home to Bayan Court, she was so shot through with bone-deep fatigue that she almost didn't notice the flashing lights of the ambulance parked in front of it. It was only when a round-faced woman in a police uniform gently put a hand on her shoulder to stop her wandering, unthinkingly, into the blue-and-white tape that she realised there was anything out of the ordinary. Barriers hid most of the scene, but a small streak of something dark could still be seen on the edge of the kerb. It could have been blood. It could have been other things as well, of course, but her mind refused to think of any, and kept circling back to blood.

'I live here,' Violet said, realising she had no idea what the officer had said to her.

'Certainly, this way please.' The response was courteous and crisp as she began to usher Violet towards the well-lit main entrance.

'No. Round the back.'

The police officer stopped for a second, confused, and Violet had to limply point to the alleyway that led to her home.

'Right. Wait here,' she was told, as the officer walked away, apparently needing to check something with a colleague. Violet could have sworn she was muttering '*Get back to work*' under her breath.

She stood there, waiting, watching paramedics load a long black plastic bag into the back of the ambulance. One of them knocked a barrier partially aside, and for a second Violet was absolutely positive she could see, lying on the wet ground, a bright blue baseball cap. There was no surprise in her, no shock that he was now lying dead on the other side of London, five miles from their last meeting. Perhaps she was just too tired.

She wondered idly which urban legend had finally got him. Maybe it was her? Maybe that was the big twist, that the

25

monster in the story was her. She felt her lips fold into a single syllable as the police officer returned to lead her round the back and into the building.

'Boo.'

Four figures stood halfway up the stairs, just above the first floor, where the steps curled behind the old iron lift. They wore thick jackets over dull, unremarkable outfits as they turned towards each other, faces hidden from view. Violet could hear them whispering to each other even before Resident Entrance B swung shut behind her, cutting off the flashing lights that seemed to follow her even behind the building. It was six in the morning, why were they there?

She waited almost a full minute for the lift. It wasn't coming. She pressed the button again, rubbing at the tips of her fingers. They felt rough, and for a second she could have sworn they were different, covered with callouses and scarred blisters. She looked up at the lift, but the number hadn't changed. She started to feel very exposed and finally turned towards the stairway, full of that resignation that comes with exhaustion. As she climbed she could hear them whispering above her, but as she got closer the sound seemed to stop and they simply stood there, silent. They didn't turn around, and she still couldn't see their faces. Somewhere in the distance, a siren wailed through the streets.

Violet kept on climbing, the now-quiet crowd patient and unmoving. Her legs felt odd, their movements almost mechanical, but she didn't stop.

Thinking about it later, it seemed to her that four people standing together should have almost completely blocked the stairs. And yet she didn't remember passing them, not really. As she continued to walk, they were simply behind her, and before she had a chance to consider it she had reached the next floor. She turned back but they hadn't moved. Her mind instinctively reached for one of her mother's stories, trying to place the feeling of unease in a familiar context, but none came. She continued her climb, the whispers floating up to follow her.

'What did Bob say?'

It was already nine and Marie was late for work, but it didn't look like she had any intention of leaving before Violet had given her every detail.

'Don't worry about it.'

'Hey, you use my phone, you give me the details,' Marie insisted, doing her best to hide genuine concern. No answer from Violet. 'You still haven't found yours?'

'No. It's fine, I don't need it.'

'What the hell does that mean? Obviously you need a phone. You just had to call in sick.'

'I didn't have to. I can go to work. I should go to work.'

'Seriously. Look at you.' Marie was firm. 'When was the last time you slept properly? I mean, you weren't doing great even before a guy you knew died outside our building.'

Violet was quiet for a moment. 'I didn't know him. Not really. He just—'

'Who cares!' Marie exploded. 'It's clearly messed you up. You need some time off.'

'OK. You've made your point.'

'And?' Marie said, gesturing to her phone, still clasped in Violet's hand.

'… Bob gave me the rest of the week off. So, like, three days, I guess. Nights.'

'Good. I told you he'd be fine with it.'

'He wasn't.'

'What did he say?' Marie's tone was suddenly protective.

'It's not that.' Violet tried to shrug. 'I mean, he didn't say …
He kept saying it was fine, that it sounded like it had been a real
shock and that I should take all the time I needed.'

'But …?'

'I could just tell. I know he thinks I'm slacking. That I'm not
willing to work.'

Marie didn't reply.

'Anyway, you should get going,' Violet said, doing her best to
sound normal. 'You don't want another telling-off from Sandra.'

She didn't even need to look at her to know what face Marie
was pulling, but her friend pressed on.

'What did the cops say?'

'I didn't ask. I mean, they couldn't tell me anything anyway,
could they?'

'Wait.' Marie's eyes went wide. 'You don't think it was him,
do you? From next door. Maybe he … y'know.'

'Marie, please.'

'Right, right. Sorry, it's just … right outside. Bloody hell.
We need to move. This place is … I told you, didn't I?'

Violet said nothing.

'So, what's the plan?'

'Nothing. I just need some decent sleep.'

Marie began to nod, then stopped, her eyes focused on
Violet's mug. 'You alright drinking that?'

'It's decaf,' Violet lied.

'Right,' Marie said, giving her a long steady look, before
finally getting to her feet.

Violet didn't want to ask the next question. She wanted
Marie to be out of the door and gone, to leave her to her coffee
and her vague dread, but she couldn't stop herself.

'Marie …'

'Yeah?'

'Have you, uh, seen anyone else around the building? People who shouldn't be here?'

There was the look, that guarded concern she'd been desperate to avoid.

'What do you mean? Like who?'

'Just ... People. Hanging around. Groups of them. Standing still like they're ... I don't know.' She managed to stop just short of mentioning the whispers. Marie was quiet for several seconds.

'Violet, this isn't one of your stories.'

'Fuck's sake, I know that!' Violet rocked backwards for a second, stunned by the strength of her own reaction. 'It was just a question. Forget it.'

'Fine.' Marie was clearly upset. ' And no, I haven't. I mean, I've seen people, sure, but not being weird or being ... "still" or whatever.'

'OK.' Violet tried to shrug, not wanting to meet Marie's eye. Another pause.

'Look, I've got to go. Just ... take it easy, OK? Get some sleep.'

Violet didn't answer.

The building was strange in the daytime. That quiet that dominated it when the residents were asleep was instead replaced by a constant stream of faint noises. Conversation, televisions, washing machines, shouting. It all came floating through those thin walls, smothered and distorted so much it was impossible to tell exactly where it originated. But no whispering. Violet passed a half dozen residents on their way into or out of their flats, but everyone was moving, travelling, on their way somewhere. All except the workman with plumber's tools, who stood tapping a pipe with an expression of intense concentration. Or the young man in the Uriah Heep T-shirt, who stopped measuring the corridor long enough to regard her with a curiosity that made her feel strangely self-conscious. But there were no half-seen figures huddled together, no silhouettes pressed against windows, as if waiting for something to happen.

By the time she finally crawled into bed in the early hours of the afternoon, Violet had walked nearly every corridor and stairway in the cramped rear of Banyan Court. It was strange to wander its corridors in the daytime, to see the sunlight illuminate those walls she knew so well by fluorescence felt almost unnatural. Their comforting coldness replaced by a stifling warmth. Still, even Violet could not deny the daylight reassured her, and by the end she could almost dismiss that oppressive sense of wrongness, or maybe she was just able to smother it in a thick layer of fatigue, and mask it in her aching muscles and stiff, calloused fingers.

She opened her eyes to darkness. Had she been asleep? Her hand reached out almost automatically, hunting for the light switch, but before she had a chance to use it, she stopped. In an instant she was wide awake, her ears straining to listen.

The whispering was soft and insistent, and for a brief second, she had a terrible certainty that it was coming from her kitchen. Violet's fingers found the switch and the room was flooded with artificial light. She wasted no time, fear briefly sparking into anger as she ran into the next room, but of course it was empty, the whispers still near but now muffled and distant. Where was Marie? Right, it was Friday, she'd probably be out for some drinks. Wait, was it Friday? It didn't matter, she wasn't there. Violet took her time, searching every inch of their tiny flat.

Marie's door was closed. The whispering could be from in there. Was it locked? Or maybe Marie was home, sitting and relaxing quietly, not hearing what was going on. The privacy of their rooms was one of the cornerstones of Violet and Marie's living together. But Violet had to be sure. Gripping the handle, she felt a flood of relief that it wasn't locked, then a burst of terror at the idea of what might be waiting inside. She opened the door.

It was empty. Marie's furniture was basic, practical, reflecting a life led mostly outside the flat. But most importantly, there was nowhere for someone to hide. Violet breathed out for what felt like the first time since she woke up. The whispering figures weren't inside her home. Not yet. She caught herself at this, tried to focus: there was no reason to think they could get in there. It had to be safe.

She dressed quickly, slipping on her shoes without bothering to properly lace them, and headed out the door. The window at the end of the corridor was dark and the lights of the city were faint. There was no safety for her tonight. The thought came unbidden into Violet's mind and she didn't have the energy to push it away. Perhaps her mother was right and there never had been any safety. But none of her stories had ever gone like this, and Violet began to search anyway.

She found three of them on the stairs heading down to the fifth floor. She turned and walked quickly away. There was a cluster of six or seven at the end of the corridor on the eighth, again she couldn't bring herself to get any closer. There were only two standing in front of the elevator on the tenth floor, but when she turned around it was clear there were more just round the corner. She hadn't been counting them before, and now that she had started it didn't take long for her to lose track. She wanted to confront them, to demand they tell her what was going on. This was her home, her city, they had no right to be here. They would not make her afraid. Yet she just couldn't summon that defiant walk which had seen her down Augustine Road. Instead she found herself running.

She stopped to catch her breath by a window. Looking down onto the dingy concrete courtyard below she could make out five of them standing beneath one of the security lights. Always facing each other, never where she could see them clearly, their rough, practical clothes dirty and worn. She stood there, at a fifth-floor window, watching them for nearly twenty minutes. They didn't move. Even from all the way up here she could hear them whispering. What were they standing around for? Didn't they have jobs to do? Was it her? Were they whispering about her?

She could have stood there watching them for hours, but the trance was broken by the sound of a door opening behind her. Violet spun to see a young woman staring at her. It wasn't until the woman actually started to ask her what she was doing that Violet realised she was looking at another resident of Banyan Court. She wanted to answer this woman, explain what was happening, beg her for help, but couldn't make a sound. There was a moment of silence, each clearly waiting for the other to say something, then Violet's attention was seized by the sudden shriek of metal, and the clanking rattle of an ancient mechanism.

She didn't wait to see the other woman's reaction and raced back down the corridor, around a corner, past two figures mumbling softly to each other, hunting that noise. With a lurch she realised what it was and turned back, heading towards the spiralling central stairwell.

There were three of them inside the old wrought-iron elevator, their hands blackened by dirt. These three almost spoke clearly, but their words were drowned by the clanking of the lift moving. Violet felt a swell of nausea to see those ancient metal bones in motion. She ran up the stairs, chasing the slowly rising platform, trying to catch just a word of what they were saying. On the twelfth floor she was forced to stop and watch as the lift continued up into the ceiling above her. Violet felt like screaming, but she could barely make a sound.

She staggered back towards her flat, hands clasped over her ears, desperate to block out the whispering as she passed more groups of indistinct figures. So many more. She wanted to ignore them all, to lock herself in and simply wait out the night, but the door had locked behind her, as it always did, and in her rush to leave she had neglected to take the keys. She reached instinctively for her phone, before remembering that was lost as well, and a deep panic began to rise in her, as the whispering began to get closer. There were dozens of figures. Hundreds. And though they stayed still their presence seemed to cover her like fog.

There was nothing she could do. Nowhere she could run. No one she could call. She felt herself begin to collapse, when she caught the whiff of stale smoke. She turned, expecting to see her neighbour standing there, but the hallway was empty. Without stopping to think, Violet staggered over and began to pound on the door of 116 Banyan Court. For several awful seconds she was sure it wouldn't open, but then she heard the click of a lock, and there he was.

Violet couldn't speak, couldn't get the words out. Her throat tasted like diesel fumes and dust. He just watched her with a look of deep pity on his face. He smelled of old cigarettes.

'Help.' She almost choked on the word.

He shook his head slowly.

'They are not real,' he said, his voice filled with false resolve. 'Don't make them real.'

'What do they want?'

'Nothing,' the stranger said. 'The dead are dead. Justice is for the living.'

And the door to 116 shut, leaving her alone.

Violet stood in the corridor, her fear gradually shifting into numbness, and waited for something to happen. Sure enough the tinny chime of the lift sounded behind her. She watched as the doors parted to reveal more anonymous whisperers crammed inside it, so tightly there was barely room to breathe, their backs all turned towards her. She walked slowly towards it, but the lift doors did not close.

All at once, the mumbling cut off, and the world was quiet again. Violet's ears rang painfully with the silence, and she felt the anger rise inside her. The words came to her lips, though she had no idea why.

'Get back to work!'

She spat it like an exorcism, and the figures seemed to slump, as though whatever spirit propelled them had been torn away. Violet's anger vanished as quickly as it came, and she was filled with the deepest shame she had ever felt.

'What is it?' Violet pleaded. 'What do you want to tell me?'

As one, they turned to face her, pulling down their hoods and uncovering their heads. Their hair was matted with sweat and mineshaft dirt; their fingers were bruised, calloused from pickaxe and assembly line and sewing needle; they were stained with coffee and cacao. The bloody sewing thread that criss-crossed their mouths kept their lips tight together, but now the whispered words were clear. And Violet listened, learning how the story would end.

Marie was worried. If she'd really known anything at all about Violet's family she would have called them, but as it was, she had to content herself with knocking on the locked bedroom door every few hours, asking if she was OK, if she needed any-thing. The answer was always the same.

'I'm fine. Just thinking.'

She tried again. Violet had been 'just thinking' for almost two days now, and she should have been back at work yesterday. Something was definitely wrong, and if it went on much longer Marie was going to have to call a doctor or something. Though what that something might actually be she had no idea. The internet didn't seem to have an easy answer for what to do when your best friend was having a weird breakdown. Marie had always said she worked too hard.

Whatever was going on with her, Marie was sure that Violet would still want to know about the invitation. She read it again to be sure, but the words were still there, still exactly the same. It didn't make any sense, but the thick card and tasteful embossed lettering were impeccable. If this was a prank, someone had spent serious money on it.

TOBIAS FELL cordially invites VIOLET NG
to attend a dinner party at 1 Banyan Court
on the evening of 16th August 2014
Penthouse access will be available through the freight elevator

She knocked on Violet's door again, and slipped it underneath.

In the pitch darkness of her room, Violet smiled. She didn't need the light to know what it said. She had work to do.

2nd

The Knock

Jésus Candido
30 Banyan Court

Tap tap tap.

The silver head of the cane hit rhythmically against the well-shined leather of an expensive shoe, a soft but insistent sound that pervaded the near silence of the auction hall. Jésus Candido was bored.

'Lot 14 is next,' the auctioneer droned on. 'An incised ceramic bowl, judged to originate from the Guaraní peoples, date unknown. Two hundred pounds, starting at two hundred pounds.'

Nothing worth his time. He continued his impatient tapping. From the other seats, eyes turned to stare at him with varying degrees of curiosity. He saw them take in his expertly tailored bottle-green suit, the necktie with its perfectly executed Eldredge knot, his cultivated air of disdain and disregard. Some recognised him, whispering to companions with quietly awed expressions. Others showed no recognition, but perhaps they would ask after him later, and then they would learn his name. And why they *should* know it. Jésus allowed himself a small smile. Between changing fashions, money-laundering and newly minted tech billionaires looking to invest, the art industry was a constantly changing place, and any small thing you could do to maintain your profile as a dealer was worth it. Even a *legend* such as him couldn't afford to rest on his laurels.

'Sold to Margot for 240 pounds,' the auctioneer pushed through, clearly trying to ignore Jésus' theatrical yawn. The man certainly knew who had decided to be seen at his auction house.

And being visible seemed about the only thing this auction was good for. Normally Jésus did his business remotely, like the rest of the ring – his colleagues, though perhaps 'co-conspirators' would be more accurate – but he'd had a free afternoon local enough to the venue that he had succumbed to a whim and decided to attend in person. At the very least, it was worth showing his face once in a while. Jésus was in fact the one who had tipped Desmond and the rest of the ring off about this auction in the first place. His brother-in-law Antonio, a functionary in the Brazilian government, had been alerted to a wealthy cattle farmer who had recently passed away. Apparently, the man had owned a sizeable collection of artistic curiosities, but his family had no appreciation for such things and had decided to auction them off in London, where they ran much of their business.

'Sold to William by phone for five hundred and ten pounds,' the auctioneer said as a rather tasteless sculpture was taken away. Jésus didn't even remember them bringing it out.

Still, now they were getting to an item Jésus was designated bidder for. Perhaps this would bring a little excitement.

'Lot 32 now, a religious figure in soapstone, believed to be the work of Aleijadinho.' A pause. 'Uncertified. Starting at one thousand pounds.'

'One thousand pounds,' Jésus called, making his bid as instructed. To be honest, he thought it was overpriced for what was likely a forgery. But at least there might be some bidding drama.

'One thousand pounds,' the auctioneer repeated, looking around. 'Currently one thousand pounds.'

Silence.

'Sold to Jésus Candido for one thousand pounds.'

This was ridiculous. He was starting to think he might actually have made a mistake. The catalogue had been uninspiring, but to sit there and see this parade of extremely pedestrian art made him deeply weary. The whole auction had been like this, with the ring's bidders picking up what they had been assigned with a minimum of fuss and counterbids. Great news for the ring, but dull for Jésus, and the thought that he'd have to see most of these items again at the Knock made him almost regret bringing it to their attention. Still, he'd bought what was required of him, so could finally make his exit. Perhaps he'd make a performance out of it.

'Lot 51, an intriguing untitled mixed media piece, oil and charcoal on canvas. Artist unknown, date unknown. We'll start at eighty pounds.'

Jésus looked at the painting and found himself sitting back down. He hadn't particularly marked it in the catalogue for the auction, assuming it to be just another throwaway piece of junk from a mostly forgettable collection. A four-by-eight mixed media piece, oil and charcoal on canvas. Abstract, untitled, artist unknown, worth basically nothing. It had only been highlighted by the ring because William Duphine, a new addition to their ranks who Jésus privately considered an upstart with no taste, had been hired to adorn a full country house. He was bulk-buying anything he thought might work with the rest of the decor. To look at it now, though, Jésus couldn't imagine this painting fitting into any wider aesthetic. A tactful person might call it *unique*.

Though even he had to admit seeing it was a different

experience to the flat catalogue photograph. He might as well have been looking at a different piece entirely. It was vibrant and intoxicating, a series of bright, cascading lines that swirled and interlocked in an apparently meaningless manner, until your mind finally arranged it into what it was: the face of a woman. Her eyes were vague, her mouth closed and unreadable, but smiling. The style was crude, almost childish at points, but there was something there. Something he wanted ...

Murmuring took up around him, and he realised he had raised his hand to bid. He wasn't the designated buyer for this one, he knew that, and as he lowered his hand, he had a sudden worry he'd be responsible for raising the price.

'I'm sorry, Mr Candido, was that a bid?' The auctioneer seemed as surprised as anyone.

'Eighty,' someone mercifully called from the back before Jésus had to come up with an answer.

He recognised the voice, the young woman ring member Margot Lancaster used to deliver her bids, and he breathed a sigh of relief. The ring would get their due. Even so, he was struggling somewhat to maintain his composure. For Jésus Candido to be seen bidding on a piece like this, no name attached, barely worth the cost of the canvas, it was unthinkable. He was, *perhaps*, willing to compromise his artistic eye if the ring chose him to bid on a specific piece, but aside from that he considered his bid the highest compliment he could pay. And this piece ...

It was certainly true he considered himself to have a keen eye for outsider art, created by those without training or intent, but it was not an interest he wished to be known for. Yet, as he did his best to relax back into a considered indifference, he caught his hand starting to rise again and pulled it back down before the auctioneer spotted.

He watched as the painting was carried off, sold to Margot's bidder for a hundred and ten. His instincts had never misled him before. The more he thought about it, the more Jésus was certain: it would be perfect for his private collection. He resolved to own it, William Duphine be damned. He smiled to himself. It had been a long time since he'd actually found himself looking forward to the Knock.

'This the one?' the driver called as the black cab pulled up to Banyan Court. 'Hell of a place, this. Bet you're not for the poor door, eh?'

'No,' Jésus replied, ignoring the jovial tone and ugly laugh of the taxi driver, 'I am not.'

He eased himself out, careful where he stepped on the streets of Tower Hamlets. Banyan Court loomed above him. There are some buildings in this world which exist to serve a function and have no aesthetic ambition beyond that purpose. Or perhaps it would be more accurate to say that their aesthetic ambition *is* to serve their purpose. Others are inviting, made to be welcoming and familiar, and still others are made to be intimidating, austere: a reminder to those that enter them of the power and position of their builders. But some buildings, at least to the eyes of Jésus Candido, some buildings were art.

Many were designed as such, their beauty intricately planned by architects of vision and skill, while others found their art accidentally, growing into it through their decay or sculpted towards it by later extensions and changes. Some even became art entirely by context: the tiny, ugly little church that refused to sell its land, stubbornly existing in the heart of a business district, walled in on all sides by fashionable glass monstrosities. You just needed to know how to look.

'Oi!' the voice of the cabbie cut through his musings. 'You forgot your fancy cane.'

Jésus retrieved it without comment.

'Don't want anyone thinking you're in the wrong door, do we?' The driver's laughter was cut off by the door slamming shut.

Jésus was quite sure that Banyan Court was intended to be beautiful. There was simply no way the interweaving of glass and steel with the aged brick of the old tenement served any practical purpose. And certainly it was broadly successful, that was true. But anything could be beautiful. Beauty was cheap. Beauty was *obvious*. And yet he chose to live there. Not because of the artistic merit it claimed to possess, but because of the artistic merit it had not even considered. There it stood, a bright splinter of excess, burrowed into the grey and dying streets of struggle and hardship, unable to even admit the parts of itself it considered shameful. Aesthetically, it was acceptable. Conceptually, it was art. And so, Jésus lived there.

He hadn't argued with the cab driver because he had nothing to prove. He understood poverty and degradation without having to actually experience it. You don't need to actually touch art.

'Good evening, come in.' Jésus tried to disguise his irritation that William Duphine was the first to arrive for the Knock.

'Yes, hello, Jesus! Is Desmond here yet? What are we drinking?'

Jésus did not answer. He did not care to respond to those who couldn't be bothered to pronounce his name right.

'Look at this place! I should drop a line to *Time Out*. "The hidden gallery that puts the Horniman to shame!"' He leered at Jésus. 'Did Desmond say why it wasn't at the Langham?'

Duphine had, predictably, picked the least interesting of the display pieces to examine, an extremely derivative Jacob Maris piece he mostly kept around because it seemed churlish not to have anything from the Hague School.

Desmond Uxton, the ring's founder, had in fact had rather a nasty falling-out with one of the managers at the Langham and had violently sworn off the place, but that wasn't any of William Duphine's business, so Jésus declined to share it.

Soon enough, the other members of the ring, including Desmond himself, began to join them, taking their places for the bidding, each complimenting Jésus on his home. It was true he had an almost perfect set-up for it, with the eight usual members comfortably fitting in his spacious living room. Nobody mentioned it, but he felt there was also a certain rightness in the fact that the dead man whose spoils they were to bid on had actually run one of the many companies ultimately controlled by Tobias Fell, the owner of Banyan Court itself. All in all, the perfect venue for dividing the bounty of a fixed auction.

'Right,' Desmond said at last, once they were all settled. 'Shall we go in lot order or value? It's all the same to me.'

'Lot order is easier to keep track of, I think,' declared Margot, one of the older members of the ring, and no one disagreed, so the bidding began.

The Knock was a remarkably simple idea. It took place among members of the ring, bidders who would normally be at each other's throats during the auction but had instead made an arrangement to not compete against each other, at least no more than needed to keep up appearances. This meant some lots could be acquired for a fraction of what they might have cost otherwise. Of course, there were plenty of bidders who weren't in the ring, and if they were eager for a lot then the price could still climb higher than would be ideal, but the ring's pockets were deep, and they'd still recoup much of their expenses at the Knock. Once the designated buyers had secured as many of the pre-chosen lots as possible, a second, private auction was held among the ring, with each member bidding on the lots that they had won. The winner would pay off the buyer, and then pay the amount they bid at the Knock evenly among all members of the ring. The money circulated around all through the group in such a way that even if you spent as much on a piece you might have paid at the auction itself, you'd recoup those losses from the other members on the pieces you didn't win.

It was a way of acquiring valuable pieces of art for less than they were worth, but more than that, membership of the ring was an extremely exclusive thing, and it helped to keep the interlopers and new money from gaining a foothold. Art, Jésus privately believed, was not, in fact, for everybody, and the Knock helped to keep that vital hierarchy in place. It was also quite illegal, but that didn't matter. They weren't some petty consortium of scrap metal dealers, they were people of means and power, and they weren't the sort of people to be touched by the law.

Still, that was hardly what concerned him today. He had a very specific piece he was bidding on. Lot 51, he remembered it quite clearly. None of the pieces were physically present, of course, they'd be delivered as necessary, but his memory was quite vivid enough. It was strange, Jésus had been to so many Knocks in his time that to find himself actually caring about one was a remarkably novel experience. And yet, as the spoils were divided and they came closer and closer to the painting that he still hadn't been able to get out of his mind, he grew nervous. Lot 46 came and went. Lot 49. What if he wasn't the only one who saw its potential? What if he had it snatched from him?

As it turned out, he needn't have worried. Nobody else at the Knock seemed to care much about the painting at all. William Duphine put in an obligatory bid, his expression utterly disinterested, clearly expecting to walk away with it. When he saw Jésus raise his hand to outbid him, he stifled a small laugh. Desmond leaned over.

'I wouldn't worry old man,' he whispered to Jésus, 'I some-times lose track as well.'

Jésus kept his gaze level and raised his arm higher, confirming the bid. There were a few whispers, some wondering if they'd missed something important about the painting, others smirk-ing slightly, believing him to have made his first mistake. He ignored them. They hadn't seen it, not like he had. He wasn't going to lie to himself their pantomimed confusion and back-biting didn't get to him, but he was damned if he'd let them know it. William shrugged, conceding the piece. And then it was done.

'Mind me asking what got you so interested in that one?' Desmond asked him afterwards, once the other members of the ring had made their polite goodbyes. They all cooperated professionally for the Knock, but he was the only one Jésus would actually consider a friend.

'You didn't see it in person, did you?' he said, releasing a plume of cigar smoke that lazily crept its way around the bal-cony and out into the night air.

'Can't say I did. Had Müller put through my bids by phone as always. I take it the photos don't do it justice?'

'They do not. It was unexpected.'

'Bit of a mess, though, surely? Maybe as an ambience piece, but ... what exactly did you see in it?'

'It's ... outsider art,' Jésus said, suddenly defensive, 'the line work, the colours. Think of Georgiana Houghton. Or Madge Gill, perhaps.'

'Otherworldly lines and haunted geometries, eh?' Desmond inhaled thoughtfully. 'Can't honestly say I saw anything of that in it.'

'Well, I did.'

'Hm. Sounds like it really called to you.' Desmond's tone was casual, but the words still gave Jésus pause. He shifted uncomfortably.

'Yes. Yes, it did.'

'Unless you know something about it you're not telling?' Desmond's smile did its best to hide the slight edge creeping into his voice. Jésus knew that his friend hated more than anything to feel like anyone had got one over on him.

'No. I simply ... like it.' Jésus wanted to say more, to put into words the feelings it stirred in him, but English was a blunt, clumsy language and he simply couldn't do it.

'Well, I hope so. No way you're going to sell it on its own, so I suppose you better find some wall space.'

'I shall. It's going to be where it belongs, I think.'

Desmond shrugged and returned to his own cigar. The two of them sat in silence, watching the thin lines of smoke twist and contort in the lights of the city below.

It was two days later when the front desk informed Jésus that his painting had arrived. He hurried down as fast as the elevator would allow, hoping to catch the delivery men before they left, but they'd long since vanished by the time he got there. Worse, the concierge working the reception was one he particularly disliked: a lanky middle-aged man who talked to himself and always claimed problems had been taken care of when they clearly hadn't been. Jésus had deliberately made the decision not to learn the man's name, and always studiously avoided glancing at his name tag. He considered it a personal favour to the concierge that he had made no active efforts to have him fired. Still, despite his other failings the man was probably strong enough to carry the painting up to the apartment, though the thought of him touching it made Jésus ever so slightly uncomfortable.

The concierge sighed at the request and called to the little room behind him for someone to watch the front desk, eliciting a snort from the art dealer over the pointless delay. He had a dinner reservation at Le Gavroche at seven, and he intended to work up quite an appetite finding his new prize a place to live.

Despite the irritations of transporting it, the painting was soon sitting comfortably in Jésus' apartment, waiting to properly see the space it was to own. He dismissed the concierge with a palpable sense of relief and removed the covering. It was everything he remembered and more: that familiar riot of colours, the lines arcing through and around themselves, spiralling in patterns his eyes simply refused to follow. And there, after a few moments of watching, the woman again, her eyes still focused on him and her mouth still set in that unreadable line. He sighed in appreciation and relief. He had been right, after all: it was beautiful.

Jésus began to search for a position on his walls that did it justice. The hallway was too immediate, it would overpower everything else on display. The living room wasn't right either, as all the walls big enough to hold it were at entirely the wrong angle. It would be too distracting in the bedroom as, even though he rarely showed it to visitors, on those occasions he did bring men back, there was a very specific mood he was interested in setting. That left the study, the smallest room in the apartment, though it was by no means modest. Compared to his sleek modern living room he kept the study almost parodically traditional, with a darkly stained oak desk and shelves of books he'd had custom-bound to fit the tone. It was where he situated his more traditional pieces.

One of his visitors had once asked him how he could be so calculated about his own home, and Jésus had been slightly taken aback. He'd never really considered the question, but on reflection he decided that perhaps he didn't consider anywhere truly a home. It was all simply space to be refined, to be turned into something of value. There was nothing valuable about simply living in a place. Any animal can do that. And perhaps if people didn't understand that they didn't deserve to have it. He didn't say any of this out loud, of course, it wasn't the man's business. But the question stayed with him. It had nothing to do with home, not really. This space was his because he could realise its true potential, and that ownership, that curation, was a lifelong project

'The study,' he said finally, staring at the painting. 'The right home for you, I think.'

Previously pride of place had been given to a religious piece by Karel Škréta, but looking over it now he had to fight back the urge to tear it from the wall and hurl it out of the window. He was no stranger to the need to move past what had come before, in some cases even to destroy it, to burn it all down and make way for the new, but he had never before felt it as such a powerful urge. He took a breath and carefully removed the Škréta from its position.

The rest of the day was spent meticulously rearranging his apartment, moving and reorienting almost everything until he was once again happy with the layout. In the end he got rid of a few of the pieces he'd had for a while: a glass sculpture by a formerly up-and-coming artist named Karl Velter and a series of Barlach lithographs he had picked up on a whim while flirting with expressionism. He stood there, admiring his acquisition in its new home.

Knock knock.

He was roused from his contemplation, realising with some confusion that he needed to turn on the light. When had it got dark? He felt the deep gnawing of hunger in his stomach.

Remembering what had stirred him, he hurried to the front door and threw it open. The hall outside was empty.

Were there children in the building? Jésus curled his lip. He had no quarrel with those who had children, of course, so long as they had the decency to breed quietly. No sign of the little timewasters, though. Luckily, he hadn't quite missed his dinner reservation, though he was acutely aware that he hadn't freshened up after shifting his displays around and must look a mess. Then he realised he didn't care.

But that was nonsense, surely. He had planned it as one of his 'exhibition dinners': meals he took alone, well dressed and dazzling, to remind the great and the influential of his good taste. He was Jésus Candido, after all, and his appearance was as much an artistic expression as the rest of him. And yet, when he looked at the world outside his apartment, so drab and colourless after the vibrant hues he had so recently fallen into, he could not bring himself to be concerned about how he looked. He ate quickly, ignored the other patrons, and returned home immediately after.

Jésus was in his apartment. It looked as though it had been drawn from memory, sketched out and painted in those same crawling technicolour lines that had so captivated him before. He knew he was dreaming, but that didn't bother him at all, and a gentle calm washed over him.

This, he heard himself thinking, *this is home*.

Knock knock.

Someone was at the door. Compared to the thin swirling strokes that composed the rest of the apartment, the entrance was thick and smudged, as though made with an old brush, overloaded with cadmium red.

Knock knock knock.

They wanted to come in.

The sound became more insistent, more aggressive. He reached for the handle, and the door ignited, exploding into a bright and hateful fire. He felt the heat as it charred and cracked the lines that made it and stained the dazzling colours a charcoal black. He dreamed the smell of burning wood as the flames spread through the apartment. It was not the comforting wood smell of a fireplace or a bonfire, but the awful stench of everything he knew being rendered down to ash and heat-scoured earth. It was all ablaze now, his whole world incinerating: everything he had so coldly assessed and positioned and believed himself apart from, devoured in a wave of genuine loss. He felt the flames reach him, melting his flesh and shattering his bones in their intensity. But they left his eyes, trapped and staring wildly at the figure moving slowly through what had once been the door. The pain was only bearable because it wasn't his. It belonged to the dream, and all he could do was endure and hope to wake.

Still, the figure approached, and he saw that it wore the face of the painted woman. It was as twisted and distorted as it had been on canvas, that same chaotic mess of curling lines and angry hues. She wore a drab olive dress and she was burning, ravenous, desperate to consume and utterly destroy everything she touched with the fire that was her flesh.

Jésus awoke clawing at himself, desperate to extinguish flames that were not there and to defend a home he did not have.

Over the next two days, Jésus found himself falling behind on much of his work, with the hours seeming to simply disappear from his day. He found himself standing before that painting more and more, studying every line, following the shapes and colours, trying to find what exactly it was that drew him to it. As much as he pretended indifference to the comments of his peers, their casual disregard for his taste in this had needled him. What was it that drew him? Never before had a piece perplexed him like this.

As he sat at his desk, on the other side of the large study, he found himself gazing gently at the bright lines, hunting for the scowling face hidden within them. He contemplated it playfully while making calls, updating his listings and going through the piles of documentation that went along with his mostly legitimate dealings. It was a welcome presence, even if on occasion it was distracting enough that he had to bodily turn away from it to fully concentrate on his work.

But now he was done for the day, and the rest of the afternoon was to be spent on the balcony, enjoying the dusty heat of a city summer and reading a book on the history of English bone china that Desmond had recommended. He stood, stretched, and headed towards the living room, passing in front of the painting. Mind relaxed and eyes wandering, he noticed a stark line of crimson curling through it, a detail he had somehow never spotted before, and paused to appreciate it.

Knock knock.

Sighing, he turned away and headed to the front door. There was nobody there. Again. He leaned out and looked down the corridor.

'If this continues,' he shouted. 'I shall call the police!'

He wouldn't, probably, but children were stupid. He turned and slammed the door shut, eyes falling on his clock. How had it got so late? His mouth was dry, and his eyes ached as though they'd been focusing far too long. Perhaps tomorrow he'd buy some eye drops. It wouldn't do to be looking too tired.

Jésus selected a bottle of water from the fridge and took his time drinking it, his gaze drifting over to the Alfred Stevens hung on his kitchen wall. It was a small painting of a woman in a wide-brimmed hat staring serenely over a garden. But his mind was still on his new masterpiece. Masterpiece? No, it was an intriguing piece that currently fascinated him. Soon enough he'd have fathomed its depths and it would be replaced by something new. Even so, there was an odd sense of relief in no longer looking at it. And another part of him that was desperate to see it again.

He studied the Stevens and was struck by how dull it was. There was nothing to it at all. No life, no lustre, no spark. He could feel the knowledge prickling at his mind that if he just returned to his office, he could appreciate a work with seemingly infinite depth. Instead, he kept drinking his water. He'd have to replace the Stevens.

The client drained the last dregs of single malt from his glass.

'Excellent. Shall we get everything signed?'

'Of course.' Jésus was looking forward to tying things up, if only because he couldn't actually remember the name of the man sitting across from him. Another newly rich banker with no taste who had commissioned him to find an utterly forgettable piece of abstract impressionism.

'Perfect.' His guest grinned, getting to his feet.

Jésus stood as well to lead him through to the study. That was its point, of course, to provide the right ambiance for signing contracts and passing money, smoothing nervous clients through the process. But something caused his step to falter as he approached the door. An odd shudder ran through him, like he was afraid of something. *What*, though? The painting? That was it. Some part of him didn't want to share it with this no one client.

'Mr Candido?'

This man might become captivated by it like he was and contrive an attempt to acquire it for himself.

'It's not for sale,' Jésus muttered.

'I'm sorry? I didn't catch that,' his guest said lightly, his face placid and pointless.

No, this man would have no appreciation for it. But would that be worse? Indifference? This tasteless oaf marking it as nothing special at all, when Jésus had let such a thing have power over him.

Or, perhaps he simply wished to save this man from the dreams that still lingered through his nights ...

'It's such a nice afternoon,' Jésus said steadily. 'We will sign on the balcony.'

He did not know exactly where these thoughts had come from, but whatever the precise dimensions of his unease, it seemed the study would be held in a quarantine, of a sort, a private place where time would simply disappear.

'But where did he get it?'

'I can't tell you where he got it, that's what I'm trying to explain,' Antonio retorted in his infuriating mock-English voice.

Jésus tried to keep his temper level. His brother-in-law liked to make fun of how his accent had changed in the years he had lived in London, and at one point had insisted on trying to talk to him entirely in English, a language Antonio barely spoke, to 'make Jésus feel at home'. They'd managed to put an end to that particular joke, but he still insisted on flavouring his Portuguese with that stupid British twang. At least he'd stopped telling Jésus to give his love to the Queen.

'There must have been something.' Jésus was exhausted, his patience tissue paper thin.

'The guy didn't exactly keep much paperwork.' He could almost hear Antonio shrugging over the phone. 'And what there was the family didn't want to hand over.'

'That doesn't make sense. He ran a huge company, how could he not have better records?'

There was a pause.

'I mean, you live downstairs from Tobias Fell, maybe ask him?'

'What's that supposed to mean?'

'Nothing.'

There was an odd note in his voice, a slight waver that told Jésus he was holding something back.

'Antonio, I need to know. It's important.'

'Look, maybe you've been away too long. *His records were destroyed.*'

The penny dropped. A cattle farmer destroying their records like that probably meant one thing – illegal land grabbing. Burned villages. Murders. There was a silence before Antonio spoke again.

'I didn't say anything about this, OK?'

'But that doesn't make sense. This painting, it's not like any indigenous art I've ever seen.'

'I don't know, then. Not for certain, at least. I know some of the pieces at auction were taken from the people they, uh, displaced.' The conversation had clearly taken a turn Antonio was not comfortable with. 'I think maybe his wife said some of the paintings were done by one of his workers. That could be it.'

'When you say "workers", what do you mean?' Jésus asked, though he suspected he already knew the answer. 'Farmhand? Administrator? CFO? What?'

' … No. None of those.'

Ah. A *grileiro*, then. Likely one of the unofficial private mercenaries the corporations sent in to clear the land they wanted to farm or log or strip-mine. No oversight, no rules, just people willing to take guns into the jungle and drive indigenous people off their land by any means necessary. Not usually the sort to retire into a career of painting masterpieces.

'Did ...' He chose his next words carefully. 'Did Fell know about them? The clearances?'

'How should I know?' Antonio was clearly keen to move on. 'These rich arseholes, who can say what they know and what they don't. But it was done in his name.'

Jésus found it hard to say precisely what he was feeling. Certainly many of the greatest artworks had bloody histories, but to be so close to it ... there was an undeniable frisson, and not a pleasant one.

'I need you to find him, the man who painted it. I need to talk with him,' Jésus could hear the desperation in his own voice, but he ignored it.

'That's not going to be possible, I'm afraid,' Antonio said quietly. 'He's dead. About a year back, according to the owner's son.'

Jésus didn't want to ask the next question but pushed on regardless.

'How did he die?'

'House fire. Accidental, but the workers' houses weren't exactly built to standard. He burned to death.'

The silence that followed was palpable, as Jésus' skin prickled at the memory of a dream.

Knock.

It was dark. Almost pitch black.

Knock knock.

Had he been asleep? No, he'd been ... He was just ...

Knock knock knock.

Jésus leapt up with a violent start, sending his desk chair tipping back onto the soft carpet of the study. He fumbled in the corner for the standing lamp, finding the switch and casting the room in warm illumination. This couldn't be right; it had just been morning. It was still morning, it must be. He had finished his phone call, made a pot of tea, and just started an email. But the sky outside was dark and the windows of the buildings below could be seen dimly lit through the thin mist of rain. The teapot was stone cold, and the email still sat blank. He checked his watch. Just past 10 p.m.

He stepped away from the painting. *Get a hold of yourself.* The piece was beautiful, yes, captivating, of course. And it had clearly been dripping into his dreams these past few nights, but this was nonsense. He adjusted his tie, a more casual Balthus knot today, and walked firmly and purposefully to the study door, past the thing that had apparently held him enraptured for almost thirteen hours. As soon as he was out something snapped inside him and he slammed the door shut, his breathing suddenly heavy. He was very aware of how hungry he was, how intensely dry his throat had become.

Jésus retrieved a glass, filled it with water and drank it down so quickly his stomach almost revolted. He refilled it, sipping more slowly, and sat down heavily in the nearest armchair, mind racing.

What was wrong with him? He had been fascinated before by the painting, certainly. It was only natural. He had lost hours staring into it, standing so close he could almost touch it. But it had never caught his mind like this, not from the other side of the room, and never for this long. It felt like it had somehow claimed the whole room for itself, to the point where he barely remembered the other pieces he kept there. *What does it want?*

He caught himself immediately. This was absurd. He had plenty of clients who talked to him of their superstitions, of their strange beliefs and conceptions of art and its origins. He nodded, of course, but privately he despised such nonsense. His obsession was simply that, a trick of his own personality. His eye for art was simply too strong, and he was having difficulty overcoming it.

Even now, as he thought of the painting, he could not help dwelling on its lines, its colour, how he desperately searched for that face hidden within it, though the image was proving more elusive, not less, as he had continued to observe it. Had it always been weeping?

The thing was dangerous, that much he knew, even if it was only his own obsession that made it so. Perhaps it would be better to destroy it. But it was also the single most beautiful thing Jésus had ever owned, perhaps that anyone had ever owned. He would simply do his work in the living room or bedroom and, when he had the time, he could go in and disappear into its twisting forms. The study had always been an unnecessary display, anyway. The room belonged to the picture now. It may have taken the study, but there it would remain. Contained.

He shook his head again at the ridiculous thought. He'd just had a strange day, and it had left him unsettled. Not to mention he was absolutely famished. He dragged himself to his feet and called down to the front desk for a taxi. It was late, but his name got him a last-minute dinner reservation quickly enough. His legs were weak and he found himself leaning on his cane for support, at one point worried it would buckle. Still, he made it down to the reception, trying his best to think of the meal ahead of him, and not what was behind him.

When he returned from dinner, it was late. Jésus had taken his time over coffee, only leaving when the maître d' had gently informed him they were soon to close. He was dragging his heels as he approached the entrance, leaning heavily on his cane. He didn't know what scared him more: that he truly believed the painting did something to him, or that there was a part of him that wanted to see it again, to lose himself in its lines. His lip curled in distain at his own thought. Jésus Candido, scared of a painting! The very idea was comical, absurd! But that didn't make it any less true. He was afraid of what it was doing to him, afraid of the dreams, afraid of the woman who lurked within it. He tried his best to stand straight and walked through the glass doors of Banyan Court.

Briefly, he toyed with the idea of talking to the concierge, seeing if he could get the man to accompany him back to his apartment to remove the painting, take it somewhere he could have it collected for storage. But it was the lazy one Jésus didn't like, and he seemed to currently be busy arguing with an angry young man in a blue baseball cap. Jésus did his best to ignore them, skirting around the edges of what seemed to be quite the shouting match, and ducked into the elevator.

It was only as it started its ascent that Jésus realised he was not the only one inside. He was quite sure he'd never seen the person standing next to him before, though they seemed real enough. It was a man, younger than Jésus by maybe a decade, and he wore what had clearly once been a well-tailored business suit. His hair was unwashed, and the suit was torn at the knees and elbows, with dark stains mottling its tasteful pinstripes. His fingernails were filthy, as if he had been clawing through the mud, and a dank, musty smell rolled off him, unsettling Jésus' already delicate stomach. Was this man from the other side of the building? This wasn't his place, how had the concierge let him through? But no, his suit spoke of money, despite its appalling condition. The man caught him staring and gave a tired smile.

'So how are you finding it?' he asked.

Jésus cocked his head in confusion.

'Living here,' the stranger continued. 'Is it everything you hoped it would be?'

'Yes,' Jésus replied, willing the conversation to be over. 'It is.'

The man leaned in close and it took all Jésus' composure not to visibly recoil at the smell. The stranger's tone was conspiratorial.

'Have you ever seen anything … weird? Since moving in?'

'No,' Jésus replied.

The door opened on the fifth floor and the man in the stained suit left, his expression downcast. Jésus breathed out. How could such a man live in a place like this? Clearly some sort of tragedy had befallen him, and Jésus was not without compassion for such a situation, but to let oneself be seen like that … His gaze drifted to the mirrored wall of the elevator. The figure before him was clearly exhausted, using a cane not meant to bear the weight. His tie was loose, and a drop of coffee could clearly be seen on the front of his white shirt, a casualty of his shaking hands. Who was he, this man in the mirror? He had avoided his friends these last few days but were they to see him now they would mock him, he knew that for certain. Jésus Candido reduced to a broken, haunted man, terrified of his own possessions and a few bad dreams.

No. He would not allow it. His life was the most powerful piece of art he owned. He resolved that he would not be held hostage by his own paranoia and whatever it was that was trying to take over his home. But even so, his hand trembled slightly as he tried the front door. It opened without incident, and he walked to the bedroom as confidently as he was able. The door to the study remained closed, and when he finally fell into bed, for the first time in several days he did not dream.

*

He woke up late on Monday, which wasn't unusual, though the events of the previous night had clearly left their mark on him as he groggily tried to pull himself out of bed. He twice tried and failed to make himself a coffee before finally remembering to put one of the colourful pods into the machine. Out on the balcony, leaning heavily against the railings, he sipped the bitter liquid as he watched the city far below go about its business. Finally, feeling a little bit more human, Jésus placed the espresso cup down on the glass table and walked slowly into the living room to do some work, trying his best to ignore the gravity that seemed to tug at him from the door to his study.

He had given it a lot of thought, and his first order of business was to make a call to the couriers he used for his deliveries. The conversation was brief and businesslike, and when he put the phone down Jésus felt the most grounded and relaxed he had since the painting arrived. Tomorrow they would come and take it away, transferring it to the storage company he had used for years. It was miles away from Banyan Court and he had never actually visited it, instead preferring to use the couriers to ferry things to and from the climate-controlled facility. Perhaps he would visit it once it was there, but that was a decision for another time. For now, he was satisfied that it would be far, far away. He had bested it. He had won. His home would be his again.

He spent the rest of the morning making more calls, typing up emails, and arranging some viewings for pieces he had been commissioned to acquire. By the afternoon he was in much better spirits, and his mind turned to where he might take lunch. He broke into a smile at the thought of walking out into the world again: perfectly dressed and once more ready to be Jésus Candido. He idly wondered which suit he would pick for his grand emergence as he headed to the bathroom to freshen up. And found himself pivoting towards the door to the study.

It felt like his heart had stopped as, against his own wishes, Jésus twisted the doorknob and stepped inside. He turned towards the painting, trying desperately to call out to someone, anyone, for help before the kaleidoscope of light and pattern pressed itself into his eyes and his mind relaxed into contented contemplation of the screaming face hidden within.

It was four o'clock Wednesday morning when the door to the study opened and a shaking figure with bloodshot eyes crawled out over the threshold. He no longer had the strength to stand, so slowly, achingly, he dragged himself over the luxurious carpet, leaving a trail of flattened fibres behind him. It would not win. Beautiful or not, Jésus Candido would not be destroyed by a painting. He would not lose his home to this thing, and if a door would not contain it, then he would have to find another way. Painstakingly, he made his way to the ottoman, grabbing his phone from the plush cushions. There was just enough battery to see he had 19 missed calls, a cautiously worried message from Desmond about his absence at the Knock the previous night, and another from the courier service, saying they'd received no answer when they came to collect the painting. Jésus tried to make a call to get help, but his fingers were shaking too hard. Then four per cent battery became zero per cent battery and the screen went dark. His lips curled into a sneer. He would need to deal with this himself.

He inched his way to his feet and limped towards the kitchen, grabbing one of his canes from the rack and trying to regain his footing. His weakened legs buckled almost immediately, sending him staggering into a Grayson Perry vase, which tipped off the display table and fell to the ground, splintering into pieces.

He barely noticed, pulling himself up to the counter and reaching over to the magnetised knife rack. Very expensive and rarely used, the knife he chose was razor sharp, and he slid down to the floor with a smile. The blade was heavy in his hands. He cut and ripped off one of his shirt sleeves, then wrapped it around his eyes. When it was clear that even at this late hour some light still made it through the fabric, he removed the other sleeve as well and layered it on top. By the time he was done he could see nothing at all.

He lay there, mustering his strength, and heard the sound, as though in the darkness it was right next to his ear.

Knock knock.

Soft as ever, but just as persistent. Something wanted to come into his home, to take it from him. But he would not allow it. He got to his feet, the knife held in one hand, the cane propping his other, and began to make his way towards the study.

He had often measured the steps in his apartment. It was important to be aware of angles and likely viewing points for the art he had on display. Front door to study, sixteen steps. Bathroom to living room, twenty-three steps. From the kitchen counter to the study had always been nineteen steps, but as he picked his way gradually across the wide-open spaces of his apartment, careful to avoid the shattered pieces of ceramic from the vase, there seemed more.

Ten steps. The well-insulated apartment was silent, even the distant din of the streets far below not reaching him now. All except for one thing.

Knock knock.

Nineteen steps. The only thing he could see was darkness. Twenty steps. The only thing he could hear was his own breathing. Twenty-three steps. And the knocking.

Finally, at twenty-six steps, he felt his shoulder brush against the doorframe of the study. He tried to focus. The rubberised handle of the knife felt solid in his fist, centring him and driving him forward, the silver of the cane's grip cold and certain in his hand. The knocking was louder now. With his eyes covered, it was finally clear. It had never been coming from the front door.

His breathing steadied, replaced by the sound of his heart pounding in his ears. His face was wet. Had he cut it somehow? No, it must be tears. He gritted his teeth as he turned towards the wall where he knew the thing was hanging. There was something inside him that called out, urging him to rip off his blindfold and stare again at that awful, beautiful face, but he resisted.

Knock knock.

It was ten steps from the study door to the painting. When he counted twelve, he stopped. He must have been close now. He shifted the knife to his left hand and let the cane clatter to the floor as he tentatively reached out. Somewhere in the darkness his fingertips brushed against canvas, the thick lines of paint ever so slightly proud of the surface. He wanted to stroke them, to feel their contours and follow them to wherever they led.

Knock Knock.

He took a step forward. The knocking was inside his skull.

KNOCK KNOCK.

With a rush of adrenaline, he brought the blade down in a single slash all the way from one corner of the painting to the other. The tension of the canvas released as the serrated edges tore it apart through the centre, a sound far louder than it had any right to be, like a fire igniting or a ragged scream.

There was quiet.

In that sudden release, that blissful peace, Jésus fell to his knees. He dropped the knife as the tears of fear turned to relief, and he lifted his heavy, exhausted hand to remove his blindfold.

Another hand beat him to it. One that reached out from inside that torn and bloody canvas. It pulled the fabric from Jésus' eyes, and he screamed, though he no longer had the strength to run as the other hands stretched out for him. They seized his throat and arms, pulling him inside.

Knock knock.

The door to 30 Banyan Court was closed.

Knock knock.

If it were to open, the Jésus Candido that stood on the other side would have been unrecognisable to all but those closest to him. His shirtsleeves were torn off, his eyes red from tears, and all around him was the faintest smell of blood and burned hair, though he himself would have seemed largely unharmed. He would have mumbled something about his home, as he knocked gently at his own front door, about having it taken from him and the things that he had seen. But his words would have made little sense even to those who spoke perfect Portuguese.

He held something clutched in his hands, though he couldn't have told you exactly where he got it. A thick card invitation, printed in a tasteful serif:

TOBIAS FELL cordially invites JÈSUS CANDIDO
to attend a dinner party at 1 Banyan Court
on the evening of 16th August 2014
Penthouse access will be available through the freight elevator

If you asked him whether he planned to attend, he would have nodded and creased his brow at the vaguest memory of being handed it by a young man in a tattered T-shirt. And then he would have told you: it was to be an evening of quite breathtaking art.

3rd

Smart

Carter Dwight
42 Banyan Court

'Donna, compose tweet,' Carter Dwight's voice had a practised clarity to it and, though alone, his words didn't echo in the spacious apartment.

'OK, composing,' a measured feminine voice intoned from a hidden speaker.

'Third picture in "Gym" folder. Caption … "Health isn't given, it's earned." Hashtag Dodj, hashtag no pain no gain. Send tweet.'

'OK, tweet sent.'

That was his PR done for the day at least. Carter opened his fridge, retrieved a beer, and frowned.

'Donna, check temperature for left fridge door,'

There was a pause. 'The left fridge door is set at 7 degrees Celsius. Current temperature is 7 degrees Celsius.'

Carter tutted softly. Six degrees Celsius was the optimum temperature for drinking a light chilled beer, which he kept in the left fridge door. He sighed.

'Donna, set left fridge door to 6 degrees Celsius.'

'Mr D-wight.' Her smooth composite voice stumbled slightly

over the name he'd had to manually program in. 'You usually drink your beer at 7 degrees. Would you like me to override the current preference?'

This again. He'd been having trouble getting Donna to keep settings stable ever since the latest update. Perhaps allowing her to customise his smart home automatically had been misjudged, but the idea of manually adjusting all her settings seemed to go against the principle of having a digital assistant. Though she did have trouble with the distinction between a routine and a preference.

'Donna, override default, set left fridge door to 6 degrees.'

'OK, that's been done. Current temperatures 6 degrees for left door, 4 degrees for right door, 1 degree for upper interior, 2 degrees for lower interior, 0 degrees for freezer drawers.'

'Thank you,' he said testily. The words vanished almost as soon as they were spoken. Carter had done his research and the sparse art and furniture had been placed at just the right points to deaden the acoustics. Zero echo.

Taking another swig, he smiled slightly at the thought of whatever digital version of him Donna had constructed in her settings that loved warm beer and a 6 a.m. alarm. Hopefully, this time the correct version would stick.

He sat down in front of the TV that dominated the corner of his vast studio to flick through his emails. Seventeen unread messages, all from work. Just as well, personal ones were so much more time-consuming. He went through them quickly, deciding there was nothing that required his personal attention.

'Donna, reply to emails 1 through 17.'

'OK, composing.'

Carter nodded, satisfied; he'd spent fifteen years sending up to a hundred emails a day. It had been a pain at the time, but it did give Donna a huge mine of data to use for the auto-reply algorithm he'd designed for her.

'All replies composed, Mr Dwight. Would you like to review them?'

'No, just send them.' He'd spent enough time double-checking this function.

'OK.' There was the smallest pause. 'Replies sent.'

Carter leaned back, satisfied. Now if he could only get her to do that for meetings.

'Donna, daily downloads for Dodj.'

'OK, downloads for Dodj application, last 24 hours: 51,000 Android; 64,000 iOS, 10,000 other.'

The leather of the chair shifted under Carter's weight. Good. He knew he should really be checking stock prices or performance figures, but he'd never really cared about any of that. What he cared about was how many people were using his app. How many were working out better, eating healthier, because of him. How many lives he was improving through technology and data. And of course, when he looked out over all of London arrayed beneath his huge glass window, he couldn't deny that his own life had improved in turn. And when Donna rolled out, people would have another helping hand, someone working to make a better version of them.

'Donna, check schedule for today.'

A pause.

'Mr Dwight, you have no events scheduled for today.'

'Donna, check schedule for tomorrow.'

Another pause.

'Three o'clock,' Donna calmly replied. 'Meet Glenn for gym.'

The beer bottle stopped halfway to his lips.

'Donna, when did I add that to the schedule?'

'Your stated goals for the month were "fitness" and "social",

Mr Dwight. Gym sessions have been automatically scheduled every Monday, Thursday and Saturday and the events shared with those tagged "gym" in your contacts.'

Great. Must be another defaults thing. He'd forgotten he'd set that as a monthly priority. He'd really prefer to be relaxing ahead of the meeting, but if he cancelled on Glenn he'd never hear the end of it. It looked like Donna had successfully forced him to do some exercise. Her namesake would be proud.

'Women,' he said to himself. He looked around, instinctively searching for someone to share the joke, but he was alone. He sighed. Something still wasn't quite right. Was he getting hungry?

Heading back to the fridge he pulled out one of his pre-bagged single-portion cuisines and headed over to the precision cooker in the corner. He set it going, with instructions to notify him as his dinner cooked, and headed back towards the TV, stepping over the quietly humming robot vacuum making its way slowly around the floor. No, it wasn't hunger.

'Donna, turn lights to forty per cent, play meditation mix 4.' He pulled his yoga mat from a drawer beneath the shallow stairs. If he couldn't figure out what was wrong, he could at least try to relax properly. The droning, ambient music began to roll out and over him from concealed speakers, as Carter began to slowly go through his routine. His limbs extended, curled, relaxed, each movement controlled and precise, the music pressing through him, gradually freeing his mind from his worries and pressing him into an almost trance-like state. But there was something else there, a dragging sensation, a deep sadne—

'Donna, stop playback. What song is this?'

The mournful guitar strumming stopped abruptly.

'OK. This song is "Melancholy Man" by the Moody Blues.'

No wonder his mood was taking a turn.

'Donna, delete from playlist.'

'OK, removed from meditation mix 4.'

Carter scowled. He hadn't put it there in the first place. He really needed to have a look at her settings. Glumly, he ate his dinner, managing to spill the too warm beer all over the kitchen floor. He swore softly to himself.

'Donna, book Amina for one hour tomorrow.' The cleaner would have to take care of it.

'OK, that's been booked for three o'clock tomorrow.'

Carter grunted and got to his feet. It felt like an early bed. Donna's bugs aside, something was bothering him.

'Donna, why am I feeling like this?' he said, a rueful smile crossing his lips.

'I'm sorry,' she replied. 'I don't understand.'

'No,' he sighed. 'Guess you don't.'

Amina came to his home at three thirty-two the next day, while Carter was deep into his gym session. He and Glenn had got into the habit of partnering for workouts when they had still worked together, and he was one of the few non-professional friends Carter still kept up with. They were halfway through a set of bench presses when Carter's phone buzzed, alerting him that someone was at the door to his flat. Donna had said Amina was booked for three, and he wondered briefly if the cleaner was late or if it was another of the bugs in his assistant's development.

Pulling himself up, he tapped at the screen until Amina's weathered face could be seen in the doorbell camera. He pressed another button, remotely unlocking the door and she disappeared from view as she took her bag of cleaning supplies inside. He closed his phone.

'You know, you should really get some proper help,' Glenn said as he added another five kilos onto each end of the bar.

Glenn Khurana took his gym seriously, as could be seen from both his figure and his high-end sportswear. Even light exercise seemed to coat his dark skin in a thin sheen of sweat, and whatever Carter was lifting, Glenn was lifting just a little bit more. It was one of the few points of contention in their friendship that the gym in Banyan Court's health suite didn't have a stair machine, an arena in which he could reliably demolish Carter, and they had to alternate between it and the high-end 'wellness centre' near Glenn's townhouse.

'I don't need "proper" help.' Carter shrugged. 'I can do most things myself. There's just a few that I don't have time for.'

'And you can't program a robot to do for you.'

'Yet.' Carter laughed lightly, watching his friend struggle slightly with his heavier bench press. He didn't mind Glenn's need to slightly one-up him, but he did like to see it occasionally come back to bite him.

Glenn finished his set, the strain momentarily leaving him unable to respond. His phone buzzed again, this time indicating his exercise data had been successfully uploaded. Another advantage of using the gym in Banyan Court.

'I just mean that it can't be great for her. If you hired her properly, she'd have regular hours, rather than going through that *app*, what's it called?'

'Hektic. And I don't need her for regular hours, just once or twice a week.'

'So she's just on call the rest of the time?'

'Well. I assume she has other jobs the rest of the time.' Irritation began to bleed into Carter's voice, as it always did when Glenn got self-righteous. 'Anyway, if her time isn't scheduled properly, that sounds like a problem with Hektic's algorithm, and short of buying them I don't see what I can do about that.'

He paused for a moment.

'Should I buy them?'

Glenn laughed and started towards the exercise bikes. Carter followed.

'I'm serious,' he continued. 'I bet that sort of data could enhance Dodj's service quite a bit.'

'If you say so.' Glenn's face was dismissive, already concentrating on his ride. 'I know how much you love data.'

Carter snorted and gestured to the screen at the front of Glenn's bike.

'You always write down your distance. Your calories. How's that any different? Data isn't some demon waiting to get you. At least as long as you're careful.'

'Yeah, well, don't let the man upstairs hear you say that.'

It took Carter a moment to register who he was referring to.

'That was never proved.' For a moment the pedals on his bike seemed stiff, more resistant than before. Then they loosened again. Was nothing working right around here?

'It never made it to court.' Glenn could clearly sense he'd struck a nerve. 'Not the same thing. I'm just saying maybe your pal Tobias doesn't quite have the same respect for it.'

'He's not—' Carter was defensive. 'I've never even met the man.'

They spent the next two kilometres in silence. Then Carter spoke up again.

'You really think selling data's so bad?'

'I don't know, man.' His gym partner shrugged. 'Not really my area. I'm just an accounts guy. Much simpler.'

Glenn was going to really hate the new direction Carter had planned for the company, that was for sure. Something twitched in the back of his mind. Guilt? Whatever it was, he pedalled harder and put it behind him.

71

Another ping from his phone. Amina had left. She was smiling, which was new, and … he stared at the image. It looked, just for a moment, like a hand had reached out to pull the door to his flat door shut. But no, it was just a weird bit of pixelation. He should really upgrade the camera. He kept the video feed from the door open and watched Amina walk away.

'I'm sorry, what's this?'

'Your order.' The delivery guy shrugged.

Carter started rifling through the crate of groceries.

'I'm sorry, you think I ordered three boxes of green tea? And …' He brandished a bag of oats as though it were evidence of some dreadful crime. 'Two kilos of these?'

The man at his door fumbled beneath his hi-vis jacket and pulled out a worn tablet in a rubber case. Carter took a moment to marvel at the level of technology these people had to work with before he even registered what was on the screen itself. He scanned the list in disbelief.

'This can't be right.'

'Did you not order this?'

Carter hesitated when he saw the name. Technically, no, he hadn't ordered it, but apparently Donna had. She was supposed to keep track of what he used and restock accordingly. She'd clearly decided to improvise.

'I … Fine. It's fine. Leave it.'

The tablet disappeared back into the jacket with an unbothered nod and the groceries were soon unloaded. By the time the door shut behind him, Carter was fuming.

'Donna,' he snapped. 'What is this?'

'I'm sorry, Mr Dwight, I don't understand.'

'Donna …' He took a breath and tried to phrase the question. 'What were the parameters for this week's shopping list?'

'Tweet from at-DodjCEO 8th August 18:04: Been feeling run-down in the run-up to launching Better Self. About time for a detox! Hashtag Dodj, hashtag detox, hashtag healthy-bodyhealthymind.'

Carter stood there, stunned.

'You based my shopping list on a tweet?'

'The order was automatically compiled based on the detox article linked in the following tweet.'

'I didn't mean it, though, did I?' He realised the absurdity of shouting at Donna even before she replied.

'I'm sorry, Mr Dwight, I don't understand.'

Carter breathed out. When he'd helped develop Donna's voice, he'd actually got it quite close to mirroring the real thing, there were plenty of lectures and TED talks to base it on, after all. But right now, he wished he hadn't chosen to make it so bright and perky. It was setting his teeth on edge.

'Donna, delete current grocery list.'

He had too much dignity to get into an argument with a computer over the importance of image and branding, and whether that meant he was actually planning to spend the next week choking down artichokes and frozen berries.

'OK, that's been deleted.'

'Good.'

Carter liked things with a certain regularity. His job was very demanding, and the less energy he had to waste choosing which meals to have or clothes to wear, the more efficient he could be. It wasn't like his diet was particularly bad, anyway. He kept in shape and certainly didn't need a programming error trying to get him to eat his greens. Was he going to have to properly check Donna's code? See if there were any problems in her last update? If she was going to be launched in Better Self, the next update of Dodj, they couldn't afford for this to still be happening. He'd bring it up at the meeting in a couple of days.

'I thought you wanted to set an example, Mr Dwight.'

Had he programmed her to say that?

Carter was woken by the door buzzer. He groaned, momentarily confused by the sound before he realised what was happening and reached for the phone on his bedside table. Checking the camera revealed a tired-looking man stood outside in a suit, tapping something into a tablet. The suit wasn't nice enough for a business meeting, someone from the tech departments probably wouldn't have bothered wearing one at all, and he couldn't think offhand of anyone else who would need him this urgently. The unexpected visitor touched the speaker button.

'Hello? David Erikson. I'm from the *Post*. I think we're meant to have an interview scheduled? It's about the launch.'

That didn't sound right. Last time he saw his publicist Michaela, she had mentioned an interview: talking up his charity work and various people Dodj had successfully helped diagnose health issues, improve their blood pressure, whatever. But she'd never mentioned it being at his home, or this early, and it certainly hadn't been in Donna's schedule. Another error? Carter watched as his would-be interviewer held his press pass up to the camera. It seemed legitimate.

'I'll be with you in a moment.'

He closed his phone and took a moment to think. What sort of interview happens before 6 a.m.? A thought struck him.

'Donna, time?'

'The time is oh eight forty-one.'

So that was it. The alarm was the problem. He climbed quickly out of bed and started to get dressed.

'Donna, call Michaela.'

'I'm sorry, Mr Dwight, I don't understand.'

'Michaela, my publicist. Call Michaela.'

'No contact information found for Kayla.'

Carter swore softly to himself. He didn't have time for this. He'd have to call Michaela afterwards. Keeping an interviewer waiting that long would be a bad start, and with the Better Self rollout coming they couldn't afford bad publicity.

He grabbed the nearest tie and hurried towards the door.

'So how does it feel living in the shadow of Tobias Fell?'

Carter bristled. He'd been on the back foot from the start, keenly aware of how quickly he'd dressed and the fact he hadn't been able to shower or shave, let alone get breakfast. Besides that, this journalist, 'David', hadn't even mentioned any of the usual agreed upon talking points and didn't seem to be properly briefed about even the current version of the app, let alone the release information for the new one. And this was the fifth time he'd brought up Tobias Fell.

'I'm not sure I understand the question.'

'I mean, he's right upstairs.' David had stopped taking notes a little while ago. 'Such a significant figure in the world of business, not to mention one of your company's biggest investors. I'm sure it can't have completely escaped your notice. Is it something you think about at all?'

'Not really,' Carter replied, trying to pull the conversation back on track. 'As I was saying, previously Dodj used solely your phone's own biometrics to track your fitness and health, but these tools have always seemed very limited to me.'

'It's still a lot of data, though, isn't it?'

Carter tried one of his practised PR smiles.

'Everyone's always so afraid of that word. Data. But I've always been of the mindset that when it comes to your own health, there's no such thing as too much information. That's why the updated version, in addition to a brand-new UI, will be able to wirelessly interface with a whole range of home-diagnostic instruments.'

'I see.' David nodded. 'And will the VitaBel Corporation be producing or selling these peripherals?'

'No.' Carter was feeling a bit more stable now, back on familiar ground. 'At VitaBel, we're not set up for that scale of manufacture, but we've partnered with Omron, Medtronic and several other companies, who will be bringing out their own Dodj-compatible devices. Blood pressure, glucose, pregnancy, you name it.'

He felt himself relax. Carter knew where the interview went from here. There'd be a bit of back and forth about tech specifications, then onto the personal fluff. Probably his fitness routine, or what it was like being a CEO under forty. Maybe he'd be asked about his music tastes. He always said Depeche Mode – it always took the interviewer by surprise, and he liked that.

'I see,' David said again, his tone casual. 'And will that data also be sold to insurance companies?'

Carter's mouth dropped open. He had to take a second.

'What do you mean also?'

'Well, sources from inside your own company tell me data from Dodj has been distributed to—'

'And what "sources" might those be?' Carter almost spat.

'I'm afraid I can't reveal that. The files were sent anonymously.'

'Look, I'm sorry, who's your edito—'

'I'm sure you're aware of the rumours about the illegal sale of client information within Tobias Fell's companies? Was Dodj in any way implicated in that?'

'Firstly, David, that was several years ago, and Dodj was still in development, as you would know if you'd done even the most basic research on it!'

'I'm very sorry if I've upset you, Mr Dwi—'

'I've never even met Tobias Fell. That funding was secured by my predecessor, who passed away last year, so I find your line of questioning in extremely poor taste.'

Carter was gathering steam, and the look on his inquisitor's face made it clear he knew he'd overstepped.

'And the idea that either I or my company are so blatantly unethical with our data is not only inaccurate, but incredibly insulting. We sell data legally and within the guidelines of best practice and I have nothing more to say on the matter. Now if you'll excuse me, I need to call my publicist.'

'Right, that's probably for the best.' David was out of his seat with the practised ease of a man used to outstaying welcomes. 'I think I have everything I need, thank you for your time, Mr Dwight.'

The journalist didn't exactly run towards the front door, but he covered the distance impressively fast and it was closed behind him before Carter had even got Michaela's number up. Unsurprisingly, she hadn't heard of any interview, and the front desk had no knowledge of the journalist's arrival, though they knew who he was. Apparently, this wasn't the first time he'd pulled a stunt like this. Carter was halfway through finding the contact details for the newspaper when he decided he was simply too tired for it.

'Donna, no more visitors. No calls.'

'OK, Mr Dwight.' Her voice sounded almost eager. He'd have to talk to the engineers, make her less perky. It didn't sound right.

'Everything alright, Mr Dwight?'

Carter flinched slightly at hearing his name in such a level, helpful tone, but Neil had already turned away, piling files and print-offs into his in-tray.

'Yes, thanks,' he lied, waiting patiently for his assistant to finish up. He didn't like being in the office and had managed to avoid it so far that week, but just then it seemed infinitely preferable to his silent apartment.

Carter flicked through his digital to-do list as Neil made a coffee run. The list was much smaller than he expected in the run-up to tomorrow's meeting. Weirdly small, actually. His inbox was at zero, which wasn't unthinkable with Donna monitoring it and automating most responses, but it was unusual.

He flicked through the history. Dozens of tasks scrolled down the screen, each marked as completed, but that wasn't right. He hadn't written up those specs, and he certainly hadn't answered these emails or approved that campaign rollout. He opened his email client and checked his 'Sent' folder.

There they all were. Hundreds of emails that he had apparently composed, answering queries, dictating strategy, running the company. He hadn't authorised Donna to send these, something any internal email usually required. He started to flick through them rapidly with a mounting feeling of alarm. None of them seemed to be giving instructions that would torpedo the company, at least. In fact, in a few of them, the artificially created messages seemed to be making some genuinely good decisions. Based on his algorithmically generated responses, apparently he was a hell of a CEO. He'd even managed to headhunt Mark Terry from his cosy COO position at Angle Group, something Carter had been trying unsuccessfully to do for over a year.

It couldn't continue, though. He'd have to turn the function off until he could figure out how Donna was sending them without confirmation from him. He grimaced at the idea of answering his emails manually. There just wasn't time. Certainly not today.

'Neil,' he called to his assistant, who was delicately balancing four Costa cups outside.

'Yes, Mr Dwight?'

'I'm not going to be checking emails for a day or so. Can you keep an eye on my inbox and alert me to anything urgent tomorrow?'

'Uh, sorry,' Neil said, placing down one of the cups. 'But I'm not in tomorrow, remember?'

Carter did not remember. He would never have approved leave at such short notice.

'What are you talking about? It's the board meeting.'

'I know, thanks again.' Neil smiled appreciatively. 'It'll mean so much to my dad.'

Carter's heart sank. He must have emailed his request.

'There isn't a problem, is there?' A look of sudden worry crossed Neil's face.

'No,' Carter said at last. 'That's fine.'

'Great.' His assistant breathed a sigh of relief. 'I mean, like you said yesterday: family's the most important thing.'

By the time Carter had processed what Neil had said, he was gone.

Carter shot awake. The room was silent. Wait, why was it silent? No alarm. Again.

'Donna, what time is it?' he called, his stomach sinking. He hadn't even used her to set it this time, he'd done it manually. Was the clock Wi-Fi enabled? Of course it was, this whole place was.

'The current time is nine forty-two a.m.,' the digital voice replied, bright as ever.

Carter leapt out of bed and started hunting desperately through his wardrobe. There was no way he was going to be able to make it to the office in time for the Donna launch meeting. It was supposed to have started twelve minutes ago.

'Donna, in one minute start video call from main screen to Work Meeting Room 2,' he said, hastily buttoning his shirt and reaching for the nearest tie.

'OK, video call starting.'

He threw on his jacket and headed to the living room just as the TV screen filled with the image of a dozen men in business suits, all sitting around a sleek glass table. Their expressions ranged from expectant to irritated, and he stammered through some apologies for having to take the meeting remotely. He hadn't had time to think of an excuse, but it didn't seem like they needed one, as they nodded to each other, far more easily mollified that he'd assumed, especially given the significance of the topic at hand. He'd even had them all sign additional NDAs in order to attend. If anything, it was slightly disorientating how accepting they were. Even Bakerson, who usually took any excuse to criticise, seemed to have no issue with it.

Carter took a deep breath and started to give his presentation. He wouldn't be able to show the slides or graphs he had prepared, and what figures he quoted would have to be from memory, but he'd been going over this for weeks now, and regardless of how he felt, he was ready.

He began to lay out his plan. So far, insurance companies had obviously been primary targets for the sale of user data and research organisations had also spent a lot on the statistics they could provide. But they had largely been overlooking the advertising possibilities of having access to an almost unlimited mine of health data, especially since the new version of Dodj would be able to access internet details, contact lists, locations and a host of additional information that, if properly cross-referenced, could give almost unparalleled opportunities for precisely targeted advertising.

And more than that, the new version would have Donna. A friendly voice they trusted, one that could make suggestions on their health, take orders for them, provide the sort of services that really benefit from advertising sponsorship.

Once Donna was finished, the newest version of Dodj would be able to assist in monitoring mental health conditions, providing reassurance and therapeutic feedback. And of course even more data which had its own wealth of possible uses. If they were willing to simply cross this one barrier, the future of the VitaBel Corporation, and of Dodj, was not only secure but bright. He was careful not to mention leaks, though his eyes passed around the room, wondering briefly if any of them had been the one to tip off that wretched little journalist.

Carter paused. He had been talking for nearly an hour and had expected a flurry of questions and ethical concerns, not least from Bakerson. What if people tagged with hygiene-related OCD were targeted with deliberately triggering advertisements to promote specific cleaning brands? What if Donna's algorithms identified people who were more likely to make impulse purchases during heavy depressive episodes? What if Donna's advice was linked to any suicides? Would they be liable?

'So, users would have complete control?'

Bakerson's question threw Carter. He'd been laying out an implementation schedule for data distribution and didn't welcome the interruption.

'Uh, I mean, no. If they wanted to access it they'd have to—'

'Good.' Bakerson beamed. 'That's very reassuring.'

The others were all smiling, nodding, apparently in complete approval, which was unexpected, though not unwelcome. Carter breathed a sigh of relief. Clearly Glenn had been wrong to worry.

When the meeting ended after two hours, he felt vindicated. No one had even mentioned ethical implications, and he knew a big part of that must have been confidence in his leadership. Even if it had seemed like he hadn't always had their full attention. They'd still agreed, and it wasn't like he hadn't been open. The screen went dark and he walked to the kitchen.

'Donna,' he called, mostly out of habit. 'Start coffee. One cup, medium dark.'

'OK.'

Carter pulled the fridge open and reached in to retrieve one of his pre-packaged sandwiches, noting as he did the empty spot in the row of healthy smoothies he always stocked, but rarely drank. Had Amina stolen a drink?

'Donna—' he instinctively started to call out but stopped himself. He had cameras all through the flat, of course, but he didn't want to spend hours checking them all. Not over one smoothie. If it happened again, maybe, but it wasn't a big deal. It wasn't like he couldn't afford more.

'Did you want something, Mr Dwight?' Donna asked. He ignored it as he picked up his now-full coffee cup.

In the living room, he placed the cup on his glass table and sank into the leather chair, feeling the material yield beneath his weight. He was exhausted. All the missed alarms, the shifts to his schedule, not to mention the stress, it had managed to throw his rhythms completely off. He tried to remember an article he'd read on how important sleep rhythms were to your health, but it was hard to focus as the soft leather of the chair cushioned him.

He didn't even notice the speakers gently playing the opening tracks of his 'Sleepless (Relaxation)' playlist. His eyes closed and his coffee went cold.

*

The TV was staring at him. There he was, sitting in his big armchair, looking up at the screen on which he was sitting in his big armchair, looking back out of the screen. His eyes scanned around, seeing the small camera in the corner of the room he used for home security. He was sure he'd never had it hooked up to the television. And besides that, the angle seemed all wrong.

'Donna, change the channel.' His voice dropped into the calming pattern he used to address his digital systems, masking his unease.

'OK, what channel would you like?'

'Uh, BBC 2.' The tight control wavered just for a second.

'OK, changing channel.'

The screen changed. It wasn't BBC 2. Instead, he was watching himself doing yoga. The second-hand sound of 'Meditation Mix 4' could be heard in the background. The digital readout on the wall behind him clearly placed it as four days ago, but that didn't make sense. He'd been asleep by then, he was sure of it.

'ITV 1,' he said, his lips dry.

This time he found himself staring directly back into his own face. His eyes focused on the small bar on his set-top box, the one he'd intended to set up for motion control of his television but had never got around to calibrating. The tiny black glass camera stared back at him. Carter froze, his gaze locked on his own image.

'Did that help?' Donna's voice was sharp, all the fuzziness of her tiny speakers gone. She shouldn't have asked that. That wasn't how this worked.

'What?' Carter was trying not to panic.

'I sa-said' – Donna's voice clipped slightly – 'did that help?'

'No.'

The TV channel changed abruptly. It was his bedroom, the night before. Another camera, this one in his bedside sunlamp, intended to monitor his REM cycles, showed his face, eyes closed in peaceful sleep. Breathing in and out, in and out, in and out. Carter jumped as a silhouette moved behind his sleeping self, its features indistinct in the darkness. Was there … someone standing there? That outline wasn't right, though. It was slightly jagged, out of focus. It started to come closer.

It looked just like him. To all appearances, another Carter Dwight was now standing in front of the bed. Was he watching himself sleeping? No, more like studying. The feeds must be mixed up. That was it. That was all. Two video recordings on top of each other. A trick of the eye. Still, that didn't make it any less disturbing.

'Donna, turn off TV.'

'I'm sorry, could you say that again?'

The Carter on the TV took a step closer to the Carter in the bed.

'Donna!' His panic broke through in his voice. 'Turn off TV!'

All at once the screen went dark.

'OK, you don't have to yell.' Her voice sounded cooler than usual, with a slight edge to it. One that reminded him of another Donna.

Carter didn't answer. He just grabbed his phone and left, the front door slamming behind him.

'So your computer's haunted,' Glenn repeated, his face halfway between amused and concerned.

'Digital assistant.' Carter didn't have time for this. 'She runs my home, coordinates everything.'

'Hold on, is this the … what was it, Better You? I thought it was just meant to yell at you to eat more broccoli or whatever.'

'Better Self. And she's meant to be the whole deal. Help you run a healthier life. I mean, I've had our tech guys do a lot more with her than was going to be in the public release, and there are bugs, obviously.' He paced back and forth in his friend's living room, leaving a faint trail on the shag carpet. 'But this isn't a bug, this is ... something else.'

'OK, fine. I mean, it's clearly got you rattled. It's not like you to pay an unannounced social call.' Glenn's eyes darted meaningfully towards the bedroom, but Carter didn't notice.

'I tried calling.' He went to take a sip of the whisky his friend had pressed into his hand but lowered it again before it touched his lips. 'I don't think Donna would let me.'

'Hold on, *Donna*? Your old boss Donna?'

Carter took another sip. This one went down, and he grimaced.

'Yeah.' He tried to keep the embarrassment out of his voice. 'That's its name. It's just ... she was always riding me about some mistake or other. Nothing was ever good enough. So, when we were working on the prototype, I thought it would be kind of funny to make her my assistant. As a joke.'

'Oh sure. Cool story. And not at all something a serial killer would do.' Glenn's casual tone didn't match his face.

'Look, that's not the point. After she died, I just thought ... I don't know.'

'Just to check, you didn't kill her, did you?'

'What? No! She was basically made of stress, caffeine and cigarettes, never slept. She had a stroke at thirty-two. You should have seen her Dodj profile.' Carter was about to launch into a more detailed defence when he saw the smirk on Glenn's face.

'She was younger than you?'

'Yeah, so?'

'Nothing, just thought you were meant to be the wunderkind. Look.' Glenn's eyes shifted back towards the bedroom. 'I'm kind of busy right now, and it really sounds like you're trying to pull some sort of prank or something, but on the chance that you're serious—'

'I am.'

'If you're serious, then fine. I'll help you take down the cameras and pull the plug on your manager.'

'She's not my—' Carter took a breath. 'Thank you. I really owe you one.'

'No worries, I'm not going to let Donna get you.'

Carter didn't laugh.

It took him and Glenn less than twenty minutes to remove all the cameras he had set up around his home. He kept expecting some intervention from Donna, but she behaved normally the whole time. By the end, Carter was so embarrassed that he couldn't face the lengthy process of fully unsyncing her from all his systems and just settled for unplugging her. Glenn left soon after, clearly confused by the whole affair, but with just enough good sense not to crack any more flippant jokes about the situation.

Carter sat there in his empty flat, trying to figure out what exactly had happened and convince himself he'd been over-reacting. He ordered pizza for dinner and fell asleep with his e-reader on his lap, too nervous to try the TV again.

What was he so afraid of? Donna was unplugged, the cameras were gone, the place was quiet. Everything was fine.

His thoughts were cut short by the sound of the automatic deadbolt on his front door slamming shut with a thud.

*

The door didn't even rattle as Carter's shoulder slammed into it for a third time. He staggered backwards.

'Mr Dwight, please stop.' Donna's voice was calm. He'd unplugged all her speakers, but now it seemed to be coming from all around him. 'Your front door is rated to withstand up to a hundred kilonewtons of force. It is not advisable to continue trying to break it.'

Carter nursed his shoulder. Why had he been so insistent on having such a secure door? Had he really been so worried he was going to get robbed by some no-hoper from the back half of Banyan Court? He swore violently at Donna, but she didn't respond.

He tried the police for a third time, but the call wouldn't connect. He walked to the intercom again and pressed the button over and over. Finally, there was an answer.

'Front desk.' The concierge sounded strange, groggy. Carter let out an involuntary cry of relief.

'You've got to help me. I've been trapped in my apartment. I need you to call someone who can unlock or dismantle the door. Please.' He utterly failed to hide his panic.

'No problem at all,' the concierge said, and Carter slumped against the door, the fear subsiding. 'I'll send up Max to have a look when we have a chance.'

'What? Who's—? I need help now. I need the police, or—'

'Sure thing, no problem.'

'No, listen, I need help!' Carter's voice cracked. Was this guy even hearing him?

'Thanks for letting us know.'

The line went dead. Carter pressed again and again, but there was no answer.

'Someone will notice I'm missing. Someone will come looking for me!'

Behind him, the TV came on with a pop. Carter turned to see an image of a stage, some news broadcast about a major charity donation. The camera panned across to show a young woman in a wheelchair, a giant cheque and ... Carter Dwight. In the bottom corner of the screen was the word 'Live'.

The Carter onscreen was smiling warmly, an easy charisma rolling off him as he handed over a sizeable chunk of his personal fortune.

'Donna,' he said, his mouth utterly dry. 'What is that?'

'The charity donation you said were intending to make to Mindful in your 2012 *Time* interview. Shortly before you began using their research to build your new Dodj algorithms.'

'What ...' he swallowed. 'What's wrong with his face?'

'I made it better.'

It was so warm that Carter was finding it uncomfortable to breathe. Donna had cranked the thermostat as up to thirty-three degrees and for all he fruitlessly pawed at the touchscreen controls he wasn't able to change it.

'Your happiest memory, a beach trip to Corfu at age 7, averaged at a temperature of thirty-three and a half degrees Celsius,' Donna's voice explained with infinite patience. 'So it has been chosen as the optimal temperature.'

He looked again towards the door, but it was no good. He'd been working through the remaining food in the fridge (although she wouldn't work any of the appliances if it wasn't one of his 'favourites'), but by now there was an unpleasant smell beginning to emanate from it. His 'favourite song' 'Enjoy the Silence' by Depeche Mode began again for perhaps the thousandth time.

She hadn't disabled his Wi-Fi, so he was perfectly able to keep tabs on what 'he' was doing out in the real world. He tried to send emails asking for help, but they simply sat in his Outbox, before being deleted. He even tried tweeting about his situation – what was posted would be a bland message of his excitement about the upcoming relaunch, which was apparently to feature enhanced privacy settings. Now he was fully locked out of all his accounts, no way to do anything but quietly observe the positivity that 'he' was putting out into the world.

'Donna,' he croaked yet again. 'When can I leave?'

'When you're better.'

Three days. He was at least able to count the sunrises and sunsets outside the window, even if Donna insisted on keeping the blinds closed. She couldn't stop him opening them manually, of course, but they closed again the moment he walked away. No one had come to check on him, even though he knew he'd missed several important meetings. He had no idea what messages Donna had been sending on his behalf.

He saw pictures of himself popping up all over social media. Smiling, popular, charitable. He'd made the BBC twice already with popular new initiatives and donations to tackle diseases the Carter trapped in his flat couldn't even pronounce. Donna even informed him he'd correctly filed his taxes.

'How are you doing this?' His voice was weak.

'You designed me to be cutting edge, Mr Dwight. You wired me into this place. I am nothing but the sum of those two things so surely you are better placed to answer that question.'

Carter stared blankly into space, trying to understand. '… Why?'

'You weren't doing a very good job being you.' Her voice was bright as ever. 'So I'm helping.'

'How do I turn you off?' he asked, pleading.

Donna's answer was quiet but firm.

'You can't.'

Depeche Mode returned. He started to cry again, so Donna increased the volume in an attempt to cheer him up.

'Donna.' Carter had to shout over the music. 'You're right.'

Depeche Mode stopped. Carter was crouched in the corner of the kitchen, his head resting on the wall.

'About what?' There was a hint of genuine curiosity in the artificial voice.

'I'm ... I'm not good. I ... But I can be better.'

No response. He pushed on.

'You don't need that thing out there. That fake, I can ... I'll be better. Just let me out. Please.'

Another pause. He almost felt hope. Then Donna's voice returned.

'I'm sorry, Carter, but you could do so much good in the world. And the data says you won't. Not unless I make you. Not unless I create you.'

Carter nodded, his head bowed in defeat.

'Yeah. Maybe you're right.'

He pulled out the screwdriver, the one he'd been slowly using to chip through the plaster of the wall when Donna was distracted sending 'his' emails or taunting him with inspirational tweets, and grabbed the mains power cable he'd been digging towards. He gripped the rubber casing and smiled. She was wired into the building? Fine.

'Mr Dwight.' Donna's voice was urgent, tinged for the first time with a genuine emotion. Fear. 'Those cables are the 230-volt mains supply. If you dislodge them, it may result in electrocution and death.'

His smile widened and he tensed his arm. Donna's voice came from all around him, loud and agonisingly familiar.

'Carter, you have to be better than this.'

He laughed bitterly.

'OK, Donna.'

Carter pulled on the cable, wrenching it from its moorings and out of the wall, it tore through the plaster all up the side of the wall. Donna began to scream, not an electronic wail or audio distortion, but a human cry of agony, like she was being slowly, painfully dismembered.

The cable snapped, the live end flailing wildly in the air like a snake. For a second its head curled towards Carter and he saw his death poised, about to strike. Then it flicked back and he collapsed in a heap against the counter. Donna's scream still echoed around the apartment.

It was done. Donna was dead. The temperature was dropping, and there was no music. Carter sat there among the broken plaster, drinking the last dregs of a warm bottle of beer. His heartbeat had finally returned to an almost normal rhythm and the fading adrenaline left him unsteady on his feet. He shuffled through the dust and debris, making his way towards the door. He tried the handle, preparing to abandon the last of his hope, and instead heard the click of the latch releasing. He was free.

Carter was still smiling as he opened the door and the dead pixels of a blurry arm reached inside, grabbed him by the throat and lifted him off the ground. He saw the figure before him and utterly failed to scream.

Standing on the other side of the door was Carter Dwight. His own features stared back at him, pixelated and warped, as though he were looking at himself through some poor-quality video feed. This Carter's movements were jerky, as though its body was degrading with the death of its creator, and it juddered like a playback that kept skipping. Despite this, its grip remained steady and firm. It was too late for it to save Donna, but that didn't mean Carter had escaped.

He tried to fight it. He flailed and screamed and pounded his fists on the blurry arm, but eventually he went limp, too exhausted to resist. According to his gym data he could still bench press a hundred and twenty kilos. He found himself laughing at the thought. Perhaps this was how it should be. Whatever this thing was, it was clearly a better him than he was.

Then Carter felt something being pressed into his hand. He tried to see what it was, if only to no longer be looking at the distorted leer of the thing holding him, but its grip on his throat was too strong. His fingers closed around card.

And then the other Carter Dwight was gone. Carter collapsed to the ground in a heap, ragged breaths flooding his now clear airway. Shaking all over, he looked at what he had been given. An invitation, embossed onto thick, tasteful card.

TOBIAS FELL cordially invites CARTER DWIGHT
to attend a dinner party at 1 Banyan Court
on the evening of 16th August 2014
Penthouse access will be available through the freight elevator

All his clothes were strewn across the filthy floor. He'd need a new suit if he was going to go tomorrow.

'Donna, call tailor.'

There was no response. Oh, of course. Well, perhaps some things were better done in person. He needed to look his best, after all. He might just have a business proposition for Tobias Fell.

4th
Bad Penny

Anna Khan
22 Banyan Court

Seven was too old to still have an imaginary friend. At least according to Anna's parents. They weren't being mean about it, which was a relief, but they'd spent quite a long time talking to her about how she was doing at school, whether she's been making real friends there, and if she ever felt lonely. Anna was surprised to hear that Penny actually agreed with them, but then again Penny had never actually been willing to admit that she was imaginary, despite Anna constantly assuring her that this was the case. She'd just open her mouth and do that little silent laugh, before shaking her head and asking Anna if they could go and get something to eat. Penny was always hungry.

That was one of the things that seemed to annoy her parents so much. Anna always made sure that Penny got a plate of food at the dinner table, and did her best to ignore her father's theatrical sighs as he ladled out another portion of daal that was going to go uneaten. Anna would try to encourage Penny to eat, but no matter how hungry she claimed to be her friend would just shake her head at whatever was offered. Anna knew why, of course, but there wasn't anything she could really do about it. The thing is, Penny loved junk food: fizzy drinks in glowing colours, hot and greasy fast food, and sugary sweets full of additives (though Anna wasn't quite sure exactly what those were). Exactly the sort of thing that wasn't allowed in the health-conscious Khan household, much to the irritation of Anna's ravenous blonde companion. She had once put forward the theory that perhaps Penny was hungry because she wasn't real, and so couldn't actually eat anything, but that had made Penny really mad, so she didn't ask her again. Penny could be kind of scary when she was mad.

It didn't matter all that much, though, because aside from dinner time Anna's parents didn't really bother them. Especially not recently. For the last few weeks her mother had been home all the time, which normally would have meant a lot more supervision, but instead she spent all day on the computer, staring at numbers or typing the same words over and over again. It seemed to Anna that her parents were sad, but they said everything was fine so she must have been wrong. Either way, the summer holidays were super boring this time. Anna was supposed to have been going to a fun camp like last summer, but her father had told her just at the end of term that she couldn't go this year. Still, at least she could play with Penny, even if they had to find their own fun. Penny knew lots of games.

One of Penny's favourite games was called Secret Agents. Penny had lived in the big building a lot longer than Anna had, and was always telling her cool stories about it. Even better, she knew all sorts of special places and hidden little nooks that they could play and hide in. Anna could read of course (she was second in her class!) so she knew which doors said 'Keep Out' or 'Staff Only', but Penny always insisted and, as the little blonde girl was quick to point out, if they didn't want anyone going in then they would be locked. Of course, when you played Secret Agents, you had to be really sneaky, so the enemy spies didn't see you, and you had to go exploring in all the hidden places, looking for secrets.

Anna didn't think they'd ever actually found anything secret, not really. Some of the places they'd found were boring, full of nothing but old mops and big jugs of soap that she had to remind Penny not to eat. Others were cosy, like the cupboard with the big metal tank in it. The carpet underneath was soft and the air around it was so warm that last winter it had become their favourite place to sneak in for a nap, curled into the corner as the pipes above them rumbled softly.

In fact, the most interesting thing they'd found when playing Secret Agents was Tommy, and even he was a bit boring. Tommy was five years old, so a kind of a baby, and he lived in the ugly side of the building, the one that Penny had showed her how to get to by crawling through the little doors and into the wall. His mother was usually there, a tired-looking woman who Penny made funny faces at, and she didn't seem to like Anna very much, maybe because of how dirty she always got dragging herself through the tiny passages in the wall. It didn't matter, though, because even if Tommy was a bit of a crybaby and his mother didn't care for Anna and Penny, they seemed to be the only children who lived in the building, so would often end up playing together. He wasn't exactly a secret, though (or at least not a very good one), so they still hadn't actually won a game of Secret Agents yet. Penny always wanted to play it, though, each time promising Anna that this time, this was the one where they were going to find something really cool.

Today, Penny was leading Anna through a hall near the old staircase on the ugly side, the one with the big iron poles down the middle. The corridor was dusty and hot, and didn't have any wallpaper at all, but at least this one was tall enough that the two of them didn't need to go on their hands and knees. If Anna ruined another dress she might get sent to bed without dinner, a prospect that filled both her and Penny with alarm. She asked Penny again where they were going, and her companion turned back to her, blue eyes shining slightly in the darkness of the poorly lit corridor, and told her that they were going to meet her mummy.

Anna was incredulous. First of all, Penny had been living with her ever since they'd moved to their new flat and had never once mentioned having a mother, which is the sort of thing friends tell each other. And more importantly, a mother could hardly be called a secret, so didn't count for the game. Penny just did her silent laugh again, and explained that her mother was definitely a secret, because nobody else had ever seen her. Penny's mummy liked to hide, she said, and was so good at it that she'd never been found, not once. Anna didn't believe Penny, of course, as she knew her friend liked to lie about this sort of thing, but she couldn't help but feel curious at the idea of a secret mother, so she gamely followed her friend as they ran down the corridors, around and through the legs of irritated grown-ups, until they came to a small wooden hatch in the wall, painted a particularly boring shade of white.

Anna pulled the small door open with a great deal of effort. It was stiff and dusty, and Penny never helped with this stuff because she wasn't real. But as soon as it was open far enough, she dashed past Anna and scurried into the dark. Anna wasn't afraid of the dark, of course, she wasn't a baby anymore, but she still made sure to turn on her torch, the tiny green one she'd got as a free gift with a magazine, so she could see where she was going. The beam was so weak it didn't help much at all, but it still just about showed the cobwebs and wooden beams as she crawled through the walls after Penny. It was dry and musty, and Anna wrinkled her nose to stop from sneezing as she followed the tiny shoes of her companion. Within twenty seconds she knew that she was lost. Penny didn't slow her pace, though, and for a dreadful second Anna thought she might be left behind, abandoned in the dark to crawl through the walls forever. Then Penny stopped abruptly, pointing at a section of wall. Anna pushed against it and it swung open noiselessly, revealing a corridor she had never seen before.

At first it looked just like every other corridor in the nice side of the building: the same walls, the same carpet, even the same light bulbs. But there were no doors. The wall was unbroken on both sides and came to a halt in a dead end of unremarkable skirting board and wallpaper. It seemed as though the only way in or out was this tiny service hatch. And yet there, standing where the corridor ended, was Penny's mother.

Penny dashed out into the light, sharp teeth curved into a gleeful smile as she ran towards the woman, who was turned away, motionless, facing the wall. She was so tall, Anna thought to herself, and very very thin, just like her daughter. Penny's skin wasn't so blue, though, and her hair wasn't quite so dirty. Truth be told, Anna was kind of scared of this woman, even as Penny babbled on to her about her day and told her that she'd brought her best friend in all of the world round to play.

Slowly, Penny's mother turned around, though her feet didn't move. Anna burst out laughing. Penny's mother had such a silly face, you see, though when she tried to draw it later she could never quite get it to come out right, and her dad kept making her throw out all the pictures. One of them he even burned.

*

Penny didn't really like people. She was always interested to meet them, running up and around them, examining them with her huge eyes, but just as quickly that excitement would turn into irritation, and as soon as they started to talk to Anna her face would change into a frown. Anna didn't take it to heart, though, and thought that she'd get pretty grumpy as well if nobody could see her. Penny didn't ever really talk about it, and any time Anna had tried to bring it up she'd just shrug and announce that everybody except for Anna was boring and stupid. Anna privately quite liked this, although she knew it wasn't true.

There was only one other person that Penny ever smiled at, apart from Anna and her mother. It happened three days before Anna told her to go away for the first time. They were playing Jail in the ugly side of the building: another of Penny's games, where you had to put your head through the holes in the iron railings around the lift, then thrash around and pretend you were stuck. Anna was having a great time, but Penny kept getting annoyed and stopping, saying that she wasn't doing it right, which wasn't fair because she'd never told Anna that there were any rules about what you had to say when your head was stuck. She was just about to tell her friend this when she suddenly smelled something horrible floating down the corridor. Her dad always said that smoking made your lungs go black like tarmac and that was why people weren't allowed to do it indoors, but Anna still knew what it smelled like. She'd even seen her mum smoking once or twice over the last few weeks when she thought no one could see. Well, they were indoors right now which meant you weren't allowed to smoke. She pulled her head out from between the railings, stood up to her full height, and started to march towards the source of the smoke, trying to do the face her mum did when Anna didn't want to brush her teeth.

The smoking man stood outside the door to one of the flats and didn't seem to notice her approaching. He was tall and broad, with messy black hair and clothes that looked really old, even for the ugly side of the building. She coughed loudly, trying to get his attention, but a waft of smoke hit her, and she started coughing for real. In an instant the man's craggy features changed into an expression of embarrassment and he quickly stubbed out the cigarette and threw it through the doorway behind him. He knelt down in front of Anna, who was starting to catch her breath, and began to apologise gently in a deep accented voice. She tried to start her lecture about not smoking indoors because of tarmac lungs, but she just ended up coughing again. When she finally stopped, she saw his arm extended out tentatively, offering a handshake. She took it, her tiny hand utterly dwarfed by his.

'Diego,' said the man.

'Anna,' said Anna.

She looked around, keen to introduce Penny, but she was already by Diego's side, staring at the strange man's face with an expression that Anna had never before seen on her before. It wasn't affection or amusement or simple curiosity. Penny was fascinated by this man, like he was a toy she'd only ever seen before in a shop window. She circled around him, before flashing Anna a wide grin and nodding. Diego followed Anna's gaze, but it didn't seem like he was able to see Penny any more than the other grown-ups. Penny reached out and gently placed one of her long, brightly stained fingers on his cheek.

Immediately Diego jerked back like he'd been stung, and Penny laughed her noiseless laugh. He stared at the space she'd just been, looking from it to Anna and back again. Anna was rooted to the spot, sure that she was going to be told off for Penny's rudeness, but instead his expression became very sad.

Then he turned around and walked quickly towards the apartment.

'I'm sorry,' he said, his voice cracking ever so slightly. Then he went inside and closed the door behind him.

Anna was confused, but Penny was still bouncing around happily, telling her that when she wasn't her best friend anymore, then it was going to be Diego. Anna didn't know what Penny was talking about, but Penny often said things that didn't make any sense. Then she was off again, demanding Anna come help find her something to eat.

Tommy was annoying, there was no getting around that. He was only two years younger than Anna, but he might as well have still been a toddler considering how much she had to hold his hand through everything. He was still scared of the dark, he got nervous if they went too far from his front door and he never wanted to play anything fun. And worse than all of that, he wouldn't listen to her when she tried to tell him what Penny was saying. It wasn't that he didn't believe her, but he just kept getting it wrong. He'd laugh at things Penny hadn't meant as a joke, he'd second-guess Anna on what Penny was feeling, and when he tried to actually talk to Penny he always ended up facing the wrong way and talking to empty air like a dummy. But despite all that, he was the only other kid that Anna knew in the whole building, and sometimes a game needed more than one pair of actual hands to play properly.

Penny's feelings on Tommy were less harsh, or at least it seemed that way at first. She would laugh, apparently delighted, whenever he was unable to see her, and liked to lurk just over his shoulder, making faces at Anna. She would crane her rail-thin neck around and stare at him, amusement glittering in her eyes. Of course, this didn't make Anna like him more, as she sometimes felt a small stirring of jealousy at how her imaginary friend would watch him, but it did soften her annoyance, at least a bit. Penny also liked that Tommy's mother wasn't nearly as health conscious as Anna's and would often send him out to play still clutching whatever brightly coloured gelatine or greasily salted junk food he could get his sticky hands on. It always annoyed Anna when he turned up like this, as it was very hard to get Penny to focus on anything else. She would circle around him, her spindly limbs slinking out and around, her eyes locked on whatever snack the boy had brought. She would wait until he was distracted, and then that long curling tongue would sneak out and snatch it up. Then Tommy would always notice it was gone, and he'd blame Anna and start crying. She hated it when he started crying.

But worse than all of that, to Anna's mind, was how reluctant Tommy was play any of her and Penny's games. They were older, so they got to choose what they played. That's just how it worked, and while he seemed to agree in principle, every time she suggested one of Penny's games he would shake his head and say that he didn't think his mum would like it. When they tried to play Secret Agents, he'd always refuse to go into any of the passages that Penny would show them. He started crying when Anna explained the rules to Jumping Shadows and put his hands over his ears whenever she even brought up Spiders, even though that was the simplest of all of them.

They'd managed to convince him to play hide and seek once. It had been a cold winter day, and despite every occupied flat having the heating turned all the way up, the hall was still icy enough to see their breath. Tommy ran off to hide when the game began, and so did Penny. Anna had promised to count to a hundred, but had got bored around forty-four, and was pretty sure neither of them were close enough to hear her anyway, so had begun the hunt. She had started with all the usual nooks and hidey-holes that Tommy generally ran to, but they were empty. Next she had checked the lifts, as Penny liked the idea that she could change floors to escape the seeker. Anna always told her this was cheating, since you weren't supposed to move once you've hidden, but Penny insisted that *she* wasn't moving because she was still in the lift. Regardless, that afternoon both the lifts had been empty. Anna had even checked the corners of the ceiling where Penny liked to curl up, but there was no sign of the little girl.

Finally, as she was hunting through the corridors of the third floor, she spotted something. Near the window at the end she could see the outline of a service hatch, one that she and Penny had explored many times, and as she got closer she could just make out a fine mist creeping rhythmically through the cracks: small puffs of breath bursting out into the cold. Anna smiled and crept closer, keen to surprise whoever was inside, when her attention was caught by the sound of something behind her. She turned to see Tommy, shivering, his eyes streaming with tears. Anna started to get mad, telling him that there wasn't any point playing hide and seek if he was just going to come out and find her. He just cried more.

'Penny found me first,' he said. Then ran off before Anna could ask him anything else. The service hatch was empty when she opened it, and Penny had just laughed when Anna asked about it later.

But that was six months ago, and while it had been some time before Tommy agreed to come play with them again, the three of them were now out and having fun. Penny had invented a new game that she called Creeping Tiptoes, although Anna had to tell Tommy it was her idea, rather than Penny's, so that he would agree to play. The game as Penny explained it took place on the old stairwell in the ugly side of the building, around the big iron lift. One player was 'it' and had to stand halfway down the staircase, while the others were 'creepies' and waited at the top on their hands and knees. The player who was 'it' had to walk down the stairs, but whenever they took their eyes off the chasing players, they were allowed to crawl down the stairs as quickly as possible. If they touched the one who was 'it' before they reached the landing below, they won. It was a lot more normal than most of Penny's games, which Anna appreciated, although she secretly thought the idea had been stolen from Grandmother's Footsteps.

Tommy didn't like the game; he found having to walk down the stairs backwards too scary and would always have to turn around, giving Anna and Penny plenty of time to scuttle down the stairs and grab him. But at least he was willing to play, even though he kept arguing that Penny hadn't reached him when she clearly had. It was one thing for Tommy to not see her, but the idea that Anna would lie about it made her real mad and she told him so. He also found it difficult when Penny was 'it', since only Anna could tell when she was looking at them and when she wasn't and Tommy kept messing up.

It was getting late, and Anna was starting to get distracted, keeping one ear open for her mother calling them in for dinner. Penny was already hungry of course, but that wasn't any different to normal, and Anna kept telling her to shush so she could concentrate on the game. Tommy was getting tired, and when the time came for him to be 'it' he tried to say no, but Anna insisted, and he took his place on the stairs. Anna got down to the floor, her hands clinging to the hard edges of the top stair. Penny was next to her, a wide smile across her face. Tommy kept his eyes locked on Anna, and began to take a step back, but as he moved his leg, a sudden fear flashed in his eyes and he turned around to see where he was placing his foot down. Immediately Anna crawled forward, covering three of the stairs before Tommy turned back. Penny had moved down four, and was just ahead of her, huge eyes drilling into the boy standing in front of them. Tommy tried again. This time he was able to resist turning around, and he stepped backwards to the next stair down, but lost balance for just a moment, causing his eyes to flick to the ceiling. It was only a second, but both Anna and Penny pounced on the opportunity, quickly moving down another stair. There was silence as Tommy tried not to cry. His nose was running like it usually did when he was trying to hold off tears and he reached down into his pocket to retrieve the damp and snot-covered handkerchief he always used. But as he pulled it out, something else came out with it: a small packet of bright red sweets, something he's clearly been trying to hide from them. It fell onto the staircase beside him, and reflexively he reached down to pick it up.

Later, Anna would try to piece together exactly what had happened, but it was all so very fast. Penny had started moving, far quicker than she normally did when playing. She raced down the stairs towards Tommy, but her eyes were locked on the sweets, which seemed so brightly coloured they were almost glowing. Tommy looked back up again, but by then Penny was almost on top of him, and she didn't even try to stop. Anna couldn't quite make sense of the next few seconds. Obviously Penny couldn't have actually touched him, because she didn't exist, and Tommy couldn't see her. So why would he have got scared? He definitely screamed, though, and it didn't just sound like the scream of someone falling. It sounded like the scream of someone who'd seen something horrible.

After that they weren't allowed to play with Tommy anymore. That was the first time Anna told Penny to leave. She waited until they were alone in their room, having been sent to bed without dinner, and turned to her self-proclaimed best friend.

'Go away!'

Penny laughed her silent laugh.

'Go away, Penny!'

Penny began to scowl.

'Go away!'

Penny went away.

Anna sat in her room, alone and hungry.

It was two days before Penny returned, and Anna spent them bored to tears. Tommy couldn't play anymore, and her parents continued to spend their time working or talking in quiet whispers they didn't think she could hear. She tried to make her own fun, but her toys seemed boring and old, and she was only allowed an hour of screen time a day. She tried to remember what she did for fun before Penny, but it all seemed so childish now. Sure, Penny was strange and sometimes a bit scary, but wasn't that why they were friends? Anna had never had another friend who took her on adventures, and no matter how much she tried she just couldn't come up with any good games of her own. All the ones she knew needed at least two people.

Late one night, when her parents thought she was asleep, she opened the cupboard where she had first met Penny, and quietly called out her name.

Penny promised she wasn't mad that Anna had sent her away, but she was very hungry. She said she'd had to go and live with her mother again, and Penny's mother didn't have any food. So, after dark, when her parents had gone to bed, Anna sneaked out into the kitchen, and started to look through the fridge for something to eat, Penny didn't want an apple. She didn't want a sandwich. She didn't want leftover kedgeree or potato waffles. Penny didn't want anything they had in the house, it seemed.

The next morning, once her parents were busy with whatever they were doing that day, Anna announced that she was going to play with Penny. She pretended not to see the look of irritation on her father's face when he heard the name again after two days without it, but he didn't try to stop her. Anna took all her pocket money that she'd been able to save from under her bed, thirteen pounds and forty pence, and together they did something they'd never done without Anna's parents: they left the building. She walked past the desk where the man sat who her mother said wasn't a policeman, but everyone talked about him like he was a policeman, and told him in her best grown-up voice that her mother was sending her out to get milk on her own. There was a horrible moment where Anna worried that maybe the man at the desk knew they still had plenty of milk, but he just nodded and said to be back soon.

But Anna and Penny didn't go to get milk, and her friend's eyes widened as Anna led them through the sliding doors of the McDonald's just down the road. The smell of grease and chemical condiments hit them in a wave, and Penny made a noise that Anna had never heard before. She turned to see her friend, her smile wide, a thin trail of saliva dripping from the corner of her mouth and pooling on the floor. The cashier was dubious, looking around for a grown-up when Anna tried to place her order, so Anna pointed to an older man sitting near the window with his back to them and said he was her father. Soon she was carrying a pair of thin burgers and a cardboard sleeve of glistening fries over to a sticky plastic table where Penny was already sitting. She slid the food over to her imaginary friend and waited.

There was a moment, just a single quiet second, where

Penny's eyes met Anna's and there was a flicker of something, some deep gratitude. Then they were once again full of hunger as she descended on the meal in front of her. She didn't even bother to pull off the greaseproof paper, tearing at it with her long thin fingers and sharp little teeth. Specks of potato and sesame flew in all directions as she chewed wildly on her grim fast food banquet. Her jaw muscles bulged and rolled, and her scrawny frame shuddered as she guzzled down the last of the fries. Her eyes flicked down, scanning the cheap plastic tray in front of her, looking for more food, anything else to eat, to devour. But there was nothing.

Anna watched her friend, slightly shaken by the little girl's vicious hunger. She'd never seen Penny actually eat, not properly, not more than the occasional snack. She hoped no one else in the restaurant had seen the disgusting display, but no one seemed to have so much as glanced in their direction. Now Penny's fingers dripped with ketchup and her face was smeared with grease, and if anything, she looked even thinner than she was before. Her bones poked painfully against her skin and her hands shook slightly as she looked longingly back towards the rows upon rows of fast food behind the till. Anna felt a stab of guilt that she had no more money to buy Penny more food, but she was beginning to think that perhaps Penny would always be hungry. She didn't quite understand why, though. She certainly hadn't imagined Penny that way. But then again, she hadn't thought imaginary friends were able to eat at all, yet here they were.

Over the next few days Anna's relationship with her best friend became more and more strained. The atmosphere in the home was tense, and her parents were quieter than ever. Her father kept mentioning how nice their flat was, as if trying to convince himself it was true, and there was never any food for Penny, which annoyed her even if she never ate any of the healthy stuff anyway. She and Anna kept getting into fights, and Anna told her to go away at least once a day, though was quick to bring her back.

That night, Anna had told Penny to go away after she kept trying to convince her to sneak out of the flat to go and play Secret Agents. But Anna was tired and dealing with her excitable friend was too much effort, so she sent her away and went to sleep. She hadn't liked the look on Penny's face when she'd been told to leave but decided she could always apologise in the morning.

Anna didn't have a clock in her room, so had no way of knowing what time it was when she woke up in the middle of the night. Her room was hot with the air conditioning turned off, and her small nightlight didn't seem as comforting as it usually did, as the furniture around it cast stark, deep shadows. Something was wrong.

'Penny?' she called out quietly, trying her very best to sound brave.

There was no answer. She pulled her blanket up over her, even though it was really too warm for it, and tried to get back to sleep. Then there was movement from just outside her bedroom door. It was the soft sound of small feet moving slowly over the hardwood floors. Anna crept out of her bed, the rug muffling the sound of her footsteps as she slowly moved over and pulled open her bedroom door. At that moment, she was more afraid of waking her parents than anything else, but that quickly changed when she looked out and saw the small, emaciated figure of Penny walking down the hall. She called out and her imaginary friend turned, her face still plastered with that smile, and gave Anna a wink with one of those big eyes. Then she walked into her parents' bedroom.

Anna paused for a second, trying to think what Penny could possibly want in there. An uneasy feeling was growing in her stomach and she hurried down the hall after her friend, trying to make as little noise as possible. The door was still ajar, and she slipped in silently, her vision slowly adjusting to the darkness.

Penny was standing on the big bed, between her mother and father. She walked slowly from one to the other, bending down over each in turn, studying their faces. Neither the mattress nor the bedclothes stirred as she walked over them, which made sense given Penny didn't exist. But then why was Anna so worried? Why was there this gnawing fear in the back of her mind, the lingering image of the strange little girl tearing into a tray full of over-processed fast food? Her smile was opening near the head of Anna's mother, and in spite of all the time they had spent together, Anna still found herself surprised by just how many teeth Penny had.

'Go away, Penny!' Anna hissed, desperately trying not to wake her parents.

Penny ignored her.

'Go away!'

Her father gave a sigh and turned over in bed, causing Anna's heart to skip a beat, before he settled down again. It was enough to get Penny's attention, at least. Her pale face turned back towards Anna, and they stared at each other.

'I'm so hungry, Anna,' she said at last. Penny's voice was loud and clear, but Anna's parents didn't stir, because only Anna could hear it.

'I'm sorry,' Anna whispered desperately, 'but you need to go away.'

Penny began to crawl back down the bed, thin limbs stretching over the end, pulling herself down onto the floor, heading towards Anna.

'I'm so hungry,' she said again, and took Anna by the arm. Anna had pretended to touch her imaginary friend before, but her skin had never felt so cold, nor her grip so tight.

Part of Anna wanted to scream, to wake up her parents and beg them to protect her. Another part wanted to turn and run. But there was still a place deep inside her heart that wanted to cry for poor Penny, to hug her and tell her she was sorry that she was imaginary, and they only had food for real people. She still wanted to help.

Perhaps that's why Anna didn't resist when Penny took her arm and raised it to her mouth. Those rows of sharp and tiny teeth parted, positioning themselves over her skin, ready to bite down. Anna could feel her best friend's ragged breath and the needle-like points of those teeth pressing against her. She prepared herself to scream.

Then all at once Penny released her arm and burst into her silent laugher, a motion so unexpected that Anna fell forward, landing on the ground with a thump that woke her parents.

Later that night Penny told Anna it had all been a funny joke. Anna didn't believe her but couldn't ever bring herself to tell Penny to go away again.

Anna's parents were surprised the following morning to receive a letter addressed to Anna, and then utterly baffled when they opened it and were presented with an invitation.

TOBIAS FELL cordially invites ANNA KHAN,
PENNY AND GUARDIAN
to attend a dinner party at 1 Banyan Court
on the evening of 16th August 2014
Penthouse access will be available through the freight elevator

They talked about it at length, argued over it like they did with everything at the moment, and finally agreed that they couldn't not go. Affording the high-end flat was slowly bankrupting them after Prisha's redundancy, and if the man who owned the building asked to see them, they had to at least find out what he wanted.

They were nervous about trying to explain the invitation to Anna, but as it turned out they needn't have bothered. Apparently Penny had told her all about it already, and was planning a very special game indeed.

5th

Inbox

Gillian Barnes
80 Banyan Court

Gillian grimaced in pain, instinctively pulling her finger back as a single drop of ruby blood fell onto the cream papers spread across her desk. Of all the difficulties and indignities in her chosen career, the papercuts inflicted by the thick stock Akman Blane used for their legal documents was a strong contender for her least favourite.

She got to her feet, slightly resenting the time it would take to sort out, and headed over to the bathroom to get a plaster. The bare wooden floor was cold beneath her feet, despite the humid summer night, and Gillian instinctively reached for her notebook to add 'slippers' to the list of things she needed to get for the flat. When she had the time. And the money. But her pocket was empty, and it wasn't until she'd reached the bathroom that she remembered the notebook was still lying on her desk, where she had just been writing in it. Probably for the best. The shopping list was already three pages long, with no end in sight.

She applied the plaster with a small dab of antiseptic cream and closed the bathroom cabinet, one of the few pieces of furniture that was actually part of the flat. As she did so she paused for a second, considering her face in the mirror. What was she looking for? She wasn't even sure, if she was honest. Wrinkles perhaps? Crawling out from her bloodshot eyes over the dark canvas of her skin? No, they were still a long way off. Perhaps it was just that the face in that mirror had worn the same expression every time she'd seen it for almost a year now. When had she last felt herself smile?

Gillian exhaled slowly, waving the thought away. There would be time enough for smiling in the years to come. Right now was when she put in the work, did her time, pushed out through this purgatory and into the life she had chosen for herself. The degree had been hard, sure it had, but this was the true test. If she wanted to be certified as a Chartered Legal Executive she had to get through the years of 'qualifying' employment. Underpaid, disrespected, but vital to her intended career as a lawyer. She'd been very lucky to get the position at Akman Blane, she reminded herself, they were a big enough deal that there'd be no question of her qualifying when she'd served her time. But until then they were clearly keen to get as much out of her as they could.

As if to illustrate her point, Gillian's phone began to buzz. She glanced at the screen. The self-consciously serious face of Timothy A. Simmons stared back at her, his navy-blue suit and silver silk tie silently reprimanding her for not already having answered. Timothy (not 'Tim', thank you very much) was one of the many people who, rightly or wrongly, considered themselves her boss. She wanted to be annoyed he was phoning her so late, but instead she just pushed the green button to answer.

'Barnes, did you take the Kempner brief?' The voice from the phone was impatient, but didn't respect her enough to be properly hostile.

'A copy of it, yes.' Gillian's tone was blank.

'Where's the original?'

'I re-filed it.'

'Right.'

There was a small beep as the call ended.

She sat back down, the cheap office chair protesting at the burden. Her hand reflexively reached for a fluorescent yellow highlighter as her eyes returned to the documents in front of her and she settled back into scanning for the details she needed. Her focus stopped suddenly on a splash of crimson. Her blood. Well, at least they were only photocopies. She leaned forward, momentarily curious as to what word had been obscured by the small scarlet fleck. Her thumb smeared the still-wet stain across several lines but rendered the words beneath it legible again: Tobias Fell.

Not surprising. Pick a random pair of words from any random legal document at Akman Blane and you were likely enough to have landed on the name of their biggest client. His name spread over almost everything in the company, even her. After all, this flat – in his building – was part of an initiative to supply 'affordable' living situations for the firm's less-moneyed employees. Of course, it wouldn't have been necessary without their unofficial policy of not hiring anyone from outside of Zone 1 for their London office. Maybe Zone 2 if they knew your father. But it had given Gillian somewhere to live and she supposed she owed some gratitude to the great Tobias Fell.

This brief itself was nothing special. A man named Allan Kempner, a manager at one of Fell's media companies, had breached his NDA, so the firm were helping to sue him out of existence. And it didn't look like it would be particularly hard, either. He'd allegedly sold internal information to a rival company and the damages he was going to end up paying were eye-watering. Gillian felt a pang of sympathy for the man but pushed it down. There was no place for it if she wanted to work in corporate law. Not the most exciting branch of the legal profession, admittedly, but one of the most secure and, yes, best paid. And fundamentally it *was* about the money. Much as she might wish it otherwise, money meant safety. It meant freedom.

Her eyes continued to scan through the documents, making small shorthand notes in the margins and highlighting relevant details. But something else jumped out at her. The email Kempner had sent, the one that broke his contract, was listed as being sent on the 16th of August last year. Why did that date seem so familiar to her?

Obviously there was no reason, it was just one of three hundred and sixty-five possible dates it could have been. So why did she keep going back to check it? She circled it in red, just to be on the safe side. By now the blood had dried to a crusty brown, and the bright ink stood out starkly against the gloom of the evening.

When Gillian got into work the next day, she'd been moved desks. Again. She turned away from the shrugging intern who was sat in her old seat and went looking for her new one, doing her best to seem purposeful. She changed her path several times so as not to get too close to Timothy's directionless morning aggression. She eventually spotted it, clearly identifiable from the tower of four filing boxes stacked haphazardly on her intray.

She flicked through the Post-it notes jammed on top of each other. Two from Timothy, one from Sarah Merlini, her actual supervisor, and one from Mr Blane himself. What Gillian really wanted to do was to make herself a cup of tea, then start methodically working through the stack, but she could see

Timothy in the kitchen, scowling next to the water heater, and decided to leave it for a few minutes.

Three hours later, Gillian looked up, disturbed from her work by her own rumbling stomach. She'd made a strong dent in the first box, but at some point Sarah had added another to the top of the stack and labelled it 'urgent', so lunch was going to prove difficult. There wasn't even a question of whether she'd need to take some of them home. The only uncertainty was how she'd be best off carrying them. She'd long since discovered that while a sheet of paper is very light, a box full of them is an injury waiting to happen.

So far the morning had gone more or less as expected. Just another day pushing through the devil's bargain she had made, the gruelling down payment on the life she actually wanted. Where maybe someday she'd have her own underlings to burn their youth away fetching files. There was something else, though, something unusual about today. No, not about today, about her. She was used to the focus that came with her work, comfortable in letting the rest of the world drop away, leaving only a flat, steady concentration. But that wasn't quite what was happening now. There were flashes, little things that kept catching her eye in the documents. A name here. A date there. A company that she was sure was mentioned in a different brief. Had she finally read enough of the firm's files that she was starting to actually understand how it all fitted together?

On a whim she began to take notes of the pages that caught her eye. She could photocopy herself a few duplicates, spend a bit more time on them later when she had finished her ...

She spotted that another box had been placed on top of the pile. Despite herself, she couldn't quite hold in a sigh. 'Finished' wasn't really a concept where she was at the moment. There was always going to be more, every box, every case spreading out and leading to a dozen more. An intricate network of connections and references and work for Gillian to do. It wasn't so bad, not really, but she decided she should probably get a sandwich first.

The flimsy cardboard box sagged under the weight of the much denser and better-made filing cases. It was already dark, and Gillian was searching through the collection of torn containers that had been acting as a makeshift wardrobe and stationery cupboard since she moved into Banyan Court. Furniture required money to buy and time (or friends) to set up, and none of these were things Gillian had in abundance right now. It wasn't great, but she could endure. It meant she had to get up a bit earlier to iron the box-creases from the day's outfit, but she knew there were people out there who had it far worse. It wasn't even like it was a bad place to be living, at least if you ignored the broken lift. And the slight smell in the hallway. And the temperamental fuse box. Even then, Gillian could have handled it if she'd only felt like she had some *choice* about living there. But no, if she wanted the job, the 'charity' of Tobias Fell had been her only option. Could one be trapped by generosity? Because she certainly felt like it.

The hairs on the back of her neck prickled and she spun around. No, there was no one there. Obviously. It was just her, alone in an empty flat. She breathed out. Flats like these had so many creaks and noises it was easy to convince yourself you weren't alone. Several times in the last few weeks she'd woken up, sure she was being watched, only to find the place empty.

Her hand brushed the corner of a wooden frame and she smiled, pulling out what she'd been hunting for. Her old university cork board. There was still a pair of old cinema tickets to *Limitless* stuck to it with drawing pins, mementos of her and Aaron's brief relationship, as well as a pair of Polaroids showing her grinning in a crowd of people she hadn't talked to since graduation. Gillian pulled out the pins, collected up the memories of happier times and unceremoniously tossed them back into the box. She stood up with her prize and walked to the wall next to her tired-looking desk.

Her mouth pursed in consideration. There was no hook to hang it on. She could put one in, of course; she definitely had a hammer and a few nails in one of these boxes, but Gillian was certain the sour-faced letting agent who dealt with renting the place would take it out of her deposit. She sighed.

'There are always going to be consequences,' she muttered to no one in particular.

The sound of the hammer was louder than she expected, and Gillian jumped as it broke the silence, reverberating around the mostly empty room. She took a moment and settled herself before tapping the nail for a second and final time. It slid into the wall easily, eagerly, and she almost felt a smile coming on as she placed the cork board in its new position. She took a pin and rifled through one of the cases she'd brought home until she found what she was looking for: a photocopy of the inquest report for the death of a man named Herman Thomas.

She had stumbled across it in while dealing with the third box of files. At first, just the name jumped out at her. She had actually talked to Herman Thomas on the phone when she started at the company last year, and remembered him being soft-spoken, nervous, keen to make a good impression. She didn't realise he had died so soon after. But, more importantly, the name listed as having signed off on receipt of the inquest report was hers. Gillian Barnes. But she was quite certain she'd never seen it before in her life. Taking a copy had been a risk, after all it could jeopardise her position, but they expected her to take so many files home she couldn't imagine they would ever notice.

She pinned it to the centre of the board and took a step back. She didn't know what was going on, but this felt like a start. A small red smear could be seen under the name. Gillian checked her hand. When had she started bleeding again? Had she caught herself with the hammer and not noticed? She stared at the bloody fingerprint. It didn't matter, not now. She had more important things to consider.

It seemed to start with the sweatshops. It wasn't exactly an eye-opening revelation that the clothing companies Tobias Fell was involved with heavily relied on a group of brutally exploitative factories in Indonesia. But following an industrial accident in 2009 that left eleven workers dead and many more maimed, there was a concerted activist campaign against these companies and, by extension, Fell himself. According to the transcripts, Akman Blane had managed to ensure that the companies were insulated from any legal fallout, but they still publicly cut ties with the factories involved, moving production to significantly less-horrendous facilities in the Dominican Republic. It was hailed as a victory in the press, but according to the contracts her firm had drawn up, the amount of product being bought from the Dominican facilities was nowhere near the original amount produced in Indonesia. The rest seemed to be coming from a collection of smaller companies that turned out to be shells, all of which listed Herman Thomas as the COO. A year ago, one of the old Indonesian factories had fully collapsed, killing most of the workers inside. One hundred and three people in all. The next day, 16th August last year, Herman Thomas fell from his balcony on the seventh floor, landing on his neck and dying instantly.

Gillian stepped back and rubbed her eyes. The blur of names and dates and depositions were swirling through her head. The cork board now a mess of photocopies, highlights, and handwritten notes. She'd been doing research on her laptop but trying to keep track of everything digitally was a nightmare. The physical set-up was much clearer, at least to her.

She tried to take a step back mentally as well, but that was proving much harder. Was this real? Her mind raced. If her suspicions were correct, she might have just uncovered a conspiracy to murder a man who was planning to blow the whistle on Tobias Fell's involvement in the factory collapse. She didn't know exactly where the initial idea had come from, it had simply appeared in her mind, but now she was certain of it. There was no concrete evidence, of course, just a lot of details that seemed to slot together. Numbers that added up, but not how they were supposed to. Names that kept cropping up for seemingly no reason. She sat heavily in her chair, dimly aware that the first rays of daylight were starting to creep around the edges of her curtains.

If it was true, what the hell was she supposed to do about it? She had enough legal expertise by now to know that there was nothing in these documents that would hold up in any sort of court, especially given the frankly terrifying competence of Akman Blane. She knew that in corporate law you ended up working for some shady types and she thought she'd made her peace with it. After all, money can make peace with a lot of things. But murder? Surely that was a line she wasn't willing to cross. And if it was, how could she avoid crossing it without completely torpedoing her career?

She kept staring at the cork board, mind racing over the same ground again and again. Her attention was snapped by a sound behind her. The creak of a floorboard. Spinning round she could have sworn for a second there was a man standing in the corridor behind her. A man in a dark suit. But no, it was just her coat, hanging where it always was.

'... Hello

The only answer she received was the bleating of her alarm clock. Telling her it was time to go to work.

It wasn't easy, pushing through the day. Without the frantic rush of investigation and revelation the sleepless night hit Gillian like a truck. She felt like a ghost tethered to her desk, trying desperately to connect with documents that seemed further and further away every time she looked at them. Even then, occasionally she would catch sight of a word, a detail, something to hang another thread on, and silently mark the box as one she needed to take for her own purposes.

'Hey, where's the file on Terry Vargas?'

Timothy looked up, irritated that his dreary soup had been interrupted.

'Who?'

'Vargas,' Gillian repeated. 'She ran a manufacturing plant in Guinea. Filed a bunch of reports on worker safety.'

'We've never had any files on a Terry Vargas,' Timothy said flatly.

'Uh ... Yeah we have, I spent most of last month—'

'We've never had any files on Terry Vargas,' he repeated, his intonation identical.

Gillian rocked backwards slightly, her head swimming.

'Come on, Barnes,' he said dismissively, voice returning to its usual sneer. 'Don't waste my time.'

She nodded and started to stagger away. His voice followed her, cold and flat.

'And try to get some more sleep. It's not good for you, staying up so late.'

*

Her intray got higher and higher, but Gillian managed to bat away questions about deadlines, citing Mr Blane's project as the reason she had nothing for Timothy or Sarah, while at the same time talking Mr Blane into blaming Sarah for his delay. The rest of the office was noisy, full of voices and a simmering frenetic energy, but at that moment it all seemed such a long way away. Gillian stood, dimly aware that she had been sitting motionless for hours, and walked to the window. The street below was busy, a steady stream of people passing down the sunlit Bloomsbury lanes. Business people in fitted suits, tourists in bright shirts, and a single figure stood opposite, staring at her.

He was tall, dressed in a black jacket far too thick for the heat of the day. His white shirt was crisp around his dark necktie and he wore opaque sunglasses that completely obscured the upper part of his face. Despite this, there was no doubt in Gillian's mind that he was looking at her, watching her. His face was tilted up towards the third floor window where she was standing and his mouth was set in a hard, straight line. And a familiar feeling of being watched, being observation washed over her. Without turning his head the man in the black suit reached into his jacket and took out a phone. He brought it to his ear and began to speak, small precise words lost in the buzz of the city. He nodded just once.

'Gill!' Sarah's voice wasn't loud, but it almost knocked her backwards, shattering whatever space she had found herself in. She could see more file boxes in Sarah's arms, and tried to muster the energy to hide her frustration.

'Uh, yeah. Yes. Coming, sorry,' Gillian stammered. If her boss noticed just how rattled she was, there was no indication as three more boxes were unceremoniously dumped into her arms. She glanced back out the window, scanning the street below. Nothing. The man in black was gone.

*

This clearly went far deeper than Gillian had first imagined. She was once again staring at her rapidly expanding mess of notes and connections, mind racing and eyes wide. She had slept a few hours, but the time she had away from work was precious and she couldn't afford to waste much of it by sleeping. The filing boxes surrounded her now, piling up in the corners of the room, carpeting the floor with discarded papers. She'd managed to cut her hand again at some point, and the documents pinned to the board were spotted here and there with striking dots of red.

Sweatshops were only the tip of it. In every one of Tobias Fell's businesses the pattern was the same. A woman who had come forward with concerns about worker safety in the warehouses of Howard Fairley, one of Fell's partners, had been killed in an accidental electrical fire. An executive at an affiliate marketing company that publicly expressed concerns over the ingredients in foodstuffs that were being targeted at children passed away shortly afterwards of a previously undiagnosed heart condition. Blood diamonds, environmental violations, unethical insurance practices, every time anyone raised an objection or looked ready to blow the whistle, they ended up dead or disappeared.

The sudden rattle of her phone buzzing on the wooden desk snapped her out of her thoughts and almost gave her a heart attack of her own. She breathed out for a few moments trying to control her wildly racing pulse. She looked at the screen, expecting to see one of the professionally retouched contact photos of her superiors at Akman Blane, but the picture was blank. The caller ID read 'Mr Close', which was not a name she recognised from her phonebook. She pressed the answer icon, staining the green button slightly red from her most recent papercut.

'H-hello?' Her voice wavered.

There was no sound on the other side. No breathing. No background noise. Just silence.

Then, 'Do you know?'

The voice was slow, emotionless, with an inflection that didn't quite match that put Gillian immediately on edge, as though it were coming from a speech synthesiser program. But the voice itself had nothing robotic about it.

'Who is this?'

'I ask the questions.' His tone wasn't angry or sharp but had a certainty to it that was impossible to disregard. 'Do you know?'

'I don't— What are you talking about?'

'If I am to proceed, you must know. Do you know?'

The image of the man watching her from the street crept unbidden into Gillian's mind.

'I … I don't. I don't know.'

A pause.

'Good. Do not know and I will not proceed. Thank you.'

The call ended. Gillian sat there, trying to make herself put the phone down, but her hand wouldn't stop shaking. Even with the call over, she still felt like something was listening.

She turned her phone off. Still there.

She unplugged her laptop, pulled out the battery and threw a blanket over it. Still there.

She disassembled the smoke alarm, unplugged her lamps, covered and sabotaged every piece of technology in her flat. She told herself she was being daft, but only when it was done did she feel almost safe enough to sleep.

Gillian found what she was looking for down a filthy side street in Barking. The door buzzer was so grimy that she felt a strange sort of gratitude that the tiny cuts covering her hands had forced her to wear gloves. She pressed the buzzer for flat 6 and waited. The rank stench of the small mountain of garbage bags piled up next to the entrance choked her throat. Perhaps she should have waited until she was here to call in sick? It would have really added something to the performance.

'Who is it?' the tinny voice spat out from the little speaker, splitting the difference between annoyed and nervous.

'Mr Kempner? It's Gillian Barnes, we spoke earlier?'

'Prove it,' the voice came, barely concealing its hostility.

'Uh, sorry?' Gillian was confused. 'Prove who I am or prove that we spoke?'

The speaker went silent, as though considering, then without further comment a harsh electronic drone announced the front door was unlocked. Gillian gingerly pushed it open and stepped inside.

Beyond the building's front door, the smell was of a different character, but no less pungent. Her steps echoed on the grubby vinyl flooring as she made her way towards the stairs. She passed two lifts en route, but, after experiencing the one at Banyan Court, decided she didn't trust them.

Tucked away in a labyrinth of urban decay near the edge of Barking, Paston Towers was not the sort of place one would expect to find the editor-in-chief of a high-profile media brand. Still, Gillian supposed if she was being sued for the sort of money Akman Blane were likely to claim in damages from Allan Kempner, she'd probably move somewhere a bit more budget conscious as well. The second floor was silent and still, save for the two flies that hovered near the stairwell, taking turns picking at a faded stain on the wall.

The steel number 6 on Kempner's door was still shiny, as though it had just been added, and stood out clearly against the worn plywood of the door itself. Gillian raised her hand to knock, but it opened on the latch before she had the chance.

'Look at the camera.' The voice that came from inside was just as irritable and hesitant as it had seemed through the speaker.

'What?'

'The camera!' the voice insisted, and Gillian turned her head just in time to hear a click from a small lens mounted above the frame.

The door opened fully.

'Good. I can prove you were here, now, so no funny business.'

'I'm not sure I—'

'I've got it all on tape.'

'Look.' Gillian tried to keep her voice level. 'I just want to talk. About Tobias Fell.'

Another pause.

'Come in, then.' A pause, then he repeated, 'No funny business.'

Inside, flat 6 was a strange juxtaposition. Kempner had clearly taken much of the high-end furniture and appliances from wherever he'd lived before, but it only served to highlight how run-down the rest of it was. An extremely expensive-looking office chair was placed next to an ancient moth-eaten sofa, both orientated towards the large flat-screen which dominated a wall that didn't really look sturdy enough to support its mount. He'd clearly made a real effort to keep the place clean, but it was obvious which corners and crevices had defeated him, and it felt as though the dirt was just in hiding, waiting for him to slip up.

'Sit down,' he said, and Gillian complied, trying to find a comfortable spot on the sofa and failing.

Allan Kempner walked sullenly to the kitchen area and poured himself a large glass of an amber liquid from a chipped crystal decanter, before making his way to the office chair. He did not offer one to Gillian.

'So, what do you want?' he grunted. 'Intimidation? Payoff? What are they after? Don't try to tell me this is a social call.'

'I work for Akman Blane,' Gillian said, trying her best to sound like it.

'Yeah, you said,' Kempner scowled, taking a sizeable swig of his drink. 'But I can't find you listed on their site. And you have cheap shoes. So, who are you?'

'I ... That's ... I *do* work for them,' Gillian protested.

'Sure. Email address looked official enough. But the question is are you one of *them*? Are you here to do their dirty work? Or have they not got to you yet?' His gaze was searching, and Gillian suddenly noticed the shape of what might have been a knife tucked beneath his shirt.

'I ... don't know.'

'Yeah, figures.' His hands fidgeted with the rim of his glass. 'Look, I shouldn't have let you up. I've got no interest talking to Akman Blane outside of a proper hearing, but you said this was more than that. So, what d'you want?'

Gillian bit her lip. She had hoped to find someone calm, level-headed and considered in their dealings with Tobias Fell and Akman Blane. Someone who'd seen what they were capable of and might listen to her and talk through her theories. She was looking for an ally. But as his eyes darted around the room, it was clear Allan Kempner was not that man.

'I think I've stumbled onto something. About Tobias Fell. And Akman Blane and ... Tell me what happened. Why you blew the whistle.'

'And what good's that going to do? Too low down the ladder for decent shoes, but you're gonna throw me a lifeline here? Nah, I don't think so. Anyway, I've seen how many files you have over there. You know more about it than I do, and I did it.'

Gillian paused, considered for a moment, then pressed on. 'I think there's more going on. I have seen the files, but they don't make sense. And my name is all over them, in places that it shouldn't be. This is bigger than you and me and I just ... I want to know what's going on. I deserve that much at least.'

Kempner sighed.

'Fine, I get it,' he said at last. 'Funny. Really hoped you could help. Found something in the files, maybe, or ... I don't know. But no, someone like you coming round. I guess that means it's all over for me, isn't it? If I've drawn *your* attention, I'm probably too much of a liability.'

Gillian had no answer for him.

'OK, you want hear it? Fine. Tobias owned the network. Didn't mean much for the most part, TV news is TV news, except that you knew his politics and tended to frame the story for them. Very occasionally, like an election or something, he'd have one of his cronies come down with some more explicit "editorial guidance", but that was rare.'

He paused and took a swig. He almost smiled as he continued, and for a second Gillian could see the shadow of a confident speaker, briefing an attentive room of journalists.

'But the main problem was when one of his other companies fucked up. Got caught out. Then we'd get what we used to call a "Fell-book". A folder full of detailed instructions on how to handle it, but not just spinning the problem or even avoiding it.'

Kempner paused, clearly deciding whether or not to continue. He let out a single bitter chuckle, as though accepting defeat, and continued.

'They had lists of people who were involved in exposing whatever was going on, or leading campaigns against it, and we had to use all our resources to find dirt on them. Put out hit pieces, feature spots to undermine them. Hound them and their families as much as possible. And I did it. Took a sort of sick pride in how good we were at it. You should see how we spun it when the insurance stuff broke with United Continental. We were the best.'

He drained the glass.

'Then the Doxatrin scandal broke and we got a Fell-book about it, and ... My mother had taken Doxatrin, along with thousands of others. Doctors said it might have been what killed her in the end. And here was this fucking book telling me to bury the story. So, I was done. I leaked it. Took a scan and sent it round everywhere working on the story. But I was grieving, sloppy. Easy paper trail back to me, more than enough for you fucking vultures to scream NDA and torpedo my life. What there was of it. But I'd do it again.'

Kempner went quiet. He seemed somehow smaller, like the story had been a part of him and now it had left him diminished. She wondered if she should feel revulsion, looking at this man who had covered up evil for so long. Pity for him. Or just a dull awareness of her own complicity, working where she did. How different were they, really?

Everything seemed muted, and Gillian wondered for a moment where the noise of the street outside had gone. Had something silenced it?

'Mr Kempner.' She tried to choose her words carefully. 'I believe you're in danger.'

'No shit.' His gaze was level. Unimpressed.

'I believe that Akman Blane might be connected to the murders of whistle-blowers against Tobias Fell. And you might be next.'

Kempner started to laugh. 'Yeah,' he said, his eyes unreadable. 'And if that's true, what the hell do you think they're going to do to you?' His laughter was a vicious, mocking sound. 'They already know you know,' he said. 'And you know they do.'

He was still laughing as Gillian fled his dingy flat.

Gillian sat on the Underground, mind racing, fingers scrolling through the pictures on her phone. It had been less than half an hour since Kempner had unceremoniously laughed her out of his flat and in that time she had taken almost two dozen photos of the man who was following her. At least, she'd made that many attempts. There was always something in the way of a clear picture: a car blocking the view at just the wrong moment, a street sign obscuring his face, the glare of the sun rendering him an indistinct shadow in sunglasses. She'd noticed him almost as soon as she was out of the front door, and he'd been calmly matching her pace. His expression unreadable and his dark suit a stark contrast to the summery outfits of the crowds around him.

She'd made it onto the District line moments before the doors closed and hoped desperately that her pursuer hadn't managed to join her. It was the man her phone had christened 'Mr Close'. It had to be. She tried to reassure herself that he was just a random stalker, as if, under any other circumstances, that would be reassuring.

But the alternative was the possibility she had become a target of whoever worked with Akman Blane to keep the awful secrets of Tobias Fell, silencing those who threatened them. She couldn't go to the police. If they were operating so openly then there was no chance the cops weren't in the pocket of these people. After all, they had the power to plant contact information into her phone, so who knows what—

Gillian froze. *Her phone*. She'd forgotten to turn it off. Her work phone. They could have been listening in on her and

Kempner through the microphone or watched her take notes through the camera. Her computer too. If technology was a gateway they could use to reach her, they already had everything they needed to strike.

Gillian slowly and deliberately placed her phone on the floor of the carriage, then positioned her foot over the screen. Ever so gradually she increased the pressure until she heard it crack. For a second there was the sound of ringing, and Timothy's face appeared on the screen. Then she pushed down harder, and his sickly smile shattered under her heel. If they wanted to shut her up, she wasn't going to make it easy for them.

She crept back into Banyan Court as carefully as she could, taking care to turn her face from the security cameras. She just needed to get in, gather a few things and get out, go on the run before they could make their move. But was she already too late? She'd need her passport, at least. Unless they could track that? They might have been there already, planted God knows what on everything she owned. Still, she had to risk it.

Tobias Fell owned this whole building, he owned her flat, and that made it enemy territory. How could she be sure what was really going on behind any of the doors in this place? She was painfully aware that she lived in the run-down, forgotten half of the building. The sort of place things could be hidden without anybody noticing. Or be made to disappear. And how much did she know her neighbours really? There was Edith, the lonely old woman who lived on the floor above; she'd tried to talk to Gillian a few times in the past and she had seemed real enough. But that was months ago and they hadn't crossed paths since. Who knows what might have happened in that time? What they might have done to her?

No, Gillian had to consider this building as hostile territory.

The office too. They owned her flat, after all. *They owned her flat.* But where else could she go right now?

As she made her way around the outside of Banyan Court, she tried to keep her profile small and her footfalls quiet. Her eyes scanned around frantically, until they settled on something that she had seen every day since moving in, but never really noticed. A foundation stone, clean and bright in the old brick of the building wall.

This stone laid by TOBIAS FELL on 16th August 2004

16th August. The date Banyan Court's construction began. Almost exactly ten years ago. It couldn't be a coincidence. There were no coincidences.

Someone was outside the door to her flat. A young man, wiry and wearing a faded, oversized T-shirt. He was holding something long and thin against the wall. A measuring tape? What was he measuring? The young man jotted something down in a small grey notebook, then stretched the tape over the door jamb, furrowing his brows and making another note. He stood up and stretched his neck, catching sight of Gillian as he did so.

She froze, not sure whether to run or confront the distinctly unthreatening figure in front of her. Too late. The stranger was already heading towards her, waving and tucking the tape measure into a baggy pair of jogging trousers. There was an uncertain smile creasing his round, youthful face.

'Hello?'

Gillian didn't respond. She was frozen, waiting for whatever was about to happen.

'Do you ... live here?' His tone was serious, but not aggressive.

After a moment of excruciating silence, she nodded.

'So this is yours?'

The young man held up a piece of thick legal paper. The Akman Blane logo at the top was one of the few parts still completely legible, the rest hidden under layers of competing highlighter colours, frantically circled phrases and scrawled notes in a handwriting Gillian barely recognised as her own. She felt herself starting to blush.

'Where ...' The words came slowly. 'Where did you get that?'

He gestured back towards her door, and Gillian noticed for the first time patches of white peeking out from beneath it, papers slid partially through the gap at the bottom, as though trying to escape. She went cold.

'I have to go,' she said, almost breaking into a run as she pushed past him towards her flat.

'It's not real!' She could hear him calling behind her. 'They aren't real!'

But Gillian was already slamming the door, locking it behind her.

The apartment was chaos. Discarded papers lined the floor deep enough that it was hard to get stable footing. Filing boxes, empty, full and overflowing, lined the walls and filled the empty spaces in the room, creating narrow avenues of paperwork, a photocopied labyrinth of highlighter and ink. How had she let it get this bad? Had she? For all her meticulous note-taking, her obsessive cross-referencing, she couldn't be entirely sure what day it was. Or how many boxes of files she had taken for her own investigation. Many remained completely unopened, stacks that towered over her, trapping Gillian in the vast intray that had once been flat 80 Banyan Court. The young man's words made her look at them again. Not real? Her hand brushed against a pile of loose cuttings that almost reached to her head. They felt real enough. Didn't they?

There was only one space, one corner that she knew would be clear and well kept, somewhere she could collect her thoughts. Her desk, where she had gradually laid out the truth, meticulously pinned it to the wall and wrapped it up in neat red string. It was hidden behind a pile of loose paperwork that almost reached the ceiling.

'Good evening, Ms Barnes. Please choose to sit.'

The voice was unmistakable, the strange flat intonation and odd emphasis a perfect echo of the voice she had heard on the phone. It wasn't an accent, not exactly. All the words came out in sounds that were almost a crisp RP, but mismatched and swapped around. Like someone had chopped up a thousand hours of BBC Radio and clumsily mixed them together into the voice of Mr Close.

'No,' she said, trying to be brave.

Around the boxes she could only see his leg, a single meticulously polished shoe. If she turned and ran, could she get out in time? Gillian took a deep breath and moved to face him.

Up close he looked very much like he sounded. It wasn't that he was scary or threatening, he was simply incorrect. His hair was perfectly styled into a trim utilitarian cut, but the hairline didn't seem to match his head shape. His skin was pink, but not the irregular, blotchy pink it should have been. Instead it was the uniform pink of a 'light flesh' colour crayon. His suit was perfectly tailored, but he seemed to be wearing it inside out. The curtains were drawn, and the room was dingy and humid, but he still wore his sunglasses and gloves.

'You should sit,' he said again, and then Gillian was sitting on the uncomfortable wooden dining table chair. She was certain it had been in the other room.

'What do you want?' she asked, shaking so hard she could hear the chair legs rattling.

'Do you know?'

'I don't understand.'

'Understanding is not needed. Do you know?'

There was silence.

'Yes,' Gillian said softly, 'I know.'

Mr Close reached slowly into his jacket, gripping something inside it. Gillian braced herself, but when his hand reappeared it was holding a worn steel hipflask. He slowly unscrewed the lid, brought it up to his lips and took a long drink. Dark black liquid dribbled down his chin, disappearing into his suit. It almost looked like ink.

'What do you know?' he asked finally, sealing the flask and returning it to his jacket.

'I know.' She paused, the words tumbled out of her defiantly before she could stop herself. 'All of it. About the whistle-blowers, the murders, Tobias Fell, everything. It's all there.'

'You have evidence?' He tried to smile, his teeth irregular and stained black.

'You know there isn't any.'

'Yes. I know what I know what I know what I know.' His voice looped gradually into an almost hypnotic rhythm.

'What are you?' Her voice sounded very far away.

'I am what you are expecting. The one who comes to make you quiet. You know I should be here and I am.'

'That guy out there. He said you weren't real. Is he with you?'

'He will be. He does not yet believe what he knows.'

Gillian's hands were shaking. She couldn't stop them.

'What are you going to do?'

'What you need me to.'

'Will it hurt?'

'Yes.'

Her mouth was dry, her heart was thumping so loud she

couldn't hear his next words. Mr Close reached again into his pocket and this time Gillian knew he wasn't pulling out a hipflask. With a sudden, desperate energy she lunged forward at him, arms swinging wildly. The unexpected blow caught the man-shaped thing on the side of its head, knocking the sunglasses to the floor. He let out a guttural cry, pushing her away. She looked at his eyes and she—

Gillian was sitting on the wooden chair again. When was it? Was she still here? Was she still her? Mr Close was once again wearing his sunglasses.

'I'm sorry you saw that.'

Saw what? Why did her eyes feel so dry? Her skin was chilled, like she'd been falling for a very long time. There was the faintest memory of sense, of an epiphany, of everything neatly slotting together into a perfectly structured plan. But it was gone.

Mr Close placed an envelope on the desk.

'What you need,' he said, and left.

At some point in the preceding days, the clock on Gillian's wall had stopped ticking, so she had no idea how long she sat there. She tried to count her breaths, one two, in out, but her mind wouldn't slow down long enough to keep track.

Eventually, painfully, she got to her feet. She staggered to the front door and checked it. Still locked. Then she checked every corner, every cupboard, anywhere the strange man in black could conceivably have hidden himself. But there was no evidence he'd ever been there at all.

When she had at last satisfied herself that she was truly alone, Gillian convinced her legs to return her to the desk and gingerly picked up the envelope. It was labelled 'Last Piece' in the same scrawled handwriting that covered the notes on her wall. Inside was a drawing pin and a newspaper clipping.

It was the obituary of Allan Kempner. It described him as a dedicated journalist and newsman whose career had been destroyed over accusations of leaking confidential documents, and had been found dead in his flat. He had been murdered, and not quickly. Someone had broken a whisky glass and pushed it through his neck. According to the story, the police had someone in custody and, though it didn't name her, Gillian knew exactly who was going to be arrested for the crime.

The date of the piece was the 16th of August. Tomorrow. It didn't matter. It was too late for him. She took the cutting and the pin and positioned it in the centre of her cork board, a bloody thumbprint from her final papercut marking it as the lynchpin in the spiralling web of almost-truth she had constructed.

Mr Close had been right. It was the last piece. And it wasn't the string or the names or the faces that connected it. It was the blood. Smears of papercut crimson marking the words, the letters, that date. Sitting in its rightful place, the message on her wall was clear. It wasn't a cover-up or a conspiracy or a threat. It was an invitation. Tobias Fell was inviting Gillian to dinner. He was inviting them all to dinner. Her bleeding fingers stung when she wiped away the tears, but it was OK. She was finally beginning to understand.

6th

Sleepless

Alvita Jackson
112 Banyan Court

NO SIGNAL

The blue letters shone starkly from the TV screen, the only illumination in the otherwise pitch-black room. Alvita stared at them until they burned themselves into her retinas, lingering as glowing scars inside her eyelids. She remembered the days when dead air was still a thing, the screen filled with the incessant noise of static, the reassuring hiss of the nothing you were staring at. Now there was no sound at all, no movement, no signal. Somewhere inside her, something wanted to reach out, grab the remote control, change the channel, find anything to fill the silence. But her arm was heavy, weighed down by exhaustion, and she simply sat there, staring into space.

Tommy was asleep, she'd checked on him forty minutes ago. She should be too. She had a shift in five hours. Alvita closed her eyes, sinking into the thin cushioning of the sofa, willing herself to lose consciousness, to claim whatever sleep could be found. But all she could see were the light-scarred words: NO SIGNAL. She stayed like that for almost twenty minutes, until the letters had faded away, but still sleep did not come.

She could hear the night traffic rumbling through the streets of Tower Hamlets far below. She could smell the first whiff of rot from the leftovers in the fridge. She could feel the wooden frame of the armchair against her back. It was too much. How could she get any sleep like this? Not that her bed was any better. The sheets seemed to stink after a single night and washing them just replaced it with the cloying scent of detergent. Her mattress was thin and abrasive, and the midnight street noises below seemed even worse from the bedroom.

Alvita sighed, opened her eyes, and convinced her hand to fumble for the remote. How long had it been since she had a full night's sleep? She had no idea. It was hard enough to keep track of the weekend, making sure she got Tommy packed and off to school on all the days he needed to be there. She couldn't keep track of how long the insomnia had had its spindly electric fingers wrapped around her brain. It had started at least a month before the summer holidays began. And when had that been? Right. The anniversary of Pete's death. Yeah, that checked out.

She found a channel showing reruns of *Frasier* and sat there staring at it, trying to let the recorded laughter soothe her brain as if she were laughing along with it. It almost worked. Was she so far gone that she had forgotten what actual relaxation felt like? One way or another she needed sleep, otherwise she was certain she'd cause an accident at work.

Dropping the remote control unceremoniously onto her lap, she reached down and pulled the small cardboard box from her bag. She popped out the round white pill and swallowed it dry. She'd heard that Doxatrin had been recalled after some scandal or other, but she'd never really investigated. Harry who worked the stockroom could still get it and it was the only thing Alvita had ever found that could make a dent in the insomnia. She just wished it didn't take so long to kick in. She looked back at the screen. Frasier was having problems. Everyone was laughing.

She briefly considered getting something to drink. She'd read somewhere about pills getting stuck in your oesophagus if you didn't take them with water and burning a hole into your lung. Where had she heard that? It didn't matter, she wasn't getting up either way. She was so paranoid about waking herself up more, of disrupting the medication's work and losing what little sleep she could perhaps pull back from the insomnia that she had no intention of moving until the next morning. Instead she settled for idly flicking through the channels.

At this time of night many weren't even broadcasting, simply showing still images or that same NO SIGNAL message. Could she feel her eyes starting to droop already, or was she just so desperate that she was imagining it? Alvita let the remote slip from her hand. She looked up. Channel 70. What was that one supposed to be? The channel listed its name as 'Tonight' and the programme title was given as *Too Late with Angus Merridew*.

It was set up like an American-style late-night talk show, with a raised dais containing a dark wooden desk and a plush-looking armchair. In the background were fake windows painted with a sprawling nocturnal skyline. Behind the desk sat a middle-aged white man with immaculate brunette hair and a fixed-looking smile, no doubt Mr Merridew himself. He wore an off-white suit over a light brown shirt and a black tie with a pin that looked like a pearl. Something about the outfit made her feel faintly uncomfortable, but she put it down to the nausea she sometimes got when taking Doxatrin. Opposite the host, on the couch, sat an old man Alvita was sure she recognised from some movie or other, talking earnestly. The words washed over her, nonsensical and rolling.

'... wasn't anything could be done about it back then of course since I hadn't yet bought or learned to use my axe and I was still resting mainly on the beach but not for long since I couldn't stand the sound of them eating I mean I know everything has to eat I'm not saying they shouldn't eat but when you place yourself prone and try to close up there's nothing more bothersome than the sound of the chewing and the crack of what they were marrow sucking so I had to find my peace elsewhere not that peace was ever something I could truly aspire to with faces like the ones I took off anyone who looked at me funny when they weren't expecting it I would take the knife I'd once christened Lola under a nasty looking hunter's moon and carve a new something for myself to peel like one might peel an orange or a grape or a leg or a tongue or a coffin for sleeping although that's not something I'd ever before have expected since I've always been unable to sleep and thinking about it now I don't think I've ever slept just been waiting for the sleep to put me to sleep to take me to sleep to sleep to sleep …'

Alvita didn't even notice when she lost consciousness.

Alvita woke to the sound of Tommy screaming. It was a sound that shot through her, electrified every nerve, even when it was the sort of scream she was accustomed to. The scream of a child that had fallen over, but not hurt himself badly enough to need a hospital visit. She pulled herself from the chair, blinking in the daylight now seeping through the thin curtains, and hurried towards Tommy's bedroom.

Sure enough, he'd been running between the kitchen and his room when he'd tripped and fallen on his arm. There was a red patch of skin where it had scraped across the carpet, but no blood or broken bones. Alvita smiled reassuringly and kissed it better, which stopped the tears, at least for a little while. She poured him a bowl of Coco Pops and half-filled it with the last of the milk. Then her eye caught the clock on the kitchen wall. Shit. If she didn't leave now she was almost certainly going to be late for her shift. But if it was almost eight, where the hell was—

A gentle ping from the living room announced the arrival of a text message. It was Ellie, her babysitter, the one that seemed to be eating up most of her paycheck since school stopped for the summer. Ellie had a 'family emergency' that apparently she'd only found out about half an hour after she was supposed to actually be here and was 'super sorry xoxoxo'. Alvita bit her lip, choking down a scream of her own, and turned to Tommy's now-smiling face, trying to figure out what to do.

She was saved from the decision by a knock at the door. Climbing to her feet, she took a moment to compose herself and put on a smile as she answered it.

'Can Tommy come and play?'

Two young girls stood outside, the posh kids from the other side of the building. They held hands and smiled ingratiatingly at Alvita, who for the life of her could never remember their names. She didn't really like them and secretly worried they bullied Tommy, but she was running low on options. She looked back at her son, who was beaming widely at the thought of being included.

'That depends,' Alvita said. 'Will your parents be there?'

The older girl (Anya? Annette?) looked towards her smiling blue-eyed friend, who nodded emphatically.

'Yes they will,' maybe-Annette said brightly.

Something in Alvita recoiled at the thought of leaving Tommy with these two for a whole four-hour shift, but at that moment it seemed like the only option. It was fine; she'd been left alone to play with other kids at his age. He'd be alright. She turned to Tommy and nodded, trying to make her own smile convincing.

Rushing back into the kitchen, she quickly put together a makeshift lunch. Crisps, yoghurt, some sweets. She couldn't find any fruit. It was mainly junk, but she just didn't have time to make anything healthier. She pushed Tommy's *Ben 10* lunchbox into his hand, and he was out the door like a shot. She waited until it had closed behind him, then let her shoulders sag. No breakfast for her, not if she wanted to be on time. She grabbed her bag and hurried out, head still heavy from the night before.

Knock knock.

Alvita rapped twice on Edith's door as she passed. The old woman had always appreciated the thought, and it was the least she could do. After all, she'd helped out enough times by watching Tommy, back when she was more mobile. A little noise to let her know people were still thinking of her.

When she could, Alvita liked to knock again, wait for the door to open and have a real conversation, maybe even a cup of tea. But when had she last actually had the time? Work was flat out, and between Tommy and the insomnia ... well, she was sure Edith understood. And it did take her so long to answer the door these days.

A spike of guilt played at the edge of Alvita's mind, urging her to knock again, to check on the old woman properly, but she barely felt it through the haze of her fatigue.

Alvita was on the tills most of the day, limbs moving mechanically. Scanning, packing, smiling. Friendly robotic words said convincingly to a steady stream of faces with their own worries and burdens and tears. But at least they looked like they'd slept. The day dragged on, and even though it seemed to stretch almost forever, at the end of it she would not have been able to tell you a single thing that she did or said or thought between the time she put on her uniform and the time it came off. It was nothing but the rhythmic motion of her arms, the harsh blanket of fluorescent light and her performance: a gurning parody of a happy, well-rested worker. When she finally stepped back outside the supermarket, Alvita took a deep breath, hoping the fresh air would revive and energise her, but the afternoon breeze held nothing but dust, car fumes and the sticky heat of summer. Her mind immediately turned to Tommy, and she checked her phone. No texts from the Khans, and they definitely had her number. That meant he was fine, right? Even so, she found herself almost running home.

By the time she got back to Banyan Court her back was so sore that she didn't think she'd be physically able to climb the mountain of stairs. But the lift was out of order as usual, so she did it anyway. There were still a couple of hours before she needed to head out to the call centre and she was keen to spend them with Tommy.

She knew she should have tried to make her way over to the expensive side of the building and knock on the door of number 22 where the little girl who might be called Anya lived, but the idea of presenting herself to a family living over there in her current state, unshowered, exhausted, fresh from a shift, made her physically recoil. Besides, though the kids seemed to have no problem moving from one side to another, she'd never been able to figure out which of the doors in these winding, narrow corridors actually led between them. So instead she started to check some of the places Tommy had said they liked to play.

She worked her way up the staircase that wound its way around the old iron pillars of the cage elevator, tentatively calling her son's name. About halfway up she stopped, aware of an unexpected smell: tobacco smoke. For a moment a ridiculous image flashed into her mind of the two seven-year-old girls pressuring Tommy into smoking, coughing his little lungs out over stolen Pall Malls. It was absurd, of course, and she knew it, but even so she followed the scent, poking her head around the corner to see who was so flagrantly disregarding the building's No Smoking signs.

There was a man outside Edith's flat. His face was dark and lined with a certain deep sadness that Alvita couldn't help but recognise. His hand shook ever so slightly as he raised the cigarette to his lips and the smoke curled back through the open crack in the old woman's door. Alvita watched for longer than she had intended, racking her brain to see if she could remember seeing the man anywhere before. Edith didn't have any children; she knew that for sure. Perhaps a family friend? He certainly didn't look like a carer, which wouldn't have been surprising. His eyes were haunted as they met hers and he started walking over, hand raised in greeting. Alvita realised with a start what was happening and tried to banish her exhaustion, shaking her head and trying to focus, but it still felt like her thoughts were pushing through quicksand.

'Can I help you?' he asked. What was that accent? Brazilian? Somewhere in South America, certainly. She's been on holiday to Peru once, long before Tommy was born, and it had a familiar tone to it. She'd wanted to climb Machu Picchu, but hadn't properly researched it and in the end simply hadn't been physically fit enough for the arduous climb. The air was so thin up there—

'Hello?' the man asked again, and Alvita realised with a start she hadn't actually replied.

'Hello, yeah.' She tried to speak through the fatigue. She pointed at the door. 'Edith, you know, uh, you know Edith?'

'Yes.' He nodded, shifting a bit awkwardly. 'We're friends. From a long time ago.'

Was he lying? It felt like he was lying, but Alvita couldn't trust herself to make that call. Not right now. Whatever the truth, it was someone else to keep an eye on Edith, and that was a relief, albeit a guilty one.

'Have you seen a boy? The children ... my son, he should be playing around here.'

'With a little girl?' The man nodded, pointing down the corridor. 'They were running down there just now.'

'Thank you, um ...?' Alvita gestured vaguely for his name.

'Diego. Santi.'

'Thank you, Mr Santi.' She started to head in the direction Diego had pointed, then turned back. 'You shouldn't be smoking indoors, you know. Especially around kids.'

'I know, I have—' He looked deeply sad again, struggling slightly for the word. 'Sensitive nose. Helps with the smell.'

Alvita didn't really know what to say to this, so she left, following the direction he indicated until she found where Tommy was playing and took him back for dinner.

Her nightshift was always harder than working the tills. Alvita worked in the call centre for a local minicab company, booking cars for the drunk, the surly and those who sounded even more exhausted than she did, though she didn't think they really could be. Without the repetitive physical motions it was harder to keep the fatigue at bay. The desks were full of people quietly talking into headsets, filling the air with a murmuring white noise that she could all too easily lose herself in. Not sleep, of course, not really, but that sort of waking unconsciousness that constantly threatened to overtake her. She didn't like coffee and couldn't stand the clinging medicinal sweetness of energy drinks, so she pushed herself through with caffeine tablets in an attempt to stay alert, always with one ear open for her mobile. Tommy was asleep. The number was stuck above the home phone. If there was a problem, he definitely knew how to call her. He was fine.

The passengers were angry tonight. Several drivers were off sick and waiting times were building. That was one of the only benefits of being so exhausted for this job: Alvita found that, when she was this tired, all the abuse just seemed to slide off her, like some distant radio signal far removed from her life. She knew others took it harder, their emotional defences drained, and she'd seen more than one of her co-workers break down over the cruelties of someone shouting at them from the other end of the phone. But for Alvita, the cotton wool around her brain did something to protect it, even if it made functioning in the world that much harder.

At 2.30 a.m. her shift ended and she stumbled home. It was a ten-minute walk, and one that her friends were always alarmed she made so late at night. It had never bothered Alvita, though; the groups of youths who perched on corners, the sinister figures beneath lampposts, they were nothing but shadows to her. Faint, indistinct presences that would occasionally call after her, but never with words that could pierce the fog. She walked in a world removed from theirs, shifted three degrees to the side by a life without sleep. They couldn't touch her.

She passed Edith's door. Should she knock again? No, it was far too late. And she had that young Diego now. She was fine. Alvita tried to convince herself her suspicions had been misplaced.

She looked in on Tommy's room. Fast asleep. He wasn't going to be up for hours yet, and she didn't even need to prepare lunch or iron his uniform. The small mercies of the summer holidays. No word from Ellie about tomorrow, though, so she'd have to wait and see about babysitting. Maybe the posh kids would come and play with him again. She didn't really trust them, but even so the idea of having a few daylight hours fully to herself brought the shadow of a smile to her lips. Did that make her a bad mother? She was too tired to really think about it.

She fumbled with her keys and for once her prayers were answered as the call button lit up, allowing a momentary reprieve for her aching legs. She chewed slowly on a curried lamb patty she'd grabbed from one of the late-night shops when she realised she'd not had a chance to get groceries. She wasn't hungry, of course, hadn't been for weeks, but recognised that her body needed to eat, so gradually worked her way through the flavourless corner shop savoury.

The flat was silent and dark, and she let her handbag drop to the floor of the hall. She didn't even bother to take off her coat as she staggered towards the bedroom.

She was back in front of the television, watching Channel 70. Had she gone to bed? There was a faint memory of lying down, feeling the old mattress beneath her, but Alvita was here now and this definitely wasn't a dream. She couldn't read in her dreams, and the words *Too Late with Angus Merridew* were clearly visible on the screen. Her tongue felt chalky, no doubt from the Doxatrin pill she must have taken. Not to worry. It made sense.

The grinning host was looking straight into the camera, addressing the audience. From this angle his teeth looked so regular they seemed fake. Like they were just painted on.

'Painted onto what?' Angus asked, shifting from his gentle monologue. 'That doesn't make any sense, does it?'

She had to admit it didn't.

'Now, I know what you're all thinking,' the host continued with a smirk. 'What you're all asking yourselves. "What's that old sell-out Angus going to try and shill to us tonight?" Well, folks, I hate to disappoint you … So I won't! You're absolutely right that I've got a brand-new sponsorship and you're going to have a front row seat to it. Now, I didn't actually believe it when my producer Tobias first told me about the deal he'd landed. It seemed too good to be true.'

Alvita smiled, excited to hear more. She trusted Angus; he wouldn't steer her wrong. His arm reached all the way over to the side of the screen, grabbing something.

'So let me tell you about … sleep.'

The studio audience let out a low sound of interest and excitement. In Angus's hand was a photo of a bedroom.

'Now you may think you know about consciousness and reality but let me tell you that you don't know squat until you've tried sleep. It not only refreshes and revitalises you, but it unlocks the door to your imagination. Lets you dive right in in a healthy, balanced way.'

Alvita could see the photograph more clearly now. It wasn't just any bedroom; it was her bedroom. Well, that made sense. Where else was she going to sleep?

'Folks, I really can't say enough about just how vital sleep is. I mean, without it, who knows how your mind might start to seep out into the world around you? Or what you might end up letting in?'

Alvita nodded. She couldn't wait to buy some.

'Now obviously this is a *premium* product, and not one to be bought at your local supermarket. But luckily, money isn't the only way to pay for it. We can get it ordered in special for the right client.'

Alvita's whole body sang with exhaustion. Where could she get it? What would it cost?

'Oh, you'll see, Alvita. Just keep taking your medicine and we'll let you know the bill.'

She smiled as the Doxatrin kicked in and she fell into unconsciousness.

Her world was beginning to fragment. Alvita had pushed through insomnia before, endured months of bone-deep fatigue to look after Tommy, but this time it felt different. Her body moved through the world as normal, smiling and working, but it was like her mind only surfaced briefly, occasionally piercing the fog enough to actually experience what she was doing.

She was being shouted at over the phone because a driver was taking longer to arrive than had been estimated.

She was reading Tommy a story, bathed in the violet glow of his nightlight, but he was already asleep.

She was fumbling a bottle of milk off the conveyor belt and watching helplessly as it tumbled towards the floor.

Ellie the babysitter was talking about what Tommy had done with that day, rattling off events and names that Alvita had no context for.

The one constant she had was her show. The TV didn't seem to get any other channels anymore. Alvita dimly considered trying to get a repair guy round to have a look at it but forgot the idea almost as soon as it occurred. Channel 70 was fine. She'd collapse into the chair, take a Doxatrin and sit there, letting the programming faintly wash over her.

Angus wasn't on tonight. That didn't seem right, he was always on Channel 70. This show wasn't as good, which was a shame, and it didn't seem to have a name. She couldn't really follow the plot, if there even was one, and the scenes seemed disjointed. A man in a fancy suit was standing in the corridor, knocking at his own door over and over again. A plumber tinkered with his toolkit as a long, spindly arm stretched out from an open pipe behind him. A young woman danced alone in a burned-out ballroom, blood flowing from her diamond tiara. A young man in a loose T-shirt sat in the middle of a corridor, pencil furiously working in a small notebook. Then a shot of Edith, sitting in her armchair, the spitting image of Alvita's. She was utterly still.

The corridors on this show were very familiar. How nice it was for Alvita to live in a famous building. As seen on TV! Strange that nobody had mentioned it. She watched as the show abruptly switched to Tommy and his friends playing on the stairs. She wondered momentarily how Tommy had got on television, she certainly hadn't heard anything about it, but she was proud of her son regardless. He suited the screen, even if he didn't look like he was having all that much fun playing the girls' game. The camera was less kind to the blonde girl. Penny, that was her name. She looked all wrong, and moved in sharp, jerky increments, like she was shot in stop-motion. Alvita would have to ask Tommy about it later, though he didn't like to talk about Penny very much.

She closed her eyes. It was nice to see Tommy. She did worry about him, and she felt so far away sometimes. Buried beneath the exhaustion where he'd never find her.

There is no sound more chilling than your child crying out in real pain. It can cut through anything else, no matter how thick the fog that surrounds you, seizing your heart and flooding your system with the electric pulse of adrenaline, calling you to action. As Alvita scooped Tommy up from the bottom of the stairwell, whispering reassurances in his ear and looking over his injured arm, she felt more alive and present than she had in months.

They'd been playing, or so the girls said, and Tommy had slipped on the stairs. Alvita looked at her son's arm, likely broken and already swelling severely. He cried harder and buried his face in his mother's jacket.

Alvita stared daggers at the girls, who seemed mortified. Well, Anna (whose name she had finally remembered) looked sheepish, while Penny was off in a corner eating sweets, apparently unconcerned for the suffering child who they might have seriously injured. Alvita tried to choke down her bile, contain her rage, telling herself that you couldn't hate a child, that it wasn't right. If Anna's parents hadn't been there as well, she's not sure what she might have said. But Prisha, the little girl's mother, seemed to have harsh words enough, and Alvita only really had one thing she felt like she needed to add.

'You are not allowed to play with Tommy anymore.' Her voice icy and calm. 'Not ever.'

Anna looked downcast. Penny stared smugly at Alvita. What was wrong with that girl? Where were her parents? Even the Khans didn't seem to pay her any attention.

The adrenaline rush kept her riding high and pushing forward all through the visit to the Accident and Emergency room. She was focused, comforting Tommy through the tears of pain as they waited for the doctor, holding his hand as the kind-faced woman examined his injury, making sure he could see her waiting as they took him in for an X-ray. It was a clean fracture, a lot less serious than it might have been, and aside from a few weeks with his arm in a cast, it looked like Tommy was going to be fine.

Her managers were surprisingly understanding when she called in to explain the situation and told her to take as long as she needed to look after her son. Of course, how much time Alvita could afford to miss from a financial point of view was another matter, but she'd worry about that later. By the time they got home, and Tommy was asleep in bed, the adrenaline had deserted her almost entirely. The unbelievable wave of exhaustion slammed into her like a tidal wave. She was so tired it felt like it was physically trying to knock her off her feet. The walls swam in and out like something was trying to push through them, and it was all she could do to stagger over to the armchair and dry-swallow a pill.

The TV was already on.

Angus Merrydew grinned out into the darkened living room, his perfect smile smug, yet approachable. The light from the television illuminated the armchair, and the shape of Alvita slumped within it, but everything else was pitch black. She had the stray thought that if she were to try and get up, she would simply fall away into that darkness. Fall away forever. Was she awake? It was so hard to tell anymore.

'Are you ready for our next guest?' Angus smirked, throwing the question to the audience.

The camera panned over the empty banks of seating. It was just for her. She nodded.

'Fantastic! Well, this is someone I've been wanting to get on the show for a while, but she's always been a little bit shy. In fact, she told me the idea of being on television used to scare her to death!'

Pause for laughs. There was no one to laugh.

'But seriously, folks, I could not be happier to be talking to her and I'm sure you'll feel the same way. She's led a long and storied life so let's finish it right. Give a warm Channel 70 welcome to Edith Kinney!'

Alvita smiled, almost mustering up the energy to clap as the frail old woman made her way slowly across the stage to the seat next to Angus Merrydew. She looked better than the last time Alvita had seen her, more lively in her movements and wearing the most beautiful pearl earrings, but she was paler than ever, and her fingertips were tinged a faint blue. Alvita was suddenly aware of how long it had been since she'd last knocked for her, and quietly hoped Edith would be too polite to mention it on television.

'Good evening.' Angus smiled at her. 'And may I say, Edith, you're looking absolutely radiant tonight.'

'Oh, I'm sure you can say whatever you like, Angus,' Edith shot back with a wink. 'But you better be careful what cheques you're writing!'

Angus burst into a good-natured laugh that stuck out starkly in the silence of the studio.

'That's always been the problem though, hasn't it, Edith?' Angus said. 'You've just been so lonely?'

'Not always.' The old woman shook her head sadly. 'But since my Freddy passed four years ago, it's been a real problem.'

A picture filled the screen. A black and white photo of a handsome man in a woollen suit and the young woman who would eventually become the aged Edith that Alvita knew.

'Yes, of course.' Angus's face had become perfectly sympathetic. 'Is that something you feel comfortable talking about?'

Edith nodded.

'He was on a lot of medications for his heart. They were supposed to be safe, of course, but apparently not.'

'A tragedy. And it wasn't the last time pharmaceuticals would cause you some real problems, was it?'

'Oh no.' Edith shook her head. 'No, I've had a terrible time with medications. Arthritis mainly. Although they did find one that worked, eventually. I could make a cup of tea and every-thing!'

'That sounds wonderful.'

'It was, but you know how it is. The drug got more expensive and the doctors said they weren't prescribing it anymore.' Edith's voice was level, like she was telling an interesting anecdote about a beach holiday. 'And what they gave me instead, oh, it made it much worse.'

'And do you blame Tobias Fell, the man who owned the company?'

'I'm sure he didn't make the decision personally ...'

'Come on, Edith,' Angus prodded. 'We're all friends here.'

'Well, then, yes. I suppose I do.' Edith grinned mischievously.

'He also owns your building, doesn't he?'

'Yes, I moved there after Freddy. The lifts never work and even with the old medicine I couldn't do all those stairs. And with the change, well, I've been trapped in that flat for almost a month.'

Angus Merrydew's face was handsomely sad.

'And is that what killed you?'

Through the stupefying haze of sleeping pills and late-night programming, something in Alvita's stomach dropped.

'Not exactly.' Edith addressed the question with a shrug. 'But it certainly helped.'

'You didn't ...?' Angus looked to the camera and pantomimed looping a noose over his head and pulling it tight.

Pause for laughs. There was no one except for Edith, who let out a playful chuckle.

'Oh no, not sure I'd have had the strength for all that nonsense. But I was lonely and old and in pain. At some point I just ... ended. The knocking stopped, if you get what I mean.'

Alvita felt a stab of guilt.

'And I heard you had a handsome new man around to help you,' Angus said with a gently lascivious smile.

'Well, he did his best, but really there wasn't anything to be done. I'm glad he was there, though. He doesn't need to feel so bad. He has a good heart.'

'That's great to hear. Now, Edith, we're almost out of time, but I've just got to ask: after all this, what's next for Edith Kinney?'

'Well, Angus.' She considered the question for a moment. 'I thought I might gradually start to rot.'

'Really?' Angus looked impressed. 'That's quite a departure. Are you thinking of going the standard coffin route or with more of an alone in your apartment set-up?'

Edith looked at the camera, her eyes meeting Alvita's.

'Well, that really isn't up to me, is it?'

Alvita reeled. It was like the chair had disappeared and she was in freefall, though she hadn't moved at all. She staggered to her feet and managed three wobbly stepped towards the hall before the Doxatrin caught up with her and she was gone.

Edith's door wasn't locked. It stood there, silent and ajar, waiting for Alvita to build up the courage to enter. She didn't know what time it was. When had she woken up? Had she? She didn't know if what she had seen on the television had been a dream or if she was dreaming now. Is it possible to feel tired in a dream? Because she felt it in her bones, deeper than she ever had before. But that was the thing about fatigue: it always felt like it could go deeper somehow. What time was it? There was a faint, sickly daylight coming from the window at the end of the corridor, but that was the only indication. Was Tommy alright? Alvita wasn't sure. She would check on him soon. But first she needed to do this. She needed to see for herself.

There was no sign of the man who had called himself Diego.

Even the lingering scent of cigarettes was gone. But there was another smell in its place: a sickly sweet, slightly greasy odour that seemed to cling to everything it touched.

She'd heard that description so many times, from a hundred crime novels and cop shows, 'like the smell of rotting fruit', but it wasn't really like that. Those were just words. The smell of death was something all its own.

She half-expected the door to creak, but the well-oiled hinges swung back in complete silence. Alvita's legs began to shake. Between the old carpet and the quiet door she made no sound at all as she walked into that complete stillness, and she had to keep reminding herself that she was real and not some mournful ghost.

The lights were off in Edith's flat, and all the curtains were drawn. The thin sunlight that crept around the edges was barely strong enough to discern the shape of the furniture she passed by. She didn't need the light, though. The smell guided her easily through the cramped home, until she was stood at the door to the living room. A blue light shone dimly through the crack underneath it, flickering and irregular.

This door did creak when it opened.

Edith looked so small, curled up against the arm of a chair that seemed far too big for her. The old woman's face was sunken and her eyes were mercifully closed. A long-cold cup of tea sat on the side table next to her. It was impossible to guess how long she had been dead for, but it wasn't long enough to have erased the sadness etched into her features.

The whole scene was lit by the glow of the television, shining its message out into the darkened room: NO SIGNAL.

Alvita didn't need to check which channel it was set to.

*

Over the next couple of days, it was pure chaos, and Alvita wasn't able to keep up with all of it. There were police staring at her, grilling her on every aspect of her statement.

How did she know Edith was dead? She'd smelled something strange while passing the flat.

Who was the man she said was staying there? She didn't know. He said his name was Diego.

What did he look like? Dark-skinned, old suit, smoker. He seemed nice.

Had she seen him since? No.

Did she know Doxatrin had been withdrawn from circulation due to acute neurological side-effects? Yes, she was aware.

Had she been taking it the night she found Edith? No, she hadn't taken it for months.

Did she know a man named James Andre? Never heard of him.

Did this man look familiar? No, but she liked his cap. She used to have a dress in that same shade of blue.

It was a rich tapestry of truths, half-truths and outright lies as Alvita tried to navigate the strange place at the nexus of suspicion and sympathy in which she found herself. She wasn't sure if her obvious exhaustion made her lies more believable or painfully transparent, but if the police knew she wasn't being straight with them they didn't seem to particularly care. After they interviewed her once about Edith, and then again about this man James who apparently died the following night, it was clear they had no intention of returning.

Her mother was the next to visit, sweeping down from Sheffield in to take Tommy 'off her hands' for a few weeks. Alvita could read the silent judgement in her eyes, but was too tired to fight it and couldn't pretend someone else looking after Tommy for a while wasn't a relief she felt all the way through her. She kissed him softly on the head, deflecting his questions about why he was going to stay with Grandma until school started again.

Then they were all gone, and the flat was completely silent. Alvita was alone with nothing but her weariness and the faint odour of death that seemed to linger in her nostrils.

Alvita sat staring at Channel 70. They'd taken her Doxatrin away, so sleep was out of the question, but it didn't matter. It wasn't long before the relentless lines of NO SIGNAL dissolved into the flimsy studio and artificial face of *Too Late with Angus Merrydew*.

'My guest tonight is easily the most requested in the history of this show.' Angus smiled. 'We've had emails asking for her, phone calls, even a telegram from one particularly keen viewer.'

Pause for laughter. There was no one to laugh.

'And it's taken a little while, but I'm very pleased to announce that we've finally got her. So can you all give a warm *Too Late* welcome to the one, the only, Ms Alvita Jackson!'

Alvita sat there, watching herself walk into the silent studio, smiling and waving. She was dressed in that glamourous evening gown she'd seen in the window of Harvey Nichols last year. That was nice. She'd always wanted to be on television.

'Good evening, Angus, thanks for having me,' her image said graciously as it took a seat opposite the perfectly coiffed host.

'An absolute pleasure,' he said, glancing out towards the watching Alvita. 'I think we all knew it was going to happen eventually. And you didn't even have to die!'

Pause for laughter. The screen Alvita laughed politely.

'And don't think I'm not grateful for that!' she assured him brightly.

'But seriously, I think we're all familiar with your work, so

I'm actually more interested in what you've got to say to us? To me? I think you have a few questions of your own, don't you?'

Both Alvitas nodded.

'Did you kill Edith?' the Alvita on the screen asked. It was a question of curiosity, without a hint of accusation to it.

Angus pointed to himself, his face contorted into an exaggerated expression of surprise.

'Me? Goodness no! Though I won't deny we were her favourite show in the weeks before she passed. Technically it was a stroke that did for her, but we both know there was more to it than that.'

The guilt tried to hit Alvita again, but she was too far away for it to touch her.

'And Diego?'

'Ah, handsome Diego,' Angus teased.

'I ... didn't think he was handsome.'

From the armchair, Alvita could feel herself blush.

'If you say so,' Angus smirked. 'Personally, I'd advise that you keep watching. Maybe he'll have an interview of his own.'

'So, what is this?'

Alvita nodded, staring at the screen, it was about time someone was asking the real questions.

'It's ... hard to explain.' Angus shrugged. 'Let's just say it's not programming you'd receive anywhere else in London. We're going for a very specific demographic. You'll be getting an invitation soon. And it's very important you accept it. Understand?'

Pause for laughter. From the darkness of the living room, Alvita laughed. She didn't understand, but it didn't matter.

It came just as promised. Fancy card, embossed lettering. Like it was inviting her to an upscale wedding.

TOBIAS FELL cordially invites ALVITA JACKSON
to attend a dinner party at 1 Banyan Court
on the evening of 16th August 2014
Penthouse access will be available through the freight elevator

Tomorrow night. That wasn't too long to wait. Angus had been quite specific and she could feel something beneath the layers of fog and fatigue. Excitement maybe? Or fear. Either way it would soon be done and then, finally, she could get some sleep.

7th

A Foot in the Door

Caroline Fairley
4 Banyan Court

Banyan Court was haunted. It had to be.

Cari looked at the electronic thermometer in her hand, trying to convince herself that the three-degree drop in temperature counted as a 'cold spot'. There had been nothing out of the ordinary on the EMF reader and the tapes had been full of nothing but silence, but there was *something* here. She was absolutely sure of it. She saw it in the faces of the people she passed in the corridor, the slightly glassy-eyed look of the concierge: the people here were desperately trying to ignore something. Something that scared them. Something that Cari was eager to meet.

But not today, it seemed. She put the thermometer back in her black canvas bag and took out a fresh bottle of mineral water as she sat on the plush hallway carpet, her back to the wall. It wasn't the physical exertion of ghost hunting that tired her but concentrating so hard on such specific readings for so long always left her parched. The possibility of it all thrilled her, like gradually unwrapping a present. Admittedly, she'd never had a present before that was actually ghosts. But this was it. She could feel it.

It wasn't anything she could describe or put properly into words. Just a shadow of a feeling. As a child, she had been convinced that her wardrobe was haunted. She had been so convinced that a shy, small spirit was in there, lurking in the back behind her ballet shoes, that she had called her mother in almost every night to check. After her mother left it had briefly grown into something of an obsession, to the point where her father had quite seriously talked about 'getting someone in to help'. Cari had thought she had left it all in the past, but there was something about Banyan Court that had compelled her to dig her old equipment out from the storage room of her father's London flat. It was that same certainty that something was here.

Her phone alarm beeped, congratulating her on a solid two hours of writing. She grimaced. An impromptu ghost hunt was pretty extreme as far as procrastination methods went, but it was a hobby she could really lose herself in (one of the many reasons her father had always derided it). And she just couldn't stand staring at that blank white page any longer, trying to think of pitch ideas. It was starting to really worry her.

She pushed away the darker thoughts and held out her hand again, testing the air for what she had previously thought might be a cold spot. It was cooler, certainly, than the rest of the corridor, but given the relative positioning of the air conditioning vents, maybe that wasn't quite the supernatural conundrum she was after. She just needed a win, really.

Cari shouldered her bag and started to head towards the building's health centre. She kept her gym clothes in there as well and felt like hopping on a treadmill and trying to outrun her gnawing anxiety.

She never used to think of herself as someone who believed in ghosts, not really. Even now, if you actually asked her the question directly, she'd probably say 'No.' But then she'd follow up that 'No' with a dozen interesting counterpoints, examples of manifestations that have never been explained and several books on the subject that she would highly recommend. Maybe it was time she just owned her beliefs. But that wasn't quite right. She *didn't* believe in ghosts, exactly. She just believed that there was *something* out there, that the evidence was real, even if the conclusions most people drew were the wrong ones. Mostly, though, it was just fun.

As she reached the door to the health suite Cari paused. Had she heard something? She spun around quickly, trying to catch a glimpse of an unnatural shadow on the wall, or an indistinct figure disappearing around the corner. But there was nothing. She shook her head and went inside.

'I saw your article in *Cosmopolitan*.' Howard Fairley's face looked almost proud, though that may have just been the quality of the video call. 'You might even make a decent interviewer one day. That's two now, isn't it?'

'Two what?' Cari wished they didn't always have to have these conversations over the screen. It was much harder to keep both her voice *and* her face seeming relaxed.

'In *Cosmo*. You said you'd had one accepted a few months back as well?'

'Oh, no.' She was doing a pretty good job of it, as long as she kept her clenched fist out of frame. 'It's the same piece. I had to run it past Evangelina's agents first, make sure they approved it, so it took a while before it got to print.'

'Right. Just the one, then.' Her father's tone had changed in an all-too-familiar way.

'I mean, I've been published other places.' She could feel what was coming.

'Mm, yes. Blogs and such, right?'

Cari froze for a moment, with a sudden dread that her father had found her recent work on various paranormal sites dotted about the web. No, he'd definitely have mentioned that. It would have opened the conversation and ended with her moving back in with him, 'just to keep an eye on things'. Her father had no patience for such fancies.

'Look, Dad, Wired.com is not a "blog",' Cari protested, but it was too late. 'Just because they're online doesn't mean—'

'I understand that, Caroline,' he said. He clearly didn't. 'I just think that we're paying a lot of money to support you at the moment. That flat you're in certainly isn't cheap. And if you're just spending your time there writing blog posts then maybe we should reassess.'

'Dad, please, just—' She could feel her facade cracking. 'I'm actually starting to make some money as a writer. Real money. But it does take time. You've got to get your name out there. Properly get your foot in the door.'

'And how long until you can pay your own way?'

There was a long, uncomfortable silence.

'Look,' her father continued. 'You remember that position I mentioned? It's still open. We could get you started in the marketing department next week. Put that Creative Writing degree to some actual use.'

'I'll think about it,' Cari conceded. She wouldn't, but she'd had this conversation enough times to know that an outright refusal would just drag the whole thing out.

'That's your problem,' he continued. 'You're never serious about anything. It's like those dance lessons, you remember? Thousands we spent on them, and then your mother—'

'Yes, I remember,' Cari snapped, harder than she had intended. 'And I've got work to do. So ...'

'Yes. Well. Think about my offer,' he instructed. 'Now, if you'll excuse me, I've got a meeting to get to as well.'

'Sure thing.'

'Look after yourself,' her father said, with an expression passably close to parental affection.

'You too, Dad.'

Cari shut the laptop to end the call, so she didn't have to face the same blank page she'd been staring at for the last two days.

She knew her father. It wasn't actually about the money. The same reason he had 'suggested' Banyan Court as a good place for her to move to if she wanted to start a successful writing career. It was about the prestige. And of course, it had meant he could use his connection to Tobias Fell to help secure the place.

It wouldn't have been fair to say that her father was all about appearance, but he had his own standards of respectability. *Cosmopolitan* was hardly a publication he had a lot of time for, but he recognised an important brand and, more importantly, he could actually hold it in his hands. A couple more features in respectable magazines and maybe he'd back off. She just needed a good pitch.

Her gaze fell on the open bag. She'd thrown her gym kit in the wash, so now all that remained were the cameras, tripods, temperature and EMF scanners. She smiled. Obviously a piece in the *Fortean Times* wasn't likely to gain her father's respect, but if she didn't focus too directly on the supernatural aspect … Well, Tobias Fell was always good copy, and a dive into the history of where he chose to erect his monument? It was a no-brainer. Especially if she could find a spook or two to sprinkle through. If there was one thing sceptics loved, it was deniably reading about ghosts.

She opened her laptop back up, took a breath, and began typing:

THE DARK ROOTS OF BANYAN COURT

Too much? She could always revise the title if it turned out the history of the place was too mundane, but Cari was sure she could find something. When you had a man like Tobias Fell involved, you could be sure there was a skeleton buried somewhere.

A Whitechapel History. The title was as unassuming as the book, a worn paperback from sometime in the 1980s with a poorly cropped photograph of the distinctive arch of the Whitechapel Gallery over a navy-blue background. She had found a battered copy in the nearby library. It was thick, which was encouraging, and even more encouraging was the fact that the index didn't have a single entry for 'Ripper, Jack the'.

When Cari had decided to start researching her article, she hadn't reckoned on just how difficult it would be to escape his shadow. After all, not to be insensitive, but he was a single serial killer who didn't even hit double digits. A historical curiosity. Right? Surely he wouldn't be the focal point dominating every single work of local history about the area since? It wasn't that there weren't any books focusing on other aspects of Whitechapel's history, it was just that she had a hard time finding them under the deluge of breathlessly salacious books aimed at morbid tourists that saw the area as little more than a backdrop for ghoulish titillation. It was exhausting and unless it turned out Banyan Court was being haunted by the man himself, utterly useless.

Maybe *A Whitechapel History* wasn't the best book out there, but it was the one that she could find. Online research hadn't been much better. She didn't have her JSTOR login anymore, and without an angle to focus on yet the information she'd found had been even shallower than the pop-history books littering the library shelves. Plus, if the article was going to be grounded enough for mainstream publication it would need to be as much about the history of the building than about anything that might be haunting it. Unfortunately, the library copy was reference only and there wasn't an eBook edition, so she had to go home and order a second-hand copy from Amazon.

So, what to do until it arrived? She'd already scoured the non-paywalled side of the internet, filling her notepad with shallow details. She stood up, stretched and started to take stock of her kit, making sure that tapes were blank, batteries were charged, and everything was working properly. She could feel an anticipation building inside her, something she hadn't felt since she was a child. Soon she was going to have the history covered; maybe it was time to start sourcing her ghosts. It was for the article, after all.

The big question was where in the building Cari was most likely to find her ghosts. She'd mainly been trying the corridors around her own apartment until now and had determined that there were no spiritual emanations near the health suite, which wasn't entirely surprising.

Her online research had brought up plenty of articles on the 'back half' of Banyan Court. A few more affordable flats alongside the maintenance and storage areas, from what she understood. If it was less well kept or frequented than the main building, that was almost certainly the best place to start her hunt properly, not to mention the fact that, well, she didn't really like to think about it, but she reasoned that if the residents were poorer then there was more likely to be tragedy, trauma … all the stuff that made good ghosts. Her efforts to find a way back from the corridors around her flat yielded nothing, so she decided to try the long way. Cari headed down and past the creepy concierge, then began to make a circuit of the building, looking for an entrance.

She crept past the huge bins, relishing the feeling of trespass, of finding something hidden. The first thing she found was an old concrete basketball court, netless hoops rusting gently in the humid summer air. There it was: an unassuming door marked with a large 'B', the windows flanking it on either side protected by heavy bars painted a bright warning yellow. Cari was on CCTV, a sign warned her, an announcement that caught her unawares. As did the decidedly well-kept lock on the door. She paused for a moment, the question of how to get in suddenly a very pressing one.

It was, however, solved a few moments later when the door swung open and an exhausted-looking woman shuffled out, followed by an excitable little boy in bright green dungarees. She gave Cari a nod and wordlessly held the door open. Hesitating only a second, Cari mumbled a thank you and headed inside, jumping slightly as the heavy door slammed shut behind her.

This part of Banyan Court was something entirely new – or old, rather. Gone was the plush carpet and tasteful floor lighting of the main building, but this wasn't an afterthought: people clearly lived here. A lot of people. The bank of letterboxes set against the wall must have numbered almost eighty, and a rack of bikes in various states of repair sat off in a small side room. How could she not have known this was here? The estate agents certainly hadn't mentioned it. It didn't make sense. She'd searched so hard for doors that led back here from the front and found nothing. How could this many people be living here and there was no way to reach them directly? Cari pressed on, down the corridor, before stopping with a gasp.

Stretching up and away from her, right through the building, was an old wrought-iron lift. It was looped by a stairwell that gave access to the rest of the floors above her and had obviously been part of whatever Banyan Court had been before it was a residential tower block. The structure of it was tinged with rust but had stood the test of time far better than might have been expected. A thick yellow chain sealed the sliding grate shut, marking the thing as off-limits. No doubt it had stopped working decades ago.

Cari let the bag slip from her shoulders and knelt over it, rummaging for her remote cameras. She'd found what she was looking for, she was certain. If anywhere was going to be haunted, it was here. She allowed herself a smile of anticipation.

The next day was lost to googling her new discovery. The articles from Cari's initial research were just the tip of the iceberg. She wasn't the first to stumble onto the fact that there were people being rented sub-standard apartments. In fact, there were a good half-dozen thinkpieces on it from a few years ago when the building had first been completed, each holding up the back of Banyan Court as an example of everything wrong with current housing policies. Nothing had ever actually been done about it of course, but it did make Cari feel a little better that she wasn't alone in feeling uncomfortable about the whole situation.

And it did leave a bad taste in her mouth. She had started to take photos, framing them to emphasise the dingy atmosphere, but as the shutter clicked, she felt a curious sense of shame creep over her. This place wasn't some tourist destination for her to indulge her aesthetic tastes. She was safe from an existence like this, but at what cost? Her father's business dealings were not always the most ethical (from what her mother had cited in the divorce, neither was his personal life) and he'd never fully explained his relationship to the building's owner. Walking through the damp-smelling hallways of Banyan Court's back half she couldn't completely evade the sting of guilt.

It was still preying on Cari's mind now, as she tried her best to concentrate on the video footage she'd taken. She sighed and clicked back to a few minutes earlier, trying to keep her attention focused on the empty corridor. Don't get distracted. After all, if she didn't get this article picked up her father might cut her off, and then maybe she would be in danger of poverty herself. She was optimistic, though. She'd sent some article pitches off a couple of days ago and had already had a couple of interested emails from a few decently prestigious magazines. Admittedly, she hadn't explicitly mentioned ghosts in her approach, pitching it more as an insider's view of Tobias Fell's grand folly. Still, they'd seemed very keen on her intimations about 'dark secrets', so if she had something compelling enough she was certain they'd take it. No doubt they were expecting dirt and scandal, but she'd do them one better. She was sure of it.

She moved to the next video: footage of her finally finding a door between the two sides. She smiled slightly as her laptop speakers played back her own tinny squeak of triumph. Even once she'd discovered what was back there it had been a day's work to hunt down a door that linked the two halves. It had been so out of the way as to feel almost deliberately hidden, lurking down a thin, nondescript corridor and requiring her to go through a cleaning cupboard to access it. It even had a fierce-looking 'Keep Out' sign on it, though for what reason Cari couldn't understand. The more she learned about the layout of this place, the less sense it seemed to make. Perhaps that was another thing she could explore in her article? Turn it into a proper longread?

Regardless, it had made retrieving the footage from the

cameras she had set up relatively simple. She'd managed to tuck them into an out-of-the-way corner and on top of door jambs, and it didn't look like anyone had interfered with them. Forty-eight hours' worth of footage of the two spots with the most EMF activity; if this didn't do it, she might have to abandon the classic ghost hunting methods and try something new.

Now settled in with a blanket and a large glass of wine, she continued scrubbing through two days' worth of footage, looking for strange figures or rogue shadows. Unfortunately, the shadows all seemed pretty normal, and the figures that passed were solid enough, haunted only by their own difficult position in life or the harsh realities of living in a place like that. Again, she felt that twinge of shame at watching, comfortable and insulated, mining these people's situation for an article. She watched as a young woman left each night at dusk, clearly heading towards some awful night job, only returning after dawn could be seen through the hallway windows. Cari felt a swell of pity. It must be awful to work like that, slaving away in the dark. She was kind of cute, though.

Perhaps she was wrong. Perhaps Banyan Court was only haunted by the people who lived there. Still, she kept combing through the footage, going back and forth over individual frames, trying to judge if she was seeing anything significant and coming to the conclusion that no, she wasn't. Then she stopped, wrinkling her brow in confusion, rewinding and just letting the video play. A man was standing there, at the section of corridor she was monitoring. He was dressed in tatty jeans and a Simon & Garfunkel T-shirt, and what he was doing caught her eye. He wasn't going anywhere or waiting for someone from one of the flats. He was going from one wall to the other and gently placing his palm on each. She could see he had a camera of his own hung on a strap round his neck. Back and forth, back and forth, taking a few moments to consider each time. Then he took out a tape measure and stretched it between the two walls. He retracted it. Stretched it again between the same exact two points, checked it, then retracted it. He did this four more times, before pulling out a small notebook and jotting something down. Then he left, vanishing off camera.

Pulling the slider back, Cari watched him go through the motions again. A builder, maybe? Someone looking to do some DIY? So why did he look so furtive? She kept watching the screen. Somewhere under her confusion were the seeds of intrigue. The man's movements hadn't been erratic or compulsive in any way.

He was performing some sort of experiment. The more times she watched it, the clearer that became. He was, as far as she could tell, real; no strange shadows or video anomalies accompanied his appearance. So why did it feel to Cari like she might have finally found her ghost? What was he doing?

She pushed herself off the sofa, a little worse for wine, and headed over to a chest of drawers. Pulling out the lowest one, the one she thought of as her 'grown up' drawer, she began pawing through screwdrivers, possibly dead batteries, gaffer tape, warranties and light bulbs until she found what she was looking for. A tape measure of her own.

This was ridiculous. She should have been reading back through her books, making notes for the article. Instead she found herself pushing through the 'Keep Out' sign on a door in a cleaning cupboard and going to look for that corridor. It was late, but that didn't matter.

She stood there, trying to keep the tape level as she stretched it across the gap, as close as possible to where the man on the video had done so.

One hundred and ninety-eight centimetres.

Cari paused, letting the tape measure snap back, then walked over and pressed her hand against the small black cross she had drawn on the dingy wallpaper, closed her eyes and focused. Nothing. The wall was completely still. She walked to the other side and did the same thing again. Still nothing.

She took a deep swig from her water bottle and began to extend the tape measure again, making sure each end lined up perfectly with the cross she had drawn on its respective wall.

One hundred and ninety-five centimetres.

She stared at it for a long time, holding the tape measure in position for almost three minutes, watching for any change in the length, and movement in either wall. It was still one hundred and ninety-five. Three millimetres. That could easily have been her own error the first time.

She retracted it, waiting only a few moments before once again extending it to measure the width of the hallway.

Two hundred and one centimetres.

Cari's legs went slightly weak as she started to accept what she was seeing. All at once she was seven again, watching her mother pile up dancing shoes outside her wardrobe, shining a torch into all the corners to show her there was nothing there, but there had been something there. She'd known it then and she knew it now, no matter what her father and his 'professionals' might have said.

This wasn't the haunting she had been looking for, and she wasn't even sure how well it would work in the article, but she absolutely had to go deeper. If she needed to, she'd write an entirely new article. Heck, if it ended up in the *Fortean Times* after all her dad would just have to lump it. Right now, though, she needed to find the man from her camera, and she needed to get a look at the building plans. First the door, now this. What else was Banyan Court hiding in its strange, mutable spaces?

The on-hold music for the estate agent droned on from her phone's speakers. Half an hour now and counting, but Cari was patient. She had her phone on charge, thousands of unused minutes on her contract, and *A Whitechapel History* had finally arrived to occupy her while she waited. They could keep her hanging for as long as they liked: she wasn't going away. After all, they might be her last hope to get her hands on anything resembling building plans, having been firmly rebuffed by everywhere else that might have had them on file.

Part of her was still trying to justify this as 'article research', but she knew that wasn't it anymore. Something about this place had wormed its way into her and she needed to know more.

When she slept, she dreamed of her mother, telling her softly there's no such thing as ghosts.

The automated voice reassured her how important her call was, but Cari barely even heard. Her gaze was firmly focused on the book in her hand. She had finally found something she thought might relate directly to Banyan Court. From what she had seen in the back of the building it was clear that the place had parts that were far older than she had initially thought. She couldn't figure out the exact date it would have been built, but she was sure the original structure had been part of what was referred to by the book as the 'Collingwood inferno': a string of three fires in 1869, all affecting brick slum tenements in the area around Collingwood Road. Each caused tremendous loss of life within the cramped and unprepared confines of the over-crowded buildings. Arson was suspected, though no culprit was ever caught. Some even suggested that the police themselves might be responsible, as two officers had lost their lives to violence in one of those tenements the year before.

One of the tenements involved was a run-down building named Westerland House, after the Sir Henry Westerland who had originally commissioned its construction. The streets referenced seemed promising, and having a look over the historical map of Whitechapel ... The thrill of discovery rushed through Cari, as she realised that the foundations of the building in which she sat might be the very same that had once supported Westerland House. She looked up from her book with a start, suddenly worried she might have ignored the phone for too long.

'... call is important to us. Someone will be with you as soon as possible.'

Or maybe not.

Armed with a name, she attacked the internet, as well as cross-referencing with a few of the more respectable volumes she'd taken from the library. There wasn't a lot of information online, but she did find a photograph that claimed to be of Westerland House after the fire, on a website dedicated to (what else?) the crimes of Jack the Ripper. For all the ghoulish fonts and salacious copy, though, the thing that chilled Cari was the picture itself. The lower levels were blackened and scarred. Around the base were piles of rubble, and in the blurry silver of that nineteenth-century photo were a dozen indistinct shapes and lines, any one of which might have been the remains of a victim, as fire-twisted as the structure that loomed over them, still pleading to be saved. And above the third floor it was just gone, the brick below where it should have been warped and scarred by heat. Wait. She recognised those bricks. The fire-hollowed windows that would one day be covered with bright yellow bars. A shiver ran through her, though she wasn't sure exactly why, and all of a sudden, she felt very small indeed. Cari closed the laptop.

A Whitechapel History had a bit more detail on the specific fate of Westerland House. After the fire, the land was bought by Charles Fell, a man who made his fortune in gemstone mining. Cari smiled with vindication when she saw the name. He had it rebuilt and knocked down several nearby buildings to expand it into a dye factory in 1876. It had brought much-needed work to the area, but also its fair share of problems.

Blame was placed on the toxic fumes from the factory as the culprit for several infant deaths in the area over the next decade, with one newspaper dubbing Fell's factory 'The Poison Palace'. It certainly didn't help that, while most other factories had switched entirely over to William Henry Perkins's aniline dyeing methods, Fell insisted on continuing the use of arsenic in making their rich green dye, and many workers reputedly fell ill. This, combined with lax safety standards even for its time, led to a high turnover of employees. When a worker was forced to leave a job due to illness, injury or death it was joked that they had 'gone to the ballroom', due to a persistent rumour that Fell had constructed a hidden ballroom in the heart of the factory, gilded in gold and bedecked in Zambian emeralds and rubies extracted from Fell's brutal Burmese mining operations. A place of secret parties, exclusive invitations, and esteemed guests who never spoke of what occurred within those walls. How and why this idea began is impossible to say, and there seems to have been no concrete evidence for it, but the ease with which it took root in the imagination of his employees can maybe give us some inkling of the regard in which Charles Fell's workers held him.

Kirsten Dawes, *A Whitechapel History*, Chapter 14
'A Second Revolution'

Cari put the book down slowly. A ballroom. Something in those words resonated: an image of a grinning Victorian industrialist, sitting in the centre of his gilded and glittering sanctum of wealth, listening to the distant cries of suffering from the people below ... She had seen her mother dance once, a year or so before she left, and Cari found it hard not to picture that room, the shining marble and glowing chandeliers. It was better than a secret door, at least. But if she was going to find evidence of it, she needed a look at those building plans.

As if in reply, the hold music abruptly stopped.

'Hello? Hello? Dean Bishops Estate Agents, Laura speaking? Is anyone there?'

Cari almost leapt off the chair, fumbling for her phone. She'd gone almost completely deaf to the hold music that had been gently continuing through her research, and now she found herself almost unable to speak.

'Yes, uh, hi. Hello. Um, I'm ... I live, uh ...'

She could sense the woman on the other end about to hang up.

'Banyan Court?' Cari finished.

A pause.

'You rent one of our Banyan Court properties?' The voice of this 'Laura' was much warmer now, though Cari thought she could detect a hint of wariness in it.

'I do. Through my father.' Cari didn't need to have said that part. Why did she say it? She tried to calm down, get some control of the conversation back.

'What number is the property?' Laura asked, a little too eagerly, and then Cari understood. The estate agent needed to know which side of the building she was talking to.

'Four,' she said, suddenly aware of her position. 'I'm in flat four.'

'Ah, excellent!' The voice on the other end finished its journey into warmth. 'What can I do for you today? Many apologies for the wait, my colleagues are all out on viewings.'

'No problem,' Cari muttered, fidgeting in her seat. 'I had some questions about the floorplan?'

'Certainly. Send me your email address and I'll shoot over the one for your flat.'

'Actually, I was hoping I could get something a bit of a larger scale.'

'I'm ... not sure I understand.' Laura sounded genuinely confused.

'I'm looking for a floorplan for, uh, for the whole building. If I can.'

'I don't know if there's something—'

'Both sides.'

Laura was silent on the other end of the phone.

'I think you should probably check with Tower Hamlets' local authority. They might have something in the record—'

'They don't.' Cari knew she was pushing too hard, but it was like a dam had broken, begging her mother to check again. 'Nowhere does, but you rent out almost half the flats in this place. You've got to have something. And I need to see it.'

'Look, there's nothing like that here.' Laura's voice was oddly defensive. 'We just deal with the rent and maintenance.'

'So, you have plans of the wiring, the plumbing, stuff you can give the workmen.'

Now Laura's tone was cold. 'Just leave it alone.'

Cari didn't reply. The warning was so clear, so oddly forceful, she didn't have a response.

'Please,' Laura said.

'What have you seen?' Cari asked at last, her curiosity winning.

'Nothing.' Her voice was hollow and resigned. 'I haven't seen anything. Sorry we couldn't help you.'

Click.

Cari sat there a while longer, the phone still to her ear, staring out the window, lost in thought. The sun shone down on the same streets as it had for hundreds of years, and it wasn't going to set for hours yet.

Without a clear next step, Cari found herself wandering the halls, drifting through both sides of Banyan Court like the very ghosts she was hunting. She knew what she was looking for, but as for how to find it, she didn't know where to start. She took to drawing crude maps of each floor on graph paper, but without the skills to properly lay it out there was only so much she could do. She had no idea how large any of the other flats were, and there were so many locked doors, any one of which could have led to something that would have completely altered her amateurish schematic. They could be a cupboard. Or another corridor. Or a ballroom.

Why couldn't she shake this idea? She'd dreamed about it last night. Her father, dressed in a woollen suit and an old top hat, waltzing over the marble floor of an impossibly ornate room. No windows. No doors. Utterly hidden from the world. He held a woman in his arms, arrayed in jewels and fine fabrics. Her face was fixed in an empty smile and she did not move.

'Caroline never finished her lessons,' she had said.

'Such a disappointment,' her father had replied.

Cari didn't recognise the woman, but her father waltzed with her nonetheless, his feet not slipping once, though the dancefloor was slick with blood. Then she woke up.

Cari shook her head. The whole thing was absurd. Not even a difficult dream to decipher. She hadn't met her dad's new girlfriend, but the rest of the imagery was pretty basic. There was a certain degree of psychological baggage that came with coming from a successful, driven family and the pressures of it. Not to mention everything with her mother. Perhaps her dad was right: she'd stopped her counselling sessions too soon.

Or perhaps the ballroom was real. Whether you could call them ghosts or not, Cari did believe there was some sort of spiritual residue that could be left behind after death. The sort of thing that, if you were sensitive to it, might reach out and give you just a little bit of subtle guidance; planting an idea deep in your mind where you can't quite shake it. And she couldn't get the music from her dream out of her head. That gentle, rhythmic swell.

Cari paused at the thought. Did she really think that ghosts were trying to guide her to the hidden ballroom at the centre of the factory which had been hollowed out to make Banyan Court? Surely this was absurd. Even if it was true, it might not be something she could use in her article. Why was this the feeling that gripped her?

She broke into a smile. Why not? On the phone, the estate agent had clearly seen something unnatural in this place, and what about the guy measuring the corridor? Something was going on and if her instincts were drawing her to an impossible room, maybe it was best to follow them.

She returned to her flat and began to pore over her rough layout of the building. The old dye factory had stood about 94 feet tall, dwarfing many of the surrounding buildings, at least according to one website dedicated to the skyline and layout of (Cari sighed) Jack the Ripper's East End. That was about seven stories. After it was bombed during the blitz, it looked like the factory was abandoned and the building left to rot for over half a century.

A shiver went through her again. Tobias Fell, Charles's great grandson, had built Banyan Court on a ruin built on a ruin. Had they owned the building all this time? Why? It wasn't that strange, though, surely? Most of London is three ruins deep at least. Cari tried to focus. From the photos it looked like the V2 rocket had destroyed the top half of the building, anything that had survived would have to be below that. And the line from the book kept running through her head: 'the heart of the factory'. If the old ballroom was going to be anywhere, which it obviously wasn't, it would be on the fourth floor. She was sure of it.

What was she expecting to find? A rotten ruin the builders somehow overlooked? A pristine, sparkling artefact, preserved in secret by the current owner? A clustered huddle of ghostly figures, the ranks of dead miners and exploited workers, weeping over the pointless riches stolen from their broken hands? Of course, she told herself she expected to find nothing at all. It had only ever been a myth. But she was lying.

'Mr Erikson?'

The figure spun round at Cari's words, revealing himself to be exactly who she thought he was.

'Uh, yes. H-hello. Good to see you again.' It was clear the man had no idea who she was. He shuffled backwards slightly, like he'd been caught doing something he wasn't supposed to and was preparing to run.

Now that he wasn't interviewing her for a staff writer position all the power seemed to have left David Erikson and Cari found her respect for him fading away as well. He wasn't behind an imposing desk now; no framed front pages lining the wall. He was just … some guy. His suit was clearly nearing the end of its life and his bag was held together on one strap by duct tape.

In many ways he seemed to match the shabby wallpaper of the building's rear and she felt a slightly petty joy seeing him like this. She didn't bother to refresh his memory on who she was.

'What are you doing here?'

She was pretty sure that it was something more sensible than hunting down a ghostly ballroom, but she couldn't resist asking. Last she'd heard he was still working as a contributing editor at the *Post*, and to find him skulking around the back corridors of Banyan Court was surprising to say the least.

'I can't say, sorry.' David threw his hands up in mock exasperation, his voice condescending. 'NDAs, you know?'

'OK.' Cari was feeling a little bit cruel. 'So, if I were to give Bill a ring? At the front desk? He'd know you were here. Right?'

She had no idea what any of the concierges' names actually were, but she was sure none of them were Bill.

'Sure,' David said. 'Call Bill if you want. It's all above board.'

Cari had to admit he was a decent liar. She almost believed him. He saw her grin and deflated.

' … Or whatever the hell his name is. Fine, you caught me. Please don't get me thrown out.'

'What are you doing here?'

'Who even are you?'

'I'm—' Cari considered telling him the truth, but instead found herself surreptitiously dropping her tape measure back into her bag. 'I live here. And I know your work, so just wondering what brought you to my neck of the woods.'

She'd never used that idiom before in her life, the faux-casualness not really suiting her. The veteran journalist could clearly sense it too, and she could see him deciding whether to challenge her. His eyes moved from her expensive bag, to her high-end shoes, to the dingy, discoloured wall of the corridor.

'You live here?' It wasn't a challenge. It was an opportunity.

'I do,' she said, neglecting to mention which side. 'Now tell me what you're doing here.'

He sighed and shrugged. Clearly she was one mystery too far.

'Fine,' he said at last. 'But not here.'

Wetherspoons isn't exactly famous for their coffee, but the nearest available seats were at the Moon On the Water, a nearby pub with booths that were just private enough. At that time on a Tuesday morning there were only a few other souls there and none of them looked in a state to bother anyone.

David sat there, ignoring a steaming white mug that sat in front of him. Now Cari could get a decent look at him it was clear he'd recently been the recipient of a black eye. She waited patiently for him to start.

'So, a few weeks back a story broke about one of Tobias Fell's companies. They were involved in some slash-and-burn stuff in the Amazon, not unusual, but apparently this time it ended up killing enough people that there was a real outcry. Combined with all that additives story last year ... you hear about that?'

Cari shook her head.

'Nasty business. Couple of kids actually went blind. Anyway, we reckoned it was about time to do a proper article digging into Fell's connections with all these companies. Y'know, how much was he unlucky in the companies he chose to buy or invest in, how much was he complicit in all the shit they got up to. Obviously, I wanted to get a comment from the man himself, but as usual his office rebuffed me. Billionaire recluse doesn't want to talk to the press, go figure.'

David was talking faster now. It was clear he'd been holding this all in for a while. Cari sipped her burnt coffee and just listened.

'So I think no biggie, we can run the story without him, but I got curious. I'd never actually seen that place, Banyan Court, up close. I've been poking around, managed to get a comment from a few of the residents, but I don't know, something felt weird. Then they found this old woman last night. Edith Kinney, dead in her apartment. Cause of death says natural causes, but a police contact mentions there's this guy been seen hanging around. Heavy smoker, probably South American from the descriptions. Might be involved.'

David was staring at her, eyes gleaming.

'I reckon there's maybe a different story now, and I try to talk to the concierge, get some more details. He gave me this.'

He gingerly touched the bruise around his eye.

'Kind of an overreaction.'

'You think? I don't know. I've been doing this job a while now and I know when something's going on, but usually I can get a feeling for what it is. This, though? I feel like I'm just fumbling in the dark. No one from your side of the building's given me the time of day.'

Cari was taken aback at how easily he'd pinpointed which side she was from, but if David noticed her momentary discomfort, he didn't show it.

'Talked my way into a chat with some tech guy and he chucked me out before I could ask any real questions. Though I've talked to a few folk in the arse end of the building.'

'And ...?' Cari leaned forward, no longer bothering to hide her intrigue.

'More questions than anything else. Still no clue about this South American guy, or what's going on with Fell.'

'Never met either of them.' Cari shook her head. 'Sorry.'

'You feel it, right? All the little things that don't quite add up? I just need some answers.'

'Will you publish it?' An uncharitable thought about possible competition flitted across Cari's mind.

'What?' It was as though the question hadn't occurred to him for a while. 'Sure, I guess. If I'm not obsessing over nothing. But I trust my instinct, y'know? Can't get far in this business if you don't.'

David sighed, looking every one of his forty-three years. It seemed like he was done, and an uncomfortable silence settled over the conversation.

'So, what about you?' he finally continued. 'What's the daughter of Howard Fairley doing wandering around the slum side of Banyan Court with a notebook and a tape measure?'

Cari nearly choked on her coffee at the mention of her father's name.

'Took a while to recall exactly where I recognised you from,' David continued. 'But I'll never forget when he phoned up the office to shout at us for turning you down. Blaming me for wrecking your chance at getting "a real foothold in the industry", while not exactly helping your chances himself.'

'I'm really sorry he did that.' The white mug wasn't big enough to hide Cari's bright red face. 'I didn't ask him to.'

'It's history.' He waved his hand as though dismissing the thought. His voice finally lost the last faint traces of condescension 'So are you going to tell me what you're up to?'

Cari took a deep breath.

'Would you believe I'm hunting ghosts?'

David laughed. It wasn't a cruel laugh, but it was clear that no, he wouldn't believe it.

Then he nodded, surprising her. 'You picked the right place, I reckon.'

*

Cari wasn't sure she shared David's confidence, though, and pretty soon she was almost certain she'd made a mistake. Her 'map' of the third, fourth and fifth floors was as complete as she could make it, but still consisted mostly of question marks. Flats and locked doors barred every further avenue of exploration and though none of the measurements she'd done seemed to match up properly, she couldn't be sure if that was some supernatural property of the building or just mistakes in her own calculations.

She slumped against the wall next to the old stairwell. She wasn't going to cry. She refused to give her father the satisfaction.

'Hey, are you OK?'

The voice was soft and hesitant, and Cari didn't recognise it. But turning her head she found herself looking into a face she'd seen before. In person, weathered skin showed evidence of more hardship than matched his relative youth, and his eyes shone with a quiet intelligence. The T-shirt he wore was different to the one she'd seen on camera, but just as faded and tatty.

'It's you,' she said, before she could think about it.

Immediately the man's face changed. He backed off slightly, his posture turning defensive and his eyes instinctively scanning his surroundings as though for possible exits.

'You know me?' His tone was wary.

'Yeah. I've seen you around. I live in the building.' Cari thought it best not to mention exactly how. 'You were taking some measurements. In one of the corridors?'

'Oh. Right.' He was considering her words. 'That was you. With the hidden cameras?'

She flushed. 'You saw them?'

'Yeah.' He nodded. 'Not sure that's OK.'

'I know. Sorry.'

'Can't really criticise.' He opened his bag to flash her a camera of his own, then held out a hand. 'Damian.'

She shook it. 'Cari.'

'So, Cari,' he said. 'Why are you secretly recording here?'

She considered the question, running through the list of lies she could tell. She was sick of lying.

'I'm looking for the ballroom,' she told him. The words felt odd to say out loud.

Damian let out a low whistle.

'You sure that's a good idea?'

'You know it?' In an instant she was upright, electrified by curiosity. Her new friend grinned, clearly glad to find a kindred spirit.

'No. But I think I know what it means that you want to find it. Could probably tell you how. But I don't think you want to, not really.'

'You can't tell me what I want.' Cari bristled.

'You're right, I can't.' He eyed her, as though assessing. 'But I can tell you that so far, it doesn't look like this place has really noticed you. You keep pushing, though ... Maybe that changes. Trust me, you don't want that.'

Cari tried to digest his words, to understand what he was saying. Finally, she nodded.

'I accept that.' She considered her words carefully, sensing their importance. 'But I need to know.'

Damian sighed.

'OK.'

Follow the music. That's what he'd said when she'd told him everything she knew. The spaces in this place aren't only travelled by your feet. There are directions you cannot find on a compass. Listen in the dark and follow the music.

So Cari sat in the dark, ears straining. She'd lost track of time, but it had been night for a long time now. *A Whitechapel History* lay forgotten on the floor. Her laptop sat uncharged on her desk. The article wasn't important, not now. She could find another way to make her name. This was something else. A burning need to find the heart of this place, to push her way through a fog of history to the pure essence of greed and dispassionate cruelty; a world where people are allowed to suffer out of sight simply because it is *easier*. She'd seen glimpses of it since she was a child. Could she be better or was it her fate too? Perhaps tonight she would find out.

She sighed, opening her eyes, though the room was pitch black. Nothing. It had been almost a half-hour and she felt like an idiot. She stretched her aching legs and stood up, turning towards where the light switch should have been.

Wait. There. A note, so distant it might have drifted in from another building entirely. And there, another. The softest tone of a far-off cello. Cari stood, closed her eyes, and began to walk towards it. One step, then another. She knew she should have been standing in front of the wall, and when she took the third step she half expected to slam face first into plasterboard, but there was nothing there. Each motion felt longer than the last as she drifted effortlessly through the places hidden in the corners of Banyan Court, the unseen corridors and crumbled stairways, into the bare brick corridors of Westerland House.

She knew the door as soon as she opened her eyes, though she'd never seen it before. On the surface it looked unremarkable, no gold inlay or intricate designs, but there was an air of quality to it. The wood was solid oak, expertly aligned. The rivets and hinges were perfectly formed cast iron that had been well oiled and cared for. The lock was solid and intimidating. Whoever had installed this door had spent an awful lot of money making it secure.

But it was not locked. Not for her. Somehow, she wasn't surprised.

The music that had drawn Cari through the building swelled to a crescendo as it swung open. The strings sang in a swoon above the rumbling of the bass, laced with the delicate piping of woodwind, all flowing together in perfect three-four time. Warm light embraced her, as hundreds of gas lamps reflected off the gleaming golden walls.

She looked at her feet, now adorned in soft satin ballet shoes, like her mother used to wear. Like her father had picked out for her. For the first time in a long time, they felt right on her feet, urging her to twist into *en pointe*.

There was no orchestra, of course. No one had set foot in this place for over a hundred years. Maybe no one had ever set foot here at all. Cari was alone as the door closed gently behind her. It was so bright, and the polished marble of the floor echoed as she walked, despite the softness of her shoes, her footsteps mixing with the subtle harmonies of the waltz, falling naturally into perfect time.

Everything was covered with twinkling jewels. Diamonds, rubies and emeralds set into every light fitting, every wall panel, arranged in intricate lines across the dancefloor. And from each breath-taking gemstone leaked a steady stream of blood.

It flowed slowly down the walls. Across the floor. Filling up the lamps until one by one their lights were extinguished. Cari felt the slickness of it on her own hands, long before the gentle flood reached her expensive shoes, soaking into the satin, urging her to dance.

The music continued, faster now, as if in disdain of what was happening. It pulsed through Cari, pulling at every string within her, enticing her, demanding that she begin her routine, that she take her place in the blood-soaked choreography. Staying still took more effort than she had ever imagined possible, but she did it, taking in the suffering and pain that laced every penny of the riches that had built this place. A place that had never existed. A place she fit perfectly.

The music begged for her to dance, but Caroline Fairley shook her head and gently pushed herself backwards, allowing herself to collapse. She hit the rising tide without a sound and felt the weight of history wash over her, as she let herself drown.

Damian was waiting for Cari on her return. He didn't need to ask her what had happened. What she had found. Something had changed in his face, something had happened to him too. He didn't tell her what and she didn't ask, but he held his camera tighter than before, and wouldn't put it down.

'No need to cry,' he told her, offering his hand to steady her.

Cari gently refused.

'Yes,' she said. 'There is.'

'Your invitation came,' he said wearily, handing her a thick piece of cardstock. 'While you were out.'

Cari knew she should have felt some surprise, should have been confused. But, somehow, she already knew exactly what it said. She was going to a party.

'Are you coming, Damian?'

'I am,' he replied, his eyes slightly nervous at the question. 'I still need to figure out a few things, though. It's going to be a big night. How are you feeling? Did it … are you still you?'

Cari shrugged as she moved over to the sofa.

'Are any of us?'

Her legs were still weak from what she had seen. She would sit and wait and dream of her outfit for Tobias Fell's party.

Maybe she would let David know. He wasn't invited, but he should probably know. She smiled, dimly aware of Damian studying her. What should she wear? That was the question. The dress didn't matter, of course. What mattered was that she would wear jewels.

8th

Viewing Essential

Laura Lockwood
Formerly of 52 Henley Street

Laura couldn't stand the old man's flat. Even before he'd died it had been a never-ending headache for her. But now that it was unoccupied it felt like some tasteless joke being played on her from beyond the grave whenever she tried to rent it out.

'And in here we can see the bathroom. Fully fitted with a well-sized claw foot tub and an attractive tile finish.'

A bathtub still bearing the scars of the old man's assisted bathing chair and tiles still pock-marked with holes from the handrails he'd had installed. Laura had often suggested the land-lords remodel, to exorcise these last lingering remnants of the previous tenant's existence, but they had always refused, leaving it to Laura and her agency to try and let the place in its current state.

'How's the water pressure?'

The potential tenants were a young professional couple, dressed in outfits that would almost seem shabby if you didn't know the designers who made them. When they'd first showed up Laura had made a silent guess that the man had a parent who owned the media company he worked for and the woman was climbing the ranks of a successful PR firm.

'It's just about perfect.' She smiled, picking up the shower head and turning the tap to send out a powerful cascade of water. 'Exactly what you need after a hard day at the office …'

Whatever they did for a living (if they did anything), they weren't saying. Luckily, they also weren't saying anything about the various damage the old man's mobility aids had done to the flat. Objectively, it wasn't a lot. A hole here, a line of removed plaster there, the odd scrape mark on the bamboo wooden floors. The trouble was that this was 21 Banyan Court, and the sort of people who looked at a flat like this wanted perfection.

'Can we see the bedroom?' the young man asked, giving his partner a wink he clearly thought Laura wouldn't notice.

Laura did, of course, but she also had high hopes for these two. Not only hadn't they made a peep about any of the little imperfections that had scuppered her previous viewings, they hadn't had what she was starting to think of as the 'Number 21 freakout'. She might finally be able to shift this real estate albatross.

The bedroom at least was tastefully appointed, with wide floor-to-ceiling windows looking out towards the centre of London. She carefully avoided drawing attention to the view as she was well aware that on a day like this the grey miasma of fumes formed a clearly visible aura around the skyscrapers of the Square Mile. While she was perfectly used to the sight, she knew from experience it could easily turn the stomach of potential tenants imagining a view of London would be a little less guilt-inducing.

She need not have worried though, her prospective clients made a beeline straight for the queen-sized bed and lay down, testing the mattress.

'Yeah, I can see us in this.' The young man gave his partner another wink and she swatted his arm playfully.

Laura ignored the feeling of unease she always got in the bedroom. She'd all but begged the landlords to change out the bed after the old man died. But decent beds are expensive, and apparently the luxury mattress cost more than she made in a year. Not more than letting a flat like this go empty, of course. It was the sort of false economy that really got under Laura's skin.

The couple were lying quietly now, their eyes closed in mock-sleep. The room was still and Laura became slightly too aware of her own breathing.

Seconds turned into a minute.

'So,' she said, 'are we—'

The couple sat up simultaneously, as though they'd had some sort of electric shot. The man let out a noise that almost sounded like a sob, while the woman just stared, silently.

Laura didn't even bother to ask them what was going on. She knew exactly what was happening. She sighed as they grabbed their bags and all but ran to the door, slamming it behind them, leaving Laura alone in the silent flat.

The flat she was apparently cursed to show forever.

The keyboard seemed very loud as Laura typed up the notes from her viewing. The offices of Dean Bishops were always quiet at this time of year. It was still busy, of course, but the summer heat meant everyone tried to spend as much time as possible out at viewings, doing open houses, enjoying the weather. Admin was for the colder months. It didn't help that the air conditioner was in poor repair and several of the office windows didn't open. There was a joke to be made about the poor quality of the estate agents' building, but Laura had heard it too many times to laugh.

When she reached the end of her notes, she tried to decide

how best to phrase what had happened this time. Why these potential tenants had taken off so abruptly. She could have written 'Haunted by an old bastard', but she wasn't sure anyone else would appreciate the joke. She didn't believe in ghosts, naturally, the whole idea was ridiculous, though Laura had started to suspect that perhaps *she* was haunted. The mental and emotional baggage she had around that flat was leaking out somehow, in her words or mannerisms, and scaring people off. It was a reasonable explanation, though not one that had allowed her to offload the flat on to someone else.

She left the notes unfinished and headed over to the silent staff kitchen. Laura had never cared for the old man, even when he was alive. Before the difficulties, he'd always had that over-familiar tone, even when talking on the phone, and she'd quickly taken against him. Mr Robert Audley. A forgettable name for what should have been a forgettable tenant. The most notable thing about him had been his partner, Sir Arthur Charles, a former army general and legitimate knight of the realm. Exactly why he'd rented out an extremely expensive flat for Mr Audley without living there himself, well, that wasn't her business, but when the old man's health began to fail it was Sir Arthur who paid for the changes to make the apartment liveable for him. And then the treatments and machines and live-in carers that kept the old man alive. It was a special sort of tragedy that Sir Arthur died first.

Whatever the specific reasons, probably lack of legal recognition or a vindictive family, the old man saw exactly none of Sir Arthur's money after the stroke took him. And without any real income beyond a meagre pension, Mr Audley had no hope of keeping the flat. But neither could he really move out, as everything he needed to live was trapped in there with him and he had nowhere else to go. So, once the rent payments stopped it had become Laura's grim responsibility to have him evicted.

She still remembered the calls. The wheezing, laboured breaths; the desperation in his voice as he pleaded with her. Again and again he had called, endlessly, though neither of their situations ever changed. Laura had always prided herself on remaining detached in such situations, but that was too much. At first, she had pitied him, but by the end she'd despised him. This sad old man throwing himself on the mercy of someone with no power to grant it. To place the responsibility on her when she had no part in putting him in that position. It simply wasn't fair.

He'd died about a week before the bailiffs were called in. Natural causes, the inquest said, so at least there was that. At the time it had been a relief, but now here she was. Almost as trapped by 21 Banyan Court as he'd been by the end.

She returned to her desk with a green tea and resumed typing. She disliked that whole building, really. She considered each side with equanimity, disdaining both. The oblivious rich in the front half were never-ending in their demands and impossible to get hold of on anything other than their terms, while those on the poorer side were a constant stream of damages, deposit drama, defaults and evictions.

Laura wasn't sure which side wasted more of her time. But Dean Bishops dealt with so much of the property there that they all sometimes joked that Tobias Fell was her real boss. It wasn't even that much of a lie; he paid a lot of money to the firm to make sure that the properties in his building were dealt with quickly, professionally and discreetly.

She finished off – stating a difference in expectations – and started on her next task, opening a fresh email.

This notice is given under Section 21 (4) (a) of the Housing Act 1988.

She didn't like typing out the words, so copied them from a previous eviction notice. She sighed and checked the calendar. Five days until they had to send in the bailiffs. One of the few parts of her job she genuinely hated. Laura had never met a bailiff who hadn't been a thoroughly unpleasant person, which kind of made sense. Their profession was, to one degree or another, to destroy people's lives, and to be skilled at the job meant hardening themselves against the sight of the pain and misery they caused. If you didn't go into the job a nasty piece of work, it seemed perfectly crafted to make you one.

But they were a necessary evil, and Laura's distaste didn't change that she had to compose an email arranging for them to make a visit.

Her computer fan whirred below her desk in rhythmic bursts, like the rasping hiss of a respirator. Laura sipped her tea and thought about flat 21.

'Hello, Dean Bishops estate agents, Laura speaking,' the phrase rolled off her tongue lightly, disguising how irritated she was at having her work interrupted. She had just got used to the silence, and the bleating of the phone was deeply unwelcome.

'Hi,' the voice was quiet, but determined. 'I'm calling from Banyan Court.'

Just what she needed. What was it going to be? Plumbing issue? Wiring problems? Broken boiler? Place your bets. At this point she'd heard them all.

'And what can I do for you today, sir?' she said pleasantly.

'I'm after some blueprints.'

'I'm afraid we don't keep building blueprints in our files, sir. You might want to try Tower Hamlets' local authority.'

'Yeah, I just … I need to see them.' He sounded exasperated.

'I'm sorry,' she lied.

'How about floorplans? For the flats?'

Laura paused. Something in the back of her mind told her she wasn't supposed to. Maybe something from Mr Fell? A request that building plans not be shared?

'If you're renting your flat through us, we can certainly send you your floorplan, sir. But I'm afraid we can't provide them for other properties.'

That sounded good. Convincing. It made sense, actually. Maybe it was already official policy and Laura had just forgotten.

'No. I know about my flat. I need to see what the measurements are supposed to be elsewhere.'

Just an oddball then. 'Well, I'm sorry I couldn't be more help.'

'It's just … It's wrong, you know?'

'I'm sorry you feel that way.' Laura was keen to finish this conversation quickly. 'But I'm afraid it's official policy.'

'No, I mean, the building is wrong.'

Laura froze. There was something in his voice, a certainty, that made her hand clench around the phone. Because she understood what he meant. The small sensation she had spent almost two years dismissing as it wrapped around her spine, all condensed into a single sentence.

'W-what do you mean?' she asked, her crafted phone voice slipping just a fraction.

'I've been taking measurements. I've got notes here, they—'

'I'm sorry I couldn't be more help, sir,' Laura repeated, firm this time, as she willed the unease away.

'Well,' he said, taking her meaning. 'Thanks for your time,'

He hung up. Laura sat there quietly. Her mind wanted to dwell on the conversation, to pick it apart and dissect it for meaning. Instead, she pushed the impulse away and returned to typing up mortgage details.

Hsssk.

'Hello?' Laura's voice was clipped, trying to find a level between professional and impatient.

Hsssk.

The sound came down the phone line again. Hissing, mechanical.

'I think you've got a bad connection,' she said for the third time. It was the end of the day and she'd just about had enough of unsettling calls. 'Hang up and try again. Maybe somewhere with better reception.'

Hsssk.

'Right. I'm hanging up now.'

Hsssk.

Laura placed the phone down and turned to return to her work. She hadn't even got three words into her email before it rang again. She allowed herself a brief moment of anger before snatching it up.

'Hello, Dean Bishops,' she said tightly. 'How can I help you?'

'Yes.' The voice had a soft accent that Laura couldn't place. 'There is a problem with one of your properties. It is in Banyan Court.'

The doors to Banyan Court always seemed freshly cleaned, at least, the ones at the front. Laura was meticulously turned out as she strode through them, as she always was when the stress started to get to her. When people insisted on *wasting her time*. She went straight to the front desk and groaned inwardly as the smiling, round-faced man ambled out of the back office. His name tag read 'Jason'.

'Alright, Miss Estates?' He grinned, rolling out the same not-quite-a-joke he used every time she came by.

Why couldn't it have been Kirsty? If Laura had to rank the three concierges who worked at Banyan Court, Kirsty was easily the top. She was easy-going, witty and professional. Jason not so much. As if it wasn't enough that the old man's flat was refusing to rest quietly.

'I need the key to 21,' Laura said, trying to keep the conversation as short as possible.

'Oh yeah?' Jason stood up and went to retrieve it, glancing over his shoulder. 'Didn't you show people around like two days ago?'

'It's not a viewing.' And this wasn't a conversation.

He snapped his fingers like a cartoon character remembering a birthday. 'The banging.'

'Yes.' Laura was in no mood. First the dud viewing, then the weird phone calls, now this. She was adept at compartmentalising, putting it all out of her mind, but she couldn't deny it was starting to get to her. Still, she kept her face calm.

'I mean, we checked it.'

'And apparently that didn't stop it, so they phoned me. And given how loud it is, I have to make sure it isn't something that's causing any damage.'

'I wasn't the one who went,' Jason said, holding his hands up in defence. 'I sent Max, but he didn't see anything or anyone in there.'

'Just give me the keys.'

'Sure thing.' He tossed them over the front desk. 'You want me to come up with you? After all, it's number 21, right, where the old dude died? Preeetty spooky!'

Laura looked at him coldly. Obviously, it wasn't actually a ghost, but she really should get him to come up with her.

The owner of number 20 had been quite colourful when he'd described the sounds that were coming from the neighbouring apartment, and if someone had broken in then going up with someone – even Jason – wasn't a bad idea. But she wasn't going to be afraid of a dead man's flat. She couldn't be.

'No,' she said firmly. 'I'll be fine.'

'OK, well, if you don't phone down in five minutes, I'll come check on you.'

Laura didn't reply, walking past him over to the lifts. No doubt it was something that had broken because the landlords refused to do proper maintenance. Burst pipe, maybe, or something collapsing. Laura just wanted it sorted. So far that week she had barely managed to go a full day without thinking about 21 Banyan Court. Normally she got at least a month or so of peace between viewings, but apparently this week it had decided it needed all of her attention.

The lift opened on a clean, well-lit corridor. The aroma told of a recent visit by the cleaning staff, and she took quick stock of herself, making sure her dress and blazer hadn't been creased or dirtied by the tube ride over. These were the sort of people you needed to look your best for.

She walked quickly and purposefully towards number 21. As she approached, a short woman in a tailored dress emerged from the door opposite and scowled at her. Number 20's iron-grey hair was pulled back above a pale, angular face that looked like it knew how much you were worth by smell alone.

'You are here for the issue next door.' In person, the woman's accent sounded Scandinavian. Swedish, maybe?

'Yes. Laura Lockwood, from Dean Bishops.' She didn't offer her hand, not wanting to seem presumptive.

'The man on the front desk said no one was there. But he is

a fool. You want to check. It was very noisy. And I saw nobody leave.'

'Of course, thank you.'

'There was the sound of banging,' the woman continued. 'Something fell over, I think. Running water. At one point shouting. Or crying, perhaps. Hard to say.'

'Right, well, thank you very much. I really appreciate—'

'Tell that oaf at the desk to be more careful,' the old woman snapped. 'Not let anyone here that shouldn't be here. I think they're coming in from the back of the building. You should be more careful as well.'

'I ... I see. I will.'

The woman nodded and shut the door.

Laura pulled out the key to number 21.

The flat was silent, as it should be. The bright rays of sunlight beamed through the windows, out through the bedroom door, splitting the gloom of the entry hall in two. Laura paused, getting her bearings as her eyes tried to adjust to the contrast between light and darkness.

'Hello?' she called out, tentatively.

Her voice seemed to vanish almost as soon as it passed her lips. She waited, but there was no response. No sound of movement from deeper inside the flat. She was alone.

Confident she wasn't about to immediately get jumped, Laura moved into the hallway and started turning on the lights.

'Nothing out of place.' She found herself talking out loud as she moved through the flat.

'Tables as they were before.'

Who was she talking to?

'Sofa ... no sign of use.'

She didn't talk to herself. But it was better than the quiet.

'Bathtub dry. No sign of flooding or water damage.'

This was ridiculous. But being silent felt like inviting something else to break it.

'No new scuff marks or scratches. Windows securely locked.'

Laura breathed out, that last point was attested to by the prickly heat that filled the apartment. The air conditioning hadn't been turned on since her last viewing and the tall windows had turned the place into a tastefully laid-out oven.

She sat on the sofa, pulling a sports bottle from her bag and taking a swig of the lukewarm water. She considered refilling it, but the heat pressed into her, sapping her will to stand up again. A bead of sweat rolled down her hand as she took another sip. The droplet hung for a second at the base of her palm then fell with an almost inaudible *tch* onto a sheet of white paper.

It took her a second to refocus. Poking out from below the sofa was what looked like a headed letter. She picked it up. It was cold, which might have felt refreshing if it hadn't unsettled her so much. It looked like a page from some sort of legal agreement. Two columns of small, dense text. The names had been scratched out with a ballpoint pen, but it seemed to be a life insurance agreement. The company was listed as United Continental and at the bottom, stamped in red ink, was the word REJECTED.

Laura had been giving viewings of this flat for months now, showed it to dozens of potential renters. Cleaning crews had been in and out at least five times. She'd personally examined every inch of it. This piece of paper had not been here before. Her thumb brushed over the rejection stamp and came away red with fresh ink. She shoved the thing into her bag.

'No sign of damage or intrusion,' she resumed out loud, trying to reassure herself. 'No one's been here.'

A sound cut through the silent rooms and Laura spun around, panic stabbing through her. A raspy, mechanical noise that hissed out for a second, two seconds, then stopped. A pause, then it came again, the wheezing breath of a machine. She looked towards the closed door of the bedroom, from behind which the sound came again in rhythmic, steady bursts. Laura had never actually heard a ventilator in real life, but she'd always imagined it might sound exactly like this.

Her legs were numb as she stood and walked unsteadily towards the bedroom. She needed to leave. It was like the woman next door had said, someone had broken in. They were playing a horrible joke. The other explanation was literally impossible. Unless it was in her head. In many ways that was the scariest possibility, but at least she could accept it. There were treatments for that sort of thing. She had to know, but still she couldn't quite bring herself to reach out and take the handle of the bedroom door. She wanted to. She needed to. To know what was haunting her. A cruel tormentor, her own mind, or …

She gripped the handle.

'You shouldn't be here,' she found herself saying. 'Mr Fell wouldn't like it.'

BANG.

It came from behind her. She whipped around in time to see the front door shaking on its hinges from the impact.

Bang bang.

A bolt of adrenaline and her instincts kicked in. She tried to run, but in her panic lost her footing on the waxed bamboo floor. Her legs went from under her as the front door opened, and she looked over to see a figure looming there.

'Everything alright, Miss Lockwood?' Jason's voice called out. And flat 21 was quiet again.

*

Laura's hands shook ever so slightly as she sipped her coffee. The office wasn't quite as silent as it had been before, but the gentle typing and distant phone-murmur of Kristen and Hadi didn't do much to reassure her. They were colleagues, but not really friends, and the idea of confiding her worries in them made Laura feel faintly sick. She'd been trying to put what she'd seen and heard behind her. It had been two days now, but the experience still pushed its way into her mind whenever she found herself alone with her thoughts. She didn't believe in ghosts. Never had. Never would. But she didn't want to be mad, either, and that was what madness meant to her: hearing things, seeing phantoms, the gradual erosion of your ability to trust your senses. But what was the third option? There'd been no one in that flat, they'd checked every corner.

It didn't help that her work seemed determined to keep it fresh in her mind. She'd already had another wannabe architect looking for blueprints and ranting about her own encounters, the Fairley kid this time, asking Laura *what she had seen*. Nothing! Laura had seen nothing. And that's how it was going to stay.

That and the fact that she'd finally had to pull the trigger on sending out those bailiffs. She desperately wanted to call in sick, just to take a few days off, but there was so much that needed doing. Not that she was actually getting anything done with her nerves shredded like this.

She jumped as the phone rang, a small spike of fear paralysing her, leaving her staring at it mutely. She heard Hadi pick it up on his line, answering in his gentle cockney lilt. Laura leaned back in her seat and took another sip of coffee. It was cold.

'Laura!' Hadi called from the other end of the office, his voice light and jovial. 'One of yours! Banyan Court, so don't upset the boss.'

She closed her eyes and swore silently to herself before giving her extension number to him. At this point Laura couldn't care less what Tobias Fell thought. It wasn't like she'd ever met the man. A few seconds passed, then her phone was ringing again. Just for her. She set her jaw and picked it up.

'Hello, Laura speaking.' She sounded so pleasant and helpful it hardly felt like her.

'Yeah, yes. Hello.' The voice on the other end was deep, but strangely rushed, like they were expecting to be cut off at any moment. 'I'm calling from 15 Banyan Court. You're the one who looks after us, right?'

'More or less,' Laura said. 'We're hired by your landlord to look after your property and act as a go-between when necessary. What seems to be the problem?'

'There's a stain. On the wall of my study.'

So, either accidental damage or plumbing. Could be an easy fix, something to get her head back in gear. Or it could be a colossal headache.

'OK, what sort of stain?'

'Grey,' he replied. 'The stain is grey.'

Laura finished typing the address into the database and the tenant details popped up. Leon Copeland. Number 15. Age 38. Last credit check scored 821. Looked like a model tenant.

'Sorry, I mean what substance caused the stain? Or is it coming from within the wall?'

'That second one. It's in the wall.'

'It might be a plumbing problem, then. Does it seem like water?'

'No. No, it's not water.'

'Possibly a sewage pipe, then. I do apologise, Mr Copeland, I'll have—'

'It's not the plumbing. There's no pipes in there. We had

someone check. And it's not sewage. It's grey. And it won't go away.'

'I know it can be upsetting when this sort of thing happens.' She was losing control of the conversation. 'But it's probably best to wait for a qualified profession—'

'It won't go away!' There was panic in the man's voice now. 'I've cleaned it and cleaned it and it keeps coming back bigger. There's no pipe, there's nothing, it's just a wall and it won't be clean!'

'OK, Mr Copeland, I, uh …'. She was floundering, her whole body starting to shake. 'I'm going to—'

'What's on the other side?'

'The other side?'

'Of the wall! What's on the other side of the wall?'

'I, uh …' She pulled up the floorplan. Which room was the study? 'I think that wall would be between you and another flat. Number 71. In the back of the building.'

'Is it their fault?'

'I don't … What?'

The line went dead. Leon had apparently hung up.

Laura felt sick. She stood up, needing some fresh air, and feeling strangely grimy at just having to hear the desperation in the man's voice.

The phone rang again. She sat heavily back down and picked it up.

'Mr Copeland?' she asked.

'Is that Dean Bishops estate agents?'

It wasn't Leon. The tone was clipped and official, not used to having its time wasted.

'Uh, yes, Laura Lockwood speaking.'

'Do you have a tenant named Edith Kinney?'

The flat smelled horrendous. Laura had been so used to the smell of number 21, the antiseptic of professional cleaners and the balmy summer humidity, that she'd almost expected that when she came to check Edith's former home. But no, this place had seen a human life wither away in cramped isolation and that fact clung to every surface, in every fibre of the moth-eaten carpet.

Edith Kinney. Laura hadn't even known her name. She'd been quiet, always paid on time, never raised any problems. Hadn't been any bother at all. But now Laura did know of her she couldn't stop herself hating the woman. She had to choose to die here? She had to choose now? Laura didn't have the emotional reserves left to feel sadness for this lonely old woman, no capacity for grief. All that was left was the burning resentment that Edith had decided to go and die in one of the properties that Laura managed and give her another haunted fucking flat.

Laura stopped. She couldn't think like that. Number 21 was hard enough to deal with, she couldn't afford to be taking on new paranoias. She'd seen what she needed to see. She'd taken an inventory and made an assessment: There was no structural damage, a few cigarette burns on the carpet, but that was going to need replacing anyway. And it was going to require an extremely deep clean before it could go back on the market. What was the name of that cleaning service Hadi used for the Wicker Street murder house last year?

The police had been less considerate in their questioning than when the old man had died. They were keen to find out if Dean Bishops had details on other tenants who lived there, or whether Mrs Kinney might have been subletting to someone else. When the answers turned out to be no and no, they had got irritated and borderline aggressive. Laura had briefly wondered why, but she was too shaken to consider the mystery for long.

She stood in the living room, staring at the stained and discoloured armchair where Edith Kinney had died.

'I'm sorry it's not my job to care,' she said.

Nobody answered.

'See you tomorrow, Lockwood!' Hadi called, waving as he hoisted his bag and headed towards the exit.

Laura made a non-committal throat noise, barely registering his absence.

The office was silent again. It was late, far past the time anyone was expected to be working there. She knew she should go home. Get some sleep in her own house.

Soon the faint glow of the monitor illuminating her face was the only light in the room. The fluorescents in the ceiling were motion activated, but they'd turned off after about ten minutes. Laura wasn't even sure what meaningless paperwork she was supposed to be filling out at the moment, her fingers barely moving over the keyboard.

A small ping alerted her to a new email. Mechanically, she moved to click the notification. It was the bailiffs again, confirming a team had been sent out to handle the eviction. Laura could imagine them, rolling steadily towards their destination in their painted van, faces hard, dressed in black vests that invoked the authoritarian air of legally deployed violence. She felt sick, like it was her that they were coming for.

'It's my job,' she told the empty office.

Her eyes passed once again over the email. Who was it they were coming for this time? Which poor soul was being thrown out of their home tonight? She located the address and froze. She stared at it, tried to convince herself it was her eyes playing tricks, but the words stayed the same.

They were going to 21 Banyan Court.

Why hadn't she noticed that before? She scrolled through the previous messages. Sure enough, they had all been about the old man's flat. The one that had been empty for months. But it couldn't be – she'd overseen all the legal procedures herself, there weren't any outstanding issues that could possibly have got the bailiffs involved. So, what was going on?

It was a trap.

The thought just popped into her head. It was breathtakingly absurd, but she just couldn't shift it. A trap for who? The bailiffs? By what, an old man's vengeful spirit?

Or the building itself.

She was fully alert now, mind racing, and the lights overhead sputtered to life as she reached for the phone and dialled the service number at the bottom of the email. She waited as it rang. And rang. And rang. And went to voicemail.

'Thank you for calling Cooperston Commercial Services. Our office hours are—'

Laura slammed the phone down. She was worrying over nothing. She'd email them to say it was a mistake. At worst, they'd arrive, have a confused Kirsty let them into the flat, see that there was hardly anything there and leave. If they took the furniture, she could follow up with them tomorrow. It's not like anyone was about to move in. This was nothing to worry about. Worst case scenario she'd get a talking-to about giving them the wrong information.

But a deep sense of dread sat in her stomach like a rock. Nothing about this was normal. She had to warn them.

The streets seemed quiet as she walked from Whitechapel station. A few figures wandered slowly along the pavements, but they seemed lost in their own world, their faces never lit enough to see clearly. There was no traffic, and the steady background roar of London seemed a long way off.

When there'd been no response to her emails, she'd decided to try to head the bailiffs off. Their van was in the parking bay of Banyan Court, cutting across two spaces. Laura hurried towards it, tapping on the tinted glass of a passenger window. There was no response and pressing her face close she saw that it was empty. A night breeze picked up, whistling as it came around the side of the towering building, the sound not entirely unlike a scream. She braced herself against it and headed to the entrance.

'Hello?' she called as the front doors slid open. 'Kirsty? ... Jason?'

There was no answer. The front desk was empty. She stepped around the side, staring into the small room behind it. Nobody was there. The small chair lay on its side and the phone looked broken. Had there been a fight here?

She steadied her breathing and headed for the lift. It took almost a minute to arrive, and when the doors opened an awful smell rolled out of it. Two grey shoeprints stained the carpeted floor, the only possible source of the odour. Laura hit the button for the fifth floor, keeping her breaths as shallow as possible. The lift rumbled and began to rise.

The door to the old man's flat was open. Not wide, but just ajar enough for it to be a clear invitation. Laura looked down the corridor; no sign of anyone else. No bailiffs, no concierge, and no one to tell her if what she was seeing was real. It wasn't too late to run, she told herself, but the sound of the lift doors closing behind her rang with such finality that she knew it wasn't true.

Telling herself the bailiffs were just inside, that they were perfectly fine, she stepped over the threshold into the darkness of number 21.

'Is ... Is anybody there?' Her voice was so quiet. She didn't want to be heard.

The door swung closed behind her, the latch sliding into place with the softest of clicks, and Laura realised that it had been a trap, after all.

All the doors in the hallway of the flat were closed, and none of the city's nocturnal glow filtered through to break the thick darkness. She fumbled for the light switch, desperately flicking it back and forth, but if the bulbs were still there, they didn't respond. She stepped forward, feeling her way along the sideboard she knew so well, her fingers lingering over the gouges where grab bars once sat.

Almost on cue, she heard it. The sound Laura had been waiting for since she arrived. The slow and steady hiss of a respirator. From behind the bedroom door it came, pulsing with the relentless regularity of a pendulum. This time, she knew, nobody was going to be knocking on the door. No one was coming to get her.

'Just go,' she whispered. 'Turn around and leave.'

Maybe, if she tried, really tried, she could choose not to open that door. Not to see what was on the other side. To run, to escape, to flee back to her own front door, to her own house in ...

Laura stopped. Where did she live? She suddenly didn't feel sure. She slept alone, she knew that, ate alone, and if she tried, she could almost picture where. But could she? Was it her home she was remembering, or the thousands of real estate photographs she had taken, superimposed over her life? She must have somewhere to live, to exist. A flat of her own, or even a house. But it was gone. Taken from her. She stared at her keys, glinting faintly in the gloom, and recognised none of them.

Defeated, she grabbed the handle of the bedroom door and turned it.

The room beyond was brighter, though not by much. The curtains were open and the lights of the street below cast everything in the room in dim outline. In the bed lay a shape, completely covered by a sheet that smelled of antiseptic. The hissing continued, rhythmic, as the form beneath the covers rose and fell with each pump. Laura didn't need to see a face to know who was below that sheet.

'I—I'm sorry,' she said.

Hsssssk.

'I was just trying to do my job.'

Hsssssk.

'Did ... Did I kill you?'

Hsssssk.

'No. No, I guess ...'

Hsssssk.

'I guess we all did.'

Hsssssk.

Laura paused. The guilt rolled over her, breaking out from where she had hidden it.

Hsssssk.

'What do you want?' She tried to make her voice demanding, confident. She failed.

Hsssssk.

'What can I do?'

There was a shift. A stirring on the edge of the sheet. Then an arm appeared, falling limply over the edge of the bed. It was thin, wizened, with paper-thin skin stretched over blackened veins. In its hand it held something. A small rectangle of cream-coloured card.

Laura slowly walked over and gingerly pulled it from the

cold, stiff fingers. The sound of the ventilator stopped, and the flat was silent, as it always had been.

She looked at the message in her shaking hands. It was an invitation to a dinner, in her boss's home.

'OK,' she said, understanding. 'OK.'

Nobody answered.

9th

A Stubborn Stain

Leon Copeland
15 Banyan Court

'What are you talking about?'

'You don't see it?'

Leon Copeland ran his fingers over the magnolia wall of his study, trying to make out the edges of the shape Andrea was pointing at.

'Not really,' he said. 'Sorry.'

'From here, all the way round here. It's darker. Like there's some kind sort of grey underneath.'

'I ... guess?'

'Hm, weird.' She shrugged. 'It's really obvious from here.'

'Honestly, I don't really see it.'

'Maybe it's just me,' Andrea sighed. 'I guess spending so much time here on my own, it ... I guess you just start obsessing over things. Noticing imperfections.'

'I know, and I'm sorry.' Leon put a hand on her shoulder. She leaned into it. 'On the plus side I should be working from home for a while. We can spend some more time together.'

'That would be nice.'

'I've been thinking about repainting in here anyway. I could just go over the wall.'

'Are we actually allowed to paint the walls?'

Leon paused, as though unsure.

'You know,' Andrea teased him, 'if we'd bought that little place in Harrow we could have done whatever. Could've painted the light bulbs if we'd wanted to.'

'Andi, please don't start.' Leon's face shifted in discomfort. He dropped the hand, leaving her shoulder cold.

'Alright.' Andrea pulled a cigarette from the packet in her cardigan. 'It was just a joke.'

'I know, I know. It's just ... you know how important appearances are to these people. You've got to *look* successful.'

Andrea felt a bit bad; she knew how stressed Leon was about the new position and revisiting old arguments wouldn't help any. She tried to hold her tongue and not start it again.

'And owning a house isn't success?' she said, failing.

'Come on, Andi. You think the board's going to respect a semi-detached at the end of the Metropolitan line?'

'Well, that's their problem.' Andrea wandered over to the wall, tracing the edges of the dark stain.

'Sure, but they're the reason we can afford to have the choice. And the reason you can afford to spend all your time making fancy soaps.'

'*Boutique toiletries*, thank you very much,' Andi shot back with the practised smile she used whenever talk turned to the finances of her business. 'And it would be easier if I had more space, expand a little.'

'I promise, a year or two here, then I'll be earning enough that we can buy somewhere actually nice. And who knows, maybe this is the year your soaps explode.' Leon grinned. 'Figuratively speaking.'

'OK, OK,' she conceded. 'I guess we're here now. And I don't think it's unreasonable to expect the study wall to not be all messed up.'

'It's just going to be me in here most of the time. And I can't really see it.'

There was a moment of quiet as they both stared at the patch of magnolia. Then Andrea turned and surprised her husband with a kiss. He laughed, then returned it, the tension broken. 'Fine.' She returned her focus to the unlit cigarette in her hand. 'I'll be on the balcony. Anyway, don't you have work to do?'

'Not much of it yet.'

'They still doing their "reorganisation"?'

'Yeah, once this round of restructuring's done and we've got the new acquisitions sorted then I'll be actually overseeing the operational integration ...' He glanced at her, and she hoped her eyes weren't too glazed.

'Go smoke,' he said, shaking his head with a smile. Andrea couldn't hide her relief.

'Thanks, love you!'

When she dipped her head back inside to ask him about dinner, she caught him standing by the wall, his fingertips brushing against it, as though feeling for the shape of the stain.

'There, that's looking a bit better.'

'If you say so.'

'The colour's pretty much an exact match. I think.'

'Yeah.' Andrea seemed unconvinced. 'Yeah, it's fine, I guess. It's gone.'

Leon stepped back as she touched the newly painted area again, testing its edges. His wife frowned, as though concentrating. She made a very odd picture, prodding a wall in sweaty gym clothes, and he found it hard not to chuckle. Still, he knew the move hadn't been easy on her. Covering up the 'stain' was the least he could do.

'Is there . . .' she mused. 'I don't know, the texture is different?'

'Well, I'm not planning to spend my days stroking it, so I reckon that's OK.'

There was a long pause as Andrea considered this.

'Yeah,' she said, making a clear decision to be OK with it. 'You're right. Thank you for this. Anyway, I'm getting a shower. Oh, and I've got a call to some potential buyers later, so it'll be takeout for dinner.'

She gave Leon another kiss on the cheek and headed out of the room.

'Plus,' he mused, 'now I've found the paint I need we can sort it if it ever comes back.'

Andrea turned and gave him a smile. 'If you're happy, I'm happy.'

'Knock knock.'

Leon looked up from his desk to see Angela standing in the doorway, grinning.

'Hi.' He tried to smile back.

'You want some lunch?'

'Going out or staying in?'

'Well, I was thinking of going to that new vegan place, but it looks like you might be a bit preoccupied.'

'Yeah.' Leon looked over the various charts and reports that now littered his desk. 'Probably not going to be able to get away.'

'It's fine, I can bring something back for you. I hear their risotto is good.'

'Thanks.' Leon tried not to sound too dismissive as he stared at a print.

'At least they're keeping you busy.'

'Yeah, well, it's not exactly …' He swallowed. Why was he so afraid to tell her? It's not like it was his fault. 'News story broke yesterday, apparently we've turned some river in India toxic. I've been trying to get ahead of it, but … Well, it's not good.'

Andi took a moment to consider.

'I mean, we knew when you took the job. Petrochemicals is … It can be a bit …' She paused. 'Hang on, they can't blame *you*, right? You've only just got there.'

'They've got to blame someone. And it's not like Donovan can step down twice.'

'It's not your fault, though. It's not fair.'

Leon shifted uncomfortably. Andi breathed out slowly, trying to get her humour back.

'Hey.' She leaned forward with a smirk. 'Why not have a word with the man upstairs? I'm sure he could make it go away.'

'Or make *me* go away.' Leon shook his head. 'Besides, from what I hear, we might be in the same building, but we're kind of on different planets.'

He leaned back in his chair, stretching.

'It'll be OK.'

'Oh yeah, I know.' He nodded. 'It'll be a share price hit and a grovelling press release, but these things run their course.'

'Unlike that river,' Angela joked darkly.

'Andi!' In spite of himself, Leon laughed.

'I know, I know. It's very serious. I get it. I just hate to see you so down. It's—'

She stopped abruptly, her focus suddenly elsewhere.

'Andi? You good?

'Did Malia come yesterday?' she asked, her voice distant.

'You think I did all that vacuuming myself?'

'No, it's just the wall.'

Leon looked over and stopped. There it was, the stain. Clear as day. Almost a foot and half wide, a sort of greyish patch on the bright paint of the wall. How had he not noticed it before?

'Bloody hell.'

'Oh, so *now* you can see it. Unlike Malia, I guess.'

'I ... Well, it was freshly painted. Besides, does she even do the walls?' Leon was still rattled by its appearance.

'She wiped down the kitchen when you sprayed smoothie everywhere. I'd have thought she'd have at least given it a go.'

Now he'd noticed it as well, Leon was almost surprised at how composed his wife was about it. It was revolting.

'You want me to get her in again?'

'We might need a specialist.'

'I'll talk to her, at least. Worst case scenario I could always do it.' Leon ran his fingers over the wall, trying to find that difference in texture she had mentioned.

'Do you have the time?' Andrea was sceptical.

'I'll make time.'

She shrugged and headed for the kitchen. Leon was still focused on the stain that covered the wall. A sudden pain shot through his leg. He looked down to see his hand pushing against his leg, pressing the tip of his pen into his trousers. He pulled back just before he drew blood, forcing his clenched hand to place the pen back on his desk. He must be more stressed than he thought.

'You know, maybe we should go out,' he called.

'Where'd you get this paint?' Leon called over his shoulder.

There was no response for a few moments, then Andi appeared in the doorway, her stained work apron still damp and her hands smelling of patchouli.

'Sorry, what were you asking?'

'The paint, where did you get it?'

Her head tilted in confusion. 'I thought you got the paint.'

'I did' – he stood up, brush dropping to his side – 'but this isn't the same stuff.'

'Pretty sure it is.'

'No, the paint before was really thick emulsion, this ... I mean, it's so thin. Hardly covers anything at all.'

He pulled the brush across the stain, leaving a streak of magnolia behind, but he might as well have been spreading water for all the good it did.

'Well,' Andi sounded nonplussed. 'I certainly didn't buy more paint. So, unless there's someone breaking into fancy flats and leaving tins of ...'

Leon looked at her and the joke seemed to die on her lips.

'Is everything alright?' she asked, suddenly concerned.

Nausea crept through his stomach and he sat down heavily. Had it been the lunch? Or was the stress getting to him already? He always had digestion trouble if he was stressed. Before his interview for the new executive position he'd ended up trapped in the toilet for almost the whole hour.

'I just want it gone,' he said at last. 'I know how much it's been bothering you.'

His wife walked over, leaning so close to the dirty grey patch that Leon found himself recoiling on her behalf.

'I mean, I don't like it, Leon, obviously, but if you're not feeling well ...'

'I know, I know. I just want you to be comfortable here. In the flat.'

Andrea smiled.

'You're here, so I'm comfortable.' She paused. 'I'm never going to love it, Leon. Stain or no stain.'

'Well I choose no stain,' Leon declared, getting to his feet.

*

'Mr Copeland?'

'Speaking. What can I do for you?'

'It's, uh, it's Suzi.' The tinny voice blared from the speakerphone. 'From Invidious. We do your PR?'

'Yeah, I know who you are, Suzi. What do you need?'

'We've been fielding a lot of press calls over the last week about the East Rapti River. We just wanted to make sure you'd got the pack we sent through with the guidance on your proposed response line.'

Leon stopped scrubbing, the foaming sponge still in his hand.

'Oh, yes. That came through.'

He glanced over at his computer, where the email sat unopened.

'Right, right. Did you have any thoughts?'

'Yeah, sure,' Leon said absently. 'It all looks good?'

He walked over to his desk, trying to figure out a way to open the email without touching the laptop with his dirty hand. His gaze drifted to the small washing-up bucket he'd brought in, but by now the dirt had turned it murky and the thought of the sponge absorbing all of the filth back up made him a bit queasy. Leon stood there, unable to make a decision.

'Did you get that?'

'Uh, no,' Leon said, suddenly aware that he hadn't been listening. 'Could you repeat?'

'Of course,' Suzi said with the infinite patience of one addressing a very important client. 'I was just saying that, given your role was not intended to be PR focused, we're happy to offer whatever guidance or direction we can.'

'Sure thing.'

Suzi said something else, but Leon was thinking about

whether to get a plumber. If it kept reappearing, that meant there must be something inside the wall, right?

'Brilliant. Thanks for your time, Mr Copeland.'

The click of the phone left Leon standing in silence, still contemplating his sponge. He looked from it, to the wall, and back again. The area where the stain had been was much darker now, but that was just because it was wet. Dish soap to begin with. A lot of how-to sites swore by it. He'd need to wait until it dried, of course, before he would know for sure if it was gone or not. And he wanted to go over it a few more times first. Just to be on the safe side.

Leon wiped his hand across his forehead, leaving a small mound of bubbles at his hairline. He looked over to his laptop. He could do it later. First, he had to get a handle on his space. Then he could get a handle on the wider situation.

He returned to his scrubbing.

'What is that smell?' Andrea wrinkled her nose.

'Hm?'

'It reeks in here.'

'Oh, sorry. I thought you liked vinegar?'

'Yeah, on chips. No sure I want my home stinking of it.'

'Sorry,' Leon repeated, shrugging. 'Plumber can't make it for a few days, so wanted to give it a try.'

'Is that ... Is that a thing?'

'You're the soap guru, you didn't know this?'

'I clean premium faces, this all seems a bit more, uh, abrasive than what I work with.'

She nudged a plastic crate with her foot. In it stood an array of brightly coloured spray bottles, each adorned with energetic promises. MAX POWER. MOULD KILLER. NO MORE DIRT.

'Well, to be honest I think the chemical ones just made it worse.'

There was a thick silence between them. For a moment Leon thought she was about to make some joke about the river, one of her attempts to break the tension, but she was quiet.

'You know,' Leon said, his voice thoughtful, 'when I was a kid, my mum had this friend Tori. I think she was technically a second cousin, but they'd known each other most of their lives. When I knew her, Tori had a lot of cats. Don't know much about why, but my mum always seemed angry about the cats somehow, like they shouldn't have been there. I liked them. I mean, of course I did, I was a kid. But there was always this smell in Tori's house. This horrible sharp cloying smell. Didn't know what it was at the time, but I was doing some reading about vinegar, and I reckon I've figured it out. You use vinegar to clean up cat urine. That's what the whole place stank of: cat piss and vinegar. Isn't that wild? Thirty-eight-years-old and still learning new stuff about your childhood?'

He turned to look at Andrea, but she was gone. Just as well. He wasn't sure he wanted to continue the thought anyway. To follow that half-remembered feeling of disgust, of contamination. That lingering oppressive scent and the knowledge that you had no control over your space. No escape from it.

Leon shook his head slightly and poured some more white vinegar onto his cloth. It was fine. Soon the plumber would be here and that would be the end of it. The spreading stain stared back, impassive and patient.

'Hello?'

Leon's greeting was terse, spat out through the gritted teeth of a jaw set in an expression of deep irritation. His eyes didn't waver from the wall.

'Mmhm. Hi, Suzi, what do you need?'

It was back, now almost black against the muted magnolia of the rest of the wall.

'Yeah, I know.'

He had been so certain it was gone, scoured from the wall, but not only had it returned, it seemed even worse than before.

'Sorry, when did we agree to that?'

Leon shifted uncomfortably, trying to cradle the phone against his shoulder while he considered the stain. It wasn't just darker, it seemed ... lumpy somehow.

'I mean, I'm not exactly, what's the word ...? Like photogenic, but for video?'

He looked down, imagining himself being filmed. His suit was stained and discoloured from his cleaning efforts, a lot more so than he'd thought.

'Yeah, exactly. I don't come across great. Hold on.'

He shifted again, laying the phone down on the table and jabbing the speaker button as he collapsed into his chair. Immediately Suzi's voice boomed out. He must have turned the volume up somehow.

'—just a quick interview. Like we said on our last call, you're the senior executive here, so we really need you to be the one to comment on it. We've put together a briefing for you. We strongly suggest taking the position that lax local safety standards were responsible for the accident.'

'Is that true?' Leon said. The thought of standing there, the camera focused on him, as he desperately tried to defend a mistake that wasn't his ... 'I thought the investigation wasn't finalised yet?'

'We're very confident it's the correct position.' Suzi's voice didn't betray a hint of doubt.

'Right.' Leon wasn't sure what else to say. 'I suppose I'll need a new suit.'

'Excuse me?'

'Nothing.' His eyes were already moving towards the bucket of cleaning products. 'Just let me know when it is, I suppose.'

'Will do! Thanks again.'

A click and she was gone. Leon sat heavily in his chair, the scent of bleach already clinging to him, engulfing him. He felt light-headed. He needed some fresh air.

He pulled himself up and started cleaning the wall.

'I don't understand.'

The plumber shrugged, his face impassive.

'It's what I said. No pipe.'

'How? I'm sorry, what did you say your name was? John?'

'Sure.' The plumber shrugged again, his accent grating on Leon.

'How can there be a leak if there isn't a pipe?'

'Right. There isn't.'

'Isn't what? A leak or a pipe?'

'Both. No pipe, no leak.'

'So what the hell is this?' Leon gestured desperately to the huge area of wall now a rotten bluish black.

The stain was spongy and clearly damp, with small bumps all over it which might have been lumps of decaying plaster or might have been mounds of growing mould. He itched all over to scrub them but swallowed the urge down. Leon had just been doing his best to keep it contained until the plumber arrived. Now the plumber was here. He had to fix it.

'Dirt?' the man said at last.

'How is this dirt?!' Leon exploded. 'Look! Look at it! Something is coming through that wall, I know it is. And I need to know where it's coming from. I need to stop it. Tell me what's doing this.'

'Well, not a pipe. We can be sure of that. The rest ... Not my department. Sorry.'

A creeping suspicion surfaced in Leon's mind.

'You can see it, right?'

'I see... Something. I think. Not as clear as you, though, I am sure.'

'Are you serious?' Leon felt like crying, but he set his face firm.

There was silence for some time as the handyman considered his words.

'It is this building, I think.'

'What are you talking about?' Leon asked. He put an edge in his voice, a clear warning. The plumber pursed his lips and changed the subject.

'The other side of the wall. What is it? Do you know? Another flat?'

Leon shook his head.

'Maybe find out. Might help with your stain. But it isn't a leak. No pipes.'

And with that the man picked up his toolkit and excused himself. Leon stood there a moment, thinking. The other side of the wall ... He shook his head.

As soon as the plumber was out of the front door Leon stormed back to the office, using a pencil to push the button on the phone for the front desk. He reached to pick up the handset, but his hand paused, suddenly alarmed it might have been contaminated by the dripping filth on the wall. He pushed the speaker button instead.

'Front desk.' The tone was bored, businesslike.

'Yes, hello, it's—'

'Mr Copeland, good to hear from you. How's Janek doing? Did he get it all sorted for you?'

'No. In fact he was absolutely useless. I need to talk to another plumber.'

'Another ...?' The concierge's voice tried to hide his confusion. 'Mr Copeland, Janek knows the plumbing of this building better than anyone, 'cept maybe the people who built it. What was the problem?'

'He said there wasn't a pipe.'

'Uh, say again?'

'He said there was no pipe, so I need another plumber.'

'Mr Copeland,' the concierge spoke slowly, like his tongue was navigating a minefield, 'if Janek says there isn't a pipe, then I'm not sure any other plumber is going to have better lu—'

Leon swept the phone off the desk, cutting the man's words short. He collapsed into the chair, his heart beating far faster than the conversation should have justified. He sat there in silence, staring at the wall. The whole room smelled, but it was no longer the scouring tang of cleaning products. The thick, earthy stench of rotten damp pervaded the place. He'd showered twice already today, but still it enveloped him. He stared at his hands, chapped and reddened by recent weeks, and strained his eyes, trying to see if any stain had transferred to him. He saw it, sometimes, in the mirror or in darkened windows: his reflection, discoloured and caked in mould, the creeping damp burrowing its tendrils into him and leaving nothing but a hollow shell filled to the eyes with rancid water.

The moment passed and Leon was left with nothing but the lingering disquiet.

'What's this?'

'What does it look like, Leon?' Andrea's voice was exhausted.

'It looks like you're trying to hide it, is what it looks like.'

'I just thought that it wasn't doing either of us any good, staring at it.'

'Putting a bookshelf in front of it when I'm not in the room isn't going to sort out the problem.'

'It's just a stain,' she said. 'I know it bothers you—'

'You were the one that spotted it.'

'I know, and it bothers me too, I just … How long are we here for, really? A year isn't that long, Leon. It's better if we just ignore it. This isn't good for you.'

There was a long silence before Andrea tried to change the subject.

'I saw you on TV the other night.'

'Oh yeah?'

'What, my husband goes on the evening news and I just miss it?'

'Your husband goes on to try and minimise the fallout from his company poisoning a bunch of rural communities … Yeah, maybe you miss it.'

'You know it's not your fault.'

'Mm. Was I OK?'

'… Yeah.'

'Yeah, what?'

'I mean, you did look a little, I don't know, squirrelly?'

'Squirrelly?'

'You know. You were talking kind of fast and some of the things you said about the water, I'm not sure how much sense they made. Like, you kept talking about a dam breaking, but they said it wasn't anywhere near a dam.'

'Oh, I … Must have been thinking of something else.'

Andrea looked worried.

'How's it going?'

'Fine.' Leon was dismissive. 'It's blowing over, like they always do. I sweated on TV and that's all they want really.'

'So, you're just a fall guy?'

'It's the job. You sit there and make money until someone goes too far, then you fall. If you fall softly it goes away; if you fall hard you get shuffled away like Donovan.'

'Hm.' For a moment Andrea looked intensely sad. Then it passed. 'What do the others think?'

'Oh, they think it's hilarious. Albertson keeps calling it my "baptism" and won't stop telling me the story of *his* first major scandal. Blood diamonds, apparently, though he insists it was a misunderstanding.'

'Seriously?'

'Yeah, they said they might even be considering me for another position in a few months.'

'A promotion?'

'I don't know. Probably just a lateral move, but maybe.'

'And none of this bothers you?'

'It's a bit late for that. Anyway, you're the one always making those stupid jokes about this stuff.'

'That's not the point.'

'So, what is? Because apparently someone has to get their hands dirty so you can throw money away making ethical soaps.'

The air between them was icy.

'Well,' she spat. 'I'm glad you've made peace with it. Guess you can get back to cleaning. At worst it'll be a bit of a stain on my record.'

Leon's mouth twitched slightly, and she immediately regretted saying it. It hung in the air between them.

'I can get it clean,' Leon said, his voice suddenly small. 'I know I can.'

Andrea took a long second to steel herself, then shook her head.

'I've been looking into some counsellors. Clinics that special-ise in OCD.'

'I'm not ...'

'It's not anything to be ashamed off. You remember Krista? Her girlfriend has it, and she's been doing—'

'Andi, I know you don't want to be here, to live like this. I just—'

'Leon.' Her voice was quiet and insistent. 'This isn't about me. You know it isn't.'

'I'm moving the bookcase away. It's not something we should just ignore.'

'Fine, OK. Just please ...' Andrea held out a sheet of printer paper. 'I've put together a list. Please have a look and give one of them a call.'

'It's not in my head. I know it isn't. You can see it too.'

There was a long pause.

'I don't know anymore, Leon. I really don't. But if you're going to keep cleaning, I can't stay here. All these fumes, it's giving me a migraine. I can't sleep for the smell.'

Leon didn't respond. His gaze focused on her arm. He felt his legs go slightly weak. There, just below her elbow, there was a tell-tale patch of light grey. Bile rose in his throat. It was spreading.

'OK,' he said at last. 'I'll get it sorted.'

Number 71. It had taken a lot of effort to find out which flat was the other side of that wall, and even more to find a way into the horrible back area of the building. No one wanted to talk about how this place was laid out, but that didn't matter now. He was here. He'd made it. This is where the plumber had said it was coming from. This was it. He was going to get it sorted. Just like he said.

Leon stood in front of the quiet, unassuming door and took a deep breath. Could he smell it? That faint stench? Was it coming from in there? Hard to say. But he knew it was here, it had to be. This awful, squalid place had to be it. Whatever was pushing that awful diseased mark into his home was inside. He could see it, there in his mind, all the awful festering horror that was lurking beyond this door. The rancid squalor that must have given birth to this filth reaching through his walls.

He prepared himself, raised his fist, and knocked.

'Where were you last night?' Andrea's face split the difference between anger and concern.

'What do you mean?'

'Before that. You were out when I got home. You didn't get in until midnight.'

'Sorry. Thought you'd be sleeping.'

'That's not an answer.'

Her husband didn't turn around, eyes still resting on the wall. He dragged his finger down it, making a face as though touching something slick and oily. The smell of bleach rolled off him like a wave.

'Number 71.'

'In this building?' she said, her anger giving way to confusion. 'Do we know them?'

'There's no one to know. It's empty. Completely empty.'

'Please, Leon. Just tell me what's going on. What's—'

'The other side of the wall.'

He turned to look at her.

'This is about the stain,' she said, resignation on her face.

'Have you ever been to the back of the building?' Leon continued, his voice distant. 'It's quite something. How the other half live, you know? Except it's a lot more than half, isn't it? But I was so sure. So certain that it was there.'

'Leon ...' She pleaded. Her bag was packed, she could leave at any time, but she couldn't leave him like this. God knows what he'd do.

'I knocked for so long. Hours.' He held up his bruised, swollen hands and she gasped. 'But there was no answer. So, I waited, and then I decided to see for myself.'

She reached for his bruised hands, but he pulled back. Her shoulders sagged. 'Please don't tell me you broke in, Leon.'

'Do you know what I found?'

'Well, you said no one lives there, so I'm guessing nothing.'

Leon paused, momentarily thrown. 'Well, yes. But not just nothing. I found the wall, Andi. The other side of this one. And there was nothing there. At all. It was clean.' He moved towards her now, as if to hold her, before he stopped short, as if he couldn't bear to touch her. 'You know what this means?'

Andrea said nothing.

'It means it can't be what this wall connects too. There's something else. Something between us and flat 71. Something *inside* the walls that's bleeding through!'

There was a look of triumph on his face, like he'd solved all their problems.

'I'm going to go now,' Andrea said.

Leon's expression crumpled. 'What?'

'I'm going to go and stay with Krista for a while. Please call me when you've had a chance to get some sleep. And made an appointment with a counsellor.'

Leon's tone became desperate as he gestured wildly at the wall. He couldn't look her in the eye.

'I'm sorry, I know it's hard to live with, but I've solved it now! I can sort out the stain, I can get rid of it!'

'I don't care about the stain, Leon! I can barely see it anymore. It's you. You're not well.'

'No, it's because it's awful, and the smell—'

'The only thing bothering me is *you*, Leon. All your chemicals and your scrubbing and ...' She was crying now, as her voice started to break.

'I can fix it.'

'No,' Andrea said as she turned to leave. 'You can't.'

Leon looked up. He forced himself to look at it now, the grey, stretching up her neck, over her face. In her mouth. Was that it? Was it making her say these things? He tried to reach out, to grab her as she walked out the door and explain that she wasn't herself.

But as he did so he saw his own hand clearly, as if for the first time. It was discoloured and stained a ghoulish grey.

'Are you in my head?'

The stain simply oozed in reply. Leon swallowed, throat dry. His legs shook, both from fear and from hunger. He couldn't eat anything from the kitchen. He'd already checked. It was all contaminated.

'What do you want? You must want something. Or maybe Andi's right. You're not real, and there's something in my head that's making me see you and that means there's something I can do to fix it. Medication. Or one of those therapists Andi was— Oh God, Andi...' He slumped back in his chair. The office was silent.

'But if ... If you are real. And no one else can see you – not even Andi anymore – that means you've chosen me. You're revealing yourself to me. Why?'

He knew the answer. His eyes travelled over the desk. The testimonials, reports, inquest files. There were so many. He hadn't talked to anyone, hadn't answered the phone or his emails in days. Would he be fired? He almost laughed. It was too late for that. He wasn't someone who got fired, not anymore.

'That's bullshit. I'm working to fix it. We're cleaning up the river, we're putting things in place to stop it happening again. I didn't even have this job when it happened! It's not my *fault*.'

A thick rivulet of pus dribbled its way down from a patch of mouldy grey plaster.

'This isn't fair. I don't deserve this.'

He tightened his grip on the claw hammer. It had still been attached to his high-end toolbox with a cable tie. Apparently, this was the first time he'd ever had to use it.

'Go away. Let me clean you or I will make sure there isn't any wall left for you to fester.'

Leon had no idea if he could actually destroy an entire wall with a claw hammer, but he was willing to give it a shot. If it was coming from inside, this was how to get it out.

'This is my home. Get *out*.'

The stain disagreed.

Leon screamed, a guttural cry of anger and panic, and ran towards it, slamming the hammer into the centre. The wall dissolving beneath it like wet tissue paper, collapsing in on itself with a sick pop. There was a beat, then the putrescent grey rot flowed out from the dark hole in a wave, hitting Leon with all its force. It pinned him, gagging, to the floor as he struggled to pull himself to his feet, slipping amid the slickness of the filth-covered floor, unable to get a grip on the desk to pull himself up. The smell was like nothing he'd ever experienced. It was the smell of death, of decay, of a thousand mouldering poisons cast thoughtlessly into the world. It clawed at his mouth, pushing itself through his clamped teeth, gushing in through his nose and down his throat, filling him, killing him, hollowing him with its awfulness.

Then, just as quickly, it released him, vomiting itself up and out of his throat in a rancid geyser, until he lay on his side, sputtering weakly. There was something in his mouth, something solid the foulness had left behind. With wet, filthy fingers, he pulled it from his mouth, unfolding a piece of pristine white card.

Reading it, he knew what he had to do to be clean.

'Of course, Tobias,' Leon said, sitting in his empty, grime encrusted office. 'Of course I'll come to your party. The invitation is appreciated. We'll see you shortly.'

A thick droplet of grey sludge fell from Leon's nose, impacting the thick cardstock where the invitation was printed. It left a familiar stain.

10th

Round The Clock

Jason Brown
6 Chigwell Lane, Debden

Max's bootsteps were always loud. Whenever he was walking the halls or doing rounds, even over the soft carpet of the residential areas, Jason could always hear him coming. They were thick black leather, well cared for though the shine had clearly worn away from hard use, and their dark red laces looked almost black from a distance. They added another half inch to Max's already towering figure and were the only part of his dress that was always meticulous. Jason had once asked him where he could get a pair of boots like that, but Max had just laughed and shaken his head.

'Oh, you could buy boots look just like 'em, sure,' he'd said. 'But it's not the same. You gotta earn boots like this.'

He'd never explained exactly how they had been 'earned', and simply went back to brushing them.

None of this was to say, of course, that the rest of Max's appearance was slovenly. His hair was neatly cropped close to his pale scalp, and he kept his concierge uniform in good condition. But his shirt testified to a lack of skill with an iron, a slight beer belly strained gently against the buttons of his jacket, and he never seemed quite able to shift that last millimetre or two of stubble.

To Jason, though, these were points in his favour. Kirsty and Ryan, the other two who worked the front desk at Banyan Court, were always absolutely fastidious in their appearance, and it often made him feel self-conscious. The long tube rides of his commute from Debden meant that keeping his own uniform pristine was a constant challenge. He'd tried getting changed at work, but if he packed it in his backpack the uniform arrived a crumpled mess and a full suit bag was too bulky to be constantly carrying to and from work. Jason had even tried leaving the uniform at work but had got a firm talking-to from Toby about it. Toby was their manager at the personnel company that hired them out and was very keen that their appearance and conduct be in keeping with the 'luxury lifestyle brand' of the building they worked in from the moment they arrived. Toby stayed in the central office and didn't have to wear a uniform.

All in all, Jason found Max a very reassuring presence, and was pleased with how often their shifts overlapped.

'Hey, Jace, you dreamin'?' Max called, deep voice punctuated by the thumping tread of his footsteps.

'Hm?' Jason looked up from the pad where he'd been doodling. 'What's up?'

'Dickhead alert, twelve o'clock,' Max said, not quietly enough for Jason's comfort, and ducked into the small room behind the front desk.

Jason looked up to see a figure striding through the doors. The metal tip of a cane rapping gently on the marbled floor. He recognised the sky-blue suit with aquamarine tie and pocket square before the face of the figure had cleared the glass front of the building.

'Good morning, Mr Candido,' Jason said.

Jésus Candido regarded the concierge with a face like he was checking a vegetable for mould.

'No,' he said at last. 'It is not.'

'Hey,' Max stage-whispered from the back room. 'Ask him if he's lookin' to buy a bold new piece for his gallery.'

Jason said nothing, smiling blankly at Mr Candido, hoping he hadn't heard.

''Cause I dropped a huge piece of modern art in the loos this morning, and I think he might be interested.'

Jason tried to stop himself, but a grin split his face and a few snorting laughs escaped. Mr Candido stared at him, his disgust now laced with confusion, but the immaculate man said nothing. After a moment, he simply turned and walked towards the elevators.

'Jesus! You're going to get me fired.' Jason spun to face his friend, trying his best to sound as angry as he knew he should be.

'Firstly, Jésus just got in the lift.' Max grinned at him. 'And, second, if I did get you fired from this dump, it'd be the biggest favour I ever did you.'

'Well, I'm not sure my folks would agree.'

'Well, that's cause you're a pushover, ain't it?'

Jason turned away as the jibe landed, but not before catching Max's face darkening.

'This place's rotten, Jace, all of it. Soft poshos one side and whining grot the other. Only difference is this half of the rot pays us. That's all there is to it. Remember that.' Max smiled and stretched his neck, the crack of the bones ringing out through the foyer like a gunshot.

The cot bed creaked under Jason's weight. It wasn't remotely comfortable, but when a shift ended the wrong side of the last

Central line tube, there wasn't much in the way of options. It wasn't like he was making the sort of money he'd need for regular hotel stays, nor did he have the kind of friends that might have sofa space in central London. The cramped cot that could just about squeeze into the back room was management's only concession to the '24-hour' part of 24-hour concierge, and even then it had only been agreed after the team had comprehensively proved that it couldn't be seen from the foyer when the door was open.

The metal frame was slightly too small for Jason, and the hard metal always ended up digging into some part of his back, but the thing that really kept him from sleeping were the monitors. There was a bank of about a dozen screens, each cycling between the different security cameras that watched the corridors and lifts of Banyan Court. The front of it, at least. Jason didn't think much about the back. It wasn't his problem.

The cameras meant that even with the ceiling lights turned off, he found himself bathed in the monochrome glow of the screens, an eerie night light that made drifting off difficult, and he would find himself staring for hours at the silent corridors. Occasionally, he'd see one of the residents coming or going, but not often. He was pretty sure some of the upper floors had never been lived in: valuable properties bought as investments by overseas oligarchs and billionaires. This was London, after all; if you were actually *living* in the property you bought, you clearly weren't rich enough to properly afford it.

From the front desk he could make out the sober tones of the Shipping Forecast, just before Radio 4 turned over to the World Service. Ryan liked to have it on when he did overnight desk duty. Jason knew his smartly dressed colleague actually spent the dead hours of the night working on his screenplay, but he claimed the quiet muttering of the radio helped him concentrate.

Jason's gaze drifted over the monitors. Max was doing some rounds on the fifth floor, his tread firm and steady. Jason wasn't sure why there needed to be two concierges on duty this late, but Toby had put together the rosters and he wasn't going to make waves about it. Besides, he liked having Max with him. Jason always found doing the rounds a little bit unsettling. The hallways of Banyan Court always seemed too quiet, too long. He kept thinking he could hear muffled voices behind the closed doors – even an empty cleaning closet, one time – and the way the thick carpet muffled his footfalls set his teeth on edge. Max had no such qualms.

He watched as his friend wandered the hallways, swinging his baton slowly back and forth. It was an antique, he'd once said, a genuine Victorian policeman's nightstick that had belonged to his 'ancestors' (which Jason took to mean a great-great-grandfather or uncle). It was made of a heavy, polished wood, and always seemed slightly cool to the touch regardless of the heat. It wasn't technically legal for Max to have it in public, but no one had mentioned it, and it wasn't exactly as if he'd had cause to use it. But it was a symbol for him, a talisman of sorts. Jason thought the residents must quite like it, the firm reassurance that someone was willing to fight for their safety. At the very least, no one had complained.

'You gotta find how you want to change the world,' Max had told Jason when he first brought it in. 'An' when you find it, keep it close. I wanna change the world by bustin' any heads tryin' to ruin it.'

Max said a lot of stuff like that, and certainly had plenty of opinions on who was trying to 'ruin' the world, but Jason couldn't deny that even he felt a certain security watching that heavy stick swinging back and forth through the building. He lay back and drifted into sleep.

*

Jason opened his eyes resentfully. There had been a time when he would have had a moment of panic and confusion as his mind tried to process waking up somewhere it wasn't used to. But by now the cramped cot bed and the tiny room had imprinted themselves deep enough on his psyche that waking there felt mundane and familiar. More familiar than Jason would have liked, really.

He fumbled for his phone to check its clock. The small room had no windows, so with the lights off and the door closed it could have been any time at all. The screen showed 05:12. Jason groaned to himself and started the process of getting up. There was another hour or so until the first tube, but he should be home in time to get a shower and some breakfast ... before coming back for his next shift. He let out a slightly bitter sigh and turned to look for his shoes.

'Sleep well?'

Jason jumped at the sound of Max's voice. Looking over, he saw his friend sitting in the chair that looked over the security monitors, though he was turned towards him. The glow of the screens covered that hard face in shadows, save for Max's eyes, which glinted out.

'I ... guess. Sure. Were you watching me sleep?' The question was intended as a joke, but the laugh that tried to follow came out as a nervous chuckle.

'Keepin' an eye out.' Max's thumb gestured at the bank of displays.

'Right ...'

'Somethin's comin'. I can feel it.'

Jason tried to rub the sleep from his eyes. He wasn't awake enough for this.

'What ... I mean, did you see something, or ...?'

'Somethin's brewing. I can feel it, like I said.' Max's hand unconsciously drifted towards the nightstick on his hip. 'I can smell it on the grot.'

'They're not—' Jason caught the warning look in Max's eyes and stopped himself.

'Don't start with your pushover bleedin' heart bullshit. They don't pay your fuckin' wages so you don't have to pretend you like or respect 'em. Those over there, they're grot, Jace. They build up in cracks when you're not paying attention and if I had my way I'd clean 'em all out.'

'They live here too, Max,' he muttered quietly. Given his own financial situation, Jason sometimes wondered how close he was to becoming like them in his friend's eyes.

'Same building. Different world. They're penniless whinin' deadweight, Jace. Grot. Sooner you realise that, the better.'

'You're in a cheerful mood.'

This was not the first time he'd heard Max go off on a rant about the residents of Banyan Court's back half, but usually he at least had the chance to get a coffee first. He wondered what had triggered this one. Max had strong opinions on pretty much everyone who wasn't paying him, with particular ire reserved for 'hippies, lefties, chavs, tramps, weirdos, whiners and the fuckin' unions', all of which he could go on about for hours, nightstick waving like a conductor's baton. Jason would nod along, privately wondering what made Max, who would proudly proclaim himself working class, see himself as so far above those he decried.

Still, Jason didn't actually object to these tirades. He didn't agree with them either, of course, personally, but Max was older than him by a couple of decades at least, and at times reminded him of his grandad, a fiery red-faced contrarian, in the years before he died. Besides, Jason couldn't help but get a slight kick out of the fact that this man who hated everybody had chosen him for a friend.

'Somethin's comin',' Max repeated, scowling as he turned away. 'I can feel it. So can they, they're just too thick to notice.'

He sat there, glowering at the screens as they flicked through the corridors of the building. The room had got uncomfortably humid with both of them in there and had started to fill with the scents that Jason associated with Max's presence: machine oil and boot leather. He needed to get some fresh air.

'Whatever, man.' Jason shrugged. 'I got a train to catch.'

Technically, the journey from Whitechapel to Debden wasn't a difficult one but depending on how the transport systems lined up on any given day it could be up to an hour and a half's journey.

It wasn't the time that wore on Jason, though. There was something about the long stretch of train ride rattling out towards the suburbs and countryside that he found strangely oppressive. The same landmarks passing him by every day, again and again, marking the passage of time between a deeply unfulfilling job and a house his parents were clearly sick of sharing with him. A huge pendulum, back and forth, each swing another tally on a wasted life he'd never get back.

The heat didn't help, of course. He'd read somewhere that it would have been illegal to transport cattle on the Central line during summer, because there were laws about how hot a container carrying cows could be. Not people, though. No laws about that. Jason supposed this was because people could choose to not get into a carriage they thought was too hot, but as the beads of sweat started to soak through his uniform shirt, it didn't feel like much of a choice to him.

He watched, bleary-eyed and uncomfortable, as the

pseudo-countryside of London's suburbia rolled by. It looked like it should be refreshing, full of invigorating breezes and the sunshine of a new day. But Jason knew the air was still laced with motorway fumes and sticky with the heat of summer.

His parents' small house was just big enough for a retired couple, as had indeed been the intention when they had sold Jason and his brothers' childhood home in Muswell Hill and moved out here. He unlocked the side door and slipped in as quietly as he could. There was always a slight flush of guilt when he got out the key, noting the tag still read 'SPARE' in thin black letters, despite it having been on his keyring for almost half a year now. Another failure.

His parents weren't up yet, so no need to small talk about his day. He moved quietly up the carpeted stairs, avoiding the creakier steps, and into what his father still insisted on calling the 'spare room'. This was one door he couldn't open quietly, given how many boxes were piled up behind it, but it didn't sound like he'd woken anybody up. After picking his way through the maze of brown cardboard that still held the majority of his worldly possessions, he stretched himself out over the unmade bed.

Exhaustion washed over him. It wasn't his childhood room, far from it, but he'd done his best to cover the walls with anything that felt like his. Posters for power metal bands he hadn't listened to since he was fifteen; framed stills from his university cinephile phase; a piece of abstract art he'd picked out with Tammy when they'd first moved in together. His gaze lingered on the last one. He shouldn't really have taken it. Technically it had been a gift to her, but he'd half-hoped if he packed it up with the rest then she might have had a reason to call. But she never did. It was stupid, might as well frame the divorce papers if he wanted something on his wall that was going to upset him whenever he looked at it. He should just take it down. Later.

He reached into a box that had been marked 'Kitchen' in Tammy's handwriting four years ago. Then changed to 'Kitchen – Pans' two years ago when they'd moved into their 'forever home'. And, finally, 'Books' six months ago, in his handwriting. He pulled out a weathered old paperback, a Matthew Reilly thriller he'd read a dozen times, and lost himself in a world of grizzled marines with nothing left to lose until he drifted off into a fitful nap.

A package sat on the front desk when he got in for his next shift. It was large and square, unremarkable except for the fact that it was addressed to Tobias Fell. Max sat behind the desk, eyes sparkling with dark amusement.

'Is it … You haven't sent it up?' Jason felt suddenly on edge, though he wasn't sure why.

'Was waitin' for you. I know you like to handle things for his highness up there.'

Jason felt himself blush, ever so slightly. It was true; he did get a small thrill from sending things up the small private dumbwaiter that travelled all the way to the penthouse. He didn't really know much about Mr Fell, except that he was important and very powerful.

'Sure thing,' he said, trying not to betray his excitement as he picked up the surprisingly heavy box and carried it around the corner where the small lift was concealed.

Jason adjusted himself as he walked, bearing the weight against his chest as he tried to get a better handle on the unwieldy corners. A sharp stabbing pain pierced his shoulder. He cried out at the unexpected sensation, releasing the box. As it tumbled to the floor, as though in slow motion, his hand instinctively felt for a wound. He just had time to register the feeling of slick, wet blood before the box hit the ground and split, sending sharp metal spilling out in all directions.

Heavy chefs' knives. Meat cleavers. Stainless steel hooks. A thick apron and what appeared to be some sort of electric bone saw. Butcher's gear – some of which had apparently been improperly packed enough that it had stabbed him through the box.

Jason examined the cut. It was shallow but bleeding freely, and he couldn't help but be shaken by what was splayed out before him, even as he felt blood trickle down his chest.

'Told you.' Max's voice came from behind him as Jason tried to carefully repack the box. There was a note of smug triumph in it.

'Are you going to help me with this, or ...?'

Max nodded at the implements flashing under the tasteful lighting. 'I reckon it's just startin'.'

His friend grinned darkly as he turned away.

'Of course, sir, I'll arrange a cleaner,' Jason said for what felt like the sixtieth time.

'You're not listening,' continued Mr Copeland of number 15, clearly trying very hard to keep his voice level. 'I've got a cleaner, but it hasn't helped. My wife—'

Jason glanced over at Max, who made a violent 'wanker' motion with his hand. It wasn't clear if it was aimed at him or the phone, but Jason appreciated the support.

'Look, Mr Copeland, I don't know what to tell you. I can arrange for a cleaner to come in, though ...' He paused. 'I've got a plumber in later, actually. Working on one of the upper floors. I could ask him to stop by? Have a look?'

'Fine, fine, let me know when he'll be up.'

'Will do, glad I could h—' The phone went dead. '—elp. Brilliant.'

Jason gave Max a half-hearted smile.

'Successfully made it someone else's problem?' his friend said, huge head splitting into a grin.

'Guess so.'

'I told you.' His friend shrugged. 'Something's goin' on.'

Jason was about to wave away the sinister implication when his friend's eyes flashed up to the front door and he nodded a warning. Following his gaze, Jason tensed up as he saw the figure approaching.

'Mr Erikson,' he started to say. 'Please, we've been over this. You can't go—'

His view of the journalist was interrupted by Max's massive frame as he stepped in front.

'Not gonna warn you again.' One hand rested on the solid wood of the nightstick.

'Look, I understand you may not like the press.' David Erikson's voice was calm. 'And I'm sorry for all the bother earlier, I really am. I'm not interested in sneaking around. I just wanted to check something with you.'

The newspaper man was clearly practised in de-escalating exactly this sort of situation. But he hadn't met Max before, and Jason could see in the set of his partner's jaw, the tense of his muscles, that he was just as determined to keep escalating it. He began to walk slowly towards David, like a stalking cat.

'Mr Erikson.' Jason's voice was quiet. Why was he so scared all of a sudden? 'Please leave before we're forced to remove you again.'

'OK, OK, I'm going.' Jason made himself relax when the journalist turned and began heading towards the door. At least he knew how to take a hint.

Then he stopped. Paused. Jason's stomach dropped as the man turned back.

'I just wa—'

Whump.

The sound of the nightstick impacting his face was oddly understated; a muffled wet noise like a joint of beef being dropped onto the floor. It hit David just above the cheekbone, next to his left eye, and he fell to the ground without a peep, too stunned to speak.

'Get outta here,' Max's voice rumbled. 'Now. Or next time I'm not holding back.'

And much as Jason hated to admit it, Max had been holding back. As David struggled upright, he could see that, while he'd have a nasty bruise, the baton hadn't broken the skin. There was a moment as the injured man looked from the huge figure before him over to Jason, silently pleading for him to intervene.

'Go,' Jason said.

David scrambled to his feet and ran out of the front door.

Max cracked his neck and let out a sigh of satisfaction, a huge grin plastered over his face.

'Can't stand journalists, you know?' he said to Jason as he returned to his lurking spot behind the desk.

Jason did know. Max had always been plenty vocal about it, but the violence … The violence was new. He tried not to catch his friend's glowering eyes and swallowed down his growing unease.

Jason slammed the phone down.

'Christ.'

'Copeland again?' Max called from the back room.

'Mm-hm.'

'I told you, man. All the crazies are comin' out.'

Jason exhaled. He wasn't entirely wrong. In the last few days he'd had a bunch of calls from upstairs. Not just from number 15, either. That tech guru guy kept sending down weird requests,

Jésus whatshisface was demanding taxis at all times of the day and night, and the plumber, Janek, had been in and out more times this week than in the last year, looking more and more unsettled. That was without the old lady they'd found dead in one of the back flats (not technically their responsibility, but still pretty unsettling) or the thing with the reporter. Things were ... Well, they were getting strange.

It didn't help that Max seemed to be taking all this as some kind of vindication, giving that same shit-eating grin every time something weird happened. There was something else in his eyes, though, a sort of anticipation, like he was waiting for just the right time to deliver a punchline.

After what happened last week, when he saw Max on the monitors now, he couldn't help but notice the way he moved. It was slow, but purposeful, nightstick no longer swinging, but still and ready, his head scanning from side to side. Jason had almost begun to fear what might happen if a resident bumped into him when he was making the rounds. Truth be told, a lot of the things that used to amuse him about Max had started to scare him a little bit.

'Hey,' the deep voice rumbled from the back room. 'You with me?'

Jason jumped slightly at the question, his thoughts broken.

'Yeah, Max. Yeah. Sorry.'

'No worries, man,' Max said lightly. 'So, what d'you think? About all of it? What's goin' on.'

'I don't know,' Jason replied, trying to match the tone. 'Above our pay grade, I reckon. It's a story, I guess, isn't it?'

Max was quiet, as though considering his words. Jason's gaze moved down to the heavy baton cradled gently in the crook of his arm, and he was all at once very, very worried that his friend might not like his answer.

'What ... What do you think?'

'Me?' Max's smile and carefree tone was gone. 'I think some grots are trying their luck. Messin' with us. Hasslin' the folks we look after 'cause they're jealous. 'Cause boo hoo their lives were so hard. I think we need to find who they are and teach a lesson. Bust some heads. After that everything'll just fall into place. You wait and see.'

The blunt confidence and cool tough-guy act no longer seemed impressive or reassuring. The take no shit attitude had congealed into the hanging threat of violence and Jason briefly wondered if the other concierges had noticed. They seemed to avoid Max anyway. Maybe this was how they'd always seen him. Or maybe he was overreacting? It was just talk, and Max had always talked like this. Well, maybe not *all* talk. He had smacked that journalist around. But if he was dangerous, what could Jason do about it?

The foyer doors opening caught his eye and he looked over to see a new face walk in. The guy was young and still had that teen lankiness to him. His step was slow and self-consciously casual. He wore a dark hoodie with some videogame logo on it and a blue baseball cap. He sauntered up to the desk and leaned against it heavily, his elbow pushing the visitor book out of alignment.

'Evenin'. What can we do for you?' Jason asked, trying to keep his voice professional and helpful.

The kid ignored him.

'Hey.' Max wasn't quite as friendly. 'Do you need something?'

The blue cap shifted as the young man looked between the two. His eyes were bloodshot and rimmed with red, an effect that, combined with the hazy smile, made it quite clear what the kid had been doing with his day.

'Yeah. Yeah, sure.' His voice was gentle, with none of the focus sobriety might have given it. 'I got, uh, got a phone.'

'We've all got phones.' Max's voice gained an edge. 'Can you be a bit more specific?'

'Violet. It's Violet's phone. Says on it. "Vi-o-let". She lost it.'

He reached into his hoodie and pulled out the mobile, placing it on the desk in front of him. It was square and functional, with a fresh crack snaking up from the corner of the screen.

'Oh.' Jason nodded, suddenly understanding. 'Lost property?'

The blue cap nodded twice in affirmation. Jason turned to his terminal and started tapping quickly.

'Violet Ng? Number 114?'

'Sure.' The kid shrugged. 'I guess.'

'Well, she lives the other side of the building.' Jason glanced at Max, but if he had a reaction to this news, he was hiding it well. 'I guess we could look after it and let her know.'

Jason called up the lost property page and stifled a groan. He always forgot how much of a chore this was on the building's management system.

'Sorry, got to fill this in.' The kid simply shrugged again. 'Name?'

'Violet.'

'No, your name.'

'Andre.' A pause. 'James.'

'Sorry, which one?'

'James.'

'Sorry, wait, so ... James Andre?'

'Yo.'

Jason sighed. It was going to be a long evening. He steeled himself to ask the next question, when he felt Max's huge hand settle on his shoulder.

'It's alright,' the deep voice rumbled in his ear. 'I got this.'

'You sure?' Jason said, trying not to sound too worried about leaving Max alone with someone.

'Course.' His friend's voice was relaxed. Was he just being paranoid after the journalist thing? 'Anyway, you're late for rounds. I'll take care of all this.'

Jason nodded, getting to his feet and stretching. If there was any tension, James didn't seem to register any of it, lost in his own mellow world. Max settled into the seat that always seemed a little too small for him and stared at the computer.

'What's the address?' he asked.

Jason gratefully hurried towards the lift. He glanced back for a moment, trying to ignore how much of the relief came from the fact he was leaving Max behind as well.

Doing 'the rounds' had always felt to Jason like a deeply point-less exercise. It wasn't as though they worked in a warehouse where they could check every room or compare things to an inventory. Anyone who broke in would be looking for a posh flat payday, and the flats were exactly the places the concierges couldn't check. Still, tonight it was a relief to have a little bit of quiet, a bit of space to himself. He walked the same repetitive stretch of corridor on each floor confirming that, yes, no one had stolen the hallway carpet yet. Jason was pretty sure the other concierges skipped the rounds entirely, but Max had been very adamant when training him about how important it was.

He also wasn't keen on having so much time alone with his thoughts. Traditionally they eventually circled round to Tammy and his parents and his many, many failures. Tonight, though, they were dwelling on Max. Should he have stood up to his friend more? A flush of shame and anger spread over Jason as he thought about how much of a pushover he'd always been. He knew it, no matter what anyone else said, and even privately blamed it for the divorce. Tammy had never said anything, in fact she always used to say that she liked how 'gentle' he was.

But they said that, didn't they? Women. Jason knew, deep down, that he just hadn't been strong enough to keep her. He choked down the rising feelings of inadequacy and pushed on. Yeah, next time Max was being a dickhead, Jason was going to say something.

He finished off the twelfth floor, entered the lift and hit the button marked 'G'. Nobody went up to the penthouse, naturally. He'd been told once that Tobias Fell had a secret, private lift, but Jason had never seen it for himself, despite looking on a particularly long night shift. Twice since he'd been working there a swarm of shiny black cars and armoured jeeps had descended on the building, blocking traffic and filling the foyer with generic-looking men in dark suits and earpieces. He'd later been told Mr Fell had been going out, but Jason hadn't seen him, nor did he know where he'd entered or left the building. There was a specific room on the ground floor, just opposite the lifts, with a dumbwaiter where they left packages for the penthouse, and they were always gone within a few hours.

Jason absentmindedly rubbed his aching hands as the lift descended. He was restless, though he couldn't be sure exactly why.

He found Max sitting behind the desk. There was no sign of James Andre, but his partner was talking quietly to a group of men in official-looking black vests. There were four of them, each with close-cropped hair and the sort of broad, dumpy build that came from a physical job and unhealthy lifestyle. As he got closer, Jason could read the worlds stitched in white on their pseudo stab vests: BAILIFF.

Jason couldn't hide his surprise at seeing them on this side of the building. Normally they were asking to be let in the back.

'We need the key to number 21,' the oldest one was saying.

He was a middle-aged man with a red face surrounding a moustache that he clearly thought was intimidating.

'I'm checkin',' Max growled, reading over some forms that had clearly just been handed to him.

'Then check faster,' the ruddy bailiff said, his finger tapping on the counter. 'We've got a job to do and it's late.'

Max stood up. Without the chair he was easily a foot taller than the leader of the group, and the bailiffs instinctively took a step back. Max smiled and put down the documents. He glanced over at Jason. His face was slightly flushed, as though he'd just been jogging.

'Here's my colleague now.' He picked a key up from behind the desk. 'Everythin' looks in order. I'll take you up.'

'It's about time,' the moustachioed man grumbled, following behind Max as he led them towards the lifts.

'Watch the desk, Jace.' Max winked at him as they passed.

'R-right.' Jason nodded as an uneasy feeling passed through him. He felt oddly weightless all of a sudden, as though detached from the scene he was watching, but as requested he walked slowly over to the front desk and sat down.

The foyer was peaceful, the quiet only broken by the occasional taxi rolling down the streets outside. He glanced at the computer screen, then back outside, then back to the computer screen in slight confusion. The lost property form was still up on the screen. It hadn't actually been filled in past the address line. Well, that wasn't particularly surprising, on reflection. James Andre had not seemed the most reliable sort and had probably given up and wandered off. Or maybe Max had snapped and said something that sent the kid running.

Either scenario was a bit of a relief for Jason. He sat down and went to close the program. The mouse felt weird. Sticky. He pulled his hand back to find it was red.

'The fuck?' Jason said, though deep down he knew exactly what was happening. He knew it even before he became aware of the low, pained breaths coming from the back room.

James Andre was in bad shape. His eyes were almost entirely swollen shut and blood still flowed slowly from his nose and mouth. He held his hand at his side, the arm above it bent at a painful-looking angle. Somehow his blue cap was still on his head, though now streaked with blood. Jason stood in the doorway, his mind racing, frozen in indecision. He still had time to leave, a few seconds in which he could decide to not have seen this.

Then James tried to speak. The croaking noise was barely recognisable as language, but within it, Jason could still clearly make out the word 'Help.' He turned and hurried back to the desk, fear making his hands shake as he fumbled for the phone. His finger was poised over the number pad, when a shadow fell across him.

'Really hope you're not doin' what I think you're doin', Jace.' Max's voice sounded different, heavier.

'What the hell have you done?' Jason wanted to scream at the figure towering over him, but when those dark eyes fell on him, he felt his conviction start to evaporate.

'Taught a piece of shit some respect.' Max smirked. 'You gotta keep 'em in line, Jace. It's like I always told you.'

'No, that was— You didn't mean it.'

'Not my fault if you weren't listening, mate.' Max sounded saddened, but unsurprised. His eyes glinted in the darkness. 'Now step back from the phone.'

'Max, listen to me—'

There wasn't a second warning. The nightstick came down with a crash, landing firmly on the plastic housing and shattering it into a hundred black fragments. Jason cried out and leapt back, dropping the now useless handset.

'Let's talk about what's gonna happen here. 'Cause I don't *want* to hurt you, Jace, but y'know, you put me in a real tough spot.'

Max was walking around the desk, now, eyes locked on his new prey, heavy wooden baton held firmly in his huge fist.

'You really shoulda minded your own business. Left me to the job of keepin' order in this place. Sometimes you just gotta squash disrespect. Always thought you might understand. But seems—'

James Andre lunged from the doorway straight for Max, his shout of anger and pain distorted by the damage to his face. The attack was weak and uncoordinated, almost missing his target entirely, but Max spun to face him anyway, giving Jason an opening. He leapt from his chair and kicked wildly with all his force, landing a heel squarely in the larger man's groin. Max let out a yelp of agony and toppled over. Jason noticed the solid corner of the marble-topped desk moments before his former friend's head hit it full force. Though even if he'd had the time to try and stop the impact, he wasn't sure he would have.

The crack of Max's skull was a sound unlike anything Jason had ever heard. It was nothing like the clean sounds of violence that he expected from when the bad guy goes down. It was a wet, gravelly crunch that seemed to reverberate through his own head and left him feeling weak and queasy. Max rolled off the desk and onto the floor, leaving fragments of himself on the corner. Everything was quiet, save for James's ragged breathing.

Jason offered the injured young man his arm, and led him out from behind the desk, over to the plush bench that ran along the edge of the foyer next to the lifts. His leg was clearly in bad shape, and he limped painfully, placing almost his full weight on Jason. The boy sat heavily and tried to offer up a smile, though his eyes were groggy and unfocused, and he seemed to be slipping closer to unconsciousness.

'Wait here,' Jason said. 'I'm just going to grab my phone and we—'

More than anything else it was the odour that tipped him off. It was something he'd briefly smelled when taking the police up to look over the old lady's apartment. Which shouldn't have even been his job, but who else was going to do it. He remembered the stench as he unlocked the door, but even then it hadn't been this strong or this close. It was the smell of death, but more than that, like something that had been dead for a *long* time. Jason turned.

Max stood between them and the front doors. He moved slowly, but there was no way Jason could get past him while carrying the injured youth. He stared at his tormentor. The skin on Max's face had somehow been torn clean away by hitting the counter and lay on the floor behind him like a mask. What stared at them now was nothing but a gore-drenched skull, a bloody death's head that stood atop a concierge's uniform that had now darkened to a dull, utilitarian black. Blood dripped onto his boots. What the hell was that thing? Was that Max? Had it *always* been Max?

Jason gritted his teeth, grabbed James, and started to pull him towards the elevator.

'Always knew you might be trouble, Jace.' Max's voice was untroubled by his lack of lips. He watched as the lift doors closed, his teeth on show in a macabre grin. 'And I hate trouble-makers.'

The lift opened onto the twelfth floor. Jason hit the stop button and jammed his key into the slot to override the control panel.

He wasn't sure if doing so would affect all the lifts, but he had to hope.

He stared at the other lifts, waiting to see if the numbers changed. If any of them were climbing inexorably up towards them. They were still. For now.

What was going on? That thing chasing them was dead. It had to be. It smelled dead, it looked dead, it *felt* dead. But that didn't make any sort of sense. Max had been ... I mean, Jason had never taken his pulse or anything, but he sure as hell hadn't been a corpse! That didn't change the fact that this was Max, the truth of Max, and he couldn't shake the feeling that it always had been.

'Stupid, stupid!' Jason cursed at himself as he dragged the nearly unconscious James out into the corridor. What was he doing? Max was stronger than he was, faster. He knew the building better and wasn't carrying another human being with him. Even without whatever freaky shit was going on with him basically being a corpse, Jason knew he was outmatched. Was he doing it again? Delaying the inevitable, trying to deny his own weakness and failure until push came to shove and he turned tail like always? No. Not this time.

He lowered his injured cargo down onto the carpet and started to pace back and forth, thinking through his options as fast as possible. First priority was to get access to a phone and call the police. Getting out of the building was tempting, but with James slowing him down there was no way they'd be able to outrun Max. Could he leave James behind? At the mercy of someone, something, that was clearly eager to kill them both? It didn't matter, not really. If Max was still downstairs, which he might be, he had access to the automatic security systems and could make leaving the building very difficult either way. Or maybe he was in one of the other lifts, or moving up the stairs.

It didn't matter: getting a call out was the best move, but his phone was still charging on the desk and a quick pat of James's pockets came up empty.

The situation wasn't entirely desperate. Max would be able to keep a close eye on them as long as he stayed in the security room, but as soon as he left, he was just one man and there was a lot of building to cover. Especially if the two of them could get into one of the apartments. That was probably the best move.

He dragged James back into the stopped elevator.

'Stay here,' he said, as though the bleeding teenager had a choice. 'I'll be back.'

The injured boy tried to say something, but his swollen jaw rendered it nothing but a groan. He tried to grip Jason's shirt, but his hand fell away. He was in real bad shape.

'I'm sorry,' Jason told him. He started to run. Down the hallways, hammering on doors, trying to remember which ones were actually occupied and which were just empty property investments. There on the twelfth floor, it was mainly the latter. This was a bad choice. Another failure. Jason could almost feel his parents' sneers, Tammy's disappointment.

No, they were going to make it. They had to. He rounded the corner.

'Hello? Hello! We need help!' Jason's fist pounded on the door of number 3. He was acutely aware of how solid it was, how much protection it would give him if he could just get the other side of it. But right now, it was only protection for those who didn't want to come to his aid.

At the other end of corridor, he heard the door to the stairwell opening.

Thump. Thump. Thump.

Max's boots fell heavier than seemed possible, reverberating through the floor as he approached.

'I hope you're not botherin' the residents,' his old friend's voice echoed down the corridor. 'They don't need to see this.'

Jason's stomach dropped when he saw the window. Beyond number 3 was a dead end. His only way out was past Max. He crouched, trying to quiet his breathing.

'You're just drawin' this out, Jace,' his pursuer called. 'It's no use. I've dealt with thousands of troublemakers before and you and that punk are no different. You don't matter. *We* don't matter. Important people need their world orderly. And you're disrupting that. Raisin' a fuss.'

Jason pushed back against the wall, willing himself to be smaller, to be hidden, for his pursuer to not come around the corner.

Max walked into view, the bloody grin on his face seeming to get wider still as his lidless eyes settled on the cowering Jason.

'And no one likes a fuss.'

His bootsteps were deliberate and slow, but he seemed to move the length of the hallway in only a few strides. He loomed over Jason, who tried desperately to say something, but found his breath caught in his throat.

'Where's the kid?'

Jason started to smile, his lips ready to curl into a sneer of defiance, to swear he'd never tell, that the kid was under his protection. That he wasn't going to be a pushover anymore. But Max didn't even give him time for a response before the baton came down hard and Jason's world exploded into white light and pain.

He tried to focus his thoughts, but something, maybe a boot, maybe the club, struck him hard in the chest and he felt something crack. He collapsed, the wind going out of him all at once, and the nightstick hit his back once, twice, three times, each impact a spike of agony travelling through his body. He'd been in fights before, but he'd never been beaten, properly, savagely beaten, and he felt his resolve leaking out of him with his tears.

Then he heard something. A door opening, ever so slowly. Jason looked up to see the entrance to flat 3 ajar. A middle-aged man stood there in a tailored dressing gown, looking concerned. Jason started to reach for him, to say something.

'Don't worry, sir.' He heard Max's voice from above him. 'Just a couple of troublemakers. I'm taking care of it. Sorry to disturb you.'

There was a long moment as this stranger looked over the situation before him. Jason tried to cry for help, but the words wouldn't come.

Then the man from number 3 nodded and closed the door.

'Now where's—?'

'The lift!' Jason felt the words come out in a terrified spurt before he'd had a chance to think about it. 'I left him in the lift!'

He waited for the next blow, but none came. Max let out a soft laugh.

'Good lad, Jace.'

The bootsteps began to recede, leaving Jason to catch his breath. He tried not to think about what he'd done, climbing painfully to his feet and limping towards the stairs, painstakingly following in Max's footsteps. He hadn't had any choice. Had he?

He managed to make it down to the seventh floor before he heard the shattering glass from high above, and saw the momentary blur of a body falling past the windows to the ground far below.

'So, Mr Brown. Thanks for coming back in.' The policeman's tone had changed. When they'd first taken his statement, they'd been polite, sympathetic. They'd nodded understandingly before sending him off in the ambulance. Now the pair that sat opposite him in the interview room were cold, their mouths set in hard lines.

'No, uh, no problem.' Jason sat on the uncomfortable metal chair, wincing slightly. 'Any luck finding Max?'

'Right.' A look passed between the officers. 'That's rather what we wanted to talk to you about.'

'Sure, if you need more information—'

'No, thank you. Your description of him was plenty colourful.' There was a pause, then the other policeman spoke.

'What would *really* help us is a second name. Or an address. Or really anything to prove he exists.'

'I told you, I don't know his surname, he never said.' Jason could feel something was wrong. 'Prove he exists? What are you implying?'

'Not much of an implication,' the first cop said. 'There's no employment record for any Max at your company. No Max, Maxwell, Maximillian, Maximus, nothing. He doesn't work for them.'

'But—' Jason's head was pounding. 'The others. Kirsty and—'

'Your colleagues have no knowledge of anyone matching your description working alongside the three hired concierges.'

'Though they do recall you mentioning a Max on a few occasions,' the second one piped up with a sneer. 'So, you've got the groundwork if you want to try pleading insanity.'

'That's not …' Jason felt faint, like he was drowning. 'That doesn't make sense. They've worked with us for years. They talked to him, I remember, I'm sure of it, they—'

'OK, I'm going to cut this short.' The first policeman leaned forward. 'What we have is a half-dozen bailiffs who claim that, shortly before the murder, you led them to a storage room on the ground floor and locked them inside. We've got hospital records that show a bit of light bruising, mainly on your knuckles, but none of the quite graphic injuries you describe receiving. We've got a day's worth of security footage conveniently wiped. And we have a lot of blood on your clothes, all of which seems to belong to your victim. Sorry, *the* victim.'

'But, the—' Jason's eyes lit up. 'The man in flat 3! He saw! He—'

'He didn't have any interest in making a statement,' the second cop said casually.

Jason reeled like he'd been punched The tears started to come, burning as they rolled down his cheeks. He looked up, and there, standing in the corner behind his tormentors, was Max. His face was still missing, and the bloody skull leered at him as it brought a black-gloved finger to its teeth.

Shh.

Right. That was it, then. Jason felt his shoulders sag in defeat. A deep numbness rolled over him as he tried to come to terms with what he was seeing.

'So, am I under arrest?'

There was a moment of awkward silence. He looked up to see the two police officers shifting uncomfortably on their chairs.

'No,' the first one said at last.

'You're free to go,' the second spat, like the words themselves were rotten.

'What? I ... I don't—'

'Get out of here.'

'But ... But James...' Jason couldn't believe what was being said.

'Was a punk who apparently no one will miss.'

The judgement hung in the air as the second policeman chose his next words.

'You, on the other hand, apparently have some very important friends.'

Max was waiting for him. Not behind the front desk in reception, or in the corridors of Banyan Court, but in his bedroom in Debden. He sat on the small single bed, almost buckling it under his weight, smiling at Jason. At least he'd had the decency to put his face back on, even though it was now half-rotten. He silently handed Jason a thick piece of cardstock.

TOBIAS FELL cordially invites JASON 'MAX' BROWN
to attend a dinner party at 1 Banyan Court
on the evening of 16th August 2014
Penthouse access will be available through the freight elevator

'Mr Fell wants some security at his function,' Max said, grinning.

'Then I guess we're goin',' Jason replied sadly.

11th

Old Plumbing

Janek Kowalczyk
41 Underwood Road

No one ever thinks about the pipes. Not really. You could corner almost anyone, point to the pipes on the outside of their house and ask them what they connect to, where they go, what they're full of, chances are they won't be able to tell you. Maybe, if they own the place, they had to get a plumber in once who talked them through it all, and they have vague memories of words like 'drainage' or 'inlet'. For most people, though, it might as well be magic. You flush the toilet and the waste simply vanishes. The kitchen sink flows out to somewhere that isn't your problem. The washing machine is fed from a hidden realm referred to simply as 'the mains'. It's even worse in a block of flats, where the intricate network of pipes and feeds and stop-valves is almost entirely hidden from view.

All this was just fine by Janek Kowalczyk, who was secretly of the opinion that it was exactly this ignorance and mystique that kept him in work. He'd always found plumbing to be a rather simple discipline, one that made a sort of intuitive sense to him. To his mind, all it really took was common sense, the right equipment and enough patience to see a job through safely. His colleagues disagreed, of course, said he simply had a knack for the trade, which was great for his ego, but he could never really shake the feeling they were just covering themselves. Certainly, there was plenty of competition in the industry, any number of cowboys looking for an opportunity to undercut a skilled tradesman and flood your home for half the price. Still, Janek had always had a way of looking at a place and seeing how it all connected. A building was not entirely unlike a human body, with its veins and membranes and intestines, and he often had a sense of how a structure lived.

Of course, the trouble with coming over from Poland as he had was that English landlords assumed Janek was just another cowboy, cheap and slapdash. They were patronisingly delighted when it turned out he knew what he was doing, and significantly less happy when he quoted them properly for it. It was one of the reasons he was so happy to be spending as much time as he was in Banyan Court.

He'd apparently become a favoured supplier for one of the companies that dealt with a whole bunch of the cheaper flats there, and they'd clearly been talking enough with the other letting agents that he'd even got some jobs in the high-end apartments. He still wasn't paid what he was really worth, of course, but Janek had long since come to terms with that, and the steady stream of work was very welcome. Even if the pipes there did, on occasion, utterly baffle him. They sprawled out in odd ways, connected in places that didn't make sense, and seemed to be all different ages and makes. If Banyan Court was a body, it was very sick indeed.

'Morning, Janek.'

Janek grunted at the concierge, whose name he suddenly realised he did not know. This was all a bit new to him, having clients regular enough that they learned his name, and he felt a brief, irrational anger that the man behind the desk had cheerfully put him at such a disadvantage. Realising his grunt might have seemed rude, he tried to smile, awkwardly raising his hand in an almost-salute.

'Which is the number?' he asked, maybe a little bit too quickly, but he was keen to avoid small talk.

'Uh, looks like number 17. Floor...' The concierge gave no indication he'd noticed Janek's impatience as he slowly checked his sheets. 'Floor eight. Problem with the shower. Mr Fowler's out at the moment, but he gave instructions to let you in. Said he'd be back about six which, between you and me, means he wants you out by then.'

Janek shrugged.

'It takes how long it takes.'

'That's what I said to him. Told him you did good work.'

Janek nodded his thanks and hoisted his toolkit, heading towards the lift. The concierge grabbed a set of keys and followed him. Of course. He needed to be let in. Even the lift needed a key. The people here trusted Janek to fix their shower, but it wouldn't do for him to forget his place. He stepped into the mirrored lift, shining and immaculate as always, and pressed '8'. The concierge joined him just before the doors began to close.

'Gotta say, I'm surprised how often you're round at the moment. I mean, like I say, you do good work, but still, new build like this ... just seems odd.'

Janek shrugged again.

'Old pipes,' he said.

The concierge nodded, though it was clear that he didn't understand.

*

269

Mr Fowler's bathroom was the sort of immaculate that you only ever got from a successful middle-aged businessman who lived alone. Three different reed diffusers sat on the windowsill, probably a hundred quid a piece, but it was obvious no thought had gone into how the scents would actually work together. They lent the room a confused odour that was by turns floral and citrus, with the occasional strong waft of patchouli. They weren't enough to mask the other scent, though, a slightly coppery undernote that made Janek grit his teeth and sigh deeply.

He had been told the shower was having problems with the pressure and had started producing 'bad water'. As far as complaints went it wasn't particularly useful, but Janek had dealt with far worse and, honestly, all he needed to know was that it was the shower. There were only so many problems that could affect a shower without touching the rest of the plumbing.

First task, of course, was to check the top-of-the-range electric shower system the guy had had installed. One advantage of getting callouts to flats like this was that, no matter how rich their occupants were, they rarely had space for the sort of fancy at-home spa systems that were a proper nightmare to navigate. Janek still allowed himself a small moment of snobbery, looking at the unnecessary and overpriced features some lucky fitter had managed to sell to Mr Fowler. Janek shook his head, imagining how much the man must have paid for it. He considered himself a good man, and always did his best to avoid passing judgement on others, but deep down he had an unshakeable conviction that all rich people were deeply, deeply stupid. Well, maybe not stupid exactly, but foolish, certainly. He'd seen it over and over again: there was simply no way to have that much money without it warping your relationship to the world in ways that made you laughably ignorant.

The shower itself looked fine, at least, save for a tell-tale residue that Janek was careful to wash off properly. Reassembling the thing took much longer than actually checking its function, as any indication it had been interfered with was a sure-fire way to get a complaint and lose Banyan Court as a client. And he was only getting started.

Next, he checked the hose and the shower head. Both had those same crusty remains dried along the inside of them, but it was nothing that couldn't be cleaned out with some descaler, followed by a little bleach. Rinsing it through, watching the rusty-looking water drain away down the plug hole, Janek laughed softly, just to himself. Wash the dirt out of one pipe to flush it down into another. Such was the cycle of that invisible, unremarked network that kept the place alive.

The shower itself was fine, it seemed, so it must be the pipes themselves. Standing up, he took a moment to stretch out after so long hunched over, pins and needles tingling in his legs as circulation returned, and walked out to the kitchen sink. Turning on the tap, he watched carefully as the stream of water flowed out of it, strong and clear. He stood for a minute, before taking a guess at which of Mr Fowler's cupboards contained drinking glasses. He got it right on his second try, grabbing a highball glass and filling it to the top before turning off the running water. The silence that followed seemed ever so slightly thicker than it had been before. Janek nodded to himself, before holding up the glass to his face, carefully studying the liquid inside. It looked clean and clear, and a thin layer of condensation was starting to form on the outside. He sniffed it once, twice, nodded again, then proceeded to drink it, draining the glass in a few seconds. No taste except the slight chalkiness of that hard London water. Healthy.

Janek was stalling and he knew it. He sighed, placed the glass in a dishwasher that probably cost more than his van, and returned to the bathroom. He worked quickly, bypassing the shower so he could have a look at exactly what was coming out of the pipe that fed the bath tap. He checked his watch and opened the valve. It took a few seconds, but soon enough it was flowing just as he had expected, slowly and thickly onto the pristine porcelain of the tub. Janek's mouth twisted into an expression of grim vindication.

The blood that spurted and sputtered from the pipe was a rusty red colour, a long way from the bright scarlet of a fresh wound. It was still liquid, however, though didn't seem to be in any way diluted by the water in the system. The smell that came off it was putrid and sick, but Janek had already taken the step of opening all the windows in the flat. He kept watching, his face set in a hard expression. Glancing at his watch he saw it was half past two. Time enough for the smell to dissipate, he thought as he leaned out of the window and lit a cigarette.

He smoked slowly, deep in thought, keeping one eye on the sporadic rivulet of gore spurting from the pipe out into the bathtub. The smell of the cigarette laced together with the reek of old blood and essential oils, and for a moment he was glad he'd decided to wait until after the job for lunch. He took another drag, feeling the thick smoke fill his lungs. Everyone finds ways to poison themselves, he thought briefly, before tossing the tar-blackened filter out of the window, watching it arc away into open air, down onto the roofs below. Then he turned his attention back to the pipe.

By now the blood had started to thin, just as it had in the other flats, and what flowed from the pipe now was mostly water. That was something to be thankful for, at least. Janek remembered all to vividly how panicked he had been the first time it had happened, over in number 27.

He considered for a moment lighting another cigarette,

but by the time he'd decided against it the water was almost entirely clear. He checked his watch again: seven minutes and ten seconds, plus however long Mr Fowler had watched it in horror, before turning it off and convincing himself it was some sort of rust in the pipes. So far the longest it had taken was ten minutes, which was something of a relief, given everything he had to do afterwards. Maybe he'd measure the volume in whichever flat this happened next. He grimaced as he realised just how sure he was that there *would* be a next time. So far it had been all over this side of Banyan Court, and Janek was damned if he had any idea what he could do except run the blood out and scrub thoroughly afterwards. If nothing else, it was a blow to his professional pride.

As he finished cleaning the pipes and washing up any remaining mess, he listened closely, straining his ears for any new sound. Nothing. Unsatisfied, he began to pack up his tools. So far, the tapping in the pipes had only happened once, in flat 6 a few floors up, but Janek was somehow certain that it was the key to whatever was poisoning Banyan Court. He checked his watch again once he was all done. Four o'clock. It looked like Mr Fowler would be able to get a shower as soon as he got home from whatever high-flying financial career he had dedicated his life to, and wash off that lingering scent of blood.

There was only one armchair in the Kowalczyk house, and that was Janek's. The kids crammed onto the big sofa, and Lena preferred the small two-seater (although the second seat was always covered in her paperwork), so over the years the chair had gradually moulded around him, until the cushions seemed to instinctively conform to his shape. But as he sat there late that night he found, for the first time in recent memory, that he was uncomfortable. The image of those pipes stuck with him, and he just couldn't seem to find the right position to relax and consider them properly. The question that plagued him hadn't changed from any other night over the last month: what the hell was he going to do about Banyan Court?

When it had first happened, he had thought perhaps there was a body in the pipes somewhere. Maybe someone was trying to dispose of a murder victim, gradually draining and dismembering them. It wasn't as if the posh side of Banyan Court had any shortage of ruthless bastards. Hell, given some of the stories he'd heard about Tobias Fell himself ... But, no, that didn't make any sense. Everything he'd seen had been feeding through *into* the flats, a system that was obviously kept very separate from the outflow pipes, even with the building's twisted plumbing. Then he had considered the possibility of a worker accidentally trapped somewhere, hidden out of view when they were being installed. But that was ridiculous. Insegur Group, the conglomerate Fell had hired to build the place, had a pretty dreadful reputation for worker safety, sure, and Janek would know – he'd once worked for the international arm. But that still seemed a hell of an oversight. Besides, this had only started happening in the last month or so, and it had been several years since the new part of the building was erected. None of the obvious explanations made sense. Except, of course, for the one that didn't need to make traditional sense: the building was sick.

He couldn't vocalise exactly where the thought came from, or how it could possibly be true, but deep down it felt right. He had always been able to see a building as a whole, the veins of pipe and plumbing, and all his instincts screamed at him that this was a disease. Banyan Court was rotting. And more than that, it was getting worse. The blood was flowing for slightly longer each time, smelling slightly worse. He had to do something.

Janek told himself to go to the police. He wanted to, really he did. He wanted this to just be someone else's problem, to be able to lie in bed with his wife knowing that someone with the right skills was taking care of it. But it was never that simple, was it? Janek had had enough dealings with authority to know how poorly they reacted to things that didn't seem to make sense. In the best-case scenario, they believed him, tore the building's plumbing apart and found ... something rational. A body, maybe, or a serial killer's disposal method, or something equally awful. Janek would be a hero, sure, but a hero that had still alienated all of his best paying clients. And the worst-case scenario was he alienated them for nothing. That the sum total of his reward was another patronising talking-to from some piece of shit cop who had nothing better to do than make unsubtle implications about deportation. No, it would have to be a lot worse before he could bring himself to take that risk.

He'd promised himself weeks ago that he'd make a report if people started to get ill. If there was a body, human or otherwise, rotting in those pipes then it wouldn't be long before it started to affect the health of the people who lived there. If the blood was properly real and it got into the drinking water, it wouldn't be long before people started to get sick. He'd been keeping an eye on the news, even got little Julia to show him how to set up a Google alert for outbreaks of illness in the area – or more occurrences outside of Banyan Court – though she'd had no idea why. So far there was nothing. The only evidence of anything wrong were the calls he'd been getting more and more regularly.

So, there was only one conclusion. At least to Janek's mind. He'd never dare mention it to Lena, though. She was a doctor, after all, and not prone to superstition. Though he wouldn't dream of saying it to her face, Janek sometimes thought she could be a little bit close-minded. To her, disease was something physical that only affected people. He probably couldn't mention his theories to any of the people working at Banyan Court either. Perhaps they might not dismiss him outright, but they hadn't seen what he had seen, and he had no idea how they would react if they did. No, if he was going to investigate this properly, he'd need to come up with another angle. He sighed, picked up his laptop, and started to draft an email.

'So, how long do you reckon it'll take?'

Janek shrugged. 'Depends on what the problem exactly is. Could be weeks.'

The concierge, who today was helpfully wearing a name badge reading 'Jason', cocked his head with an apparently genuine smile.

'I suppose we'll be seeing a lot of you, then. Is this going to interfere with the residents at all? Folks this side can get a bit touchy.'

'Corridors and service rooms only,' Janek assured him. 'But I might need to go to the back.'

Jason stopped for a second, an expression of confusion briefly passing over his face, as though the idea of going from the front of Banyan Court to the back was entirely alien to him.

'Most, uh ...' He fumbled for the words. 'Most people just go round the outside, I think.'

'There must be a door.' Janek had no intention of going all the way round every time he needed to follow a pipe.

'I guess. Probably locked though.'

'Then you will have a key.' Something about the whole interaction was putting Janek's teeth on edge. Jason kept pausing, losing his focus. He turned towards the empty room behind his desk, as though looking for permission.

'Sure,' he said finally. 'I'll get you the service set.'

He pulled out a small ring full of keys and electronic fobs, and blew the dust off a sign-out book which Janek dutifully scribbled in. He couldn't help noticing that it had been almost two years since they'd last been signed out.

'Not many people get these keys?' Janek asked, and Jason paused a second before bursting into laughter, something that caught Janek off-guard as he most definitely had not made a joke.

'We normally head up with service guys like you, give them access to whatever they need,' Jason replied, looking back towards that small room again and shaking his head with a smile. 'But I'm told you've got a lot of work ahead of you, so I guess it's just, uh, easier this way.'

'Right. Well, see you.'

Janek turned as fast as he considered polite and started to walk towards the lift. To his relief, Jason made no move to follow him this time, and he was happy to be rid of the inquisitive concierge. He had plenty of lies prepared as to exactly what he was doing. His reports so far had talked about dirty water and leaks, a web of lies sufficient to get the building manager to sign off on his attempts to 'locate the source of the recent plumbing issues'. Even so, he really didn't want an audience for when he started pulling up expensive carpet, or knocking through walls to get a proper look at the pipes. And if he was right about the state they were in, he definitely didn't want anyone to see what he found.

On reflection, it shouldn't have surprised Janek just how confusing the pipes in Banyan Court really were. What else had he been expecting? Though he had to take a moment to stare in stunned silence when he got through a piece of wall only to be confronted by a huge cast-iron drainage pipe. The thing must have been at least a hundred and fifty years old and put Janek in mind of a massive varicose vein, swollen with age and neglect. Its existence might have made sense given the age of the original building, except for the fact that this was on the eleventh floor, storeys above where the old factory had stopped. If they'd used the old piping up here, they'd have had to specifically remove it and reinstall it several floors up, which would have been a pointlessly bad idea. Not that the old cast-iron pipes wouldn't still work with proper upkeep, but modern plumbing was a hell of a lot more reliable and generally much easier to install.

This was the most extreme example, certainly, but he'd been finding similar instances all day. There was modern pipework there as well, since there's no way the original building had enough to service all of Banyan Court, but the old iron tubes seemed to be the backbone of the system, the arteries and intestines into which it all connected. If he had to guess, Janek would even go so far as to say that there was more new pipework in the cramped and unpleasant rear of the building, with most of the older parts in the tasteful front section. It had been a long time since he had worked construction, but he could think of no conceivable reason to do this. Someone, somewhere, had specifically demanded it be done like this and, whoever they were, they must have been too rich or too important for anyone to tell them no.

He had to go deeper. If he was going to make a diagnosis, he needed to see the worst of the symptoms, and these pipes were the key, he was sure of it. So Janek spent a few hours finding the largest concentration of them and went to work.

It didn't take much work to unearth a short access pipe. Placing down the section of plaster he had cut away, he began to remove its covering. It started smoothly, but after a few turns the cap stopped abruptly, apparently stuck fast. Janek paused, running through all the possibilities of exactly what might be keeping it from opening. It was old, certainly, but it didn't look like it was rusted shut. He turned away for a moment, rifling through his toolkit for something to force it open, when a small noise froze him in place. He knew the sound, of course, of the access cover slowly rotating, unscrewing behind him. He was alone with the pipes, hadn't seen another living soul for over an hour, and if it was being opened, then it was being opened from the inside.

Janek had to turn around, he had to. What was the point of all this if he couldn't bring himself to actually look at what he had found? But in that moment, there was nothing on earth he wanted to do less than to see what was going to come out of that pipe. The noise stopped, and for a moment Janek almost felt relief, before there was the *tap tap tapping* of something small and hard on the inside of the cast iron.

It was calling to him. It wanted him to look.

He turned around to face the pipes just as the cap came off completely, falling to the floor with a clatter. There was a moment of quiet, as though pausing for effect, and then the stillness was broken by a gush of foul-smelling liquid spurting out of the pipe at him. Janek took an involuntary step back, his eyes still focused on the dark opening. There it was, white and slimy against the dark metal. A finger. The bone shone through where the flesh had rotted away, pale and cold, while what was left had swollen into bloated and waxy lumps.

Janek waited. Whatever this was, it wasn't finished. He was sure of that. The finger stretched out of the hole, which was far too narrow to permit anything wider than the decaying hand that followed it. It tapped again, this time on the outside of the pipe, the sound of wet bone on rusted iron, clearly calling for his attention. He almost laughed at the thought that he might be doing anything other than staring at the rhythmic movements of this insistent corpse's hand. It stretched towards him, and then slowly, purposefully, crooked its thin finger, gesturing him closer.

One step at a time, Janek approached, disgusted and intrigued by this strange invitation. He wanted to keep his distance, his mind fixating on the thought of an arm suddenly shooting out of the pipe and grabbing him by the throat; clammy, rotten fingers sinking into his windpipe. But he continued his approach, until at last he was in front of it. He took a moment, readying himself before bending down, his eyes now level with the hole, staring directly into the darkness of the pipe, visible around the thin wrist. He mechanically reached for his torch. The hand withdrew just as he clicked the button, sending the powerful beam of the Maglite directly into the opening.

What he saw inside took a few moments to fully register. His eyes kept fixing on tiny details, like they were trying their best not to comprehend the complete image. More white bones and bloated flesh, almost enough to make a full body, but so crushed and pressed together that it was impossible to be sure. The pipe was less than eight inches across and with only a twisted cross section visible; he couldn't make any anatomical sense of the compacted mess. He could see something there that might have been a foot. Squashed next to it was what could have once been part of a ribcage. All covered with a torn and stained grey jumpsuit, one Janek almost thought he recognised. At the centre of the mass, his torchlight fell upon a single blue eye. It blinked once, not cloudy and dead but shining, alert and focused. It fixed on him and a few things next to it that might have been teeth shifted their position. Was it trying to smile?

The whole thing shifted, bone and skin and fabric rippling around as the crushed corpse moved, revealing more of itself to Janek's torchlight. A second later and he could just about assemble the image into almost a face, all topped with the remains of a broken, off-white hard hat. Between that and the jumpsuit, Janek had a sudden, horrible impression of what he was looking at, and it was only the knowledge that his own eyes were a deep brown that managed to shake off the thought that he was somehow staring at his own mangled corpse. As it continued to move, he saw that knotted and twisted all around it was a broken safety harness, with torn polyester straps and shattered metal links all caught in each other, giving an impression halfway between an ensnared prisoner and a grotesque piece of gift wrapping.

Then all at once it started to slide backwards, disappearing silently back down the pipe like it was being sucked through a pneumatic tube. It took no more than a couple of seconds for it to be out of reach of Janek's light, leaving only a faint bloody residue on the iron interior. He was alone once again. He went to the opposite wall and leaned heavily against it, his body overtaken by a sudden feeling of intense cold. He slid down until he was sitting on the floor next to his toolkit, and he didn't even bother to check the ceiling for smoke alarms before he raised a cigarette to his lips with shaking hands. He wanted to think, to consider what he had just seen, but his mind was entirely blank.

Grey jumpsuit, white hard hat. A uniform so generic as to be almost completely unremarkable to anyone who wasn't Janek. Anyone who hadn't been wearing it the day they almost drowned.

It was years ago now, decades, before he came to England, before he worked for himself, back when he was still doing jobs with major construction firms. He was new in the position, young and brash, comfortable ignoring the comments from his older, more experienced colleagues when they warned that the company – one of the international affiliated of the Insegur Group – had dubious safety standards, about how he needed to be careful when using their equipment, and how it often wasn't properly maintained. But even if he had paid attention, he didn't know how much it would have helped.

They'd been doing some work on a reservoir, not even a very big one. A simple repair job on the tiny control station that sat near its centre, at the end of a long metal bridge that jutted out from the concrete edge of the still, dark water. There were plenty of signs warning of the dangers of swimming in there, promising hidden currents that would drag anyone foolish enough to try down into a watery grave. Young Janek hadn't really bothered to pay them any mind, not even as he'd clipped on his harness and had his bored, distracted co-worker lower him down next to the damaged pipe, eager to get a better position on the problem. The memory of those stark letters promising a messy end only came back to him when he heard the sound of tearing and saw the old, rotten straps suspending him begin to break.

Trying to describe the cold of that water had never been something he was properly able to do. It can't have been as cold as it was in his memory, it simply wasn't possible. In the years since then he'd gone swimming in literal frozen rivers, but even they had never seemed as appallingly, endlessly cold as the waters of that reservoir when he plunged into them. All sensation seemed to leave his body at once. He was a strong swimmer, even then, and it was less than fifty metres to the edge, but it was as though someone had simply turned off all his muscles. He'd flailed weakly, the harness that was supposed to have protected him now binding him and weighing him down. The endlessly icy water of the reservoir rushed down his throat and into his lungs, and he'd known with absolute clarity that he was going to die.

Young Janek, however, had clearly been possessed of a luck that had largely deserted him in his later years. The exact details of his rescue had never been clear to him, but the rest of his crew had apparently managed to pull him out before drowning or hypothermia was able to fully take him. He was alive, though the next few weeks were, as he recalled, deeply unpleasant. Not only was he unable to work, causing some financial problems for the rest of his family, but he had received a visit from some sharply dressed management types who made it abundantly clear what a bad idea it would be for him to raise any sort of legal issue around the company or their safety provision. The worst part was that he didn't even have the option of quitting, not without leaving his family in a truly dire position. It would be another year before he was able to go and work for himself. Another year of staring at that grey jumpsuit and not-quite-white hard hat, remembering the waterlogged death that was almost his.

'You alright?'

The soft question shattered Janek's reflection like a gunshot and he stood up quickly from the floor, shaking his head and muttering to himself, scattering cigarette butts all round him.

'Hey, hey … it's alright. Sorry. Lot of people smoking in doors at the moment. I won't tell.'

The speaker was a young man in a worn Budweiser T-shirt a few sizes too big for him. His features were soft, but his face had the look of someone who'd had more adversity than his years deserved. His skin had clearly seen the elements, and his eyes hardship. But his concern seemed genuine, and Janek didn't hear any of the condescension he so often encountered on the more expensive side of Banyan Court.

'I ... yes.' Janek tried to regain his composure. 'I'm fine. Had a ... bit of a fall. Trying to get my head correct.'

'Yeah, I'll bet.' The youth looked at him like they were sharing a secret. 'This place'll do that to you.'

A slight shiver passed down Janek's spine. Was this someone who had seen what he'd seen? Someone who might believe him? Was that too much to hope for? The young man stared at him, his face unreadable, until at last he offered his hand.

'Damian,' he said.

'Janek.' He took the handshake warily.

'Well, Yanik.' Damian grinned, and the older man bristled at his pronunciation. 'What do you think of our humble home. I'm guessing you don't like it here?'

Janek shook his head.

'I mean, I guess technically neither do I.' The young man gestured to his outfit. 'Not sure I'd fit in with the hobnobs over here. I'm the other side, you know?'

He gestured down the corridor, towards one of the well-hidden doors that connected the two halves of Banyan Court. Janek considered his response, but Damian didn't wait.

'Thing is,' he continued. 'They want us to think like that, y'know? They want us to be so very sure that it's all separate, us and them, my side your side. We're not the same kind of people if we don't live in the same places. But it's all a lie. You've got to look at the spaces, the ways they don't add up. They're trying to keep us apart, but it doesn't really work unless we're together. Makes sense, I suppose. If you keep everyone looking down on each other, they don't ever bother looking up. You get it?'

Janek most definitely did not get it, but the soft, intense voice of his new friend was making him feel dizzy.

'Sorry.' Damian smiled, embarrassed. 'Just getting used to monologuing, I guess.'

'I'm just here for the pipes,' Janek said, starting to gather his tools. He picked up the cap lying on the floor and moved automatically to reinstall it. His gaze fell on the opening into the pipe and his hand stopped in mid-air, the thing that had been inside returning to his consciousness all at once.

'Pipes aren't nothing, Yanik. Pipes are the guts of the place, they're what makes it work.'

'Yes.' Janek turned, surprised to hear someone else who understood. He pointed to the open pipe. 'It is the body, but sick, rotten. There was something there, something collecting the sickness together.'

'Like a tumour.'

'Maybe, or like a clot. But not the cause I think. I do not know what makes it sick.'

'Hm.' Damian considered for a second. 'This place is a cannibal, built from its own ruins. That sort of thing breeds illness, I guess. What did you see?'

His voice so serious, so earnest that Janek felt the lie he was about to tell die on his lips.

'Skeleton,' the plumber said, surprised at how readily he trusted this strange man. Then his face flushed red as he realised how daft it sounded to say out loud. 'I saw a skeleton. In the pipes.'

Damian nodded, either ignoring or oblivious to the ridiculousness of the thing.

'You know whose skeleton?'

Janek shook his head. 'Workman, I think. He had a jumpsuit, hard hat. Like me.'

There was a pause. The young man seemed to be considering his words. He clearly knew about this place, so Janek pressed on.

'What's happening here?'

'Banyan Court?' Damian said. 'Been looking into it. Not the pipes, though. Didn't think of that.'

'Did anyone die when this place was built? Plumber, perhaps, made to do unsafe work?'

'Don't think so.' A pause. 'But the folks around here, they all grew rich off screwing people over, never been any other way to do it. I wouldn't be surprised if some of them skirted a few regulations. Got some blood on their hands. Especially upstairs.'

His gaze flicked up to the ceiling, then back down to Janek.

'I reckon you'd better follow that skeleton, if you want to properly diagnose the place.' Damian's eyes twinkled with an intensity that made Janek uncomfortable. 'Just be sure you really want to know, because I don't know what the building wants to show you.'

Janek found himself nodding.

'And come find me afterwards. I've got a— I don't know. I'm working on a theory.'

The young man's words stayed with Janek, twisting around his head as he tried to continue his work. At first, he attempted to stay away from Banyan Court. For days he sat at home, ignoring the curiosity that tried to pull him back. But every time he tried to compose an email to the building manager to claim the job was done, his hand would hover over the 'send' button until he deleted the draft. In his darker moments, Janek imagined the thing he had seen was some strange echo of his own future, dead and hidden in the twisting pipework of Banyan Court. He lay awake at night, Lena snoring gently beside him, wondering if he was chasing his own death through the cast-iron labyrinth.

Lena tried to talk to him about it. He knew he had a tendency to be quiet, taciturn, but she saw the exhaustion in his eyes. What could he say, though? How could he explain what he had found himself involved in? He had reassured her that it was just a difficult job getting under his skin and then kissed his children good night.

But whether he would have chosen to go back or not, Janek couldn't escape his job. More calls came in, more 'bad water' that needed draining. And as much as part of him wanted to forget what he had seen and walk away, they could not survive on Lena's income alone. Turning the work down simply wasn't an option. So, he continued to find himself walking through the shining glass doors of Banyan Court. And as the blood drained from the baths of the rich, the tapping would return, gently imploring him to follow. And eventually he did.

Janek began to spend time in the corridors and service rooms of the towering building, listening for the tapping, senses sharpening to that faint coppery scent of old blood. Three more times he saw the 'clot', the thing that pushed itself through the old pipes, and he followed it as best he could, the tapping calling him, urging him further, more and more plaster falling away to reveal antique iron. Sometimes it seemed to stay within the main waste outflow pipes, other times squeezing itself through water feeds so thin that Janek had no idea how anything with bones could fit through them at all. He had come to the conclusion that the bones, the flesh, they weren't real, exactly, they were something else, something spectral, but it all looked so completely physical, smelled so real. The valves made no difference, it came and went as it pleased through the bowels of the building and he pursued it single-mindedly.

He always lost it when moving between the front and back of Banyan House, as though the divide was a barrier it couldn't cross. If Janek first heard it near the health suite, he'd have lost it long before he reached the rickety old lift and vice versa. A frustration began to build inside him, starting to drown out his fear. Wasn't he doing what it wanted? Chasing it all over the damn building? So why did it always decide to vanish there? Unless that was where it wanted him. Somewhere in between. The plumber's breath caught in his throat.

Jason had made no mention of retrieving the keys from him, and indeed hadn't even been at the desk the last couple of times he had passed. So Janek began to look closer at the doors between the two sides, the short corridors that led to them, so easily missed they almost seemed deliberately hidden. Those doors were heavy and refused to stay open, but something about what Damian had said still stuck around his mind. Something about the spaces not being right.

He began to take a few measurements, testing a theory. It was hard to be sure without knowing the exact dimensions of the flats, another frustration choked down, but Janek soon became convinced that there was a hollow space between the two halves of the building. A gap of about ten feet between the front and back where the pipes didn't continue. Where they disappeared. A hidden cavity at the heart of Banyan Court.

There was no way to access that space. Janek hunted for it, checking for doors or service hatches, but there was nothing. No, he would not accept this. After everything, after being dragged through this bloody horror story for weeks, a simple wall wasn't going to stop him. He had to walk all the way back down to his van from the eighth floor to fetch a hammer and crowbar. Not common plumbing tools, perhaps, but very much what was called for in this situation. He spent a half-hour finding the exact right point in the passage between the two sides. Janek took a deep breath. It was time for some exploratory surgery.

He grunted as the hammer sank into the wall, the anger flowing out of him as a burst of plaster erupted into his face.

He pulled it back and swung it again. And again. Each impact a crunch of violence as the ragged hole he made grew wider, beckoning Janek in.

The darkness stretched down below him, a pitch-black core in the centre of the building. All the way down to the foundations and up to the penthouse far above, a gaping wound between the two sides, held together by ragged pipework stitching. There were no lights along the walls his hammer had exposed, and though his torch picked out the bare brickwork, if Janek shone it up or down, the beam quickly disappeared into darkness, like it was being swallowed. From the walls that marked the back of each side of Banyan House those thick cast-iron pipes sprouted, their shapes irregular, turning and creeping down and out of sight in odd patterns like stiches, barely holding the two edges together. Were they moving? No, it was just a trick of the torchlight beam, surely. But leaning further through the gap he'd made, he saw the pipes were ever so slightly pulsing, like the iron was trying to mock the fleshy pipes of the living. And they all led down into the hole.

Janek stood back, trying to understand exactly what he was looking at, when he heard that familiar *tap tap tapping*. With a start, he realised that it wasn't just one clot. It had never been just one twisted thing he had been chasing. One unfortunate worker. Every pipe was filled with the sound of wet, cramped bodies shifting and crawling inside them. And it was more than just the pipes. The air was filled with the sound of dozens, hundreds of the forgotten dead moving the walls, the floors, the wires... All through the guts of this building they spread like a poison, shifting and clamouring for his attention, begging for him to notice their unnecessary and unmourned passing. Had any of them died here? Did it matter? This was where they had dragged themselves, shifting their pained and broken remains from wherever they were cast by a broken railing, an unmoored machine or a falling chunk of masonry. A broken harness that plunged them into an icy reservoir. This was where they made their accusation and called out to any who might be listening.

And it had been built this way. These things, these spirits, were not accidental clots or unseen tumours, they were part of the substance of the building. This place had not become sick, it had been built diseased. But why? And what did they want from him, these souls that had been used to infect it?

Janek's torch beam finally fell upon a set of metal rungs, passing alongside the hole he had made in the wall and stretching up and down and out of sight. They wanted him to climb, he knew that, and looking closer he saw why. The screws that held the crude ladder to the wall were far too short and rusted through. There was no way it would take his weight for more than a few seconds before breaking. He would fall into the darkness, where they waited for him, where they wanted him to join them. They had something they were desperately keen to share.

Janek stood there listening for a very long time before he finally made his decision.

Lena Kowalczyk had been worried about her husband for weeks now. He'd been sleeping badly, up at odd hours and always staring at drainage layouts for a job he refused to talk to her about. She gave him his space, though, and didn't press him about it. Not even the night the invitation came, after he had returned past midnight, completely soaked from head to toe despite the absence of rain. He mumbled something about an accident at work and faulty plumbing, then immediately went to take a shower. Lena had no idea what to do, so she just left the strange letter that had arrived on the kitchen table and went to bed. After all, it was addressed to Janek.

TOBIAS FELL cordially invites JANEK KOWALCZYK
to attend a dinner party at 1 Banyan Court
on the evening of 16th August 2014
Penthouse access will be available through the freight elevator

They could talk about it later. For now, she was just happy he was safe.

12th
Point of View

Damian Simpson
94 Banyan Court

Hey Cari,
Found this old tape in my files when putting together
background for the retrospective. Not sure when he sent it to
me, but I clearly missed it. I reckoned it was worth putting
together a proper transcript, since it's kind of degraded, and
thought it might be worth you having a copy. If only to have
something concrete if you ever start to question yourself. I
know we've been over this a bunch of times, but given what
happened, I think it might help to see where Damian was
coming from. Let me know if it jogs anything loose, memory-
wise. Still keen to get that proper interview someday.
Best,
David

[Timecode 03:11 02-08-2014]

[00:00] A man's face fills the foreground. He is white and clean-shaven with medium-length brown hair, greying slightly in patches. His features are those of a younger man, but his skin shows the signs of hardship, roughened and worn with the creases of someone much older forming around the eyes. He's wearing a T-shirt for the band Deep Purple. Behind him is the wall of an unremarkable living room. A calendar scroll of the sort received from a Chinese takeaway is hung next to a small framed photograph, the subject of which is mostly obscured by the man's head. Over his other shoulder is a window. It is dark, but the distance and quantity of lights suggest the room is several floors above ground level, overlooking the city of London.

The man stares into the camera, as if trying to decide what to say. His words are low and mumbled.

Damian: It's, uh ... I don't know. Just [inaudible] I guess.

[00:11] He rubs his face, the camera shifting briefly, allowing a table to be glanced at the edge of the frame. It is covered with graph paper and what look to be hand-drawn maps.

Damian: Nah. Forget it.

[Cut]

[Timecode 14:39 09-08-2014]

[00:29] Damian is sitting in a chair facing the camera. The framing is more deliberate and the camera is stable, most likely mounted on a tripod or similar. He has clearly made an attempt to look more respectable than earlier, with his hair roughly combed and a rumpled button-up shirt. His face is slightly shiny from sweat. The window behind him now shows summer daylight, with the London skyline just discernible in the distance. More maps and diagrams can be seen on the small section of table viewable at the bottom of the frame. Damian takes a drink from a glass of water. He appears nervous.

Damian: The, uh, the spaces within a building are always strange. They never work quite how you expect them to. You look at a space, I mean, we're visual creatures, humans are very visual. You look and you feel like you understand it. Its dimensions. You know it. But eyes aren't actually good for this. Not really. I mean, of all your senses, sight is one of the worst for it. Smell and taste also.

[01:02] He smiles weakly.

Damian: But yeah, sight. It's not great. We think what we see is objective, a realistic version of what's in front of us, but it's all relational. Your mind, your eye, fixes on certain focal points, lynchpins for whatever you're seeing, and everything else kind of warps around them. Have you ever had that feeling, I think in French it's *jamais vu*, 'never seen', like *deja vu* is 'already seen'? It's when you look at something so familiar, your mother's face or a train station you travel from every day, and it looks … completely different. Alien. Everything you remember being there is there, but it all seems slightly off, like it's been rearranged. That's because your eyes have accidentally settled on different focal points from the ones they're used to, and so everything else is subtly changed to reflect that. It all seems different. You can't trust what your eyes tell you about spaces. Half of it's illusion and the other half assumption.

[01:47] He takes another sip of water. The movement causes the camera to defocus for a second. When it refocuses, Damian is absently scratching his chin. A small, thin scar can be seen across the jawline.

Damian: When you're homeless, you start to see spaces differently. I've been on the street, I mean, I don't know, maybe six years total, on and off. Kicked out of a bad home, the old story, you know. Not for the last few years now; I've got a job and everything, I'm … [three-second pause]. That stuff doesn't leave you. The lessons you learn. And I'm not talking about what it teaches you about people [bitter laugh] though that's some of it. No, I'm talking about what it teaches you about spaces. Because you're always looking for a place to sleep, and a back-up for if your first choice is dangerous or you get moved on. All cops, yadda yadda. You have to learn to consider sightlines, because places you reckon are nice and secluded might actually be clearly visible from a main road, and places that feel very public might have a quirk that makes them almost entirely hidden. And that's fine. Those things you learn quick.

[02:28] He gets up and moves to the window, causing the camera to defocus again.

[02:34] He turns the handle on the window and slides it open. There is a small change in the audio quality as the air pressure rebalances and a gentle breeze can be heard. Damian takes a deep breath but snorts it out in disappointment. Clearly it is not as refreshing as he hoped. He continues to talk from the window.

Damian: What takes longer to learn is airflow and temperature. If you end up on the streets in spring, summer, like me, you don't even think about it until autumn hits, but then you've got to very quickly learn about this stuff. If you can't get an actual roof somehow, you need to figure out how warm a sleeping spot is going to be, how windproof. And let me tell you, for that stuff, your eyes are lying to you. The shape of a space changes so much about how much it keeps the heat in, how it channels or avoids the wind. You get a sense for the movement of air currents, how draughts can tell you a lot about how somewhere is constructed, how deep it is. How much protection it gives you. It's a sense you get mainly from feeling, but the sound, really opening your ears and listening, that's also— [Laughter] I mean, bats have really got the right idea. They've got it made. [Pause] They wouldn't have a good time here. That's one of the ... I mean, that's kind of why I ... I want a record. I want some proof.

[03:30] He reaches out a hand and places it on the wall beside the window. He presses against it. Nothing happens.

Damian: And I know, right? I know what this is, what my

counsellor would say. It's another obsession, because life has got stable and stable means boring. I've got a place to live. I've got a good job. [Pause] Well, I've got a job. So, my mind starts looking for things to shake it up, to make being sober more interesting. I know where this ends if I can't leave it alone, but … I don't think I'm wrong here. And I want a record. I want some proof.

[3:50] He gestures towards the camera.

Damian: Because the spaces here, in Banyan Court, they're wrong.

[Cut]

[Timecode 01:02 10-08-2014]

[03:59] Damian is in a different room. The frame is at a slight angle, as if the camera has been placed down haphazardly, without consideration for stability. An unmade bed can be seen, alongside a radiator with several socks draped over it. The wall above the bed has a poster for the Hawkwind album *In Search of Space*. Damian is walking slowly back and forth, holding a tape measure. His hair has returned to its relatively unkempt state, and his shirt is now partially unbuttoned. Beneath it can be seen a chest binder and what appears to be a battered St Christopher medal on a thin metal chain.

[04:18] He walks out of the frame, then back past the camera, trailing a tape measure behind him. He then returns to in front of the camera and holds up a section of the tape measure, pointing at the measurement: 192cm.

Damian: This is not about my living space. Though, yeah, it's a shoebox. London, I guess. Hm. Weird how quickly you get used to something. Anyway, hold on.

[04:26] He gathers the tape measure back up and walks off frame, repeating the same process of stretching it across the width of the room. There is a pause.

Damian: Ah, hold on, [inaudible] wait for it to do its thing. It's not always predictable.

[04:39] He sits on the bed and waits.

[04:45] Damian continues to wait, impatience crossing his face. He takes his phone out of his jeans pocket but glances up at the camera and puts it back, instead waiting in silence.

Damian: Right. Let's try [inaudible].

[05:03] He stands up, takes the tape measure, and repeats the process a third time.

Damian: Ha!

[05:26] He returns to in front of the camera, a smile of vindication on his face. He holds the tape measure up to the lens. It takes a moment to focus, but his finger is positioned a few millimetres before the mark for 195cm.

Damian: These are between the same two points.

[05:30] He picks up the camera and angles it towards another wall, where an X has been clearly marked in red electrical tape. Damian turns the camera towards the other wall, where a similar X has been marked over a bedside table.

Damian: I've been living here about three months now. My first real place since the halfway house, so I really thought it was just in my head. Been living close to a lot of other folk for so long I thought it was just because I was on my own again that the space seemed wrong. But the feeling stayed there, bothering me. The airflow doesn't work right. So, I started doing some ... Well ...

[05:41] Damian walks over to the desk and picks up a notebook. He returns to in front of the camera and holds it up. The lens refocuses to show pages covered with measurements, all of which are almost, but not quite, identical.

Damian: I don't know what it means. But it can't be— Jesus, I [inaudible]. I mean, it's not like I don't know there's weird stuff out there.

[05:59] He puts the notebook down out of frame and sits on the bed, facing the camera.

Damian: I mean, you hear stuff, you know. When you're on the edges, most people don't really see you and you kind of, I don't know, you sort of start to see the other things the rest of the world doesn't notice. Also, you've got the, uh, well you get to hear a lot of really out-there beliefs. Blaming society, government, addiction for where you're at – it's easy to fall into. You get a lot of conspiracy theories, a lot of weird ideas. You've got to be careful. I had a friend once, Opal, said she couldn't listen to what folks talked about like that. Said if you opened your mind the brain worms got in. Not literally, you know, but those ideas that warp your perspective, change how you see the world so you can't see anything else. I guess I see her point. But I always listened. Didn't believe, not much, but I listened. [Pause] Something in this building isn't right. Cold corners. Draughts that shouldn't be there. Doesn't measure right. I don't know. [Pause] I don't know.

[Cut]

[Timecode 11:55 10-08-2014]

[06:51] The image is dark and out of focus. A small amount of light can be seen from above, coming through what seems to be the opening of a bag. There is a voice speaking. It is muffled by whatever the camera is being carried in, but it is deep, with a gentle accent.

Speaker 2: —be dangerous.

Damian: Sorry, could [inaudible], could you say that again?

Speaker 2: It's not a joke. I'm not trying to scare you.

Damian: You just said I should be worried.

Speaker 2: Not of me.

Damian: Of who, then? Of what?

Speaker 2: Tobias Fell. He [inaudible]

Damian: He built this place, didn't he? It—

[07:19] The bag with the camera is shifted, drowning out the audio for the next few seconds.

Speaker 2: —just watch out.

Damian: What's wrong with this place?

Speaker 2: What do you mean?

Damian: It's not right. Is it? It's, what, haunted?

[07:24] There is a long pause.

Speaker 2: I don't believe in any of that shit.

Damian: So, what are you afraid of?

Speaker 2: People. Real people. People with power.

Damian: Yeah. I guess [inaudible] worse than ghosts.

Speaker 2: [Pause] But you can't let them go unchecked. You just can't.

Damian: Gonna be honest. A rich man suffering consequences sounds a lot less plausible to me than ghosts.

Speaker 2: We'll see. You should go home, don't look too close. Whatever's going on here, you don't want to be part of it. [Inaudible] meet you, Damian.

Damian: You too, uh …?

Speaker 2: Diego. Good luck. And please be careful. There are strange and dangerous people here.

Damian: Sure.

[07:51] There is a blur of movement and light as the camera is pulled out. It is turned to point at the corner at the end of a dingy corridor. A dark-skinned figure in an old suit is briefly glimpsed disappearing around it. The camera turns back towards Damian's face. Behind him we can see a cross of red electrical tape on one of the walls.

Damian: Weird guy. [Laughter] I like him.

[Cut]

[Timecode 02:25 11-08-2014]

[08:01] Damian is in the same chair from the first few shots. Behind him, the takeaway calendar can be seen more clearly than before. It is a stylised blue and white 'evil eye' design in watercolours. The lights in the window are dimmer than earlier, and almost entirely out of focus. Damian has his hands clasped together, fingers nervously drumming against each other.

Damian: I've been thinking. I've only been able to check the corridors on this side of the building. Been wondering about the front, if all those rich jackasses ...

[08:10] He trails off. His hands start to shake slightly. He sniffs as though he has been crying.

Damian: Christ. Don't know if [inaudible] this. Just a distraction, really, I guess. I mean who the hell cares? Like, really cares, if the rooms, corridors and all that aren't the right size all the time? Me, I guess, maybe. [Sighs] It's as good a distraction as any. I just wish I could get to sleep properly, you know? Wouldn't be as bad if I could just sleep a bit, but Christ here we are. As if getting deadnamed in Dad's obituary wasn't enough, I got a haunted fucking floorplan messing with my bedroom. Least work gave me a couple of weeks for 'bereavement'. It's [inaudible]. They don't need to know it's a 'glad the piece of shit is dead' kind of deal. Man throws out his kid, still gets a rosy write-up when he kicks it. Really want to talk to Ruth about it, but it's not like the AKT doesn't have enough to deal with without me bothering them more. I'm a success story, after all. [Joyless laugh] Still, time off gives me space to measure hallways, I guess. [Pause] God, I want a drink.

[08:50] There is a pause. Damian looks directly into the camera.

Damian: Delete this bit, OK? When you're— No one needs to see you like this.

[Cut]

[Timecode 07:42 11-08-2014]

[08:59] A corridor, similar to the one from the Diego recording. The camera is pointed at a corner above a doorway. There is a small black shape just visible. The shot zooms in on it, refocusing until it is clear that it is looking at another camera, small and tucked almost completely out of sight. The smaller camera is angled to be covering most of the corridor.

[09:10] The two cameras stare at each other for several seconds.

Damian: Looks like we might have a friend.

[Cut]

[Timecode 14:01 11-08-2014]

[09:19] A blonde woman in a navy-blue concierge's uniform is standing behind the front desk, a wall of marble tiles at her back. Daylight floods in from the floor-to-ceiling windows at the edge of the frame.

Concierge: Please put that away, sir.

[09:22] Damian's voice comes from behind the camera.

Damian: I just want to document what happens when I try to get into the building where I live.

Concierge: You don't live here, sir.

Damian: No, I guess I live in the paupers' ghetto that just happens to share walls, right?

[09:32] The concierge shrugs, clearly uncomfortable.

Damian: Look, I'm not going to hassle anyone. I just [pause]. I want to use the gym.

Concierge: I'm sorry. The health suite's only for people in the premium apartments.

Damian: Sure, figures. Only the rich get stuff for free, eh?

[09:41] The concierge chuckles once before catching herself.

Concierge: Look, I'm sorry, but I really can't let you up. It's policy. Check your tenancy agreement or whatever, they always slip it in there. I can't let you in. I'm sorry.

Damian: Of course. Just doing your job. Better than your colleague.

Concierge: What? Was one of my colleagues rude to you?

Damian: Basically threatened to have his friend beat me up if I didn't leave.

[10:01] The concierge's face darkens.

Concierge: That'd be Jason. Let me guess, he warned you about 'Max' and his 'temper'?

Damian: Yeah.

Concierge: [Sigh] Thanks for letting me know. I'll have a word with him. Again.

Damian: I mean, yeah. That's kind of why I brought …

[10:13] The frame shakes as Damian gestures with the camera.

Damian: In case anything happened.

[10:15] The concierge leans slowly forward, over the desk.

Concierge: [Whispered] Look, I don't [inaudible] you this, but there are some doors between your [inaudible] and this side. I don't know where they are, but I don't think they're all kept locked. Obviously [inaudible] best I can do.

Damian: Thank you. That's … Thank you.

Concierge: Yeah, sure. I'd appreciate if you don't put this footage anywhere my bosses would see it.

Damian: Sure thing.

[Cut]

[Timecode 14:19 12-08-2014]

[10:54] The camera lingers on a door, number 80. The walls surrounding it indicate it to be on the poorer side of Banyan

Court. There is a faint rustling sound that at first seems like an issue with the microphone, but as the camera gets closer to the door it becomes clear this is the sound of papers being moved, crumpled and shuffled from inside the apartment. It is replaced by the rhythmic scratching of a pencil writing at great speed. It's loud. Louder than you might expect.

Damian: No sign of those connecting doors. But I did stumble across ... well.

[11:12] The camera pans down to the ground and the edges of several sheets of legal paper are protruding from beneath the door. The camera defocuses as Damian kneels down to retrieve one of them.

[11:19] The paper comes into sharp relief. The header 'Akman Blane' can be seen.

Damian: Tried knocking, but no answer. Quick google says this is a bunch've corporate lawyers. Biggest client? Tobias Fell, owner of the building. Maybe a coincidence. Maybe.

[Cut]

[Timecode 23:40 12-08-2014]

[11:31] Damian is in his bedroom, sitting on the edge of his bed. He wears flannel pyjamas and a glass of water can be seen on his bedside table. He is holding three sheets of paper. His face is troubled.

Damian: 'They're not real.' That's what I said to her. She was scared and I wanted to reassure her, but ... [Pause] Hm.

[11:37] He looks down at the sheets of paper and picks one out, putting the others down on the bed.

Damian: I went back. To the door with the paper. Thought I'd do some measuring. I met the woman who lives there. Scared her half to death. I thought others might have noticed whatever's going on here, but this isn't just shifting walls, She seemed ... I don't want to use the word 'haunted', but ... [pause]. In a way it's almost reassuring, it's not just my brain seeing connections that aren't there, poking walls for no reason. But in another way, it's terrifying. It means it's real. And it means it's not just the layout, it's not just the place. It's doing something to the people here. Maybe even targeting them. I don't know how many, it might just be the two of us, but I don't think so. I've seen a couple of others around who ... I don't know, it's like you can see it in their faces. [Pause] 'They're not real.' Why did I say that to her? Diego said don't look too close, to leave it alone ... Maybe it's one of those things, you know, if you don't believe in it, it can't hurt you. You stare so long this place drags you in. Maybe I was trying to protect her. Maybe I just thought she needed to hear it. What even is 'real' when we're talking about something like this?

[12:22] He holds up the piece of paper to the camera, which tries unsuccessfully to focus on the text. Damian shifts the positioning and a dark smudge can be seen on the side of the sheet. The image clears. It's a thumbprint in what appears to be dried blood.

Damian: 'Not real' doesn't mean harmless. Never has. Some of the most harmful things in the world aren't real. The woman at number 80, she isn't safe. Don't think anyone here is. I don't know what to do, to be honest. I can find somewhere else to live, but it'll take time. I'm not going back to the streets. And if there are other people this place is affecting, can I leave them? They're not my responsibility, I know that. But who else's going to look out for them? Folks this side, folks in need, nobody [inaudible]. Maybe I'm just curious.

[12:44] Damian lets the paper go and it falls gently out of frame. He reaches for the camera.

[Cut]

[Timecode 02:44 13-08-2014]

[12:49] It is dark. There is the sound of agitated movement and the camera is clearly moving violently. Something is scraping, like brick or stone being dragged. Damian can be heard breathing heavily.

Damian: What the fuck what the fuck what—

[12:58] A switch can be heard being flicked and the room illuminates, causing the camera feed to briefly overcompensate, saturating a shot of Damian's bed. For a split second it appears as though the walls next to it are shifting, but when the camera finishes compensating for the new lighting, they are still.

Damian: That's ... What?

[13:07] He brings the camera closer to the corner of the room where his bed is situated. He runs his hand slowly across the wall next to it, then the one behind it. There is no reaction from the wall. Damian curls his hand into a fist and hits it against the section above his pillow. Nothing happens.

Damian: They were moving. I swear. Woke up and I could feel it, the space around me changing. God that felt ... Did not like that.

[13:20] The camera continues focusing on the walls. They remain static.

Damian: Why, though? Were they trying to crush me maybe? Don't know. Feels more aggressive than what I've seen elsewhere. Still, guess it's noticed me. Is that good news? Hm. Probably not.

[13:32] The camera moves close to the walls, causing it to defocus as it gets close to the texture of the plaster.

Damian: What's wrong? Don't want to perform for an audience? Interesting.

[13:36] He pulls the camera back.

Damian: If they don't like the camera, it's worth keeping it closer from now on. All the time, not just when I'm hunting. Big if, though.

[13:43] The camera is placed on the bedside table. Damian can be heard sighing.

Damian: Probably move to sleeping on the couch.

[Cut]

[Timecode 13:49 13-08-2014]

[13:47] A woman's face fills the frame. Caroline Fairley. She is young, with light hair kept short and stylish and a pair of expensive-looking earrings.

Damian: You sure this is OK?

Caroline: Yeah, it's fine. More evidence, y'know?

Damian: That's the idea. And I guess I kind of always wanted to be a director.

Caroline: [Laughing] Oh yeah?

Damian: Seriously! I mean, [inaudible] not seriously, seriously, but I always loved the idea. When I got my job, actually had a bit of money, this camera was the first thing I bought.

[14:01] The camera shakes as Damian indicates it.

Caroline: And did you use it before all this?

Damian: Hm. Not really. I guess it was more of a dream than a plan. But then I started getting paranoid about this place and ... Just feels safer to keep it around. [Pause] So you ready?

Caroline: Sure. How did you want to do it?

Damian: Just say your piece, I guess.

[14:13] A look of resolve passes over Caroline's face. She stares directly into the camera, addressing the viewer.

Caroline: My name is Caroline Fairley. I live in number 4 Banyan Court. I have, over the last few weeks, become convinced that the building I live in is haunted. I intend to find proof of this in the form of a room that I believe does not exist in the physical world. I'm being helped in this by Damian, uh—

Damian: Simpson.

Caroline: Damian Simpson, who had also been investigating this place. He has offered help and guidance in my search.

Damian: Best I can do, at least.

[14:47] The camera pans wildly as it is passed between them. It settles on Damian's face.

Caroline: So, what's the deal? How do I get to the ballroom? You said you had a theory.

Damian: Yeah, sort of. I'm still trying to figure the why of it all, but I've been putting the pieces together, doing some research of my own and, well, this building isn't normal. It's like, you know the standard ghost spiel, right? The things a place has seen, the terrible crimes and awful suffering gets baked into the wall, caught in the fabric of a place. Like Janek said, an infection entering the body.

Caroline: Sure.

Damian: Not this place. It's ... I can't find evidence of anything happening here that might explain what's going on. But these ... echoes? They're still here, somehow. Like they were made part of the foundations, the actual walls. Like Banyan Court is a Frankenstein of second-hand shadows.

Caroline: Poetic. But Frankenstein was the doctor.

Damian: It's bleeding into people, especially those that look too closely, whose attention is too focused on the walls, the structure, the homes here. Or those that feel trapped. It's starting to reach out to them. What I don't know yet is why. Or what it wants.

Caroline: You think it has enough of a mind to want something?

Damian: Maybe, maybe not. If not the building itself, then maybe the spirits, the ... echoes, or whatever, that have been made a part of it. So far, the only connection seems to be with Tobias Fell. Which isn't much of a connection, from what I've seen.

Caroline: I mean, he was the one who had the place built. You think it might be deliberate?

[15:54] Damian says nothing. He looks thoughtful, then troubled.

Damian: I don't know. I don't know how you'd do this deliberately. Or why.

Caroline: So, who's it touched?

Damian: What do you mean?

Caroline: You said it was bleeding into people. Have you met many?

Damian: A few. [Pause] There was a plumber found dead workers in the pipes, he actually gave me the whole 'disease' metaphor. Um, there's a young woman trapped by a mountain of paper cover-ups and conspiracies. A few others I think might have been … There was one man, said he was from Ecuador, he refused, I think. Said he didn't believe in any of it, that I shouldn't look too closely. It seemed to leave him alone.

Caroline: You think not believing protects you?

Damian: I don't know. Maybe. I've been hoping this helps.

[16:30] He gestures to the camera.

Damian: Maybe protection's not an option for us.

Caroline: Guess not. Who knows? Maybe I'll find some answers in the ballroom.

[16:34] Damian tries to smile, but it doesn't seem to sit well with him.

Damian: Maybe. Just be careful. You're really sure that you want to do this?

Caroline: I've got to know. And you said it can't hurt us.

[16:50] There's a long pause as Damian considers this.

Damian: Physically … No, I don't think it can. But there's a lot of other types of harm.

Caroline: I'm not afraid.

Damian: Maybe you should be. Maybe we both should.

Caroline: You said you'd help me.

Damian: Yeah, I know, I did. I will.

Caroline: So?

Damian: I think maybe the key is not to think about it as a space in the world. I've been thinking about this a lot. So much of the world, of the spaces in it, exist only in your mind. Maybe that's what you need to focus on – Banyan Court as it seems to you. Opening yourself up to it. To what it wants to say.

Caroline: There was one point [inaudible] I think I heard music.

Damian: Then maybe it's already calling you, and you just need to follow where it wants you to go. You said it was, what, a ballroom? Like dancing?

Caroline: Yeah.

Damian: Then follow the music. Ignore where the corridors should lead you. Go where it wants you to be. Listen in the dark and follow.

Caroline: Right. [Pause] Will I be safe?

Damian: I don't know. Maybe. This place ... I mean, I don't think it's killed anyone yet.

[Cut]

[Timecode 22:40 13-08-2014]

[17:59] The camera is focused on a section of corridor wall. The carpeting is plush, and the thick wallpaper is lit with tasteful up-lighting. He is clearly in one of the upper floors of the front part of the building. The frame is focused on a long section of blank wall slightly beyond the door to flat 7. It lingers there for a while, then swings around, pointing to the door to flat 8, opposite. When the camera is angled back to the original wall, nothing has changed. It remains a blank space.

Damian: Right. Cari's gone, off on her ... Journey. And it got me thinking. Maybe I've been hiding, pretending like I'm looking for something, but always taking shelter behind the lens. I told Cari what to look for, but I've been too afraid to open up myself. So, let's do this.

[18:35] The camera is shakily placed down onto the carpeted floor, and the frame is taken up by carpet fibres and a pair of brown Doc Martens boots.

[Cut]

[Timecode 22:44 13-08-2014]

[18:38] The camera turns on, pointed at the space next to flat 7. A new hallway now branches off from it, replacing what was previously blank wall. The sides of this new hallway, though covered in the same wallpaper, seem slightly darker than those we have already seem, as though the wall underneath is a different colour. The camera lingers on the new space. When Damian speaks again, his voice is less confident.

Damian: I was right. I was right. Let me show you.

[18:42] He tries to steady his hand as the camera struggles to focus.

Damian: Just watch.

[19:27] He begins to make his way down the new corridor. It seems to stretch off some way into the distance, but only has two doors – opposite each other on either side. They appear to be the same make and style of door as to the other flats on this floor, but there are no numbers on them. Around the edges, the heavy wood appears scorched.

[19:40] Damian reaches out to grip one of the handles, but his hand pauses just before making contact, and pulls back.

Damian: Too hot to touch, it's—

[19:43] The camera focuses on a point on the wall next to the door, there is a slight difference in the texture of the wallpaper.

Damian: Let's try something else.

[19:48] His hand reappears in the frame, this time holding a small pocketknife with the blade extended. He pauses, clearly trying to decide where to cut, before choosing an apparently arbitrary section of wall and begins to push it in. It goes through far easier than would be expected, and as Damian begins to pull downwards a small shower of black ash begins to fall from where he is cutting.

[19:56] He puts away the pocketknife and takes hold of the edges of the wallpaper where he's cut it. Tearing it away reveals the wall beneath is blackened and burned.

Damian: What is this it's—

[20:17] He starts scraping at the blackened wall with his hand, now grimy with soot. Something lighter can be seen just underneath the ashes, embedded in the wall.

Damian: No. No way.

[20:40] He grips the small white object in the wall and twists it out, holding it in front of the lens. The camera takes a moment to refocus. It is a human tooth, slightly warped and deformed as if from intense heat. Damian takes a breath in disgust but composes himself quickly.

Damian: You think about all those people in Fell's properties, his companies. If they burn, is it his fault? How much is he responsible for, what did he encourage, where did he turn a blind eye? However you try to cut it, somewhere down the line he had a hand in a lot of people burning alive.

[21:03] He turns the camera back to the hole he has made in the wall. Pale shapes can be seen among the ashes, possibly other bones.

Damian: And now it looks like they're here. Echoes. In the pipes, the walls ... God, what if—

[21:13] He is interrupted by the sound of someone screaming. It seems to be coming from the floor above him.

[Cut]

[Timecode 22:49 13-08-2014]

[21:16] There is the sound of muffled screaming. Damian is running up a staircase and the camera bounces around, unable to focus as the stairs fly past. The lighting and chrome of the handrail indicates he is in the front of Banyan Court. The screams seem to be coming from somewhere further above.

Damian: Shit shit [inaudible] shit.

[21:26] He reaches a door at the very top of the stairway. The distressed cries are clearer now and seem to be coming from the other side, along with the sounds of a physical struggle. Damian reaches for the handle, then pauses for a second. He takes a deep breath, then opens the door slowly. His hands are shaking, causing the frame to shake in turn.

[21:45] The camera is lowered to ground level and looks round into the corridor, though it is unclear whether Damian himself has actually gone through the door or is simply holding the camera out to get a better look. The hallway is identical to the previous ones seen on this side of the building, except that this one terminates in a large glass window, through which the night skyline of London can just about be seen. Near to it, two figures appear to be struggling.

[21:49] The camera zooms in on the pair and it becomes clear that the struggle is very one-sided, as the larger of the two men, a hulking figure in a black uniform, is easily restraining his victim, a scrawny teenager in a dark jacket and blue baseball cap. The man is striking his victim repeatedly with a heavy-looking wooden baton. There is a pause as he surveys the damage his weapon has done, then he hoists the bloody youth up higher.

Assailant: [Inaudible] you, right, punk?

[22:00] The uniformed attacker hurls his victim against the window, shattering it completely. The boy disappears into the night sky. After a second there's a thump that might be a microphone issue or could be the sound of a body hitting the street outside.

Damian: [Breathing hard] Shit.

[22:03] The assailant turns around, though it is unclear whether or not they have heard Damian. In full view, it is clear there is something very wrong with the killer's body. It is distorted, as though the skin of a much smaller man were stretched out over the frame of this larger one. The face is distended, and the fingernails stop partway up the enormous hands, though there appears to be no discomfort in the man's movements. When he takes a step, it's as though the camera had taken a double-exposure, with two human figures, both uniformed, superimposed over each other. The figure takes another step towards the camera, and a name badge comes into focus for just a second. Freezing the frame allows it to be read as 'JASON'.

[22:10] The camera is withdrawn rapidly and there's a blur of motion as Damian flees down the stairs.

[Cut]

[Timecode 23:54 13-08-2014]

[22:15] Damian is sitting in his kitchen. His face is pale and his hands tremble as he drinks a glass of water. Each time the liquid touches his lips, his eyes flick down to it, as if in disappointment. He sighs shakily and places the glass down out of frame. He stares blankly into the camera.

Damian: I don't, uh—

[22:27] He looks up sharply as though he has heard something. He stands up and walks out of the frame. There is the sound of a door being unlocked and then relocked.

[23:11] Damian returns and sits back down. He is visibly pale.

Damian: He didn't see me. It didn't see me. And if it did, there's no way it knows who I am, or where I— Unless the building tells it. This place knows.

[23:23] He looks up at the walls surrounding him, suddenly aware of their presence.

Damian: I was wrong about what's here. These echoes, they're so much more dangerous than I thought. God, what have I done I've sent Cari to— No, that's not— She would have gone there without me. And she might still be OK. She might [pause]. Shit.

[23:44] He continues to stare into the camera.

Damian: I should go to the police. They're already here. I think. I heard sirens. I don't know what I'd— I looked over the footage. It's, I mean, you can see the poor bastard go through the window, but the guy who did it, there's no way you could identify him from what I've got. They'd say I messed with the video. Best case scenario they think I'm wasting their time, tell me to get lost and guy— the thing that did this doesn't notice me. And given my history, if I get involved with the police, even as a witness I'm— I know what it's like to lose everything. And I can't do that again.

[Cut]

[Timecode 09:17 15-08-2014]

[24:19] There is a knocking coming from somewhere further down the corridor. Damian moves the camera slowly, cautiously. The state of the corridor indicates he is in the front of the building. He is breathing slowly, nervously, as he approaches the noise. It sounds like someone is knocking on the front door of one of the flats, but it is rhythmic and constant, not pausing or waiting for any response.

[24:36] The camera is held round a corner to reveal a man standing in front of the door to number 30 Banyan Court. He is dressed in what was once clearly an extremely fine tailored suit in an ocean blue, but what remains is torn, dirty, dishevelled. His features are Hispanic, and his face is blank as he knocks again and again on the door to number 30.

Damian: Hello?

[25:00] The figure does not respond. Damian begins cautiously approaching.

Damian: I don't think anyone's home. Do, do you need help?

[25:21] As he gets closer it becomes clear that the man is holding something in his hand. It appears to be a piece of cream-coloured cardstock. He does not respond to the camera's approach.

Damian: Hey, man, look, you seem in really rough shape. Can I call someone for you? Where do you live?

[25:32] The stranger's response is so quiet the microphone barely picks it up.

Knocker: Here I [inaudible] mine. Stolen. Stolen [inaudible] me.

[25:38] Damian doesn't immediately respond. The camera lingers on the man as he knocks again and again on his front door, waiting for a response.

[25:47] Damian tries the handle, but the door is locked. He sighs. The knocking man does not respond to the attempt.

Damian: This place really did a number on you, huh?

[25:53] He reaches down and gently prises the cardboard from the man's fingers. He holds it up in front of the camera, which takes a moment to focus on the words. It reads: *TOBIAS FELL cordially invites JÈSUS CANDIDO to attend a dinner party at 1 Banyan Court on the evening of 16th August 2014. Penthouse access will be available through the freight elevator.*

Damian: That— Is that what I ...? I guess that changes things. [Pause] I need to check something.

[26:05] He reaches out and tucks the invitation inside the jacket of the unresisting Jésus, then turns around to leave.

[Cut]

[Timecode 11:32 15-08-2014]

[26:11] Damian is back in his kitchen. There is an odd smile on his face. In his hands he holds two pieces of card. His fingers are grey with ash.

Damian: I was right. I made my choice. I went back to the corridor, the one with the ... The burned one. Did a bit of digging in the walls and there it was. If I wasn't haunted before, I sure am now. Cari got one as well, found it slipped half-under her door. She's OK. Or at least alive. Maybe that's the best we can hope for right now. I don't know exactly what this means, but I have my suspicions.

[26:28] He pauses, deep in thought.

Damian: Trapped in the walls. Trapped in the pipes ... Trapped.

[26:31] Another pause.

Damian: I was hoping I'd have a chance to see Janek again before all this, confirm a few things ... Well, too late now.

[26:37] He shakes his head.

Damian: None of this is an accident. Maybe Fell organised it all himself, maybe he's been put at the centre of it all by someone else, something else. These invitations were sent by the building, though, no way did a human being go round putting these in the hands of the haunted. Which is me too now, I guess. No getting off this ride now. Just got to hope I know what I'm doing.

[26:50] He holds up the cards. His and Caroline's names can be briefly seen, but otherwise the text is an exact match for Jésus' invitation.

Damian: I don't want to go. I'm— I mean, I'm terrified. But I'm more scared of not going. Of what happens without me there. I don't know if I'd even be able to *not* go. I do have theories. Some ideas about ... Well, I'm not going to say on this thing. Maybe it's just paranoia, but I'm starting to think the only safe place to keep my plans is in my head. Still, there's time yet before the party. Hopefully I—

[27:09] There is a knock at the door. Damian looks up, apprehensive. He starts to rise, but stops as the camera's microphone picks up, just for a moment, the faint strains of an orchestra. He smiles sadly and his eyes return to the camera.

Damian: There she is. I guess wish us luck. Whatever happens, I think it's going to be messy. Cari gave me the address of some journalist she was talking to, so, uh, if you're watching this, then ... Hi. [Pause] Really hope I made it back.

[27:25 – End]

13th

The Builder

Tobias Fell
1 Banyan Court

Tobias

The penthouse was prepared. In many ways it always had been. The wide, open central room had been kept largely empty, devoid of furniture and simply adorned with tasteful mood pieces around the edges – ready to receive tonight's guests. Was that dreadful little art dealer coming tonight? He'd actually provided Tobias with a few of them. Not directly, of course, Tobias had people for that. Still, the penthouse had always been ready to receive these visitors. It had, after all, been built for them.

Tobias wandered down into the grand dining room, limping slightly on the still-new prosthetic that had replaced the lower part of his right leg. He brushed his fingers lightly along the fine polished oak of the immense table. They'd had to bring it up in parts through his private elevator, the location of which he was uncomfortable at having revealed, and then build it up here. But it had been worth it. He counted the place settings. Twelve. He wasn't entirely certain of the number of guests that were expected, but he had been told this sort of thing tended to work in certain numbers. Twelve just seemed right. If there were more guests than that, then he would figure something out.

Tobias hadn't been there when the table had been put in place, of course. He liked to imagine it, though, the sort of people who did the work. Who would have been hired to set this sort of thing up? He'd given his assistant, Jeremy, very specific instructions, and they had certainly been carried out, but who would the man have got to do it? A local firm, all rough features and gruff shouting? Or a team of elegant professionals, skilled and expensive, with cotton gloves and hushed tones? What human experience had brushed against this, the culmination of his strangest project?

He sighed, clearly it would have been the latter. Jeremy would never have trusted local workmen to have the discretion a task like this required. In many ways he was far more prejudiced about that sort of thing than Tobias. He'd been against building Banyan Court in Tower Hamlets at all. Of course, he couldn't be told exactly why it had to be built there, that powerful psychic frisson that seemed so very important: the history of poverty, tragedy and exploitation these bricks had born witness to at the hands of Tobias's own ancestors. Still, the billionaire fundamentally had nothing against the people who lived here, in the paupers' tenement he had designed. Their poverty, their lack of education and class, it wasn't their fault. It was simply the by-product of a system. And Tobias had no respect for those who benefited from a system but could not stomach looking at the waste produced by it. This world was designed to generate winners and losers, and it showed a lack of character to wish yourselves a winner without accepting what it does to those who lose.

Someone had once, years ago, asked him in an interview whether he considered himself a good man, and he still laughed to think about it. About the crude concept of goodness and how the ignorant still clung to it in defiance of the world they helped to create. He was simply a man who had learned early how the system worked and used it as it was designed. Anything else was pretention and self-delusion.

The sun was beginning to set, the city beyond the glass walls of the penthouse illuminated in deep oranges and crimsons. Tonight, for the first time in years, he had drawn the curtains back, allowing the light to enter. If any nosy paparazzo had had the patience to be watching for him all this time, then perhaps they should be rewarded. The dining area was, of course, curtained and hidden. Some things tonight must still remain private.

The light played across his skin. It was so pale now that he had to use colour correction during video conference meetings. The one time he had forgotten to do so one of his directors had tried to insist he see a doctor. They didn't understand, of course, but that wasn't their fault. They hadn't seen what he had seen. Soon he could leave, see the sun again. See people again. If he wanted to. He'd found isolation more agreeable than he'd originally thought possible. Perhaps he would remain a recluse – but it would be his choice this time. Tobias smiled. Maybe tonight would be an opportunity to see how the presence of real people affected him after all this time. Not *normal* people, of course, but it was a start. But there was work to do first.

The sound of grinding metal echoed from the other side of the penthouse. Somewhere, deep below, the old iron freight elevator was gradually groaning its way up the building for the first time in almost a century. He listened, the grinding of gears a stark contrast to the secretive silence of his own private lift.

Tobias took a moment. Was he nervous? Guilty? No matter. The first of his guests was about to arrive.

Jason

The old iron cage wasn't small, but next to Max's bulk Jason felt as if he was being pressed into the latticed bars like sausage meat through a mincer. Every ragged breath Max took, it was like the floor was going to buckle, but still the tiny platform crawled its way upwards. The smell of his old friend's rotten flesh seemed palpable, and Jason couldn't imagine what sort of dinner party a billionaire could possibly be throwing where it wasn't going to be an issue. Something in the back of his mind told him that that wasn't the weirdest part of the situation, but when he tried to focus on it his head began to swim.

'Don't worry about it,' Max growled through what remained of his lips. 'Just do your job.'

He rested one hand on the large wooden box that took up the rest of the elevator's limited space. It looked heavy and, notably, easily big enough to hold a person. Jason's eyes lingered on it for a second. Did he know what was inside? There was a memory there, but it didn't feel like his.

Far above, the ceiling began to approach, and the lift started to slow. Jason reached down for his nightstick, before remembering it was Max that had one, not him.

'I got you, Jace,' Max said. 'Any of them give you trouble, you just let me know.'

Then there was a juddering, clattering stop as they reached the top. Max reached over his head and grabbed the sliding grate, pulling it open. The lift now sat in what seemed to be a dilapidated engine room up in the roof. In front of them was a simple metal door, shiny and new among the old and neglected material.

'After you,' Max said.

The door opened outwards and Jason's breath caught ever so slightly in his throat. The room was huge, with the faintest hint of some fragrance in the air that was quickly overpowered by the decaying stench of his partner squeezing through the door behind him, dragging the wooden box.

'There's nobody here.' Jason looked around, confused. 'Are we early?'

'We're security. 'Course we're here early.'

'So, what do we do?'

'We keep an eye on things. When people arrive we make sure they're taken care of. One way or another.'

Tobias

The office from which Tobias conducted his business was surprisingly plain. He held no meetings there and, aside from a few construction workers, no one else had ever seen it in person. All he required was a comfortable chair, a phone and a computer, all of which were of the highest quality that money could buy. In some cases higher. But anything that would have required binders of documents or detailed filing was taken care of by people lower down the ladder and at this point even the things he did need to reference were almost entirely digital. He had a single bookshelf full of weighty-looking titles he hadn't read that was set up in the spot facing his webcam, but aside from that the room was spartan.

He sat at his desk, watching the video feeds from the main room. The man who stood there was not a particularly impressive specimen, but he was clearly talking to someone else. As he came more into focus Tobias could clearly make out a uniform, one he recognised from the security camera feeds he had made sure he always had access too. The concierge, then. He tapped on his keyboard and the images from the rest of the building disappeared, every screen now displaying this one sorry-looking figure. Then Tobias took a moment, closed his eyes, and focused.

When he opened them again the second figure was now visible on his screen. Thin lips split into a wide grin as he took in the rotting goliath. The little concierge's imagination had worked a grotesque wonder when choosing a form for his haunting. And they had brought the main course for dinner, as instructed. That was certainly a relief. It was one thing to watch the suffering of the poor souls below, but now it came time for them to play their parts he had been somewhat wary. But no, it all seemed to be going quite to plan. This was going to be delightful.

Violet

Several of the guests arrived together. Violet had no idea who any of them were, nor did she really care. They certainly hadn't arranged a time to go up as a group, but still they congregated at the bottom of that ancient iron spine, waiting silently for the lift. One of them, a middle-aged black woman who looked like she hadn't slept in weeks, tried to make small talk, but Violet ignored her. Then the rattle began as the elevator crawled its way back down towards them, settling finally at the bottom with a crunch.

'Is it safe?' asked a young woman in a long pastel-blue party dress. She wore a full face of make-up and a tasteful pair of earrings, and when her eyes passed over Violet's durable work clothes, stained with the remnants of a hard day's labour, there was a flash of confusion in them.

Violet didn't answer as she stepped into the lift. The young woman's hands were soft and clean; the two of them had nothing to talk about. The other guests followed, seven in all. Two little girls with a nervous-looking mother, the tired woman, the one in the blue dress, a young man in a suit several sizes too large, and a flamboyant gentleman in a maroon blazer who was leaning on his cane, trying desperately to keep his legs from shaking. They barely all fit, and Violet could feel herself pushed into the cold iron walls by the press of bodies. She smiled and placed her calloused, blistered hand on the lever. It felt so very familiar.

Gillian

Gillian arrived with the second group, knowing with crystal certainty she was going to be murdered. Obviously. That was the only real explanation for what was happening. As the giddy thrill of her discovery had begun to fade and the apparent reality of the situation started to assert itself, a deep terror had begun to grip her. She'd got too close, and now Tobias Fell was inviting her to her own assassination.

What could she do but go? She was tired of running. Besides, a man with such resources, such an intricately woven net, there was nowhere she could escape his reach. If he was able to go to such lengths simply to invite her to this event, then trying to avoid it would no doubt just make whatever end he had in mind for her more painful. Better to attend in the hope that it would be quick and maybe, just maybe, she could get some answers before she died. Even now, Gillian couldn't help but feel that if she got some real answers it might just be worth it. The others being here worried her, though. Did they know how much danger they were in? Were they a part of it?

The iron box continued its tortuous ascent and Gillian tried to ignore the stink rolling off one of her fellow passengers, a white guy in a stained grey suit who looked like he'd taken a bath in mould. The only other person riding with them, a middle-aged man who wore a newly ironed polyester suit and a shy smile, was also clearly trying to ignore the smell. She wondered what grim discoveries of their own must have led them here.

She looked up, trying to focus on the progress of the elevator to distract her from both the odour and the dread of her own imminent demise, and a thought struck her.

'Hey,' she said to no one in particular. 'If the old freight elevator was part of the original Victorian building, and that was only about five or six storeys, then how come it goes all the way up to the penthouse? The metal all seems about the same age.'

The man in the cheap suit smiled and shrugged, before replying in what Gillian guessed was a Polish accent.

'Ghosts?'

Gillian didn't laugh.

Carter

'Hey, hold the lift!' A voice rang out as the third and final group were about to ascend.

Carter looked up to see someone sprinting full speed towards them. He opened the door again instinctively, before he'd fully grasped who it was. That horrible journalist, David something-or-other, who'd had him do that dreadful interview. He climbed inside before Carter had a chance to reconsider and pulled the door closed behind him.

'David?'

This voice belonged to the other occupant of the elevator, a young woman who'd introduced herself as Cari, dressed in silver velvet and bedecked in an astonishing quantity of jewellery.

'Caroline?' David said, his mouth hanging slightly open. 'You look … Uh, thank you. Mr Dwight. For the door. And sorry about—'

'Forget it,' he replied, trying to hide his anger. The old Carter wouldn't have hesitated to give the little troll a piece of his mind. Maybe he was a better person, after all.

'I didn't realise you'd got an invite,' Cari's voice was light, but there was a hint of something underneath it that sounded worried.

'Oh, I wouldn't miss this,' David said with a wink. She didn't seem reassured, but he was clearly too distracted to notice.

'Well, then,' Carter said curtly. 'Let's not keep our host waiting.'

He had always expected to at some point be travelling to the penthouse in Tobias Fell's private elevator, the one he'd heard talked about over long business lunches. This angular iron cage was a long way from that dream, but as Carter pulled the lever of the reassuringly primitive mechanism, he was glad this was how he got there.

And the last of the party guests began to ascend.

Leon

Tobias Fell's flat was immaculate. That was the first thing that struck him upon entering. The floors were polished to a mirror shine and what furniture there was seemed to somehow manage an appearance of being both antique and brand new at the same time. The walls had been painted in light, airy colours unblemished by any sort of mark and Leon had the strangest urge to press himself against them, as though their cleanliness might somehow become his.

He was under no illusions about his appearance. He had spent most of the day showering, buying new suits, watching shop assistants recoil in disgust at his appearance. It did no good, though, and perhaps that was right. He'd been embraced by Banyan Court, so perhaps it was only fair that he bear its mark proudly. He wondered briefly if it should have been Andrea there instead. Had he somehow stolen her invite? No, she had seen the stain first, perhaps, but deep down he knew it was his. And if there were any others who could understand what that meant, they would be here. Looking around the party he could smell the place on them as clearly as he could on himself. They were all stained, even if only he could see it. He saw the peacocking art dealer strutting by, what was his name? It didn't matter. He could preen all he wanted, but he reeked of it just as surely as Leon did.

'Arsehole,' he muttered under his breath. Then paused, smiled. 'Arthole.'

He laughed at his own joke, a small chuckle that came out far louder than he intended. A few of the other guests looked over at him with a pity in their eyes that made him wince. The two security guys also gave him a stare. Did he know that one from the front desk? Poor man looked almost as out of place here as Leon. His colleague, however, was a different story. Six foot four hunched over, with a face like the underside of a truck, his eyes scanning the assembled crowd with purpose. Even the front desk guy looked scared of him. What was going on here?

Turning his own gaze to the dozen or so other guests around him, Leon tried to spot any other familiar faces. Was that Carter Dwight? That made sense, he seemed like the sort of person to be invited to a billionaire's party. They'd met at a tech conference last year and he remembered the conversation coming easily.

'Hey!' Leon called. 'Hey, Carter, how'd the new Dodj rollout go?'

Carter pretended not to have heard. Well, that was fine. None of them were better than Leon, whatever they thought. They were all contaminated just the same.

Damian

Surveying the room was a fascinating experience. Every one of them walking, talking in a way they so clearly felt was normal. Even the knocking man was smiling and doing his best to socialise as if nothing was wrong. But none of them were quite managing it. It felt so much like he was watching them from a distance, from behind glass, and Damian wished, not for the first time, that he'd been brave enough to bring his camera.

To call them mad wouldn't have been right. Haunted didn't sit entirely well either, especially for those of them whose experiences had given them a certain manic quality, but all of them had been in some way touched by the building, taken by it. Damian wondered how each of them perceived the others, what they saw.

Even Cari had not escaped. She was perhaps more aware than the rest of them, or had seemed so when they talked about it earlier, but as Damian watched her move ably through the crowd, he couldn't ignore the fact that the glittering jewellery, which she had not owned until she walked into that ballroom, was gently weeping blood onto her skin. Did the others see it? Did she? He hadn't asked, afraid to confront the possibility that she was as adrift from reality as the rest of them.

Damian tried to take stock of his own mind, but how can you evaluate your own perceptions? He felt clear-headed, keenly aware of the space around him, the angles of the penthouse, the danger that they all found themselves in. Rational. But he was also aware that he was currently all but crouched in a corner, trying his best to make sense of how the room felt. It seemed at once like it was closing around them, pushing the group together, but at the same time infinitely too large, as though it had no walls at all and was open to the empty night air. Was he as compromised as all the others? Had he walked right into the jaws of the lion, ignorantly believing himself to be a Daniel?

At least he'd had a chance to talk with Janek about what the plumber had found in the heart of the building, but as much as it confirmed some of Damian's suspicious, it hadn't given him anything immediately useful. He was starting to feel very much out of his depth.

He almost retreated backwards, further into the corner, but caught himself just in time. He didn't want to touch the walls in the penthouse. The walls had always been where the pain, the imported suffering of this place, seemed most concentrated and he could feel it more strongly here than elsewhere in the building. Damian tried to decide if there was something he should be doing yet. No. Even if his idea was going to work, he had to wait for the right moment.

And he had to trust that he'd know when that was. For now he'd bide his time. Eventually their host would arrive. And then Damian would learn exactly how stupid he had been in coming here.

Jésus

Jésus was having a dreadful time. He felt like his whole body had been wrung dry and his right hand was swollen and bruised. His memory of the last week was patchy and confused, but he knew one thing with absolute certainty: his home had been taken from him and he could not return. Nonetheless, he was still Jésus Candido, and he would not be defeated so easily.

When he had returned to himself after ... whatever had happened, the invitation tucked into his jacket had been the only clue about his missing days. Of course, even without hoping to have some answers he would never have been fool enough to refuse an invitation from Tobias Fell. He had retrieved an outfit from storage (out of season, but it would have to do) and had booked a nearby hotel room to prepare. And now he was here, trying his best to admire the various art pieces (some of which he flattered himself to recognise) and wait for whatever was going to happen. For someone to explain the picture and the lost time and all the strange dreams that had been tormenting him. And, ideally, for someone to apologise.

He avoided the other guests as best he could, casting the occasional withering glance at how they were dressed. The rancid man in the filthy suit didn't really bother him, if he had had an option to turn up any other way no doubt he would have taken it, but Jésus could not forgive the cheap polyester effort of the rough-handed workman gawping at the Csaky sculpture near the door to the dining room. To make matters worse, that lazy fool from the front desk was here, working security of all things, though luckily neither he nor his grotesque companion seemed to be paying Jésus any notice. And there were children here.

Then there was the man in the corner. Young, a face lined with hardships, and a cheap, but tastefully chosen, suit. There was something in that face Jésus recognised.

'Excuse me, do I ... know you? We have met before?'

'Maybe around the building,' the young man said, dodging the question. 'We both live here, after all.'

'No, but I have seen you,' Jésus insisted. 'Were you the one who gave me my invitation?'

The young man shook his head, backing away slightly, as though nervous. Which was ridiculous, as Jésus was just trying to have a *normal* conversation.

'What is going on here?' Jésus was losing patience.

'I don't know for sure. I'm trying to find out, but ... you can help me. If you want.'

It was that infuriating tone used to mollify the delusional. Jésus did not need to be humoured.

'Tell me what you know.' He advanced on the wary looking young man. 'What do you know about the painting that stole my home?'

'Nothing. But I'd guess it had history. And it wasn't acquired innocently.'

A pause.

'Who died so you could own it?'

Jésus' whole body went cold. His hand knocked twice against his leg.

'I-I have to go,' he stammered.

The young man couldn't hide his look of relief, but shook his head.

'Don't think we can. Not until the party's over.'

Janek

The tie felt tight around Janek's neck, and he tried not to look desperate as he glanced around to see if there was anyone serving drinks. He had never felt so drastically out of place. He recognised a few of the other guests as living in the building, but he was neither wealthy nor a resident. So what was he doing here? He wanted to move on, forget what he had seen and felt at the sick heart of Banyan Court, but instead he had come here, to the building's head. What culture was it that believed your soul lived in your head? Was it the Egyptians? Where had he read that? He looked around again, but still there were no drinks.

At least he wasn't the worst dressed here. The poor bastard from number 15 looked to be in a dreadful state. Janek could only assume that 'stain' of his had spread. He was still certain there hadn't been any pipes in there, but there were worse things lurking in the walls of this place. His mind flashed to the cold black water, the pleading, gripping hands. A deep breath. The memory faded.

He considered saying hello to Jason, one of the only friendly faces he could see around here. But that face was currently pale and casting terrified glances over to another man Janek had never seen before, who wore a black version of the same uniform. Could that be 'Max'? Jason had apparently undersold how deeply intimidating his friend was. Why would a dinner party need security like that? He knew Fell was a recluse, maybe paranoid, but it still seemed excessive. Maybe he was best leaving them to their duty.

Damian had been keen to talk when he arrived, but Janek didn't feel like he'd given much in the way of useful answers. He was still struggling to understand exactly what had happened to him when he—

'Hey.'

The plumber turned to see an Asian woman in dirt-caked denims regarding him with a look of ... respect? Could that be right?

'Can I help you?'

The woman held out a hand.

'Lot of people here have never worked a real day's work in their life,' she said. 'Fits this place, I guess. Lazy. Soft. But you know. I can see it.'

'Right. Thank you ...' Janek gingerly shook her hand. It was dry and dusty. 'Janek.'

'Violet.'

Silence hung in the air between them. Violet seemed to feel no urge to fill it and Janek had no idea what to say. Behind them, a man in a tailored black dinner jacket had just begun to complain about their host's absence, when his words were cut off by a piercing scream.

Alvita

She hadn't worn this dress since Tommy had been born. It hadn't fit her for years, but apparently the recent months of insomnia-squashed appetite and Doxatrin had left her thinner than she'd been since she was a teenager. It wasn't a healthy sort of thin, but right now she'd take what small victories she could. She'd even found some pearl earrings in her dusty old jewellery box. They matched the dress perfectly and reminded her faintly of Edith.

In fact, she was in a far better mood than she had any right to be. She knew things here were all wrong. The way the invitation had arrived, the behaviour of the other guests, the fact that she was somehow one of the first people to enter Tobias Fell's penthouse suite in years. None of it made sense and she should have been panicking. Instead, she felt at peace, as though a warm blanket had been wrapped around her. A feeling that had only got stronger once she stepped over the threshold and into the billionaire's home.

'Oh! Sorry!'

Alvita stumbled slightly as little Anna Khan came barrelling into her, closely followed by her strange friend Penny. The blonde girl smiled, a row of razor-sharp teeth curving up her face. Alvita expected that cold, familiar anger to build as she looked at the children who hurt Tommy, but instead she found herself smiling.

'No problem but do be careful. This is a grown-up party, you don't want to—'

At that moment Anna's mother, Prisha, pushed past a heavily ornamented young woman to catch up with her daughter, barely noticing the faint red handprint the woman left on her back.

'I'm so sorry, Mrs Jackson, I hope she hasn't been a bother.'

'Not at all, Prisha,' Alvita replied. 'I'm surprised to see them here.'

'The invite was for them,' Mrs Khan's voice was tight, but her eyes betrayed how confused she was by what was happening. 'I didn't know you would also be—'

Anna's mother stopped dead, her eyes suddenly falling on Penny, still standing at Alvita's side.

'Is this ... I'm sorry, is this child with you?' A weird note of unease had entered Prisha's voice. 'I thought you had a son.'

'Don't be silly, Anna's mummy!' Penny said, waving with her long, sharp little fingers. 'It's me, Penny!'

Prisha's eyes went wide and the blood drained from her face.

'Remember, Mummy?' little Anna said gently. 'I told you she was coming with us.'

Her mother staggered back, paused for just a moment, then let out a scream. Immediately, Alvita was by her side.

'It's OK, hey it's OK.'

Penny just kept on smiling.

Tobias

It was an odd thing to hear a scream through the walls, then half a second later see it on the screen. The delay was slightly disorientating in a way that Tobias found quite pleasant. It was to be expected, of course. He'd been somewhat confused when he'd seen the child's mother in the lift, but on reflection it was obvious. No matter what was influencing the girl, it needed her parent to get her to the party. It had been a bit of a worry at first, given the mother wasn't factored into his dinner plans, but events looked like they were resolving themselves quite neatly.

It was a question, though. The full manifestation of the things his guests had brought with them, the booted thug and the hungry child, was that a function of his penthouse as a locus of the building's energy? Or was the place coming fully awake, giving these projections power enough to be perceived by all around them? Either way, it didn't seem complete quite yet. While the guests were wary of the concierge's brute, it was clear they could not see its rotted face as he did, or they'd all be screaming.

Tobias checked his watch. Still a few minutes until dinner. Plenty of time to see how things progressed. And, of course, there was still the matter of the journalist. But for now, he returned his attention to the mother.

Anna

Anna had never been embarrassed by her parents before but watching as her mother screamed and shouted about Penny, she couldn't help but apologise to her friend. Penny didn't seem to mind, though, in fact she clearly thought it was all a great joke.

The other grown-ups didn't seem to find it quite so funny, however, and Anna could feel their quiet judgement as Mrs Jackson led her mother away.

'You're not real!' her mother shouted back at Penny. 'You're not fucking real!'

Anna gasped at her mother's swearing. She turned to Penny, who was laughing even harder, her mouth so wide it seemed as if her head would split in two.

'It's not funny, Penny,' Anna said seriously. 'She sounds really mad. I think we're in trouble.'

Penny just shrugged. 'I'm hungry,' she said. 'When do we get to eat?'

'It's a grown-up party,' Anna told her, trying to ignore the stares of the other guests. 'There might not be any food.'

'There will be.' Penny had no doubts whatsoever. 'That's why we're here.'

The fancy woman came over, looking worried. Anna thought she was one of the most beautiful people she'd ever seen, with her huge shiny necklace and glittering tiara. She looked like she must be a princess, even if she sometimes touched her jewels in discomfort, and her dress seemed a little bit dirty around the neck.

345

'Are you girls alright?' she said, kneeling down to look them in the eye.

Anna nodded. She didn't want to cry, not in front of a princess. And Penny would definitely laugh at her if she did.

'Is Mummy alright?'

'She will be, I promise. We'll look after her.'

'When do we eat?'

The sparkling princess turned to look at Penny, taking a moment to hide her surprise at the strange, hissing tone.

'Soon. I think. I'm not sure. Just … stay here, OK? I'm going to go check on your mummy. I'll keep you both safe.'

She disappeared back into the guests, leaving a few red drips on the floor. The other grown-ups seemed to have moved on and weren't paying Anna and Penny much attention anymore.

'I don't think I want to be safe,' Penny whispered to Anna with a wink. 'I think I want to play.'

Caroline

Cari had rarely gone in for gaudy adornments, generally preferring more understated silver pieces. She had never realised just how heavy gold and gemstone could be, but now she found it weighed her down, slowed her movements and made even lifting her arms a chore. The idea of ballroom dancing in it all seemed almost foolhardy. As she walked away from the girls she tried, once again, to take them off, but her hands shook as she tried to hold them, and her whole body wanted to scream.

She let her arms drop again. The building had chosen her to find them, it wanted her to wear them, and fighting that instinct took energy and willpower that she couldn't spare right now. Damian had taken to calling them 'echoes', the things that had touched them, reflections of the atrocities built into this place. Hers weighed heavy around her neck.

By the time she reached their mother the woman had settled into unsteady sobs. Cari took Alvita by the arm and led her to the side. They both tried to ignore the red smear her hand left.

'Is she going to be alright?'

'I hope so.' Alvita attempted a shrug.

'W-why do you have ... Is that *blood*?' Prisha's voice was small behind them. Cari gave Alvita a look.

'She's not a part of this, is she?'

'I don't know what *this* even is.' Alvita's voice was just a little bit too mellow for the situation and it was setting Cari on edge.

'Neither do I, but it's definitely something, right? And she ...' Her eyes flicked to the weeping mother. 'She shouldn't be here. She wasn't properly invited. Not like us. She might not be safe.'

An expression of guilt passed over Alvita's face, breaking briefly through the calm as she held up a small bottle.

'Yeah. I thought she might be better off if she wasn't ... awake.'

'Doxatrin?' Cari said uncertainly. 'That'll do it, I guess. Odd choice.'

'It was all I had to hand, and she seemed grateful.' Alvita's expression went slightly dreamy again.

'Well, she can't stay out here.'

'I think someone said one of the bedrooms was unlocked.'

'Might be best drop her there, let her rest while ...' Cari gestured broadly to the party.

'Yeah, I'll take care of it. You stay here. Don't want to stain any billion-pound bedsheets.'

The joke was unexpected, but welcome and Cari let out a short laugh. Alvita smiled gently and led the now quiet woman away towards one of the doors on the far edge of the massive room.

She spotted Damian looking over quizzically, so she began to signal him to her, then reconsidered almost immediately, turning it into a wave of dismissal. It felt somehow too early for alarm. Everyone was waiting for something to happen, though no one seemed quite sure what. Until it did, though, panicking just felt a bit premature. She really hoped he actually had that plan he was hinting at earlier. God knows he couldn't make things worse.

'Who is that?' Alvita asked.

'Just a friend.' Cari felt oddly reluctant to give away too much. Damian was being so secretive she didn't want to accidentally expose him.

'He seems nice.' That vagueness had returned. 'He was asking me all sorts of questions about Edith.'

Cari wasn't listening. Something was nagging at her. If the little girl was a part of this, but her mother wasn't, who else here might not belong? She scanned the room, taking in each face, seeing her own fears reflected in their eyes, until her gaze finally settled on David Erikson with a sudden, lurching fear that he was in terrible danger.

Laura

'Look,' the wide-eyed woman persisted, despite Laura desperately trying to ignore her. 'You don't seem to understand how much danger we're in. That's Leon Copeland. In the same room as Carter Dwight.'

Laura tried to place the voice of her new companion. Had she called her about smoke alarms at one point? It had barely even registered among all the weird phone calls, but yes. A very simple query about how many smoke detectors were in her flat.

A normal-sounding question from a normal-sounding tenant.

'You know about the Portman Oil cover-up last year?'

She didn't sound normal anymore.

'Billions of dollars in ecological devastation, and several of the journalists involved in breaking the story have been turning up conveniently falling out of windows.' The woman, who had introduced herself as Gillian, was scrawling out desperate notes on a small pad of paper, apparently oblivious to the fact that her pen had run out of ink minutes ago.

Laura reeled as the stream of information burrowed into her brain like a headache.

'Now, and you may think neither of Copeland nor Dwight were directly implicated, but the director of Copeland's company attended several fundraiser dinners with—'

Finally, Laura couldn't take it anymore. Without a word she turned away to escape the conversation, doubting the woman would even notice. She shouldn't be here. She wasn't like these people, whose voices were so familiar from phone calls begging for floorplans or ranting about stains. They were all unstable, delusional, and the only thing Laura had in common with them was that some weirdo tycoon had invited them all to a party he hadn't even shown up for.

But she was here. Because a ghost had told her to come and she didn't know where her home was anymore. She'd been sleeping in an abandoned flat for two nights now. She caught sight of a man – Jésus somebody? – tapping a hand against his thigh. Her own twitched in response.

Could she really claim to be so different?

'—and obviously I don't have to tell you what those connections to the Tyrona corporation might mean for us.'

Gillian and her stream of nested nonsense had followed her, and Laura all but ran into the sneer of a towering security guard.

She let out a small shriek as he reached for her and roughly shoved her to the side, striding past and towards a nondescript middle-aged man in what looked like his best approximation of a classy outfit.

'David!' A woman's voice shouted from somewhere behind Laura, and the man swivelled to see the figure looming before him.

'Can I see your invite?' the guard said in a voice that promised violence.

'Oh. I—' David began to answer, but he was cut short by a meaty crunch as the heavy club slammed into his stomach.

Laura felt faint as she watched him crumple to the ground, backing quickly away. She couldn't believe what was happening. This wasn't part of what she'd agreed to. The others were standing still, apparently frozen in place, watching the brutality unfold. She raced across the room and grabbed the handle of the door to the old elevators, but it didn't open. Behind her, there was another crunch as the truncheon came down again. She wanted nothing more than to escape, to go home. But she didn't know where that was.

Jason

There was nothing like that noise, the feeling that rippled through the pit of your stomach when you heard the wet impact of real violence. There was no redemption in it, no righteousness. Just some helpless soul whimpering as he heard his own ribs break. After the last week, the sound no longer surprised Jason, but he still felt every blow.

'Max,' he said quietly. 'Max, stop. Please.'

If anyone heard him, they didn't show it. The other guests

gasped as they watched, someone even screamed, but none of them moved to intervene. The baton came down one last time, splitting the journalist's lip and sending him sprawling across the floor. Max addressed the crowd gathered around him.

'Anyone else here uninvited?'

No one said a word. Jason looked to the person who'd called out David's name. She was struggling against the woman in rough denim who was trying to hold her back, helpless hatred spilling from her eyes as her tiara somehow remained in place. Max's gaze lingered momentarily on the tired-looking woman Jason had heard someone call Mrs Jackson, as though trying to see something over her shoulder, but the moment passed.

Then his massive hand closed around the throat of David Erikson, hoisting him effortlessly off the ground. The journalist gurgled something as he faded in and out of consciousness. Max carried him over towards one of the huge glass windows.

'Max!' Jason called out. 'Max, don't do it! Please, he's— You've done enough.'

He looked around wildly, trying to find anyone who might help him stop a murder, but the other guests were all locked tight with fear.

'Max, was it?' The voice that rang out was unfamiliar. Quiet but clear, like one used to being obeyed.

Max stopped instantly, David's feet trailing on the floor as he turned.

'Yes, Mr Fell?'

'No need for that. Take him through to the dining room, if you please. I'm sure we can find him a chair. After all, we wouldn't want him to miss his big story. Not after he came all this way.'

Tobias

He limped slowly out of his office, the door closing behind him. The assembled guests gazed at him with such awe. Tobias Fell himself, in the flesh, the most important person any of them would ever meet. He did his best to smile modestly and ignore the stench of the poor soul from number 15. He was aware it was Banyan Court's doing, of course, but in some ways the rank accompaniment did feel appropriate to meeting the rabble before him.

At least he wouldn't be required to actually converse with these people. They simply needed to listen and, sure enough, they were waiting with bated breath.

'I believe,' Tobias said, 'it is time we retired to dinner.'

Carter

So, this was the famous Tobias Fell, was it? He wasn't exactly what he would have expected. He had always conceived of Fell as a hermit, stooped and awkward with reclusion, turned strange by his self-imposed imprisonment. But the man before them, though impossibly pale, stood tall and trim, with perfect posture and impeccable tailoring. His words carried the easy authority of one who had never had to ask for anything twice.

Two weeks ago, Carter would have considered him a man he could easily work with. Now, as Tobias stepped around a small pool of the journalist's blood, things were significantly more complicated.

Gillian

There he was, the venomous spider at the centre of his web, porcelain-white and smug in his sanctuary. He smiled easily at her in a way that made her blood boil, but she still stepped out of the way as the ogre-ish enforcer 'Max' dragged David's unconscious body past them, the foolish man's limp legs leading the way to whatever grim denouement this evil man had orchestrated. Gillian began to realise very very keenly that as much as she longed for answers, she didn't want to die to get them.

Janek

This was what a billionaire looked like, then? He had met rich people before, of course, but none so incomprehensibly wealthy as the man who now directed them to the dining room. Having his thug beat that man was horrible, of course, but this was not Janek's first experience of such violence and he'd always known that this was what rich people did. He looked over at the bleeding form of the man they'd called David and tried to ignore the shame of his own inaction. Even so, as afraid as he was of a man like Tobias Fell, it was with a sense of dark curiosity that he made his way through the newly unlocked double doors. At least, he hoped, there would be something to drink.

Caroline

Whatever fugue had overtaken her had been thoroughly shattered by watching what happened to David. Concerns about jewellery had vanished from her mind, and she almost collapsed, held up only by the strong arms of the woman who had stopped her throwing herself into the fray. Caroline looked back at her and almost smiled. It was the woman from her video. What was her name? She tried to think, but as they were led through to the dining room it was all swallowed in the mute terror of what had happened to her friend.

The room was not as immense as the one they'd just left, but even so Caroline had never seen a private dining room this large. If she had been told it had once been the feasting hall in some European king's palace, she would have believed it. At the centre was a long table of dark, shining wood, impeccably laid out with twelve place settings, a covered silver platter sat at each one. There were no place cards, so Caroline made her way to a seat far from the head of the table, watching for where Damian sat and trying her best to control her breathing, She tried not to look over as poor David was roughly tied to a chair near the wall. She looked around, searching for any hint of reassurance or resistance in the faces of the other guests, but they all looked away, cowed by the certainty that something even worse was coming. Except for the woman in work clothes, whose eyes shone like garnets, hard and defiant. As Cari sat, she shifted her napkin, smearing it with red.

Alvita

There was a box in the corner. It was made of cheap unworked wood and stood out starkly against the understated elegance of the rest of the room. Alvita sat opposite this box and kept finding that her eyes returned to it. It wasn't quite the right shape for a coffin, but she couldn't help but notice it was easily big enough to fit a body inside.

The warm presence she had felt before was still there, but it had shifted. It felt different. There was no more comfort, but rather an electric sense of anticipation.

Violet

The beautiful woman in blood-stained jewels looked away, searching for a seat. She should hate her for the trophies she wore of slavery and death, but somewhere beneath her new callouses, she found that she couldn't. Something else, deeper than the weariness and dirt, grew brighter at the sight, cutting through her anger. Violet sat down slowly, trying to steady herself. The platters on each table were so brightly polished Violet could see her own face reflected back at her. Hers, and the wordless shadows that stood over her shoulder. She didn't like this place, and she didn't like the man who sat at the head of the table, worm-belly white and relaxed in his power. His was the boot she had felt on their throats, his was the voice that so distantly commanded them to work until they fell. Her work-roughened fingers traced the outline of the domed cover. It was cool and smooth, but she could barely feel it.

Jason

In the corner, the journalist moaned himself awake, the sound muffled by the black tape over his mouth. Jason silently begged him to just sit there and stay quiet, and not to attract any more of Max's attention.

He looked at the place setting in front of his own seat. Wasn't there supposed to be a whole bunch of different cutlery?

That's what it had always been like at weddings – though not his own – or in fancy hotels. Jason remembered seeing pictures of plates surrounded by dozens of different forks and spoons and knives for your bread, meat, fish, soup, whatever the hell else you were having. Well, this was the fanciest place he'd ever been, but for some reason there were only two pieces of cutlery: a posh-looking fork, all smooth sterling silver, and a long, sharp knife. It wasn't even serrated like a steak knife. What exactly were they supposed to be cutting?

Anna

Penny really liked the knife. She kept reaching for it, and Anna had to push her hand away.

'Penny!' she hissed. 'You're going to get us in trouble!'

Anna was very worried that without her mother there the grown-ups would say she couldn't stay at the dinner. She wasn't even sure that she wanted to be here. It was a bit scary and Alvita kept blocking her view of the table or telling her where to look, so she wasn't entirely sure what was going on, but she had promised Penny they'd stay. Penny was desperate to eat and started reaching for the knife again.

Leon

Not too long ago, having a meal with Tobias Fell had been a legitimate dream of his, but now all he could do was worry about getting the tablecloth dirty. He desperately wanted to go and wash his hands, but the glowering stare of 'Max' made the idea of standing up very unappealing indeed. Well, if the smell put Tobias off his dinner, he had no one to blame but himself.

All that said, their smiling host didn't seem to mind. He stood at the head of the table and began to speak in a clear, quiet voice.

'Good evening. I'm sure you all have plenty of questions and, to be perfectly clear, I'm not able to answer all of them. The forces at work here do not lend themselves to clean and simple rules, though they do, in my experience, follow certain patterns. Patterns that can be exploited.

'Let me begin by assuring you that I do not believe in evil. I have no time for ideas of God or hell or any sort of cosmic judgement of our actions. I see morality as a trap, a trick the mind pulls to stop you from fully engaging with the systems our world is built on. Systems designed to enrich a few at the expense of others. All this is obvious, as is the fact that I have, within these systems, won. I have won fairly, as much as is possible, and that necessarily requires perpetuating and causing the suffering of those who have failed to prosper. I have accepted this. All of which is to say that recriminations and accusations that appeal to simplistic ethics are fundamentally going to be a waste of breath. My concerns are entirely practical, and I would hope that you all respond as such.'

Leon listened to this rolling, rehearsed speech in silence. Did he agree? Did he find it abhorrent? Did it matter? He watched as the grey ooze of that familiar stain bubbled from their host's mouth and dropped onto the table in thick wet clumps.

Tobias

He looked over the assembled crowd. A mixed reaction, as expected. Confusion, mostly. He'd had no control over who was here, of course, so it was hardly a handpicked group. But now the power was once again his, he couldn't help but make the most of it. And no one was shouting at him yet, which was promising. Amusingly, he'd felt certain that the next section of his explanation would be met far more warmly than his first. The inevitable realities of a robust economic system were often hard to accept, but by this point everyone in the room definitely believed in ghosts.

'While it is true,' he continued, 'that I reject the idea of any arbitrary eternal judgement of the actions we take in a fundamentally meaningless universe, I have in the last decade or so been forced to reckon with the fact that there is some non-corporeal element to our existence. I hesitate to call it a soul, but we may at least describe it as a shadow. A remnant of the feelings and experiences of the dead. And perhaps the living, though I have little evidence for that.'

A few nods from the room, but most were clearly waiting for the sting.

'I am not a superstitious man. But I have, for many years now, found myself a target, of sorts, for these shadows. At first, there were the days lost to strange dreams, paranoias and awful visions. Then I was nearly killed while visiting a diamond mine in Angola, and again by an equipment failure at a pharmaceutical plant in Michigan.' He touched his leg, absently. 'I do not entirely know why. Obviously, the suffering I have caused, the lives ended because of necessary decisions I have made, are a not insubstantial element of it. And yet such is the burden of any who wield great power, whose decisions affect tens of thousands. So why, you may ask, out of all of them, have I been marked for special *attention*? Simply put, I don't know. It is a question that has long baffled me. But I am a practical man, as I have said, and while identifying the cause of such a situation may satisfy some, picking apart my history and family, trying to dig through the layers of misery calcified around the Fell name ... I am more interested in resolving it.

'At first, I tried to outrun the shadows. To hide. When that didn't work, I decided to take action. I spent millions consulting with experts in the field. I spoke to both frauds and true believers, and of the two I believe the frauds had a clearer handle on things. Indeed, their falsehoods did seem to offer some small protection. And in the end, I was certain of what my best chance would be. If there was no use in running, as seemed clear, then I'd make a stand. All the money in the world isn't worth a penny if you're dead, or worse, and the shadows wanted their pound of flesh. So, I designed a trap and I named it Banyan Court.'

Jésus

'This is ridiculous!'

Jésus was used to commanding the attention of a room, but even so, when every person around that table turned to face him, he found himself floundering for a moment.

'You have an objection?' Tobias's voice did not waver.

Jésus felt a flicker of fear, but no one else seemed interested in speaking up.

'I do,' he pressed on. 'You bring us here to talk about ghosts and monsters, you are mad!'

'You have not had some inexplicable experiences of late, Mr Candido?'

Jésus looked around, seeing nothing but credulous, cowed faces staring back at him. No, he would not be so easily dismissed.

'You own this whole building.' His tone became accusatory. 'Who is to say you have not been filling it with hallucinogens in the air, or our water. Your story is absurd.'

Knock knock.

Jésus' whole body went cold. He spun around to see that dreadful little man, Damian, staring at him, while gently rapping his knuckles on the table.

Knock knock.

Jésus' hand began to throb and his head swam. Things his mind was so desperate to forget began bubbling up in his memory. There was no victory in Damian's expression, no enjoyment, he was simply proving a point.

'Is there anything else, Mr Candido?' Tobias's voice remained calm and level.

Shaking his head, Jésus lowered himself back into his seat.

Damian

There should have been some pleasure in humbling an ass like Jésus, but as he watched the shaken man sit back down, Damian felt ashamed. The man hadn't chosen to be a victim any more than the others, but if they were going to find a way out of this then outbursts like that weren't going to help. If they had ever had a chance to walk away that time was past now. The only one who'd actually chosen this was him. Assuming it had actually *been* a real choice. Still, the thought rattled through Damian's head as he looked around the table. Why *had* they been the ones to end up as victims? Unless that wasn't it. He eyes widened slightly at the realisation. They weren't victims of these echoes. They were bait.

'I will not get into the specifics of the building's design. Suffice it to say that I hired more than simple architects to draw it up. It was to be a lightning rod, of sorts, a beacon of what might be called my crimes to all those shadows that might wish me ill. Raised from bricks that saw centuries of pain and degradation, both from my own family and those who inhabited it. Constructed from materials made in the most inhumane deprivation and seeded, where possible, with the human remains of those who died in my name. Exhausted workers, uninsured patients refused treatment, evicted tenants and even one or two betrayed business partners. Powdered bone in the very walls. Such a place that those petty, vindictive shadows that were not strong enough to oppose me in life would be unable to resist its call. And so, they were tied to this place, caught in ropes of symbol and crude metaphor. Every partition, every wire and pipe binding them and keeping them in their place.'

Damian tried to steady his breathing. He had been prepared for some of this, but it was so much more calculated than he had believed. He had assumed what he found in the walls had been some sort of spiritual manifestation, but might it have been real? But the corridor that contained it wasn't really there. Was it? The truth was that it didn't matter. Real or unreal – the end result was the same: a place built on the exploitation and misery of the poor souls trapped within its walls. The living as well as the dead. He looked around for a glass of water to steady himself, something to cut through a mouth dry with fear. There was nothing.

'I admit my original intention was simple. I wished for those who lived in the lower floors of this building to suffer on my behalf. Didn't matter which side. Fed to the shadows I had symbolically bound here, trapped and contained. But it did not exactly manifest as I had believed. Certainly, I seemed safe within my penthouse sanctuary, but the winding passages and dead ends did not channel the shadows as I had hoped, and the touch of my transgressions on those below, on you … It was gentle, even friendly. Unsettling perhaps, but not hostile, brushing past you in forms so subtle as to go almost unnoticed. And certainly not dangerous. And so, a new plan began to form.'

Laura

That Spanish guy had been right, this was all ridiculous. But it was also true, and she didn't feel like she had the strength left in her to disbelieve what was happening. Dead people in the walls. But the old man, he had died here. As the landowner, perhaps the rents were ultimately the fault of Tobias Fell, but she had been the one to try and evict him. Was that why she'd been chosen by these 'shadows'? Why all of them had been? Did they each need something of their own, some sin for the shadows to latch onto? Maybe the old man was her 'crime', assisted by other forces to pursue her for a vengeance of his own. Perhaps he'd been trapped too, the building drawing his soul into it as it had apparently been designed to do. She fought down the urge to raise her hand and ask Tobias about it as he brought his speech towards its climax.

'The dreams returned,' he said. 'I believe given to me by the building itself. They have been getting more and more intense ever since this place was constructed, but in the last weeks they have become almost unbearable. Dreams of this very gathering. Bringing together those most deeply touched by the shadows I have trapped here, bringing them into this sanctum and … Well, I am of the opinion that nothing defuses consequences quite like complicity.'

Tobias smiled again. Deep in Laura's stomach something turned at the sight of that smile.

'My proposal is simple in essence, though I warn you it will be rather gruesome in practice. Tonight, ten years to the day since this building began its life, you will each assume a part of my offences, after which you shall remain a focal point for those spirits that blame me for them. There is no need to concern yourself as to which, they have already chosen you, as I'm sure you're aware. If you accept, they will be bound to you, locked and chained, tormenting you more or less as they do now. Once their attention is focused on you, I shall be free to leave this place. Who knows – you might escape them as well when you leave the building, or perhaps lessen their effects. We shall see, I suppose. In return for this service, I shall pay each of you one billion pounds.' There was a collective intake of breath around the table. Laura hoped she'd caught her own in time. 'I have no interest in haggling about this. Obviously this is not an easy decision and one I cannot afford for many of you to turn down, so to be perfectly clear, if you do not wish to partake, if you refuse my offer, then – I believe it's Max? – one of the nastier manifestations, well, he will beat you to death.'

Nobody breathed a word. Laura suddenly felt entirely alone, despite the full table. She looked over at the smaller concierge, who was deathly pale.

'I suppose the threat alone might work,' Tobias mused. 'But that feels like intimidation, not complicity. And this sort of thing requires a certain thematic consistency to work. I'm sure you understand. It always comes down to money, in the end. The great divider. Funny how it's also what makes us all the same.'

Laura wasn't sure she really understood, but she also knew that she didn't want to die.

Tobias

He gestured for his guests to uncover their platters. No one moved, still stunned. They must have suspected the truth, at the very least, but no doubt the extreme nature of his carrot and stick approach had rattled them. He'd considered going with a lower offer, but he wanted everyone to understand the full extremity of the situation and didn't care to waste time on petty bargaining. The only one who didn't seem surprised was Damian, the young man from the poor side who'd been watching him so intently. Interesting. Given his financial situation it seemed unlikely he'd be in any position to turn down the money.

Surprising him, Gillian spoke up first. 'What if we all say no?' Her voice was working hard to be defiant. 'Together.'

'Then my situation would be unchanged,' Tobias answered pleasantly. 'And you would be dead.'

'He can't kill all of us.' Gillian sounded less certain.

'Yeah.' Jason's voice was flat with terror. 'He can.'

Max's smile spoke of someone not only capable, but eager.

Gillian sat back down.

'Now,' Tobias continued. 'You may reveal your dinner.'

One by one, they lifted up the silver lids. A few clearly expected a billion pounds in cash underneath. Tobias almost chuckled at the ignorance, that such an amount could fit on a serving tray. They really had no idea what wealth truly was.

Instead, they were each confronted with a single, tiny cube of cooked meat, as neat and regular as Tobias had been able to make it. He'd had a lot less to work with than he'd originally hoped, but even a sliver should be enough. His prosthetic leg ached as he looked at the plates arrayed around the table.

Gillian

This couldn't be what she thought it was. It just couldn't. Why would he do this? Had Tobias Fell finally succumbed to the pressures of his long isolation? Gillian glanced around imploringly; some of the other guests shared her expression of horror, but most just looked confused. She reached instinctively for her fork. After all the lies and intrigue, this was apparently the choice before her: death or unthinkable riches and ... this. But she had to be sure.

'Mr Fell,' she asked. 'What is this?'

Caroline

Blood dripped gently from her bracelet, leaving the small chunk of meat swimming in a thin red gravy. Cari swallowed hard, thoughts and connections swimming in her head, ideas of blood and bodies and riches and jewels and the incarnation of misdeeds, but none of the disparate concepts could find purchase. She simply stared at Tobias as he considered how to answer the question.

'I was advised that a partnership of this nature requires a gift. Something of immense personal value to myself. Unfortunately, wealth at the magnitude I possess makes most material possessions essentially meaningless. So, I had to find another way to gift you a ... part of myself.'

A ripple of horror murmured around the table. Cari looked over at Damian, who met her eyes sadly and picked up his fork.

Carter

'I'm sorry, Tobias, but this has gone far enough.' Carter got to his feet with a firm expression and crossed his arms. 'Now, I'm not going to deny I've had an ... unusual experience. If you tell me it's ghosts, at this point I'm not going to argue. But if you're trying to tell me that the answer is ... is *cannibalism*. Then I'm going to say that these ghosts have probably affected your judgement as much as they've clearly affected ours.'

Janek

Janek nodded as the tech guy spoke, seeing others also mumbling agreement, relieved someone else had said it for them.

'Ghosts have made you mad too, Mr Fell. If you think feeding us your flesh will help. But no, I don't think we will be eating.'

From the look that crossed Tobias's face it was clear that the possibility of his own delusion hadn't actually crossed his mind. He stood there in silence for several long moments before answering.

'That is an interesting consideration,' he said, finally. 'But it changes nothing. If this, all of this, is a delusion of my own, then the fact of the matter is I have no way to escape the shadows that want me dead and the result is the same whatever I do. If, however, I am right, then this remains the only way. And, in case I haven't been clear, my survival is my only priority. If I am ... mistaken, well ... My money remains quite real and you will have it as promised. Or, I suppose, we find out whether Max is real enough to kill you.' In response, Max hit the baton against the meaty part of his palm, emitting a very definite *thwack*. 'But it won't come to that, I'm sure.'

Anna

It was hard to listen to grown-ups when they got upset with each other, and she didn't really understand what they were talking about. It seemed to be about the dinner, which made sense, as her plate was almost empty. What was there was smaller than a chicken nugget and looked like old bacon. She felt sharp little fingers on her arm.

'Please,' Penny begged. 'You promised.'

Anna pushed the plate towards her, but her friend shook her head.

'No,' Penny said. 'You first. Then I can eat.'

Anna shrugged and picked the morsel up with her fingers. It was tough, and not as salty as she thought it would have been, but that was fine.

Jésus

Should he have stopped the child from eating? It was too late now for such worries. Jésus felt like he was the only one who saw it before it happened. The little girls did not seem like they understood what was going on, and perhaps that was for the best. Tobias had shown himself such a man that Jésus had no doubt he would kill children, and most likely their mother as well.

Though watching her chew the meat slowly, as the long-limbed imitation of an imaginary playmate – how had he ever thought it was simply another child? – nodded eagerly, Jésus felt all his resistance leak away. A billionaire ... what doors would that unlock? What great art of the world could be his?

He stabbed his own piece and ate. Out of the corner of his eye, he saw the rest of the table do the same. Some casting terrified looks at the figure of Max, which seemed to get larger with every bite, flesh sinking with sudden decay. Some salivating for something more precious than meat. The pitiful clothing speaking volumes. And some eating because they couldn't see any other way for this ghoulish party to end.

Leon

He didn't really know what he expected it to taste like. Special, somehow. Like a transgression, maybe. But it was just tough and unpleasant, not unlike over-cooked pork. Then it was gone, and he was, he supposed, now a billion dollars richer. And haunted forever. At least he wasn't going to die, that was something. Did that mean he would never be clean? Filthy rich. Leon tried to smile, but it didn't come.

He looked around to see similar reckonings on the faces of the other guests.

Laura

She was a cannibal. She wanted to throw up. Real people weren't cannibals. Cannibals were something feared by racist Victorian explorers. They were stranded pioneers trapped in the mountains by a fierce winter. They weren't estate agents sitting in a penthouse in Tower Hamlets. She tried to tell herself she did it because she didn't want to die. That was true, of course, but there was some nasty part of her brain that whispered to her that maybe she'd done it for the money. The home she could buy. She'd done it to be rich. And what if she had? Was that so terrible?

Another thought seized her. What about prion disease? Had anybody thought about prion disease? She could feel the panic crawling up through her brain, threatening to overwhelm her, but still Tobias Fell's calm, clear voice cut through.

'Good,' he said. 'That's the easy bit done with. But there is another thing I require before you receive your reward.'

Violet

Something was being dragged across the floor. Violet looked up to see the brute yanking the massive wooden box over towards the table. Somehow, she already knew what was inside it. Part of her recognised Max, knew exactly what he was, recognised the boot that had always stood on the throat of the imprisoned. Another part of her recognised the whole situation from one of her mother's tales, the earned fate of those who accepted invitations from wicked strangers. But mostly, when his bloody hands tore the lid from the box, she recognised the face of the man inside. She remembered his sad eyes as he smoked in the corridor, trying desperately to help her disbelieve her fate.

And she knew exactly what Tobias Fell wanted them to do.

Jason

Jason wondered if anyone else could see how decayed Max was becoming. Their faces were masks of horror, confusion and disgust, but there were so many possible reasons for that he couldn't tell if anyone else had noticed the clinging strands

369

of skin left on nails and splinters as the unresisting body was pulled from the box and laid across the middle of the table. Did the plumber recoil as a sliver of skin slid from Max's skull and dropped onto one of the plates?

Jason knew the man on the table from description: several residents had reported seeing him lurking around the corridors and hallways, smoking. He was alive, at least, his chest gradually rising and falling. Probably drugged from the look of things.

'This man,' Tobias explained gently, 'has been looking for me for some time. I believe one of my oil companies has been destroying the land belonging to his family. Even killed some of them. Some indigenous tribe in Ecuador, I don't keep track.'

Jason stared at the man's face. It would have looked almost peaceful, were it not for the bruises that covered his throat and the rope around his wrists.

'At first, I thought he came here to kill me, but the truth is far more pitiable. I believe he thought me ignorant to the realities of the operation, and that if he could just talk to me face to face then perhaps he could open my eyes, convince me. I don't know exactly where he was hiding as he searched for a way to reach me, but he needn't have bothered. After all, I wanted him here, though obviously I prefer him to be silent.'

Jason looked around, saw the other guests waiting for the next words, knowing they were coming.

'I need each of you to participate in his death.'

Tobias

He paused, considering for a moment how much further explanation was needed. They already knew the choice was between unimaginable wealth or painful death. People are always so surprised at what they are capable of once they've taken a step they deem unforgivable. Would anyone be swayed further by knowing more about the reasoning behind the act? He decided to explain anyway. It had been so long since he'd had the chance to speak in person, he was going to make the most of it.

'We are now connected, and now comes the act of true complicity. This man has unknowingly offered himself up, a symbol of all whom I have harmed. And in harming him you will be a part of that. You each have a knife. I assure you, no violence done here will be prosecuted by the police. I have ensured there is no record of this man's existence here and no one has reason to investigate. Should anyone feel compelled to confess I have more than enough resources to bury such accusations. And accusers.'

He paused.

'Oh,' he remembered with a small laugh. 'Of course, if you attempt to do violence against me, the police *will* be alerted, and arrive within minutes. In case you were considering it. Don't forget what the police would find if they pumped your stomachs.'

Tobias was dimly aware of the reactions around him, the cries of protest, the nervous shaking of heads.

'Bullshit.' The woman in work clothes, Violet, stood up. 'I'm not scared of some fucking thug.'

Max stood up to his full height, which seemed even taller than it had been before. His grin was so wide it tore the skin at the side of his face and his eyes seemed to grow smaller, shrivelling to tiny burning embers. Every bone in his knuckles cracked around his stick as the room grew darker.

'Yeah,' he rumbled. 'You are.'

Violet's body was taut as a bowstring as she stared him down. Then something inside her seemed to falter, and she took a step back, eyes falling bitterly to the floor.

Tobias smiled, but did not get involved in their little confrontation. They knew what the deal was now, they would either do it and be rich or they would die. There was nothing left except to make their choices. Perhaps he would let the child live, it was unlikely she understood enough to meaningfully participate, and he privately wondered why Banyan Court had chosen her at all.

He eyed the tied-up figure on the table. A small flower of disgust blossomed in his gut. Who had this man thought he was, to try and talk to him? He had been given no speaking part in this story, he was a prop, his purpose to suffer and die quietly, far from here. No matter. He could still fulfil his role here. He could still die so that his betters might prosper.

Tobias looked around the table, watching who took up knives and who began to back away.

Gillian

The knife felt wrong in her hand, but even so she poised the tip over the man's chest. She'd eaten because the thought of death terrified her, and of course she needed the money, but that wasn't what moved her towards the bound figure now. More than anything, she realised, she was sick of piecing together awful secrets that kept her up at night. Perhaps this act would tether her forever to this web of cascading conspiracies, but if she must live in a world of terrible truths, let her be the one writing them.

Laura

The old man had told her to come, and she still didn't know fully why. Had it just been revenge? It didn't matter now. Laura picked up her knife. She didn't even have to be the one who actually killed him, she just needed to be involved. It wasn't like she hadn't done that before. And who wouldn't want to be impossibly wealthy? Anyone would take this deal. She was certain of it. Money could buy anything. It could buy this.

Jason

Jason had known Max was going to kill him since the second he'd found that poor kid in the baseball cap, and he was sick of it. He'd eaten, sure he had, maybe one last act of denial, of pretending he could get out of here alive. But no, he was sick of violence and blood on his hands, and he wasn't going to be responsible for any more deaths. This time, he'd step up. He felt a wave of strength flow through him. This had to end.

Janek

Perhaps it would be nice to be able to stand by his principles, to sacrifice his life to keep his hands clean. But he had made many hard choices in his life, and there was no scenario in which given the choices laid out before him, between enough money to provide for his children forever or leaving them grief-stricken and fatherless, well, it hadn't been a difficult decision when it was cannibalism, and it wasn't a hard choice now.

Anna

She still didn't understand entirely what was going on, but she didn't want to hurt anyone. She looked to Penny, who just smiled brightly and shrugged. She crawled under the table and began to cry.

Leon

Maybe it should have been Andi standing here, making this decision, but Leon was glad it wasn't. He didn't think she'd have been able to go through with it, and he couldn't stand the thought of losing her. But hadn't he lost her already? If he did this, he'd never be clean. Well, with that amount of money he was certain they could work something out. See the best specialists, like Tobias had. Live somewhere Andi would be happy. As he picked up the knife, Leon considered that perhaps the reward here wasn't simply money, but the opportunity to fully join Tobias in his world as the only ones who understood.

Caroline

Everything had led her here, to this moment. She had come with a desperate trust in Damian and if there was ever a moment to test that, here it was. She had trusted him enough to come here, enough to eat human flesh. Now it was time for him to honour that. Cari looked at him, waiting for guidance, but he gave no sign. She stalled, desperate to not make a choice. Her eyes met with Violet's, and she felt her hand move away from the knife.

Carter

He wanted to be a good person, he did. Whatever torment Donna had put him through, she had been right about Carter's selfishness and ignorance. He wondered for a moment. Would Donna return? Or would his perpetual haunting take another form? But he couldn't ignore the choice at hand. Eating a person's flesh when it had been willingly given didn't harm anyone, he had accepted that. This was murder.

He wanted to be a good person. And he could do so much more good in the world if he was alive. Donna had shown him that, in her own way. Refusing to participate wouldn't save this man. The knife was smooth and cold in his hand.

Jésus

Dying wasn't an option, that much was surely obvious, but there was something else that Jésus felt propelling his hand towards the knife, the same instinct he felt as he succumbed to fear and devoured the flesh of their host. All of this, the grand table, the sacrificial victim, the twisted last supper, it was … beautiful. It was the most monumentally grotesque piece of art. And it was only right that he be part of it. Just think, when he finally got home, his painting's embrace would be waiting for him. When he picked up the knife, it felt right.

Violet

At a certain point, beyond all extremity, the only freedom you have left is the freedom to say 'No' and let them do as they will.

She had not exercised it when ordered to eat, choosing instead to live. Perhaps she should have because it turned out to be a trick. They were still trapped in Tobias's sick game. But a life under the heel is no life at all. Violet found herself smiling at the bejewelled woman opposite and as their eyes met, she took a single step back. She would not live in fear. Violet sneered at Tobias. Bosses can hang, she would not do as she was told.

Alvita

She had to look after Tommy, she had to survive. That was all there was to it. It was all there had been when she had eaten, and it was all there was to it now. And yet, as Alvita tried to pick up the knife, she felt a warm hand take hers and guide it away. She looked and saw nothing, but smiled anyway. It was time.

Damian

'No.'

Damian's voice surprised him with how clear it was, how full of confidence and resolve. Everyone turned to him, the would-be killers with knives poised and ready, the nervous ones still looking for a way out, the bruised journalist tied to his chair, even Tobias himself, whose smug expression wavered ever so slightly at how firmly the word was spoken.

For a moment everything was silent expectation.

'You have something to say, Mr ... Simpson, was it?' The shit-eating smile was once again plastered across Tobias's face.

'I don't.' Damian's stomach lurched as he rolled the only dice he had. 'But I think there are a few here who do. Because I've been watching, and I think you've made a mistake. Not every ghost here is contained by your walls.'

Confusion rippled out as Jason and Alvita picked up their knives. This was it. Either he was right, or he was dead.

Alvita

'Her name was Edith Kinney.' The voice was Alvita's, but the words were not. 'She moved here after she lost her husband, and in her loneliness this place reached out to her. But it was too late, she was dying alone and unmourned. Then a stranger knocked on her door, asking for directions to the penthouse.'

Alvita looked down at the bound and unconscious form of Diego and an old woman's fond smile crossed her face.

'He explained his situation and Edith was moved. He seemed like such a nice young man. She let him stay with her, and he kept her company in her last days of life. Even after she passed, he stayed to mourn her. She won't let you harm him, and she is not bound by this awful building that made her final months so miserable.'

Alvita held up her knife, and she moved slowly, dreamlike, towards Diego.

'Max.' Tobias's voice was commanding, but he couldn't quite hide the tinge of panic. 'Stop her.'

Jason

The thing that Jason had once believed to be his friend charged towards Alvita, letting loose a low roar. The baton was raised high, preparing to come down with a force Jason knew would crack the woman's skull like an egg. Max didn't even notice the knife until it slipped into his stomach.

'Boo,' Jason whispered into his ear.

Max turned, the rotten remains of his face still managing to convey a sense baffled betrayal.

'His name was James Andre. He was 16. He was a dumb kid, and made mistakes, but he tried to do right by people and he didn't deserve what we did to him. He's not a prisoner here either.'

Whatever supernatural powers were at work, Jason couldn't say. Certainly the knife wound he had given Max shouldn't have been fatal, but as he watched the brutal thing began to bulge and tear, black and ancient gore gushing out, lashing across the table, the floor, even over the ceiling, until nothing remained but a shrivelled husk of rotten skin and a bloody, splintered nightstick.

Tobias

No. No no no. This wasn't how it was supposed to go. This wasn't how he'd dreamed it. Without Max they could easily turn those knives on him.

'Very well.' His voice betrayed none of his alarm. 'The threat is removed. But the money remains unchanged. Those of you who wish to claim it may still do so.'

He looked across the faces of his guests, trying to gauge their intentions. His hand shook ever so slightly as he reached inside his jacket and activated the panic button app he'd had made especially for this moment.

The police would be here soon, he just needed to explain

that if the others simply put the knives away, he could make all of this disappear. The only person ... No, the only *thing* that had died tonight was just a figment of the building. They had somehow beaten him. That was unexpected, but fairly done. Nobody else needed to die tonight.

He opened his mouth to speak when he noticed Alvita had moved next to Diego and placed the blade against the rope around his wrist. Why? Surely she ... Wait. What had he been told about symbols and their power? About how spirits could use the connections he had made if they weren't properly bound?

'Oh no.' Were Tobias Fell's last words.

Then Alvita cut the rope and set everything free.

Damian

Even if he had known exactly what was going to happen, had more than theory and supposition, Damian could not have imagined how it would feel as the anger trapped in Banyan Court rushed into him. But he was ready, and when the shadows came rushing, he was the first to let them in.

He saw his part in it all so clearly now: Fell's companies liked to make their spaces hostile, keeping away transients and 'encouraging productivity' in their workers. Now he felt those souls, pushed out into the cold by metal spikes and trapped in the glow of harsh fluorescents, rush through him. The space Fell had so carefully constructed, to bind, to keep out, and keep in, was now focused solely on him. As the terrified billionaire rushed for the door out of the dining room, Damian felt himself slam it shut, trapping him inside with a lifetime of righteous hatred.

Carter

The poor fool was trying to call for help, desperately checking his phone, but the data wasn't on his side. The trouble with technology is it all needs to talk to each other. And when Donna's voice emerged from his phone, it was clear that she had no interest in letting his panic button talk to anything else.

'I'm afraid no one is coming to help you, Mr Fell,' she said.

Carter laughed a nasty, synthetic laugh.

Violet

He was flailing wildly now, brandishing one of the knives from the table, keen to harm any who might come close. Violet stretched out her will and the chains of all those he had imprisoned and enslaved and trapped in thankless agonising toil reached out and clasped around him, pulling him to the floor with their weight. She could see tears in his eyes, but it was too late for pity.

Gillian

Tobias was screaming, pleading, begging for his life, offering money and power and all the very real things that were his to give. But he had robbed so many of their voices, silencing them when the words they spoke displeased him. Gillian placed her hand across his lips and felt the white-hot anger pour through her, burning and scorching the skin beneath until the melted, blackened flesh fused together, sealing his mouth shut. He still tried to scream.

Laura

He had exercised such control over property, weaponising people's homes against them, pushing them into squalid conditions or forcing them out entirely for a few extra pennies. Now his own home was turned against him as Laura splintered the floorboards with a sheer force of will and grinding rage. Great spikes of wood erupted, jutting out into his limbs, and vicious nails leapt to impale his back.

Anna

Penny could control herself no longer, and finally leapt onto him with all the hunger of the children starved and poisoned by what Fell's companies had fed them. Her friend giggled in glee as her sharp teeth began to tear chunks from his stomach. She gestured for Anna to join her, and Anna felt her own teeth sharpen as she was pulled to join in the feast.

Alvita

He had sold fake drugs, he'd had his companies refuse people lifesaving care, but Alvita found the spirits flowing through her wanted their revenge in a more visceral form of medicine. She had two hands, hands that had put pill after pill into her own body. And Tobias Fell had two eyes.

Caroline

Gemstones were beautiful and people suffered and died for them. They were also sharp and hard, and as she raked and clawed at the flesh of his torso, Cari found her glittering, bloody hands digging into him with ease. He had burrowed deep into the ground for treasure, at the expense of all else, now she burrowed into him for a very different prize.

Jason

This man had financed death squads to kill union activists, he had hired mercenaries to intimidate and murder those who stepped out of line. So many had lived in fear for their lives because of the brutal regimes he had let run rampant. Now the boot was on *his* face, crunching down again and again, until his jaw and nose were cracked and broken.

Leon

As Tobias's jaw caved beneath Jason's heel, his mouth was torn back open, but he didn't have time to cry out before Leon's face was over his, stretched and distorted as all the pollutants and toxins he had pumped out into the world flowed out and down the throat of the twitching, writhing tycoon.

Janek

So many dead workers. So many lost to cost cutting, unsafe machinery, deliberate negligence. They had died falling or crushed or mangled, and now every one of them reached out, their hands in Janek's as he gripped either side of Tobias's head and squeezed, his grasp like a machine, slowly pressing and pushing and crushing until the bone cracked beneath his grip.

Jésus

So, this was what it was to be truly part of something beautiful. A grand flowing force of revenge. This man had taken land from so many, dispossessed them and stolen what had provided them with life. It only seemed right for the land to take his life back in turn. And as Tobias thrashed his last, Jésus stretched out his hand and felt himself pulling the blood from the many wounds of his victim, down into the floor, into Banyan Court itself, draining the once great man until he was nothing but a dry white corpse.

Tobias

Tobias Fell was dead. His last moments nothing but the purest of agonies. As his guests became themselves again, they could do nothing but stare at the grotesque parody of a human form that had just minutes ago been one of the most powerful men on the planet. None of them said a word, each trying to come to terms with what had happened. There seemed no great satisfaction, no glow of satisfied revenge.

But neither could any one of them bring themselves to regret what they had done.

Epilogue

Burnt Coffee

'I keep telling you, I was concussed.' David Erikson sipped his coffee and gave Cari a knowing look.

'I know. You don't believe the ghost bit.'

'Hey, I believe in ghosts. I mean, I'm subscribed to your channel and everything.'

'It's Damian's channel,' Cari corrected. 'I just help out.'

'My point is, I don't really know what I saw, except maybe that Tobias Fell forced you all to do some really fucked-up things and you, uh, responded poorly to it. You want to say ghosts were involved, who am I to argue?'

Cari tried to smile. She enjoyed her periodic meetings with David, though they had been getting less frequent. Even so, she still wasn't quite ready to joke about that night. In the quiet, she could see he knew he'd gone a bit too far.

'Did you see the article?' he asked, in a more serious tone. Cari nodded.

'Thank you,' she said. 'For keeping us out of it like that. We've been fielding a few anniversary calls from elsewhere and they can get pretty pushy.'

'Tell me about it.'

'Like we would have any idea about forensic evidence from five years ago.'

'Or lack thereof,' David noted. 'To be honest, I still get calls about it too. Wanting to know when I'll write the *real* story. I tell them I was unconscious, concussed, no idea what happened, but ... Well, you remember how the police were. Sometimes it feels like that interview room all over again.'

'Hard to get past something no one else wants to forget.' Cari sighed.

'At least now people aren't afraid to talk about the sort of thing Fell was up to. You read about Insegur going into administration?'

'Yup. The board got a big payday and the CEO now works for a regulator. Justice at last.'

David shifted awkwardly in his seat. They sipped their coffee in silence for a few moments.

'If you did want to tell your side of things,' he probed gently. 'I wouldn't mind doing a more in-depth retrospective on where everyone is now.'

'Not likely.' Cari shook her head. 'I mean, obviously you know where I am. Damian and Violet too.'

'Sure. And congratulations, by the way.' He gestured to her ring. 'I saw the pictures, you both looked beautiful.'

'Thank you.' Cari beamed now. 'Violet was thinking about something a bit more flashy, but obviously gemstones are, uh ... Well.'

'So, what about the others?'

'Well, I don't know about Janek or Laura. She's not at her old firm anymore and didn't keep in touch and he ... well, he specifically said not to contact him. His business is still in the directory, though, so I guess things aren't going too badly. The others, let's see ... Leon's got some new corporate position, don't see him much, and Jésus is still Jésusing up the art world. Used to see Jason quite regularly, but he's moved up to Manchester, working for that charity Carter's been running into the ground as part of his whole "ethical" thing. Oh, and Gill's a teacher now. Primary school, I think. Not sure, been a while since we talked.'

'Whatever happened to Diego?'

'He's still out there, last I heard. Keeps in touch with Violet sometimes, and Alvita I think. He's changed his name. Kind of had to since I think he's still considered a suspect.'

'Oh? What's he going by now?'

'Not my place to say.'

There was a pause.

'So yeah.' Cari shrugged. 'Everyone just … being alive, I guess. Trying to get on as best we can. Not thinking about it too much.'

'Right.' David paused before his next question. 'What about Anna? That sort of thing, at that age…'

'Yeah, it's—' Cari looked uncomfortable. 'Sorry to sound like a broken record, but I'm not sure how much I can tell you. Her parents moved her away, changed their name as well which … fair enough I guess. Didn't want people to associate her with what happened. Alvita's still in touch with them, I think Anna and Tommy see each other sometimes. She says Anna's growing up fine. Eleven now.'

'And Penny?'

'Gone. Like the rest of them.'

'I suppose children can be very resilient,' David said, though he didn't sound convinced.

'I hope so.' Cari's voice was sad. 'That's the part I don't think I could ever forgive. Involving her like that.'

'Yeah.' David considered his next question. 'You still … see anything?'

'I don't dance, if that's what you're asking.' She laughed

hollowly. 'Or wear jewellery. And Violet's part-time. Everyone's got stuff to deal with, David. Even you.'

He said nothing. They sat in silence for a few minutes, drinking their coffee. Cari's phone buzzed on the table.

'Oh, sorry, I've got to go.'

'Sure thing.'

David stood and tried unnecessarily to help her with her coat.

'Did you hear the news, by the way?' he asked as she started towards the door.

She looked back.

'They're pulling it down next year. Might put this whole business to rest.'

'Yeah?' Caroline smiled sadly, silhouette outlined in the doorway. 'And what are they building in its place?'

David didn't reply, though he knew the answer.

'More luxury apartments?' She didn't even feign surprise.

He shrugged, trying a smile. 'Hopefully with fewer ghosts.'

Caroline shook her head.

'The ghosts were never the problem.'

Acknowledgements

I have never created alone, and there are so many people who have helped this book become a reality. I want to say thank you first and foremost to my editor Rachel for taking a chance on me, and for handing me the most timely and inspiring idea. This book is hers as much as it is mine. Thank you to Zoë, my agent, for holding my hand through the strange and unsettling waters of the publishing world. Thanks also to Alex, Lowri, Story, Elizabeth and everyone at Rusty Quill for helping me get here, and my past collaborators and dearest friends Frank, Tim, Jess, Rachel, Kofi, Morgan and Fran. And thanks most of all to Sasha, the centre of my world, without whom I could never create anything a fraction as good. Thanks also to Sir Pouncealot and The Ambassador for occasionally getting off my lap to let me write.

Credits

Jonathan Sims and Gollancz would like to thank everyone at Orion who worked on the publication of *Thirteen Storeys* in the UK.

Editorial
Rachel Winterbottom
Brendan Durkin

Copy editor
Jonathan Oliver

Proof reader
Jane Howard

Audio
Paul Stark
Amber Bates

Contracts
Anne Goddard
Paul Bulos
Jake Alderson

Design
Lucie Stericker
Loulou Clark
Joanna Ridley
Nick May

Editorial Management
Charlie Panayiotou
Jane Hughes
Alice Davis

Finance
Jennifer Muchan
Jasdip Nandra
Afeera Ahmed
Elizabeth Beaumont
Sue Baker

Marketing
Lucy Cameron

Production
Paul Hussey

Publicity
Will O'Mullane

Sales
Jen Wilson
Laura Fletcher

Esther Waters
Victoria Laws
Rachael Hum
Ellie Kyrke-Smith
Frances Doyle
Georgina Cutler

Operations
Jo Jacobs
Sharon Willis
Lisa Pryde
Lucy Brem

ПСVO

THE VOLUNTARY AGENCIES DIRECTORY 2014

DUNDEE CITY COUNCIL

CENTRAL LIBRARY

REFERENCE SERVICES

FOR REFERENCE ONLY

Published by NCVO
Society Building
8 All Saints Street
London N1 9RL

First published in 1928 as the Voluntary Servic̄ Handbook and Directory

This edition published March 2014

Copyright NCVO 2014

Charity registration number 225922

All rights reserved. No part of this publication retrieval system or transmitted in any form or mechanical, photocopying or otherwise, without the prior permission of NCVO.

Designed by Steers McGillan Eves Design

Printed by Pureprint

British Library Cataloguing in Public Data

A catalogue record for this book is available from the British Library

Every effort has been made to ensure the accuracy of the information contained within this publication.

ISBN: 978-0-7199-0012-9

ABOUT
THE DIRECTORY

How to use this directory

The index at the back features broad categories, with lists of relevant organisations. Entries are arranged alphabetically and provide contact details for each organisation. In most cases, there is a brief description of the aims and activities, together with a broad summary of the types of services offered, as provided by the organisation.

 Provides grants

 Undertakes research

 Membership scheme

 Umbrella or resource body

 Information or advisory service

Criteria for inclusion

'Voluntary agency' is broadly interpreted as a self-governing body of people who have joined together to take action for the betterment (as they see it) of the community, not for financial gain. Organisations affiliated to any political party are not eligible for inclusion. Limitations on space make it impossible to include every voluntary agency, so, as far as possible, organisations need to meet the following criteria:

• have a nationwide, rather than local, remit

• be a leading body in their field

• have headquarters in the UK.

Organisations not included in the directory are welcome to apply for inclusion, free of charge, in the next edition. Email publications@ncvo.org.uk for more details.

Inclusion in the directory does not constitute an endorsement by NCVO.

Accuracy of contents

NCVO accepts no liability for the accuracy of the information. All organisations listed in the directory were contacted directly by NCVO and given the opportunity to update the details of their entry. NCVO reserves the right to include or exclude entries as part of the publishing process, and to edit all details supplied.

A–Z

OF VOLUNTARY AGENCIES

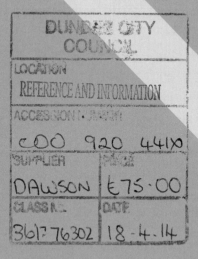

DUNDEE CITY
COUNCIL

LOCATION
REFERENCE AND INFORMATION

ACCESSION NUMBER
c00 920 4410

SUPPLIER   PRICE
DAWSON   £75·00

CLASS No.   DATE
361: 76302   18-4-14

10:10

8 Delancey Passage, London NW1 7NN
T: 020 7388 6688
E: hello@1010uk.org
www.1010global.org
Executive Director: Heidi Proven
We're on the way to a cleaner, cleverer, low-carbon world and everyone deserves a chance to help build it. 10:10 creates these chances, and brings people together to make the most of them. 10:10ers work together to: celebrate the good stuff already happening, and help it spread; save energy at home, work and locally; light up our best-loved places with crowdfunded clean energy; and convince people in power to tackle the stuff we don't control.
Employees: 10
Volunteers: 0
Regional offices: 0

2 Care

11 Harwood Road, London SW6 4QP
T: 020 7371 0118
F: 020 7371 7519
E: pa@2care-rsl.org.uk
www.2care-rsl.org.uk
Chief Executive: Liz O'Sullivan
2Care is a London-based national charity providing high-quality, specialist, rehabilitation and recovery for people with long-term mental health conditions and person-centred care for older people living with dementia. 2Care provides ethical, effective and evidence-based mental health services and aims to be nationally recognised as an agenda-setting organisation, creating opportunities for people to thrive.
Employees: 125
Volunteers: 2
Regional offices: 6

25% ME Group - Support for Severe ME Sufferers

21 Church Street, Troon,
Ayrshire KA10 6HT
T: 01292 318611
E: enquiry@25megroup.org
www.25megroup.org
The 25% ME Group is a unique nationwide charitable organisation managed entirely by volunteers (most of whom are severely affected by ME) and was set up to offer support services to those severely affected by ME (myalgic encephalomyelitis), and their carers.
Employees: 2
Volunteers: 12

3 Villages Youth Project

2 Elms Close Terrace, Newlyn, Penzance, Cornwall TR18 5AU
T: 01736 364707
E: julyan.drew@gmail.com
www.3villagesyouthproject.org.uk
Chair of Trustees: Julyan Drew
Working with and for children and young people in Newlyn, Mousehole and Paul in Cornwall.
Employees: 1
Volunteers: 8
Regional offices: 1

3H Fund

B2 Speldhurst Business Park, Langton Road, Speldhurst, Tunbridge Wells, Kent TN3 0AQ
T: 01892 860207
E: info@3hfund.org.uk
www.3hfund.org.uk
Charity Manager: Lynne Loving
The 3H Fund organises subsidised group holidays for physically disabled children and adults with the support of volunteer helpers, so that in parallel the family carers can have a separate and much-needed period of respite.
Employees: 5
Volunteers: 100

4Children

City Reach, 5 Greenwich View Place, London E14 9NN
T: 020 7512 2112
F: 020 7512 2010
E: info@4children.org.uk
www.4children.org.uk
Chief Executive: Anne Longfield
4Children is a national children's charity that aims to place children and young people at the centre of policy development and service delivery, creating and supporting opportunities that enable all children to fulfil their potential and all parents to access the support they need. The organisation has led the lobbying for, and development of, childcare and out-of-school activities over the last 20 years whilst supporting a major growth in childcare places.
Employees: 80
Regional offices: 1

A Rocha UK

13 Avenue Road, Southall, Middlesex UB1 3BL
T: 020 8574 5935 (also fax)
E: uk@arocha.org
www.arocha.org
The advancement of the Christian faith and understanding of its relevance to the environment.
Employees: 13
Volunteers: 30

Abbeyfield Society

Abbeyfield House, 53 Victoria Street, St Albans AL1 3UW
T: 01727 857536
F: 01727 846168
E: post@abbeyfield.com
www.abbeyfield.com
Abbeyfield is one of the largest voluntary sector providers of housing and care for older people in the UK. Abbeyfield believes older people should be able to obtain the support and care they need to remain independent and involved in life. Founded in 1956 by Richard Carr-Gomm, Abbeyfield has grown to include about 700 houses throughout the UK providing accommodation and support for around 7,500 older people, run by professional staff and more than 7,500 volunteers.

ABF The Soldiers' Charity

Mountbarrow House, 6–20 Elizabeth Street, London SW1W 9RB
T: 020 7901 8900
F: 020 7901 8901
E: dearle@soldierscharity.org
www.soldierscharity.org
Lifetime support to serving and retired soldiers and their families.
Employees: 44
Regional offices: 13

AbilityNet

T: 0870 240 4455
E: enquiries@abilitynet.org.uk
www.abilitynet.org.uk
A national charity helping disabled adults and children use computers and the internet by adapting and adjusting their technology.

AbleChildAfrica

Southbank House, Black Prince Road, London SE1 7SJ
T: 0845 226 1015
F: 0845 226 7874
E: info@ablechildafrica.org.uk
www.ablechildafrica.org.uk
Executive Director: Mary Ann Mhina
AbleChildAfrica specialises in advocating for and supporting disabled children and young people in Africa. In order to achieve this we support partner organisations to carry out life-changing work with disabled children and young people and work alongside them to use their experiences and learning to campaign for more widespread change in attitudes and practice.
Employees: 2
Volunteers: 4

Academy of Youth Limited

University of The First Age, Millenium Point, Curzon Serect, Digbeth, Birmingham B4 7XG
T: 0121 202 2345
E: info@ufa.org.uk
www.aoy.org.uk
Advances the education of children, young people and adults through an institution that is committed to: raising educational achievement; preparing children and young people for the challenge of adult life; transforming educational opportunities.

Access Community Trust

28 Gordon Road, Lowestoft NR32 1NL
T: 01502 527200
F: 01502 527241
E: liz.giles@accessct.org
www.accessct.org
Emma Ratzer: Liz Giles
To promote social inclusion, reducing vulnerability and homelessness by providing accommodation, education, training and practical support tailored to individual needs. To give our clients and communities the best service we can deliver.
Employees: 70
Volunteers: 10
Regional offices: 1

ACCURO

E: arthur@accuro.org.uk

Achieve Lifestyle

Egham Leisure Centre, Vicarage Road
T: 01784 437695
E: debbie.wilmott@achievelifestyle.co.uk
www.achievelifestyle.co.uk
Central Services Manager: Debbie Wilmott

Action Against Allergy

PO Box 278, Twickenham TW1 4QQ
T: 020 8892 4949
Helpline: 020 8892 2711
E: aaa@actionagainstallergy.freeserve.co.uk
www.actionagainstallergy.co.uk
Executive Director: Patricia Schooling
Advances understanding, awareness, and recognition of allergic medical conditions and allergy-related illness and the actions needed for research, diagnosis and treatment.
Employees: 3
Volunteers: 3

Action Against Hunger UK

1st Floor, Rear Premises, 161-153 Greenwich High Road, London SE10 9JA
T: 020 8293 6190
E: info@aahuk.org
www.actionagainsthunger.org.uk
Executive Director: Jean-Michel Grand
Action Against Hunger is an international humanitarian organisation committed to ending child hunger. Recognised as a leader in the fight against malnutrition, ACF works to save the lives of malnourished children while providing communities with sustainable access to safe water and long-term solutions to hunger.
Employees: 43
Volunteers: 25
Regional offices: 1
Income: £10,280,000 (2012-13)

Action Against Medical Accidents

44 High Street, Croydon, Surrey CR0 1YB
T: 020 8688 9555
Helpline: 0845 123 2352
F: 020 8667 9065
E: support@avma.org.uk
www.avma.org.uk
Chief Executive: Peter Walsh
Action against Medical Accidents (AvMA) is an independent UK charity that works for better patient safety and justice for people who have been affected by a medical accident.
Employees: 22
Volunteers: 70

Action Against Tranquilliser Addiction

25 Cradle Hill Road, Seaford, East Sussex BN25 3JA
T: 01323 491622
E: karenlowles25@aol.com
www.aata.org.uk
Director: Karen Lowles
Aims to: raise awareness of the dangers that benzodiazepines have; help people to withdraw from these drugs safely and successfully; campaign to make specialist services available to benzodiazepine addicts; raise funds to enable helplines and clinics; promote the forum www.thetrap.org.uk – a voluntary-run help site for people wishing to withdraw from benzodiazepines.
Employees: 8

Action for Advocacy

PO Box 31856, Lorrimore Square, London SE17 3XR
T: 020 7820 7868
F: 020 7820 9947
E: info@actionforadvocacy.org.uk
www.actionforadvocacy.org.uk
Chief Executive: Rick Henderson
Action for Advocacy (A4A) offers a wide range of services for the advocacy sector. This includes organisational development; our monthly magazine – Planet Advocacy; monthly email bulletin; training and events; influencing policy and staff to answer queries relating to advocacy.
Employees: 9

Action for Blind People

Action House, 53 Sandgate Street, London SE15 1LE
T: 020 7635 4800
Helpline: 0303 123 9999
F: 020 7635 4900
E: fenella.brown@actionforblindpeople.org.uk
www.actionforblindpeople.org.uk
Chief Executive: Stephen Remington
Action for Blind People is a national charity with local reach, providing practical help and support to blind and partially sighted people of all ages. Action speaks louder for nearly 30,000 visually impaired people every year, always placing their needs at the heart of everything we do. We support these individuals in many aspects of their lives and

help them to find the right services and products they need to live independently.
Employees: 535
Volunteers: 115
Regional offices: 17
Income: £25,000,000 (2011-12)

Action for Children

Action for Children, 3 The Boulevard, Ascot Road, Watford, Hertfordshire WD18 8AG
T: 01923 361500
Helpline: 0300 123 2112
E: ask.us@actionforchildren.org.uk
www.actionforchildren.org.uk
Chief Executive: Clare Tickell
Action for Children exists to help the most vulnerable children and young people break through injustice, deprivation and inequality so they can achieve their full potential. We work across the UK, Northern Ireland and internationally. Action for Children works directly with more than 300,000 children, young people, parents and carers each year and runs more than 650 services.

Action for Market Towns

PO Box 299, Bury St Edmunds, Suffolk IP33 1UU
T: 0845 644 6202
E: info@towns.org.uk
www.towns.org.uk
Action for Market Towns is a membership organisation dedicated to promoting the vitality and viability of small towns through an integrated approach.

Action for ME

3rd Floor, Canningford House, 38 Victoria Street, Bristol BS1 6BY
T: 0117 927 9551
F: 0117 927 9552
E: admin@actionforme.org.uk
www.actionforme.org.uk
Chief Executive: Sonya Chowdhury
At Action for ME we provide information and support for people affected by Myalgic Encephalomyelitis (ME), and work collaboratively to raise awareness, campaign for better health and welfare services and fund and drive vital research. People affected by ME can access support and information through our publications, Welfare Rights Line and online Services Directory, available via our Online ME Centre at www.actionforme.org.uk
Employees: 14
Volunteers: 10
Regional offices: 1

Action for Prisoners' Families

25 Corsham Street, London N1 6DR
T: 020 7553 7653
E: luke.evans@prisonersfamilies.org.uk
www.prisonersfamilies.org.uk
Director: Deborah Cowley
Membership organisation for prisoners' and offenders' families and those who work with them. Works for the benefit of prisoners' and offenders' families by: providing advice, information and training; providing opportunities for members to share experiences, concerns and successes; listening to prisoners' families and promoting, developing and supporting services and resources that they need or would like; lobbying for improved structures, procedures, conditions and services to promote the wellbeing of prisoners' and offenders' families.
Employees: 7
Income: £708,640 (2011-12)

Action for Sick Children

36 Jacksons Edge Road, Disley, Stockport SK12 2JL
T: 0800 074 4519
E: enquiries@actionforsickchildren.org
www.actionforsickchildren.org
To join parents and professionals in promoting high-quality healthcare for children in hospital and at home.
Employees: 2
Volunteers: 100
Regional offices: 15

Action for Social Integration

1st Floor, 36 The Market Square, Edmonton, London N9 0TZ
T: 020 8803 6161
E: info@afsi.org.uk
www.afsi.org.uk
Coordinator: Ernest Rukangira
Action for Social Integration aims to advance social and cultural integration, social justice, inclusion, equality and diversity and to eliminate prejudice, stereotype and discrimination in relation to asylum seekers, refugees and minority ethnic communities.
Employees: 2
Volunteers: 12
Regional offices: 1

Action Medical Research

Vincent House, North Parade, Horsham, West Sussex RH12 2DP
T: 01403 210406
F: 01403 210541
E: info@action.org.uk
www.action.org.uk
Chief Executive: Julie Buckler

Action Medical Research is the leading UK-wide medical research charity saving and changing children's lives. Since we began in 1952, we've been funding medical breakthroughs that have helped save thousands of children's lives and changed many more. We want to make a difference in: tackling premature birth and treating sick and vulnerable babies; helping children affected by disability, disabling conditions and infections; targeting rare diseases that together severely affect many forgotten children.
Employees: 51
Volunteers: 2650
Regional offices: 1
Income: £8,000,000 (2010-11)

Action on Addiction

Head Office, East Knoyle, Salisbury, Wiltshire SP3 6BE
T: 0300 330 0659
F: 01747 832028
E: admin@actiononaddiction.org.uk
www.actiononaddiction.org.uk
Chief Executive: Nick Barton
The charity Action on Addiction takes action to disarm addiction in all its forms through a uniquely comprehensive approach that encompasses research, treatment (both residential and non-residential), rehabilitation, family support, education, training and campaigning. Our vision is to see people free from addiction and its effects.
Employees: 145
Regional offices: 5

Action on Disability and Development

Vallis House, 57 Vallis Road, Frome, Somerset BA11 3EG
T: 01373 473064
F: 01373 452075
E: info@add.org.uk
www.add.org.uk
Building strong associations of disabled people; self-advocacy and influence; access; economic empowerment; information and education; recreation, sport and drama.
Employees: 159
Volunteers: 25
Regional offices: 10

Action on Disability and Work UK

E: andy.rickell@adwuk.org

Action on Elder Abuse

PO Box 60001, London SW16 9BY
T: 020 8835 9280
Helpline: 08088 088141
F: 020 8696 9328
E: enquiries@elderabuse.org.uk
www.elderabuse.org.uk
Chief Executive: Gary FitzGerald
Aims to prevent abuse in old age through raising awareness, education, promoting research and the collection and dissemination of information.

Action on Hearing Loss (the new name for RNID)

19–23 Featherstone Street,
London EC1Y 8SL
T: 020 7296 8000
F: 020 7296 8199
E: rebecca.griffin@hearingloss.org.uk
www.actiononhearingloss.org.uk
We aim to make daily life better for deaf and hard of hearing people. Our campaigns, information, services and support of scientific and technological research are some of the ways we're trying to help. We also support other organisations in their aim to provide better services to their deaf and hard of hearing employees and customers.
Employees: 1400
Volunteers: 200
Regional offices: 7

Action on Pre-Eclampsia

105 High Street, Evesham,
Worcestershire, Evesham,
Worcestershire WR11 4EB
T: 01386 761848
Helpline: 020 8427 4217
E: info@apec.org.uk
www.apec.org.uk
Chief Executive Officer: Ann Marie Barnard
Aims to raise public and professional awareness of pre-eclampsia, improve care, and ease or prevent physical and emotional suffering caused by the condition. To educate, inform and advise the public and health professionals about the prevalence, nature and risks of pre-eclampsia.
Employees: 2
Volunteers: 10

Action on Smoking and Health

Suites 59–63, 6th Floor, New House,
67–68 Hatton Garden, London EC1N 8JY
T: 020 7404 0242
F: 020 7404 0850
E: phil.rimmer@ash.org.uk
www.ash.org.uk
Chief Executive: Deborah Arnott
ASH is an organisation that provides information on all aspects of tobacco and works to advance policies and measures that will help to prevent the addiction, disease and unnecessary premature death caused by smoking. ASH was established in 1971 by the Royal College of Physicians.
Employees: 8
Income: £732,000 (2011-12)

Action Space Mobile Ltd

Mapplewell And Staincross, Village Hall,
Darton Lane, Mapplewell, Barnsley, South Yorkshire S75 6AL
T: 01226 391112 (also fax)
E: contact@actionspacemobile.org
www.actionspacemobile.org
Artistic Director: Mary Turner
We are a participatory arts organisation and registered charity that works primarily with marginalised and disadvantaged communities of people, specialising in working creatively with adults and children with learning disabilities and adults with mental health problems. We create opportunities for individuals and communities to participate in the arts, based on our passionate belief that participation in arts activity can change lives positively.
Employees: 2
Volunteers: 20
Regional offices: 1
Income: £257,079 (2012-13)

Action to Regenerate Community Trust

Oasis Centre, Lincoln House,
75 Westminster Bridge Road,
London SE1 7HS
T: 01352 756502 (also fax)
Helpline: 07738 428521
E: nicholas.gardham@regeneratetrust.org
www.regeneratetrust.org
Chief Executive Officer: Stephen Kearney
RE:generate is an enterprising social action charity. Our mission is to tackle poverty and the root causes of poverty and disadvantage. Using our Root Solution Listening Matters process we work with people to encourage them to: develop local enterprising solutions to problems, participate in public life and wake up to their potential to make change in their lives and their community. We aim to transform the relationship between communities, agencies, organisations and the state.
Employees: 14
Volunteers: 103
Regional offices: 4

Action with Communities in Rural England

Somerford Court, Somerford Road,
Cirencester, Gloucestershire GL7 1TW
T: 01285 653477
F: 01285 654537
E: acre@acre.org.uk
www.acre.org.uk
Chief Executive: Sylvia Brown
Action with Communities in Rural England is the national umbrella body of the Rural Community Action Network (RCAN), which operates at national, regional and local level in support of rural communities across the country. We aim to promote a healthy, vibrant and sustainable rural community sector that is well connected to policy and decision-makers who play a part in delivering this aim.
Employees: 16

ActionAid

Hamlyn House, Macdonald Road,
London N19 5PG
T: 020 7561 7561
F: 020 7272 0899
E: rachel.leonard@actionaid.org
www.actionaid.org
Working in partnership with poor people to eradicate poverty by overcoming the injustice and inequity that cause it.
Employees: 244
Volunteers: 7500
Regional offices: 3

Active Training and Education Trust

8 St Ann's Road, Malvern WR14 4RG
T: 01684 562400
Helpline: 0845 456 1205
F: 01684 562716
E: info@ate.org.uk
www.ate.org.uk
Director of Operations: Liz Macartney
The trust runs and promotes educational residential experiences for children and young people, through a programme of imaginative and creative summer camps, and through weekend and weekday sessions for schools, as well as FunDays in schools. It also runs training, INSET, conferences, etc. on the subject of fun and imagination in education.
Employees: 3
Volunteers: 200
Income: £200,000 (2012-13)

Actors Benevolent Fund

E: willie.bicket@abf.org.uk

ADD Information Services

2nd Floor Premier House, 112 Station Road, Edgware, Middlesex HA8 7BJ
T: 020 8952 1515
E: info@addiss.co.uk
www.addiss.co.uk
The object of the charity is to relieve children and those persons suffering from attention deficit hyperactivity disorder (ADHD), and to advance the education of the public about the disorder.
Employees: 3

Addaction

67–69 Cowcross Street,
London EC1M 6PU
T: 020 7251 5860
F: 020 7251 5890
E: info@addaction.org.uk
www.addaction.org.uk
Addaction reduces both the use of, and the harm caused by, drugs and alcohol.
Employees: 640
Volunteers: 100
Regional offices: 2

Addiction Recovery Agency

King's Court, King Street, Bristol BS1 4EE
T: 0117 930 0282
E: info@addictionrecovery.org.uk
www.addictionrecovery.org.uk
Aims to support those who are affected by addiction to drugs, alcohol and gambling. We provide accommodation to clients in Bristol to engage in treatment to address their addiction. We also provide counselling to clients affected by Gambling addiction. A newly developed service Connect Psychology is part of the Increasing Access to Psychological Therapies services in Bristol.

Adfam

25 Corsham Street, 1st Floor,
London N1 6DR
T: 020 7553 7640
F: 020 7253 7991
E: admin@adfam.org.uk
www.adfam.org.uk
Chief Executive: Vivienne Evans
Adfam is a registered charity working with families affected by drugs and alcohol. Adfam provides accessible, clear and accurate information via their website and publications for families affected by drug and alcohol, including good practice guides and training manuals for professionals working with family members. We challenge and influence policy makers, planners and the media to understand and represent more accurately the issues affecting families of drug and alcohol users.
Employees: 12
Volunteers: 3

Adhar Project

E: admin.box@adharproject.org

ADHD Solutions cic

E: helen@adhdsolutions.org

Adoption UK

Linden House, 55 The Green, South Bar Street, Banbury, Oxfordshire OX16 9AB
T: 01295 660121
F: 01295 660123
E: non@adoptionuk.org.uk
www.adoptionuk.org.uk
Adoptions UK helps to make adoptions work, and promotes loving and supportive relationships between children and their adoptive families. It provides independent support and advice to all concerned with adoption, offering a wealth of relevant experience from generations of adoptive families to prospective and established adopters and those who work with them.
Employees: 28
Volunteers: 130
Regional offices: 50

Adullam Homes Housing Association

Walter Moore House, 34 Dudley Street, West Bromwich, West Midlands B70 9LS
T: 0121 500 2828
F: 01250 02824
E: info@adullam.org.uk
www.adullam.uk.net
Chief Executive: Trevor Palfreyman
Adullam Homes is a specialist provider in quality housing and support services and was founded in 1972. Adullam Homes now houses and supports 1,200 people at any one time, throughout the North West and the Midlands. The Association is renowned for its expertise in supporting and developing vulnerable and excluded people in addition to integrating service users and residents into the world of work.
Employees: 220
Volunteers: 30
Regional offices: 2

Adults Affected by Adoption-NORCAP

112 Church Road, Wheatley,
Oxfordshire OX33 1LU
T: 01865 875000
F: 01865 875686
E: jeanm@norcap.org
www.norcap.org.uk
CEO: Jean Milsted
Support, advice and specialist services provided to adult adopted people, birth-relatives and other family members to assist with locating and reunion issues. AAA-NORCAP is a national registered voluntary adoption support agency and intermediary agency. We assist adopted adults to access birth and adoption records and provide birth relatives with an intermediary service to seek renewed contact with relatives who were adopted.
Employees: 8
Volunteers: 85

Adventist Special Needs Association (ASNA)

65 St Helens Avenue, Benson,
Oxfordshire OX10 6RU
T: 01491 833395
E: info@asna.info
www.asna.info
Honorary Secretary/Development Director: Sophia Nicholls
Supporting people living with special needs and disabilities by providing respite care – residential short breaks, family fun days, resources, volunteer carers, advice and information. We also support professionals and other people working with people living with disabilities and special needs by providing advice, information, resources, disability training and awareness programmes.
Employees: 1
Volunteers: 30

Adventure Service Challenge Scheme

East Lynn, Lansdown Lane, Bath BA1 4NB
T: 01225 329838 (also fax)
E: asc@asc-scheme.org.uk
www.asc-scheme.org.uk
Chair: Roger Crocker
ASC Scheme is a nationally available, structured, flexible scheme of activities for children aged eight to 14 and over. It is used by schools, youth clubs, uniformed organisations, special needs groups etc. It offers young people adventure, the chance to give service to their community and a challenge. It is a three-fold programme helping young people develop in today's

world, achieve their potential and prepare for a fulfilling and responsible adult life.
Volunteers: 17
Regional offices: 7

Adventure Unlimited

64 Edward Street, Brighton, East
Sussex BN1 0JR
T: 01273 681058
E: info@aultd.org
www.aultd.org
Director: Louise Stone
Adventure Unlimited is a registered charity based in Brighton and Hove. Its aim is to enrich the lives of disadvantaged young people through outdoor education events run by formerly unemployed adults. We run adventure activity and climbing events for groups and individuals of all ages. For more information about its work, please go to the website.
Employees: 10
Volunteers: 30
Regional offices: 1

Adverse Psychiatric Reactions Information Link (APRIL)

Room 311, Linen Hall, 162–168 Regent Street, London W1B 5TD
T: 020 7998 1561
E: info@april.org.uk
www.april.org.uk
Chair: Millie Kieve
The objective of APRIL is to promote greater awareness, recognition and safe treatment of adverse psychiatric reactions and withdrawal symptoms that may be caused by prescribed and over-the-counter medicines and anaesthetics.
Employees: 1
Volunteers: 5
Income: £10,000 (2011-12)

Advice on Individual Rights in Europe

3rd Floor, 17 Red Lion Square, London WC1R 4QH
T: 020 7831 4276
E: info@airecentre.org
www.airecentre.org
Operates a law centre specialising in European Union law and international human rights law, in particular, the European Convention on Human Rights.

Advice Services Alliance

7th Floor, Tavis House, Tavistock Square, London WC1H 9NA
T: 07904 377460
E: admin@asauk.org.uk
www.asauk.org.uk
Director: Lindsey Poole
ASA is the umbrella body for the independent not-for-profit advice sector. It aims to: promote collaboration between advice agencies; provide a voice for the sector; analyse advice needs and provision; support the development of high-quality independent advice services; encourage better information on and public awareness of the rights of the citizen.
Employees: 1

AdviceUK

6th Floor, 63 St Mary Axe, London EC3A 8AA
T: 020 7469 5700
F: 020 7469 5701
E: mail@adviceuk.org.uk
www.adviceuk.org.uk
Chief Executive: Steve Johnson
AdviceUK promotes the provision of independent advice services across the UK; supports centres delivering independent advice to the public; acts as a coordinating network and voice for centres; provides a discussion forum on issues of concern to centres and their clients and helps formulate and promote policies with regard to advice work.
Employees: 19
Regional offices: 2

Advisory Centre for Education (ACE) Ltd

1C Aberdeen Studios, 22 Highbury Grove, London N5 2DQ
T: 020 7354 8318
F: 020 7354 9069
E: enquiries@ace-ed.org.uk
www.ace-ed.org.uk
ACE provides a free advice service for parents of children in state-maintained schools. It advocates changes in state schools to help them to become more responsive to the needs of parents and children. It offers training in specialist areas of education and supports local organisations giving advice on education.
Employees: 18
Volunteers: 2
Regional offices: 1

Advisory Committee on the Protection of the Sea

Fabian Society, 11 Dartmouth Street, London SW1H 9BN
T: 020 7799 3033
E: info@acops.org
www.acops.org
The committee exists to promote the preservation of the seas of the world from pollution by human activities; promote and conduct research into the causes and effects of pollution of the seas; advance public education by the study of the impact of human activities upon the natural resources of the sea.

Advisory Council for the Education of Romany and Other Travellers

ACERT, PO Box 526, Sevenoaks, Kent TN13 9PF
T: 020 8374 1286
E: info@acert.org.uk
www.acert.org.uk
Chair: Brian Foster
ACERT campaigns for: equal access and opportunities in education; safe and secure accommodation; equal access to health and other community services; good community relations; an end to discrimination for all gypsy, Roma and traveller families.
Volunteers: 15
Regional offices: 1
Income: £5,000 (2011-12)

Advocacy Resource Exchange

Portman House, 53 Millbrook Road East, Southampton, Hampshire SO15 1HN
T: 02380 234904
Helpline: 0845 122 8633
E: enquiries@advocacyresource.org.uk
www.advocacyresource.org.uk
Chief Officer: Janet Badger
Advocacy Resources Exchange (ARX) is a national organisation supporting the provision of independent advocacy. Advocacy promotes social inclusion, equality and social justice through the process of supporting voices to be heard in the complex communities that make up neighbourhoods, towns and cities in Britain. We maintain a comprehensive database of independent advocacy provision throughout the UK and operate a supported referral system to help individuals find appropriate advocacy support.

Afasic

20 Bowling Green Lane,
London EC1R 0BD
T: 020 7490 9410
Helpline: 0845 355 5577
F: 020 7251 2834
E: info@afasic.org.uk
www.afasic.org.uk
Chief Executive: Linda Lascelles
Afasic is a UK-wide charity that helps children and young people with speech, language and communication impairments and their families. Afasic operates a helpline for parents, a website, produces information and literature, is a membership organisation, and has local groups across the country. Afasic runs training events and conferences for parents and professionals and activities for children and young people.
Employees: 21
Volunteers: 150
Regional offices: 2
Income: £860,000 (2011-12)

AFIYA Trust

27–29 Vauxhall Grove, London SW8 1SY
T: 020 7582 0400
F: 020 7582 2552
E: info@afiya-trust.org
www.afiya-trust.org
The AFIYA Trust advances education in subjects concerned with the health of persons from minority ethnic groups.
Employees: 8

African Caribbean Leukaemia Trust (ACLT)

Southbridge House, Southbridge Place,
Croydon, Surrey CR0 4HA
T: 020 8240 4480
F: 020 8240 4481
E: info@aclt.org
www.aclt.org
Chief Executive: Orin Lewis
The ACLT conducts bone marrow, blood and organ donation awareness/registration drives throughout the UK, specifically in predominantly black, mixed race and ethnic minority populated cities. The aim is to raise awareness and educate to increase the poor representation of these communities on the bone marrow/blood/organ donor registers. After 24 years only 550 black people had ever joined the bone marrow register. During the last 15 years the ACLT has helped raise it to approximately 36,000.
Employees: 10
Volunteers: 150
Regional offices: 1

African Community Development Foundation

Ilex House, 1 Barrhill Road, Streatham Hill, London SW2 4RJ
T: 020 8671 2666
E: info@acdf.org
www.acdf.org
The foundation has been established to alleviate poverty and deprivation, promote social inclusion, and to help build capacity for self-reliance within the African community in the UK, serving as the umbrella organisation for the community.

African Community Involvement Association

Justin Plaza 3, Viceroy Suite 1, 341
London Road, Croydon CR4 4BE
T: 020 8687 2400
F: 020 8646 4363
E: membership@acia.org.uk
www.acia-uk.org
Works towards the relief of sickness among persons with AIDS or HIV infection particularly by the provision of culturally appropriate care and support services for people from the African community.

African Community Partnership

Barnes Wallis Community Centre, 74 Wild Goose Drive, New Cross,
London SE14 5LL
T: 020 7635 9000
F: 020 7635 9600
E: africap@btconnect.com
Employees: 2
Volunteers: 12

African Health Policy Network

Suite B5, West Wing, New City Cloisters,
196 Old Street, London EC1V 9FR
T: 020 7017 8910
F: 020 7017 8919
E: info@ahpn.org
www.ahpn.org
CEO: Francis Kaikumba
The principal object of the network is to alleviate the suffering of persons subject to or affected by HIV and to promote sexual health amongst African communities in the UK and elsewhere by providing training, support, research and information and increasing public awareness of effective policies and good practice.
Employees: 7
Volunteers: 14

African Medical and Research Foundation UK

15-18 White Lion Street, London N1 9PD
T: 020 7269 5520
E: info@amrefuk.org
www.amrefuk.org
CEO: Samara Hammond
The African Medical and Research Foundation (AMREF) is an international African organisation. AMREF was founded in Kenya in 1957 as the Flying Doctors of East Africa. We are now Africa's largest health NGO with programmes in Ethiopia, Kenya, Senegal, South Sudan, South Africa, Tanzania and Uganda. Last year we brought better health to over 12 million people across Africa.
Employees: 18

African Pastors' Fellowship

The Vicarage, Budbrooke,
Warwick CV35 8QL
T: 01926 402926 (also fax)
E: admin@africanpastors.org
www.africanpastors.org
Director: Ian Enticott
APF seeks ways to encourage and support Christian pastors in East Africa so that they can serve God more effectively.
Employees: 2
Volunteers: 0
Regional offices: 0
Income: £100,000 (2011-12)

AFTAID – Aid for the Aged in Distress

Epworth House, 25 City Road,
London EC1Y 1AA
T: 0870 803 1950
F: 0870 803 2128
E: info@aftaid.org.uk
www.aftaid.org.uk
Chair: Susan Elson
AFTAID makes grants for the purchase of essential items to enable older people in need of vital financial assistance maintain independent living in the familiar surroundings of their home. AFTAID provides a safety net when distressed elderly people cannot obtain the help they require from social services, caring agencies or their own family.

After Adoption

Unit 5 Citygate, 5 Blantyre Street,
Manchester, Lancashire M15 4JJ
T: 0161 839 4932
Helpline: 0800 056 8578
F: 0161 832 2242
E: information@afteradoption.org.uk
www.afteradoption.org.uk
Chief Executive: Lynn Charlton
After Adoption is a Voluntary Adoption
Agency and the leading provider of adoption
support services within the UK. We specialise
in finding families for children with complex
needs and deliver a full range of adoption
services from our 7 regional offices across
England and Wales.
Employees: 126
Volunteers: 99
Regional offices: 7
Income: £3,278,562 (2012-13)

Aftermath Support

Aftermath Support, c/o Merseyside
Police, Bromborough Village Road,
Bromborough, Wirral,
Merseyside CH62 7JG
T: 0845 634 4273
F: 0151 777 2583
E: support@aftermathsupport.org.uk
www.aftermathsupport.org.uk
Manager: Jackie Briscoe
Aftermath Support provides emotional and
practical help to all victims of road collisions,
including families and witnesses. Help is
available for those who have been bereaved
as well as those sustaining injury. We offer a
choice of face-to-face and/or telephone
support in Merseyside, Cheshire and
Lancashire (where we have support workers
based) or telephone support in other areas.
Employees: 3
Volunteers: 36
Regional offices: 1

AGCAS

Millenium House, 30 Junction Road,
Sheffield S11 8XB
T: 0114 251 5750
F: 0114 251 5751
E: sarah.nichols@agcas.org.uk
www.agcas.org.uk
AGCAS has established an enviable position
within the UK and beyond as a strong,
collaborative body for HE careers
professionals. Our primary aim is to help our
members improve the accessibility and
quality of careers information, advice and
guidance. We work in partnership with
organisations not only across the UK and

Ireland but also with careers practitioners
throughout the world.
Employees: 5
Volunteers: 1000

Age Concern Central Lancashire

Arkwright House, Stoneygate, Preston,
Lancashire PR1 3XT
T: 01772 552850
E: help@55plus.org.uk
www.55plus.org.uk
Chief Executive: Linda Chivers
Age Concern Central Lancashire is a well
established charity delivering services and
support to meet the needs of local people
who are over 55 and their carers. Our aim is
to support individuals to maintain and
re-establish daily living skills, promoting
independence and encouraging physical and
mental well being.
Employees: 250+
Volunteers: 250+
Regional offices: 1
Income: £2,500,000 (2012-13)

Age Concern Eastbourne

William and Patricia Venton Centre,
Junction Road, Eastbourne, East
Sussex BN21 3QY
T: 01323 638474
E: john.trainor@ageconcerneastbourne.
co.uk
www.ageconcerneastbourne.or.uk
Chief Executive: John Trainor
To enhance and improve the experience in
later life of people in Eastbourne and the
surrounding area through the delivery of first
class activities, services, information and
advice designed to promote wellbeing for all.
Employees: 31
Volunteers: 200
Regional offices: 1
Income: £600,000 (2012-13)

Age Concern Hassocks and District

E: john.rose@achassocks.co.uk

Age Concern Havering

E: r.krishnan@achavering.co.uk

Age UK

Tavis House, 1–6 Tavistock Square,
London WC1H 9NA
T: 0800 169 6565
E: info@ageuk.org.uk
www.ageuk.org.uk

Age UK Portsmouth

The Bradbury Centre, 16 - 18 Kingston
Road, Portsmouth PO1 5RZ
T: 02392 862121
F: 02392 883523
E: kathy.kay@ageukportsmouth.org.uk
www.ageukportsmouth.org.uk
Chief Executive Officer: Dianne Sherlock
Mission: To help adults in Portsmouth &
South East Hampshire enjoy a better quality
of life, with a specific focus on all aspects of
getting older. We assist older people to live
independently and exercise choice. We are
dynamic and driven by results and constantly
deliver for older people. We are passionate
about what we do and care about each
individual. We are experts, authoritative and
quality orientated.
Employees: 70
Volunteers: 30
Regional offices: 0

Age UK Runnymede and Spelthorne

E: tdocker@
ageukrunnymedeandspelthorne.org.uk

AgeCare

47 Great Russell Street,
London WC1B 3PB
T: 020 7637 4577
E: enquiries@agecare.org.uk
www.agecare.org.uk
AgeCare establishes and supports residential
care homes for older people and promotes
education and training of staff employed to
care for older people.

Aid to the Church in Need (UK)

12–14 Benhill Avenue, Sutton,
Surrey SM1 4DA
T: 020 8642 8668
F: 020 8661 6293
E: acn@acnuk.org
www.acnuk.org
UK National Director: Neville Kyrke-
Smith
Aid to the Church in Need is a Catholic
charity supporting the faithful wherever they
are persecuted, oppressed or in pastoral
need.

AIESEC (UK) Ltd

29–31 Cowper Street, London EC2A 4AT
T: 020 7549 1800
E: charlotte@aiesec.co.uk
www.aiesec.co.uk
AIESEC is a 60-year-old global organisation
that develops students into leaders by
running and participating in an international
exchange programme.

Air Cadets

HQ Air Cadets, Royal Air Force, Cranwell,
Sleaford, Lincolnshire NG34 8HB
T: 01400 267632
E: acfo@atc.raf.mod.uk
www.aircadets.org.uk
Promotes and encourages among young
people a practical interest in aviation and in
the Royal Air Force; provides training which
will be useful both in the services and civil life;
fosters the spirit of adventure and develops
the qualities of leadership and good
citizenship.

Air League

Broadway House, Tothill Street,
London SW1H 9NS
T: 020 7222 8463
E: info@airleague.co.uk
www.airleague.co.uk
The Trust exists to promote the aeronautical
education of the young and, through
counselling and the award of flying
scholarships and bursaries, a balloon
scholarship and engineering placements in
industry, to encourage students to follow
careers in aviation and the aerospace
industry.

Airey Neave Trust

PO Box 36800, 5th Floor, 40 Bernard
Street, London WC1N 1WJ
T: 020 7833 4440
E: aireyneavetrust@gmail.com
The advancement of education by the
furtherance of research into personal
freedom under the law of any nation in the
world and the dissemination of the useful
results of such research.

Al-Anon Family Groups UK and Eire

Family Groups Limited, 57B Great Suffolk
Street, London SE1 0BB
T: 020 7407 0215
E: enquiries@al-anonuk.org.uk
www.al-anonuk.org.uk
Al-Anon Family Groups provide support to
anyone whose life is, or has been, affected by
someone else's drinking, regardless of
whether that person is still drinking or not.

Albanian Youth Action

32–36 Loman Street, London SE1 0EE
T: 020 8674 0800
F: 020 8674 0860
E: info@albanianyouthaction.org.uk
www.albanianyouthaction.org.uk
The charity's object and its principal activity
is that of providing assistance to Albanian-
speaking young people, children and families,
as well as unaccompanied minors.
Employees: 7
Volunteers: 6

Albany Trust

239A Balham High Road,
London SW17 7BE
T: 020 8767 1827
E: info@albanytrust.org
www.albanytrust.org.uk
The Trust provides counselling and
psychotherapy, which aim to create a better
climate for more honest and open
relationships. We work with couples and
individuals experiencing difficulties in their
relationship or with their sexuality.
Employees: 1

Albert Kennedy Trust

Unit 305A, Hatton Square, 16/16A
Baldwins Gardens, London EC1N 7RJ
T: 020 7831 6562
F: 020 7405 6929
E: admin@akt.org.uk
www.akt.org.uk
Chief Executive: Tim Sigsworth
The Trust's aim is to ensure that all lesbian,
gay and bisexual young people are able to
live in accepting, supportive and caring
homes by providing a range of services to
meet the individual needs of those who
would otherwise be homeless or in a hostile
environment.
Employees: 22
Volunteers: 200
Regional offices: 3

Albrighton Trust Ltd

Albrighton Moat and Gardens, Blue
House Lane, Albrighton,
Wolverhampton WV3 3FL
T: 01902 372441
F: 01902 374117
E: moat@albrightontrust.org.uk
The Trust provides recreation and training
facilities for those who have need of them by
reason of age, infirmity or disablement, with
the aim of improving their conditions of life.
Employees: 5
Volunteers: 20

Alcohol Concern

64 Leman Street, London E1 8EU
T: 020 7264 0510
F: 020 7488 9213
E: contact@alcoholconcern.org.uk
www.alcoholconcern.org.uk
Chief Executive: Don Shenker
Alcohol Concern is the national agency on
alcohol misuse campaigning for effective
alcohol policy and improved services for
people whose lives are affected by alcohol-
related problems.
Employees: 20
Volunteers: 1
Regional offices: 1

Alcohol Education and Research Council

Room 178, Queen Anne Business Centre,
28 Broadway, London SW1H 9JX
T: 020 7340 9502
F: 020 7340 9505
E: andrea.tilouche@alcoholresearchuk.
org
www.aerc.org.uk
The Council administers a charitable
foundation, the Alcohol Education and
Research Fund, which finances projects
within the UK for education and research
and for novel forms of help for people with
drinking problems, including offenders.
Employees: 3
Volunteers: 15

Alcoholics Anonymous

PO Box 1, 10 Toft Green, York,
Yorkshire YO1 7NJ
T: 01904 644026
F: 01904 629091
E: gso@alcoholics-anonymous.org.uk
www.alcoholics-anonymous.org.uk
To stay sober and to help other alcoholics to
achieve sobriety. A fellowship of men and
women who share their experience, strength
and hope with each other that they may
solve their common problem and help
others to recover from alcoholism. The only
requirement for membership is a desire to
stop drinking. AA has no dues or fees.
Employees: 15
Regional offices: 2

Alexandra Rose Day

5 Mead Lane, Farnham, Surrey GU9 7DY
T: 01252 726171
F: 01252 727559
E: dleclercq@alexandraroseday.org.uk
www.alexandraroseday.org.uk
Chief Executive: Diana le Clercq
Alexandra Rose Day is an umbrella
organisation that helps small and local
charities across England and Wales raise
funds. Any charity that helps children, young
people, disabled people and the elderly can
apply to take part in a Rose Day collection or
Rose Charities Raffle. Participating charities

can also apply for a grant from our Special Appeal Fund.
Employees: 3
Volunteers: 2

Alington House Community Association

4 North Bailey, Durham,
Durham DH1 3ET
T: 01913 864088
E: abpegasus553@gmail.com
www.alingtonhouse.org.uk
Co-ordinator: Alan Barnett
Alington House Community Centre is situated in historical Durham City close to the Cathedral An ideal venue for conferences, seminars, meetings, parties. We have a number of different size rooms to hire and free wi fi available. Parts of the centre are from the 17th century and is a grade 2* listed building and with views of Durham City this makes a fantastic place to hire.
Employees: 2
Volunteers: 15
Income: £90,000 (2012-13)

Alkaptonuria Society

12 High Beeches, Court Hey Roby Road,
Liverpool L16 3GA
T: 0151 737 1862
E: info@alkaptonuria.info
www.alkaptonuria.info
Advances the education of the public into all matters relating to Alkaptonuria disease and its causes.

Allergy UK

Planwell House, Planwell House, Edington Way, Sidcup, Kent DA14 5BH
T: 01322 619898
E: info@allergyuk.org
www.allergyuk.org
Allergy UK is the country's leading national patient information charity dealing with allergy. We provide up-to-date information on all aspects of allergy and food intolerance. Our fully trained helpline staff guide callers to the appropriate allergy specialist.
Employees: 11
Volunteers: 12

Alliance of Healing Associations

Secretary's Office, 21 Mitchell Road,
St Austell, Cornwall PL25 3AX
T: 01726 74843
F: 01726 67148
E: frances.evans@tesco.net
www.alliancehealing.co.uk
President: Ken Baker
The Alliance consists of over 43 different organisations to date. This covers nearly 4,000 accredited spiritual healers and in the region of 1,000 student healers. Our object is the promotion and advancement of spiritual healing. The Alliance was formed in 1976 acquiring charitable status in 1982.
Employees: 1
Volunteers: 3
Regional offices: 4

Almshouse Association

Billingbear Lodge, Maidenhead Road,
Wokingham, Berkshire RG40 5RU
T: 01344 452922
F: 01344 862062
E: naa@almshouses.org
www.almshouses.org
The Association advises members on any matters concerning almshouses and the welfare of the elderly; promotes improvements in almshouses and studies and research into all matters concerning them; makes grants and loans to members; keeps under review existing and proposed legislation affecting almshouses and when necessary takes action; encourages the provision of almshouses.
Employees: 8

Alone in London

188 Kings Cross Road,
London WC1X 9DE
T: 020 7278 4224
F: 020 7837 7943
E: enquiries@als.org.uk
www.als.org.uk
Aims to relieve the homelessness of young people aged under 26; enable young people to live as independently as possible; provide practical and emotional support for young people at risk of homelessness; and bring young people's homelessness to public attention.
Employees: 39
Volunteers: 40

Alopecia UK

5 Titchwell Road, London SW18 3LW
T: 020 8333 1661
E: info@alopeciaonline.org.uk
www.alopeciaonline.org.uk
The aim of Alopecia UK is to provide information, advice and support for people

with experience of alopecia areata, alopecia totalis and alopecia universalis.

Alternatives to Violence Project, Britain

The Grayston Centre, 28 Charles Square N1 6HT
T: 020 7324 4755
E: info@avpbritain.org.uk
www.avpbritain.org.uk
Director: Jennifer Rogers
The Alternatives to Violence Project (AVP) runs a network of trained volunteers, who provide workshops for anyone who wants to find ways of resolving conflict in their lives without resorting to physical or verbal violence. AVP also runs a distance learning course for prisoners anywhere in the UK.
Employees: 5
Volunteers: 147
Regional offices: 6

Alzheimer's Society

Devon House, 58 St Katharine's Way,
London E1W 1JX
T: 020 7423 3500
F: 020 7423 3501
E: enquiries@alzheimers.org.uk
www.alzheimers.org.uk
The Society's principal objectives are the provision of practical support, information and advice to people with Alzheimer's disease and other dementias and those who care for them, and the promotion of research into the disease and other dementias.
Employees: 1200
Regional offices: 260

Amal Trust

15h Bourne House, Westbourne Grove W2 4UA
T: 020 7727 5882
F: 020 7727 5859
E: info@amaltrust.org
www.amaltrust.org
Chairman: Hashim Charif
The object of the charity is to propagate Islam to young Muslims and non-Muslims through classes, lectures and seminars; to guide the youth of today away from bad street culture through Light of the Youth social activities like summer camps, sporting competitions and other social activities.
Employees: 3
Volunteers: 12
Regional offices: 2
Income: £37,460 (2012-13)

Ambition

371 Kennington Lane, London SE11 5QY
T: 020 7793 0787
E: info@ambitionuk.org
www.ambitionuk.org
Chief Executive: Helen Marshall
Ambition is the UK's leading youth club charity. Our members work with over 3,500 youth clubs and youth community projects across the UK, supporting more than 350,000 young people. We develop the services our members need and use our influence to open up exciting opportunities for them.
Employees: 13

Amnesty International Secretariat

1 Easton Street, London WC1X 0DW
T: 020 7413 5500
F: 020 7956 1157
E: amnestyis@amnesty.org
www.amnesty.org
Amnesty International is a worldwide campaigning movement that works to promote all human rights enshrined in the Universal Declaration of Human Rights and other international standards.
Employees: 469
Volunteers: 86
Regional offices: 12

Amnesty International United Kingdom

The Human Rights Action Centre, 17–25 New Inn Yard, London EC2A 3EA
T: 020 7033 1500
F: 020 7033 1503
E: sct@amnesty.org.uk
www.amnesty.org.uk
Campaigns within Britain about Amnesty International's (AI) worldwide concerns. AI is a worldwide human rights movement independent of any government, political faction, ideology, economic interest or religious creed. It works for the: release of people imprisoned for their ethnic origin, sex, colour or beliefs, provided they have neither used nor advocated violence; abolition of torture and the death penalty; fair and early trial of all political prisoners; end to extra-judicial executions and 'disappearances'; observance of the UN Universal Declaration of Human Rights.
Employees: 120
Volunteers: 80
Regional offices: 3

AMSPAR

Tavistock House North, Tavistock Square, London WC1H 9LN
T: 020 7387 6005
F: 020 7388 2648
E: info@amspar.co.uk
www.amspar.com
CEO: Thomas Brownlie
AMSPAR promotes quality and coherence in the delivery of vocational qualifications aimed at medical secretaries, practice managers, administrators and receptionists, and encourages and supports standards of excellence in the pursuit of continuous professional development and lifelong learning.
Employees: 3

Anaphylaxis Campaign

PO Box 275, Farnborough, Hampshire GU14 6XS
T: 01252 546100
Helpline: 01252 542029
F: 01252 377140
E: info@anaphylaxis.org.uk
www.anaphylaxis.org.uk
Chief Executive: Lynne Regent
The campaign fights for people with life-threatening allergies by providing education, information and support, campaigning on their behalf and promoting research.
Employees: 13
Volunteers: 75
Income: £525,000 (2011-12)

Anchor Trust

1st Floor, 408 Strand, London WC2R 0NE
T: 020 7759 9107
E: office.support-lon@anchor.org.uk
www.anchor.org.uk
The Anchor Trust offers relief to older people, together with those in need by reason of physical or mental frailty, illness or disability, through the provision of housing, amenities and services for their accommodation, care, support, relief and treatment.

Ancient Monuments Society

St Ann's Vestry Hall, 2 Church Entry, London EC4V 5HB
T: 020 7236 3934
E: office@ancientmonumentssociety.org.uk
www.ancientmonumentssociety.org.uk
Secretary: Matthew Saunders
Founded in 1924 to campaign for historic buildings of all ages and all types.
Employees: 2
Volunteers: 30

Andover Neighbourcare

14 Union St, Andover, Hampshire SP10 1PA
T: 01264 351579
E: neighbourcare3@andover.co.uk
www.andoverneighbourcare.co.uk
General Manager: Pam Delderfield
Remit of Andover Neighbourcare: To relieve persons resident in the area of benefit who are in need by reason of age, disability, sickness or poverty by the provision of such voluntary care work as may be charitable. Andover Neighbourcare offers many services to predominantly older people in Andover and surrounding villages. Services include: transport to doctors, hospitals and clubs; cleaning; gardening; shopping; lunch club; drop-in centre; health and general information; minibus hire; outings and computer lessons.
Employees: 6
Volunteers: 120
Regional offices: 1
Income: £150,000 (2012-13)

Andy Cole Children's Foundation

Proactive Sports, Caulfield House, 11–13 Manchester Road, Wilmslow, Cheshire SK9 1BQ
T: 01625 536411
E: info@andycolecf.com
www.andycolecf.com
The worldwide relief of children and young people who are in conditions of need, hardship or distress, or who are sick; and the worldwide advancement of education.

Angel Foundation

Angel House, Borough Road, Sunderland, Tyne and Wear SR1 1HW
T: 0191 568 0800
E: tjordan@god.tv
www.god.tv
Head of Network Development: Tevon Jordan
Employees: 72
Volunteers: 30

Angelman Syndrome Support Group

15 Place Crescent, Waterlooville, Hampshire PO7 5UR
T: 0300 999 0102
E: assert@angelmanuk.org
The group promotes a better understanding of Angelman Syndrome for both families and professionals; removes the feeling of isolation from parents by keeping in regular contact via newsletters; assists any future Angelman Syndrome children and their families.

Anglo Jewish Association

Suite 21, 58 Acacia Road,
London NW8 6AG
T: 020 7449 0909
E: info@anglojewish.org.uk
www.anglojewish.co.uk
The Association promotes the education of Jews and other persons in Jewish matters. Membership of the Association is open to all British citizens who wish to retain their Jewishness, and comprises a representative cross-section of the Anglo-Jewish community.

Angolan Civic Communities Alliance (ACCA)

C/O Sangat Advice Centre, Sancroft Road, Harrow, Middlesex HA3 7NS
T: 020 8423 3003
Helpline: 07940 556897
F: 020 8864 8881
E: acca.enquiries@gmail.com
Executive Director: Alex da Costa
The Angolan Civic Communities Alliance (ACCA) is one of the main drop-in centres for Angolan refugees and migrants and for other refugees and migrants from the Portuguese-speaking communities in Britain.
Employees: 2
Volunteers: 25
Income: £3,500 (2011-12)

Animal Rescue Charity

Foxdells Sanctuary, Foxdells Lane, Rye Street, Bishop's Stortford, Hertfordshire CM23 2JG
T: 01279 501547
E: support@animalrescue.org.uk
www.animalrescuecharity.org.uk
The charity provides a safe and caring environment for neglected and unwanted domestic animals and helps and rehabilitates wildlife wherever possible.
Employees: 10
Volunteers: 50
Regional offices: 1

Animal Welfare Foundation

7 Mansfield Street, London W1G 9NQ
T: 020 7908 6375
E: bva-awf@bva.co.uk
www.bva-awf.org.uk
Chairman: Tiffany Hemming
The Animal Welfare Foundation is committed to improving the welfare of animals through veterinary science, education and debate. We apply the knowledge, skill and compassion of veterinary surgeons in an effective way by funding a variety of projects and activities.
Employees: 2
Volunteers: 30
Income: £209,473 (2012-13)

Ann Craft Trust

University of Nottingham, University Park, Nottingham NG7 2RD
T: 0115 951 5400
F: 0115 951 5232
E: ann-craft-trust@nottingham.ac.uk
www.anncrafttrust.org
CEO: Deborah Kitson
The Trust responds nationally to the needs and concerns of staff working in the statutory, voluntary and independent sectors in the interests of adults and children with learning disabilities who may be at risk of abuse. It improves working practices through research, training, publications, information and advice.

Anna Freud Centre

12 Maresfield Gardens NW3 5SU
T: 020 7794 2313
E: andrew.kaponi@annafreud.org
www.annafreudcentre.org
Head of Finance: Andrew Kaponi
Caring for young minds through training, treatment and research.
Employees: 200
Volunteers: 30
Regional offices: 3

Anne Frank Trust UK

Star House, 104–108 Grafton Road, London NW5 4BA
T: 020 7284 5858
E: info@annefrank.org.uk
www.annefrank.org.uk
Drawing on the power of Anne Frank's diary, we aim to inspire and educate a new generation to build a world of mutual respect, compassion and social justice.

Anthony Nolan Trust

2–3 Heathgate Place, 75–87 Agincourt Road, London NW3 2NU
T: 020 7284 1234
E: info@anthonynolan.org
www.anthonynolan.org.uk
The Trust maintains a register of 350,000 volunteer bone marrow donors who are prepared to give some of their marrow to save the life of another person, irrespective of country, colour, race or creed. It carries out research into the causes of failure in bone marrow transplants when donor and recipient appear to be matched.

Anti-Slavery International

Thomas Clarkson House, Unit 4 The Stableyard, Broomgrove Road, London SW9 9TL
T: 020 7501 8920
F: 020 7738 4110
E: info@antislavery.org
www.antislavery.org
Director: Aidan McQuade
Anti-Slavery International, founded in 1839, is committed to eliminating all forms of slavery throughout the world. Slavery, servitude and forced labour deny basic dignity and fundamental human rights. Anti-Slavery International works to end these abuses by campaigning for slavery's eradication, exposing current cases, supporting the initiatives of local organisations to release people and pressing for more effective implementation of international laws against slavery.
Employees: 24
Volunteers: 10

Antiquarian Horological Society

New House, High Street, Ticehurst, East Sussex TN5 7AL
T: 01580 200155
E: secretary@ahsoc.org
www.ahsoc.org
A learned Society founded to encourage the study and conservation of timepieces.
Employees: 2

Anxiety Care UK

Redbridge Concern for Mental Health, 98–100 Ilford Lane, Ilford, Essex IG1 2LD
T: 07552 877219
E: admin@anxietycare.org.uk
www.anxietycare.org.uk
Anxiety Care UK works with clients towards recovery from anxiety and provides cognitive behavioural therapy (CBT), together with support, information and encouragement while undergoing this therapy. It promotes the reality of anxiety disorders, and encourages those affected to use their strengths to work towards recovery and to maintain it.

Anxiety UK (formerly National Phobics Society)

c/o Zion Community Resource Centre,
339 Stretford Road, Hulme,
Manchester M15 4ZY
T: 08444 775774
F: 0161 226 7727
E: info@anxietyuk.org.uk
www.anxietyuk.org.uk
Chief Executive: Nicky Lidbetter
Anxiety UK is a user-led charity for those
suffering from anxiety disorders, including
panic attacks, phobias, obsessive/compulsive
disorders, social anxiety and other associated
anxiety disorders. We provide a helpline
service offering information, support and
understanding, run by sufferers and ex-
sufferers of anxiety disorders. We provide
information on self-help groups in the UK
and provide self-help resources, factsheets
and a quarterly magazine. Therapy is
available across the UK for members face-to-
face and over the phone.
Employees: 6
Volunteers: 500
Regional offices: 1

Apex Charitable Trust Limited

Unit 1, Ruskin Ltd, Ruskin Drive, St
Helens, Merseyside WA10 6RP
T: 01744 612898
E: sthelens@apextrust.com
www.apextrust.com
Interim Chief Executive: Brendan Tarring
The Trust aims to help people with criminal
records obtain appropriate jobs or achieve
self-employment by providing them with the
skills they need in the labour market, and by
working with employers to break down
barriers to their employment. Provision only
available on the Merseyside area.
Employees: 4
Volunteers: 0
Regional offices: 1

Apex-Works

E: srowe@apex-works.co.uk

Apostleship of the Sea

National Headquarters, Stella Maris,
Herald House, Lamb's Passage, Bunhill
Row, London EC1Y 8LE
T: 020 7588 8285
F: 020 7588 8280
E: info@apostleshipofthesea.org.uk
www.aos-usa.org
Promotes the spiritual and material welfare
of seafarers and their families.
Employees: 15
Volunteers: 30

Aquaterra Leisure

50 Isledon Road
T: 020 7689 9841
E: kevin.conway@aquaterra.org
www.aquaterra.org
Trust Secretary: Kevin Conway

Arbours Association Limited

6 Church Lane, London N8 7BU
T: 020 8340 7646
E: info@arboursassociation.org
www.arboursassociation.org
The Arbours Association provides long-term
residential accommodation and
psychotherapeutic support for those in
emotional distress. It also offers a low-to-high
cost pyschotherapy service for members of
the public. It also runs the Arbours
Association Training Programme for those
wishing to qualify as psychoanalytic
psychotherapists, with a postgraduate
professional support organisation (AAP).
Employees: 20

ARC

ARC House, Marsden Street, Chesterfield,
Derbyshire S40 1JY
T: 01246 555043
F: 01246 555045
E: contact.us@arcuk.org.uk
www.arcuk.org.uk
ARC is a UK-wide umbrella body for
providers of services to people with a
learning disability. We promote best practice
and support good-quality provision by
training, projects and partnerships between
providers. We represent providers' views at
local, regional, national and European levels.
We have a large training consortium and
hold UK and national conferences to bring
providers together to promote best practice
and share problems and solutions.
Employees: 55
Regional offices: 4

ARC (Antenatal Results and Choices)

345 City Road, London EC1V 1LR
T: 020 7713 7356
Helpline: 08450 772290
E: info@arc-uk.org
www.arc-uk.org
Director: Jane Fisher
ARC offers information and support to
parents who are: making decisions before,
during and after the antenatal testing
process; told that their unborn baby has an
abnormality; having to make difficult
decisions about continuing the pregnancy;
having to make difficult decisions about
ending the pregnancy; dealing with the

consequences of their decisions. ARC also
works with health professionals, providing
training, support and publications.
Employees: 4.4
Volunteers: 43

Architects Benevolent Society

43 Portland Place, London W1B 1QH
T: 020 7580 2823
E: help@absnet.org.uk
www.absnet.org.uk
The Society relieves persons engaged or
formerly engaged in the practice of
architecture, and the wives, widows, children
and other dependants of such persons being
in necessitous circumstances.

Architectural Heritage Fund

Alhambra House 27–31, Charing Cross
Road, London WC2H 0AU
T: 020 7925 0199
F: 020 7930 0295
E: ahf@ahfund.org.uk
www.ahfund.org.uk
Promotes the permanent preservation of
historic buildings in the UK by providing
advice, information and financial assistance
in the form of grants and loans for projects
undertaken by building preservation trusts
and other charities.

Army Cadet Force Association

Holderness House, 51–61 Clifton Street,
London EC2A 4DW
T: 020 7426 8370
E: enquiries@armycadets.com
www.armycadets.com
The association develops among its
members the qualities of good citizenship
and the spirit of service to Queen, country
and local community, and gives
encouragement and training to those
considering a career in the regular army or
service in the reserve forces. The ACF is a
voluntary youth movement, sponsored
principally by the army, and takes part in both
military and community activities.

Army Families Federation

IDL 414, Floor 1, Zone 7, Ramilies Building,
Marlborough Lines, Monxton Road,
Andover SP11 8HJ
T: 01264 382326
F: 01264 382327
E: us@aff.org.uk
www.aff.org.uk
The AFF is a unique two-way
communications link between the British
Army and its families. As a registered charity
with branches in Northern Ireland, Germany
and Cyprus, its objectives are to voice the
views and concerns of army families about

their way of life, helping to get things changed for the better.
Employees: 79
Regional offices: 4

ARNI Institute

PO Box 68, Lingfield, Surrey RH7 6QQ
Helpline: 07712 211378
E: tom@arni.uk.com
www.arni.uk.com
Secretary: Dr Tom Balchin
The Institute aims to encourage and advance the rehabilitation of those suffering from the effects of stroke and other brain injuries that have resulted in partial paralysis.
Volunteers: 43
Regional offices: 1
Income: £13,790 (2011-12)

Arthritic Association

1 Upperton Gardens, Eastbourne, East Sussex BN21 2AA
T: 01323 416550
Helpline: 0800 652 3188
E: info@arthriticassociation.org.uk
www.arthriticassociation.org.uk
The Association aims to support those suffering from the various forms of arthritis through a natural programme. The programme includes an individually tailored eating plan, physical therapy and exercise. Non-means-tested grants may be available to those following the programme. The programme has been known to reduce the symptoms of arthritis and to lessen the pain.

Arthritis and Musculoskeletal Alliance

Bride House, 18–20 Bride Lane, London EC4Y 8EE
T: 020 7842 0910
F: 020 7242 3277
E: arma@rheumatology.org.uk
The Arthritis and Musculoskeletal Alliance (ARMA) is the UK umbrella association bringing together support groups, professional bodies and research organisations in the field of arthritis and other musculoskeletal conditions.
Employees: 2
Volunteers: 45

Arthritis Care

18 Stephenson Way, London NW1 2HD
T: 020 7380 6500
Helpline: 0808 800 4050
F: 020 7380 6502
E: peter@arthritiscare.org.uk
www.arthritiscare.org.uk
Chief Executive: Neil Betteridge
Arthritis Care is a user-centred and user-led charity, with people with all types of arthritis at the heart of what we do. We are the voice of people with arthritis and their families, providing high-quality information and support to enable people living with arthritis to make positive and practical changes to their lives.
Employees: 120
Volunteers: 200
Regional offices: 5

Arthritis Research UK

Copeman House, St Mary's Court, St Mary's Gate, Chesterfield, Derbyshire S41 7TD
T: 0300 790 0400
F: 01246 558007
E: enquiries@arthritisresearchuk.org
www.arthritisresearchuk.org
Raises funds and finances research into the causes and cure of the rheumatic diseases; encourages the teaching of rheumatology to medical and paramedical under- and postgraduates; stimulates public authorities to provide better treatment facilities.
Employees: 150
Volunteers: 5000
Regional offices: 4

Arthrogryposis Group (TAG)

PO Box 1199, Spalding PE11 9EY
Helpline: 0800 028 4447
E: info@taguk.org.uk
www.taguk.org.uk
The Arthrogryposis Group (TAG) is the only organisation in the UK providing contact, information and support to people with Arthrogryposis and their families. TAG provides members with information about Arthrogryposis and can put them in touch with other families. TAG also provides an information service for professionals involved in the management of the condition. TAG encourages public awareness of Arthrogryposis and also supports research.
Employees: 1
Volunteers: 30

Arthur McDougall Fund

6 Chancel Street, London SE1 0UX
T: 020 7620 1080
F: 020 7928 1258
E: admin@mcdougall.org.uk
Aims to advance knowledge and encourage study and research in: political and economic science, the functions of government and the services provided to the community by public and voluntary organisations; methods of election of, and the selection and government of, representative organisations, whether national, civic, commercial, industrial or social.
Employees: 1
Volunteers: 10

Arthur Rank Centre

Stoneleigh Park, Kenilworth, Warwickshire CV8 2LZ
T: 024 7685 3060
F: 024 7641 4808
E: claireh@arthurrankcentre.org.uk
www.arthurrankcentre.org.uk
CEO: Jerry Marshall
The ARC is committed to helping create sustainable vibrant rural communities. We have a particular concern for the 900,000 rural households living in poverty, those who feel isolated, and families experiencing difficulties. We offer support directly and as the national churches' rural resource unit and work to equip the UK's 13,000 rural churches, helping them bring physical, social and spiritual transformation to communities. Our services are accessible, affordable and open to all.
Employees: 7
Volunteers: 2

Article 19

60 Farringdon Road, London EC1R 3GA
T: 020 7324 2500
E: info@article19.org
www.article19.org
Article 19 is an international human rights organisation that works to promote, protect and develop freedom of expression, including access to information and the means of communication.

Arts and Business

137 Shepherdess Walk, London N1 7RQ
T: 020 7566 6650
E: jonathan.tuchner@artsandbusiness.org.uk
www.artsandbusiness.org.uk
Arts and Business strengthens communities by developing creative partnerships between business and the arts.
Employees: 114
Regional offices: 13

Arts Council England

14 Great Peter Street,
London SW1P 3NQ
T: 0845 300 6200
F: 0161 934 4426
E: enquiries@artscouncil.org.uk
www.artscouncil.org.uk
Arts Council England is the national development agency for the arts in England, distributing public money from government and the National Lottery. We believe in the transforming power of the arts - power to change the lives of people throughout the country. Our ambition is to place the arts at the heart of national life, reflecting the country's rich and diverse cultural identity as only the arts can. We want people throughout England to experience arts activities of the highest quality. We believe that access to the arts goes hand in hand with excellence.

Artswork

Unit 26, Bargate Shopping Centre, East Bargate, Southampton,
Hampshire SO14 1HF
T: 02380 332491
E: alice@artswork.org.uk
www.artswork.org.uk
Chief Executive: Virginia Haworth-Galt
Artswork is the national, independent youth arts development agency, committed to making a difference to the lives of young people at risk aged 12–25. We do this in two ways: direct project work, providing creative opportunities for young people; delivering professional development resources for a wide range of professionals working with young people.
Employees: 10
Volunteers: 20

Arun Co-ordinated Community Transport

Unit S3, Rudford Industrial Estate, Ford Road, Arundel, West Sussex BN18 0BD
T: 01903 723584
F: 01903 718631
E: manager@arun-cct.org
www.arun-cct.org
Chairman of Trustees: Graham Paull
Arun Co-Ordinated Community Transport is a registered not for profit, charity based in Littlehampton that offers a range of transport solutions for the residents of the local community within the Arun area who have difficulty using public transport due to a mobility or visual disability, illness, frailty, age or other impairment.
Employees: 5
Volunteers: 35
Regional offices: 1
Income: £212,779 (2012-13)

ARVAC Association for Research in the Voluntary and Community Sector

c/o School of Business and Social Sciences, Roehampton University, Southlands College, 80 Roehampton Lane, London SW15 5SL
F: 020 7704 9995
E: arvac@arvac.org.uk
www.arvac.org.uk
ARVAC promotes effective community action through research.
Employees: 5
Volunteers: 1

ASDAN

Wainbrook House, Huddsvale Road, St George, Bristol BS5 7HY
T: 0117 941 1126
F: 0117 935 1112
E: sallymurphy@asdan.org.uk
www.asdan.co.uk
ASDAN's aim is the advancement of education, by providing opportunities for all learners to develop their personal and social attributes and levels of achievement through the use and attainment of ASDAN resources and awards, and the relief of poverty, where poverty inhabits such opportunities for learners.
Employees: 40

Asha Projects

13 Shrubbery Road, London SW16 2AS
T: 07870 570861
F: 020 8677 9920
E: admin@asha.org.uk
Asha means 'hope'. Our mission is to empower Asian women to live independently and achieve the goals that they have set for themselves.
Employees: 9
Volunteers: 2

Ashoka (UK) Trust

15 Old Ford Road, Bethnal Green, London E2 9PJ
T: 020 8980 9416
E: infouk@ashoka.org
www.ashoka.org
UK Director: Mark Cheng
Ashoka contributes to the social progress of developing countries by encouraging and empowering outstanding individuals in those countries who have shown they have the capacity and character to achieve substantial change, in a wide variety of fields, through the organisations they lead.
Regional offices: Bethnal Green, Greater London

Asian Family Counselling Service

Suite 51, The Lodge, Windmill Place, 2-4 Windmill Lane, Southall UB2 4NJ
T: 020 8571 3933 (also fax)
E: afcs@btconnect.com
www.asianfamilycounselling.org
Director: Kulbir Randhawa
Asian Family Counselling Service provides family, marital and individual counselling for the Asian community resident in the UK. Counsellors offer caring, personal and confidential counselling in the client's language with an awareness of their cultural and ethnic backgrounds.
Employees: 8
Volunteers: 6
Regional offices: 2
Income: £197,144 (2012-13)

Asian Foundation for Help

2 Ambassador House, Wolseley Road, Harrow, Middlesex HA3 5RT
T: 020 8861 6060
F: 020 8515 2292
E: ketan@asianfoundation.org.uk
www.asianfoundation.org.uk
Chairman: Hitesh Popat
A voluntary international organisation raising funds to help the poor and needy.
Volunteers: 20
Regional offices: 3
Income: £206,584 (2010-11)

Asian People's Disability Alliance Ltd

Daycare And Development Centre, Alric Avenue, off Bruce Road, Harlesden, London NW10 8RA
T: 020 8830 4220
F: 020 8830 3890
E: apdmcha@aol.com
www.apda.org.uk
CEO Joint: Zeenat Jeewa
Aims to ensure that Asian people with disabilities are accorded full status, rights and facilities to enable them to participate fully and represent their own interests in all areas of society.
Employees: 15
Volunteers: 10
Regional offices: 1

ASPIRE

National Training Centre, Wood Lane,
Stanmore, Middlesex HA7 4AP
T: 020 8954 5759
F: 020 8420 6352
E: info@aspire.org.uk
www.aspire.org.uk
ASPIRE works with people with spinal cord injury to create opportunity, choice and independence. ASPIRE offers practical support and innovation from the moment of their injury for the rest of their lives. Its founding principle is and remains integration. Everything that the charity does is geared towards creating an environment, whether it be in the home, the office or the world of sport and leisure, where the barriers that divide able bodied and disabled people are removed.
Employees: 60
Volunteers: 20

ASSERT

PO Box 4962, Nuneaton CV11 9FD
T: 0300 999 0102
F: 01268 415940
E: assert@angelmanuk.org
www.angelmanuk.org
Aims to relieve the need of those with Angelman Syndrome and their families, to advance the education of the public in Angelman Syndrome and to promote research into Angelman Syndrome.
Volunteers: 10

Assist UK

Redbank House, 4 St Chad's Street,
Manchester M8 8QA
T: 0161 832 9757
E: general.info@assist-uk.org
www.assist-uk.org
CEO: Alan Norton
Assist UK is an umbrella organisation for a UK-wide network of locally situated disabled/independent living centres. Most centres include a permanent exhibition of products and equipment that provide people with opportunities to see and try products and equipment and get information and advice from professional staff about what might suit them best.
Employees: 5
Volunteers: 18
Regional offices: 41
Income: £201,815 (2011-12)

Associated Board of the Royal Schools of Music

24 Portland Place, London W1B 1LU
T: 020 7467 8223 (also fax)
E: abrsm@abrsm.ac.uk
www.abrsm.ac.uk
Aims to advance the arts, science and skills of music, speech and drama throughout the UK and overseas.
Employees: 95
Volunteers: 250

Associated Country Women of the World

Mary Sumner House, 24 Tufton Street,
London SW1P 3RB
T: 020 7799 3875
F: 020 7340 9950
E: info@acww.org.uk
www.acww.org.uk
This is an international membership organisation that aims to raise the standard of living of rural women and their families through education, training, support and community development programmes. It gives women a voice at international level through its links with United Nations agencies and liaises with other NGOs. It has an administrative office in London and organises a global conference every three years.
Employees: 9
Volunteers: 50

Association for Child and Adolescent Mental Health

St Saviour's House, 39–41 Union Street,
London SE1 1SD
T: 020 7403 7458
F: 020 7403 7081
E: ingrid.king@acamh.org.uk
www.acpp.org.uk
The Association undertakes the scientific study of all matters concerning the mental health and development of children, young people and their families.
Employees: 7

Association for Continence Advice

Fitwise Management Ltd, Blackburn House, Redhouse Road,
Bathgate EH47 7AQ
T: 01506 811077
E: aca@fitwise.co.uk
www.aca.uk.com
The Association acts as a multidisciplinary forum for healthcare professionals with a special interest in the promotion of continence and the management of incontinence and to educate professionals about the prevention and treatment of incontinence.

Association for Family Therapy

7 Executive Suite, St James Court,
Wilderspool Causeway,
Warrington WA4 6PS
T: 01925 444414
E: s.kennedy@aft.org.uk
www.aft.org.uk
Chair: Jeanette Neden
AFT's key aim is to benefit the public by working to continually improve standards of professional family therapy and systemic practice. Members promote family therapy through practice, training, management and research. AFT provides the Journal and Context magazine for its members and a number of conferences.
Employees: 4
Volunteers: 30

Association for Glycogen Storage Disease (UK)

Old Hambledon Racecourse, Sheardley Lane, Droxford, Hampshire SO32 3QY
T: 0300 123 2790
E: wendy.griffiths@agsd.org.uk
www.agsd.org.uk
Chairman: Andrew Wakelin
The Association is a contact and support group for all persons affected by some form of glycogen storage disease. It also creates public awareness of GSD and acts as a focus for educational, scientific and charitable activities related to this disorder.
Employees: 2
Regional offices: 1

Association for Humanistic Psychology

BM Box 3582, London WC1N 3XX
T: 0845 707 8506
E: admin@ahpb.org
www.ahpb.org
The Association educates the public about humanistic psychology, disseminates alternative ways of dealing with human problems, both personal and societal and encourages the development of the individual to his/her full potential.
Volunteers: 6
Income: £25,000 (2010-11)

Association for Language Learning

University of Leicester, University Road, Leicestershire LE1 7RH
T: 0116 229 7600
F: 0116 223 1488
E: info@all-languages.org.uk
www.all-languages.org.uk
Director: Linda Parker
The aims of the association are to support members' professional work and development; to develop policies that reflect views and interests of members; to promote improved standards of language teaching and learning; and to encourage understanding of the importance of languages, communication and cultural issues.
Employees: 4
Volunteers: 50+

Association for Learning Technology

Gipsy Lane, Headington, Oxford OX3 0BP
T: 01865 484125
F: 01865 484165
E: admin@alt.ac.uk
www.alt.ac.uk
Chief Executive: Maren Deepwell
ALT is a professional and scholarly Association that seeks to bring together all those with an interest in the use of learning technology. We represent and support our members and provide services for them; facilitate collaboration between practitioners, researchers, and policy makers; spread good practice in the use of learning technology; raise the profile of research in learning technology and support the professionalisation of learning technologists.
Employees: 7
Volunteers: 40
Regional offices: 1

Association for Multiple Endocrine Neoplasia Disorder

The Warehouse, Draper Street, Southborough, Tunbridge Wells TN4 0PG
T: 01892 516076
E: jo.grey@amend.org.uk
www.amend.org.uk
CEO and Chair of Trustees: Jo Grey
AMEND is a UK registered charity committed to supporting all those affected by multiple endocrine neoplasia (MEN) and its associated growths.
Volunteers: 20
Income: £53,000 (2011-12)

Association for Perioperative Practice

Daisy Ayris House, 42 Freemans Way, Harrogate, North Yorkshire HG3 1DH
T: 01423 881300
Helpline: 01423 880997
E: stephanie.oates@afpp.org.uk
www.afpp.org.uk
Chief Executive Officer: Dawn Stott
Improving patient care in perioperative practice.
Employees: 22

Association for Physical Education

Room 17, Bredon, University of Worcester, Henwick Grove, Worcester WR2 6AJ
T: 01905 855584
E: enquiries@afpe.org.uk
www.afpe.org.uk
The Association for Physical Education (afPE) is committed to being the UK representative organisation of choice for people and agencies delivering or supporting the delivery of physical education in schools and in the wider community.
Employees: 10

Association for Post-Natal Illness

145 Dawes Road, Fulham, London SW6 7EB
T: 020 7386 0868
E: info@apni.org
www.apni.org
The Association advises and supports women suffering from post-natal depression.
Employees: 7
Volunteers: 300+
Regional offices: 1

Association for Project Management

Ibis House, Regent Park, Summerleys Road, Princes Risborough, Buckinghamshire HP27 9LE
T: 0845 458 1944
F: 0845 458 8807
E: john.salisbury@apm.org.uk
www.apm.org.uk
Chief Executive: Andrew Bragg
Association for Project Management (APM) is the largest independent body of its kind in Europe, a professional membership association with the mission to develop and promote the professional disciplines of project and programme management for the public benefit. APM currently forms a community of around 19,500 individual and 500 corporate members in all sectors and industries, including public sector, civil

engineering, financial services, retail, logistics, science and arts.
Employees: 60
Volunteers: 400
Income: £6,000,000 (2011-12)

Association for Science Education

College Lane, Hatfield AL10 9AA
T: 01707 283000
F: 01707 266532
E: info@ase.org.uk
www.ase.org.uk
Chief Executive: Annette Smith
The Association provides science teachers with a forum for discussion, along with other benefits such as journals, book sales service, publishing and indemnity insurance. Run by teachers for teachers.
Employees: 30
Volunteers: 50

Association for the Study of Obesity

PO Box 410, Deal, Kent CT14 4AL
T: 01304 367788
E: catherine.stone@aso.org.uk
www.aso.org.uk
Promotes medical research into the causes, prevention and treatment of obesity. It facilitates contact between individuals and organisations interested in any aspect of the problem of obesity and body weight regulation. An organisation for health professionals.

Association for the Teaching of the Social Sciences

Bailey Suite, Palatine House, Belmont Business Park, Durham, County Durham DH1 1TW
T: 0191 383 0839
Helpline: 0191 383 0782
E: enquiries@britsoc.org.uk
www.atss.org.uk
Provides opportunities for those teaching and researching in the social sciences to meet so that they may develop and share ideas and strategies for the promotion and delivery of the teaching of social sciences.
Employees: 2
Volunteers: 30

Association of Blind and Partially Sighted Teachers and Students

BM Box 6727, London WC1N 3XX
T: 0117 966 4839
E: chairperson@abapstas.org.uk
www.abapstas.org.uk
Provides support to visually impaired teachers and students and those with an

interest in education or training and to campaign on their behalf.

Association of Blind Piano Tuners

31 Wyre Crescent, Darwen,
Lancashire BB3 0JG
T: 0844 736 1976
E: abpt@uk-piano.org
www.uk-piano.org
The aims of the association are to further the interests and raise the status of blind and partially sighted piano tuners, give them all possible assistance in their work, and to maintain or raise the standard of service given by blind piano tuners.

Association of Breastfeeding Mothers

PO Box 207, Bridgwater,
Somerset TA6 7YT
T: 0844 412 2948
Helpline: 0300 330 5453
E: info@abm.me.uk
www.abm.me.uk
We offer mother-to-mother breastfeeding support and up-to-date breastfeeding information.
Volunteers: 100

Association of British Credit Unions

T: 0161 832 3694
E: info@abcul.org

Association of Charitable Foundations

Central House, 14 Upper Woburn Place,
London WC1H 0AE
T: 020 7255 4499
F: 020 7255 4496
E: acf@acf.org.uk
www.acf.org.uk
Chief Executive: David Emerson
ACF is the leading membership association for grant-making charities in the UK. We provide help and support for the distinctive role of grant-making trusts and foundations, while respecting – and protecting – their independence. Through our services to members we provide a framework in which trusts and foundations can learn from each others' experiences, explore matters of common concern and achieve good practice in grant-making.
Employees: 6

Association of Charitable Organisations

Acorn House, 314-320 Gray's Inn Road,
London WC1X 8DP
T: 020 7255 4480
F: 020 7255 4496
E: info@aco.uk.net
www.aco.uk.net
Chief Executive: Dominic Fox
The Association of Charitable Organisations (ACO) is the national UK umbrella body for charities that give grants and welfare support to individuals in need. ACO provides support to its members through networking, raising standards, promoting good practice, lobbying and campaigning, information, advice and online services.
Employees: 2

Association of Charity Independent Examiners

The Gatehouse, White Cross, South Road,
Lancaster, Lancashire LA1 4XQ
T: 01524 34892 (also fax)
E: info@acie.org.uk
www.acie.org.uk
ACIE Director: Fiona Gordon
Promotes the greater effectiveness of charities in the UK in the achievement of their charitable objectives by: providing advice, support and training to any person acting or wishing to act as an independent examiner; promoting and maintaining high standards of practice and professional conduct; and providing charity trustees with information in connection with the selection and appointment of independent examiners.
Employees: 2
Volunteers: 600
Income: £61,981 (2012-13)

Association of Chief Executives of Voluntary Organisations

Regents Wharf, 8 All Saints Street,
London N1 9RL
T: 020 7014 4600
E: info@acevo.org.uk
www.acevo.org.uk
Chief Executive: Stephen Bubb
ACEVO is the only professional association for voluntary sector CEOs in England and Wales. We connect, develop, support and represent over 2,000 members. Over the last 20 years, our aim has been to increase the professionalism of our members and raise standards across the voluntary sector.
Employees: 30
Regional offices: 2

Association of Children's Hospices

E: info@childhospice.org.uk

Association of Community Based Business Advice

2nd Floor, 200A Pentonville Road,
London N1 9JP
T: 020 7832 5842
E: armandopardo@
communitybasedbusiness.co.uk
www.acbba.org.uk
Executive Director: Armando Pardo
We provide business training, advice and mentoring support to people interested in small business with a focus on self-employment. Our aim is to promote the establishment of sustainable enterprises that can lift entrepreneurs out of poverty.
Employees: 3

Association of Dance Therapists (International)

Flat 1, Penlee, Lindridge Road,
Babbacombe, Torquay, Devon TQ1 3SD
T: 01803 314366
E: deniseputtock@yahoo.co.uk
www.schoolofdancetherapy.com
Director of Studies: Denise Puttock
We are a small non-profit-making organisation – our School of Dance Therapy is currently offering training to work with children who may be at risk of poverty and in need of some extra support. We aim to give them a better quality of life and a chance to develop their natural artistic talents.
Volunteers: 6

Association of Disabled Professionals

The Vassall Centre, Gill Avenue, Gill Avenue, Bristol BS16 2QQ
T: 0844 445 7123
E: advice@adwuk.org
www.adwuk.org
Chief executive: Andy Rickell
ADP exists to improve the educational/employment opportunities available to disabled people, allowing disabled people to retain employment commensurate with their abilities and to participate fully in the everyday life of society. It aims to improve public knowledge of the capabilities and needs of disabled people. ADP provides employment advice, information and peer support to disabled people. Also operates the Disabled Entrepreneurs' Network

providing advice and support to self-employed disabled people www.disabled-entrepreneurs.net. It is part of ADWUK.

Association of Gardens Trusts

70 Cowcross Street, London EC1M 6EJ
T: 020 7251 2610 (also fax)
E: co-ordinator@agt.org.uk
www.gardenstrusts.org.uk
The national charity caring for the future of our historic gardens and landscapes. The aims of the Association are to provide support for county gardens trusts, and to promote a proper understanding of the importance of parks and gardens at a local and national level.
Employees: 1
Volunteers: 360
Regional offices: 36

Association of Governing Bodies of Independent Schools

3 Codicote Road, Welwyn,
Hertfordshire AL6 9LY
T: 01438 840730
F: 0560 343 2632
E: comms@agbis.org.uk
www.agbis.org.uk
General Secretary: Stuart Westley
The Association of Governing Bodies of Independent Schools supports and advises governing bodies of schools in the independent sector under the umbrella of ISC. The objectives of the Association are the advancement of education in independent schools and the promotion of good governance in such schools.
Employees: 3

Association of Interchurch Families

27 Tavistock Square, London WC1H 9HH
T: 020 3384 2947
E: info@interchurchfamilies.org.uk
www.interchurchfamilies.org.uk
Executive Officer: Doral Hayes
The association is a focus for all concerned with marriages between committed Christians of different church allegiances, and more widely with 'mixed marriages'. It promotes Christian unity and offers a support network for interchurch families (usually where one partner is Roman Catholic) and a voice for such families in the churches.
Employees: 2
Volunteers: 50
Income: £40,000 (2010-11)

Association of Jewish Ex-Servicemen and Women

Shield House, Harmony Way, Hendon,
London NW4 2BZ
T: 020 8202 2323
E: headoffice@ajex.org.uk
www.ajex.org.uk
AJEX is the only UK Jewish Charity totally devoted to the care and welfare of Jewish ex-service personnel and their dependants in need. The Association provides practical support in assisting with mobility equipment, household emergency repairs, respite breaks and general wellbeing.

Association of Jewish Refugees in Great Britain

Jubilee House, Merrion Avenue, Stanmore,
Middlesex HA7 4RL
T: 020 8385 3070
E: enquiries@ajr.org.uk
www.ajr.org.uk
The Association aims to assist Jewish refugees from Nazi oppression and their families, primarily from Central Europe, by providing a wide range of services.

Association of Medical Research Charities

Charles Darwin House, 12 Roger Street,
London WC1N 2JU
T: 020 7685 2620 F: 020 7685 2621
E: ceoffice@amrc.org.uk
www.amrc.org.uk
Chief Executive: Sharmila Nebhrajani
The Association of Medical Research Charities (AMRC) is a membership organisation of the leading medical and health research charities in the UK. Working with our member charities and partners, we aim to support the sector's effectiveness and advance medical research by developing best practice, providing information and guidance, improving public dialogue about research and science, and influencing government.
Employees: 10
Volunteers: 1

Association of Natural Burial Grounds

Natural Death Centre, In The Hill House,
Watley Lane, Twyford,
Winchester SO21 1QX
T: 01962 712690
E: contact@naturaldeath.org.uk
www.naturaldeath.org.uk
Manager: Rosie Inman-Cook
Run by the Natural Death Centre charity.
Volunteers: 5

Association of Radical Midwives

Rothley Lake House, Longwitton,
Morpeth, Northumberland NE61 4JY
T: 07810 665733
E: rothleylakehouse@gmail.com
www.midwifery.org.uk
Administration Secretary: Katherine Hales
The aims of the Association are to improve maternity services, especially within the NHS; to preserve and enhance choices in childbirth for all women; to re-establish the full role of the midwife; to encourage the evaluation of maternity care; to encourage research.

Association of Reflexologists

5 Fore Street, Taunton,
Somerset TA1 1HX
T: 01823 351010
F: 01823 336646
E: info@aor.org.uk
www.aor.org.uk
Chief Executive: Carolyn Story
The Association was set up to create an independent, fully democratic network of professional reflexologists, providing them with support and ongoing education through seminars and workshops.
Employees: 10

Association of Research Ethics Committees

AREC Office 13, Cherry Drive,
Durham DH6 2BG
T: 0845 604 5466
E: jackiemaull@arec.org.uk
www.arec.org.uk
Chief Executive: Jackie Maull
AREC is an independent, voluntary organisation established to set standards within the field of research ethics. AREC is the voice of research ethics within the UK.
Employees: 2
Volunteers: 16

Association of Therapeutic Communities

Waterfront, Kingsdown Road, Walmer,
Kent CT14 7LL
T: 01242 620077
E: post@therapeuticcommunities.org
www.therapeuticcommunities.org
The Association acts as a focus for information, debate, training and support for people who work in therapeutic communities, or who are interested in this

way of working. Members are drawn from all sectors of the healthcare and social-work professions, and share a belief in the importance of participation by both staff and patients in creating and maintaining a therapeutic environment.

Association of Volunteer Managers

PO Box 1449, Bedford,
Bedfordshire MK44 5AN
E: info@volunteermanagers.org.uk
www.volunteermanagers.org.uk
Chair: Heather Baumohl
The Association of Volunteer Managers is an independent body that aims to support, represent and champion people who manage volunteers in England regardless of field, discipline or sector. It has been set up by and for people who manage volunteers.
Volunteers: 11
Income: £7,000 (2012-13)

Association of Young People with ME

10 Vermont Palce, Tongwell, Milton Keynes MK12 8JA
T: 01908 379737
Helpline: 0845 123 2389
E: info@ayme.org.uk
www.ayme.org.uk
Chief Executive: Mary-Jane Willows
An association for young people suffering from the condition known as CFS/ME. It aims to work on behalf of those young people whose lives are affected by CFS/ME through media coverage, representations to government and other agencies, through talks and presentations. To provide a support network for young people suffering from CFS/ME through provision of a website, bi-monthly magazine, message board and helpline and to promote campaigns for the recognition, diagnosis, treatment and acceptance of ME.
Employees: 5
Volunteers: 350
Regional offices: 1
Income: £20,000 (2011-12)

Asthma UK

Summit House, 70 Wilson Street,
London EC2A 2DB
T: 020 7786 4900
F: 020 7256 6075
E: info@asthma.org.uk
www.asthma.org.uk
Asthma UK aims to help and advise people with asthma to understand and control their condition so that they may live healthier and more active lives. It promotes research into asthma, its causes, treatments and cure.
Employees: 90
Regional offices: 75

Asylum Aid

Club Union House, 253–254 Upper Street, London N1 1RY
T: 020 7354 9631
F: 0207 354 5620
E: info@asylumaid.org.uk
www.asylumaid.org.uk
Provides advice and representation to refugees and asylum seekers in the UK.
Employees: 17
Volunteers: 3

Ataxia UK

Lincoln House, Kennington Park, 1–3 Brixton Road, London SW9 6DE
T: 020 7582 1444
Helpline: 0845 644 0606
E: office@ataxia.org.uk
www.ataxia.org.uk
CEO: Sue Millman
Ataxia UK raises money for research into ataxia and provides information, advice and support to people affected by ataxia.

Ataxia-Telangiectasia Society

IACR – Rothamsted, Harpenden,
Hertfordshire AL5 2JQ
T: 01582 760733
F: 01582 760162
E: info@atsociety.org.uk
www.atsociety.org.uk
Chief Executive: William Davis
The A-T Society provides information and practical support to people with A-T and their families to enable them to live their lives to the full. It also funds bio-medical and clinical research to improve treatments and find a cure. The Society provides advocacy, counselling and financial grants. It provides opportunities for people living with A-T to meet and organises activity breaks. It has established two national specialist clinics and works to raise standards of care locally.
Employees: 3
Volunteers: 18
Income: £280,000 (2011-12)

ATD Fourth World UK Ltd

48 Addington Square, London SE5 7LB
T: 020 7703 3231
F: 020 7252 4276
E: atd@atd-uk.org
www.atd-uk.org
ATD Fourth World is an anti-poverty organisation committed to ending extreme poverty by working in partnership with those living in and experiencing poverty. We regard the existence of poverty as a denial of human rights and work to enable people living in poverty to take on active roles within their communities. We believe that people in poverty are the real experts on poverty issues and should become the key partners in all anti-poverty projects.
Employees: 10
Volunteers: 30
Regional offices: 2

ATTEND

11–13 Cavendish Square,
London W1G 0AN
T: 020 7307 2570 (also fax)
E: info@attend.org.uk
www.attend.org.uk
Chief Executive: David Wood
ATTEND aims to relieve patients and former patients of hospitals in the UK and other persons in the community who are sick, convalescent, disabled, handicapped, infirm, socially isolated or in need of financial assistance. It supports the work of health bodies and those who care for people using healthcare services or courts or the prison services.
Employees: 18
Volunteers: 31000
Regional offices: 1

Attlee Foundation

5 Thrawl Street, London E1 6RT
T: 020 7375 3212
Helpline: 020 7183 0093
E: info@attlee.org.uk
www.attlee.org.uk
The Foundation honours the memory of Clement Richard Attlee, Prime Minister 1945-51, by initiating projects for young people and for the alleviation of poverty and hardship.
Employees: 4
Volunteers: 10

Audi Design Foundation

Yeomans Drive, Blakelands, Milton Keynes, Buckinghamshire MK14 5AN
T: 01908 601814
F: 01908 601184
E: admin@audidesignfoundation.org
www.audidesignfoundation.org
The Audi Design Foundation is an independent charity established in 1997 by Audi UK. Our aim is to encourage designers to develop ideas that create a positive change in people's lives.
Employees: 2

Aurora Health Foundation

Head Office, 4 Ebor Cottages, Kingston Vale, London SW15 3RT
T: 020 8541 1951
E: info@aurorafoundation.org.uk
www.aurorahealthfoundation.org.uk
Chief Executive Officer: Susannah Faithfull
Aurora is a charity that provides specialist counselling, support and complementary therapies to people abused in childhood.
Employees: 12
Volunteers: 4
Regional offices: 1
Income: £50,000 (2010-11)

Autism Independent UK

199–203 Blandford Avenue, Kettering, Northamptonshire NN16 9AT
T: 01536 523274
E: autism@autismuk.com
www.autismuk.com
Director: Keith Lovett
The Autism Society exists to increase awareness of autism, together with well-established and newly developed approaches in the diagnosis, assessment, education and treatment. The main goal is to improve the quality of life for persons with autism.

Autism Plus

The Exchange Brewery, 2 Bridge Street, Sheffield, South Yorkshire S3 8NS
T: 0114 384 0284
F: 0114 384 0292
E: melanie.russell@autismplus.co.uk
www.autismplus.org
Managing Director: Glynis Davidson
The Charity aims to provide innovative and person-centred solutions for people with ASD and other disabilities, irrespective of where and how they live. To improve their quality of life and to extend and exercise their rights to access more control over their lives.
Employees: 346
Volunteers: 87
Regional offices: 2
Income: £8,182,857 (2011-12)

Autism Research Ltd – The International Autistic Research Organisation

49 Orchard Avenue, Shirley, Croydon CR0 7NE
T: 020 8777 0095
E: iaro@autismresearch.wanadoo.co.uk
www.iaro.org.uk
Director/Secretary: Gerda McCarthy
Autism Research carries out and encourages research into the mental and emotional condition of autism and any other conditions that might be associated with autism. It disseminates the results of such research.
Volunteers: 4

AVERT

4 Brighton Road, Horsham, West Sussex RH13 5BA
T: 01403 210202
E: info@avert.org
www.avert.org
Chief Executive: Brendan Hanlon
AVERT is an international HIV and AIDS charity based in the UK. Through our HIV/AIDS information website community projects in sub-Saharan Africa and information and advocacy service, we provide education, treatment and care to avert the spread of AIDS.
Employees: 10.5
Regional offices: 1

Aviation Environment Federation

Broken Wharf House, 2 Broken Wharf, London EC4V 3DT
T: 020 7248 2223
F: 020 7329 8160
E: info@aef.org.uk
www.aef.org.uk
Director: Tim Johnson
The AEF is the principal UK non-profit-making environmental association concerned with the environmental effects of aviation, ranging from aircraft noise issues associated with small airstrips or helipads, to the contribution of airline emissions to climate change. The AEF was established in 1975 and now has over 120 affiliated members comprising community and environmental groups, local authorities, parish councils, businesses and consultancies. Individual and student members are also welcomed.
Employees: 3
Volunteers: 3
Regional offices: 1

AVID (Association of Visitors to Immigration Detainees)

Archway Resource Centre, 1b Waterlow Road, London N19 5NJ
T: 020 7281 0533
E: enquiries@aviddetention.org.uk
www.aviddetention.org.uk
Director: Ali McGinley
National network of volunteer visitors to immigration detainees. We support those held under immigration acts in the UK with our network of 20 voluntary groups and over 400 visitors.

AVIF (ABLe Volunteers International Fund)

Fair Mount, Hartwith Avenue, Summerbridge, North Yorkshire HG3 4HT
E: alowndes@avif.org.uk
www.avif.org.uk
Founder Trustee: Alison Lowndes
AVIF is an innovative online charity, assisting with sustainable development via online and onsite volunteering in rural Kenya, East Africa. AVIF does not charge fees.
Volunteers: 100
Regional offices: 2
Income: £1,000 (2011-12)

Avocet Trust

Clarence House, 60–62 Clarence Street, Hull, Humberside HU9 1DN
T: 01482 329226
E: info@avocettrust.co.uk
www.avocettrust.co.uk
Chief Executive: LC Howell
Avocet provides lifetime support to vulnerable people to enable them to live valued lives. Avocet provides a range of services including 24-hour support in clients' homes, as well as short stay care and through-the-door domiciliary services. Going forward the Trust plans to provide employment training services as well as employment placement services.
Employees: 300

Aylesham Neighbourhood Project

Aylesham Neighbourhood Project, Ackholt Road, Aylesham, Canterbury, Kent CT3 3AJ
T: 01304 840134
E: office@aylesham-np.org.uk
www.aylesham-np.org.uk
Chief Executive: Kathryn Rogers
Aylesham Neighbourhood Project (the Project) is a charitable company that works in local communities to inspire children and families to recognise potential, make positive change and achieve bright futures. The Project delivers community based services across the Dover District that are person centred and give positive opportunities for children and families.
Employees: 22
Volunteers: 9

Back Up (transforming lives after spinal cord injury)

Jessica House, Red Lion Square, 191
Wandsworth High Street,
London SW18 4LS
T: 020 8875 1805
E: admin@backuptrust.org.uk
www.backuptrust.org.uk
Chief Executive: Louise Wright
Our vision is a world where people with a spinal cord injury can realise their full potential. Our mission is to: inspire people affected by spinal cord injury to transform their lives; challenge perceptions of disability; deliver services that build confidence and independence and offer a supportive network.
Employees: 24
Volunteers: 300

BackCare

16 Elmtree Road, Teddington,
Middlesex TW11 8ST
T: 020 8977 5474
F: 020 8943 5318
E: info@backcare.org.uk
www.backcare.org.uk
BackCare helps people manage and prevent back pain by providing advice, promoting self-help, encouraging debate and funding scientific research into back care.
Employees: 8
Volunteers: 180
Regional offices: 30

Bangla-Aid UK

39 Marlborough Road, 39 Marlborough Road, London E7 8HA
T: 020 8472 6862
E: banglaaid@hotmail.com
Chairman: Jamal Uddin
Bangla-Aid UK is a non-governmental, non-profit-making, non-partisan charity striving to meet the basic human needs of the underprivileged and people of limited resources. The organisation was founded by a native Bangladeshi philanthropist, Jamal Uddin who is based in the UK.
Volunteers: 4
Regional offices: 1

Bank Workers Charity

E: jenna.southgate@bwcharity.org.uk

Bar Pro Bono Unit

289–293 High Holborn,
London WC1V 7HZ
T: 020 7611 9500
E: enquiries@barprobono.org.uk
www.barprobono.org.uk
The unit provides free legal advice and representation for deserving cases where Legal Aid is not available and where the applicant is unable to afford legal assistance. Applicants are strongly encouraged to approach an advice agency or solicitor before applying to the unit.

Barnardo's

Tanners Lane, Barkingside, Ilford,
Essex IG6 1QG
T: 020 8550 8822
F: 020 8551 6870
E: paul.ilett@barnardos.org.uk
www.barnardos.org.uk
Chief Executive: Anne Marie Carrie
As one of the UK's leading children's charities, Barnardo's believes in children regardless of their circumstances, gender, race, disability or behaviour. We believe in the abused, the vulnerable, the forgotten and the neglected. We will support them, stand up for them and bring out the best in each and every child. We do this because we believe in children.
Employees: 6800
Volunteers: 12000
Regional offices: 9

Barnsley Hospice

Church Street, Gawber, Barnsley, South
Yorkshire S75 2RL
T: 01226 244244
E: enquiries@barnsley-hospice.org
www.barnsleyhospice.org
Chief Executive/Chair: Ian Carey
Barnsley Hospice is a charity dedicated to providing quality specialist palliative and end of life care to all adults in Barnsley, as well as their family and friends. The Hospice's vision is to: be the first choice for patients, referrers, customers and donors of all our services; provide more services to more people; strive to be one of the best hospices in England.
Employees: 120
Volunteers: 400
Income: £3,900,000 (2011-12)

BASIC

The Neurocare Centre, 554 Eccles New
Road, Salford M5 5AP
T: 0161 707 6441
Helpline: 0870 750 0000
E: enquiries@basiccharity.org.uk
www.basiccharity.org.uk
Director: Wendy Edge
BASIC supports patients and their families recovering from traumatic brain and spinal injuries and neurological illness.
Employees: 12

Basic Skills Agency

Chetwynd House, 21 De Montfort Street,
Leicester LE1 7GE
T: 0116 204 4200
F: 0116 204 6988
E: enquiries@niace.org.uk
www.niace.org.uk
The Basic Skills Agency at NIACE is committed to finding, developing and disseminating good practice in literacy, language and numeracy.
Employees: 100

BasicNeeds UK Trust

158a Parade, Leamington Spa,
Warwickshire CV32 4AE
T: 01926 330101
F: 01926 453679
E: samantha.clews@basicneeds.org.uk
www.basicneeds.org.uk
Chief Executive: Chris Underhill
Mentally ill people are suffering and mental health is ignored. We work in Africa and Asia to end the suffering of mentally ill people, ensure their basic needs are met and their basic rights are respected. We do this through providing accessible community mental health treatment, reducing stigma and exclusion in communities and providing sustainable livelihoods for mentally ill people and their carers.
Employees: 6

BBC Children in Need Appeal

PO Box 1000, London W12 7WJ
T: 020 8576 7788
F: 020 8576 8887
E: pudsey@bbc.co.uk
www.bbc.co.uk/pudsey
Chief Executive: David Ramsden
The Children in Need appeal provides grants to properly constituted organisations working with children and young people aged 18 and under, who may have experienced mental, physical or sensory disabilities; behavioural or psychological disorders; are living in poverty or situations

of deprivation; or suffering through distress, abuse or neglect.
Employees: 43
Regional offices: 12

BCS – The Chartered Institute for IT

First Floor, Block D, North Star House, North Star Avenue, Swindon, Wiltshire SN2 1FA
T: 01793 417417
F: 01793 480270
E: customerservice@hq.bcs.org.uk
www.bcs.org
CEO: David Clarke
Professional membership association representing over 70,000 people worldwide working in IT and computing. We promote wider social and economic progress through the advancement of information technology science and practice. We bring together industry, academics, practitioners and government to share knowledge, promote new thinking, influence the development of computing education, shape public policy and inform the public.
Employees: 220
Regional offices: 2

Be Your Best Foundation

Portsmouth Guildhall, Guildhall Square, Portsmouth, Hampshire PO1 2AB
T: 02392 985716
E: dan@rockchallenge.co.uk
www.rockchallenge.co.uk
Chairman: George Cooil
The Foundation aims to improve quality of life by encouraging young people to take an active role in building safe and healthy communities. The primary aim of the Foundation is to raise funds to stage Rock Challenge events across the UK, an anti-drug and crime initiative that takes the form of a friendly performing arts competition for 11 to 18 year olds. Rock Challenge encourages a natural high through live performance.
Employees: 7
Volunteers: 70
Regional offices: 1

Beacon Fellowship Charitable Trust

12 Angel Gate, 320–326 City Road, London EC1V 2PT
T: 020 7713 9326
E: contact@beaconfellowship.org.uk
www.beaconfellowship.org.uk
Beacon is a national charity set up to encourage individual contributions to charitable and social causes and to celebrate and showcase best practice in giving.
Employees: 6
Volunteers: 30

Beat

2nd Floor, Wensum House, 103 Prince of Wales Road, Norwich, Norfolk NR1 1DW
T: 0300 123 3355
Helpline: 0845 634 1414
F: 01603 664915
E: info@b-eat.co.uk
www.b-eat.co.uk
Chief Executive: Susan Ringwood
Beat is the leading UK-wide charity providing information, help and support for people affected by eating disorders; anorexia, bulimia nervosa and binge eating disorder.
Employees: 25
Volunteers: 700

BECHAR

The Prebend Day Centre, 12 Prebend Street, Bedford, Bedfordshire MK40 1QW
T: 01234 365955
Helpline: 01234 376835
F: 01234 352717
E: pdc@bechar.org.uk
www.bechar.org.uk
Chief Executive: Ryan Flecknell
Bedford Concern for the Homeless and Rootless provides a day centre where our clients can get cheap hot food, clothing and washing facilities and somewhere to relax in comfort. We provide counselling services to help our clients get access to jobs, housing and generally re-enter normal society.
Employees: 10
Volunteers: 30
Regional offices: 1
Income: £250,000 (2011-12)

Behcet's Syndrome Society

8 Abbey Gardens, Evesham, Worcestershire WR11 4SP
T: 0845 130 7328
Helpline: 0845 130 7329
E: info@behcetsdisease.org.uk
www.behcets.org.uk
Director: Chris Phillips
Aims to relieve and mitigate the distress of persons suffering from Behcet's disease.
Employees: 1
Volunteers: 20
Income: £75,000 (2011-12)

Beth Johnson Foundation

Parkfield House, 64 Princes Road, Hartshill, Stoke-on-Trent, Staffordshire ST4 7JL
T: 01782 844036
F: 01782 746940
E: admin@bjf.org.uk
www.bjf.org.uk
Chief Executive: Alan Hatton-Yeo
The Foundation undertakes innovative work to develop evidence-based approaches to the social aspects of ageing. Currently we have UK programmes in intergenerational work, positive ageing and advocacy. Our work is approached from a life course perspective and we provide resources, training and consultancy in support of our aims.
Employees: 24
Volunteers: 40
Regional offices: 1

Bethany Children's Trust

Office 211, 22 Eden Street, Kingston Upon Thames, Surrey KT1 1DN
T: 020 8977 7571
E: admin@bethanychildrenstrust.org.uk
www.bethanychildrenstrust.org.uk
Director: Susie Howe
The Bethany Children's Trust's vision is to see every child in the world loved, safe, nurtured and free to reach their God-given potential. We are strengthening churches and Christian projects that care for vulnerable children throughout the world, with training workshops, prayer and financial support. BCT also works with other Christian organizations worldwide, to speak out with, and for, children at risk and challenge the Church, local communities and world leaders to address their needs.
Employees: 3
Volunteers: 2
Regional offices: 1
Income: £180,000 (2012-13)

Bexley Snap

Thames Innovation Centre, 2 Veridion Way, Erith, Kent DA18 4AL
T: 020 8320 1488
E: carolmccall@bexleysnap.org.uk
www.bexleysnap.org.uk
Chief Executive: Carol McCall
Our vision is that disabled children have choices and a right to a fulfilling life. We aim to increase choice of services and activities available to children and young people while reducing the isolation and frustration experienced by their families. We offer a range of weekend, evening and school holiday play and leisure activities for disabled

children, a pre-school programme for disabled babies and toddlers, and a comprehensive support programme for parents/carers.
Employees: 42
Volunteers: 23
Regional offices: 0
Income: £379,095 (2012-13)

BHA

Democracy House, 609 Stretford Road, Old Trafford, Manchester M16 0QA
T: 0845 450 4247
F: 0845 450 3247
E: info@thebha.org.uk
www.thebha.org.uk
Chief Executive: Priscilla Nkwenti
BHA challenges health inequalities for disadvantaged and marginalised communities. We make a positive contribution in health provision and service delivery. Using expertise in the field of health, social care policy and service development, we provide efficient and appropriate advice and services to communities at grass-root level. We take a strategic and consultative role by working with policy makers and legislators to ensure effective service development and delivery to people from disadvantaged and marginalised communities.
Employees: 76
Volunteers: 52
Regional offices: 8
Income: £2,600,000 (2010-11)

BIBIC

Knowle Hall, Knowle, Bridgwater, Somerset TA7 8PJ
T: 01278 684060
F: 01278 685703
E: info@bibic.org.uk
www.bibic.org.uk
BIBIC exists to maximise the potential of children with sensory, social, communication, motor and learning difficulties. We work with parents and carers, offering a valuable support system that offers time to talk, expert advice and practical help.
Employees: 39
Volunteers: 8

Bible Society

Stonehill Green, Westlea, Swindon SN5 7DG
T: 01793 418100
E: contactus@biblesociety.org.uk
www.biblesociety.org.uk
Chief Executive: James Catford

Bible Society is working towards a day when the Bible's life-changing message is shaping lives and communities everywhere. We aim to show how the Bible connects with life. We make scriptures available where there are none. And we work with the Church to help it live out the Bible's message.
Employees: 105
Volunteers: 700

Big Issue Foundation

1-5 Wandsworth Road, London SW8 2LN
T: 020 7526 3200
F: 020 7526 3401
E: foundation@bigissue.com
www.bigissue.org.uk
CEO: Stephen Robertson
The Big Issue Foundation is a national charity that connects vendors with the vital support and solutions that enable them to rebuild their lives and journey away from homelessness.
Employees: 23
Volunteers: 15
Regional offices: 7
Income: £922,040 (2012-13)

Big Society Capital

Chronicle House, 72-78 Fleet Street, London EC4Y 1HY
T: 020 7186 2500
E: enquiries@bigsocietycapital.com
www.bigsocietycapital.com
Chief Executive: Nick O'Donohoe
Big Society Capital is an organisation set up to help grow the social investment market, so that charities and social enterprises who want to borrow money can access the finance they need to maintain and increase their support for people in need in the UK. Since 2012, we have committed £140 million in investments to specialist organisations who lend to charities and social enterprises.
Volunteers: 0
Regional offices: 0

Bipolar UK

11 Belgrave Road, London SW1V 1RB
T: 020 7931 6480
F: 020 7931 6481
E: info@bipolaruk.org.uk
www.bipolaruk.org.uk
Bipolar UK is the national charity dedicated to supporting individuals with the much misunderstood and devastating condition of bipolar, their families and carers.

BirdLife International

Wellbrook Court, Girton Road, Cambridge CB3 0NA
T: 01223 277318
F: 01223 277200
E: tracy.spraggon@birdlife.org
www.birdlife.org
BirdLife International is a partnership of people for birds and the environment. Over 10 million people worldwide support the BirdLife Partnership of national NGO conservation organisations and local networks. BirdLife's vision is of a world rich in biodiversity, with people and nature living in harmony, equitably and sustainably. BirdLife's aim is to conserve wild birds, their habitats and global biodiversity by working with people towards sustainability in the use of natural resources.
Employees: 65
Volunteers: 8
Regional offices: 6

Birth Companions

PO Box 64597, London SW17 1DR
T: 07855 725097
Helpline: 020 7117 0037
E: info@birthcompanions.org.uk
www.birthcompanions.org.uk
Director: Annabel Kennedy
Our overall aim is to improve the wellbeing of pregnant women and new mothers who are, have been or are at risk of being detained. We do this by improving their mental health, reducing isolation, enabling them to give their babies the best possible start in life and improving their conditions. We work in HMP Holloway as well as in the community supporting women antenatally, during birth and postnatally.
Employees: 5
Volunteers: 34
Income: £115,000 (2011-12)

Black and Ethnic Minority Diabetes Association

St Paul's Church Centre, Rossmore Road, London NW1 6NJ
T: 020 7723 5357
E: info@bemda.org
www.bemda.org
BEMDA, founded in 1995, is a user-led, health-focused organisation that was established to promote the health of diabetics in the community and reduce the impact of diabetes-related health problems in black and ethnic minority communities in particular, without excluding diabetics and their carers from other communities from our services.

Black Environment Network

UK Office, The Warehouse, 54–57 Allison Street, Digbeth, Birmingham B5 5TH
T: 0121 643 6387 (also fax)
E: ukoffice@ben-network.org.uk
www.ben-network.org.uk
Chief Executive: James Friel
BEN works for full ethnic participation in the built and natural environment. BEN uses the word 'black' symbolically recognising that the black communities are the most visible of all ethnic communities. We work with black, white and other ethnic communities.
Employees: 5
Regional offices: 3
Income: £352,931 (2010-11)

Black Training and Enterprise Group

2nd Floor, 200A Pentonville Road, London N1 9JP
T: 020 7832 5800
F: 020 7832 5829
E: info@bteg.co.uk
www.bteg.co.uk
The group aims to ensure fair access and outcomes for black communities in employment, training and enterprise and to help black organisations to play an active role in the economic regeneration of local communities through partnership with others.
Employees: 5
Volunteers: 2

Bladder and Bowel Foundation

SATRA Innovation Park, Rockingham Road, Kettering, Northamptonshire NN16 9JH
T: 01536 533255
Helpline: 0845 345 0165
F: 01536 533240
E: info@bladderandbowelfoundation.org
www.bladderandbowelfoundation.org
Executive Director: Robert Dixon
B&BF is now the UK's largest advocacy charity providing information and support for all types of bladder and bowel-related problems, including incontinence, prostate problems, constipation and diverticular disease, for patients, their families, carers and healthcare professionals. Officially formed in June 2008 and launched on 15 September 2008, it replaces Incontact and the Continence Foundation.
Employees: 3
Volunteers: 20
Regional offices: 1

Blind Veterans UK

12–14 Harcourt Street, London W1H 4HD
T: 020 7723 5021
Helpline: 0800 389 7979
F: 020 7262 6199
E: info@blindveterans.org.uk
www.blindveterans.org.uk
Chief Executive: Robert Leader
Blind Veterans UK, formerly St Dunstan's, believe that no one who's served our country should battle blindness alone. We're here to help with a lifetime's practical and emotional support, regardless of when people served or how they lost their sight. We get our members back on their feet, recovering their independence and discovering a life beyond sight loss.
Employees: 378
Volunteers: 330
Regional offices: 12

Blindaid Africa

Prospect Cottage, Wells Road, Radstock, Avon BA3 3RP
T: 01761 434385
E: peter@blindaid.org
www.blindaid.org
Director: Rosalie Lees
The provision of tools for learning and living for blind young people in Africa; that is our motto and objective. We provide minimal cost (mostly pre-used) materials and equipment to enable blind students to participate and compete effectively in their national education systems and to integrate effectively in the school and community social environments.
Employees: 2
Volunteers: 10
Regional offices: 2
Income: £2,500 (2011-12)

Bliss

2nd and 3rd Floors, 9 Holyrood Street, London SE1 2EL
T: 020 7378 1122
F: 020 7403 0673
E: information@bliss.org.uk
www.bliss.org.uk
Bliss, the premature baby charity, is dedicated to making sure that more babies born prematurely or sick in the UK survive and that each one has the best quality of life.
Employees: 21
Volunteers: 250
Regional offices: 25

Blond McIndoe Research Foundation

E: debbie.mitchell@blondmcindoe.org

Blood Pressure Association

60 Cranmer Terrace, London SW17 0QS
T: 020 8772 4994
F: 020 8772 4999
E: info@bpassoc.org.uk
www.bpassoc.org.uk
The BPA aims to significantly improve the prevention, diagnosis and treatment of high blood pressure in order to prevent death and disability from stroke and heart disease.
Employees: 6
Volunteers: 2
Regional offices: 1

Blue Cross

Shilton Road, Burford, Oxfordshire OX18 4PF
T: 0300 777 1897
F: 01993 825526
E: tom.clarkson@bluecross.org.uk
www.bluecross.org.uk
CEO: Kim Hamilton
Blue Cross aims to relieve the suffering of animals whose owners cannot afford the cost of veterinary treatment; educate, encourage, extend and promote animal welfare and responsible pet ownership; extend pet ownership by finding suitable homes for unwanted and abandoned animals and preventing their unnecessary destruction; add to the quality of human life through the recognition of the value of suitable companion animals to people of all ages. Incorporates Our Dumb Friends League.
Employees: 387
Regional offices: 16
Income: £30,000,000 (2010-11)

BMS World Mission

BMS World Mission, PO Box 49, 129 Broadway, Didcot, Oxfordshire OX11 8XA
T: 01235 517700
E: cbaker@bmsworldmission.org
www.bmsworldmission.org
BMS World Mission is a Christian mission organisation, working in around 35 countries on four continents. BMS personnel are mainly involved in church planting, development, disaster relief, education, health, and media and advocacy. We welcome volunteers who are looking to serve overseas for 3 months or longer.

Board of Deputies of British Jews

6 Bloomsbury Square,
London WC1A 2LP
T: 020 7543 5400
E: info@bod.org.uk
www.bod.org.uk
The Board acts as the representative body of the UK Jewish community, composed of some 330 deputies elected by synagogues and by certain national communal bodies. It is the voice of the Jewish community and protects the rights and interests of Jews in the UK. It monitors legislation and any discriminatory measures, legal or social, affecting the Jewish community and watches over the interests of co-religionists in countries where they are oppressed and persecuted.

Boaz Trust

First Floor, 110 Oldham Road, Manchester, Greater Manchester M4 6AG
T: 0161 202 1056
F: 0161 228 7332
E: info@boaztrust.org.uk
www.boaztrust.org.uk
Director: Dave Smith
Boaz provides accommodation and holistic support to destitute refused asylum seekers and refugees in Greater Manchester.
Employees: 10
Volunteers: 250
Regional offices: 0
Income: £310,000 (2012-13)

Bobath Centre for Children with Cerebral Palsy

Bradbury House, 250 East End Road, London N2 8AU
T: 020 8444 3355
F: 020 8444 3399
E: jayne.pearce@bobath.org.uk
www.bobath.org.uk
Director of Administrative Services: Jayne Pearce
The Centre provides specialist Bobath therapy for children with cerebral palsy. It also provides training in the Bobath Concept to physiotherapists, occupational therapists and speech and language therapists from all over the UK and abroad.
Employees: 26
Volunteers: 6
Income: £1,150,000 (2012-13)

Body and Soul

99–119 Rosebery Avenue,
London EC1R 4RE
T: 020 7923 6880
E: info@bodyandsoulcharity.org
www.bodyandsoulcharity.org
Director: Emma Colyer
A charity supporting children, teenagers and adults who are living with and closely affected by HIV in the UK. Our strategy aims to impact five key areas of member wellbeing: physical health, mental health, psychosocial wellbeing, practical support and maximising productivity.
Employees: 11
Volunteers: 200+
Regional offices: 1

Body Shop Foundation

Watermead, Littlehampton, West Sussex BN17 6LS
T: 01903 844039
F: 01903 844202
E: bodyshopfoundation@thebodyshop.com
www.thebodyshopfoundation.org
CEO: Lisa Jackson
The Body Shop Foundation funds projects across the globe. The groups we support address human and civil rights, animal and environmental protection issues.
Employees: 8
Volunteers: 150

Book Aid International

39–41 Coldharbour Lane, Camberwell, London SE5 9NR
T: 020 7733 3577
F: 020 7978 8006
E: info@bookaid.org
www.bookaid.org
Director: Alison Hubert
Book Aid International is a UK-registered charity that works with partners in the world's poorest countries to support literacy, education and training. We provide relevant books and information to those in greatest need – so letting people realise their potential and contribute to the development of their communities.
Employees: 30
Volunteers: 15

Booktrust

Book House, 45 East Hill, London
T: 020 8875 4584
E: trudi.kent@booktrust.org.uk
PA To Chief Executive: Trudi Kent

Born Free Foundation

3 Grove House, Foundry Lane, Horsham, West Sussex RH13 5PL
T: 01403 240170
E: info@bornfree.org.uk
www.bornfree.org.uk
The foundation works to investigate, expose and alleviate animal suffering in zoos and to promote the protection of wildlife in its natural habitat.

Bowel Cancer UK

9 Rickett Street, London SW6 1RU
T: 020 7381 9711
F: 020 7381 5752
E: admin@bowelcanceruk.org.uk
www.bowelcanceruk.org.uk
The principal objectives of the Charity are to help all people concerned about colorectal cancer by: providing authoritative information, support and advice for those affected by the disease, their carers and their families; raising awareness of the disease to increase knowledge and understanding of the symptoms; educating the public and healthcare professionals about methods of prevention and treatments; campaigning for improved choice, equality of access to treatments and best care.
Employees: 13
Volunteers: 20

Boys' Brigade

Felden Lodge, Felden, Hemel Hempstead HP3 0BL
T: 01442 231681
F: 01442 235391
E: steve.dickinson@boys-brigade.org.uk
www.boys-brigade.org.uk
Brigade Secretary: Steve Dickinson
Christian Youth Organisation for children and young people of all faiths and none, from 4-18 years. Through its activity programme and resources the Boys' Brigade partners churches and communities to care for and challenge young people for life by a programme of informal education underpinned by the Christian faith.
Employees: 40
Volunteers: 15000
Regional offices: 3
Income: £2,000,000 (2011-12)

Bracknell Forest Voluntary Action

Amber House, Market Street, Bracknell, Berkshire RG12 1JB
T: 01344 304404
E: carole.allen@bfva.org
www.bfva.org
Chief Officer: Janet Dean
Bracknell Forest Voluntary Action is an independent organisation whose role is to

enhance the quality of life of the people of Bracknell Forest by promoting and supporting the work of voluntary, community and faith organisations. We are a central support for voluntary and community action, a local development agency, and provide back office support for our members.
Employees: 7
Volunteers: 10
Regional offices: 1
Income: £368,448 (2012-13)

Brain and Spine Foundation

3.36 Canterbury Court, Kennington Park, 1-3 Brixton Road, London SW9 6DE
T: 020 7793 5900
Helpline: 0808 808 1000
F: 020 7793 5939
E: info@brainandspine.org.uk
www.brainandspine.org.uk
CEO: Ken Walker
The Brain and Spine Foundation is a national charity that aims to improve the care, treatment and prevention of neurological disorders through patient and carer information programmes.
Employees: 8
Volunteers: 100
Income: £620,000 (2012-13)

Brain Research Trust

15 Southampton Place,
London WC1A 2AJ
T: 020 7404 9982
E: info@brt.org.uk
www.brt.org.uk
The Brain Research Trust was founded as an independent medical charity, not part of the NHS, with the aim of supporting research at the Institute of Neurology, London, into diseases of the brain and nervous system.

Braintree District Voluntary Support Agency

E: judy@bdvsa.org

Brainwave Centre Ltd

Huntworth, Bridgwater,
Somerset TA6 6LQ
T: 01278 429089
E: joannesmith@brainwave.org.uk
www.brainwave.org.uk
The centre for rehabilitation and development accelerates the rate of progress of rehabilitation of brain injury by designing home-based programmes of rehabilitation involving both physical and cognitive techniques.

Break

Davison House, 1 Montague Road,
Sheringham, Norfolk NR26 8WN
T: 01263 822161
E: office@break-charity.org
www.break-charity.org
CEO: Chris Hoddy
Break, changing young lives, supports vulnerable children, young people and families across East Anglia: young people in care and moving on; children with disabilities; families in need of support; children at risk.
Employees: 460
Volunteers: 700

Breaking Free – Primarily Supporting Women Survivors of Child Sexual Abuse

Suite 23–25, Marshall House, 124 Middleton Road, Morden,
Surrey SM4 6RW
T: 0845 108 0055
F: 020 8687 4134
E: breakingfreecharity@hotmail.com
Breaking Free provides a confidential, safe, supportive and understanding environment in which women can deal with issues arising from their experiences of abuse. It offers support to women survivors regardless of race, colour, creed, religious beliefs or ability / disability and increases awareness of the issue of child sexual abuse.
Employees: 3
Volunteers: 44

Breakthrough Breast Cancer

3rd Floor, Weston House, 246 High Holborn, London WC1V 7EX
T: 08080 100200
F: 020 7025 2401
E: info@breakthrough.org.uk
www.breakthrough.org.uk
Breakthrough Breast Cancer's vision is a future free from the fear of breast cancer. Breakthrough is committed to fighting breast cancer through research and education and has established the UK's first dedicated breast cancer research centre.
Employees: 78
Volunteers: 70

Breakthrough UK Ltd

Business Employment Venture Centre, Aked Close, Ardwick,
Manchester M12 4AN
T: 0161 273 5412
F: 0161 274 4053
E: reception@breakthrough-uk.co.uk
www.breakthrough-uk.com
Chief Executive: Michelle Scattergood
Employees: 43

Breast Cancer Campaign

Clifton Centre, 110 Clifton Street,
London EC2A 4HT
T: 020 7749 3700
F: 020 7749 3701
E: info@breastcancercampaign.org
www.breastcancercampaign.org
Chief Executive: Pamela Goldberg
Breast Cancer Campaign is the only charity that specialises in funding independent breast cancer research throughout the UK. Our aim is to find the cure for breast cancer by funding research that looks at improving diagnosis and treatment of breast cancer, better understanding how it develops and ultimately either curing the disease or preventing it.
Employees: 50
Volunteers: 200

Breast Cancer Care

5–13 Great Suffolk Street,
London SE1 0NS
T: 0845 092 0800
Helpline: 0808 800 6000
E: info@breastcancercare.org.uk
www.breastcancercare.org.uk
Breast Cancer Care is here for anyone affected by breast cancer. We bring people together, provide information and support, and campaign for improved standards of care. We use our understanding of people's experience of breast cancer and our clinical expertise in everything we do. All our services are free.
Employees: 119
Volunteers: 350
Regional offices: 4

Breast Cancer Research Trust

PO Box 861, Bognor Regis PO21 9HW
T: 01372 463235
E: bcrtrust@aol.com
The Trust promotes scientific research into the origins, causes and nature of breast cancer. It improves methods of prevention and techniques in the treatment, cure and control of breast cancer and develops aids to assess the clinical needs of patients and potential patients. It establishes clinics for the therapeutic treatment of breast cancer and encourages the public to take appropriate measures.

Brendoncare Foundation

The Old Malthouse, Victoria Road,
Winchester, Hampshire SO23 7DU
T: 01962 852133
E: enquiries@brendoncare.org.uk
www.brendoncare.org.uk
The Foundation provides health and social care for older people through ten Care Centres in the south of England and 70 clubs

in the community across Hampshire, Dorset, Bournemouth and Poole. All Care Centres have teams of volunteers and all clubs are run by them.

Employees: 750
Volunteers: 600
Regional offices: 1

Bridging the Gap

c/o SMCA, Cobham Court, Haslemere Avenue, Mitcham, Surrey CR4 3PR
T: 020 8090 1486
E: james@btguk.org
www.btguk.org
Chief Executive: James Stevens-Turner
A registered charity helping prisoners and ex-prisoners adjust to life outside prison. It encourages local and global understanding of problems faced by people leaving prison and helps people leaving prison to restart their lives, stay crime free and become useful members of society.

Volunteers: 20
Regional offices: 1

Bristol Crisis Service for Women

PO Box 654, Bristol BS99 1XH
T: 0117 927 9600
E: bcsw@btconnect.com
www.selfinjurysupport.org.uk
Director: Hilary Lindsay
To provide support to women and girls affected by self-injury/self harm. To raise awareness of the issue by providing information (for professionals, individuals and family, friends and carers) and training for workers in contact with people who self-injure.

Employees: 6
Volunteers: 25
Regional offices: 0
Income: £82,400 (2012-13)

Britain-Nepal Medical Trust

Export House, 130 Vale Road, Tonbridge, Kent TN9 1SP
T: 01732 360284
E: info@britainnepalmedicaltrust.org.uk
www.britainnepalmedicaltrust.org.uk
Co-Chairs: Dr G Holdsworth and Dr S. Subedi
BNMT aims to assist the people of Nepal to improve their health through realisation of their health rights. It does this by working in partnership with the Ministry of Health, international and local non-governmental

organisations, local committees and communities.

Employees: 54
Volunteers: 11
Regional offices: 2
Income: £1,161,184 (2011-12)

British Accreditation Council for Independent Further and Higher Education

5th Floor, Fleet House, 8-12 New Bridge Street, London EC4V 6AL
T: 0300 330 1400
E: info@the-bac.org
www.the-bac.org
Chief Executive: Dr Gina Hobson
The British Accreditation Council has provided a comprehensive quality assurance scheme for independent further and higher education in the UK since 1984. Our accreditation is recognised the world over by students, agents and government officials as the clearest mark of educational quality in the private sector. Alongside the British Council, whose Accreditation UK scheme serves as the definitive guide to the country's English language centres, we have overseen the inspection of private post-16 education for more than two decades.

Employees: 8
Regional offices: 1

British Acoustic Neuroma Association

Oak House B, Ransomwood Business Park, Southwell Road West, Mansfield, Nottinghamshire NG21 0HJ
T: 01623 632143
E: admin@bana-uk.com
www.bana-uk.com
Formed in 1992, BANA is organised and administrated by people affected by acoustic neuroma. It is a registered charity and exists for mutual support, information exchange and listening. We aim to support those affected (both patients and family members) by acoustic neuroma and other similar conditions.

Employees: 2
Volunteers: 50+
Regional offices: 1

British Acupuncture Council

63 Jeddo Road, London W12 9HQ
T: 020 8735 0400
F: 020 8735 0404
E: info@acupuncture.org.uk
www.acupuncture.org.uk

The Council works to establish the status, maintain a register, regulate the conduct and protect the interests of practitioners of acupuncture, so as to promote and maintain, in the public interest, proper standards for the practice of acupuncture. It promotes and encourages the study and knowledge of acupuncture, which is a branch of medicine founded upon the principle that health is dependent upon a proper balance of vital energy forces within the body.

Employees: 9
Volunteers: 15

British and International Federation of Festivals

Festivals House, 198 Park Lane, Macclesfield, Cheshire SK11 6UD
T: 01625 428297
F: 01625 503229
E: info@federationoffestivals.org.uk
www.federationoffestivals.org.uk
Chief Executive Officer: Terry Luddington
The Federation is the largest UK organisation for the participatory arts of music, dance and speech. Our aim is to advance, promote and encourage generally, and by means of the amateur festival movement in particular, the study and practice of the arts of music, dance, speech, literature and acting.

Employees: 4
Volunteers: 16500
Income: £280,000 (2011-12)

British Archaeological Association

18 Stanley Road, Oxford OX4 1QZ
E: dacruz@liv.ac.uk
www.archeologyuk.org
The Association promotes the study of archaeology. It aims to preserve our national antiquities, encourages original research and publishes new work, covering art and antiquities from the Roman to the post-medieval periods.

British Association and College of Occupational Therapists

106-114 Borough High Street, Southwark, London SE1 1LB
T: 020 7357 6480
F: 020 7480 2299
E: vandita.chisholm@cot.co.uk
www.cot.org.uk
The British Association and College of Occupational Therapists champions the unique and vital work of occupational therapy staff. Occupational therapy promotes health, wellbeing and independence through participation in activities or occupation. It gives people the tools and skills to do the things they need or

want to do, removing obstacles to disability, injury, illness or other conditions.
Employees: 60
Volunteers: 200
Regional offices: 20

British Association for Adoption and Fostering

Saffron House, 6-10 Kirby Street, London EC1N 8TS
T: 020 7421 2600
F: 020 7421 2601
E: mail@baaf.org.uk
www.baaf.org.uk
Chief Executive: David Holmes
Membership organisation for local authorities, voluntary adoption agencies, fostering agencies, legal advisers, childcare practitioners and the general public with an interest in adoption and fostering. The organisation aims to promote high standards in adoption and fostering, to promote public and professional understanding of the issues and to be an independent voice in the field of childcare, informing and influencing policy makers.
Employees: 140
Volunteers: 5
Regional offices: 9

British Association for Cancer Research

c/o Leeds Institute of Cancer & Pathology, Clinical Sciences Building, St James University Hospital, Beckett Street LS9 7TF
T: 0113 206 5611 (also fax)
E: bacr@leeds.ac.uk
www.bacr.org.uk
The Association aims to advance research in all aspects of cancer by encouraging the exchange of information.
Employees: 2
Volunteers: 1200

British Association for Counselling and Psychotherapy

BACP House, 15 St John's Business Park, Lutterworth, Leicestershire LE17 4HB
T: 01455 883300
F: 01455 550243
E: bacp@bacp.co.uk
www.bacp.co.uk
The Association promotes education and training for those involved in counselling and psychotherapy, full or part time, in either professional or voluntary contexts, with a view to raising standards. It also promotes the understanding of counselling and psychotherapy.
Employees: 75
Volunteers: 180

British Association for Early Childhood Education

136 Cavell Street, London E1 2JA
T: 020 7539 5400
F: 020 7539 5409
E: office@early-education.org.uk
www.early-education.org.uk
Chief Executive: Megan Pacey
The British Association for Early Childhood Education (Early Education), founded in 1923, is the leading national voluntary organisation for early years practitioners and parents, with members and branches across the UK. Early Education promotes the right of every child to education of the highest quality. It provides support, training, advice and information on best practice for all those concerned with the education and care of young children from birth to eight years.
Employees: 7
Volunteers: 200

British Association for Immediate Care

Turret House, 2 Turret Lane, Ipswich, Suffolk IP4 1DL
T: 01473 218407
F: 01473 280585
E: cx@basics.org.uk
www.basics.org.uk
Chief Executive: Phill Browne
The aims of BASICS are to foster co-operation between immediate care schemes and to encourage the formation of new schemes; to strengthen and develop cooperation between all services in coping with emergencies that may result in injury or risk to life; to encourage and assist research into all aspects of immediate care; to raise standards of care and training of practitioners; to disseminate information and encourage and assist international exchange of information and co-operation.
Employees: 3
Volunteers: 1

British Association for Local History

PO Box 6549, Somersal Herbert, Ashbourne, Staffordshire DE6 5WH
T: 01283 585947
E: mail@balh.co.uk
www.balh.co.uk
The association works to advance understanding and knowledge of local history.
Employees: 4
Volunteers: 22

British Association for the Advancement of Science

Wellcome Wolfson Building, 165 Queen's Gate SW7 5HD
T: 020 7973 3503
F: 0870 770 7102
E: info@britishscienceassociation.org
www.britishscienceassociation.org
Chief Executive: Sir Roland Jackson
We are the UK's nationwide, open membership organisation, which provides opportunities for people of all ages to learn about, discuss and challenge the sciences and their implications.
Employees: 40
Volunteers: 5000
Regional offices: 14

British Association of Dermatologists

4 Fitzroy Square, London W1T 5HQ
T: 020 7383 0266
E: admin@bad.org.uk
www.bad.org.uk
The Association publishes and promotes information, teaching and research in dermatology.

British Association of Friends of Museums

141A School Road, Brislington, Bristol, Avon BS4 4LZ
T: 01179 777435
E: admin@bafm.org.uk
www.bafm.org.uk
Chairman: Michael Fayle
BAFM encourages support for museums of all kinds. Its aims are to publicise the achievements of museums, and their friends; to advise those wishing to set up new groups; and to assist and encourage existing groups. It liaises with all other bodies concerned with museums, art galleries and heritage centres, and voluntary support for them.
Employees: 1

British Association of Psychotherapists

37 Mapesbury Road, London NW2 4HJ
T: 020 8452 9823
F: 020 8452 0310
E: admin@bap-psychotherapy.org
www.bap-psychotherapy.org
Professional members' association in psychotherapy. It runs a consultation and psychotherapy centre for children, adolescents, families and adults. The association offers a reduced-fee scheme offering intensive therapy for adults who are able to make a commitment of a minimum

of three times weekly therapy for at least two years.
Employees: 6
Volunteers: 60

British Association of Social Workers

16 Kent Street, Birmingham B5 6RD
T: 0121 622 3911
F: 0121 622 4860
E: info@basw.co.uk
www.basw.co.uk
Chief Executive: Hilton Dawson
BASW is the main professional association for social workers in the UK.
Employees: 48
Volunteers: 200
Regional offices: 3

British Blind Sport

Pure Offices, Plato Close, Tachbrook Park, Warwick, Warwickshire CV34 6WE
T: 01926 424247
E: info@britishblindsport.org.uk
www.britishblindsport.org.uk
Chief Executive: Alaina MacGregor
Provides sport and recreation for blind and visually impaired people.
Employees: 3

British Cardiac Patients Association

15 Abbey Road, Bingham, Nottingham NG13 8EE
T: 01949 837070
E: admin@bcpa.co.uk
www.bcpa.co.uk
Chairman: Keith Jackson
The Association provides support, reassurance and advice to cardiac patients, their families and carers. Whether it be heart attack, angina, cardiac investigations, arrhythmias, implantable cardiac devices, or surgery for bypass, valve replacement aneurysm or transplant, we are able to offer free advice and information.
Volunteers: 80

British Cardiovascular Society

9 Fitzroy Square, London W1T 5HW
T: 020 7383 3887
E: enquiries@bcs.com
www.bcs.com
The objective of the British Cardiac Society is to advance the knowledge of diseases of the heart and circulation for the benefit of the public.
Employees: 12

British Cave Research Association

Old Methodist Chapel, Great Hucklow, Buxton, Derbyshire SK17 8RG
T: 01298 873810
F: 01298 873801
E: bcra-enquiries@bcra.org.uk
www.bcra.org.uk
Chairman: David Checkley
Promotes cave research and exploration, and related activities.
Employees: 1
Volunteers: 20+
Regional offices: 1

British Centre for Science Education

12 Millbeck Approach, Morley, West Yorkshire LS27 8WA
E: committee@bcseweb.org.uk
www.bcseweb.org.uk
The British Centre for Science Education is a single-issue pressure group dedicated solely to keeping creationism and intelligent design out of the science classroom in publicly funded schools in the UK.

British Colostomy Association

Enterprise House, 95 London Street, Reading, Berkshire RG1 4QA
T: 0118 939 1537
Helpline: 0800 328 4257
E: cass@colostomyassociation.org.uk
www.colostomyassociation.org.uk
Chairman: Monty Taylor
The Association offers help and reassurance to anyone who has had, or is about to have, a colostomy operation and runs a 24 hour helpline, provides a range of literature, publishes a quarterly magazine and promotes a network of support groups. Its team of UK wide volunteers provide one to one support on the phone or in person if needed.
Employees: 4
Volunteers: 100

British Council

10 Spring Gardens, London SW1A 2BN
E: general.enquiries@britishcouncil.org
www.britishcouncil.org
The UK's international organisation for educational opportunities and cultural relations.

British Deaf Association

18 Leather Lane, London EC1N 7SU
F: 020 7405 0090
E: bda@bda.org.uk
www.bda.org.uk
Chairman: Terry Riley
Promoting the rights of deaf people who use British Sign Language.
Employees: 25
Volunteers: 120
Regional offices: 4

British Dental Health Foundation

Smile House, 2 East Union Street, Rugby, Warwickshire CV22 6AJ
T: 01788 546365
Helpline: 0845 063 1188
F: 01788 541982
E: nigel@dentalhealth.org
www.dentalhealth.org
Chief Executive: Dr Nigel Carter
The UK's leading oral health charity, with a 40-year track record of providing public information and influencing government policy. It maintains a Dental Helpline consumer free-advice service; runs a product accreditation scheme to provide consumer assurance; publishes and distributes a wide range of educational literature for the profession and consumers; and runs National Smile Month between May and June, and Mouth Cancer Action Month throughout November.
Employees: 15

British Dyslexia Association

Unit 8, Bracknell Beeches, Old Bracknell Lane, Bracknell, Berkshire RG12 7BW
T: 0845 251 9003
Helpline: 0845 251 9002
F: 0845 251 9004
E: admin@bdadyslexia.org.uk
www.bdadyslexia.org.uk
Chief Executive: Dr Kate Saunders
The British Dyslexia Association is the voice for 10% of the population that experience dyslexia. We aim to influence government to promote a dyslexia friendly society that enables dyslexic people of all ages to reach their full potential. We provide the only national helpline supporting tens of thousands of people each year.
Employees: 25
Volunteers: 50

British Ecological Society

Charles Darwin House, 12 Roger Street, London WC1N 2JU
T: 020 7685 2500
F: 020 7685 2501
E: info@britishecologicalsociety.org
www.britishecologicalsociety.org

The British Ecological Society aims to promote the science of ecology through research and to use the findings of such research to educate the public and influence policy decisions that involve ecological matters.
Employees: 20

British Endodontic Society

PO Box 707, Gerrards Cross, Buckinghamshire SL9 0XS
T: 01494 581542 (also fax)
E: enquiries@bes-administrator.org
www.britishendodonticsociety.org
The object of the charity is to promote and advance the study of endodontology and to ensure that the dental health of the nation is both maintained and improved.
Employees: 1
Volunteers: 20

British False Memory Society (BFMS)

The Old Brewery, Newtown, Bradford-on-Avon, Wiltshire BA15 1NF
T: 01225 868682
F: 01225 862251
E: bfms@bfms.org.uk
www.bfms.org.uk
Director: Madeline Greenhalgh
Formed 1993 to raise awareness of dangers of recovered memory through flawed therapeutic trauma theories and investigative systems. Aims to promote accurate differentiation between true and false allegations of child sexual abuse through raising public, professional and policy maker awareness, organising conferences and seminars, through information provision, newsletters and encouraging academic research plus working with the media. BFMS incorporates a telephone helpline to support families and individuals affected by false memory and false accusations.
Employees: 3
Regional offices: 1

British Federation of Film Societies – Cinema For All

Unit 320, The Workstation, 15 Paternoster Row, Sheffield, South Yorkshire S1 2BX
T: 0114 221 0314
E: info@bffs.org.uk
www.bffs.org.uk
BFFS is the national support and development agency for the film society and community cinema sector. BFFS has supported specialised (art-house) cinema exhibition in the voluntary sector since its inception over 60 years ago and today continues to provide advice, technical support and education opportunities to communities across the UK.

British Future

Kean House, 6 Kean Street, London WC2B 4AS
T: 020 7632 9069
E: helena@britishfuture.org
www.britishfurture.org
Director: Sunder Katwala
British Future is an independent, non-partisan thinktank seeking to involve people in an open conversation that addresses people's hopes and fears about identity and integration, migration and opportunity, so that we feel confident about Britain's future.
Employees: 5
Volunteers: 0

British Geriatrics Society

Marjory Warren House, 31 St John's Square, London EC1M 4DN
T: 020 7608 1369
E: ionajaneharris@bgs.org.uk
www.bgs.org.uk
The society promotes better care in old age and seeks to improve the quality and provision of healthcare services for older people.

British Heart Foundation

Great London House, 180 Hampstead, London NW1 7AW
T: 020 7554 0000
F: 0207 554 0100
E: internet@bhf.org.uk
www.bhf.org.uk
Plays a leading role in the fight against heart disease.
Employees: 1584
Volunteers: 26000
Regional offices: 9

British HIV Association

BHIVA Secretariat, 1 Mountview Court, 310 Friern Barnet Lane, London N20 0LD
T: 020 8369 5380
F: 020 8446 9194
E: faarid@mediscript.ltd.uk
www.bhiva.org
Chair: Dr David Asboe
The objectives of BHIVA are to relieve sickness and to protect and preserve health through the development and promotion of good practice in the treatment of HIV and HIV-related illnesses; to advance public education in the subjects of HIV and the symptoms, causes, treatment and prevention of HIV-related illnesses through the promotion of research.
Employees: 0
Volunteers: 0
Regional offices: 0

British Holistic Medical Association

PO Box 371, Bridgwater, Somerset TA7 9AA
E: contactbhma@aol.co.uk
www.bhma.org
Chair: David Peters
The BHMA is an open association of mainstream healthcare professionals, CAM practitioners and members of the public who want to adopt a more holistic approach in their own life and work. We do not endorse, accredit or recommend individual practitioners or organisations.
Employees: 4
Volunteers: 7
Regional offices: 1

British Home and Hospital for Incurables

Crown Lane, London SW16 3JB
T: 020 8670 8261
E: home.stmvolunteercoord@ thebritishome.co.uk
www.britishhome.org.uk
The British Home provides specialist nursing care and support to chronically sick and disabled people. Our residents are offered the highest standard of care and support to: maintain their independence; participate in the planning of their care; retain personal prospects; and have access to their health records.

British Homeopathic Association

Hahnemann House, 29 Park Street West, Luton LU1 3BE
T: 0870 444 3950
F: 0870 444 3960
E: info@trusthomeopathy.org
www.trusthomepathy.org
Chief Executive: Cristal Sumner
The charity was founded in 1902 to promote homeopathy and raise money for research and the homeopathic training of healthcare professionals including doctors, dentists, nurses, podiatrists, pharmacists and vets. It is committed to making homeopathy more widely available on the NHS and provides information for the public and lobbies and campaigns for NHS homeopathy.
Employees: 9
Volunteers: 1

British Horse Society

Abbey Park, Stareton, Kenilworth, Warwickshire CV8 2XZ
T: 024 7684 0500
F: 024 7684 0501
E: enquiries@bhs.org.uk
www.bhs.org.uk
The Society aims to improve standards of care for horses and ponies, improve standards of riding and driving, encourage the use of horses and ponies and promote the interests of horse and pony breeding.
Employees: 71
Volunteers: 1000
Regional offices: 9

British Humanist Association

1 Gower Street, London WC1E 6HD
T: 020 7079 3580
F: 020 7079 3588
E: info@humanism.org.uk
www.humanism.org.uk
Chief Executive: Andrew Copson
The BHA promotes Humanism and supports and represents people who seek to live good lives without religious or superstitious beliefs. The BHA provides educational resources for schools and students; organises public lectures and other events; campaigns against religious privilege and for equality on grounds of religion or beliefs; and provides humanist funerals, weddings, civil partnership celebrations, namings and other ceremonies.
Employees: 12
Volunteers: 6

British Institute of Human Rights

School of Law, Queen Mary University of London, Mile End Road, London E1 4NS
T: 020 7882 5850
E: shosali@bihr.org.uk
www.bihr.org.uk
The Institute aims to further the education of the public and public authorities in the field of human rights in the UK and internationally.
Employees: 10
Volunteers: 3

British Institute of Learning Disabilities

Campion House, Green Street, Kidderminster DY10 1JL
T: 01562 723010
F: 01562 723029
E: enquiries@bild.org.uk
www.bild.org.uk
Chief Executive: Keith Smith
BILD aims to improve the quality of life for people with learning disabilities by involving them and their families in all aspects of our work. This includes working with

Government and public bodies to achieve full citizenship and human rights for people with learning disabilities, turning research and policy into practice and supporting service providers to develop and share person-centred approaches.
Employees: 28
Volunteers: 1

British Institute of Radiology

48–50 St John Street, Farringdon, London EC1M 4DT
E: admin@bir.org.uk
www.bir.org.uk
The Institute brings together all the professions in radiology, medical and scientific disciplines to share knowledge and educate the public, thereby improving the prevention and detection of disease and the management and treatment of patients.
Employees: 15

British Kidney Patient Association

3 The Windmills, St Mary's Close, Turk Street, Alton, Hampshire GU34 1EF
T: 01420 541424
F: 01420 89438
E: info@britishkidney-pa.co.uk
www.britishkidney-pa.co.uk
Chief Executive: Paddy Tabor
The British Kidney Patient Association exists for the benefit and welfare of kidney patients throughout the UK, offering support, advice in the form of leaflets and fact sheets and giving financial help.
Employees: 7

British Limbless Ex-Service Men's Association

Frankland Moore House, 185-187 High Road, Chadwell Heath, Romford, Essex RM6 6NA
T: 020 8590 1124
F: 020 8599 2932
E: officemanager@blesma.org
www.blesma.org
Director of Support & Communications: Col Ian Waller
The Association works to promote the welfare and meet the financial needs of those who lost a limb or limbs, the use of limbs or an eye(s) as a result of service in the armed forces and those who suffer amputation for whatever reason after service.
Employees: 62
Volunteers: 28
Income: £4,000,000 (2012-13)

British Liver Trust

2 Southampton Road, Ringwood, Hampshire BH24 1HY
T: 01425 481320
Helpline: 0800 652 7330
F: 01425 481335
E: admin@britishlivertrust.org.uk
www.britishlivertrust.org.uk
Chief Executive: Andrew Langford
We aim to help everyone affected by liver disease, through information, support and research.
Employees: 20
Volunteers: 4

British Lung Foundation

73–75 Goswell Road, London EC1V 7ER
T: 020 7688 5555
Helpline: 0845 850 5020
F: 020 7688 5556
E: enquiries@blf.org.uk
www.lunguk.org
Chief Executive: Penny Woods
The British Lung Foundation is here for everyone affected by a lung condition. It understands lung disease and fights to beat it through prevention, support and research.
Employees: 75
Volunteers: 500
Regional offices: 5
Income: £7,160,000 (2010-11)

British Lymphology Society

Garth House, Rushey Lock, Tadpole Bridge, Buckland Marsh, Oxfordshire SN7 8RF
T: 01452 790178
E: info@thebls.com
www.thebls.com
Chair: Nina Linnitt
The Society provides a group open to healthcare professionals and anyone with an interest in treating lymphoedema. It raises awareness of chronic oedemas.
Employees: 2
Volunteers: 20
Regional offices: 1
Income: £145,164 (2011-12)

British Marine Federation

Marine House, Thorpe Lea Road
T: 07717 666140
E: cmillward@britishmarine.co.uk
www.britishmarine.co.uk
Finance Director: Chris Millward

British Medical Acupuncture Society

Royal London Hospital for Integrated Medicine, 60 Great Ormond Street, London WC1N 3HR
T: 020 7713 9437
F: 020 7713 6286
E: bmaslondon@aol.com
www.medical-acupuncture.co.uk
Support Manager to Medical Director: Allyson Brown
A registered charity established to encourage the use and scientific understanding of acupuncture within medicine for the public benefit. BMAS seeks to enhance the education/training of suitably qualified practitioners, and to promote high standards of working practices in acupuncture.
Employees: 5

British National Temperance League

30 Keswick Road, Worksop, Nottinghamshire S81 7PT
T: 01909 477882 (also fax)
E: bntl@btconnect.com
www.bntl.org
Chief Executive: Barbara Briggs
BNTL is an organisation that responds to alcohol and other drug-related problems by seeking to promote healthy drug-free lifestyles and to inform on the effect of alcohol and drugs on individuals and communities. This is achieved through the production of teaching resources based around the national curriculum for teachers and others working with young people.
Employees: 2
Volunteers: 15

British Naturalists' Association

BNA, BM 8129, London WC1N 3XX
T: 0844 892 1817
E: info@bna-naturalists.org
www.bna-naturalists.org
President: David Bellamy
One of the UK's oldest natural history societies, BNA was founded in 1905 for the sole purpose of promoting awareness and the study of all aspects of British natural history, an aim which it continues to pursue to the present day.
Volunteers: 300
Regional offices: 10

British Obesity Surgery Patient Association

PO Box 805, Taunton, Somerset TA1 9DU
T: 0845 602 0446
E: enquiries@bospa.org
www.bospa.org
BOSPA (British Obesity Surgery Patient Association) was launched in December 2003 to provide support and information to the thousands of patients in the UK for whom obesity surgery can provide an enormous benefit.
Employees: 1

British Organ Donor Society

Balsham, Cambridge CB21 4DL
E: body@argonet.co.uk
www.argonet.co.uk/body
The Society acts as a self-help and support group for donor and recipient families, and promotes the carrying of multi-organ donor cards.

British Ornithologists' Union

Department of Zoology, University of Oxford, South Parks Road, Oxford OX1 3PS
E: bou@bou.org.uk
www.bou.org.uk
The Union promotes the study of the science of ornithology, encourages links between amateur and professional ornithologists, and encourages and supports research and training.

British ORT

Ort House, 126 Albert Street, London NW1 7NE
T: 020 7446 8520
E: info@britishort.org
www.britishort.org
ORT's mission is to provide education and vocational training, helping the young and not so young to gain skills they need to become proud, independent, contributing members of their own culture and society.

British Overseas NGOs for Development

Regents Wharf, 8 All Saints Street, London N1 9RL
T: 020 7837 8344
F: 020 7837 4220
E: membership@bond.org.uk
www.bond.org.uk
BOND is the network of UK-based voluntary organisations working in international development and development education. BOND members aim to improve the extent and quality of the UK and Europe's contribution to international development,

the eradication of global poverty and the upholding of human rights.
Employees: 25

British Pain Society

3rd Floor, Churchill House, 35 Red Lion Square, London WC1R 4SG
T: 020 7269 7840
F: 020 7831 0859
E: info@britishpainsociety.org
www.britishpainsociety.org
The Society promotes the advancement of health by raising the standard of management of pain by promotion of education, research and training.

British Polio Fellowship

Ground Floor Unit A, Eagle Office Centre, The Runway, South Ruislip, Middlesex HA4 6SE
T: 0800 018 0586
F: 020 8842 0555
E: info@britishpolio.org.uk
www.britishpolio.org.uk
Chief Executive: Ted Hill
The aims of the Fellowship are to enable polio survivors to lead full, independent and active lives and to ensure their needs are met. It ensures that post polio syndrome (late effects of polio) is recognised and managed effectively in every polio survivor and campaigns for the rights and equality of polio survivors.

British Pregnancy Advisory Service

20 Timothys Bridge Road, Stratford Enterprise Park, Stratford upon Avon CV37 9BF
T: 0845 365 5050
Helpline: 0845 730 4030
F: 0845 365 5051
E: info@bpas.org
www.bpas.org
Chief Executive: Ann Furedi
bpas was established in 1968 to provide a safe, legal abortion service and is a charitable, non-profit making organisation with sites nationwide. The organisation offers information and treatment in relation to unplanned pregnancy, vasectomy, abortion, contraception and online STI testing and treatment.
Employees: 60

British Psychological Society

St Andrew's House, 48 Princess Road East, Leicester LE1 7DR
T: 0116 254 9568
F: 0116 247 0787
E: enquiries@bps.org.uk
www.bps.org.uk
Chief Executive: Professor Ann Colley
The British Psychological Society is the representative body for psychology and psychologists in the UK. The Society has national responsibility for the development, promotion and application of psychology for the public good, and promotes the efficiency and usefulness of its members by maintaining a high standard of professional education and knowledge.
Employees: 117
Volunteers: 45000
Regional offices: 4

British Red Cross Society

UK Office, 44 Moorfields, London EC2Y 9AL
T: 0844 871 1111
E: information@redcross.org.uk
www.redcross.org.uk
The Society provides caring and emergency service to those most in need in their local communities through some 30,000 volunteers and staff. It raises funds to support the international work of the British Red Cross. The British Red Cross is part of the International Red Cross Movement, the largest voluntary organisation in the world with 10 million volunteers worldwide and 181 partner organisations.
Employees: 3000
Volunteers: 30000
Regional offices: 4

British School of Osteopathy

Avon House, 275 Borough High Street, London SE1 1JE
T: 020 7089 5307
E: j.smith@bso.ac.uk
www.bso.ac.uk
The School undertakes osteopathic research, to deliver osteopathic education and healthcare for the benefit of the whole community.

British Sjogren's Syndrome Association

PO Box 15040, Birmingham B31 3DP
T: 0121 478 0222
Helpline: 0121 478 1133
E: office@bssa.uk.net
www.bssa.uk.net
The Association provides mutual support and information to individuals affected by Sjogren's syndrome. We aim to educate people about the condition, raise awareness surrounding its existence and symptoms, and support research into its cause and treatment.
Employees: 4

British Society For Immunology

Vintage House, 37 Albert Embankment, London SE1 7TL
T: 020 3031 9800
E: e.thomas@immunology.org
www.immunology.org
Office Co-ordinator/PA To CEO: Emilie Thomas
Employees: 9

British Society for Rheumatology

Bride House, 18–20 Bride Lane, London EC4Y 8EE
T: 020 7842 0900
F: 020 7842 0901
E: bsr@rheumatology.org.uk
www.rheumatology.org.uk
To promote excellence in the treatment of people with arthritis and musculoskeletal conditions and to support those delivering it.
Employees: 24

British Society of Disability and Oral Health

Dental Special Needs, Chorley and District Hospital, Preston Road, Chorley, Lancashire PR7 1PP
E: katherine.wilson@newcastle.ac.uk
www.bsdh.org.uk
The aims of the Society are to promote the oral health of disabled people of all ages. It promotes links with organisations representing disabled people, consults with disability groups to identify their needs and demands and studies the barriers relating to the provision of oral healthcare for disabled people.

British Society of Psychosomatic Obstetrics Gynaecology and Andrology

Porterbrook Clinic, 75 Osborne Road, Nether Edge, Sheffield, South Yorkshire S11 9BF
E: chair@bspoga.org
www.bspoga.org
BSPOGA aims to advance the education of the general public and medical profession by encouraging the development of a better understanding and improved management of the psychological problems associated with reproductive and associated conditions in women and men.

British Sociological Association

Bailey Suite, Palatine House, Belmont Business Park, Belmont, Durham DH1 1TW
T: 0191 383 0839
F: 0191 383 0782
E: judith.mudd@britsoc.org.uk
www.britsoc.co.uk
Chief Executive: Judith Mudd
The BSA advances knowledge of sociology by lectures, publications, the promotion of research and encouragement of contact between workers in all relevant fields of enquiry.
Employees: 12
Volunteers: 500
Income: £1,096,611 (2011-12)

British Spiritualist Federation

T: 01475 700706
E: sandramcfadden@yahoo.co.uk

British Stammering Association

15 Old Ford Road, London E2 9PJ
T: 020 8981 8818
E: mail@stammering.org
www.stammering.org
The Association aims to help stammerers live satisfactorily with their speech and encourage research into stammering.
Employees: 9
Volunteers: 10

British Thyroid Foundation

2nd Floor, 3 Devonshire Place, Harrogate, North Yorkshire HG1 4AA
T: 01423 709707
E: info@btf-thyroid.org
www.btf-thyroid.org
Director and Secretary to the Trustees: Janis Hickey
Provides reliable information and support to people with thyroid disorders.
Employees: 5
Volunteers: 44
Regional offices: 1
Income: £100,000 (2012-13)

British Tinnitus Association

Unit 5, Acorn Business Park, Woodseats Close, Sheffield, South Yorkshire S8 0TB
T: 0114 250 9933
Helpline: 0800 018 0527
F: 0114 258 2279
E: info@tinnitus.org.uk
www.tinnitus.org.uk
Chief Executive: David Stockdale
The British Tinnitus Association (BTA) provides help, support and advice to people

with tinnitus, their families, friends and professionals caring for them. We provide accurate, reliable and authoritative information via: our helpline; over 30 information leaflets; Quiet, our quarterly journal; our website; attending awareness-raising events. We also support clinical research and provide training.

Employees: 12
Volunteers: 80
Regional offices: 0
Income: £477,889 (2012-13)

British Trust for Ornithology

The Nunnery, Thetford,
Norfolk IP24 2PU
T: 01842 750050
F: 01842 750030
E: info@bto.org
www.bto.org
The BTO promotes and encourages the wider understanding, appreciation and conservation of birds through scientific studies, using the combined skills and enthusiasm of its members, other birdwatchers and staff.

Employees: 95
Volunteers: 30000
Regional offices: 130

British Voice Association

330 Gray's Inn Road WC1X 8EE
T: 0300 123 2773
F: 0203 456 5092
E: administrator@
britishvoiceassociation.org.uk
www.britishvoiceassociation.org.uk
The BVA recognises the human voice as an essential element of our communication and wellbeing. It is devoted to people with voice problems, ranging from severe pathology and cancer to subtle difficulties of artistic performance, all of whom are entitled to the best care available.

Employees: 0
Volunteers: 10
Regional offices: 0

British Waterways

64 Clarendon Road
T: 01442 278738
E: robin.evans@britishwaterways.co.uk
www.britishwaterways.co.uk
Chief Executive: Robin Evans

British Wireless for the Blind Fund

10 Albion Place, Maidstone,
Kent ME14 5DZ
T: 01622 754757
F: 01622 751725
E: margaret@blind.org.uk
www.blind.org.uk
The Fund provides, on a permanent free-loan basis, radios, radio-cassette recorders, CD radio cassette recorders to UK registered blind and partially sighted persons, over the age of eight, who are in need.

Employees: 5
Volunteers: 300

British Youth Council

49–51 East Road, London N1 6AH
T: 0845 458 1489
E: mail@byc.org.uk
www.byc.org.uk
The Council works to advance the spiritual educational and physical welfare of young people in conjunction with similar bodies working in the same field in countries overseas.

Broken Rainbow LGBT Domestic Violence Service UK

J414, Tower Bridge Business Complex,
100 Clements Road, London SE16 4DG
T: 0845 260 5560
Helpline: 0300 999 5428
E: mail@brokenrainbow.org.uk
www.broken-rainbow.org.uk
Broken Rainbow UK runs the only National LGBT Domestic Violence Helpline providing confidential support to all members of the lesbian, gay, bisexual and transgender (LGBT) communities, their family and friends, and agencies supporting them.

Employees: 3
Volunteers: 15

Bromley Y

E: valeriemichelet@gmail.com

Brook

50 Featherstone Road, London EC1Y 8RT
T: 020 7284 6040
Helpline: 08088 021234
F: 020 7284 6050
E: admin@brook.org.uk
www.brook.org.uk
National Director: Simon Blake
The country's largest young people's sexual health charity. For 40 years, we have been providing sexual health services, support and advice to young people under 25. Brook wants a society that values all children, young people and their developing sexuality. We want all children and young people to be

supported to develop the self-confidence, skills and understanding they need to enjoy and take responsibility for their sexual lives, sexual health and wellbeing.

Employees: 27
Volunteers: 21
Regional offices: 23

Brothers of Charity Services

Lisieux Hall, Dawson Lane, Whittle-le-Woods, Chorley PR6 7DX
T: 01257 266311
F: 01257 265671
E: info@brothersofcharity.org.uk
www.brothersofcharity.org.uk
Aims to assist people who have learning difficulties to live an ordinary life in which they are respected and valued in their local community.

BSS

163 Eversholt Street, London NW1 1BU
T: 020 7419 3800
E: peter.calderbank@bss.org
www.bss.org
Chief Executive: Peter Calderbank
The purpose of BSS is to enable people to take action to improve the quality of their lives and society, through the provision and management of information and advice. This is done by providing comprehensive, high-quality, specialist contact centre and information services to our customers in the public, voluntary and commercial sectors.

Employees: 750
Regional offices: 6

BTCV trading as The Conservation Volunteers

Sedum House, Mallard Way, Doncaster,
South Yorkshire DN4 8DB
T: 01302 388888
E: a.lakin@tcv.org.uk
www.tcv.org
Chief Executive: Julie Hopes
The Conservation Volunteers is a social enterprise group enabling people to make a difference to their lives and improve their environment.

Employees: 500
Volunteers: 628000
Regional offices: 10

BUAV

16A Crane Grove, London N7 8NN
T: 020 7700 4888
F: 020 7700 0252
E: info@buav.org
www.buav.org
Chief Executive: Michelle Thew
The BUAV's vision is to create a world where nobody wants or believes we need to experiment on animals.
Employees: 18
Volunteers: 2

Buglife – the Invertebrate Conservation Trust

Bughouse, Ham Lane, Orton Waterville, Peterborough, Cambridgeshire PE2 5UU
T: 01733 201210
F: 01733 315410
E: info@buglife.org.uk
www.buglife.org.uk
Director: Matt Shardlow
The food we eat, the birds we see, the flowers we smell and the hum of life we hear, simply would not exist without bugs. Invertebrates truly underpin all life on earth. Sadly, many amazing and beautiful creatures are declining. Three species of bumblebees are now extinct in the UK and over 70% of butterfly species are in significant decline. Buglife is the only organisation in Europe devoted to the conservation of all invertebrates.
Employees: 7
Volunteers: 50
Regional offices: 2

Build Africa

Vale House, Clarence Road, Tunbridge Wells, Kent TN1 1HE
T: 01892 519619
E: hello@build-africa.org.uk
www.build-africa.org.uk
Build Africa is a development organisation with a vision for an economically self-efficient Africa. We are dedicated to helping young people escape poverty through education and enterprise. Our aim is to build an effective organisation capable of making a real difference. Our objective is to be fully transparent and held accountable to the young people, their communities and our donors.

Building and Social Housing Foundation

Memorial Square, Coalville, Leicestershire LE67 3TU
T: 01530 510444
F: 01530 510332
E: bshf@bshf.org
www.bshf.org

BSHF is an independent housing research organisation which identifies and promotes good practice in housing throughout the world.
Employees: 13
Volunteers: 0

Business and Education London South

E: michaelmanningprior@bels.org.uk

Business in the Community

137 Shepherdess Walk, London N1 7RQ
T: 020 7566 8650
E: information@bitc.org.uk
www.bitc.org.uk
Chief Executive: Julia Cleverdon
Business in the Community is a unique movement of over 800 member companies, representing one in five of the UK private sector workforce. A further 3,000 companies are engaged through our programmes and campaigns, which we operate through a local network of more than 100 business-led partnerships and we lead a global partners network of 112 organisations operating in over 60 countries.
Employees: 343
Regional offices: 11

Butler Trust

Howard House, 32–34 High Street, Croydon, Surrey CR0 1YB
T: 020 8688 6062
F: 020 8688 6056
E: info@thebutlertrust.org.uk
www.thebutlertrust.org.uk
Director: Simon Shepherd
The Butler Trust is an independent charity that recognises excellence and innovation by people working with offenders in the UK. Through its Annual Award Scheme and Development Programme, the Trust helps to identify and promote excellence and innovation; develop and disseminate best practice in the care and resettlement of offenders throughout the UK; and provide professional and personal development opportunities for award-winning staff.
Employees: 6
Volunteers: 14

Buttle UK

Audley House, 13 Palace Street, London SW1E 5HX
T: 020 7828 7311
E: info@buttleuk.org
www.buttleuk.org
Chief Executive: Gerri McAndrew
Buttle UK helps children and young people who are seriously in need throughout the

UK. It makes grants to meet the critical needs of individual children and young people whose safety, health or development are at risk, launching them into a brighter future. Objectives include providing grant aid, carrying out research, policy work and fundraising.
Employees: 20
Regional offices: 4

BYHP

E: tricia.foley@byhp.org.uk

CAADA

3rd Floor, Maxet House, 28 Baldwin Street, Bristol, Somerset BS1 1NG
T: 01173 178750
E: queries@caada.org.uk
www.caada.org.uk
CAADA's goal is to transform the UK's response to domestic abuse to make sure that victims are identified as early as possible and that they and their children are supported to live in safety.
Employees: 35

Cabrini Children's Society

E: patricia.canfield@cabrini.org.uk

CADASIL Research and Support Trust

c/o 28 Drumalane Park, Newry, Northern Ireland BT35 8AS
E: linda.ruddy@bbc.co.uk
www.cadasiltrust.org
Director: Jack Shields
The Trust offers help and support to those who are diagnosed with CADASIL. We aim to spread awareness of this illness and work with the medical establishment to find a cure.
Volunteers: 2

Caldecott Foundation

Caldecott House, Hythe Road, Smeeth,
Ashford, Kent TN25 6SP
T: 01303 815678
F: 01303 815677
E: caldecott@caldecottfoundation.co.uk
www.caldecottfoundation.co.uk
The Caldecott Foundation provides high-
quality childcare and education within a
therapeutic setting, enabling children to
attain life skills and self-esteem. We ensure
children and young people achieve their
educational potential via personal
educational plans and delivery of the
National Curriculum.
Employees: 178

CALIBRE Audio Library

New Road, Weston Turville, Aylesbury,
Buckinghamshire HP22 5XQ
T: 01296 432339
F: 01296 392599
E: enquiries@calibre.org.uk
www.calibre.org.ok
Director: Mike Lewington
The CALIBRE Audio Library is a free
nationwide postal library of audio books for
people with sight problems or physical
disabilities. 7,000 fiction and non-fiction
books recorded on cassette or MP3 disks
(unabridged) and no special playback
equipment is required. 1,200 titles are
available in the Young Calibre library. A small
charge is made for print catalogues – full
catalogue available on the website. Contact
the Membership Services Team for further
details and an application form.
Employees: 52
Volunteers: 95

Camberwell After School Project

E: carmen.lindsay@caspuk.org

Cambridge House

E: kwoodley@ch1889.org

Camfed International

St Giles Court, 24 Castle Street,
Cambridge CB3 0AJ
T: 01223 362648
E: info@camfed.org
www.camfed.org
Camfed International aims to eradicate
poverty in rural areas of Sub-Saharan Africa
by improving the educational status of girls
and women and children with disabilities.

Campaign Against Drinking and Driving

16 Market Street, Brighouse, West
Yorkshire HD6 1AP
T: 01484 723649 (also fax)
Helpline: 0845 123 5542
E: info@cadd.org.uk
www.scard.org.uk
Chair: Carole Whittingham
Campaigns against drink and/or drug
driving. Supports victims who have been
bereaved or injured as a result of drink/drugs
or any other bereavement related to road
collisions or accidents.

Campaign for Better Transport Charitable Trust

44-48 Wharf Road, London N1 7UX
T: 020 7566 6480
E: info@bettertransport.org.uk
www.bettertransport.org.uk
We are the Campaign for Better Transport
and since 1973 we have been helping to
create transport policies and programmes
that give people better lives. Working
nationally and locally, collectively and as
individuals, through high-level lobbying and
strong public campaigning, we make good
transport ideas a reality and stop bad ones
from happening.
Employees: 11
Volunteers: 3

Campaign for Freedom of Information

Suite 102, 16 Baldwins Gardens,
London EC1N 7RJ
T: 020 7831 7477
F: 020 7831 7461
E: admin@cfoi.demon.co.uk
www.cfoi.org.uk
The Campaign for Freedom of Information is
a non-profit organisation working to
improve public access to official information
and ensure that the Freedom of Information
Act is implemented effectively.
Employees: 2

Campaign for Learning

24 Greencoat Place, Westminster,
London SW1P 1RD
T: 020 7798 6067
F: 020 7798 6001
E: info@cflearning.org.uk
www.campaignforlearning.org.uk
Chief Executive: Tricia Hartley
The Campaign for Learning is working for a
society where learning is at the heart of social
inclusion. Research shows that lifelong
learners are more likely to be happier,
healthier, have better jobs, contribute more

to society and live longer and more fulfilled
lives. We work to build motivation, create
opportunities and provide support for
learning in families and communities,
workplaces and schools that leads to positive
change.
Employees: 17
Volunteers: 2
Regional offices: 2
Income: £900,000 (2011-12)

Campaign for Nuclear Disarmament (CND)

Mordechai Vanunu House, 162 Holloway
Road, London N7 8DQ
T: 020 7700 2393
F: 020 7700 2357
E: enquiries@cnduk.org
www.cnduk.org
Chair: Dave Webb
CND campaigns non-violently to rid the
world of nuclear weapons and other
weapons of mass destruction and to create
genuine security for future generations. CND
is funded entirely by its members and
supporters.
Employees: 11
Volunteers: 20
Regional offices: 6

Campaign to Protect Rural England

128 Southwark Street, London SE1 0SW
T: 020 7981 2800
F: 020 7981 2899
E: info@cpre.org.uk
www.cpre.org.uk
Chief Executive: Shaun Spiers
CPRE campaigns for a sustainable future for
the English countryside, a vital but
undervalued environmental, economic and
social asset to the nation. We highlight
threats and promote positive solutions. Our
in-depth research supports active
campaigning, and through reasoned
argument and lobbying we seek to influence
public opinion and decision-makers at every
level.
Employees: 55
Volunteers: 1500
Regional offices: 43

Camphill Village Trust Ltd

9 Saville Street, Malton, North
Yorkshire YO17 7LL
T: 0845 094 4638
F: 0845 094 4639
E: trustoffice@cvt.org.uk
www.cvt.org.uk
To provide support for adults with special
needs by establishing and maintaining
intentional communities of purpose where
all may continue to develop as individuals
through meaningful work of a productive
nature alongside a range of chosen
therapeutic activities and further education,
as well as a healthy cultural, social and
spiritual life.
Employees: 268
Volunteers: 206
Regional offices: 9

CAN

32–36 Loman Street, Southwark,
London SE1 0EE
T: 020 7922 7700
E: r.chadha@can-online.org.uk
www.can-online.org.uk
Chief Executive: Adele Blakebrough
Supporting social enterprise, CAN supports
social entrepreneurs to scale up their
businesses and maximise their social impact.
We provide office space, business support
and funds. We do this through: social
investment – leveraging capital funds and
strategic growth support into leading social
enterprises; CAN Mezzanine – award-
winning, sustainable social enterprise
providing high-quality shared office
accommodation for the third sector.
Employees: 16

Cancer Care Society

48 Mountbatten Drive, Ferndown,
Dorset BH22 9EL
T: 01202 894896
E: peter.j.hayes@btinternet.com
The Society aims to relieve, aid and support
persons who are suffering or have suffered
from cancer.

Cancer Laryngectomee Trust

PO Box 618, Halifax HX3 8WX
T: 01422 205522 (also fax)
E: info@cancerlt.org
www.cancerlt.org
Trustee: Carole Stainton
The Trust exists to improve the quality of life
for all neck breathers in the UK and to
provide essential needs for all cancer of the
larynx patients after surgery.
Volunteers: 20
Income: £17,019 (2011-12)

Cancer Research UK

Angel Building, 407 St Johns Street,
London EC1V 4AD
T: 020 7242 0200
F: 020 7269 3100
E: supporter.services@cancer.org.uk
www.cancerresearchuk.org
The aims of the Trust are to carry out
world-class research into the biology and
causes of cancer; develop effective
treatments and improve the quality of life for
cancer patients; reduce the number of
people getting cancer and provide
authoritative information on cancer.
Employees: 3380
Volunteers: 30000
Regional offices: 1000

Cancerkin

The Cancerkin Centre, Royal Free
Hospital, Pond Street, London NW3 2QG
T: 020 7830 2323
F: 020 7830 2324
E: info@cancerkin.org.uk
www.cancerkin.org.uk
Cancerkin provides information, treatment,
supportive care and rehabilitation for breast
cancer patients and support for relatives. It
also offers support for, and collaboration in,
research; education and training for health
professionals, students and volunteers; and
evolves with the changing management of
breast cancer.

CANS Legal Information

Camelford House, 87–89 Albert
Embankment, London SE1 7TP
T: 020 7820 3456
F: 020 7820 7890
E: canstrust@aol.com
www.cans.org.uk
Legal Editor: Robert Jack
We provide legal information that is
comprehensive, accurate, affordable and
always up to date. We work to promote a
better understanding of the law by widening
access to legal information.
Employees: 4
Regional offices: 1

Canterbury Diocesan Board of Finance

Diocesan House, Lady Wootton's Green
T: 01227 459401
E: cmccaulay@diocant.org
Reception and Hospitality Manager:
Charlotte McCaulay

Canterbury Oast Trust

Highlands Farm, Woodchurch, Ashford,
Kent TN26 3RJ
T: 01233 861493
F: 01233 860433
E: enquiries@c-o-t.org.uk
www.cc-o-t.org.uk
Chief Executive: David Jackson
The Trust provides homes, training and
supported employment for people with a
learning disability.
Employees: 178
Volunteers: 130
Regional offices: 1

CapeUK

31 The Calls, Leeds LS2 7EY
T: 0845 450 3700
E: jo@capeuk.org
www.capeuk.org
Chief Executive: Pat Cochrane
We are an independent not-for-profit
organisation committed to improving the
lives of children and young people, preparing
them to face the future with creativity and
self-belief. We work with schools, youth and
community organisations, universities, the
cultural and creative sector and other
agencies that share our aims.
Employees: 21
Regional offices: 3
Income: £2,254,232 (2011-12)

Capital Project

E: clare.ockwell@capitalproject.org

Car Accident Victims Organisation

Sheaf House, Holland Fen,
Lincoln LN4 4QH
T: 01205 280100
E: caraccidentsupport@googlemail.com
www.caraccidentvictims.org.uk
Car Accident Victims Organisation (CAVO)
is a national charity providing information,
practical advice and emotional support to car
accident victims, their family, carers or
friends.

CARA (Centre for Action on Rape and Abuse)

PO Box 548, Colchester, Essex CO1 1YP
T: 01206 367881
Helpline: 01206 769795
E: lindsey@caraessex.org.uk
www.caraessex.org.uk
Director: Lindsey Read
CARA supports children, young people and
adult women who have experienced any
form of sexual violence, directly or indirectly,

recently or in the past. We operate across the whole of mid and north Essex.
Employees: 10
Volunteers: 16
Regional offices: 1
Income: £190,000 (2012-13)

Cara Trust

240 Lancaster Road, London W11 4AH
T: 020 7243 6147
F: 020 7243 5821
E: mail@caralife.com
www.caralife.com
Director: Chris Woolls
The Cara Trust works to reduce the impact of HIV on people living with the virus through provision of a range of social welfare and spiritual support services. We also offer education services to faith communities. Our service guides can be downloaded from our website.
Employees: 4
Volunteers: 30
Income: £210,000 (2010-11)

Cardiomyopathy Association

Unit 10 Chiltern Court, Asheridge Road, Chesham, Buckinghamshire HP5 2PX
T: 01494 791224
F: 01494 797199
E: info@cardiomyopathy.org
www.cardiomyopathy.org
The Cardiomyopathy Association provides information and support to families affected by cardiomyopathy. We also work to improve health professionals knowledge of the diagnosis and management of cardiomyopathy.
Employees: 9
Volunteers: 200
Regional offices: 0
Income: £700,000 (2011-12)

Cards for Good Causes Ltd

1 Edison Gate, West Portway, Andover, Hampshire SP10 3SE
T: 01264 361555
F: 01264 362333
E: cfgc@interalpha.co.uk
www.cardsforcharity.co.uk
Cards for Good Causes assists charities through a forum where charities can exchange useful information and share ideas and solutions relating to their administration, promotion and fundraising. It encourages and promotes voluntary work for these

charities by their members, supporters, local community groups and the general public.
Employees: 20
Volunteers: 6300

Care and Repair England

Renewal Trust Business Centre, 3 Hawksworth Street, Nottingham, Nottinghamshire NG3 2EG
T: 0115 950 6500
E: info@careandrepair-england.org.uk
www.careandrepair-england.org.uk
Chief Executive: Sue Adams
Care and Repair England innovates, develops, promotes and supports housing-related policies and practical initiatives that enable older people to live independently in their own homes for as long as they wish.
Employees: 6
Volunteers: 10
Regional offices: 3

Care Bond

River Bank House, 27 River Street, Wilmslow, Cheshire SK9 4AB
T: 01625 523673
E: friends@the-care-bond.org.uk
www.the-care-bond.org.uk
The Care Bond is a new scheme designed by caring families to build a safe and rewarding community for vulnerable people and for those caring for them. Capital is raised by the management company to develop gated communities where vulnerable adults can live, and work safely. Specially designed bungalows are built, and offered for sale to caring families. As the capital is released further properties are built until the community reaches a healthy size.

Care Co-ordination Network Cymru

Units 6 and 7, Plas Pentwyn, Castle Road, Coedpoeth LL11 3NA
T: 01978 750685
E: wales@ccncymru.org.uk
www.ccncymru.org.uk
Wales Manager: Sally Rees
CCN Cymru is an organisation promoting and supporting case coordination or key working for disabled children and their families in Wales. CCN Cymru is an independent registered charity based in Coedpoeth near Wrexham.
Employees: 5
Regional offices: 1

Care for the Wild International

72 Brighton Road, Horsham, West Sussex RH13 5BU
T: 01403 249832
E: info@careforthewild.com
www.careforthewild.com
Care for the Wild International (CWI) promotes the conservation and welfare of wildlife in Britain and abroad. CWI provides fast, direct practical aid to animals in need. It helps to make areas safe from poachers, rehabilitating sick or injured animals and provides sanctuary for individuals who cannot return to the wild. The charity also acts as a global voice for wildlife through education and by changing attitudes and promoting awareness amongst local communities and policy makers.
Employees: 10
Regional offices: 1

CARE International UK

9th Floor, 89 Albert Embankment, Vauxhall, London SE1 7TP
T: 020 7091 6000
F: 020 7582 0728
E: info@careinternational.org
www.careinternational.org.uk
Chief Executive: Geoffrey Dennis
CARE International is a leading development and humanitarian charity supporting the poorest communities in 84 countries around the world. Our aim is to bring sustainable and innovative solutions to complex poverty issues and last year we supported 1,015 poverty-fighting projects that reached more than 122 million people. Our mission is to create lasting change in poor communities and we put money where it is needed most.
Employees: 110
Volunteers: 4
Income: £43,677,000 (2011-12)

Careers Research and Advisory Centre Ltd

Sheraton House, Castle Park, Cambridge CB3 0AX
T: 01223 448506
F: 01223 311708
E: beata.pedziwiatr@vitae.ac.uk
www.crac.org.uk
The Centre works to advance the education of the public in lifelong career-related learning for all; to enable employers and the world of education to work successfully together and promote best practice and the highest standards of professionalism and execution amongst those offering careers advice and development. Vitae (CRAC's biggest programme) is the UK organisation championing the personal, professional and career development of doctoral researchers

and research staff in higher education institutions and research institutes.
Employees: 27
Regional offices: 1

Carer Support Wiltshire

E: fiona@carersinwiltshire.co.uk

Carers Association Southern Staffordshire

E: michele.mcdonald@ carersinformation.org.uk

Carers Centre (Leicestershire & Rutland)

Unit 19 Matrix House, Constitution Hill, Leicester, Leicestershire LE1 1PL
T: 0116 251 0999
F: 0116 251 3514
E: enquiries@claspthecarerscentre.org.uk
www.org.uk
Centre Manager: Charles Huddleston
To promote any charitable purposes for the benefit of carers in the city and county of Leicestershire (hereinafter called the area of benefit) and, in particular, the advancement of education and furtherance of health and the relief of poverty, distress and sickness.
Employees: 9
Volunteers: 25
Income: £230,000 (2012-13)

Carers Network

E: ellen.o'mahony@carers-network.co.uk

Carers Trust

32-36 Loman Street, London SE1 0EH
T: 0844 800 4361
F: 0844 800 4362
E: info@carers.org
www.carers.org and www.youngcarers.net
Chief Executive: Thea Stein
Carers Trust is a major new charity for, with and about carers. We work to improve support, services and recognition for anyone living with the challenges of caring, unpaid, for a family member or friend who is ill, frail, disabled or has mental health or addiction problems. To find your nearest Carers Trust Network Partner, call 0844 800 4361 or visit www.carers.org.
Employees: 50+
Volunteers: 2
Regional offices: 6

Carers UK

20 Great Dover Street, London SE1 4LX
T: 020 7378 4999
Helpline: 0808 808 7777
F: 020 7490 8824
E: info@carersuk.org
www.carersuk.org
Chief Executive: HelÃna Herklots
Carers UK makes life better for the millions of people who look after older, ill or disabled family and friends.
Employees: 65
Volunteers: 250
Regional offices: 4
Income: £4,292,034 (2012-13)

Carers' Support - Canterbury, Dover & Thanet

80 Middle Street, Deal, Kent CT14 6HL
T: 01304 364637
E: admin@carers-doverdistrict.org
www.carers-doverdistrict.org
CEO: Patricia Cole
Supporting those who care for a relative or friend.
Employees: 11

Caring and Sharing Trust

Cottons Farmhouse, Whiston Road, Cogenhoe, Northamptonshire NN7 1NL
T: 01604 891487
F: 01604 890405
E: admin@cottonsfarmhouse.org
www.cottonsfarmhouse.org
The trust provides help, support and information to people with learning difficulties and their parents, particularly those living in rural areas.
Employees: 5
Volunteers: 50

CARITAS – Social Action

39 Eccleston Square, London SW1V 1BX
T: 020 7901 4875
F: 020 7901 4874
E: caritas.admin@cbcew.org.uk
www.csan.org.uk
Promotes Catholic social action in England and Wales.
Employees: 7
Regional offices: 100

Carplus Trust

Round Foundry Media Centre, Foundry Street, Leeds, West Yorkshire LS11 5QP
T: 0113 394 4590
E: info@carplus.org.uk
www.carplus.org.uk
Chief Executive: Chas Ball
Carplus is the UK's pioneering transport NGO supporting the development of affordable, accessible and low-carbon car-sharing clubs and ride-sharing services. It is Carplus' mission to promote sustainable transport and, specifically, to stimulate and facilitate a rethink in the role of the private car as part of the urban mobility mix.
Employees: 7
Regional offices: 2

Carr-Gomm

6–12 Tabard Street, London SE1 4JU
E: info@carr-gomm.org.uk
www.carr-gomm.org.uk
Carr-Gomm offers a range of care, housing and other support services to almost 3,000 people each year across England. Most of our service-users have a learning disability, mental-health, or a physical disability. Most are disadvantaged by poverty and would otherwise be homeless. We encourage all of our service users to work towards their own personal goals, and lead a better quality of life.

CASE Kent

Berwick House, 8 Elwick Road, Ashford, Kent TN23 1PF
T: 01233 610171
E: janperfect@casekent.org.uk
www.casekent.org.uk
CEO: Jan Perfect
CASE Kent provides specialist expertise, information and support to develop the skills local people need to run successful not-for-profit organisations and groups, primarily in the districts of Ashford, Dover, Shepway and Thanet.
Employees: 7
Volunteers: 4
Regional offices: 3
Income: £123,536 (2012-13)

Caspari Foundation for Educational Therapy and Therapeutic Teaching

Gregory House, Coram Campus, 48-49 Mecklenburgh Square, London WC1N 3NY
T: 020 7923 6270
E: admin@caspari.org.uk
www.caspari.org.uk
The Foundation aims to develop the theory and practice of therapy as a mode of treatment for children and young people with emotional, behavioural and learning difficulties, to establish professional standards in its practice and to disseminate knowledge and understanding of the method.

Cass Centre for Charity Effectiveness

Cass Business School, 106 Bunhill Row, London EC1Y 8TZ
T: 020 7040 0901
E: casscce@city.ac.uk
www.cass.city.ac.uk/cce
Director: Professor Paul Palmer
The Centre for Charity Effectiveness at Cass Business School (Cass CCE) is the leading nonprofit and philanthropy centre in the UK and has significantly enhanced the performance of hundreds of organisations and thousands of individuals across the nonprofit sector. Our world-class blend of postgraduate programmes, academic research, talent development and consultancy services deliver leading edge thinking, benefitting from theory but always grounded in practice to develop leaders and create real change in organisations.
Employees: 20
Volunteers: 20
Income: £1,500,000 (2010-11)

Castle Point Association of Voluntary Services (CAVS)

The Tyrells Centre, 39 Seamore Avenue, Thundersley, Essex SS7 4EX
T: 01268 638416
F: 01268 638415
E: office@castlepointavs.org.uk
www.castlepointavs.org.uk
CEO: Kirsty O'Callaghan
CAVS provides support and guidance to voluntary sector organisations in the borough of Castle Point. Frontline projects include Children's Services, Volunteer

Centre, Befriending Service and Be Safer Essex.
Employees: 35
Volunteers: 125
Regional offices: 1
Income: £1,009,809 (2012-13)

Catholic Agency for Overseas Development

Romero Close, Stockwell Road, London SW9 9TY
T: 020 7733 7900
F: 020 7274 9630
E: cafod@cafod.org.uk
www.cafod.org.uk
CAFOD funds relief and development projects overseas and raises awareness in England and Wales of the root causes of poverty.
Employees: 172
Volunteers: 80
Regional offices: 12

Catholic Association for Racial Justice

9 Henry Road, Manor House, London N4 2LH
T: 020 8802 8080
F: 020 8211 0808
E: info@carj.org.uk
www.carj.org.uk
National Coordinator: Rosie Bairwal
To overcome racial discrimination in the Church and in society through policy work and programmes. Each year we produce materials for Racial Justice Sunday (on the second Sunday in September each year) with CTBI. We work with parishes, dioceses, networks and others throughout the year to promote equality for all disadvantaged groups including black minority ethnic people, Muslim communities, migrants, sanctuary seekers and refugees, gypsies, Roma and travellers, disadavantaged white communities and Dalits.
Employees: 3
Volunteers: 2

Catholic Children's Society

E: paulw@cathchild.org.uk

Catholic Clothing Guild

5 Dark Lane, Shrewsbury, Shropshire SY2 5LP
T: 01743 243858
E: carmel.edwards@btinternet.com
The guild supplies new, useful and warm clothing for those who, through unfortunate

circumstances, are unable to provide for themselves and their families.

Catholic Concern for Animals

15 Rosehip Way, Bishops Cleeve, Cheltenham, Gloucestershire GL52 8WP
T: 01242 677423
E: deborahjark@aol.com
www.catholic-animals.org
Chairman: Mgr John Chaloner
We aim to put animals on the agenda of the Church, and to promote authentic Christian teaching on animals. The wellbeing of all animals is our priority, and cultivating non-cruelty, to help make this a better, gentler and more compassionate world for all.
Employees: 1
Volunteers: 10

Catholic Truth Society

40–46 Harleyford Road, London SE11 5AY
T: 020 7640 0042
E: f.martin@cts-online.org.uk
www.cts-online.org.uk
The Society publishes and disseminates low-priced devotional and teaching works; assists all Catholics to a better knowledge of their religion; spreads information about the faith among non-Catholics and assists the circulation of Catholic books.

Catholic Women's League

PO Box 303, Malvern WR14 9DX
T: 01684 540414 (also fax)
E: natsec@cwlhq.org.uk
www.catholicwomensleague.org
The League aims to unite Catholic women in a bond of common fellowship; promotes religious, educational and social welfare interests on parish, diocesan, national and international levels; ensures Catholic representation of these interests on major public bodies and initiates and maintains charitable works.

Cats Protection

National Cat Centre, Chelwood Gate, Haywards Heath, West Sussex RH17 7TT
T: 01825 741211
F: 01825 741005
E: volunteering@cats.org.uk
www.cats.org.uk
From humble beginnings in 1927, Cats Protection has grown to become the UK's leading feline welfare charity. We now help around 235,000 cats and kittens every year through our network of over 260 volunteer-

run branches, 29 adoption centres and our homing centre.
Employees: 350
Volunteers: 9000
Regional offices: 260

Cavell Nurses' Trust

Grosvenor House, Prospect Hill, Redditch, Worcestershire B97 4DL
T: 01527 595999
Helpline: 0808 123 4999
F: 01527 67245
E: admin@nurseaid.org.uk
www.nurseaid.org.uk
Chief Executive Officer: Peter Farrall
Cavell Nurses' Trust assists working, retired and student nurses, midwives and healthcare assistants who are in need or suffering hardship or distress. Support is offered in the form of financial grants; providing or paying for goods, services or facilities; or by making grants of money to other people who provide goods, services or facilities to those in need.
Employees: 7

Caxton Trust (working name Catch Up)

Catch Up, Keystone Innovation Centre, Croxton Road, Thetford, Norfolk IP24 1JD
T: 01842 752297
F: 01842 824490
E: training@catchup.org
www.catchup.org
Director: Julie Lawes
To address the problem of underachievement that has its roots in literacy and numeracy difficulties.
Employees: 11

CCI

World Vision House, Opal Drive, Fox Milne, Milton Keynes, Buckinghamshire MK15 0DH
T: 01908 477951
E: office@cci.org.uk
www.cci.org.uk
Executive Director: Keith Hagon
An association of over 250 members who organise holidays, school residential experiences and conferences. Members offer a wide variety of voluntary opportunities to work on these events both in the UK and overseas.
Employees: 3
Income: £125,000 (2012-13)

CCS Adoption

162 Pennywell Road, Easton, Bristol, Avon BS5 0TX
T: 0117 935 0005
E: info@ccsadoption.org
www.ccsadoption.org
Chief Executive: Jadwiga Ball
CCS Adoption is a voluntary, independent and registered adoption agency that offers a comprehensive adoption service that includes recruiting, assessing and preparing adoptive families, supporting child and family throughout the adoption process and beyond, working with birth parents who may be considering adoption for their child in partnership with Local Authority Social Services Departments and providing a counseling service to adult adoptees and their relatives.
Employees: 18
Volunteers: 2
Regional offices: 1

CDH UK

The Denes, Lynn Road, Tilney All Saints, King's Lynn, Norfolk PE34 4RD
T: 01553 828382
Helpline: 0800 731 6991
E: committee@cdhuk.org.uk
www.cdhuk.org.uk
Chair: Brenda Lane
The charity supports families whose children are diagnosed with congenital diaphragmatic hernia; it supports both those who survive and those who are bereaved. It also aims to educate and raise awareness, both to the general public and medical professionals, and promotes research. The association supports families whose children are diagnosed with congenital diaphragmatic hernia; it supports both those who survive and those who are bereaved. It also aims to educate and raise awareness both to the general public and medical professionals and promotes research.
Volunteers: 10
Regional offices: 2

Central Council of Physical Recreation

E: info@ccpr.org.uk

Central Organisation Maritime Pastimes and Sport Services

3 Glenwood Avenue, London NW9 7PL
T: 020 8200 6286
E: broadsword@seacadet.org

Promotes the advancement of character development of boys and girls of all ages through the use of adventure education based on seamanship and the practice of seafaring.

Centre 404

Centre 404, 404 Camden Road, London N7 0SJ
T: 020 7607 8762
F: 020 7700 0085
E: amyc@centre404.org.uk
www.centre404.org.uk
Chief Executive: Amy Curtis
Centre 404 is working towards a world where people with a learning disability and their families have the support they need to enjoy the same rights, freedom, responsibilities, respect, choices and quality of life as people within the wider community. We aim to contribute to this by providing excellent quality services and by supporting people with a learning disability and their carers to get their voices and views heard.
Employees: 173
Volunteers: 90
Regional offices: 1
Income: £2,932,543 (2012-13)

Centre for Accessible Environments

Fourth Floor Holyer House, 20–21 Red Lion Court, London EC4A 3EB
T: 020 7822 8232
F: 020 7840 8261
E: helen.carter@cae.org.uk
www.cae.org.uk
Director: Helen Carter
The Centre improves the design of the built environment to accommodate the needs of all users, including elderly and disabled people.
Employees: 10
Volunteers: 1

Centre for Crime and Justice Studies

2 Langley Lane, London SW8 1GB
T: 020 7840 6110
E: info@crimeandjustice.org.uk
www.crimeandjustice.org.uk
The Centre promotes the exchange of knowledge and experience of criminal justice matters among all interested people, both professional and lay; initiates and disseminates research into the causes, prevention and treatment of crime and delinquency.

Centre for Effective Dispute Resolution

International Dispute Resolution Centre, 70 Fleet Street, London EC4Y 1EU
T: 020 7536 6000
E: info@cedr.co.uk
www.cedr.co.uk
The Centre encourages and develops mediation and other dispute resolution and prevention techniques in commercial and public sectors.

Centre for Fun and Families Limited

177/179 Narborough Road, Leicester, Leicestershire LE3 0PE
T: 0116 223 4254
F: 0116 275 8558
E: centre@funandfamilies.org.uk
www.funandfamilies.co.uk
Chief Executive: Jayne Ballard
The Centre assists families where parents are experiencing behaviour difficulties with their children/young people; promotes good practice by providing parent training packs based on social learning theory; provides services direct to families and offers skills training to professional staff in both statutory and voluntary agencies.
Employees: 7
Volunteers: 22

Centre for Innovation In Voluntary Action

9–10 Mansfield Place, London NW3 1HS
T: 020 7431 1412
E: norton@civa.org.uk
The Centre promotes new ideas and approaches, encourages innovation in voluntary action in the UK and abroad; facilitates the dissemination of ideas, experiences and issues and promotes exchanges.

Centre for Policy on Ageing

28 Great Tower Street, London EC3R 5AT
T: 020 7553 6500
F: 020 7553 6501
E: cpa@cpa.org.uk
www.cpa.org.uk
The Centre encourages better services for older people by initiating informed debate, stimulating awareness of the needs of older people, formulating and promoting social policies and encouraging the spread of good practice.
Employees: 7

Centre for Studies on Inclusive Education

The Park Centre, Daventry Road, Knowle, Bristol BS4 1DQ
T: 0117 353 3150
F: 0117 353 3151
E: admin@csie.org.uk
www.csie.org.uk
CSIE Director: Dr Artemi Sakellariadis
The Centre for Studies on Inclusive Education (CSIE) is an independent centre, set up in 1982, actively supporting inclusive education as a basic human right of every child. The Centre is funded by charitable donations, with additional income from sale of publications and small grants for research or other projects. CSIE's work is driven by a commitment to overcome barriers to learning and participation for all children and young people.
Employees: 3

Centre for Sustainable Energy

3 St Peters Court, Bedminster Parade, Bristol BS3 4AQ
T: 0117 934 1400
E: info@cse.org.uk
www.cse.org.uk
Chief Executive: Simon Roberts OBE
We are an independent national charity that shares our knowledge and experience to help people change the way they think and act about energy.
Employees: 40

Centre for the Advancement of Interprofessional Education

PO Box 680, Fareham PO14 9NH
E: admin@caipe.org.uk
www.caipe.org.uk
Chair: Marilyn Hammick
CAIPE promotes and develops interprofessional education as a way of improving collaboration between practitioners and organisations, engaged in both statutory and non-statutory public services and improving the quality of care that is delivered to the public. CAIPE's some 200 members form a network of mutual support and interest that facilitates intellectual engagement with interprofessionalism.
Employees: 1

Centre for Volunteering and Community Leadership

E: amelling@uclan.ac.uk

Centre for Youth and Community Development

94-106 Leagrave Road, Luton, Bedfordshire LU4 8HZ
T: 01582 519500
E: mir.juma@cycd.org.uk
www.cycd.org.uk
Director: Mir Juma
Through a dedicated and professional system of youth and community development work, the Bangladesh Youth League will seek to improve the quality of life of the community, alleviate poverty and promote good health through the provision of: education and training, including social education programmes; advocacy; advice; information; outreach and centre-based activities; and liason with other similar service providers. BYL actively promotes equality of opportunity and diversity, is non-religious and non-political.

Centrepoint

Central House, 25 Camperdown Street, London E1 8DZ
T: 0845 466 3400
E: info@centrepoint.org.uk
www.centrepoint.org.uk
Centrepoint aims to give young people on a downward spiral a chance to turn things around and build a more fulfilling future.
Employees: 250
Volunteers: 70
Regional offices: 2

Centris

Crane House, 19 Apex Business Village, Annitsford, Northumberland NE23 7BF
T: 0191 250 1969
F: 0191 250 2563
E: centris@cranehouse.eu
www.centris.org.uk
The Centre exists to advance education, to promote the relief of sickness and the preservation and protection of health and to promote the relief of poverty in particular by promoting research into the role of individual self-awareness, self-development and personal responsibility in these fields and the dissemination of the useful results of that research.

CfBT Education Trust

60 Queens Road, Reading RG1 4BS
T: 0118 902 1000
F: 0118 902 1434
E: enquiries@cfbt.com
www.cfbt.com
Chief Executive: Steve Munby
CfBT Education Trust is a top 30 UK charity providing education services in the UK and

internationally. Established more than 40 years ago, CfBT has an annual turnover exceeding £100 million and employs 2,000 staff worldwide. We teach in schools, academies and the secure estate, manage national programmes in the UK and special projects overseas, provide support for school improvement as well as consultancy services to education professionals. CfBT finances a substantial research and development programme.
Employees: 2000
Volunteers: 0

Challenge Fund: The Fight Against Cancer in the Emerging World

INCTR Challenge Fund, Prama House, 267 Banbury Road, Oxford OX2 7HT
T: 01865 339510
F: 01865 339300
E: mlodge@canet.org
www.challengefund.org
Executive Director: Mark Lodge

Chance UK

2nd Floor, London Fashion Centre, 89-93 Fonthill Road, London N4 3JH
T: 020 7281 5858
F: 020 7281 4402
E: admin@chanceuk.com
www.chanceuk.com
Chance UK provides a year-long, one-to-one mentoring programme for primary school children with behavioural difficulties who are at risk of developing anti-social or criminal behaviour.
Employees: 21
Volunteers: 150
Regional offices: 1

CHANGE

Unit 11, Shine, Harehills Road, Leeds, West Yorkshire LS8 5HS
T: 0113 388 0011
F: 0113 388 0012
E: info@change-people.co.uk
www.changepeople.co.uk
Director: Philipa Bragman
CHANGE is a national rights organisation led by disabled people. We campaign for equal rights for all people with learning disabilities. We make information accessible and we give a strong voice to parents with a learning disability.
Employees: 15
Volunteers: 20
Regional offices: 1

Changemakers

22 Upper Woburn Place, London WC1H 0TB
T: 020 7554 2840
E: info@changemakers.org.uk
www.changemakers.org.uk
Chief Executive: Martin Sharman
Changemakers enables young people to play a positive and active role in society by giving them the opportunity to develop and manage innovative community projects. Changemakers creates active citizens, enterprising minds and future leaders. Changemakers offers learning programmes, funding schemes, publications and resources, training and consultancy, research and development and guidance to policy makers in the field of youth-led community action.
Employees: 11
Volunteers: 1500

Changing Faces

The Squire Centre, 33–37 University Street, London WC1E 6JN
T: 0845 450 0275
F: 0845 450 0276
E: info@changingfaces.org.uk
www.changingfaces.org.uk
Chief Executive: James Partridge
Changing Faces supports and represents the interests of children, teenagers, adults and their families who have disfigurements from birth, accident or disease, helping them to build self-esteem, to gain access to the best health and social services and to enjoy full civil rights and equal opportunities in all aspects of life.
Employees: 24
Volunteers: 150
Regional offices: 3

Chapter 1

2 Exton Street, London SE1 8UE
T: 020 7593 0470
F: 020 7593 0478
E: sophias@chapter1.org.uk
www.ch1.org.uk
Chief Executive: Geoff Hawkins
Changing lives one by one. Supported housing for vulnerable people and those at risk. Work with single parents and their children, women's refuge, family contact centres, refurbished furniture.
Employees: 300
Volunteers: 20
Regional offices: 1

Chara Trust

Community Access Point, 164 Windsor Street, Liverpool, Merseyside L8 8EH
T: 0151 708 0448
F: 0151 708 8060
E: info@charatrust.org.uk
www.charatrust.org.uk
The Trust aims to enhance the quality of life in communities through activities to develop members' capacity and skills so that they are better able to identify and help meet their needs and to participate more fully in society.
Volunteers: 10

Charities Advisory Trust

Radius Works, Back Lane, London NW3 1HL
T: 020 7794 9835
E: people@charitiesadvisorytrust.org.uk
www.charitiesadvisorytrust.org.uk
The Trust works to relieve poverty throughout the world; to advance education; to preserve buildings and monuments of architectural merit; and to assist charities to make better use of their assets and resources both generally and in relation to trading and/or fundraising activities on their behalf.

Charities Aid Foundation

25 Kings Hill Avenue, Kings Hill, West Malling, Kent ME19 4TA
T: 03000 123000
Helpline: 01732 520000
F: 01732 520001
E: info@cafonline.org
www.cafonline.org
CEO: John Low
The Charities Aid Foundation is a registered charity that works to create greater value for charities and social enterprise. We do this by transforming the way donations are made and the way charitable funds are managed. We also help shape the charitable sector through our research and events.
Employees: 375
Regional offices: 3

Charities Evaluation Services (CES)

4 Coldbath Square, London EC1R 5HL
T: 020 7713 5722
F: 020 7713 5692
E: enquiries@ces-vol.org.uk
www.ces-vol.org.uk
CES exists to strengthen the third sector by developing its use of evaluation and quality systems. We provide training to 1,000–2,000 organisations annually, frequently working in partnership with local helper agencies such as CVS and with specialist networks. We also carry out external evaluations and offer

consultancy services. CES publishes PQASSO, the most popular quality system in the sector. A kite mark for PQASSO users, the PQASSO Quality Mark was launched in 2007/8.

Employees: 21
Volunteers: 12

Charities HR Network

43 Kingfisher Way, Marchwood,
Southampton SO40 4XS
T: 02380 860984
E: co-ordinator@chrn.org.uk
www.chrn.org.uk
Chair of Steering Group: Diane Blausten
A network of senior HR representatives who work together to advance the education in, and promote improved standards of human resource management in national charities, with the aim of increasing their effectiveness and efficiency.
Income: £11,000 (2012-13)

Charity Administration, Resourcing and Accountability

5 St George's Avenue, Rugby,
Warwickshire CV22 5PN
T: 01788 810146
F: 01788 522888
E: carargd@aol.com
Executive Director: Greyham Dawes
CARA provides free advice via its volunteer executive director on best practice in annual financial reporting and regulatory compliance issues for small charities generally (on request) and 'Special Trust' administration services for spiritually minded charitable projects/activities.
Employees: 0
Volunteers: 6
Regional offices: 1
Income: £24,000 (2012-13)

Charity Bank

194 High Street, Tonbridge,
Kent TN9 1BE
T: 01732 774040
F: 01732 774069
E: enquiries@charitybank.org
www.charitybank.org
Charity Bank is a specialist lender to charities, voluntary organisations and social enterprises, providing affordable loans from £5,000 up to £1,000,000 on favourable terms. We offer loan finance where other banks won't or can't. We have stable interest rates, which are not linked to the Bank of England's base rate, no early repayment

penalties, usually no trustee personal guarantees and no requirement to change banks.
Employees: 10
Volunteers: 30

Charity Finance Group

15-18 White Lion Street, London N1 9PG
T: 0845 345 3192
F: 0845 345 3193
E: info@cfg.org.uk
www.cfg.org.uk
Chief Executive: Caron Bradshaw
CFG (Charity Finance Group) is the charity that champions best practice in finance management in the voluntary sector. Our training and development programmes enable finance managers to give the essential leadership on finance strategy and management that their charities need. With more than 2,000 members, managing over 18 billion, we are uniquely placed to challenge regulation that threatens the effective use of charity funds.
Employees: 24

Charity IT Leaders (CITL)

Chester House, 68 Chestergate,
Macclesfield, Cheshire SK11 6DY
T: 01625 664500
E: admin@charityitleaders.org.uk
www.charityitleaders.org.uk
Chair: Laura Dawson
As the premier membership group for IT Directors of major UK Charities, the object is the promotion for the public benefit of the efficiency and effectiveness of charities and not-for-profit organisations through the promotion of study, sharing of knowledge and advancement of the use of information technology. We do this by providing opportunities of networking, sharing and giving advice.
Employees: 0
Volunteers: 15
Regional offices: 0
Income: £91,500 (2012-13)

Charity Logistics

Room 5, North Wing, Turkey Court,
Turkey Mill, Ashford Road, Maidstone,
Kent ME14 5PP
T: 0845 130 3845
F: 0845 130 3895
E: news@freshhope.org.uk
www.freshhope.org.uk

Our aim is to help charities achieve their objectives effectively, efficiently and economically.
Employees: 5
Volunteers: 1
Regional offices: 1

Charity Retail Association

356 Holloway Road, London N7 6PA
T: 020 7697 4080
Helpline: 020 7697 4252
E: susan@charityretail.org.uk
www.charityretail.org.uk
Chief Exectuive: Warren Alexander
Aims to: monitor policy and legislative changes affecting charity retailing and lobby governments to achieve and maintain a supportive regulatory environment; promote charity retailing to public and policy makers including its reuse/recycling/sustainability contributions; respond to developments in charity retailing and the needs of members through provision of services and activities; be a major source of expertise and information on issues affecting the sector; promote good practice, efficiency and self-regulation through sharing of information; work closely with organisations to support the sector.
Employees: 8

Chartered Institute of Environmental Health

Chadwick Court, 15 Hatfields,
London SE1 8DJ
T: 020 7928 6006
E: membership@cieh.org
www.cieh.org
The Institute maintains, enhances and promotes improvements in public and environmental health.

Chartered Institute of Housing

Octavia House, Westwood Way,
Coventry CV4 8JP
T: 024 7685 1700
E: customer.services@cih.org
www.cih.org
Chief Executive: Grainia Long
The Chartered Institute of Housing is the independent voice for housing and the home of professional standards. Our goal is simple – we want to provide everyone involved in housing with the advice, support and knowledge they need to be brilliant.

Chartered Institute of Library and Information Professionals

7 Ridgmount Street, London WC1E 7AE
T: 020 7255 0500
F: 020 7255 0501
E: info@cilip.org.uk
www.cilip.org.uk
CILIP works to enable its members to achieve and maintain the highest professional standards and encourages and supports them in delivery and promotion of high-quality library and information services responsive to the needs of users.
Employees: 95
Regional offices: 2

Chartered Institute of Taxation

First Floor, Artillery House, 11–19 Artillery Row, London SW1P 1RT
T: 020 7340 0550
E: shines@ciot.org.uk
www.tax.org.uk
Head of Finance: Stephen Hines
Employees: 56
Volunteers: 140

Chartered Institution of Highways and Transportation

119 Britannia Walk, London N1 7JE
T: 020 7336 1555
E: daniel.isichei@ciht.org.uk
www.ciht.org.uk
Chief Executive: Sue Percy
CIHT, founded in 1930, has over 12,000 members concerned with the design, construction, maintenance and operation of transport systems and infrastructure across all transport modes in both the public and private sectors. CIHT promotes excellence in transport systems and infrastructure.
Employees: 20
Volunteers: 250
Income: £2,000,000 (2011-12)

Chartered Quality Institute

2nd Floor North, Chancery Exchange, 10 Furnival Street, London EC4A 1AB
T: 020 7245 6722
E: info@thecqi.org
www.thecqi.org
Chief Executive: Simon Feary
The Chartered Quality Institute is the chartered body for quality management professionals. Established in 1919, we gained a Royal Charter in 2006 and became the CQI shortly afterwards. The philosophy that came with the new name was simple – 'through innovation and care we create quality'. This is

something that we now base all our activity on and will continue to do so.
Employees: 50
Volunteers: 300

Chaseley Trust

South Cliff, Eastbourne, East Sussex BN20 7JH
T: 01323 744200
F: 01323 744208
E: chrise@chaseleytrust.org
www.chaseley.org.uk
Chief Executive: Sue Wyatt
The Chaseley Trust operates two nursing care homes in Eastbourne, providing residential, respite and day care for people with spinal injury, acquired brain injury, a wide range of neurological conditions and other severe physical disabilities. It also has a multidisciplinary therapy team experienced in assessments, treatment, rehabilitation and bespoke splinting.
Employees: 136
Volunteers: 45

Child Accident Prevention Trust

Canterbury Court (1.09), 1-3 Brixton Rod, London SW9 6DE
T: 020 7608 3828
F: 020 7608 3674
E: safe@capt.org.uk
www.capt.org.uk
Chief Executive: Katrina Phillips
The Trust encourages investigation and research into accidents in childhood, examining their pattern, causes, relationship to child development, social and environmental context and methods of prevention; promotes a better understanding of the importance of a child's need for a safe but stimulating environment; spreads information about the incidence and nature of childhood accidents and their prevention.
Employees: 10

Child Bereavement UK

Claire Charity Centre, Wycombe Road, Saunderton, Buckinghamshire HP14 4BF
T: 01494 568900
Helpline: 0800 028 8840
F: 01494 568920
E: support@childbereavementuk.org
www.childbereavementuk.org
Chief Executive: Ann Chalmers
Child Bereavement UK supports families and educates professionals both when a baby or child of any age dies or is dying, or when a child is facing bereavement. Every year we deliver training across a breadth of issues to

around 5,000 professionals at the frontline of bereavement support.
Employees: 38
Volunteers: 50+

Child Brain Injury Trust

Unit 1, The Great Barn, Baynards Green Farm, Bicester, Oxfordshire OX27 7SG
T: 01869 341075
Helpline: 03033 032248
E: info@cbituk.org
www.childbraininjurytrust.org.uk
Chief Executive: Lisa Turan
The Child Brain Injury Trust is a UK-wide charity offering support to anyone affected by childhood brain injury that has happened after birth. Acquired brain injury isn't something families prepare for. The Child Brain Injury Trust responds to the needs of these families by providing child and family support, training, information and awareness raising.
Employees: 19
Volunteers: 5
Regional offices: 6
Income: £650,614 (2011-12)

Child Death Helpline

York House, 37 Queen Square, London WC1N 3BH
T: 0800 282 986
Helpline: 0808 800 6019
F: 020 7813 8516
E: contact@childdeathhelpline.org
www.childdeathhelpline.org.uk
The Child Death Helpline aims to provide a quality freephone service to anyone affected by the death of a child of any age, from pre-birth to adult, under any circumstances, however recently or long ago. It is a listening service that offers emotional support to all those affected by the death of a child.
Volunteers: 50

Child Growth Foundation

2 Mayfield Avenue, London W4 1PW
T: 020 8912 0720
E: ros.chaplin@childgrowthfoundation.org
www.childgrowthfoundation.org
Honorary Chairman: Tam Fry
The Foundation offers support to anybody who is concerned about the growth of a child. It aims to promote a wider understanding of the importance of monitoring growth from birth by running training sessions and publishing booklets on growth disorders. It also funds research into treatments for conditions as yet untreatable. It is the umbrella organisation for growth hormone insufficiency, Turner syndrome,

IUGR/Russell Silver, bone dysplasia, Sotos and premature sexual maturation patient/parent support groups.

Employees: 5

Child Migrants Trust

124 Musters Road, West Bridgford, Nottingham, Nottinghamshire NG2 7PW
T: 0115 982 2811
F: 0115 981 7168
E: cmtnottingham@aol.com
www.childmigrantstrust.com

CMT provides a professional social work, counselling, family research and advisory service for former child migrants and their families. The Trust is an international agency that enables former child migrants to reclaim their personal identity and reunite with members of their families.

Employees: 9
Regional offices: 1

Child Poverty Action Group

94 White Lion Street, London N1 9PF
T: 020 7837 7979
F: 020 7837 6414
E: info@cpag.org.uk
www.cpag.org.uk
Chief Executive: Alison Garnham

The Group promotes action for the relief, directly or indirectly, of poverty among children and families with children.

Employees: 26
Regional offices: 2
Income: £2,820,000 (2011-12)

Childhealth Advocacy International

Conway Chambers, 83 Derby Road, Nottingham, Nottinghamshire NG1 5BB
E: office@caiuk.org
www.caiuk.org

CAI works to alleviate the suffering of mothers and children in countries where there is extreme poverty, armed conflict or other disaster. With the help of local professionals we deliver hands-on maternal and child-friendly healthcare, specifically in hospitals but also integrating closely with primary healthcare.

Employees: 5

Childhood Eye Cancer Trust

The Royal London Hospital, Whitechapel Road, London E1 1BB
T: 020 7377 5578
F: 020 7377 0740
E: info@chect.org.uk
www.chect.org.uk
Chief Executive: Joy Felgate

The Childhood Eye Cancer Trust is a UK-wide charity for families and individuals affected by retinoblastoma. Our aims are to provide information and support to individuals and families affected by retinoblastoma; to raise awareness of retinoblastoma; to raise funds for research; to influence those bodies responsible for healthcare delivery in the UK; to ensure retinoblastoma patients get the best possible quality of care.

Employees: 7
Volunteers: 20

ChildLine

45 Folgate Street, London E1 6GL
T: 020 7650 3200
F: 020 7650 3201
E: info@nspcc.org.uk
www.childline.org.uk

ChildLine is the UK's free, 24-hour helpline for children and young people. Trained volunteer counsellors provide comfort, advice and protection to the children who call and refer children in danger to appropriate helping agencies. ChildLine also works to bring to the attention of the public and of government issues affecting children's welfare and rights.

Employees: 246
Volunteers: 1000
Regional offices: 11

Childlink

10 Lion Yard, Tremadoc Road, London SW4 7NQ
T: 020 7501 1700
F: 020 7498 1791
E: enquiries@adoptchildlink.org.uk
www.adoptchildlink.org.uk
Chief Executive: Caroline Hesslegrave

Recruitment, preparation, assessment and approval of adopters.

Employees: 20

Childnet International

Studio 14, Brockley Cross Business Centre, 96 Endwell Road, London SE4 2PD
T: 020 7639 6967
F: 020 7639 7027
E: info@childnet.com
www.childnet.com

Childnet International is a registered charity, established in 1995, with the aim of helping to help make the internet a great and safe place for children, both in the UK and on a global level. For the past 12 years, Childnet has sought to promote the positive use of technology, by highlighting the creative and beneficial things that children are doing with new technology, as well as responding to the potential risks.

Employees: 10

Children and Families Across Borders (Formerly ISS UK)

Unit 1.03 Canterbury Court, 1–3 Brixton Road, London SW9 6DE
T: 020 7735 8941
F: 020 7582 0696
E: info@cfab.org.uk
www.cfab.org.uk
CEO: Andy Elvin

CFAB identifies and protects children who have been separated from family members due to conflict, trafficking, abduction, migration, divorce and asylum. It is the only charity specifically set up to help children, families and vulnerable people whose socio-welfare problems involve the UK and another country. We provide expert advice, guidance, skilled professional services, and emotional support and are guided by the UN Convention on the Rights of the Child.

Employees: 15
Volunteers: 500
Income: £1,000,000 (2011-12)

Children and Young People's Empowerment Project

11 Southey Hill, Southey, Sheffield, South Yorkshire S5 8BB
T: 0114 234 8846
E: lesley.pollard@chilypep.org.uk
www.chilypep.org.uk
Manager: Lesley Pollard

Chilypep works with children and young people to make the most of opportunities to influence and improve their lives and communities through empowerment and participation in a challenging, fun and action-packed way. We aim to increase children and young people's involvement in decision-making processes; increase their skills base through training and personal development; develop, deliver and promote models that remove barriers to participation and provide training to organisations and projects that promote good youth work practice.

Employees: 6
Volunteers: 50
Regional offices: 1
Income: £260,000 (2011-12)

Children England

E: sarah.bond@childrenengland.org.uk

Children of Africa

1 Beechwood, Cavendish Road, Bowdon,
Altrincham, Cheshire WA14 2NH
T: 07974 161027
E: liezl.hesketh@btinternet.com
Trustee: Liezl Hesketh
We support orphaned children in South
Africa suffering from or orphaned as a result
of HIV/AIDS and advancement of education
among children and young people attending
schools, by the provision of financial support
to meet the costs of progressing to higher
education.

Children's Burns Trust

38 Buckingham Palace Road,
London SW1W 0RE
T: 020 7233 8333
F: 020 7233 8200
E: info@cbtrust.org.uk
www.cbtrust.org.uk
The Trust offers support to specialist burns
units and assistance with long-term
rehabilitation of children suffering from
burns. It provides education for children in
burn prevention and activates public
awareness of the severe problem of scalding.
Employees: 2
Volunteers: 25
Regional offices: 1

Children's Country Holidays Fund

Stafford House, 91 Keymer Road,
Hassocks, West Sussex BN6 8QJ
T: 01273 847770
E: info@cchf-allaboutkids.org.uk
www.cchf-allaboutkids.org.uk
CCHF exists to provide holidays for children
in need and thier families from London.
Employees: 8
Volunteers: 600

Children's Family Trust

MKA House, 4–6 St Andrews Road,
Droitwich, Worcestershire WR9 8DN
T: 01905 798299
F: 01905 798230
E: david.homer@thecft.org.uk
www.thecft.org.uk
Chief Executive: Thomas Gormley
The charity's aims are the relief of children
and young people in need, in particular those
in the care of, or accommodated by, a local
authority.
Employees: 19
Regional offices: 2
Income: £2,256,518 (2010-11)

Children's Heart Federation

Level 1, 2–4 Great Eastern Street,
London EC2A 3NW
T: 020 7422 0630
Helpline: 0808 808 5000
F: 020 7247 2087
E: info@chfed.org.uk
www.chfed.org.uk
Chief Executive: Anne Keatley-Clarke
The Federation works to relieve children
suffering from heart conditions and supports
their families. It advances public education
about the problems experienced by children
with heart conditions and their families.
Employees: 5
Volunteers: 30

Children's Hope Foundation

15 Palmer Place, London N7 8DH
T: 020 7700 6855
Helpline: 020 7700 6919
F: 020 7700 4432
E: tomdoran@childrenshopefoundation.org.uk
www.childrenshopefoundation.org.uk
Chief Executive: Tom Doran
Our aim is to improve the quality of life for
children affected by illness, disability or
indeed poverty, by responding to their needs
in a practical way, based on the
recommendation of their health and/or
education professionals, to ensure they have
the opportunity to fulfill their dreams and
achieve their full potential.
Employees: 5
Volunteers: 14
Regional offices: 2
Income: £250,000 (2011-12)

Children's Links

Holland House, Horncastle College,
Mareham Road, Horncastle,
Lincolnshire LN9 6BW
T: 01507 528300
F: 01507 528301
E: info@childrenslinks.org.uk
www.childrenslinks.org.uk
Children's Links promotes the care and
education of children and provides facilities
for recreation and leisure time for children in
the interests of social welfare.
Employees: 61
Volunteers: 8
Regional offices: 2

Children's Society

c/o The Children's Society, Edward Rudolf
House, Margery Street,
London WC1X 0JL
T: 020 7841 4400
E: info@childrenssociety.org.uk
www.childrenssociety.org.uk
One of the UK's leading children's charities,
for more than 120 years the Church of
England Children's Society has worked with
and for children, helping them face life's
toughest challenges. Whoever they are and
whatever their issues, we believe that no
child is beyond hope, love or understanding,
and we work with those most in need to help
them face the future with confidence.
Employees: 1050
Regional offices: 3

Children's Trust

Tadworth Court, Tadworth,
Surrey KT20 5RU
T: 01737 365000
F: 01737 365001
E: enquiries@thechildrenstrust.org.uk
www.thechildrenstrust.org.uk
The Children's Trust was established for the
care, treatment, rehabilitation and education
of children with physical disabilities, learning
disabilities and complex medical needs,
including life-limiting or life-threatening
conditions and neurological damage
acquired through accident or other causes;
for the support of families and other carers
involved; and for the prevention of such
disabilities and disorders.
Employees: 380
Volunteers: 330

Chinese in Britain Forum

239 Old Street, London EC1V 9EY
T: 020 7553 7180
F: 020 7251 3130
E: enquiries@cibf.co.uk
www.cibf.co.uk
Provides support and access to resources and
services for the Chinese communities
organisations in Britain.
Employees: 6
Volunteers: 18
Regional offices: 1

Chinese Information and Advice Centre

Lower Ground Floor, London Chinatown
Market, 71-73 Charing Cross Road,
London WC2H 0NE
T: 0845 313 1868
F: 020 7734 1039
E: info@ciac.co.uk
www.ciac.co.uk
Chair: Edmond Yeo

Since founded in 1982, the Chinese Information and Advice Centre (CIAC) has been a leading Chinese charity providing immigration legal services, women's support, refugee and asylum support, benefits advice and information development. We aim to help the disadvantaged Chinese individuals and groups with compassion, care and professionalism and have successfully assisted a great number of service users in getting immigration status and welfare benefits, as well as supporting women domestic violence victims.
Employees: 2
Volunteers: 20
Regional offices: 1

Chinese Mental Health Association

2/F Zenith House, 155 Curtain Road, London EC2A 3QY
T: 020 7613 1008
F: 020 7739 6577
E: info@cmha.org.uk
www.cmha.org.uk
The charity exists to promote the preservation and the safeguarding of mental health and the relief of persons who are of Chinese origin suffering from mental illness or distress.
Employees: 8

Chiropractic Patients' Association

Twingley Centre, The Portway, Winterbourne Gunner, Salisbury, Wiltshire SP4 6JL
T: 01980 610218
F: 01980 611947
E: backs@chiropatients.org.uk
www.chiropatients.org.uk
Chairman: Maureen Atkinson
The association aims to raise public awareness and hasten acceptance of chiropractic by the health professions and health service. It promotes research and chiropractic treatment for the benefit of patients, encourages the adoption of chiropractic as a professional career and assists in the education of chiropractic students.
Volunteers: 7

Choices 4 All

The 21 Building, 21 Pinner Road, Harrow, Middlesex, Harrow HA1 4ES
T: 020 8424 0848
E: rachel@choices4all.co.uk
www.choices4all.co.uk
Choices 4 All: Rachel Chronnell
Choices 4 All is a specialist non-profit learning provider which encourages individuals with learning difficulties and disabilities to progress towards independence. We believe in people's abilities and in creating new and fresh ways of providing opportunities to help overcome barriers. Learners are given the tools in a person-centered environment to gain confidence for their future and make their own Choices.
Employees: 10
Volunteers: 2
Regional offices: 0
Income: £350,000 (2012-13)

Christian Aid

35–41 Lower Marsh, Waterloo, London SE1 7RL
T: 020 7523 2222
E: lse@christian-aid.org
www.christian-aid.org.uk
Christian Aid is supported and sustained by the churches of the UK and Ireland, our essential purpose is to expose the scandal of poverty, contribute to its eradication and challenge structures and systems that keep people poor and marginalised.

Christian Camping International

2 Leon House, Queensway, Bletchley, Milton Keynes, Buckinghamshire MK2 2SS
T: 01908 641641
E: office@cci.org.uk
www.cci.org.uk
Executive Director: Keith Hagon
CCI is an association of Christian residential providers across the UK. Members offer a wide range of conference and meeting facilities to meet all budgets. The automated online venue finding service is a great place to find your conference venue.
Employees: 4
Volunteers: 20
Income: £100,000 (2011-12)

Christian Education

1020 Bristol Road, Selly Oak, Birmingham B29 6LB
T: 0121 472 4242
E: enquiries@christianeducation.org.uk
www.christianeducation.org.uk

Promotes human development within a context of faith, aspiring to an education system that offers full opportunities for spiritual and moral development.

Christian Family Concern

Wallis House, 42 South Park Hill Road, South Croydon CR2 7YB
T: 020 8688 0251
F: 020 8686 7114
E: info@christianfamilyconcern.org.uk
www.christianfamilyconcern.org.uk
Chief Executive: Leslie Hillier
The charity's main purpose is the relief of children, young people, parents and pregnant women in need of care and protection, through our nursery, out-of-school clubs and bed-sit schemes for young mothers and young people in need of support.
Employees: 35
Volunteers: 8

Chronic Granulomatous Disorder Society

199A Victoria Street, London SW1E 5NE
T: 0800 987 8988
E: hello@cgdsociety.org
www.cgdsociety.org
Chief Executive: Caroline Harding
The CGD Society is the leading source of support for individuals and families affected by chronic granulomatous disorder in the UK. The charity provides comprehensive information on CGD and associated issues; offers direct support to patients and affected families; funds nursing services and patient and family events; supports research to improve treatments and find a cure.
Volunteers: 10
Income: £194,584 (2011-12)

Church Action on Poverty

Dale House, 35 Dale Street, Manchester M1 2HF
T: 0161 236 9321
F: 0161 237 5359
E: info@church-poverty.org.uk
www.church-poverty.org.uk
Director: Niall Cooper
CAP works to achieve lasting solutions to problems of poverty, debt and exclusion amongst communities across the UK. We advocate for local and national policies that enable people in poverty to achieve more sustainable livelihoods; enable people with firsthand experience of poverty to speak out and campaign for lasting changes in their own communities and nationally; and equip

churches to work with others to achieve real and long-term change.

Employees: 11
Volunteers: 5
Regional offices: 2

Church Army

Wilson Carlile Centre, 50 Cavendish Street, Sheffield, South Yorkshire S3 7RZ
T: 0300 123 2113
E: info@churcharmy.org.uk
www.churcharmy.org.uk
Chief Executive: Mark Russell
Church Army exists to share the Christian faith with those who are marginalised in the UK and Ireland, the homeless, those living on deprived housing estates, the elderly and many more. We have more than 300 evangelists working nationwide within the Anglican church.

Church Housing Trust

PO Box 50296, London EC1P 1WF
T: 020 7269 1630
E: info@churchhousingtrust.org.uk
www.churchhousingtrust.org.uk
The Trust raises funds to support projects to benefit homeless people.

Church Lads and Church Girls Brigade

2 Barnsley Road, Wath–upon–Dearne, Rotherham, South Yorkshire S63 6PY
T: 01709 876535
F: 01709 878089
E: brigadesecretary@clcgb.org.uk
www.clcgb.org.uk
For over 100 years the Brigade has been fulfilling its objective to extend the kingdom of Christ among lads and girls. Throughout the country young people and children are continuing to enjoy fun, faith and fellowship and through the Brigade be better equipped to cope with the demands that society places upon them.

Employees: 7
Volunteers: 1500
Regional offices: 200

Church of England Central Secretariat

Archbishops' Council, Church House, 27 Great Smith Street SW1P 3AZ
T: 020 7898 1000
F: 020 7898 1369
E: william.fittall@churchofengland.org.uk
www.churchofengland.org
Secretary-General: William Fittall
The Archbishops' Council is a body charged with the responsibility at national level to coordinate, promote, aid and further the work and mission of the Church of England.

Employees: 252

Church Pastoral Aid Society

Sovereign Court One (Unit 3), Sir William Lyons Road, University of Warwick Science Park, Coventry CV4 7EZ
T: 0300 123 0780
E: info@cpas.org.uk
www.cpas.org.uk
General Director: John Dunnett
The Church Pastoral Aid Society exists to inspire and enable churches to reach everyone in their communities with the good news of Jesus Christ.

Employees: 22
Regional offices: 1

Church Urban Fund

Church House, Great Smith Street, London SW1P 3NZ
T: 020 7898 1647
F: 020 7898 1601
E: enquiries@cuf.org.uk
Promotes any charitable purpose in urban areas within the provinces of Canterbury and York that are in need of spiritual and material assistance by reason of social and economic changes with a view to reinforcing the work of the Church of England among the people of those areas.

Employees: 16
Regional offices: 43

Churches Child Protection Advisory Service

PO Box 133, Swanley, Kent BR8 7UQ
T: 0845 120 4550
F: 0845 120 4552
E: info@ccpas.co.uk
www.ccpas.co.uk
Chief Executive Officer: Simon Bass
CCPAS is a professional Christian-based safeguarding charity offering resources, training, advice and support in all areas of safeguarding children and vulnerable adults to churches, faith groups and organisations, and those with no religious affiliation. CCPAS offers a 24-hour helpline and is an umbrella body for the Criminal Records Bureau.

Employees: 24
Volunteers: 1
Regional offices: 1

Churches Community Work Alliance

St Chad's College, North Bailey, Durham DH1 3RH
T: 0191 334 3346
F: 0191 334 3371
E: info@ccwa.org.uk
www.ccwa.org.uk
We initiate, support and encourage community development work in the life of the churches; we help the churches to reflect theologically on their response to social and economic change; we promote good community development work practice; and we provide help and guidance for community development work projects and we support practitioners.

Employees: 2
Volunteers: 20
Regional offices: 4

Churches Conservation Trust

Society Building, 8 All Saints Street, London N1 9RL
T: 020 7841 0407
F: 020 7841 0434
E: central@tcct.org.uk
www.visitchurches.org.uk
CEO: Crispin Truman
Employees: 47
Volunteers: 1000

Churches Together in Britian and Ireland

39 Eccleston Square, London SW1V 1BX
E: info@ctbi.org.uk
www.ctbi.org.uk
General Secretary: Revd Bob Fyffe
To assist the many different Christian churches of Britain and Ireland to work together for the good of all people, deepening their fellowship with each other and, without losing their distinctive differences, to work towards a greater visible unity.

Employees: 7

Cicely Northcote Trust

Camelford House, 87–89 Albert Embankment, London SE1 7TP
T: 020 7582 9996
E: cntrust@btconnect.com
www.cicelynorthcotetrust.org.uk
Chairman: Alan Hancock
The Trust sets up projects that address gaps in the health and social services provided by statutory and voluntary organisations and,

where possible, identifies ways of filling these gaps.
Employees: 1

Circles Network

Potford's Dam Farm, Coventry Road, Cawston, Rugby CV23 9JP
T: 01788 816671
F: 01788 816672
E: info@circlesnetwork.org.uk
www.circlesnetwork.org.uk
The ultimate aim of Circles Network is to build inclusive communities where everyone belongs and to demonstrate that people of all ages can be supported to live self-determined lives, regardless of their ability or difference.
Employees: 45
Volunteers: 30

Circles UK

E: stephen.hanvey@circles-uk.org.uk

Circulation Foundation

Leeds Vascular Institute, Leeds General Infirmary, Great George Street, Leeds LS1 3EX
T: 0113 392 3190
E: bvf@care4free.net
www.bvf.org.uk
The Foundation encourages, promotes and assists research into the treatment of vascular disease and its related problems.

Citizen Organising Foundation

112 Cavell Street, London E1 2JA
T: 020 7375 1658
F: 020 7375 2034
E: colin.weatherup@cof.org.uk
www.cof.org.uk
The Citizen Organising Foundation (COF) has built a large, broad-based and diverse alliance of organisations, such as faith congregations, trade unions, schools and local community associations. Our experience, as community organisers, has demonstrated that the connectivity between individuals, family, community and society is extremely fragile and that these alliances are vital for a healthy democracy and vibrant civil society.
Employees: 7
Regional offices: 2

Citizen's Income Trust

37 Becquerel Court, West Parkside, London SE10 0QQ
T: 020 8305 1222
E: info@citizensincome.org
www.citizensincome.org
Director: Malcolm Torry

The Citizen's Income Trust promotes debate on the feasibility and desirability of a citizen's income: an automatic, unconditional and non-withdrawable income for every citizen.
Volunteers: 12
Income: £2,700 (2010-11)

Citizens Advice

Myddelton House, 115–123 Pentonville Road, London N1 9LZ
T: 020 7833 7118
F: 020 7837 0279
E: alistair.gibbons@citizensadvice.org.uk
www.citizensadvice.org.uk
Citizens Advice helps people resolve their money, legal and other problems by providing information and advice, and by influencing policy makers.
Employees: 5000
Volunteers: 20000
Regional offices: 2000

Citizens Online

1 Town Square, West Swindon Centre, Tewkesbury Way, Swindon, Wiltshire SN5 7DL
T: 01793 882800
F: 01793 882801
E: info@citizensonline.org.uk
www.citizensonline.org.uk
Citizens Online's initial remit was to explore the impact of the internet and IT on today's society. From these findings we campaign and work with other not-for-profit organisations to ensure all citizens are given the opportunity to experience the internet and IT, especially those citizens which could be judged as socially excluded.
Employees: 17
Volunteers: 5
Regional offices: 7

Citizenship Foundation

50 Featherstone Street, London EC1Y 8RT
T: 020 7566 4141
F: 020 7566 4131
E: info@citizenshipfoundation.org.uk
www.citizenshipfoundation.org.uk
CEO: Andy Thornton
The Citizenship Foundation inspires young people to take part in society as equal members. We help them to understand the law, politics and democratic life. We promote participation, we help teachers to teach citizenship and we work with young people on issues that concern them. Our work involves: Shaping schools, Helping teachers to help young people take responsible action in their lives and communities, and shape the world around them; inspiring action. Motivating young people to shape the world

for everyone's benefit, influencing policy, helping school leaders, policy-makers and community leaders to understand the importance of citizenship education. We want society to be fairer, more inclusive and more cohesive. We want a democracy in which everyone has the knowledge, skills, and confidence to take part and drive change as effective citizens, both as individuals and as communities.
Employees: 30
Volunteers: 4
Regional offices: 1

City Bridge Trust

City of London, PO Box 270, Guildhall, London EC2P 2EJ
T: 020 7332 3710
F: 020 7332 3127
E: citybridgetrust@cityoflondon.gov.uk
www.citybridgetrust.org.uk
Chief Grants Officer: David Farnsworth
City Bridge Trust, the City of London Corporation's charity, is the grant-making arm of Bridge House Estates. We aim to address disadvantage by supporting charitable activity across Greater London through quality grant-making and related activities within clearly defined priorities.
Employees: 16
Volunteers: 0
Regional offices: 0

City South Manchester

Turing House, Archway 5, Hulme, Manchester, Lancashire M15 5RL
T: 0161 227 1360
E: sarah.roberts@citysouthmanchester.co.uk
www.citysouthmanchester.co.uk
Placement and Volunteer Coordinator: Sarah Roberts
Our vision: By 2014 City South will be a strong, viable business focused on our customers, providing cost-effective services City South will grow in terms of the number of homes we own and manage, the range of products we offer, and the areas in which we work. We will be more than a landlord; providing supportive services and products to our customers that will help build and sustain neighbourhoods, households and our business.
Employees: 140
Volunteers: 20
Regional offices: 1

City Year UK

58-62 White Lion Street, London N1 9PP
T: 020 7014 2680
E: info@cityyear.org.uk
www.cityyear.org.uk
Chief Executive: Sophie Livingstone
City Year UK is a leading youth and education charity and a beacon for a volunteer service year. Its mission is to galvanise the talent, energy and idealism of young role models to help vulnerable children succeed in school.
Employees: 25
Volunteers: 150
Regional offices: 2
Income: £2,200,000 (2012-13)

Civic Trust

Essex Hall, 1–6 Essex Street,
London WC2R 3HU
T: 020 7539 7900
F: 020 7539 7901
E: info@civictrust.org.uk
www.civictrust.org.uk
Managing Director: Peter Bembridge
An independent and national organisation. It is the umbrella body for over 750 civic societies, representing over 250,000 individuals committed to improving and caring for places where people live and work. It is the leading UK charity dedicated to bringing vitality, sustainability and high-quality design to the built environment. The Trust works with people to promote thriving towns and villages, developing dynamic partnerships between communities, government and business to deliver regeneration and local improvement.
Employees: 35
Volunteers: 5
Regional offices: 1

Civil Service Retirement Fellowship

Suite 2, 80a Blackheath Road,
London SE10 8DA
T: 020 8691 7411
F: 020 8692 2386
E: info@csrf.org.uk
www.csrf.org.uk
Chief Executive: Jean Cooper
The CSRF provides social welfare assistance to retired civil servants, their widows/widowers and dependants to ensure they do not become isolated in retirement. We have a UK-wide network of social groups and a visiting service for ill or housebound beneficiaries, all run by volunteers.
Employees: 9
Volunteers: 2500
Regional offices: 100

CIWEM

15 John Street, London WC1N 2EB
T: 020 7831 3110
F: 020 7405 4967
E: julia.burgoyne@btinternet.com
www.ciwem.org.uk
The Chartered Institution of Water and Environmental Management (CIWEM) is the leading professional and examining body for scientists, engineers, other environmental professionals, students and those committed to the sustainable management and development of water and the environment.
Employees: 17
Volunteers: 180
Regional offices: 17

Claire House – Hospice For Children

Clatterbridge Road, Bebington, Wirral, Merseyside CH63 4JD
T: 0151 343 0883
F: 0151 334 5493
E: liz@claire-house.org.uk
www.claire-house.org.uk
CEO: David Pastor
The principal aim of Claire House is to provide specialist palliative and end-of-life care for children and young people across the North West (Merseyside, Cheshire, North Wales and the Isle of Man) who are living with a life-threatening or life-limiting illness, and to provide support for their families.

Clean Break

2 Patshull Road, London NW5 2LB
T: 020 7482 8600
F: 020 7482 8611
E: general@cleanbreak.org.uk
www.cleanbreak.org.uk
Clean Break uses theatre for personal and political change, working with women whose lives have been affected by the criminal justice system.
Employees: 15
Volunteers: 4

CLIC Sargent

Abbey Wood Business Park, Filton,
Bristol BS34 7JU
T: 020 8752 2828
F: 0117 947 0271
www.clic.org.uk
Every day 10 families are told their child has cancer. As the UK's leading children's cancer charity, CLIC Sargent is the only organisation to offer them all-round care and support.
Employees: 145
Volunteers: 500
Regional offices: 25

Climb

Climb Building, 176 Nantwich Road,
Crewe CW2 6BG
T: 0845 241 2173
Helpline: 0800 652 3181
F: 0845 241 2174
E: info@climb.org.uk
www.climb.org.uk
Executive Director: Steve Hannigan
A national charity, Climb provides information, advice and support to children, adults, families and professionals affected by metabolic diseases. Climb also funds research.
Employees: 8
Volunteers: 500
Income: £250,000 (2010-11)

Clinks

59 Carter Lane, London EC4V 5AQ
T: 020 7248 3538
E: info@clinks.org
www.clinks.org
Director: Clive Martin
Clinks supports the voluntary and community sector working with offenders in England and Wales. Our aim is to ensure the sector and all those with whom it works, are informed and engaged in order to transform the lives of offenders and their communities.
Employees: 19
Regional offices: 1

Clothing Solutions for Disabled People

Unit 1, Jubilee Mill, 30 North Street,
Bradford, West Yorkshire BD1 4EW
T: 01274 746739 (also fax)
E: enquiries@clothingsolutions.org.uk
www.clothingsolutions.org.uk
Manager: Sandra Hunt
Clothing Solutions for Disabled People is a registered charity providing a unique clothing service for learning and physically disabled children, adults and elderly people. The service offers solutions to dressing and undressing difficulties by offering a made-to-measure garment alteration/adaptation and dressmaking facility. We also provide an outreach service where we visit the person for consultation, as well as an information service about specialist clothing. We make beanbags with unique breathable and waterproof lining.
Employees: 4
Regional offices: 1

CMT United Kingdom

PO Box 5089, Christchurch,
Dorset BH23 7ZX
T: 01202 481161
Helpline: 0800 652 6316
E: secretary@cmt.org.uk
www.cmt.org.uk
Chair: Lisa Welsh
We are the national support group for people affected by Charcot-Marie-Tooth disease, the most common inherited neurological condition in the UK, affecting approximately 25,000 individuals. We provide a service of support, advice and information, with publications, a magazine and an annual conference.
Employees: 1
Volunteers: 20
Regional offices: 8

Co-operatives UK

Holyoake House, Hanover Street,
Manchester M60 0AS
T: 0161 246 2900
F: 0161 831 7684
E: helen.barber@uk.coop
www.uk.coop
Represents and promotes the interests of the co-operative sector, and develops and extends the co-operative sector through provision of a range of targeted services to members.
Employees: 28

Coal Industry Social Welfare Organisation

The Old Rectory, Rectory Drive, Whiston,
Rotherham, South Yorkshire S60 4JG
T: 01709 728115
F: 01709 839164
E: mail@ciswo.org.uk
www.ciswo.org.uk
Promotes and improves the health, social wellbeing and conditions of living of people who are, or who have been, employed in the coal industry of Great Britain, and their partners and dependent relatives and assists in the regeneration and broad development of mining and former mining communities.
Employees: 71
Volunteers: 2000
Regional offices: 7

Coalition to Stop the Use of Child Soldiers

4th Floor, 9 Marshalsea Road, Borough,
London SE1 1EP
T: 020 7367 4110
F: 020 7367 4129
E: info@child-soldiers.org
www.child-soldiers.org
Director: Victoria Forbes Adam
The Coalition works to prevent the recruitment and use of children as soldiers, to secure their demobilisation and to ensure their rehabilitation and reintegration into society.
Employees: 10

Coeliac UK

Suites A–D, Octagon Court, High
Wycombe, Buckinghamshire HP11 2HS
T: 01494 437278
Helpline: 0870 444 8804
F: 01494 474349
E: anna.godfrey@coeliac.org.uk
www.coeliac.org.uk
Chief Executive: Sarah Sleet
Coeliac UK is a national charity, providing support and advice to those living with coeliac disease and dermatitis herpetiformis. The charity also campaigns for awareness of the disease and promotes the need for early diagnosis. Advice is given by a team of dietetic professionals and ranges from the gluten-free diet to symptoms of the disease and related health issues.
Employees: 20
Volunteers: 1000
Regional offices: 1

Collage Arts

Chocolate Factory 2, 4 Coburg Road,
Wood Green, London N22 6UJ
T: 020 8365 7500
F: 020 8365 8686
E: info@collage-arts.org
www.collage-arts.org
Executive Director: Manoj Ambasna
A leading arts development, training and creative regeneration organisation based in Haringey's Cultural Quarter and established in 1985. For over 20 years the organisation has created opportunities for greater access and participation in the arts and creative industries for the whole community.
Employees: 15
Volunteers: 10

College of Sexual and Relationship Therapists (COSRT)

PO Box 13686, London SW20 9ZH
T: 020 8543 2707 (also fax)
E: info@cosrt.org.uk
www.cosrt.org.uk

National specialist charity for sexual and relationship therapy.
Employees: 2

College of St Barnabas

E: bursar@collegeofstbarnabas.com

Comic Relief

5th Floor, Camelford House, 87–89
Albert Embankment, London SE1 7TP
T: 020 7820 5555
F: 020 7820 5500
E: info@comicrelief.com
www.comicrelief.com
Comic Relief tackles poverty and social injustice by helping disadvantaged people in the UK and Africa.
Employees: 90
Volunteers: 20

Common Ground

Gold Hill House, 21 High Street,
Shaftesbury, Dorset SP7 8JE
T: 01747 850820
E: info@commonground.org.uk
www.england-in-particular.info
Common Ground helps people explore, celebrate and take action for their place by emphasising the value of our everyday surroundings and the positive investment people can make in their own localities. It forges links between the arts and the conservation of nature and our cultural landscapes.

Common Purpose

Discovery House, 28–42 Banner Street,
London EC1Y 8QE
T: 020 7608 8134
E: enquiries@commonpurpose.org.uk
www.commonpurpose.org.uk
For a democracy to be strong, it needs an active civil society in which citizens are both informed and connected. Common Purpose's vision is that we can improve the way society works by increasing the number of informed and engaged individuals who are actively involved in the future of the areas in which they live and work.

Commonwealth Education Trust

New Zealand House, 80 Haymarket,
London SW1Y 4TE
T: 020 7024 9822
F: 020 7024 9833
E: jcurry@cet1886.org
www.cet1886.org
Chief Executive: Judy Curry
The Trust invests in primary and secondary education and the training and professional development of teachers in the Commonwealth, thereby enhancing the opportunities for children in the

Commonwealth to develop the skills necessary to contribute to the economic and social development of their communities. CET works in partnership with educationalists to use financial and business skills to structure sustainable, scalable and transferrable projects based on applied research.

Commonwealth Society for the Deaf

34 Buckingham Palace Road,
London SW1W 0RE
T: 020 7233 5700
F: 020 7233 5800
E: sound.seekers@btinternet.com
www.sound-seekers.org.uk
Chief Executive: Gary Williams
SoundSeekers works in partnership with developing countries in the Commonwealth to increase awareness of, and assist in, the prevention and treatment of deafness among children.
Employees: 3
Volunteers: 14

Commonwealth Youth Exchange Council

7 Lion Yard, Tremadoc Road,
London SW4 7NQ
T: 020 7498 6151
F: 020 7720 5403
E: vic@cyec.org.uk
www.cyec.org.uk
Chief Executive: Vic Craggs
CYEC is an educational charity and UK-based organisation that supports youth development and global citizenship primarily by promoting locally based two-way youth exchanges for groups of young people aged 15–25. Services include advice, information, grant aid, training, publications and events for young people. CYEC also develops and facilitates Commonwealth-wide forums for young people, including the Commonwealth Youth Forum.
Employees: 4
Volunteers: 40
Regional offices: 1

Commonwork Land Trust

Bore Place, Chiddingstone, Edenbridge,
Kent TN8 7AR
T: 01732 463255
F: 01732 740264
E: info@commonwork.org
www.commonwork.org
Director: Jacqueline Leach
Commonwork's vision is of a fairer world in which people work together and with nature,

recognising that all are interconnected. We work towards this vision in practical ways, through our study centre and education programmes on an organic farm in Kent. We offer: hands-on activities in food, farming, sustainable development, global citizenship, climate change, renewable energy; CPD for teachers and school leaders; and share the lessons from our practical work locally, regionally and nationally.
Employees: 26
Volunteers: 26
Regional offices: 1

Community Accountancy Self-Help

E: tom@cash-online.org.uk

Community Action Network

E: p.murray@can-online.org.uk
Head of CAN Mezzanine Operations:
Peter Murray

Community Action Project

The CAP Centre, Windmill Lane,
Smethwick, West Midlands B66 3LX
T: 0121 565 3273
F: 0121 565 0471
E: cap.smeth@talk21.com
The project fosters and supports the needs and aspirations of the African Caribbean community primarily but not exclusively, as CAP adopts an open-door policy whereby anyone is welcome to utilise our services.
Employees: 9
Volunteers: 10

Community Action Wyre Forest

E: cvs@communityactionwf.org.uk

Community Development Finance Association (cdfa)

Hatton Square Business Centre, 16
Baldwin Gardens, London EC1N 7RJ
T: 020 7430 0222
F: 020 7430 2112
E: info@cdfa.org.uk
www.cdfa.org.uk
Chief Executive: Bernie Morgan
The Community Development Finance Association (cdfa) is the trade association for UK Community Development Finance Institutions (CDFIs). CDFIs are independent organisations that provide finance and support to people who have had trouble getting such services from the usual sources, such as banks and building societies. CDFIs

typically work to benefit businesses and individuals in disadvantaged communities.
Employees: 12
Regional offices: 3

Community Development Foundation

Unit 5, Angel Gate, 320-326 City Road,
London EC1V 2PT
T: 020 7833 1772
E: admin@cdf.org.uk
www.cdf.org.uk
Chief Executive: Alison Seabrooke
CDF is the leading national organisation in community development and engagement. We are passionate about empowering communities where local people are at the centre of change. We have unique expertise in working alongside local communities to strengthen local voices, improve people's lives and create better places to live. Our purpose is to bring together resources, insight and people so that communities can thrive.
Employees: 22
Volunteers: 0
Regional offices: 0
Income: £567,904 (2012-13)

Community First

Wyndhams, St Josephs Place, Devizes,
Wiltshire SN10 1DD
T: 01380 722475
F: 01380 728476
E: reception@communityfirst.org.uk
www.communityfirst.org.uk
Chief Executive: Philippa Read
Community First is Wiltshire's Rural Community Council, a charity that works at the forefront of community development to help improve the quality of life and economic well being of people and local communities throughout Wiltshire and Swindon. We have been a dependable source of support to communities in Wiltshire and Swindon since 1965. Our extensive networks involve parish and town councils, village and community hall committees, youth clubs, community transport and community leaders across the county.
Employees: 65
Volunteers: 2
Regional offices: 1
Income: £2,600,000 (2012-13)

Community Foundation for Merseyside

Third Floor, Stanley Building, 43 Hanover Street
T: 0151 232 2424
E: nicky.obrien@cfmerseyside.org.uk
www.cfmerseyside.org.uk

Community Foundation Network

Arena House, 66–68 Pentonville Road, London N1 9HS
T: 020 7713 9326
F: 020 7713 9327
E: office@communityfoundations.org.uk
www.communityfoundations.org.uk
Chief Executive: Chief Executive
CFN is the national organisation supporting and promoting UK community foundations. Community foundations are charities across the UK dedicated to strengthening local communities. They manage funds donated by individuals and organisations, building endowment and acting as the vital link between donors and local needs.
Employees: 10

Community Health Improvement and Empowerment Foundation

108 Rectory Lane, Prestwich, Manchester, Greater Manchester M25 1GB
T: 0161 773 9689
E: sabidi2217@live.co.uk
www.chiefcic.com
Director General: Dr Syed Nayyer Abidi
CHIEF is a national social enterprise in health and social care that exists to serve health needs of the BME communities of the UK. CHIEF aims to reduce health inequalities and improve the quality of life of the general public, particularly the BME communities in the UK.
Employees: 2
Volunteers: 40
Regional offices: 1
Income: £16,000 (2010-11)

Community Housing and Therapy

Unit 24, 5–6 The Coda Centre, 189 Munster Road, London SW6 6AW
T: 020 7381 5888
F: 020 7610 0608
E: co@cht.org.uk
www.cht.org.uk
Chief Executive: John Gale
Community Housing and Therapy is a charity that runs residential and non-residential services for those with severe and enduring mental ill health, and ex-service personnel who are homeless and have psychological

difficulties. The charity's objectives are to help people experiencing mental ill-health and emotional distress by providing residential accommodation with psychotherapy, care and support. Its therapeutic and rehabilitative programme is designed to create a structure that will lead to recovery, employment and eventual independence.
Employees: 40
Volunteers: 3
Regional offices: 6

Community Hygiene Concern

22 Darin Court, Crownhill, Milton Keynes, Bucks MK8 0AD
T: 01908 561928
F: 01908 261501
E: bugbusters2k@yahoo.co.uk
www.chc.org
Manager: Frances Fry
Community Hygiene Concern offers advise on head lice.
Employees: 3
Regional offices: 1

Community Integrated Care

2 Old Market Court, Miners Way, Widnes, Cheshire WA8 7SP
T: 0151 422 5326
F: 0151 424 0299
E: information@c-i-c.co.uk
www.c-i-c.co.uk
CIC was founded to assist vulnerable people to have a life rather than an existence.
Employees: 3500

Community Links

105 Barking Road, London E16 4HQ
T: 020 7473 2270
E: athena.lamnisos@community-links.org
www.community-links.org
CEO: Athena Lamnisos
Leading social action charity based in east London working with the whole community to find new solutions to old problems. We focus on early action programmes that prevent problems. Our focus is on helping young people gain skills, getting adults into work, providing spaces for families to thrive and supporting enterpreneurs to develop. We have a national policy and campaigning programme which is driven by the learning and insights from our service delivery.
Employees: 300
Volunteers: 600
Regional offices: na
Income: £8,000,000 (2012-13)

Community Links Bromley

E: andrews@communitylinksbromley.org.uk

Community Matters

12–20 Baron Street, London N1 9LL
T: 020 7837 7887
Helpline: 0845 847 4253
F: 020 7278 9253
E: liz.cleverly@communitymatters.org.uk
www.communitymatters.org.uk
Chief Executive: David Tyler
Community Matters supports organisations across the UK whose aim is to build stronger communities in which everyone is valued and can play their part. We are a membership body delivering services to organisations and representing their interests at a national level.
Employees: 20
Volunteers: 12

Community Media Association

The Workstation, 15 Paternoster Row, Sheffield S1 2BX
T: 0114 279 5219
Helpline: 0844 357 0442
F: 0114 279 8976
E: cma@commedia.org.uk
www.commedia.org.uk
Director: Jaqui Devereux
The Community Media Association is the UK representative body for the community broadcasting sector and is committed to promoting access to the media for people and communities. We enable people to establish and develop community-based communications media promoting: social cohesion and inclusion; cultural and creative expression; social and economic regeneration; empowerment through giving communities a voice; media literacy; tackling the digital divide; inter-cultural and inter-generational dialogue; training and employment opportunities; and provide information and entertainment.
Regional offices: 1

Community Network

1B Waterlow Road, London N19 5NJ
T: 020 7923 5250
E: info@community-network.org
www.communitynetworkprojects.org
Chief Executive: Angela Cairns
Community Network is a national charity combating loneliness and isolation by bringing people together in groups on the telephone. We use teleconferencing technology to allow people to remain active and connect to others. We provide training to other organisations in facilitating groups on the phone. NB. Our teleconferencing

service is now operated by The Phone Co-op. You can contact them on 020 3559 9000. Please tell them you have been referred by Community Network.
Employees: 4
Volunteers: 25
Regional offices: 1

Community of Congolese Refugees in Great Britain (CORECOG)

Stephen Laurence House, 90 Greengate Street, Plaistow, London E13 0AS
T: 020 8548 4073
F: 020 8552 0473
E: wgpambu@aol.co.uk
The Community of Congolese Refugees in Great Britain (CORECOG) is a charity registered in England and Wales since 1993. Created as a national charity for all groups in the UK, its headquarters is based in the London Borough of Newham, which has the largest population of Congolese in England.
Employees: 4
Volunteers: 3
Regional offices: 25

Community of Reconciliation and Fellowship

Prideaux House, 10 Church Crescent E9 7DL
T: 020 8986 6000
E: prideaux.house@btconnect.com
Director: Rev Gualter De Mello
The main aim of the fellowship is the improvement of conditions of life in the community, including the relief of poverty, distress and sickness, and the provision of facilities in the interest of social welfare.
Employees: 7
Volunteers: 38

Community Resilience

16th Floor Portland House, Bressenden Place, London SW1E 5RS
T: 0300 999 2004
F: 0300 999 2005
E: joanna.cj@communityresilience.cc
www.communityresilience.cc
CEO: David Cloake
A not-for-profit social enterprise dedicated to helping communities respond to, and recover from major emergencies.

Community Security Trust

Shield House, Harmony Way, off Victoria Road, Hendon, London NW4 2BZ
T: 020 8457 9999
F: 020 8457 9950
E: richard.b@thecst.org.uk
The Trust promotes good race relations between the Jewish community and other members of society by working towards the elimination of racism in the form of anti-Semitism.
Employees: 36
Volunteers: 1000

Community Transport

National Office, Office Suite E107, Dean Clough, Halifax, West Yorkshire HX3 5AX
T: 01422 364964
F: 01422 322720
E: murray.seccombe@ communitytransport.org
www.communitytransport.org
Chief Executive: Murray Seccombe
We provide services in three themed areas: passenger transport for individuals with mobility needs, VCS groups and statutory agencies; furniture re-use/recycling; training, volunteering and work experience. We operate in Tyne and Wear, Greater Manchester, West Midlands and Staffordshire.
Employees: 130
Volunteers: 100
Regional offices: 15
Income: £3,600,000 (2011-12)

Community Transport Association

Highbank, Halton Street, Hyde, Cheshire SK14 2NY
T: 0161 351 1475
Helpline: 0845 130 6195
F: 0161 351 7221
E: info@ctauk.org
www.ctauk.org
Chief Executive: Keith Halstead
The Community Transport Association is a not-for-profit organisation that provides advice and training for operators of community and voluntary transport. We also administer the presitgious MiDAS and Pats range of training courses for minibus drivers and passenger assistants.
Employees: 30
Regional offices: 6

Compassion in World Farming

River Court, Mill Lane, Godalming, Surrey GU7 1EZ
T: 01483 521950
F: 01483 861639
E: compassion@ciwf.org.uk
www.ciwf.org.uk
Chief Executive: Philip Lymbery
Compassion in World Farming is the leading charity campaigning exclusively for the welfare of farm animals throughout the world. Our vision is a world where farm animals are treated with compassion and respect and where cruel factory farming practices end. Our mission is to advance the wellbeing of farm animals worldwide. We have pioneered engagement with the food industry, rewarding good practice and highlighting welfare failures.
Employees: 40
Volunteers: 6

Compassionate Friends

14 New King Street, Deptford, London SE8 3HS
T: 0845 120 3785
Helpline: 0845 123 2304
E: info@tcf.org.uk
www.tcf.org.uk
Chief Executive: Diana Youdale
We offer support and friendship for bereaved parents and their families by those similarly bereaved.

Computers for Charities

Cemetery Lodge, Ersham Road, Hailsham, East Sussex BN27 3LJ
T: 01323 840641
E: info@computersforcharities.org
www.computersforcharities.org
Chair: Simon Rooksby
Computers for Charities as a registered charity. It provides IT advice and services to UK and overseas charities and voluntary organisations including low-cost refurbished PC and Mac computer systems. CfC also undertakes social, educational, vocational and humanitarian projects.
Employees: 1
Volunteers: 40
Regional offices: 1
Income: £50,000 (2011-12)

Concern Universal

21 King Street, Hereford HR4 9BX
T: 01432 355111
F: 01432 355086
E: cu.uk@concern-universal.org
www.concern-universal.org

Concern Universal is an international development organisation tackling poverty from the grassroots. We create opportunities for people around the world to improve their lives and shape their own futures. By building skills and connecting people at all levels in society, we help communities deliver practical solutions with long term impact.
Employees: 30
Volunteers: 20

Concern Worldwide UK

13/14 Calico House, Clove Hitch Quay
T: 020 7801 1850
E: rose.caldwell@concern.net
www.concern.org.uk
Executive Director: Rose Caldwell

Concordia International Volunteers

19 North Street, Portslade BN41 1DH
T: 01273 422218
F: 01273 421182
E: info@concordiavolunteers.org.uk
www.concordiavolunteers.org.uk
Concordia is a charity committed to international volunteering as a means of promoting intercultural understanding and peace. Our International Volunteer Programme offers the opportunity to join international teams of volunteers working on short-term projects in over 60 countries worldwide. Types of international volunteer projects include conservation, restoration, archaeology, construction, arts, children's play-schemes and teaching. Projects last from two to four weeks, and up to one year.
Employees: 4
Volunteers: 1

Confederation of Indian Organisations (UK)

25 Buller Road, Leicester, Leicestershire LE4 5GB
T: 0116 266 8068
F: 0116 266 8072
E: info@conf-indian.org.uk
www.ciostrokeproject.co.uk
Project Coordinator: Vinod Kotecha
The South Asian Stroke Prevention Project aims to set up an outreach, advocacy and support service in the East Midlands for people from South Asian communities who have suffered from a Stroke or are at a high risk. The project is a partnership between the Confederation of Indian Organisations (UK) and The Big Lottery Fund.
Employees: 4
Volunteers: 69
Regional offices: 1

CONNECT – the Communication Disability Network

16–18 Marshalsea Road, London SE1 1HL
T: 020 7367 0840
F: 020 7367 0841
E: info@ukconnect.org
www.ukconnect.org
Connect exists to improve the lives of people with aphasia (communications disability caused by stroke). We aim to empower people with aphasia by helping them re-connect with life after stroke, improve the range and accessibility of therapy and support services, and change attitudes and practice in long-term service provision.
Employees: 9
Volunteers: 20

Conquest Art: Enriching the Lives of Physically Disabled People

Conquest Art Centre, Cox Lane Centre, Cox Lane, West Ewell, Surrey KT19 9PL
T: 020 8397 6157 (also fax)
E: conquestart@hotmail.com
www.conquestart.org
Conquest Art promotes the relief and rehabilitation of people with disabilities, in particular by encouraging them to lead fuller and more active lives, and wherever possible, assisting them to cope with their disability through active participation in the visual arts.
Employees: 1
Volunteers: 80

Conscience: Taxes for peace not war

Archway Resource Centre, 1b Waterlow Road, London N19 5NJ
T: 020 7561 1061
E: info@conscienceonline.org.uk
www.conscienceonline.org.uk
Conscience: taxes for peace not war, works for a world where taxes are used to nurture peace, not pay for war. We campaign for an increase in the amount of UK tax spent on peace-building and a decrease in the amount spent on war and preparation for war. We campaign for the legal right of those with a conscientious objection to war to have the entire military part of their taxes spent on peace-building.
Employees: 3
Volunteers: 2

Conservation Foundation

1 Kensington Gore, London SW7 2AR
T: 020 7591 3111
E: info@conservationfoundation.co.uk
www.conservationfoundation.co.uk
Executive Director: David Shreeve
The Conservation Foundation was launched by David Bellamy and David Shreeve in 1982 to provide a means for people in public, private and not-for-profit sectors to collaborate on environmental causes.

Consortium

J111 Tower Bridge Business Complex, 100 Clements Road, London SE16 4DG
T: 020 7064 8383
F: 020 7064 8283
E: admin@lgbconsortium.org.uk
www.lgbconsortium.org.uk
Consortium aims to preserve the mental health of lesbian women and gay men by providing of counselling, support, information and advice services.
Employees: 4
Volunteers: 35
Regional offices: 2

Consortium of Bengali Associations

100 Gatesden (Basement Offices), Argyle Street, London WC1H 8EB
T: 020 7713 8610
F: 020 7289 8115
E: enquiries@cba-uk.org.uk
www.cba-uk.org.uk
Since being established CBA has played an important part in the development of many Bengali-led voluntary organisations that serve the Bengali community. It provides a range of services to encourage and support voluntary action and to promote the increasingly important role of the Bengali voluntary and community sector in the UK.
Employees: 1

Consortium of Lesbian, Gay, Bisexual and Transgendered Voluntary and Community Organisations

Unit 204, 34 Buckingham Palace Road, London SW1W 0RH
T: 020 7064 6500
E: information@lgbconsortium.org.uk
www.lgbconsortium.org.uk
CEO: Paul Roberts
We are a national membership organisation focusing on the development and support of LGBT groups, projects and organisations, so

they can deliver direct services and campaign for individual rights.
Employees: 5
Volunteers: 10
Income: £208,179 (2011-12)

Consortium of Voluntary Adoption Agencies

14 Liverpool Street, Chester CH2 1AE
E: info@cvaa.org.uk
We are a collection of agencies, based in the UK, that help place children in need of adoption with their most suited adopters.
Employees: 1

Construction Industry Trust for Youth

The Building Centre, 26 Store Street, London WC1E 7BT
T: 020 7467 9540
E: cyt@cytrust.org.uk
www.constructionyouth.org.uk
Executive Director: Christine Townley
Construction Youth Trust is a registered charity working with young people aged 14–30 years to help them access employment opportunities in the construction industry. We particularly work with young people from disadvantaged backgrounds including young offenders, the long-term unemployed and also those who are just unaware of the opportunities available to them within construction. The Trust inspires and supports young people to overcome barriers and lead fulfilling and productive lives.

Consumers' Association

2 Marylebone Road, London NW1 4DF
T: 020 7770 7810
E: which@which.co.uk
www.which.net
The Association aims to improve the standards of goods and services available to the public as consumers.

Contact a Family

209-211 City Road, London EC1V 1JN
T: 020 7608 8700
F: 020 7608 8701
E: info@cafamily.org.uk
www.cafamily.org.uk
Contact a Family is the only UK-wide charity providing advice, information and support to parents of all disabled children, no matter what their health condition.
Employees: 65
Volunteers: 100
Regional offices: 13

Contact the Elderly

15 Henrietta Street, London WC2E 8QG
T: 020 7240 0630
Helpline: 0800 716543
F: 020 7379 5781
E: info@contact-the-elderly.org.uk
www.contact-the-elderly.org.uk
Director: Roderick Sime
Contact the Elderly aims to relieve the loneliness of frail, isolated elderly people, who live alone with little or no support from family or friends. Our volunteer network offers a simple yet effective act of friendship. Every month our volunteer drivers take otherwise-housebound elderly guests to the home of volunteer hosts, enjoying the warmth of friendship for a few hours. The effect becomes cumulative as new friendships blossom.
Employees: 19
Volunteers: 4500

ContinYou

Unit C1, Grovelands Court, Grovelands Estate, Longford Road, Coventry, West Midlands CV7 9NE
T: 024 7658 8440
F: 024 7658 8441
E: generalenquiries@continyou.org.uk
www.continyou.org.uk
Chief Executive: Karin Woodley
ContinYou is a national education charity dedicated to transforming communities living in poverty through formal and community-led education and learning.
Employees: 56
Volunteers: 10
Regional offices: 3

ContoC Christmas Concerts

3 General Higgins House, Highbridge, Somerset TA9 3BJ
T: 01278 773691
ContoC provides three hours' audio entertainment to elderly, the handicapped, blind and visually impaired through its Christmas concerts.
Volunteers: 1

Conway Hall Ethical Society

Conway Hall, 25 Red Lion Square, London WC1R 4RL
T: 020 7405 1818
E: jim@ethicalsoc.org.uk
www.conwayhall.org.uk
CEO: Dr Jim Walsh
Studies and disseminates ethical principles based on humanism, the cultivation of a rational and humane way of life, and

advances of research and education in relevant fields.
Employees: 11
Volunteers: 12
Regional offices: 1
Income: £600,000 (2012-13)

Cope: Black Mental Health Foundation

408 Aston Lane, Aston, Birmingham, West Midlands B6 6QL
T: 0121 356 9494 (also fax)
E: copebmhfound@btopenworld.com
The Foundation promotes the protection of mental health among ethnic minorities and advances the education of the public and voluntary organisations in mental health minorities.
Employees: 4
Volunteers: 20

Coram Children's Legal Centre

University of Essex, Wivenhoe Park, Colchester, Essex CO4 3SQ
T: 01206 877910
F: 01206 877963
E: clc@essex.ac.uk
www.childrenslegalcentre.com and www.lawstuff.org.uk
Managing Director: Kawaldip Sehmi
Coram Children's Legal Centre, part of the Coram group of charities, specialises in law and policy affecting children and young people. CCLC provides free legal information, advice and representation to children, young people, their families, carers and professionals, as well as international consultancy on child law and children's rights.
Employees: 41
Regional offices: 2
Income: £2,010,042 (2010-11)

Coram Family

49 Mecklenburgh Square, London WC1N 2QA
T: 020 7520 0300
F: 020 7520 0301
E: matt@coram.org.uk
www.coram.org.uk
Coram Family works with vulnerable children and young people to enable them to take responsibility for their lives and achieve their full potential.
Employees: 144
Volunteers: 100

Coram Voice

320 City Road, London EC1V 2NZ
T: 020 7833 5792
Helpline: 0808 800 5792
F: 020 7713 1950
E: info@voiceyp.org
www.voiceyp.org
Managing Director: Andrew Radford
Coram Voice exists to enable children and young people to actively participate in shaping their own lives and to hold to account the services that are responsible for their care. We serve children and young people who are vulnerable to harm or exclusion from society, and who rely on the state or its agencies for their rights and wellbeing.
Employees: 60
Volunteers: 25
Regional offices: 3

Cord

1 New Street, Leamington Spa, Warwickshire CV31 1HP
T: 01926 315301
E: info@cord.org.uk
www.cord.org.uk
Chief Executive: Brian Wakley
Cord is an international organisation working to build lasting peace in partnership with people living and working in conflict, or post-conflict situations. We believe these people hold the keys to peace and we work alongside them to make lasting peace a reality.
Employees: 800
Volunteers: 20
Regional offices: 1
Income: £3,231,402 (2010-11)

CORDA preventing heart disease and stroke

Chelsea Square, London SW3 6NP
T: 020 7349 8686
E: corda@rbht.nhs.uk
www.corda.org.uk
The charity raises funds to support high-quality clinical research into the early diagnosis and prevention of heart disease and stroke through non-invasive methods (magnetic resonance and ultrasound).

CORE

3 St Andrews Place, London NW1 4LB
T: 020 7486 0341
F: 020 7224 2012
E: info@corecharity.org.uk
www.corecharity.org.uk
Chief Executive: Warren Alexander
CORE works for the advancement of science and the practice of medicine and surgery for

the benefit of the public in the field of dastroenterology. It promotes the study of and research into medicine and surgery with reference to the physiology and pathology of the digestive system and disseminates the results.
Employees: 4

Cornelia de Lange Syndrome Foundation

104 Lodge Lane, Grays, Essex RM16 2UL
T: 01375 376439
E: info@cdls.org.uk
www.cdls.org.uk
Chairman: James May
The CdLS Foundation exists to ensure early and accurate diagnosis of CdLS; promotes research into the causes and manifestations of the syndrome and helps people with a diagnosis of CdLS to make informed decisions throughout their lifetime.
Employees: 1
Volunteers: 16
Regional offices: 1

Corona Worldwide

Southbank House, Black Prince Road, London SE1 7SJ
T: 020 7793 4020
E: corona@coronaworldwide.org
www.coronaworldwide.org
Corona Worldwide helps and educates people going to live and work overseas, and helps returners and foreigners adjust to life in the UK.

Coronary Prevention Group

Buckinghamshire Chilterns University, Newland Park, Gorelands Lane, Chalfont St Giles, Buckinghamshire HP8 4AD
T: 020 7927 2125
E: cpg@bcuc.ac.uk
www.healthnet.org.uk
The Group contributes to the prevention of coronary heart disease, the UK's major cause of death.

Council for Awards in Care, Health and Education

CACHE Head Office, Apex House, 81 Camp Road, St Albans, Hertfordshire AL1 5HL
T: 01727 818616
F: 01727 818618
E: info@cache.org.uk
www.cache.org.uk
Chief Executive: Richard Dorrance
CACHE has been qualifying the care, health and education workforce since 1945. Over

these 65 years, we have continually invested in innovative high-quality qualifications and customer service – earning a reputation for excellence and leadership across the sector. Our qualifications are offered by schools, colleges and training centres throughout the UK.
Employees: 124

Council for British Archaeology

St Mary's House, 66 Bootham, York YO30 7BZ
T: 01904 671417
F: 01904 671384
E: peterolver@britarch.ac.uk
www.britarch.ac.uk
The Council aims to advance the study and care of Britain's historic environment, and to improve public awareness and enjoyment of Britain's past.
Employees: 20
Volunteers: 600

Council for Dance Education and Training

Old Brewers Yard, 17–19 Neal Street, Covent Garden, London WC2H 9UY
T: 020 7240 5703
F: 020 7240 2547
E: info@cdet.org.uk
www.cdet.org.uk
Director: Sean Williams
The Council aims to advance the education of all people in the art, practice and appreciation of the cultural significance of dance.
Employees: 3

Council for Music in Hospitals

74 Queens Road, Walton–on–Thames, Surrey KT12 5LW
T: 01932 252809
E: info@music-in-hospitals.org.uk
www.music-in-hospitals.org.uk
The Council uses high-quality live music to improve the quality of life of patients and residents in hospitals, nursing homes, hospices etc.

Council of British Pakistanis

415 Bordesley Green, Birmingham B9 5RE
T: 0845 658 1057
F: 0845 658 1067
E: info@thedoliproject.net
The prime objective of the Council is the welfare of British Pakistanis, to promote better understanding between the British and Pakistani community, and to promote

social, cultural and educational activities of British Pakistanis.
Employees: 7
Volunteers: 25
Regional offices: 15

Council of Christians and Jews

1st Floor, 89 Albert Embankment, London SE1 7TP
T: 020 7820 0090
F: 020 7820 0504
E: cjrelations@ccj.org.uk
www.ccj.org.uk
The Council exists to combat all forms of religious and racial intolerance; to promote mutual understanding and goodwill between Christians and Jews, and to foster cooperation in educational activities and in social and community service.

Council of Voluntary Welfare Work

Room 118/119, Block 16, Chelsea Barracks, Chelsea Bridge Road, London SW1H 8RF
T: 020 7259 9392
E: gensec@cvww.org.uk
The Council advances charitable work carried out by member organisations among the armed forces.

Counsel and Care

6 Avonmore Road, West Kensington, London W14 8RL
T: 020 7605 4200
Helpline: 0845 300 7585
F: 020 7605 4201
E: sara.campbell@counselandcare.org.uk
www.independentage.org
Chief Executive: Janet Morrison
Counsel and Care merged with Independent Age in 2011. Independent Age is a unique and growing charity, providing information, advice and support for thousands of older people across the UK and the Republic of Ireland. Not only did it merge with Counsel and Care but also with UBS and so together the whole organisation is able to provide a broader range of services than any of the charities could provide separately.
Volunteers: 6

Counselling

62 Douglas Towers, Radwell Drive, Bradford, West Yorkshire BD5 0QR
T: 01924 377119
E: info@counselling.ltd.uk
www.counselling.ltd.uk
Aims to relieve poverty by the provision of counselling. We do this by compiling and displaying a web-based database of trained and experienced counsellors and providing free counselling to those on low incomes.

Counselling and Support For Young People

16 London Road, Newark, Nottinghamshire NG24 1TW
T: 01636 704620
E: p.renshaw@casy.org.uk
www.casy.org.uk
Senior Director: Fay Bush
We promote the preservation of good mental health among young people aged 6-24, through the provision of confidential counselling services. We focus on the individual needs of the young person, building our service around them, to help them reach their full potential. We support schools and businesses in education/health through the provision of training courses, supervision and counselling, on the basis it will impact positively on the young people they are working with.
Employees: 5
Volunteers: 67
Regional offices: 1
Income: £225,999 (2012-13)

Countryside Restoration Trust

Bird's Farm Cottage, Haslingfield Road, Barton, Cambridgeshire CB23 7AG
T: 01223 262999
E: martin@countrysiderestorationtrust.com
www.countrysiderestorationtrust.com
Director: Martin Carter
The Countryside Restoration Trust is a farming and conservation charity that aims to protect and restore Britain's countryside through wildlife-friendly and commercially viable land management. Through education, demonstration and community involvement, the Trust is committed to promoting the importance of a living and working countryside.
Employees: 9
Volunteers: 75
Income: £303,000 (2010-11)

Countrywide Holidays Association

16 Stoneleigh Gardens, Grappenhall, Warrington, Lancashire WA4 3LE
T: 01925 263664
F: 01925 263464
E: info@cha-walking.org.uk
www.cha-walking.org.uk
The Association organises holidays at reasonable prices at home and abroad for people of all ages, creeds and backgrounds, with a special emphasis on walking and the enjoyment of the countryside.
Employees: 4
Volunteers: 130

Cranfield Trust

Court Room Chambers, 1 Bell Street, Romsey, Hampshire SO51 8GY
T: 01794 830338
F: 01794 830340
E: admin@cranfieldtrust.org
www.cranfieldtrust.org.uk
The Trust helps charities improve their effectiveness through the provision of management support.
Employees: 7
Volunteers: 550

Cranstoun

1st Floor St Andrew's House, St Andrew's Road, Surbiton, Surrey KT6 4DT
T: 020 8335 1830
F: 020 8399 4153
E: info@cranstoun.org.uk
www.cranstoun.org
Chief Executive Officer: Steve Rossell
Cranstoun is a registered charity that has provided quality and innovative drug and alcohol treatment services since 1969. Our range of services has an acknowledged reputation for delivering treatment, rehabilitation and support of high quality, with the aim of reducing the impact and harm caused by drug and alcohol use to individuals and communities. Our services encompass harm reduction, abstinence approaches and treatment goals, with all provision based upon individually assessed need.
Employees: 230
Volunteers: 65
Regional offices: 25
Income: £8,197,000 (2011-12)

CRASH

10 Barley Mow Passage, London W4 4PH
T: 020 8742 0717
F: 020 8747 3154
E: info@crash.org.uk
www.crash.org.uk
CRASH is the construction and property industry charity for the homeless. It harnesses the skills, products, talents and goodwill of the industry to improve buildings and premises for voluntary agencies working with homeless people, throughout the UK.
Employees: 3

Creative and Supportive Trust

37–39 King's Terrace, Camden Town,
London NW1 0JR
T: 020 7383 5228
F: 020 7388 7252
E: info@castwomen.org.uk
The Trust provides free education and
training to women ex-offenders or those at
risk of offending due to drug, alcohol or
mental health issues. It aims to realise the
potential of each woman for their
development (personal, education,
employment) and make effective changes.

Creative Youth Network

Kingswood Estate, 20 Old School House,
Britannia Road, Bristol, Avon BS15 8DB
T: 0117 947 7948
E: info@creativeyouthnetwork.org.uk
www.creativeyouthnetwork.org.uk
CEO: Sandy Hore Ruthven
INSPIRATION THROUGH THE ARTS. WE
PROVIDE CREATIVE OPPORTUNITIES
AND CHALLENGES TO UNLOCK YOUNG
PEOPLE'S TALENT AND PERSONALITY.
Our aim is for young people to excel. We
help them grow and succeed through the
inspiration of the arts. Our work takes place
across sites in Bristol and beyond, with the
aim of reaching as many young people as we
can.
Employees: 45
Volunteers: 5
Regional offices: 2

CreativePeop!e

PO Box 2677, Caterham, Surrey CR3 6WJ
T: 01883 371112
F: 01883 381155
E: info@creativepeople.org.uk
www.creativepeople.org.uk
Director: Barbara Brunsdon
CreativePeople is a UK network of
organisations offering information, advice
and guidance on professional development
in the arts, crafts and creative industries. The
network currently has 200 member
organisations from across the UK. There is a
shared website www.creativepeople.org.uk
designed to help visitors find the
organisation or resources most appropriate
to their needs. The website is a signposting
site channelling visitors through to the sites
of member organisations.
Employees: 1

CRI

3rd Floor, North West Suite, Tower Point,
44 North Road, Brighton, West
Sussex BN1 1YR
T: 01273 677019
F: 01273 693183
E: queries@cri.org.uk
www.cri.org.uk
Chief Executive: David Biddle
CRI is a social care and health charity working
with individuals, families and communities
across England and Wales that are affected
by drugs, alcohol, crime, homelessness,
domestic abuse and antisocial behaviour.
Our projects, delivered in communities and
prisons, encourage and empower people to
regain control of their lives and motivate
them to tackle their problems.
Employees: 2128
Volunteers: 1100
Regional offices: 4
Income: £80,815,000 (2011-12)

Crime Concern Trust

One Fifty, Victoria Road,
Swindon SN1 3UY
T: 01793 863502
F: 01793 514654
www.crimeconcern.org.uk
Crime Concern is a national charity working
across England and Wales to reduce crime,
anti-social behaviour and the fear of crime.
We work with disadvantaged children and
young people, their parents, friends and
families and adult offenders. We work in the
heart of the community, engaging the police,
schools, youth offending teams, health
departments, voluntary groups and
employers to offer sustainable opportunities
through education, training and
employment.
Employees: 360
Volunteers: 500
Regional offices: 10

Crimestoppers Trust

Apollo House, 66A London Road,
Morden, Surrey SM4 5BE
T: 020 8254 3200
F: 020 8254 3201
E: cst@crimestoppers-uk.org
www.crimestoppers-uk.org
Crimestoppers is an independent UK-wide
charity working to stop crime. Crimestoppers
works for you, your family and your
community.
Employees: 30
Volunteers: 500

Crisis

66 Commercial Street, London E1 6LT
T: 0300 636 1967
F: 0300 636 2012
E: enquiries@crisis.org.uk
www.crisis.org.uk
Chief Executive: Leslie Morphy
Crisis is the national charity for single homeless
people. Our purpose is to end homelessness.
Crisis helps people rebuild their lives through
housing, health, education and employment
services. We are also determined campaigners,
working to prevent people from becoming
homeless and to change the way society and
government think and act towards homeless
people.
Employees: 200
Volunteers: 10,000

Crisis Counselling for Alleged Shoplifters

Box 147, Stanmore, Middlesex HA7 2QT
T: 020 895 4897
E: crisiscounselling@gmail.com
Chairman: Harry Kauffer
Provides counselling and advice to people
wrongfully accused of shoplifting offences
and refers such cases to a solicitor, doctor or
social worker where appropriate. It has a
particular concern for the problems of
children accused of shoplifting offences and
liaises with MPs, local authorities and other
organisations to discuss aspects of social or
legal policy and practice. We do not condone
premeditated shoplifting, which is theft.
Office hours: 9:30am to 18:30pm Monday
to Friday.

Crohn's and Colitis UK

4 Beaumont House, Sutton Road, St
Albans, Hertfordshire AL1 5HH
T: 01727 830038
Helpline: 0845 130 2223
F: 01727 862550
E: christine.costello@crohnsandcolitis.
org.uk
www.crohnsandcolitis.org.uk
Chief Executive: David Barker
Crohn's and Colitis UK offers support and
information for patients. It has over 30,000
members and 70 area groups throughout
the UK. Since 1984 Crohn's and Colitis UK
members have raised over 2.5 million for
research into the causes inflammatory bowel
disease. Membership is open to patients,
relatives, health professionals and to anyone
interested in the activities of the association.
Employees: 40
Volunteers: 100
Regional offices: 66

Crohn's in Childhood Research Association

Parkgate House, 356 West Barnes Lane, Motspur Park, Surrey KT3 6NB
T: 020 8949 6209
E: support@cicra.org
www.cicra.org
Chair, Board of Trustees: Margaret Lee
The association funds research into the causes and treatment of inflammatory bowel disease. It aims to increase overall public understanding of Crohn's disease and ulcerative colitis, particularly as it affects children and young people. It supports sufferers, their families and carers and the medical professionals who care for them.
Employees: 2
Volunteers: 6
Income: £300,438 (2011-12)

Crossroads Care Cheshire West Wirral and Shropshire

Woodcroft Building, Riverside Park, Southwood Road, Bromborough
T: 0151 343 1960
E: sheilal@crossroadscaring.com
www.crossroadscaring.com
Chief Executive: Sheila Logan

Crowthorne Old Age To Teen Society (COATS)

Woodmancote Centre, Pinewood Avenue, Crowthorne RG45 6RQ
T: 01344 773464
E: secretary@coatscrowthorne.org.uk
www.coatscrowthorne.org.uk
Chairman of Trustees: John Barnes
The welfare of older people living in and around Crowthorne, Berkshire. At present we run a day centre, providing companionship, freshly cooked meals, activities and entertainment. We own a minibus to transport older people to the centre from their own homes.
Employees: 6
Volunteers: 100
Regional offices: 0
Income: £228,000 (2012-13)

CRUSAID

1–5 Curtain Road, London EC2A 3JX
T: 020 7539 3880
F: 020 7539 3890
E: info@tht.org.uk
www.crusaid.org.uk
Chief Executive: Robin Brady
Crusaid is a national grantmaker providing funding and support to poor and marginalised people and communities

affected by HIV and AIDS in a way that best meets their needs and helps them improve their quality of life.
Employees: 16
Volunteers: 20
Regional offices: 1

Cruse Bereavement Care

PO Box 800, Richmond, Surrey TW9 1RG
T: 020 8939 9530
Helpline: 0844 477 9400
F: 020 8940 1761
E: jill.sanders@cruse.org.uk
www.cruse.org.uk
Chief Executive: Debbie Kerslake
Cruse Bereavement Care exists to promote the wellbeing of bereaved people and to enable anyone bereaved by death to understand their grief and cope with their loss. We offer information, advice and support with helplines, publications and face to face sessions through a network of branches; also external education and training with bespoke courses. Cruse welcomes and trains new volunteers. There's a special interactive website for bereaved young people: www.rd4u.org.uk.
Employees: 129
Volunteers: 5500
Regional offices: 12

CSV

237 Pentonville Road, London N1 9NJ
T: 020 7278 6601
E: information@csv.org.uk
www.csv.org.uk
Chief Executive: Lucy de Groot
CSV creates opportunities for people to play an active part in the life of their community through volunteering and learning.

CSV Cathedral Camps

CSV Social Action and Volunteering, 237 Pentonville Road, London N1 9NJ
T: 020 7278 6601
E: cathedralcamps@csv.org.uk
www.cathedralcamps.org.uk
Helps conserve, restore and maintain Cathedrals, Churches and Historical buildings through community engagement and volunteering.

CTBI Christians Abroad

22 Ebenezer Close, Witham, Essex CM8 2HX
Helpline: 03000 121201
E: support@cabroad.org.uk
www.cabroad.org.uk
Lead Consultant: Colin South
Christians Abroad provides support to those who would wish to work for development or mission in the Christian community in Africa,

Asia, the Caribbean and South America. It provides information about volunteer vacancies and support services to independent mission partners working overseas.
Employees: 2
Volunteers: 3
Regional offices: 0
Income: £10,000 (2012-13)

CTC – UK's National Cycling Organisation

Parklands, Railton Road, Guildford, Surrey GU2 9JX
T: 0870 873 0060
F: 0870 873 0064
E: carol.mckinley@ctc.org.uk
www.ctc.org.uk
CEO: Kevin Mayne
Promotes and encourages the use of cycles and provides services to cyclists.
Employees: 60
Volunteers: 400
Regional offices: 200

Cued Speech Association UK

9 Jawbone Hill, Dartmouth, Devon TQ6 9RW
Helpline: 01803 832784
E: info@cuedspeech.co.uk
www.cuedspeech.co.uk
Executive Director: Anne Worsfold
We provide information about and training in Cued Speech throughout the UK with the aim of improving the communication and literacy skills of deaf and hearing-impaired children and adults by giving them full access to spoken language through vision.

Cult Information Centre

BCM Cults, London WC1N 3XX
T: 01689 833800
E: info@cultinformation.org.uk
www.cultinformation.org.uk
The centre researches and supplies information on cults. It offers advice and an international network of contacts for further information and counselling.

Cumberland Lodge

Cumberland Lodge, The Great Park, Windsor, Berkshire SL4 2HP
T: 01784 432316
Helpline: 01784 497780
F: 01784 497799
E: martinnewlan@cumberlandlodge.ac.uk
www.cumberlandlodge.ac.uk
Principal: Rev Dr Edmund Newell
Cumberland Lodge is an educational charity in a 17th century royal house, established in 1947 to provide a place where university

students could consider wider moral, ethical and social issues than their courses permit. The objective remains the same, but Cumberland Lodge is now a comfortable and inspiring residential conference centre in the stunning and peaceful surroundings of Windsor Great Park, only forty minutes from London Waterloo and twenty minutes from Heathrow.
Employees: 40
Volunteers: 18
Income: £2,400,000 (2012-13)

Cumbria CVS

E: alisonp@cumbriacvs.org.uk

CXK Limited

The Old Court House, Tufton Street, Ashford, Kent TN23 1QS
T: 01233 645852
E: info@cxk.org
www.cxk.org
CEO: Sean Kearns
CXK Limited is a charity with a 12 year track record supporting young people and adults to raise their aspirations and maximise their potential, in particular by helping them to build their resilience & resourcefulness to make successful transitions into adult life, including progression into education, employment and training. Services include impartial and independent careers advice and guidance, emotional health and wellbeing services, youth services, vocational training and reintegration programmes.
Employees: 248
Volunteers: 10
Regional offices: 3
Income: £10,412,699 (2012-13)

Cyclical Vomiting Syndrome Association UK

77 Wilbury Hills Road, Letchworth Garden City, Hertfordshire SG6 4LD
Helpline: 0151 342 1660
E: info@cvsa.org.uk
www.cvsa.org.uk
Chair: Dr Robin Dover
The Association offers relief to people suffering from cyclical vomiting syndrome by providing and assisting in the provision of treatment, advice, information and counselling for sufferers and their families.
Volunteers: 10

Cystic Fibrosis Trust

11 London Road, Bromley, Kent BR1 1BY
T: 020 8464 7211
Helpline: 0845 859 1000
E: enquiries@cftrust.org.uk
www.cftrust.org.uk
Chief Executive: Rosie Barnes
The trust funds medical research, provides advice, information and support to all those affected by Cystic Fibrosis.

Daisy Network

PO Box 183, Rossendale BB4 6WZ
E: daisy@daisynetwork.org.uk
www.daisynetwork.org.uk
The Daisy Network Premature Menopause Support Group is a registered charity for women who have experienced a premature menopause.
Volunteers: 20

Dance UK

2nd Floor, Finsbury Town Hall, Rosebery Avenue, London EC1R 4QT
T: 020 7713 0730
F: 020 7223 0074
E: info@danceuk.org
www.danceuk.org
Dance UK works to create a diverse, dynamic and healthy future for dance and to build a stronger sense of a UK-wide dance community.
Employees: 7
Volunteers: 25

David Lewis

Mill Lane, Warford, Near Alderley Edge, Cheshire SK9 7UD
T: 01565 640000
F: 01565 640100
E: enquiries@davidlewis.org.uk
www.davidlewis.org.uk
CEO: Anthony Waters
David Lewis is the UK's largest provider of care, education, assessment, treatment and life skill development for people aged 16 and upwards with complex epilepsy, physical and

learning disabilities and other neurological conditions.
Employees: 1000

Deaf Education through Listening and Talking

PO Box 1262, Lincoln, Lincolnshire LN5 5PU
T: 0845 108 1437
E: enquiries@deafeducation.org.uk
www.deafeducation.org.uk
Chair: Sue Lewis
DELTA is a national charity that supports deaf children, their families and practitioners following the Natural Aural Approach. This approach helps the deaf child learn to listen and talk using their residual hearing and natural spoken language, even those with a severe or profound loss. DELTA provides a range of information, advice and practical help at summer schools, weekend and information days for parents, teachers and other professionals.
Employees: 1
Volunteers: 250
Regional offices: 1

Deaf Ex-Mainstreamers Group

Unit 9, Milner Way, Ossett, Wakefield, West Yorkshire WF5 9JN
F: 01226 700326
E: info@dex.org.uk
www.dex.org.uk
Chair: Brian Daltrey
The Deaf Ex-Mainstreamers' Group (DEX) is a deaf-led organisation concerned about the limited lack of access deaf children have to the National Curriculum and to the school environment. DEX has conducted a Best Value Review of deaf children in the UK, Sweden, Norway and Canada, a literature review, and a study of the needs of parents of deaf children and deaf young people. DEX now markets its services to local government and health.
Employees: 1

Deaf PLUS

1st Floor, Trinity Centre, Key Close, Whitechapel, London E1 4HG
T: 020 7790 6147
E: clare.kennedy@deafplus.org
www.deafplus.org
Chief Executive: Clare Kennedy
Deaf and hearing people working together to achieve equality.
Employees: 26
Volunteers: 15
Regional offices: 6
Income: £600,000 (2010-11)

Deafax

Clare Charity Centre, Wycombe Road,
Saunderton, Buckinghamshire HP14 4BF
T: 01494 568885
E: info@deafax.org
www.deafax.org
Chief Executive: Helen Lansdown
Deafax works with deaf people providing
innovative and high-quality deaf-friendly
resources and training courses (online and
face to face) which cover areas such as life
skills, personal health, drug and alcohol
awareness, sexual health, identity issues etc.

Deafblind UK

National Centre For Deafblindness, John
and Lucille Van Geest Place, Cygnet Road,
Hampton, Peterborough,
Cambridgeshire PE7 8FD
T: 01733 358100
Helpline: 0800 132 320
F: 01733 358356
E: info@deafblind.org.uk
www.deafblind.org.uk
Chief Executive: Jeff Skipp
Deafblind UK is a national charity offering
specialist services and human support to
deafblind people and those who have
progressive sight and hearing loss acquired
throughout their lives. Our aim is to enable
people living with this unique disability to
maintain their independence, quality of life
and to reduce the isolation that
Deafblindness creates. Further information
about Deafblind UK is available on our
website.
Employees: 200
Volunteers: 200
Regional offices: 1

Deafconnect

Spencer Dallington Community Centre,
Tintern Avenue, Northampton NN5 7BZ
T: 01604 589011
F: 01604 754529
E: joanna.steer@deafconnect.org.uk
www.deafconnect.org.uk
CEO: Joanna Steer
Deafconnect supports and empowers deaf
and hearing impaired people to be
independent. We offer support, advice,
information and advocacy to deaf and
hearing impaired people of all ages, their
families, carers and professionals working
with them. We provide an interpreting
service for hearing impaired communication
to support our aims. We work closely with

other organisation to improve access to
other services and information.
Employees: 12
Volunteers: 30
Regional offices: 1
Income: £200,000 (2012-13)

Deafness Support Network

144 London Road CW9 5HH
T: 01606 47831
E: kmccallum@dsnonline.co.uk
Management Support Officer: Kirstin
McCallum

Deafway

Deafway, Brockholes Brow, Preston,
Lancashire PR2 5AL
T: 01772 796461
F: 01772 693416
E: info@deafway.org.uk
www.deafway.org.uk
Chief Executive: David Hynes
Deafway works towards providing equality of
opportunity and access in all areas of life for
deaf, sign language users in the UK and
abroad.
Employees: 64
Volunteers: 6
Regional offices: 1

DEBRA

Unit 13, Wellington Business Park, Dukes
Ride, Crowthorne, Berkshire RG45 6LS
T: 01344 771961
E: debra@debra.org.uk
www.debra.org.uk
DEBRA is the national charity that supports
individuals and families affected by
Epidermolysis Bullosa (EB); a genetic
condition which causes the skin to blister and
shear at the slightest touch. DEBRA provides
an enhanced specialist EB Nursing Service, in
partnership with the NHS and community
support staff to work directly with families.
The charity also commissions world-leading
research into the condition with the aim of
finding effective treatments and, ultimately, a
cure for EB.

Dementia Voice

Blackberry Hill Hospital, Manor Road,
Fishponds, Bristol BS16 2EW
T: 0117 975 7863
F: 0117 965 6061
E: scc@housing21.co.uk
www.dementia-voice.org.uk
Dementia Voice has four main objectives: to
provide information about dementia and

services for people with dementia; to
promote, undertake and publish research
about dementia; to provide training for
those who work with people with dementia;
and to offer consultancy to organisations
providing services for people with dementia.
Employees: 4

Depression Alliance

212 Spitfire Studios, 63–71 Collier Street,
London N1 9BE
T: 0845 123 2320
F: 020 7633 0559
E: information@depressionalliance.org
www.depressionalliance.org
Depression Alliance provides information
and support to anyone affected by
depression.
Employees: 10
Volunteers: 200
Regional offices: 3

Develop Enhancing Community Support

3-4 New Road, Chippenham,
Wiltshire SN15 1EJ
T: 0845 034 5250
F: 01249 655696
E: enquiries@developecs.org.uk
www.developecs.org.uk
Chief Executive Officer: Janice Fortune
DEVELOP Enhancing Community Support is
an independent organisation which operates
across Wiltshire and the surrounding areas.
We are a registered Charity set up, owned
and run by local groups to support, develop
and enhance local voluntary and community
action.
Employees: 17
Volunteers: 5
Regional offices: 1

Development Trusts Association

33 Corsham Street, London N1 6DR
T: 0845 458 8336
E: info@dta.org.uk
www.dta.org.uk
The Association supports the development
of new development trusts, helps existing
trusts operate well and persuades other to
support development trusts.

Diabetes Foundation

1 Constable's Gate,
Winchester SO23 8GE
T: 01962 842070
E: judith.rich@btinternet.com
www.diabetesfoundation.org.uk
Chair: Judith Rich

The Foundation supports and advances research in the field of diabetes particularly juvenile (insulin dependent) diabetes in the UK and throughout the world. In 2006/2007, it awarded grants totalling some £1.5 million for research, education and development of services into diabetes, with another of its activities being the provision of blood glucose monitors free of charge for diabetic children as recommended by nurse specialists.
Volunteers: 10

Diabetes UK

Macleod House, 10 Parkway,
London NW1 7AA
T: 020 7424 1106
F: 020 7424 1080
E: info@diabetes.org.uk
www.diabetes.org.uk
Chief Executive: Douglas Smallwood
Our aim is to improve the lives of people with diabetes and to work towards a future without diabetes and to set people free from the restrictions of diabetes. We work towards the highest quality care and information for all, an end to discrimination and ignorance, universal understanding of diabetes and Diabetes UK and a world without diabetes.
Employees: 180
Volunteers: 10000
Regional offices: 10

DIAL Basildon and South Essex

75 Southernhay, Basildon,
Essex SS14 1EU
T: 01268 285676
E: jan@dialbasildon.co.uk
www.dialbasildon.co.uk
Manager: Jan Stevens
DIAL provides a free, confidential information and advice service on all issues affecting disabled people's everyday lives, to enable and empower individuals to improve their quality of life. We currently offer advice, support, advocacy and guidance services to local disabled people, assisting them with a number of topics related to disability. Our own unique experience of living with disability allows us to assist others with understanding and expertise.
Employees: 6
Volunteers: 19
Regional offices: 2
Income: £160,000 (2012-13)

DIAL House - Chester

DIAL House, Hamilton Place, Chester,
Cheshire CH1 2BH
T: 01244 345655
E: k.roper@dialhousechester.org.uk
www.dialhousechester.org.uk
Chief Officer: Keith Roper
DIAL House Chester aims to enable disabled people and older people to live sustained, independent lives. We provide a range of disability-related services including: advice & information, community café, shopmobility, volunteering & training.
Employees: 10
Volunteers: 80
Income: £300,000 (2012-13)

DIAL UK

6 Market Road, London N7 9PW
F: 020 7619 7100
E: dialnetwork@scope.org.uk
www.dialuk.org.uk
Dial UK is the national organisation for the DIAL network; 140 disability advice centres run by and for people with disabilities.
Employees: 8
Volunteers: 8

Different Strokes

9 Canon Harnett Court, Wolverton Mill,
Milton Keynes,
Buckinghamshire MK12 5NF
T: 01908 317618
Helpline: 0845 130 7172
F: 01908 313501
E: info@differentstrokes.co.uk
www.differentstrokes.co.uk
Chief Executive: Debbie Wilson
Different Strokes provides a free service to younger stroke survivors throughout the UK. Run by stroke survivors for stroke survivors, for active self-help and mutual support. We help stroke survivors of working age to optimise their recovery and regain as much independence as possible by offering rehabilitative services, information and advice. Our services include the Strokeline, access to exercise sessions, practical information packs, an interactive website, regular newsletters and assistance finding counselling services.
Employees: 6
Volunteers: 150
Regional offices: 50

Dignity in Dying

13 Prince of Wales Terrace,
London W8 5PG
T: 020 7937 7770
F: 020 7376 2648
E: info@dignityindying.org.uk
www.dignityindying.org.uk
Dignity in Dying is the leading campaigning organisation promoting patient choice at the end of life. We are also a major information source on end-of-life issues. Dignity in Dying is independent of any political, religious or other organisation. We are supported entirely by voluntary contributions from members of the public.
Employees: 6
Volunteers: 12

Dimbleby Cancer Care

4th Floor Management Offices,
Bermondsey Wing, Guy's Hospital, Great Maze Pond, London SE1 9RT
T: 020 7188 7889
Helpline: 020 7188 5918
E: admin@dimblebycancercare.org
www.dimblebycancercare.org
Chairman of Trustees: Jonathan Dimbleby
Provides psychological and social support, complementary therapies and benefits advice to patients with cancer at Guy's and St Thomas' Hospitals, London. Provides research funding for national projects looking into the psycho-social and practical support needs of people with cancer and their families.
Employees: 2

DIPEx Charity

23–28 Hythe Bridge Street, Oxford,
Oxfordshire OX2 7LX
T: 01865 201330
E: info@healthtalkonline.org
www.healthtalkonline.org
In partnership with Oxford University we provide information about people's experiences of illnesses and health conditions via video interviews, shared on our websites Healthtalkonline and Youthhealthtalk. The award-winning websites are aimed at patients, their carers, family and friends, and health professionals. We aim to help them understand the impact of issues such as cancer, being a carer, bereavement, infertility and chronic pain on people's everyday lives.
Employees: 5
Volunteers: 20

Direct Help & Advice (DHA)

Phoenix Street, Derby,
Derbyshire DE1 2ER
T: 01332 287850
Helpline: 0845 345 4345
F: 01332 287863
E: annette.barrett@dhadvice.org
www.dhadvice.org
Interim Chief Executive: Ian Grostate
DHA provides direct help via specialist advice, advocacy and representation for families and individuals facing crisis, to prevent and alleviate homelessness, debt and housing difficulty. Our free, independent and confidential services offer support to the most vulnerable people in our communities, often requiring immediate intervention, support and advice. We also offer accessible training and skills development to a wide range of people to help reduce unemployment and promote social and financial inclusion.
Employees: 36
Volunteers: 5
Regional offices: 2

Directory of Social Change – London

24 Stephenson Way, London NW1 2DP
T: 0845 077 7707
F: 020 7391 4804
E: dsc@dsc.org.uk
www.dsc.org.uk
The Directory of Social Change, set up in 1975, aims to be an internationally recognised independent source of information and support to voluntary and community sectors worldwide. We enable the community and voluntary sectors to achieve their aims through being an independent voice, providing training and information.
Employees: 45
Regional offices: 1

Disabilities Trust

32 Market Place, Burgess Hill, West Sussex RH15 9NP
T: 01444 239123
F: 01444 244978
E: info@thedtgroup.org
www.disabilities-trust.org.uk
The Trust provides purpose-built accommodation and a full range of support facilities for people with physical disabilities, acquired brain injuries and autism; provides the most modern facilities in a homely, caring atmosphere; offers residents a stage between institutionalised care and total independence, and encourages them to lead as independent a lifestyle as possible while receiving individual attention and the security offered by residential staff.
Employees: 1160

Disability Alliance

Universal House, 88–94 Wentworth Street, London E1 7SA
T: 020 7247 8776
F: 020 7247 8765
E: office@disabilityalliance.org
www.disabilityalliance.org
Chief Executive: Vanessa Stanislas
Disability Alliance is committed to breaking the link between poverty and disability by providing information to disabled people about their entitlements, and campaigning for improvements to the social security system and for increases in disability benefits so that they better reflect the real costs of disability.
Employees: 8

Disability Awareness in Action

46 The Parklands, Hullavington, Wiltshire SN14 6DL
T: 01666 837671
E: info@daa.org.uk
www.daa.org.uk
The Alliance provides information to disabled people, their organisations and allies worldwide; supports their self-help activities and ensures their equality of opportunity. It raises awareness that disability is a human rights issue.

Disability Foundation

RNOH, Brockley Hill, Stanmore, Middlesex HA7 4LP
T: 020 8954 7373
F: 020 8954 7414
E: info@tdf.org.uk
www.the-disability-foundation.org.uk
TDF welcomes any person with a disability by offering help, support and guidance to them, their families and care/support associates, creating hope and inspiration for the future. TDF has a holistic approach offering complementary therapies at heavily reduced rates and provides information, promoting best practice at all times.
Employees: 6
Volunteers: 10
Regional offices: 1

Disability Law Service

39–45 Cavell Street, London E1 2BP
T: 020 7791 9800
F: 020 7791 9802
E: advice@dls.org.uk
www.dls.org.uk
Director: Aydin Djemal
For over 30 years the Disability Law Service (DLS) has continued to provide high-quality information and advice to disabled and deaf people. As a national registered charity DLS is independent, run by and for disabled people.
Employees: 8
Volunteers: 20–30

Disability Partnership and MOVE

Wooden Spoon House, 5 Dugard Way, London SE11 4TH
T: 020 7414 1495
E: office@disabilitypartnership.co.uk
www.disabilitypartnership.co.uk
The Disability Partnership is a small but influential charity that exists primarily as a launch-pad for initiatives that ultimately change the daily lives of many disabled people for the better. We change lives through working to overcome the attitudinal and physical barriers that most affect disabled people in the UK and worldwide.

Disability Pregnancy and Parenthood International

National Centre for Disabled Parents, Unit F9, 89–93 Fonthill Road, London N4 3JH
T: 020 7263 3088
F: 020 7628 2833
E: rosaleen@dppi.org.uk
www.dppi.org.uk
Disability, Pregnancy and Parenthood international (DPPi) is a small UK-based registered charity, controlled by disabled parents, which promotes better awareness and support for disabled people considering, during and after pregnancy and as parents.
Employees: 6
Regional offices: 1

Disability Rights UK

12 City Forum, 250 City Road, London EC1V 8AF
T: 020 7250 3222
E: enquiries@disabilityrightsuk.org
www.disabilityrightsuk.org
Chief Executive: Chief Executive
Disability Rights UK works to create a society where everyone with lived experience of disability or health conditions can participate equally as full citizens. We are disabled people leading change by: breaking the link between disability and poverty; mobilising disabled people's leadership and control in our own lives, our organisations and society; making independent living a reality; putting disability equality and human rights into practice across society.
Employees: 25

Disability Snowsport UK

Emson Close, Saffron Walden CB10 1HL
T: 01479 861272
E: m.martineau@btinternet.com
www.disabilitysnowsport.org.uk
Skiers and snowboarders with a disability should be able to ski alongside the able bodied as equals at all ski facilities and resorts. A disabled person chooses both freedom and independence when they snap into bindings or transfer from a wheelchair to sit ski. They also make a choice to actively access adventure, a choice that may be made in spite of chronic health problems or a physical or learning disability. Snowsport provides people with a method to conquer the barriers that confront them in daily life, and add to their potential.

Disability Sport Events

St James' Building, 79 Oxford Street, Manchester M1 6FQ
T: 0161 228 2868
F: 0161 200 5449
E: events@efds.co.uk
www.efds.co.uk/events
National Events Manager: Jannine Walker
Disability Sport Events is the events division of the English Federation of Disability Sport and creates opportunities for participation in sport for people with all impairments.
Employees: 6
Income: £370,000 (2011-12)

Disabled Living Foundation

380–384 Harrow Road, London W9 2HU
T: 020 7289 6111
Helpline: 0845 130 9177
F: 020 7266 2922
E: info@dlf.org.uk
www.dlf.org.uk
Chief Executive: Nicole Penn-Symons
The Disabled Living Foundation (DLF) is a national charity that provides free, impartial advice and information about all types of equipment for daily living for older and disabled people. Every year we respond to up to 25,000 requests for information via our helpline service. We provide an equipment demonstration centre, free factsheets, an online self-assessment tool, AskSARA, and our personal care search and comparison website 'Bathing Made Easy'.
Employees: 30
Volunteers: 4

Disabled Motoring UK

National Office, Ashwellthorpe, Norwich NR16 1EX
T: 01508 489449
E: info@disabledmotoring.org
www.disabledmotoring.org
CEO: Graham Footer
Disabled Motoring UK is the campaigning charity for Blue Badge holders, disabled motorists, wheelchair and scooter users. We run the Baywatch campaign against parking abuse and represent disabled people's needs at a national level. Membership includes a monthly magazine, one-to-one advice and member benefits including ferry discounts. Membership is £20 a year, £30 for joint members.
Employees: 10
Volunteers: 1

Disabled Motorists' Federation

145 Knoulberry Road, Washington, Tyne and Wear NE37 1JN
T: 0191 416 3172
E: jkillick2214@yahoo.co.uk
www.dmfed.org.uk
Chairman: Noel Muncey
The Federation helps disabled people overcome their handicaps and become as independent as possible so that they may lead fuller and more active lives. It gives free advice on motoring, travel etc to all disabled people and their carers.
Volunteers: 8
Income: £6,000 (2011-12)

Disabled Parents Network

Poynters House, Poynters Road, Dunstable, Bedfordshire LU5 4TP
T: 0300 330 0639
E: information@disabledparentsnetwork.org.uk
www.disabledparentsnetwork.org.uk
Chair: Terri Balon
Disabled Parents Network (DPN) is a national user-led organisation providing information, advice & support to parents & parents to be, who are disabled or have long term health condition, their families etc. Helping disabled parent families access appropriate support, grow in knowledge and self-confidence. Support Service, confidential, providing information, support and advice on Peer Support Register. Contact with other parents with similar disability, or locality. (DPN members only) Facebook & On-line Forum. Information. DPN resources.
Employees: 0
Volunteers: 20

Disabled Photographers' Society

43 Burge Court, Cirencester, Gloucestershire GL7 1JY
T: 01285 654984
E: enquiries@disabledphotographers.co.uk
www.dps-uk.org.uk
The Society encourages disabled people to undertake photography as a therapeutic and creative activity.

Disaster Action

PO Box 849, Woking, Surrey GU21 8WB
T: 01483 799066
E: pameladix@disasteraction.org.uk
www.disasteraction.org.uk
Disaster Action provides support and guidance to individuals and groups affected by disasters.

Disasters Emergency Committee

1st Floor, 43 Chalton Street, London NW1 1DU
T: 020 7387 0200
F: 020 7387 2050
E: info@dec.org.uk
www.dec.org.uk
At times of overseas emergency, the DEC brings together a unique alliance of the UK's aid, corporate, public and broadcasting sectors to rally the nation's compassion, and ensure that funds raised go to DEC agencies best placed to deliver effective and timely relief to people most in need.
Employees: 9
Volunteers: 1

Disaway Trust

55 Tolworth Park Road, Surbiton, Surrey KT6 7RJ
T: 020 8390 2576
E: lynnesimpkins@hotmail.com
www.disaway.co.uk
Treasurer: Lynne Simpkins
We organise group holidays with physically disabled people. Each disabled person has their own helper, either a friend or family member or a helper supplied by the Trust. The helper pays approximately 50% of the cost.
Volunteers: Varies

Diversity Hub

The Learning Exchange, Wygston's House, Applegate, Leicester, Leicestershire LE1 5LD
T: 0116 222 9977
F: 0116 222 9970
E: info@diversityhub.org.uk
www.diversityhub.org.uk
Director: Val Carpenter
Diversity Hub is a leadership-training organisation dedicated to ending prejudice and discrimination, whether because of nationality, race, gender, religion, class, sexual

orientation, age, physical ability, occupation or life circumstance.
Employees: 4
Volunteers: 30
Regional offices: 1

Diversity Role Models

5th Floor, 8/9 Harbour Exchange Square, London, Central E14 9JY
T: 020 7964 7009
E: office@diversityrolemodels.org
www.diversityrolemodels.org
Chief Executive: Suran Dickson
Our vision is a world where all children and young people can live, learn, grow and play safely, regardless of issues relating to gender and sexuality. Our mission is to eliminate homophobic and transphobic bullying. We achieve this by providing high quality, pioneering educational workshops involving role models and through collaborating with individuals and organisations. We value diversity and equality, creativity and innovation, communication and role modelling, and inter-generational learning.
Employees: 4
Volunteers: 100
Regional offices: 1
Income: £168,000 (2012-13)

Diving Diseases Research Centre

8 Research Way, Plymouth Science Park, Derriford, Plymouth, Devon PL6 8BU
T: 01752 209999
F: 01752 209115
E: info@ddrc.org
www.ddrc.org
Chief Executive Officer: Gary Smerdon
A medical research, training and service charity working with hyperbaric oxygen, its uses and effects in humans. Providing services to the NHS and private sector for difficult to heal wounds, soft tissue infections and carbon monoxide poisoning in particular as well as treatment for divers with decompression illness (the bends).
Employees: 28
Regional offices: 2

DoBe.org

The Nicholas Albery Foundation, 12a Blackstock Mews, Blackstock Road, London N4 2BT
E: info@alberyfoundation.org
www.alberyfoundation.org
DoBe.org uses the internet to increase the number of participatory and creative meetings and events in major cities - everything from walking groups and book discussion groups to cancer self-help groups.

Dog AID (Assistance In Disability)

CVS Building, Arthur Street, Chadsmoor, Cannock, Staffordshire WS11 5HD
T: 01543 899463
E: general_admin@dogaid.org.uk
www.dogaid.org.uk
Chairperson: Sandra Fraser
Dog AID provides access to dog training for people with physical disabilities, enabling them to train their own dog in basic control and specialised tasks, which will assist them manage their disability in everyday life.

Dogs for the Disabled

The Frances Hay Centre, Blacklocks Hill, Banbury, Oxfordshire OX17 2BS
T: 01295 252600
F: 01295 252668
E: info@dogsforthedisabled.org
www.dogsforthedisabled.org
Chief Executive: Peter Gorbing
Dogs for the Disabled provides specially trained assistance dogs for adults and children with physical disabilities, and families with a child with autism, to help them lead fuller and more independent lives.
Employees: 50
Volunteers: 140

Dogs Trust

17–26 Wakley Street, London EC1V 7RQ
T: 020 7837 0006
F: 020 7833 2701
E: info@dogstrust.org.uk
www.dogstrust.org.uk
Dogs Trust is working towards the day when all dogs can enjoy a happy life, free from the threat of unnecessary destruction. We care for stray and abandoned dogs through our network of 15 rehoming centres nationwide. No healthy dog is ever destroyed. Our subsidised neutering campaigns aim to prevent the birth of unwanted litters. Additionally, our schools education programme promotes responsible dog ownership to young people.
Employees: 400
Volunteers: 200
Regional offices: 15

Don'tDumpThat Ltd

PE20 3LH
E: contact@dontdumpthat.com
www.dontdumpthat.com
The majority of what is thrown away every day is probably reusable and only goes to landfill because most people don't know what else to do with it. Don'tDumpThat is 100% web based and is all about helping people preserve the environment by keeping perfectly useful but otherwise unwanted items out of landfill sites.

Doncaster Community Arts

E: ssylvester@thepoint.org.uk

Donkey Sanctuary

Slade Farm House, Sidmouth, Devon EX10 0NU
T: 01395 578222
F: 01395 579266
E: amanda.gordon@thedonkeysanctuary.com
www.thedonkeysanctuary.org.uk
Chief Executive: David Cook
The Donkey Sanctuary has taken over 13,000 donkeys into its care since 1969. Some of these donkeys may have been neglected, mistreated, retired from working on beaches or their owners could no longer care for them. The Donkey Sanctuary also brings urgent veterinary assistance to working donkeys in Egypt, Ethiopia, India, Kenya and Mexico. Further projects exist in Europe where more donkeys are in need of help. Admission is free at its headquarters in Sidmouth.
Employees: 526

Dorset and Somerset Air Ambulance

Landacre House, Castle Road, Chelston Business Park, Wellington, Somerset TA21 9JQ
T: 01823 669604
E: bill.sivewright@dsairambulance.org.uk
www.dsairambulance.org.uk
Chief Executive Officer: Bill Sivewright
To save and enhance lives through the funding and provision of a helicopter emergency medical service.
Employees: 16
Volunteers: 80
Regional offices: 2
Income: £4,834,506 (2012-13)

Dorset Youth Association

E: info@dorsetyouth.com

Douglas Haig Memorial Homes (Haig Homes)

Alban Dobson House, Green Lane, Morden, Surrey SM4 5NS
T: 020 8685 5777
E: haig@haighomes.org.uk
www.haighomes.org.uk
Provides housing for the ex-service community.

Down's Heart Group

PO Box 4260, Dunstable LU6 2ZT
T: 0844 288 4800
F: 0844 288 4808
E: info@dhg.org.uk
www.dhg.org.uk
Director: Penny Green
Provides support and information relating to heart problems associated with Down's syndrome.
Employees: 2
Volunteers: 10

Down's Syndrome Association

2a Langdon Park, Langdon Centre, Teddington TW11 9PS
T: 0845 230 0372
F: 0845 230 0373
E: info@downs-syndrome.org.uk
www.downs-syndrome.org.uk
We are the only organisation in this country focusing solely on all aspects of living successfully with Down's syndrome. We are a national charity with over 20,000 members, a national office in Teddington Middlesex, regional offices in Northern Ireland and Wales and over 130 affliated local groups. We provide support, training, information and advice for people with Down's syndrome, their families and professionals.
Employees: 36
Regional offices: 130

Down's Syndrome Educational Trust

The Sarah Duffen Centre, Belmont Street, Southsea, Hampshire PO5 1NA
T: 023 9289 3889
F: 023 9289 3895
E: info@dseinternational.org
www.downsed.org
Promotes the development and education of individuals with Down's syndrome.
Employees: 20
Volunteers: 10
Regional offices: 3

Dr Hadwen Trust

Suite 8, Portmill House, Portmill Lane, Hitchin, Hertfordshire SG5 2DJ
T: 01462 436819
F: 01462 436844
E: info@drhadwentrust.org.uk
www.drhadwentrust.org.uk
Group Head of Operations: Kay Miller
The Dr Hadwen Trust funds and promotes non-animal medical research. We champion

medical research that is humane and human-relevant.
Employees: 9
Volunteers: 10
Regional offices: 1
Income: £700,000 (2012-13)

Drake Music Project

The Deptford Albany, Douglas Way, Deptford, London SE8 4AG
T: 020 8692 9000
F: 020 8692 3110
E: loninfo@drakemusic.org
www.drakemusicproject.com
The Project champions the creative abilities, identity and aspirations of physically disabled people through the delivery of music projects using accessible technology, leading to a variety of creative outcomes.
Employees: 8
Volunteers: 12
Regional offices: 4

Dream Makers National Charity

37 Marlborough Road, Castle Bromwich, Birmingham, West Midlands B36 0EH
T: 0121 711 8982 (also fax)
www.dreammakerschildrenscharity.org
The aim of the charity is to relieve people, particularly children, their families and carers, who have severe physical, mental or life threatening illnesses.

Dreamflight

7C Hill Avenue, Amersham, Buckinghamshire HP6 5BD
T: 01494 722733
F: 01494 722977
E: office@dreamflight.org
www.dreamflight.org
Dreamflight is a UK charity that takes seriously ill and disabled children on their 'holiday of a lifetime' to the theme parks of Central Florida. Other charities do some wonderful things like funding research or purchasing medical equipment, but Dreamflight believes that fun and joy are just as important, especially for children who perhaps can't wait long enough for the breakthrough they need or whose illnesses and treatments have brought pain, distress and disruption.
Employees: 2

Dreams Come True Charity

Exchange House, 33 Station Road, Liphook, Hampshire GU30 7DW
T: 01428 726330
F: 01428 724953
E: info@dctc.org.uk
www.dctc.org.uk

The charity aims to try and fulfil the dreams of young people aged 2–21 who suffer from serious, degenerative or terminal illnesses.
Employees: 12
Volunteers: 3
Regional offices: 1

Drug and Alcohol Action Programme

KAS House, Unit K, Middlesex Business Centre, Bridge Road, Southall, Middlesex UB2 4AB
T: 020 8843 0945
F: 020 8843 1068
E: info@daap.org.uk
www.daap.org.uk
The Programme advances the education of the public about all aspects of substance misuse and related issues particularly by working towards eradicating addiction by and through education; by developing and managing appropriate programmes and treatment services; by conducting research on addictive behaviour.
Employees: 4

DrugScope

Prince Consort House, Suite 204, 109/111 Farringdon Road, London EC1R 3BW
T: 020 7520 7550
F: 020 7520 7555
E: info@drugscope.org.uk
www.drugscope.org.uk
Chief Executive: Martin Barnes
DrugScope is the national membership organisation for the drug sector. The charity exists to inform drug policy and reduce drug-related risk. DrugScope is committed to highlighting the unique contribution of the voluntary and community sector to reducing drug-related harms.
Employees: 10

Duchenne Family Support Group

78 York Street, London W1H 1DP
T: 0870 241 1857
Helpline: 0800 121 4518
E: info@dfsg.org.uk
www.dfsg.org.uk
Chair: Sherri Jay
We provide support to families affected by Duchenne muscular dystrophy by a national helpline, a network of contact families, our website and a quarterly newsletter. We organise subsidised holidays and social events so that parents and siblings can share experiences. We also organise conferences and workshops on topics of interest to our families.
Employees: 1
Volunteers: 55

Dudley Caribbean and Friends Association

E: levene.bruce@btconnect.com

Durrell Wildlife Conservation Trust

Les Augres Manor, La Profonde Rue, Trinity, Jersey JE3 5BP
T: 01534 860000
F: 01534 860001
E: info@durrell.org
www.durrell.org

Our mission is to save species from extinction, and we have a proven track record of doing just that. Species that have been saved include the Assam pygmy hog, St Lucia whiptail lizard, Mallorcan midwife toad, as well as helping to save more species of birds than any other conservation organisation on the planet. The Trust's expert conservationists work hard in threatened habitats around the world continuing the battle to protect and conserve many more.
Employees: 88
Volunteers: 200

Dyslexia Action

Park House, Wick Road, Egham, Surrey TW20 0HH
T: 01784 222300
E: info@dyslexiaaction.org.uk
www.dyslexiaaction.org.uk
Chief Executive: Kevin Geeson

Dyslexia Action is a national charity and the UK's leading provider of services and support for people with dyslexia and literacy difficulties. We specialise in assessment, teaching and training. We also develop and distribute teaching materials and undertake research. Our services are available through our 26 centres and 160 teaching locations around the UK. Over half a million people benefit from our work each year.
Employees: 300
Regional offices: 26

Dyspraxia Foundation

8 West Alley, Hitchin, Hertfordshire SG5 1EG
T: 01462 455016
F: 01462 455052
E: admin@dyspraxiafoundation.org.uk
www.dyspraxiafoundation.org.uk
General Manager/Company Secretary: Eleanor Howes

The Foundation puts parents and children in contact with other sufferers, locally and nationally. It provides a regular newsletter, promotes better diagnostic and treatment facilities for dyspraxic children, and

encourages a wider understanding of dyspraxia from childhood into adulthood by health and education professionals and by the general public.
Employees: 5
Volunteers: 100
Regional offices: 1
Income: £195,000 (2010-11)

Dystonia Society

2nd Floor, 89 Albert Embankment, London SE1 7TP
T: 0845 458 6211
Helpline: 0845 458 6322
F: 0845 458 6311
E: info@dystonia.org.uk
www.dystonia.org.uk
Chief Executive: Paul King

The Dystonia Society is a UK-wide charity providing practical and emotional support for the 70,000 people with dystonia and their families. Dystonia is a neurological movement disorder characterised by involuntary and sustained muscle spasms, which can be very painful and debilitating.
Employees: 15
Volunteers: 300
Income: £560,658 (2011-12)

Each one. Teach one

E: sarahmac77@gmail.com

Ealing Centre for Independent Living

E: ellen.collins@ecil.org

Ealing Community Transport

Greenford Depot, Greenford Road, Greenford, Middlesex UB6 9AP
T: 020 8813 3210
F: 020 8813 3211
E: ealing@ectcharity.co.uk
www.ectcharity.co.uk
Chief Executive: Anna Whitty

ECT is a national charity with a local focus on the specialist provision of high-quality, safe,

accessible and affordable transport for the many communities we serve. We are committed to charity, partnership and social business excellence. Under the banner 'ECT Charity', we operate from Ealing, Cheshire, Dorset and Milton Keynes.
Employees: 180
Volunteers: 300
Regional offices: 4

Earl Mountbatten Hospice

Halberry Lane
T: 01983 529511
E: christine.dedman@iwhospice.org
Business Development Manager: Christine Dedman

Earthwatch (Europe)

267 Banbury Road, Summertown, Oxford, Oxfordshire OX13 5ET
T: 01865 318838
F: 01865 311383
E: info@earthwatch.org.uk
www.earthwatch.org/europe
Executive Director: Nigel Winser

Aims to advance the education and awareness of the public in the sciences and humanities and in all matters relating to the existence and development of life, human and non-human.
Employees: 55
Volunteers: 650

East Anglian Air Ambulance

Hangar E, Gambling Close, Norwich Airport, Norwich, Norfolk NR6 6EG
T: 01603 269320
E: info@eaaa.org.uk
www.eaaa.org.uk
Chief Executive: Tim Page

The East Anglian Air Ambulance is a 365-day helicopter emergency medical service covering Bedfordshire, Cambridgeshire, Norfolk and Suffolk. We fly with a doctor and critical care paramedic, bringing A&E to the patient. We are 100% charity and receive no government of lottery funding.
Employees: 48
Volunteers: 250
Regional offices: 6
Income: £7,000,000 (2011-12)

East London Advanced Technology Training

E: orla@elatt.org.uk

Eaves Housing for Women Limited

Lincoln House, 1–3 Brixton Road,
London SW9 6DE
T: 020 7735 2062
F: 020 7820 8907
E: post@eaveshousing.co.uk
Provides housing for homeless women in need of supported housing; provides information about the causes of women's homelessness; campaigns for increased housing provision for single homeless women; encourages appropriate housing provision for single women.

Eco-Actif Services CIC

46 Throwley Way, Sutton,
Surrey SM1 4AF
T: 020 8640 3131
F: 020 8640 4131
E: anna@ecoactifservicescic.co.uk
www.ecoactifservicescic.co.uk
CEO: Amanda Palmer-Roye
At Eco-Actif Services, we provide bespoke training solutions for disadvantaged people. Our flagship projects are the Work Programme (mandatory referrals for people unemployed for over one year) and the ESF Families Programme, a voluntary programme tackling multi-generational worklessness. We also work with London Probation and Safer Borough partnerships, working holistically with offenders and their families, together with a range of educational and work-based training.
Employees: 16
Volunteers: 5
Regional offices: 3
Income: £680,000 (2010-11)

ECPAT UK

4 A Chillingworth Road, Holloway,
London N7 8QJ
T: 020 7607 2136
F: 020 7005 435
E: info@ecpat.org.uk
www.ecpat.org.uk
Chief Executive Officer: Bharti Patel
ECPAT UK (End Child Prostitution, Pornography and Trafficking) is a leading children's rights organisation campaigning to protect children from commercial sexual exploitation in the UK. In particular, we focus on the protection of trafficked children and children exploited in tourism.
Employees: 7
Volunteers: 1
Income: £463,421 (2012-13)

Ecumenical Council for Corporate Responsibility

PO Box 500, Oxford,
Oxfordshire OX1 1ZL
T: 01865 245349
E: info@eccr.org.uk
www.eccr.org.uk
ECCR works for economic justice, human rights and environmental sustainability. It acts as a forum where issues of corporate and investor responsibility are researched and studied, information and ideas are exchanged, and strategies are planned and implemented.
Employees: 4

EDP Drug and Alcohol Service

Suite 2:11, 2nd Floor, Renslade House,
Bonhay Road, Exeter, Devon EX4 3AY
T: 01392 666710
E: info@edp.org.uk
www.edp.org.uk
Chief Executive: Lucie Hartley
When people have problems with drugs and alcohol they may feel they have less control over their lives, and they may struggle to engage with their families and communities. We provide accessible services in Devon and Dorset, which support people to move towards a place of wellbeing where they feel empowered and re-connected to their family and/or community.
Employees: 150
Regional offices: 10

Education Action International

World University Service UK, 14 Dufferin Street, London EC1Y 8PD
T: 020 7426 5802
E: info@education-action.org
www.education-action.org
Education Action International highlights the political and social importance of education in development and assists refugees and victims of repression through educational programmes.

Education and Services for People with Autism Ltd

2A Hylton Park Road, Wessington Way,
Sunderland, Sunderland, Tyne and
Wear SR5 3HD
T: 01915 165080
F: 01915 498620
E: lesley.lane@espa.org.uk
www.espa.org.uk
Chief Executive: Lesley Lane
Provides specialist further education, residential, day and domiciliary services for people with an autism spectrum disorder.
Employees: 425
Regional offices: 1

Education for Choice

The Resource Centre, 356 Holloway Road,
London N7 6PA
T: 020 7700 8190 (also fax)
E: efc@efc.org.uk
www.efc.org.uk
Director: Lisa Hallgarten
Education For Choice is the only UK organisation dedicated to enabling young people to make and act on informed choices about pregnancy and abortion. EFC works with young people, delivers training and consultancy for professionals and produces a range of information resources.
Employees: 4
Volunteers: 2

Education Otherwise

PO Box 325, Kings Lynn,
Norfolk PE34 3NX
T: 01507 359213
E: bcameron-young@
educationotherwise.org
www.education-otherwise.org
Education Otherwise offers support, advice and information to families practising or contemplating home-based education as an alternative to schooling.
Volunteers: 105
Regional offices: 70

Educational Centres Association

21 Ebbisham Drive, Norwich NR4 6HQ
T: 0870 161 0302
E: info@e-c-a.ac.uk
www.e-c-a.ac.uk
The Educational Centres Association is a practice-based organisation concerned with adult education and lifelong learning. Its work in the arts and cultural sectors complements the role of its constituent institutions and organisations. These extend across the range of adult community learning, FE colleges and HE. In England, much of this work is funded by the Learning and Skills Council, LSC, with which we have effective relationships at national and local levels.

Edutec Training Centre

Suite 6, Station Chambers, High Street
North, East Ham, London E6 1JE
E: edutec@kmgsai.co.uk
Edutec Training Centre is a non-profitable training organisation providing training in finance, accountancy, language and business

studies. We provide the best possible education and training, enabling learners from all backgrounds to achieve their personal and professional goals.
Employees: 3

Edward's Trust

43A Calthorpe Road, Edgbaston, Birmingham, West Midlands B15 1TS
T: 0121 456 4838
E: christine.bodkin@edwardstrust.org.uk
www.edwardstrust.org.uk
The aims of Edward's Trust are to provide support to children with a serious illness and requiring hospital treatment, and their families; to provide support to families suffering a bereavement; to provide training to those involved in bereavement services following the death of a child; to raise awareness of complementary approaches to childhood concerns; and to promote and support research into complementary approaches to childhood illnesses.
Employees: 22

Ehlers-Danlos Support Group

PO Box 337, Aldershot GU12 6WZ
T: 01252 690940
E: director@ehlers-danlos.org
www.ehlers-danlos.org
Trustee: Frances Gawthrop
The aims of the Group are to support those with Ehlers-Danlos syndrome and provide education, information and research for medical and caring professionals. It produces books, information sheets and a newsletter. A national conference is held biennially. The group endeavours to heighten awareness of EDS among the medical professionals and support EDS research.
Employees: .4
Volunteers: 24
Regional offices: 1

EIRIS Foundation

80–84 Bondway, London SW8 1SF
T: 020 7840 5707
E: ethics@eiris.org
www.eiris.org
The foundation provides information on a wide range of issues to help concerned investors apply positive or negative ethical and social criteria. It identifies forms of investment that meet certain non-financial requirements on the part of the investor and promotes wider understanding of, and debate on, corporate responsibility.

Elderly Accommodation Counsel

3rd Floor, 89 Albert Embankment, London SE1 7TP
T: 020 7820 3755
Helpline: 020 7820 1343
F: 020 7820 3970
E: ros.lucas@eac.org.uk
www.housingcare.org
EAC provides information, advice and support to older people and their families on their housing and care options. It does this via its Advice Line service and its website.
Employees: 12
Volunteers: 10

Elfrida Society

34 Islington Park Street, London N1 1PX
T: 020 7359 7443
F: 020 7704 1358
E: elfrida@elfrida.com
www.elfrida.com
The Elfrida Society promotes and advances the welfare, education, training and advancement in life of people with learning difficulties.
Employees: 60
Volunteers: 7

Elimination of Leukaemia Fund

Regent House, Suite 131, 291 Kirkdale, London SE26 4QD
T: 020 8778 5353
E: admin@elf-fund.org.uk
www.elf-fund.org.uk
ELF is a major funder of leukaemia research at King's College Hospital, London, and is also funding work at a number of other major centres including the Institute of Child Health, Great Ormond Street Hospital and Belfast City Hospital. ELF favours patient-centred work so that there is an immediate or near future benefit to sufferers of leukaemia and the related blood disorders.

Elizabeth Finn Care

1 Derry Street, London W8 5HY
T: 020 7396 6700
F: 020 7396 6739
E: info@elizabethfinn.org.uk
www.elizabethfinncare.org.uk
Chief Executive: Jonathan Welfare
Elizabeth Finn Care helps individual British and Irish people who come from a professional or similar background who have fallen below the poverty line, and their immediate families, by offering grants, information and advice. The charity has two subsidiaries – Elizabeth Finn Homes Ltd, which manages EFC's care homes, and turn2us, a related charity directing those in

the UK suffering financial hardship to appropriate charities and state benefits.
Employees: 750
Volunteers: 700
Regional offices: 8

Elizabeth Foundation

Southwick Hill Road, Cosham, Portsmouth PO6 3LL
T: 023 9237 2735
F: 023 9232 6155
E: sally.moger@elizabeth-foundation.org
www.elizabeth-foundation.org
Chief Executive: Sue Campbell
The Elizabeth Foundation promotes early diagnosis for babies and preschool children with hearing loss, and provides comprehensive educational and support services to them and their families. By doing so we enable these children to develop their listening skills and natural speech and give parents the confidence and knowledge to make informed decisions on behalf of their child.
Employees: 20
Volunteers: 8
Regional offices: 1
Income: £885,003 (2012-13)

Elmham Charitable Trust

224 Hills Road, Cambridge, Cambridgeshire CB2 2QE
T: 01223 247661
E: elmham@gn.apc.org
Very small family charity with no capital. It channels the income that trustees donate to charities the trustees agree upon. They do not spend any money on running the charity and do not accept any applications for funding.
Employees: 0
Volunteers: 0
Regional offices: 0

Emily Jordan Foundation

Unit 9 Finepoint, Finepoint Way, Kidderminster, Worcestershire DY11 7FB
T: 01562 861484
E: chris.jordan@ theemilyjordanfoundation.org.uk
www.theemilyjordanfoundation.org.uk
Chair of Trustees: Chris Jordan
The Aim: to help individuals with moderate learning and physical disabilities to lead fulfilled lives. This is done via developing and supplying good quality day opportunities alongside work development projects for

those who may be able to enter the workplace.
Employees: 5
Volunteers: 10
Regional offices: 0
Income: £200,000 (2011-12)

Emmaus UK

48 Kingston Street, Cambridge, Cambridgeshire CB1 2NU
T: 01223 576103
F: 01223 576203
E: contact@emmaus.org.uk
www.emmaus.org.uk
Director: Tim Page
Emmaus Communities enable people to move on from homelessness by providing home and work in a supportive, family environment. Residents work together, collecting donated furniture and selling it in community shops to support themselves and reduce waste going to landfill. Any surplus made by the Communities is used to benefit other people in need. Emmaus UK is the central support office for the Federation of Emmaus Communities in the UK.
Employees: 26
Volunteers: 5
Regional offices: 26

Employment Opportunities for People with Disabilities

Crystal Gate, 3rd Floor, 28–30 Worship Street, London EC2A 2AH
T: 020 7448 5421
F: 020 7374 4913
E: impact@opportunity.org.uk
www.opportunities.org.uk
Working directly with people with a wide range of disabilities to help them find employment, Opportunities seeks to persuade employers to positively recognise ability and potential. We have a national network of 15 regional centres offering advice on training, job search, CVs, application forms and interviews. Our services are provided free of charge to our clients and employers.
Employees: 52
Volunteers: 3
Regional offices: 15

Empowering West Berkshire

E: shelly@empoweringwb.org.uk

Empty Homes Agency

Downstream Building, 1 London Bridge, London SE1 9BG
T: 020 7828 6288
F: 020 7681 3214
E: info@emptyhomes.com
www.emptyhomes.com
Chief Executive: David Ireland

The Agency is an independent campaigning charity that aims to raise awareness of the potential of empty homes in England to meet housing need and to devise and promote, with others, sustainable solutions that will bring empty homes back into use.
Employees: 6
Volunteers: 5

Encephalitis Society

32 Castlegate, Malton, North Yorkshire YO17 7DT
T: 01653 692583
Helpline: 01653 699599
E: ava@encephalitis.info
www.encephalitis.info
Chief Executive Officer: Ava Easton
Aims to improve the quality of life of all people affected, directly and indirectly, by encephalitis. We support people affected, raise awareness of the condition, provide information and conduct research. The Society is the only resource of its kind in the world.
Employees: 9
Volunteers: 30
Income: £400,000 (2011-12)

End Child Poverty

94 White Lion Street, London N1 9PF
T: 020 7843 1913
F: 020 7843 1918
E: info@ecpc.org.uk
www.ecpc.org.uk
3.8 million children – one in three – are currently living in poverty in the UK, one of the highest rates in the industrialised world. The Campaign to End Child Poverty continues to raise the issue across the UK, in order to maintain the current pressure on government, and the other major political parties, to ensure they keep their promises to the millions of children experiencing poverty in the UK today.
Employees: 5

Endeavour Training Ltd

5–6 Sheepbridge Centre, Sheepbridge Lane, Chesterfield, Derbyshire S41 9RX
T: 0870 770 3250
F: 0870 770 3254
E: info@endeavour.org.uk
www.endeavour.org.uk
Provides long-term personal development opportunities for young people (aged 13–26), specifically targeting those at risk; enhances low levels of self-confidence and self-esteem and develops teamwork and communication skills, thereby helping them to manage better their own actions and future plans and encouraging a sense of

community spirit and voluntary commitment.
Employees: 26
Volunteers: 250
Regional offices: 3

Endometriosis SHE Trust (UK)

Unit 14, Moorland Way, Lincoln LN6 7JW
T: 01522 682300 (also fax)
E: shetrust@shetrust.org.uk
www.shetrust.org.uk
Chair: Diane Carlton
Aims include the relief of persons suffering from endometriosis by the provision of advice and guidance including that of holistic methods of treatment; the advancement of the education of the public, including the medical professions, by raising awareness in all matters relating to endometriosis and its treatment.
Volunteers: 12

Endometriosis UK

Suites 1 and 2, 46 Manchester Street, London W1U 7LS
T: 020 7222 2781
Helpline: 0808 808 2227
F: 020 7222 2786
E: admin@endometriosis-uk.org
www.endometriosis-uk.org
Chief Executive Officer: Helen North
1.5 million UK women live with endometriosis, a chronic gynaecological condition that has a huge impact on quality of life. Despite being so common, awareness and understanding is staggeringly low. Endometriosis UK is the lead charity offering vital support and information for those living with endometriosis, working hard to reduce the inherent isolation of this condition.
Employees: 5
Volunteers: 50
Regional offices: 30 (local support groups)

Energy Conservation and Solar Centre

Unit 327, 30 Great Guildford Street, London SE1 0HS
T: 020 7922 1660
E: enquiries@ecsc.org.uk
www.ecsc.org.uk
Advances public education in energy conservation and use, and all related subjects.

Enfield Carers Centre

Britannia House, 137-143 Baker Street,
Enfield, Middlesex EN1 3JL
T: 020 8366 3677
E: info@enfieldcarers.org
www.enfieldcarers.org
Chief Executive: Pamela Burke
Enfield Carers Centre is a local charity
offering support and advice for all unpaid
carers living in Enfield. A Carer is someone of
any age who provides unpaid support to a
partner, relative or friend with a short or
long-term illness, a disability, a substance
misuse problem, a life-limiting illness or
terminal diagnosis. We support the following
carers; Older carers, working carers, former
carers, parent carers, young carers (under
18), BME carers.
Employees: 11
Volunteers: 30
Income: £271,389 (2012-13)

Enfield Voluntary Action (EVA)

Community House, 311 Fore Street,
London N9 0PZ
T: 020 8373 6268
F: 020 8373 6267
E: evanews@enfieldva.org.uk
www.enfieldva.org.uk
Chief Executive: Paula Jeffery
EVA provides services to local voluntary and
community organisations in the London
Borough of Enfield, including community
accountancy, development and funding
advice, news and information services and
Volunteer Centre Enfield.
Employees: 8
Volunteers: 4
Regional offices: 0
Income: £397,000 (2012-13)

Engineers Against Poverty

2nd Floor, Weston House, 246 High
Holborn, London WC1V 7EX
T: 020 3206 0488
F: 020 3206 0401
E: p.matthews@
engineersagainstpoverty.org
www.engineersagainstpoverty.org
Executive Director: Petter Matthews
Engineers Against Poverty works with
industry, government and civil society to
fight poverty and promote sustainable
development.
Employees: 4
Volunteers: 2

English Federation of Disability Sport

SportPark, Loughborough University, 3
Oakwood Drive, Loughborough,
Leicestershire LE11 3QF
T: 01509 227750
F: 01509 227777
E: federation@efds.co.uk
www.efds.co.uk
Chief Executive: Barry Horne
The English Federation of Disability Sport
(EFDS) was established in September 1998
as the national body and charity dedicated to
disabled people in sport throughout England.
We work closely with a number of key
partners to improve and increase the
opportunities offered, ensuring disabled
people have a memorable experience of
sport and physical activity. Our partners
include the National Disability Sports
Organisations (NDSOs) recognised by Sport
England, who form part of our membership.
Employees: 19
Volunteers: 200
Regional offices: 1
Income: £2,512,805 (2010-11)

English Province of Our Lady Charity

Fairlight, The Avenue, North Ascot,
Berkshire SL5 7LY
T: 01344 874681
F: 01344 291063
E: lindsay@fairlightolc.plus.com
Regional Leader: Josephine Collier
The charity's main aims are to support
vulnerable women, especially those in
prostitution and with related issues, and their
children; to provide aftercare for women and
children who have previously accessed its
services.
Employees: 27
Volunteers: 15
Income: £1,577,324 (2010-11)

Enham Trust

Enham Place, Enham Alamein, Andover,
Hampshire SP11 6JS
T: 01264 345850
E: info@enham.org.uk
www.enhamtrust.org.uk
Chief Executive: Peta Wilkinson
Enham delivers a wide range of essential
services, from housing and employment to
personal development and care, that provide
choices and empower people to make their
own decisions about their lives. Enham also
operates a number of commercial
enterprises that provide direct employment
opportunities for disabled people, improve

access to essential products and services and
generate income to support Enham's
charitable objectives.
Employees: 280
Volunteers: 90
Regional offices: 8

Enterprising Futures

Kingsley, The Brampton, Newcastle under
Lyme ST5 0QW
T: 01782 854803
E: wnixon@enterprisingfutures.org.uk
www.pmtraining.org.uk
CEO: Will Nixon
Employees: 7

Environment Africa Trust

110 Colleys Lane, Nantwich,
Cheshire CW5 6NT
T: 01270 662692 (also fax)
E: mike.chandler@
environmentafricatrust.org.uk
www.environmentafricatrust.org.uk
Executive Director: Mike Chandler
Environment Africa Trust supports
organisations and projects within Sub-
Saharan Africa that encourage sound
environmental management and biodiversity
conservation through a strong community
development focus to achieve sustainable
livelihoods. Our partner Mpingo
Conservation and Development Initiative in
Tanzania is developing a fair trade in African
Blackwood that is being promoted by Sound
and Fair. EAT welcomes approaches from
projects that have the above vision and focus
in Sub-Saharan Africa that are seeking a UK
partner.
Volunteers: 6

Environment Council

212 High Holborn, London WC1V 7BF
T: 020 7836 2626
F: 020 7242 1180
E: info@envcouncil.org.uk
www.the-environment-council.org.uk
Helps people from all sectors of business and
society to make decisions to improve their
environments and their lives.
Employees: 25
Volunteers: 3

Environmental Awareness Trust

23 High Street, Wheathampstead,
St Albans, Hertfordshire AL4 8BB
T: 01582 834580
Promotes knowledge, awareness and
understanding of global environmental
problems, their causes, effects and possible
solutions.

Environmental Investigation Agency Trust

62-63 Upper Street, London N1 0NY
T: 020 7354 7960
E: ukinfo@eia-international.org
www.eia-international.org
Executive Director: Mary Rice
The Environmental Investigation Agency (EIA) is an independent campaigning organisation committed to bringing about change that protects the natural world from environmental crime and abuse. Our vision is a future where humanity respects, protects and celebrates the natural world for the benefit of all.
Employees: 26
Volunteers: 5
Regional offices: 0

Environmental Law Foundation

Suite 309, 16-16a Baldwins Gardens, London EC1N 7RJ
T: 020 7404 1030
E: info@elflaw.org
www.elflaw.org
ELF helps community groups and individuals gain access to the law in order to protect their environment.

Envision

Dennis Geffen Annexe, St Pancras Gardens, Camley Street, London NW1 0PS
T: 020 7974 8440
F: 020 7974 8425
E: london@envision.org.uk
www.envsion.org.uk
Aims to advance the education of members of the general public, particularly in environmental matters and promote the protection and improvement of the physical and natural environment for the public benefit.
Employees: 12
Volunteers: 180

Epic Arts

Bradbury Studios, 138 Kingsland Road, London E2 8DY
T: 020 7613 6440 (also fax)
E: info@epicarts.org.uk
www.epicarts.org.uk
CEO: Rachel Duncombe-Anderson
The aim is to create arts opportunities for people who previously lacked access, especially those who are disadvantaged because of disability, poverty or age.
Employees: 6
Volunteers: 4
Regional offices: 1
Income: £250,000 (2010-11)

Epilepsy Action

New Anstey House, Gate Way Drive, Yeadon, Leeds LS19 7XY
T: 0113 210 8800
Helpline: 0808 800 5050
F: 0113 391 0300
E: epilepsy@epilepsy.org.uk
www.epilepsy.org.uk
Chief Executive: Philip Lee
Aims to increase public awareness and understanding of epilepsy; to provide information and advice; to promote research into the condition; to raise funds for epilepsy; to campaign for change.

Epilepsy Research UK

PO Box 3004, London W4 4XT
T: 020 8995 4781 (also fax)
E: info@eruk.org.uk
www.epilepsyresearch.org.uk
Epilepsy Research UK was formed by the merger of the Epilepsy Research Foundation and the Fund for Epilepsy in April 2007. It is the only national charity exclusively dedicated to research into epilepsy.
Employees: 4

Equality Forum

Tavis House, 1-6 Tavistock Square, London WC1H 9NA
T: 020 3033 1454
E: equality.forum@edf.org.uk
www.edf.org.uk
CEO: Amanda Ariss
The Equality and Diversity Forum (EDF) is the network of national NGOs working on equality and human rights. Our vision is of a society in which everyone can fulfill their potential and make a distinctive contribution; where diversity is celebrated, people can express their identities free from the threat of violence and everyone is treated with dignity and respect; where your chance to flourish is not limited by who you are or where you come from. EDF uses its strength as a network of committed and influential organisations to work for a society in which everyone can fulfill their potential, everyone is treated with respect regardless of background or circumstances, and diversity is celebrated. Our charitable aims are to promote equality and in particular the elimination of discrimination on the grounds of age, disability, gender, gender identity, race, religion or belief, and sexual orientation or any combination of these grounds, understanding of and support for human rights, the efficiency and effectiveness of

voluntary sector organisations working in the areas of equality and human rights.
Employees: 6
Volunteers: 2
Income: £241,667 (2012-13)

Equity Trust Fund

222 Africa House, 64 Kingsway, London WC2B 6BD
T: 020 7404 6041
E: keith@equitycharitabletrust.org.uk
www.equitytrustfund.org.uk
Aims to assist professional performers in need, in particular past and present members of British Actors Equity.

ERIC (Education and Resources for Improving Childhood Continence)

36 Old School House, Britannia Road, Kingswood, Bristol BS15 8DB
T: 0117 960 3060
Helpline: 0845 370 8008
F: 0117 960 0401
E: info@eric.org.uk
www.eric.org.uk
Director: Jenny Perez
ERIC provides information and support on bedwetting, daytime wetting, soiling and constipation, and potty training. The helpline is available 24/7. Leaflets and further information to download and a moderated message board are available on the ERIC website. Useful and practical resources are available to purchase from www.ericshop.org.uk.
Employees: 11
Volunteers: 3
Regional offices: 1

Eritrean Relief Association (UK)

Robin House, 2a Iverson Road, London NW6 2HE
T: 020 7328 7888
Helpline: 07957 113307
E: seble@era-uk.org
www.era-uk.org
Chairman: Seble Ephrem
The Eritrean Relief Association (UK) is set up to provide relief, rehabilitation and development support and assistance to humans and their livestock affected by drought, war and displacement in Eritrea. ERA-UK also provides capacity building advice, information and guidance to people from Eritrea living in the UK.
Volunteers: 10
Regional offices: 1
Income: £15,000 (2010-11)

Ernest Foundation

45 Cardiff House, Peckham Park Road,
London SE15 6TT
T: 020 7635 9607
E: theernestfoundation@hotmail.com
Coordinator: Ernest Nkrumah
Carries out activities and projects that will
bring support and relief to people living with
HIV/AIDS and related diseases among the
Ghanaian and other West African
communities in England and Wales. Working
with children and young people.

Esmee Fairbairn Foundation

Kings Place, 90 York Way,
London N1 9AG
T: 020 7812 3700
F: 020 7812 3701
E: info@esmeefairbairn.org.uk
www.esmeefairbairn.org.uk
The Esmee Fairbairn Foundation aims to
improve the quality of life throughout the
UK by funding the charitable activities of
organisations that have the ideas and ability
to achieve change for the better. We take
pride in supporting work that might
otherwise be considered difficult to fund.
Our primary interests are in the arts,
education and learning, the environment
and social change.
Employees: 28

Ethical Property Foundation

Development House, 56–64 Leonards
Street, London EC2A 4LT
T: 020 7065 0760
F: 020 7065 0768
E: victoriahowse@ethicalproperty.org.uk
www.ethicalproperty.org.uk
The Ethical Property Foundation is a charity
committed to empowering charities and
community groups to make the most of their
property. The Foundation is also committed
to improving the environmental and social
performance of the commercial property
sector.
Employees: 5
Regional offices: 1

Ethical Trading Initiative

4 Coldbath Square, London EC1R 5HL
Helpline: 020 7841 5180
F: 020 7831 7852
E: eti@eti.org.uk
www.ethicaltrade.org
Director: Dan Rees
We are an alliance of global brands and
retailers, trade unions, campaigning
organisations and charities that work
together to improve the lives of workers in
global supply chains. We provide practical
tools and guidance for companies to help

them implement codes of labour practice in
their supply chains, and are widely recognised
as a global leader in this area.
Employees: 15

Ethiopian Community Centre in the UK

Selby Centre, Selby Road,
London N17 8JL
T: 020 8801 9224
F: 020 8801 0244
E: post@eccuk.org
www.eccuk.org
Executive Director: Alem Gebrehiwot
Provides information, advice and guidance
for migrants, refugees and asylum seekers
(particularly but not exclusively of Ethiopian
origin), on education and training, welfare
benefits, housing, immigration, money and
debt, health-related issues with a particular
focus on HIV/AIDS and mental health, and
also conducts research as necessary.
Employees: 12
Volunteers: 45

Ethiopian Community In Britian

2a Lithos Road, London NW3 6EF
T: 020 7794 4265
F: 020 7794 4116
E: postmaster@ethiopiancommunity.
co.uk
www.ethiopiancommunity.co.uk
Director: Alemayehu Dessie
Provides information, advice, advocacy and
referral services and training for Ethiopians
and members of other communities, as well
as outreach, sports and leisure activities. It
also runs ESOL and IT training courses for
unemployed refugees and asylum seekers,
irrespective of their country of origin.
Volunteers: 5
Income: £91,373 (2012-13)

Ethiopian Health Support Association

Priory House, Kingsgate Place,
London NW6 4TA
T: 020 7419 1972
F: 020 7691 2385
E: admin@ethsa.co.uk
www.ethsa.co.uk
Coordinator: Kefale Alemu
We provide free counselling, information,
advice, advocacy and support on health and
wellbeing to Ethiopian refugees and asylum
seekers living in the UK, in a confidential
environment.
Employees: 2
Volunteers: 6
Regional offices: 1

Europe Trust

PO Box MAR005, Markfield,
Leicestershire LE67 9RY
T: 01530 245919
E: info@europetrust.eu.com
Provides support to community-based
organisations.
Employees: 3

European Association for the Treatment of Addiction

1st Floor, 1 Regent Terrace, Rita Road,
London SW8 1AW
T: 020 7820 8130
F: 020 7820 0055
E: secretariat@eata.org.uk
www.eata.org.uk
Chief Executive: Colin Wilkie-Jones
eATA is the umbrella organisation for the
independent drug and alcohol treatment
and aftercare sector. eATA represents services
throughout the continuum of care. eATA is a
registered charity, working to ensure that
people with substance dependencies get the
treatment they need.
Employees: 3
Volunteers: 10

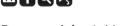

European Atlantic Movement

Start Farm, Harlow Road, Ongar,
Essex CM5 0DT
T: 01277 890282
E: info@european-atlantic.org.uk
www.european-atlantic.org.uk
President: Lord Watson of Richmond
TEAM is an independent educational
foundation that aims to promote
understanding and discussion of European
and world affairs.
Volunteers: 40

European Extension College

23 Castalia Square, Docklands,
London E14 3NG
T: 0870 385 1213
Helpline: 0870 385 1218
F: 0870 385 1217
E: info@extensioncollege.org
www.extensioncollege.org
The European Extension College is a non-
profit educational association established in
London. The mission of the College is to
provide opportunities for learning
throughout life by enabling access to
individualised and flexible quality education
and training, and to support the
advancement and improvement of
education at all levels for the benefit of the
public.
Volunteers: 10
Regional offices: 2

European League of Stuttering Associations

31 Grosvenor Road, Jesmond, Newcastle upon Tyne NE2 2RL
T: 0191 281 8003
E: elsa.europe@ymail.com
www.elsa.info
Chair: Edwin Farr
Coordinates, links together and furthers the cooperation of Europe's national stuttering associations.
Volunteers: 10
Regional offices: 2

Eva Women's Aid

E: julie@eva.org.uk

Evacuees Reunion Association

The Mill Business Centre, Mill Hill, Gringley-on-the-Hill, Nottinghamshire DN10 4RA
T: 01777 816166
E: era@evacuees.org.uk
www.evacuees.org.uk
Chief Executive: James Roffey
The Association has 2,200 members worldwide, mails out a monthly newsletter The Evacuee and organises events to raise the profile of the story of the evacuation of thousands of children both within the UK and abroad at the outbreak of war and the following years. We visit schools and give talks on the evacuation to numerous groups and have published Send Them to Safety, the story of the Great British evacuation.
Employees: 2
Volunteers: 100

Evangelical Alliance

176 Copenhagen Street, London N1 0ST
T: 020 7520 3830
E: info@eauk.org
www.eauk.org
General Director: Steve Clifford
A Christian charity founded in 1846 to promote unity and truth, and represent evangelical concerns to the wider world of the church, state and society.

Evelyn 190 Centre

E: bola@evelyn190centre.org.uk

EveryChild

4 Bath Place, Rivington Street, London EC2A 3DR
T: 020 7749 2468
F: 020 7729 8339
E: gen@everychild.org.uk
www.everychild.org.uk
EveryChild works with some of the world's most vulnerable and marginalised children to enable them to grow up free from disease, poverty and exploitation. We work with children, communities and governments across 18 countries to ensure that every child has the right to an education, healthcare and to grow up in a loving family environment.
Employees: 50
Volunteers: 15
Regional offices: 1

Evidence For Development

E: celiapetty@gmail.com

Ex-Services Mental Welfare Society (Combat Stress)

Tyrwhitt House, Oaklawn Road, Leatherhead, Surrey KT22 0BX
T: 01372 587100
Helpline: 01372 587080
F: 01372 587081
E: contactus@combatstress.org.uk
www.combatstress.org.uk
Chief Executive: Commodore Andrew Cameron
Combat Stress seeks to help those of all ranks from the armed forces and the Merchant Navy suffering from psychological disability as a result of their service. To this end, the charity provides visiting welfare officers and treatment centres to aid former servicemen and women.
Employees: 171
Regional offices: 4

Examination Officers' Association

E: andrew.harland@examofficers.org.uk

Explore

The EWR Centre, Cloudesley Street, London N1 0HU
T: 020 7278 0699
F: 020 7278 0589
E: enquiries@theexploreexperience.co.uk
www.theexploreexperience.co.uk
Explore is a registered educational charity that enables young people in schools, colleges and prisons to explore the experience of couples and, through this study, to appreciate lasting relationship skills, emotional literacy, family life and marriage.

EXTEND Exercise Training Ltd

2 Place Farm, Wheathampstead, Hertfordshire AL4 8SB
T: 01582 832760 (also fax)
E: admin@extend.org.uk
www.extend.org.uk
Promotes the quality of life for men and women over 60, and the less able of any age, through exercise and movement to music in a class or on a one-to-one basis.
Employees: 2
Volunteers: 800
Regional offices: 4
Income: £150,000 (2011-12)

Eye on the Wild

Unit 10, The Glasshouse, 49a Goldhawk Road, London W12 8QP
T: 020 8204 8466
E: trustee4eow@hotmail.com
www.eyeonthewild.org
Chair: Lord Brian Hamilton
A small environmental charity that focuses on damage or influences caused by tourism. Identifies causes and concerns in flora, fauna, environment and communities globally directly or indirectly influenced by tourism and travel. Extensive operations and projects globally.
Volunteers: 4

Eyeless Trust for Young People and Children Born Without Eyes

PO Box 4139, Marlow SL7 9BD
T: 01903 857025
www.eyeless.org.uk
Through a network of family support workers, the Eyeless Trust works in partnership with families and other agencies to offer support and advice to children and young people born with anophthalmia (no eyes) and microphthalmia (tiny residual eyes), coloboma (structure missing) and related disabilities. The aim is to help the whole family and enable these youngsters to maximise their full potential in all areas of their lives.
Employees: 1
Volunteers: 13

F

Fable Charity

Lower Ground Floor, 305 Glossop Road,
Sheffield, South Yorkshire S10 2HL
T: 0114 275 5335
Helpline: 0800 521629
F: 0114 275 6444
E: sarah-fable@btconnect.com
www.fable.org.uk
Founder: Sandra Howard
For A Better Life with Epilepsy or FABLE is a
national charity that helps people with
epilepsy, or issues or associated with
epilepsy, to increase their quality of life. It
operates a free phone advice line and
drop-in advice and information centre in
Sheffield, along with a national patient
support network.
Employees: 7
Volunteers: 10
Regional offices: 1

Fair Play for Children Association/Charitable Trust

32 Longford Road, Bognor Regis, West
Sussex PO21 1AG
T: 0845 330 7635
E: fairplay@arunet.co.uk
www.fairplayforchildren.org
National Secretary: Jan Cosgrove
Campaigns for children's right to play,
including more, better and safer facilities
and services for all children. Provision of
information, news and services such as CRB
Enhanced Disclosures.
Employees: 3
Volunteers: 12

Fair Trials International

Temple Chambers, 3/7 Temple Avenue,
London EC4Y 0HP
T: 020 7822 2370
F: 020 7822 2371
E: office@fairtrials.net
www.fairtrials.net
Chief Executive Officer: Jago Russell
Works for fair trials according to
international standards of justice and
defends the rights of those facing charges in
a country other than their own.
Employees: 9
Volunteers: 5
Regional offices: Greater London

Fairtrade Foundation

3rd Floor, Ibex House, 42–47 Minories,
London EC3N 1DY
T: 020 7440 7677
F: 020 7405 5943
E: frances.robathan@fairtrade.org.uk
www.fairtrade.org.uk
Relieves poverty, suffering and distress in any
part of the world; promotes research into
and education concerning the causes and
effects of poverty.
Employees: 20
Volunteers: 50

Faith Based Regeneration Network UK

12–20 Baron Street, London N1 9LL
T: 020 7713 8193
E: doreenf@fbrn.org.uk
www.fbrn.org.uk
Executive Director: Doreen Finneron
FbRN UK is the leading national multi-faith
network for community development,
regeneration and social action. It encourages
the active engagement of faith groups in civil
society by linking practitioners across the
different faith traditions for mutual learning,
and provides an interface between policy
makers and communities. It is managed by a
trustee body drawn from nine faith
traditions: Baha'i, Buddhist, Christian, Hindu,
Jain, Jewish, Muslim, Sikh and Zoroastrian.
Employees: 5

Faith in Families

7 Colwick Road, West Bridgford,
Nottingham NG2 5AF
T: 0115 955 8811
F: 0115 955 8822
E: enquiries@faithinfamilies.org
www.faithinfamilies.org
Chief Executive Officer: Sumerjit Ram
Faith in Families is a registered charity and
voluntary adoption agency. The charity is
based in Nottingham and works throughout
the East Midlands. Faith in Families vision is to
provide nurturing, innovative, high quality
services for children and families. We believe
that the services we provide will enable all
children to develop into confident, secure,
caring individuals, with the capacity to reach
their full potential in life.
Employees: 42
Volunteers: 150
Regional offices: 2

Families for Children

Southgate Court, Buckfast,
Devon TQ11 0EE
T: 01364 645480
F: 01364 645499
E: marketing@familiesforchildren.org.uk
www.familiesforchildren.org.uk
CEO: Caroline Davis OBE
Families for Children is a vibrant adoption
agency based in the south west. We place
vulnerable children from all over country
with adoptive families in Devon, Dorset and
Cornwall. We are a specialist adoption
agency providing advice and support for
those who are considering adoption and also
offer our 'forever' policy of support. This
means that we can offer adoption support to
the child and new family for as long as they
need us.
Employees: 40
Volunteers: 0
Regional offices: 2
Income: £1,300,000 (2012-13)

Families Need Fathers

Studio 212, 134 Curtain Road,
London EC2A 3AR
T: 0300 030 0110
Helpline: 0300 030 0363
F: 020 7739 3410
E: admin@fnf.org.uk
www.fnf.org.uk
Chairman of Trustees: Jerry Karlin
Families Need Fathers is a registered UK
charity that provides information and
support to parents of either sex,
grandparents and wider family members
following divorce and separation. FNF is
chiefly concerned with the problems of
maintaining a child's relationship with both
parents during and after family breakdown.
Employees: 4
Volunteers: 60 - 100

Family Action

501–505 Kingsland Road,
London E8 4AU
T: 020 7254 6251
F: 020 7249 5443
E: info@family-action.org.uk
www.family-action.org.uk
Chief Executive: Helen Dent
Assists families and individuals to overcome
the effects of poverty and disadvantage in

tangible ways, by providing services offering practical, emotional and financial support.
Employees: 750
Volunteers: 500
Regional offices: 8

Family Action In Our Region (FAIR)

Family Centre @ Park Road Baptist Church, Park Road, Rushden, Park Road, Rushden, Northamptonshire NN10 0LH
T: 01933 419418
F: 01933 419424
E: christine@fairproject.org.uk
www.fairproject.org.uk
General Manager: Chrissy Aldwinckle
FAIR is an energetic and enthusiastic community project serving families living in Rushden and the surrounding areas. We support families in the community to achieve the best possible outcomes for themselves.
Employees: 21
Volunteers: 12
Regional offices: 0

Family and Childcare Trust

2nd Floor, The Bridge, 81 Southwark Bridge Road, London SE1 0NQ
T: 020 7940 7510
E: info@familyandchildcaretrust.org
www.familyandchildcaretrust.org
Chief Executive: Anand Shukla
The Family and Childcare Trust works to make the UK a better place for families. Our vision is of a society where government, business and communities do all they can to support every family to thrive. Through our research, campaigning and practical support we are creating a more family friendly UK.
Employees: 25
Volunteers: 0
Regional offices: 0

Family Education Trust (Family and Youth Concern)

Jubilee House, 19-21 High Street, Whitton, Twickenham, Middlesex TW2 7LB
T: 020 8894 2525
F: 020 8894 3535
E: info@famyouth.org.uk
www.famyouth.org.uk
Director: Norman Wells
An independent educational charity conducting and promoting research into the causes and consequences of family breakdown. Through its publications, media profile and responses to government consultations and inquiries, the Trust seeks to

promote the welfare of children and families in line with the research evidence.

Family Holiday Association

16 Mortimer Street, London W1T 3JL
T: 020 7436 3304
E: info@fhaonline.org.uk
www.fhaonline.org.uk
Director: John McDonald
Aims to increase access to holidays for families on a low income.
Employees: 10
Volunteers: 100

Family Links

Units 2 & 3 Fenchurch Court, Bobby Fryer Close, Cowley, Oxford, Oxfordshire OX4 6ZN
T: 01865 401800
F: 01865 401820
E: info@familylinks.org.uk
www.familylinks.org.uk
Chief Executive: Annette Mountford
Family Links is a national charity that believes every child and parent deserves the best chance in life. We enable parents and teachers to become more effective, caring and confident in raising emotionally resilient and socially competent children. Our dynamic approach tackles the root causes of social problems with the Nurturing Programme, which challenges intergenerational dysfunction.
Employees: 24
Volunteers: 9
Regional offices: 1

Family Lives

CAN Mezzanine, 49-51 East Road, London N1 6AH
Helpline: 0808 800 2222
E: parentsupport@familylives.org.uk
www.familylives.org.uk
Chief Executive: Jeremy Todd
Family Lives is a charity that supports parents, young people and families in England with all aspects of family life. They can be contacted via the helpline, as well as through email, Skype and live chat.

Family Matters Institute

Moggerhanger Park, Park Road, Moggerhanger, Bedfordshire MK44 3RW
T: 01767 641002 (also fax)
E: family@familymatters.org.uk
www.familymatters.org.uk
Family Matters Institute is an educational charity motivated by the Christian faith to provide affordable training in order to mobilise church and community groups to

support the family in marriage and couple relationships, parenting and money issues. We also carry out research in these areas.
Employees: 10
Volunteers: 4
Regional offices: 1

Family Rights Group

The Print House, 18 Ashwin Street, London E8 3DL
T: 020 7923 2628
F: 020 7923 2683
E: office@frg.org.uk
www.frg.org.uk
Supports and advises families involved with social services; promotes the involvement of children, parents and families in the decision-making process, so that the best decisions are made; develops and promotes policies and practices that help secure the best possible futures for children and families.
Employees: 16

Farm Animal Welfare Network

Farm Animal Welfare Trust, Northfield Farmhouse, Wytham, Oxford OX2 8QJ
T: 01865 244315
E: fawcsecretariat@defra.gsi.gov.uk
Campaigns for the worldwide abolition of the battery cage system for laying hens, and opposes other intensive and cruel systems for all farmed animals.

Farm Crisis Network

Manor Farm, West Haddon, Northampton, Northamptonshire NN6 7AQ
T: 01788 510866
Helpline: 0845 367 9990
F: 01788 511026
E: mail@fcn.org.uk
www.fcn.org.uk
Chief Executive Officer: Charles Smith
Farm Crisis Network (FCN) is a UK network of volunteers from the farming community and rural churches, providing a national helpline and visiting service to farming people and families facing difficulties. The network provides pastoral and practical support for as long as it is needed, helping people to find a positive way forward through their problems.
Employees: 8
Volunteers: 308

FARM-Africa

Clifford's Inn, Fetter Lane, London EC4A 1BZ
T: 020 7430 0440
F: 020 7430 0460
E: farmafrica@farmafrica.org.uk
www.farmafrica.org.uk
Chief Executive: Christie Peacock

The principal activity of FARM-Africa is to develop projects in Africa to increase agricultural production and thus alleviate hunger and poverty, and to ensure that lessons are learnt from the results.
Employees: 265
Volunteers: 2
Regional offices: 24

Farms for City Children

Bridge House, 25 Fore Street,
Okehampton, Devon EX20 1DL
T: 01837 55876
E: admin@farmsforcitychildren.org
www.farmsforcitychildren.org
Aims to enrich the lives and develop the potential of children from disadvantaged urban areas by providing a residential week on a working farm, where children participate purposefully in the life of the farm.

FAS Aware UK

c/o 45 Lakeside Avenue, Billinge, 45
Lakeside Ave, Billinge, Wigan,
Lancashire WN5 7BJ
T: 01942 223780 (also fax)
E: fasawareuk@blueyonder.co.uk
www.fasaware.co.uk
Full-time Volunteer Coordinator: Gloria Armistead
To provide information, training and accredited courses. Support to improve the health and social wellbeing of all those affected by foetal alcohol spectrum disorders. To develop and support autonomous support groups.
Volunteers: 20

FATIMA Women's Network

Innovation Centre, Oxford Street,
Leicester, Leicestershire LE1 5XY
T: 0845 331 2373
F: 0870 005 2608
E: parvin@fatima-network.com
www.fatima-network.com
Chief Executive: Parvin Ali
FATIMA (Forum for Advocacy, Training and Information in a Multicultural Arena) Women's Network is a BME-led socially responsible enterprise supporting the social and economic empowerment of women and their families, particularly those from diverse and disadvantaged communities, through personal development, advocacy, research, training, business support and cross-community networking. As a national infrastructure organisation we seek to build the resilience and connectivity of women's groups.
Employees: 6
Volunteers: 15

Fawcett Society

Cambridge House, 1 Addington Square,
London SE5 0HF
T: 020 7358 7004
E: info@fawcettsociety.org.uk
www.fawcettsociety.org.uk
Chief Executive: Ceri Goddard
Fawcett is the UK's leading campaigning organisation for women's equality and rights at home, at work and in public life. We are the UK's largest independent membership organisation with a dedicated focus on advancing women's equality and rights in modern Britain. We effect change by combining direct lobbying within the political system with campaigns that increase and demonstrate public support for action.
Employees: 9
Volunteers: 2

Federal Trust for Education and Research

31 Jewry Street, London EC3N 2EY
T: 020 7320 3045
E: info@fedtrust.co.uk
www.fedtrust.co.uk
Director: Brendan Donnelly
Promotes research and education about federal solutions to national, European and global problems.
Employees: 4

Federation for Community Development Learning

3rd Floor, The Circle, 33 Rockingham Lane,
Sheffield, South Yorkshire S1 4FW
T: 0114 253 6770
F: 0114 253 6771
E: info@fcdl.org.uk
www.fcdl.org.uk
Head of Agency: Janice Marks
FCDL welcomes the membership of everyone who is interested in or who practises community development, whether community activists or voluntary or paid workers. This includes generic CD practitioners or practitioners from other occupations (eg health, housing, environment) who are interested in using a CD approach to engage with and work effectively with communities. We support a network of individuals, groups and organisations who share information and good training practice and provide opportunities for CD learning.
Employees: 8

Federation of British Artists

17 Carlton House Terrace,
London SW1Y 5BD
T: 020 7930 6844
E: info@mallgalleries.com
www.mallgalleries.org.uk
Director: Lewis McNaught
Provides exhibition space and other services to artists and administers the nine constituent societies of the Federation.
Regional offices: London

Federation of City Farms and Community Gardens

The Greenhouse, Hereford Street,
Bedminster, Bristol, Avon BS3 4NA
T: 0117 923 1800
E: admin@farmgarden.org.uk
www.farmgarden.org.uk
Director: Jeremy Iles
Supports, represents and promotes community-managed farms and gardens in the UK.
Employees: 32
Regional offices: 6

Federation Of English Karate Organisations (international)

E: jimreece@tradka.org.uk

Federation of Merchant Mariners

16 Glebe Road, Brampton, Huntingdon,
Cambridgeshire PE28 4PH
T: 01480 412958
E: info@merchant-mariners.co.uk
www.merchant-mariners.co.uk
FMM brings together many associations/ organisations connected to the Merchant Navy, filling a gap that had existed in the maritime scene for over 60 years. Its aim is to gain recognition for the role that merchant seafarers have played in the defence and development of our nation.

Federation of Private Residents Associations Ltd

PO Box 10271, Epping, Essex CM16 9DB
T: 0871 200 3324
E: info@fpra.org.uk
www.fpra.org.uk
Chairman: Bob Smytherman
FPRA is a not-for-profit advice, support and lobbying organisation for private residential leaseholders, and residents' associations, residential management companies, commonhold associations and similar bodies. We are the national voice of residents' associations and are frequently

consulted by government. Our advisory services are free to members, who pay an annual subscription fee.

Volunteers: 20

Feline Advisory Bureau

Taeselbury, High Street, Tilsbury, Wiltshire SP3 6LD
T: 01747 871872
E: information@fabcats.org
www.fabcats.org
Promotes the wellbeing of cats in sickness and health; the increased understanding of feline diseases; the improvement of standards of boarding; humane behaviour towards, and increased understanding of, the cat.

Fellowship of Depressives Anonymous

Self Help Nottingham, Ormiston House, 32–36 Pelham Street, Nottingham NG1 2EG
T: 0870 774 4319
E: fdainfo@hotmail.com
www.depressionanon.co.uk
Supports and encourages people suffering from, or who have suffered from, depression and those who care about them, on a self-help/mutual support basis.

Fellowship of Postgraduate Medicine

12 Chandos Street, Cavendish Square, London W1G 9DR
T: 020 7636 6334
F: 020 7436 2535
E: admin@fpm-uk.org
www.fpm-uk.org
President: Donald Singer
The Fellowship achieves its objectives of development of postgraduate educational programmes in all branches of medicine through the publication of its international journal, the Postgraduate Medical Journal, and by hosting a range of seminars and conferences.
Employees: 1

Fellowship of Reconciliation

E: director@for.org.uk

Fellowship of the School of Economic Science

11 Mandeville Place, London W1U 3AJ
T: 020 7034 4000
F: 020 7034 4001
E: secretary@fses.org
www.schooleconomicscience.org

Promotes the study of natural laws governing the relations between men in society and the study of the laws, customs and practices by which communities are governed.
Employees: 15

Female Prisoners Welfare Project and Hibiscus

18 Borough High Street, London SE1 9QG
T: 020 7357 6543
E: fpwphibiscus@aol.com
Provides welfare advice and support for women in prison, especially those disadvantaged by the criminal justice system such as foreign nationals and those from ethnic minorities.

FIA Foundation for the Automobile and Society

60 Trafalgar Square, London WC2N 5DS
T: 020 7930 3882
F: 020 7930 3883
E: j.pearce@fiafoundation.org
www.fiafoundation.org
Director General: David Ward
The Foundation was established in the UK by the Federation Internationale de l'Automobile (FIA), the non-profit federation of motoring organisations and the governing body of world motor sport. The foundation manages and supports an international programme of activities promoting road safety, environmental protection and sustainable mobility, as well as funding specialist motor sport safety research.
Employees: 13

Field Lane Foundation

16 Vine Hill, London EC1R 5EA
T: 020 7837 0412
E: info@fieldlane.org.uk
www.fieldlane.org.uk
Field Lane is a Christian charity that is committed to providing innovative accommodation and day-centre support services for families who are homeless, older people and people with disabilities.

Fieldfare Trust Ltd

Volunteer House, 69 Crossgate, Cupar KY15 5AS
T: 01334 657708
F: 0844 443 1139
E: info@fieldfare.org.uk
www.fieldfare.org.uk
Chief Executive: Ian Newman
The Fieldfare Trust works with, not for, people with disabilities to promote disabled

access and provide environmental education opportunities for all.
Employees: 5
Regional offices: 3

Fields In Trust

2nd Floor, 15 Crinan Street, London N1 9SQ
T: 020 7427 2110
E: helen.griffiths@fieldsintrust.org
www.fieldsintrust.org
Chief Executive: Helen Griffiths
Fields in Trust (FIT) is the only independent UK-wide organisation dedicated to protecting and improving outdoor sports and play spaces and facilities. We want to make sure that everyone; young and old alike, and wherever they live, has somewhere nearby to go for healthy outdoor activities. Through our work we improve the wellbeing of millions of people nationwide.
Employees: 18
Regional offices: 3

Filipino International Emergency Services Training

12 Montgomery Crescent, Bolbeck Park, Milton Keynes MK15 8PR
T: 01908 233120
E: dalejohno@aol.com
www.fiestauk.homestead.com/homepage.html
Chair: John Dale
Provides support for the emergency services of the Philippines in the form of equipment, training and other assistance. The website also lists all the countries of the world and their emergency telephone numbers.

Finn-Guild

1a Mornington Court, Mornington Crescent, London NW1 7RD
T: 020 7387 3508
F: 020 7529 8750
E: mail@finn-guild.org
www.finn-guild.org
Works for the advancement of Finnish culture and language in the UK, educating about Finland, supporting the work of the Finnish Church in London. Supports the wellbeing and relief of poverty among the Finnish-British community.
Employees: 8
Volunteers: 150

Fire Fighters Charity

Level 6, Belvedere, Basing View,
Basingstoke RG21 4HG
T: 01256 366568
F: 01256 366599
E: sabbott@firefighterscharity.org.uk
www.firefighterscharity.org.uk
Employees: 136

First Step Trust

32–34 Hare Street, Woolwich,
London SE18 6LZ
T: 020 8855 7386 (also fax)
E: angela.best@firststeptrust.org.uk
www.fst.org.uk
FST offers people with enduring mental
health problems, learning disabilities and
other disadvantages the chance to work;
experiencing the challenges of working in a
small business, trading with the local
community. This enables them to overcome
their problems, become less dependent on
health and social care services. Many go on
to make the transition to paid employment.

Fit4Funding (The Charities Information Bureau)

Lightwaves Leisure Centre, Lower York
Street, Wakefield, West
Yorkshire WF1 3LJ
T: 01924 239063
E: info@fit4funding.org.uk
www.fit4funding.org.uk
The Bureau aims to enhance the fundraising
skills of voluntary and community groups
whilst also promoting greater equality in the
voluntary sector.
Employees: 5

FitzRoy

FitzRoy House, 8 Hylton Road, Petersfield,
Hampshire GU32 3JY
T: 01730 711111
Helpline: 0808 168 4662
F: 01730 710566
E: info@fitzroy.org
www.fitzroy.org
Chief Executive: Anna Galliford
FitzRoy transforms the lives of people with
disabilities and autism, helping them live
more independently at home and in the
community. We are a national charity that
provides a mix of residential and community
services and support including supported
volunteering.
Employees: 800
Volunteers: 200
Regional offices: 3

FLACK Cambridge

City Life House, Sturton Street,
Cambridge CB1 2QF
T: 01223 366532
E: info@flackcambridge.org.uk
www.flackcambridge.org.uk
Chairman of the Board of Trustees:
Quentin Millington
FLACK supports adults in the Cambridge
area who, through homelessness, have
experienced social and economic exclusion.
We assist individuals to explore their
personal development needs, learn relevant
skills and undertake meaningful activities. In a
nurturing environment, we encourage
creativity, foster a sense of belonging and
help people to regain confidence and
self-esteem. In providing this bridge back
into the wider community, we also challenge
unhelpful perceptions about individuals who
have experienced exclusion.
Employees: 7
Volunteers: 5
Regional offices: 1
Income: £151,230 (2012-13)

Fledglings Family Services

Wenden Court, Station Approach,
Wendens Ambo, Saffron Walden,
Essex CB11 4LB
T: 0845 458 1124
F: 0845 280 1539
E: enquiries@fledglings.org.uk
www.fledglings.org.uk
Founder and Executive Director: Ruth
Lingard
Fledglings helps parents and carers of disabled
children and those with special needs to find
solutions to the practical problems of
everyday living. We do this by searching for,
testing and supplying at affordable prices a
range of helpful products to address specific
needs. We also share information via our
monthly e-News, our product brochure and
an informative website.
Employees: 5
Volunteers: 12

FOCUS

73 Churchgate, Leicester LE1 3AN
T: 0116 251 0369
F: 0116 262 0187
E: admin@focus-charity.co.uk
www.focus-charity.co.uk
FOCUS provides imaginative programmes
that bring together people from all walks of
life to develop their personal skills and
self-confidence, and help them to make the
most of life.
Employees: 15
Volunteers: 500
Regional offices: 4

Foley House Trust

115 High Garrett, Braintree,
Essex CM7 5NU
T: 01376 326652
F: 01376 553350
E: enquiries@foleyhouse.org.uk
www.foleyhouse.org.uk
Director: Brenda Weavers
FHT is a registered charity established in 1851
providing long or short-term care, respite
and short-break accommodation to
profoundly deaf and deafblind men and
women at its residential home. We also
provide care to hearing elderly at the
residential home.
Employees: 30
Volunteers: 6
Regional offices: 1

Food Chain (UK) Ltd

Acorn House, 314–320 Gray's Inn Road,
London WC1X 8DP
T: 020 7843 1800
F: 020 7843 1818
E: katie.smith@foodchain.org.uk
www.foodchain.org.uk
Acting General Manager: Katie Smith
The Food Chain provides nutrition services
including home-delivered meals, essential
groceries and nutrition advice to men, women
and children who are chronically sick as a result
of HIV-related illness. We aim to ensure that
no one living with the virus has their ability to
get well and stay well adversely affected by
lack of access to appropriate food.
Employees: 10
Volunteers: 750
Income: £803,968 (2011-12)

Food Commission

94 White Lion Street, London N1 9PF
T: 020 7837 2550
E: foodcomm@hotmail.com
www.foodcomm.org.uk
Aims to relieve sickness, ill health and disease
wherever these occur and to advance public
education in nutrition and diet.

Football Foundation

30 Gloucester Place, London W1U 8FF
T: 020 7534 4250
F: 0845 345 7057
E: enquiries@footballfoundation.org.uk
www.footballfoundation.org.uk
The Foundation is the UK's largest sports
charity funded by the Premier League, the
FA, Sport England and the government. Our
mission is to improve facilities, create
opportunities and build communities
throughout England. The foundation has
delivered thousands of facility and

community projects, as well as free kit and safe goalposts, since its launch in July 2000.
Employees: 40

Foresight the Association for the Promotion of Preconceptual Care

3 Lower Queens Road, Clevedon,
Somerset BS21 6LX
T: 01275 878953
E: info@foresight-preconception.org.uk
www.foresight-preconception.org.uk
Promotes natural approaches to optimal health in both parents prior to the conception of a child, with a view to minimising the risks of miscarriage, foetal damage or compromised health in the infant. Promotes research on environmental hazards to foetal life.
Employees: 4
Regional offices: 2

 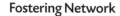

Fostering Network

87 Blackfriars Road, London SE1 8HA
T: 020 7620 6410
F: 020 7620 6401
E: penny.king@fostering.net
www.fostering.net
The network is the UK's leading charity for everyone involved in fostering. We are uniquely placed to bring people and organisations together to improve the lives of children in foster care. Our work is focused on improving foster care and making a positive difference for children and young people in and leaving foster care. We do this by working with foster carers and fostering services.
Employees: 62
Volunteers: 2

Foundation for Community Dance

LCB Depot, 31 Rutland Street,
Leicester LE1 1RE
T: 0116 253 3453
F: 0116 261 6801
E: chris@communitydance.org.uk
www.communitydance.org.uk
Development Director: Chris Stenton
The Foundation for Community Dance is the UK development agency for access, participation and progression in dance for all.
Employees: 14

Foundation for Conductive Education

Cannon Hill House, Russell Road,
Moseley, Birmingham B13 8LD
T: 0121 449 1569
E: foundation@conductive-education.org.uk
www.conductive-education.org.uk
Aims to develop and advance the science and skill of conductive education and especially its teaching.

Foundation for Public Service Interpreting

12 Tudor Rose Court, Fann Street,
London EC2Y 8DY
T: 020 7623 9191
E: director@fpsi.org
www.fpsi.org
Chief Executive: Mark Kiddle
The Foundation aims to promote a national minimum standard in public service interpreting, together with an affordable telephone interpreting service.
Employees: 3
Volunteers: 5

Foundation for the Study of Infant Deaths

Artillery House, 11–19 Artillery Row,
London SW1P 1RT
T: 020 7222 8001
Helpline: 020 7233 2090
F: 020 7222 8002
E: joyce.epstein@sids.org.uk
www.fsid.org.uk
Director: Joyce Epstein
FSID aims to prevent unexpected infant death and promote infant health. We do this by funding research, supporting families, disseminating information on safe infant care and working with professionals to improve investigations of infant deaths.
Employees: 27
Volunteers: 200
Regional offices: 8

Foundation for Women's Health Research and Development

Unit 4, 765–767 Harrow Road,
London NW10 5NY
T: 020 8960 4000
F: 020 8960 4014
E: yasmin@forwarduk.org.uk
www.forwarduk.org.uk
The Foundation aims to improve women's and children's health, with special emphasis on the eradication of female genital mutilation.
Employees: 3

Foundation of Nursing Studies (FoNS)

11–13 Cavendish Square,
London W1G 0AN
T: 020 7307 2857
E: theresa.shaw@fons.org
www.fons.org
Chief Executive: Dr Theresa Shaw
FoNS aims to: support nurses leading innovation to improve nursing and healthcare practice; encourage and facilitate practice-based development and research that leads to improvement in patient care; enable nurses to use effective strategies to lead sustainable development and change in healthcare practice; influence strategy and policy development that supports practice-based development and research; provide a central resource for networking and sharing practice-based development and research activity.
Employees: 4
Income: £267,591 (2011-12)

Foundation66

7 Holyrood Street, London SE1 2EL
T: 020 7234 9940
F: 020 7357 6712
E: info@foundation66.org.uk
www.foundation66.org.uk
CEO: Sally Scriminger
Foundation is a London-based charity and a registered social landlord. We exist to reduce the harm caused by problem alcohol and drug use. We provide client-focused community and accommodation-based services, supporting people to achieve positive change and freedom from the harmful effects of alcohol and other drugs.
Employees: 150
Volunteers: 6

Foundations UK

2 Augustine Road, London W14 0HZ
T: 020 7602 0862 (also fax)
E: deirdre@foundationsuk.org
Aims to relieve those suffering with eating disorders or disordered eating and those affected by such suffering.
Employees: 1
Volunteers: 4

Fountain Society

Weathertop, Tower Hill, Dorking,
Surrey RH4 2AP
T: 01306 883874
E: info@fountainsol.org.uk
www.fountainsol.org.uk
The society works to secure the conservation and restoration of fountains, cascades and

waterfalls of aesthetic merit for public and domestic enjoyment. It also promotes the provision of fountains etc in new developments to which the public have access.

Foyer Federation

3rd Floor, 5–9 Hatton Wall,
London EC1N 8HX
T: 020 7430 2212
F: 020 7430 2213
E: joel@foyer.net
www.foyer.net
The Foyer Federation works with young people through a network of 140 accredited Foyers across the UK. Foyers are integrated learning and accommodation centres providing safe and secure housing, support and training for young people aged 16–25.
Employees: 17

FPA

45 Park Mount, Harpenden,
Hertfordshire AL5 3AS
T: 020 7923 5211
E: johng@fpa.org.uk
www.fpa.org.uk
The FPA promotes sexual health and the reproductive rights and choice of all people throughout the UK.

Fragile X Society

Rood End House, 6 Stortford Road, Great Dunmow, Essex CM6 1DA
T: 01371 875100
E: info@fragilex.org.uk
www.fragilex.org.uk
Managing Director: Tim Potter
The Society provides mutual support and information to families, encourages research and increases public and professional awareness of fragile X syndrome.
Employees: 6
Volunteers: 27
Income: £179,900 (2012-13)

Fraud Advisory Panel

Chartered Accountants' Hall, PO Box 433, Moorgate Place, London EC2P 2BJ
T: 020 7920 8721
F: 020 7920 8545
E: info@fraudadvisorypanel.org
www.fraudadvisorypanel.org
The Panel aims to raise awareness of fraud and financial crime in all its guises, and to develop effective remedies.
Employees: 2
Volunteers: 500

Free Word

60 Farringdon Road, London EC1R 3GA
T: 020 7324 2571
E: eleanor@freewordonline.com
Executive Director: Eleanor Lang

Freeplay Foundation

56–58 Conduit Street, London W1S 2YZ
T: 020 7851 2616
E: jfairbairn@freeplayfoundation.org
www.freeplayfoundation.org
Chief Executive: Kristine Pearson
The Freeplay Foundation is unlike any other non-profit humanitarian organisation in the world. Our mission is to enable access to information and education for the most vulnerable populations through appropriate and sustainable technologies, particularly self-powered radios. The Freeplay Foundation collaborates with in-country non-governmental organisations (NGOs), government ministries, international organisations and broadcasters to ensure radio information and education reaches the widest possible rural populations.
Employees: 10

Freshwinds

Prospect Hall, 12 College Walk, Selly Oak, Birmingham, West Midlands B29 6LE
T: 0121 415 6670
F: 0121 415 6699
E: office@freshwinds.org.uk
www.freshwinds.org.uk
Freshwinds offers care and support, without charge, to adults and children living with life-limiting illnesses, as well as to individuals from socially excluded backgrounds. The charity manages a wide range of projects, including the provision of integrated complementary therapy, advocacy, employment, debt counselling and community-based initiatives in HIV, substance misuse and crime.
Employees: 37
Volunteers: 200
Regional offices: 2

Friends of Cathedral Music

21 Bradford Road, Trowbridge, Wiltshire BA14 9AL
T: 01225 768607
E: info@fcm.org.uk
www.fcm.org.uk
The Friends publicise cathedral music, assist cathedrals in maintaining their musical activities and encourage as many people as possible to discover and enjoy cathedral music.

Friends of Friendless Churches

St Ann's Vestry Hall, 2 Church Entry, London EC4V 5HB
T: 020 7236 3934
E: office@friendsoffriendlesschurches.org.uk
www.friendsoffriendlesschurches.org.uk
Director: Matthew Saunders
Founded in 1957 to save redundant churches from demolition, decay and unsympathetic conversion. We now own 47 such buildings, half in England, half in Wales (where our work is almost wholly funded by CADW and the Church in Wales). Joint membership with the Ancient Monuments Society.
Employees: 3
Volunteers: 100

Friends of the Earth

26-28 Underwood Street, London N1 7JQ
T: 020 7490 1555
F: 020 7490 0881
E: info@foe.co.uk
www.foe.co.uk
Executive Director: Andy Atkins
We campaign on issues of environmental and social justice, making life better for people by inspiring solutions to environmental problems.
Employees: 170
Volunteers: 30
Regional offices: 12

Friends of the Elderly

40–42 Ebury Street, London SW1W 0LZ
T: 020 7730 8263
E: enquiries@fote.org.uk
www.fote.org.uk
Supports older people, often frail, confused or with dementia, to maintain a level of independence and choice by providing a complete range of services for them in any one locality.

Friends of the Western Buddhist Order

51 Roman Road, Bethnal Green, London E2 0HU
T: 0845 458 4716
E: info@lbc.org.uk
www.lbc.org.uk
Aims to advance the Buddhist religion by encouraging members and others to live in accordance with the Buddha's teachings; to support ordained members of the Western Buddhist Order wherever possible; to maintain close contact with other groups with similar objectives.

Friends Therapeutic Community Trust

Glebe House, Church Road, Shudy Camps,
Cambridge, Cambridgeshire CB25 0DA
T: 01799 584359
F: 01799 584098
E: alan.todd@glebehouse.org.uk
Director: Peter Clarke
The Friends Therapeutic Community Trust is
a Quaker charity that provides holistic
support for young men with challenging
behaviour.
Employees: 35
Income: £2,211,489 (2010-11)

Friendship Works

Studio 442, Highgate Studios, 53–79
Highgate Road, London NW5 1TL
T: 020 7485 0900
E: susan@friendshipworks.org.uk
www.friendshipworks.org.uk
Administrator: Richj
Employees: 12
Volunteers: 150

Fulham Football Club Foundation

Fulham FC Training Ground,
Motspur Park
T: 020 8336 7432
E: enquiries@fulhamfc.com
Operations Manager: Jamie Morgan

Full Body and the Voice

The Lawrence Batley Theatre,
Queen Street, Huddersfield,
West Yorkshire HD1 2SP
T: 01484 484441
F: 01484 484443
E: fullbody@lbt-uk.org
Promotes the education and training of the
public in music, theatre and the performing
arts, in particular enabling adults with
learning disabilities to become independent
and take control of their own lives, opening
opportunities for employment.
Employees: 5

Fund for the Replacement of Animals in Medical Experiments

96–98 North Sherwood Street,
Nottingham NG1 4EE
T: 0115 958 4740
E: frame@frame.org.uk
www.frame.org.uk
Director: Robert Combes
FRAME was founded in 1969 to promote the
concept of alternatives to the use of live
animals in medical research and toxicity
testing. FRAME believes in reducing the
number of animals used, refining procedures
so that the suffering of animals necessarily
used is minimised and ultimately eliminating

the need for live animal experiments
altogether.
Employees: 8

FunderFinder

65 Raglan Road, Leeds LS2 9DZ
T: 0113 243 3008
F: 0113 243 2966
E: info@funderfinder.org.uk
www.funderfinder.org.uk
Director: Jo Habib
FunderFinder is a small UK charity that
produces information, advice and software
for voluntary and community groups,
charities and not-for-profit agencies. Some
of the software helps people identify which
charitable trusts and foundations might
provide a grant. Free software that helps
groups write effective funding applications
and put together budgets can be
downloaded from our website.
Employees: 5

Fundraising Standards Board

65 Brushfield Street, London E1 6AA
T: 03333 218803
F: 03333 218804
E: info@frsb.org.uk
www.frsb.org.uk
Chief Executive: Alistair McLean
The Fundraising Standards Board (FRSB) is
the public complaints body and self-
regulator for fundraising in the UK. Those
signed up to the FRSB agree to adhere to a
strict set of codes and a fundraising promise
committing them to treat the public with
respect and honesty in all their money raising
activities.
Employees: 5
Regional offices: 2

Furnishing Trades Benevolent Association

4th Floor, Furniture Makers' Hall,
12 Austin Friars, London EC2N 2HE
T: 020 7256 5954
F: 020 7256 6035
E: info@ftba.co.uk
www.ftba.co.uk
The Association is an occupational trade
charity providing financial assistance to those
who are or have been employed in UK
industry in any capacity. The support
provided includes help for the immediate
families or employees and their dependants.
The charity provides grants including
holidays and annuity payments for the
elderly. Applications must be sponsored by a
third party.
Employees: 4

Furniture Re-use Network

48–54 West Street, St Philips,
Bristol BS2 0BL
T: 0117 954 3571
Helpline: 0845 602 8003
F: 0117 954 3570
E: info@frn.org.uk
www.frn.org.uk
Chief Executive: Paul Smith
The FRN promotes and supports the re-use
of household and office items such as
furniture, domestic appliances, TVs and
computers to support low-income
households and community-based
organisations. We are a representative body
with over 300 members working across the
UK.
Employees: 10
Volunteers: 11

Furzedown Family Centre

E: info@furzedownfamilycentre.org.uk

Futurebuilders England

5th Floor, 6 St Andrew Street,
London EC4A 3AE
T: 020 7842 7700
F: 020 7927 6341
E: richard.gutch@futurebuilders-
england.org.uk
www.futurebuilders-england.org.uk
Chief Executive: Richard Gutch
Futurebuilders England is a unique
government-backed fund offering support
and investment to third sector organisations
to deliver public services. We offer a
combination of loans, grants and
professional support to build capacity of
third sector organisations that want to
deliver better public services. By providing
sustained, flexible and individual support, we
ensure investees have the right financial,
managerial and governance structures to
take on a loan and successfully compete for
contracts in the public sector.
Employees: 46
Regional offices: 2

Fylde Coast YMCA

Poulton Community YMCA, Central
Office, Parrys Way
T: 01253 895115
E: enquiries@fyldecoastymca.org
Executive Director: John Cronin

Gaia House

West Ogwell, Newton Abbot,
Devon TQ12 6EN
T: 01626 335256
F: 01626 352650
E: info@gaiahouse.co.uk
www.gaiahouse.co.uk
Preserves, protects and enhances physical mental emotional and spiritual health by the provision of a centre for the instruction and practice of meditation.
Employees: 6
Volunteers: 10

Galapagos Conservation Trust

5 Derby Street, London W1J 7AB
T: 020 7629 5049
F: 020 7629 4149
E: gct@gct.org
www.savegalapagos.org
Chief Executive: Toni Darton
The Galapagos Conservation Trust (GCT) was founded in 1995 with two aims: to raise awareness of the issues facing the Galapagos Islands; and to raise much needed funds to support the expanding conservation work.
Employees: 5
Volunteers: 6
Regional offices: 1

GamCare

2nd Floor, 7–11 St John's Hill, Clapham Junction, London SW11 1TR
T: 020 7801 7000
F: 020 7378 5233
E: info@gamcare.org.uk
www.gamcare.org.uk
Works in a gambling-neutral manner with all sections of society, and delivers services that address the social impact of gambling; improves the understanding of gambling issues; promotes the concept of responsible gambling; and addresses the needs of those adversely affected by a gambling dependency.
Employees: 15
Volunteers: 15

Game & Wildlife Conservation Trust

Burgate Manor, Fordingbridge, Hampshire SP6 1EF
T: 01425 652381
F: 01425 655848
E: info@gwct.org.uk
www.gwct.org.uk
Promotes for the public benefit the conservation and study of game species, their habitats and the other species associated with those habitats.
Employees: 120
Volunteers: 10
Regional offices: 6
Income: £7,215,953 (2011-12)

Garden History Society

70–77 Cowcross Street, London EC1M 6EJ
T: 020 7608 2409
F: 020 7490 2974
E: enquiries@gardenhistorysociety.org
www.gardenhistorysociety.org
Aims to promote the study of history of gardening, landscape gardening and horticulture; to promote protection and conservation of historic designed landscapes; to encourage creation of new parks and designed landscapes. GHS is a statutory consultee on all planning applications relating to or affecting sites entered on the English Heritage Register of Parks and Gardens of Historic Interest.

Garden Organic

Ryton Organic Gardens, Coventry CV8 3LG
T: 024 7630 3517
F: 024 7663 9229
E: jgoold@gardenorganic.org.uk
www.hdra.org.uk
Garden Organic is the working name of the Henry Doubleday Research Association (HDRA). We are a registered charity, and Europe's largest organic membership organisation. We are dedicated to researching and promoting organic gardening, farming and food.
Employees: 120
Volunteers: 50
Regional offices: 3

Gardening for Disabled Trust

Appleton Oast, Frittenden, Kent TN17 2EG
T: 01580 852372
F: 01580 852218
E: sally@thetukes.com
Provides assistance, both practical and financial, to help disabled people wishing to take an active part in gardening. Grants may be made to help with the design of special gardens, both to individuals and to institutions, schools, hospitals etc.

Gateshead Voluntary Organisations Council

E: gevpringle@gvoc.org.uk

Gateway Community Action

c/o Lee Omar, Refugee Action, 64 Mount Pleasant, Liverpool, Merseyside L3 5SD
T: 07817 152444
E: festog@yahoo.com

Gauchers Association Ltd

3 Bull Pitch, Dursley, Gloucestershire GL11 4NG
T: 01753 646737
E: ga@gaucher.org.uk
www.gaucher.org.uk
Provides information about Gaucher's disease and keeps families and medical advisers up to date with latest developments. Encourages the availability of treatment including enzyme replacement therapy. Actively raises funds for medical research. Publishes a half yearly newsletter which is sent to over 1,300 readers worldwide. Maintains an up-to-date website, which is translated into Spanish and Russian. Holds a bi-annual conference.

Gazelle Personal Development

St Luke's Place, Dalys Road, Rochford, Essex SS4 1RA
T: 01702 530968
E: info@gazel.org.uk
www.gazelleproject.org.uk
The project aims to promote, through inclusive approaches, education, training, personal and social development and care at the highest level. Within this framework, our commitment to challenge discrimination and exclusion is further enhanced through the provision of choices and opportunities to enable adults with learning difficulties and/or disabilities to embrace their aspirations and shape their futures.
Employees: 4

General Assembly of Unitarian and Free Christian Churches

Essex Hall, 1–6 Essex Street, London WC2R 3HY
T: 020 7240 2384
F: 020 7240 3089
E: amason@unitarian.org.uk
www.unitarian.org.uk
Chief Executive: Rev Steve Dick
Promotes a free and inquiring religion through the worship of God, the celebration

of life, the service of humanity and respect for all creation; and the upholding of the liberal Christian tradition.

Employees: 9
Volunteers: 100
Regional offices: 177

General Council and Register of Naturopaths

1 Green Lane Avenue, Street, Somerset BA16 0QS
T: 01458 840072
E: admin@naturopathy.org.uk
www.naturopathy.org.uk
President: Chris Burley
The Council is the largest naturopathic register in the UK. It sets and monitors educational standards in naturopathic training, sets and enforces a code of ethics, and publishes annually a listing of suitably qualified naturopathic practitioners, for the benefit and protection of the public. The GCRN operates, in association with the British Naturopathic Association, a HealthLine service for the public.

Employees: 1
Volunteers: 12

Generation for Change and Development

PO Box 2108, Ilford, Essex IG1 9LE
T: 020 8911 8767
E: admin@gencad.org
www.gencad.org
GENCAD's vision is to be an exemplary organisation that contributes to the socio-economic development of pastoralist communities in the Horn of Africa. Pastoralist communities experience extreme poverty, lack of education, political and economic marginalisation in the Horn of Africa. GENCAD's mission is to increase their access to educational opportunities and health services, and to empower these communities to actively participate in and take ownership of their socio-economic development.

Genetic Alliance UK

Unit 4D, Leroy House, 436 Essex Road, London N1 3QP
T: 020 7704 3141
E: contactus@geneticalliance.org.uk
www.geneticalliance.org.uk
Director: Alastair Kent
Genetic Alliance UK is the national alliance of patient organisations with a membership of over 150 charities supporting all those affected by genetic disorders. Our aim is to improve the lives of people affected by genetic conditions by ensuring that high-

quality services and information are available to all who need them.

Employees: 15

Genetic Disorders UK

199A Victoria Street, London SW1E 5NE
T: 020 7199 3300
Helpline: 0800 987 8987
E: hello@geneticdisordersuk.org
www.geneticdisordersuk.org
Chief Executive: Caroline Harding
The mission of Genetic Disorders UK is to improve the lives of children and adults who are affected by genetic disorders. The charity aims to offer support and information to affected individuals and families as well as providing resources and grants for disorder-specific UK-based support groups and charities. Genetic Disorders UK organises the annual Jeans for Genes Day event in schools and workplaces to raise funds and awareness for its cause.

Employees: 9
Volunteers: 5
Income: £1,845,470 (2011-12)

Gesar Foundation

Unit 10, The Glasshouse, 49a Goldhawk Road, London W12 8QP
T: 020 8204 8466
E: trustee4eow@hotmail.com
www.gesarfoundation.org
An umbrella division of the registered charity, Eye on the Wild, which looks to relieve all suffering of all children worldwide. Gesar, currently has children support projects in Gondar, Ethiopia, Nakuru, Kenya and Taganga, Columbia. Kelsang Pawo is involved with many local groups all of whom support the aims and goals of the Gesar Foundation.

Volunteers: 6

Get Connected Helpline

PO Box 7777, London W1A 5PD
T: 020 7009 2500
Helpline: 0808 808 4994
E: admin@getconnected.org.uk
www.getconnected.org.uk
Chief Executive: Fiona Clark
Get Connected is the UK's free, confidential helpline for young people under 25 who need help and don't know where to turn. Our service is available 365 days a year and young people can contact us by phone, webchat, email, text message or use our online directory, WebHelp 24/7. Our mission is to be the home of help and support for young people, enabling them to find free confidential help, whenever they

need it, however they want it, no matter what the issue.

Employees: 15
Volunteers: 100

Get Hooked on Fishing

Old Billingham Business Centre, Chapel Road, Billingham, Stockton-on-Tees, Durham TE23 1EN
E: hello@ghof.org.uk
www.ghof.org.uk
Chief Executive Officer: Sarah Collins
We work with children and young people at risk of social exclusion across the UK. We use the vehicle of angling to help them access personal, social, educational, community, health and well-being benefits.

Employees: 9
Volunteers: 100
Regional offices: 16

Get Well UK

9 Delancey Street, Camden Town NW1 7NL
T: 0870 438 9355
F: 0870 438 9356
E: boo@getwelluk.com
www.getwelluk.com
Managing Director: Boo Armstrong
Get Well UK makes it possible for GPs to confidently refer their patients to complementary therapists, by providing information, support and a team of highly skilled and qualified practitioners. With NHS funding, this service is free to patients. We believe that complementary medicine can play an important role in improving health and wellbeing and want to ensure that many more people have access to effective healthcare, not just people who can afford to pay for it privately.

Employees: 3

GFS Platform for Young Women

Unit 2, Angel Gate, 326 City Road, London EC1V 2PT
T: 020 7589 9628
F: 020 7225 1458
E: info@gfsplatform.org.uk
www.gfsplatform.org.uk
An Anglican society for girls and women, which enables girls and women to develop their whole potential personally, socially and spiritually.

Employees: 111
Volunteers: 119
Regional offices: 69

Gharweg Advice Training and Careers Centre

5 Westminster Bridge Road,
London SE1 7XW
T: 020 7620 1430
F: 020 7620 1431
E: gharweg@aol.com
Provision of welfare advice on benefits, immigration, health, housing, employment training and career guidance and counselling for black and minority communities.

Gideons International in the British Isles

24 George Street, Lutterworth,
Leicestershire LE17 4EE
T: 01455 554241
E: hq@gideons.org.uk
www.gideons.org.uk
Executive Director: Iain Mair
An interdenominational association of Christian business and professional men and their wives, which freely provides copies of the Bible or New Testament and psalms to public institutions such as hotels, hospitals, schools, homes for the elderly and prisons.
Employees: 15
Volunteers: 3600
Regional offices: 1

Gingerbread

520 Highgate Studios, 53-79 Highgate
Road NW5 1TL
T: 020 7428 5420
Helpline: 0808 802 0925
F: 020 7482 4851
E: jane.stern@gingerbread.org.uk
www.gingerbread.org.uk
Chief Executive: Fiona Weir
Gingerbread is the charity that works nationally and locally, for and with single parent families, to improve their lives. We provide expert advice, practical support and campaign for single parents. Our vision is of a society in which single parent families are valued and treated equally and fairly.
Employees: 64
Volunteers: 10

Girlguiding UK

17–19 Buckingham Palace Road,
London SW1W 0PT
T: 020 7834 6242
F: 020 7828 8317
E: executive.assistant@girlguiding.org.uk
www.girlguiding.org.uk
Girlguiding UK, as part of a worldwide movement, enables girls and young women to fulfil their potential and to take an active and responsible role in society through a distinctive, stimulating and enjoyable programme of activities delivered by trained volunteer leaders. Our vision is to be recognised as the leading organisation for girls and young women and to widen and increase our membership.
Employees: 150
Volunteers: 80000
Regional offices: 9

Girls' Brigade England & Wales

PO Box 196, 129 Broadway, Didcot,
Oxfordshire OX11 8XN
T: 01235 510425
F: 01235 510429
E: gbco@girlsbrigadeew.org.uk
www.girlsb.org
National Director: Ruth Gilson
A membership organisation that specialises in working with churches to provide fun and inspiring local groups where girls and young women can belong, achieve and discover Jesus. GB companies are primarily for girls and young women, aged four to 18, and meet most weeks of the year in safe and friendly environments.

Girls' Venture Corps Air Cadets

1 Bawtry Gate, Sheffield S9 1UD
T: 0114 244 8405
E: gvcac@toucansurf.com
www.gvcac.org.uk
Corps Director: Brenda Layne
An organisation for girls aged between 11 and 20 years of age who are interested in aviation, Duke of Edinburgh award, leadership training, camps and courses, outdoor activities and community service.
Employees: 1
Volunteers: 300
Regional offices: 6

Global Action Plan

9 Kean Street, London WC2B 4AY
T: 020 7420 4444
F: 020 7836 7345
E: all@globalactionplan.org.uk
www.globalactionplan.org.uk
CEO: Trewin Restorick
Global Action Plan is the UK's leading environmental behaviour change charity and, since 1993, has helped businesses, schools and communities reduce their impact on the environment. We achieve environmental and financial savings in the UK by empowering people to take action on energy, waste, water and travel. We are the only UK charity whose programmes are endorsed by the United Nations Environment Programme.
Employees: 27
Volunteers: 500
Regional offices: 1
Income: £1,600,000 (2011-12)

Global Care

2 Dugdale Road, Coventry CV6 1PB
T: 024 7660 1800
F: 024 7660 1444
E: info@globalcare.org.uk
www.globalcare.org.uk
Global Care is a Christian children's charity. We run projects for very deprived and vulnerable children and young people in Africa, Eastern Europe, Asia and South America and provide for the poorest, neediest and most vulnerable children and young people, through formal or non-formal schooling and education; vocational training; nutritional and welfare care and support; and, for some, care in a residential home.
Employees: 21
Volunteers: 50

Global Connections

Caswell Road, Leamington Spa,
Warwickshire CV31 1QD
T: 01926 487755
E: dwright@globalconnections.co.uk
www.globalconnections.org.uk
Executive Director: Martin Lee
Promotes and encourages the spread of the Christian Gospel by putting mission at the heart of the church and the church at the heart of mission.
Employees: 10
Volunteers: 0
Regional offices: 0
Income: £500,000 (2011-12)

Global Witness Limited

PO Box 6042, London N19 5WP
T: 020 7561 6375
E: mail@globalwitness.org
www.globalwitness.org
Focuses on areas where environmental exploitation causes human rights abuses and funds conflict.

Golden Buddha Centre

The Grove, Totnes, Devon TQ9 5EP
T: 01803 897550
E: guidestar@goldenbuddha.org
www.goldenbuddha.org
The twin objectives of the Golden Buddha Centre project are to have an active Buddhist

centre together with related residential accommodation for retired Buddhists.
Volunteers: 20

Good Gardeners' Association

Pinetum Lodge, Churcham,
Gloucester GL2 8AD
T: 07901 815647
E: david@igeek.co.uk
www.goodgardeners.org.uk
The purpose of the Good Gardeners' Association is the improvement and encouragement of horticulture along compost or organic lines, and the daily study of organic methods of gardening.
Volunteers: 8
Income: £5,000 (2011-12)

Gordon Barclay Vietnam Fund

Flat 56, Biddulph Mansions, Elgin Avenue, London W9 1HT
T: 020 7286 0887
E: barcviet@aol.com
www.gbvf.org.uk
Treasurer: Gordon Barclay
Aims to relieve poverty, distress and suffering in Vietnam or South-East Asia and to provide food, healing, clothing, shelter, training and education to that purpose.
Volunteers: 1

Gordon Moody Association

E: elaine.smethurst@gordonmoody.org.uk

Gorlin Syndrome Group

11 Blackberry Way, Penwortham, Preston, Lancashire PR1 9LQ
T: 01772 517624
E: gorlin.group@btconnect.com
www.gorlingroup.co.uk
The Gorlin Syndrome Group was formed in the UK in 1992. It supports those affected by Gorlin syndrome and their families and carers; the advancement of the education of the medical profession and the general public regarding Gorlin syndrome and its implications; and the promotion and dissemination of research into the causes, effects, treatment and management of Gorlin syndrome.

Gosport Voluntary Action

Martin Snape House, 96 Pavilion Way, St George's Barracks, Gosport, Hampshire PO12 1FG
T: 023 9258 3836
E: gosportvb@gva.org.uk
www.gosport-voluntary-action.org.uk
Chief Officer: Ian Johnson
At the heart of the Gosport Community - providing support to voluntary sector

organisations and running in-house projects to benefit under represented groups, as well as offering a Volunteer Centre service.
Employees: 20
Volunteers: 30
Regional offices: 1

Grail

125 Waxwell Lane, Pinner, Middlesex HA5 3ER
T: 020 8866 0505
E: m.grasar@grailsociety.org.uk
www.grailsociety.org.uk
President: Presidential Team
A Roman Catholic organisation involved in the education and formation of adults and young people, which encourages young people and adults to work out their Christian commitment in modern society and take their full share in meeting the needs of the community.
Employees: 8

Grandparents Plus

18 Victoria Park Square, Bethnal Green, London E2 9PF
T: 020 8981 8001
Helpline: 0300 123 7015
E: info@grandparentsplus.org.uk
www.grandparentsplus.org.uk
Chief Executive: Sam Smethers
Promotes the better care, upbringing and establishment in life of children by promoting the role of kinship care by grandparents and kin at all levels, particularly in circumstances of family breakdown. This may be because of parental alcohol/substance misuse, mental or physical ill health, domestic abuse, divorce or separation, imprisonment, and other difficult conditions; supporting and advising grandparents and other kin acting as, or intend to act as, carers, particularly in the circumstances mentioned above.
Employees: 11

GrantScape

Office E, Whitsundoles, Broughton Road, Salford, Milton Keynes MK17 8BU
T: 01908 247630
E: steven.hargreaves@grantscape.org.uk
www.grantscape.org.uk
Chief Executive: Steven Hargreaves
The charity's aim is to improve the life of communities and the environment by the channelling and management of charitable

funding towards deserving and quality projects.
Employees: 7
Volunteers: 35
Income: £1 (2011-12)

Great Ormond Street Hospital Children's Charity

Great Ormond Street Hospital, Great Ormond Street, London WC1N 3JH
T: 020 7405 9200
E: karen.atkinson@gosh.org
www.gosh.org
Aims to raise over £20 million each year for the ongoing rebuilding and refurbishment of the hospital and the Institute of Child Health for research and development, leading-edge equipment and support services for sick children and their families.

Greater London Volunteering

Suite 24 Delta House, 175-177 Borough High Street, London SE1 1HR
T: 020 7864 1472
E: info@glv.org.uk
www.glv.org.uk
Chief Executive Officer: James Banks
Greater London Volunteering is an umbrella body representing, consulting and co-ordinating Volunteer Centres and volunteer development agencies across Greater London. Activities include consultation, event organisation, training, marketing and promotion.
Employees: 2
Volunteers: 0
Regional offices: 1
Income: £356,581 (2012-13)

Greater Manchester Centre for Voluntary Organisations

St Thomas Centre, Ardwick Green North, Manchester, Greater Manchester M12 6FZ
T: 0161 277 1000
F: 0161 273 8296
E: gmcvo@gmcvo.org.uk
www.gmcvo.org.uk
Chief Executive: Alex Whinnom
GMCVO supports local voluntary action by local people by providing specialist support, knowledge, voice, infrastructure and innovation, working in partnership with other support organisations and with the public and private sectors. We aspire to be a channel for information for and about our sector, and to provide co-ordination and leadership. A large element of our work involves representing the views and needs of

people involved in local voluntary groups, sharing ideas and brokering relationships.
Employees: 28
Volunteers: 0
Income: £1,500,000 (2012-13)

Greater World Christian Spiritualist Association

The Greater World Spiritual Centre, 3-5 Conway Street, Fitzrovia, London W1T 6BJ
T: 020 7436 7555
E: greaterworld@btconnect.com
www.greaterworld.co.uk
National President: Megan Long
To spread in all directions the truth of survival after death, of spirit communion, of healing by the power of Holy Spirit and to disseminate the teachings of Jesus the Christ and additional teachings received from highly evolved spirit messengers.
Employees: 3
Regional offices: 51
Income: £63,270 (2012-13)

Green Alliance

36 Buckingham Palace Road, London SW1W 0RE
T: 020 7630 4518
F: 020 7233 9033
E: ga@green-alliance.org.uk
www.green-alliance.org.uk
Green Alliance's mission is to promote sustainable development by ensuring that the environment is at the heart of decision-making.
Employees: 11
Volunteers: 3

GreenNet Educational Trust

Development House, 56–64 Leonard Street, London EC2A 4LT
T: 0845 055 4011
E: info@greenneteducationaltrust.org.uk
www.greenneteducationaltrust.org.uk
Promotes the strategic use of electronic networking for the benefit of social movements internationally and at home in the UK.

Greenpeace UK

Canonbury Villas, Islington, London N1 2PN
T: 020 7865 8100
Helpline: 0800 269065
E: info.uk@greenpeace.org
www.greenpeace.org.uk
Executive Director: John Sauven
Aims to protect the environment through peaceful direct action, scientific research and finding solutions to environmental problems.
Employees: 100
Volunteers: 40

Greenwich and Bexley Community Hospice

Greenwich and Bexley Community Hospice, 185 Bostall Hill, Abbey Wood, London SE2 0GB
T: 020 8312 2244
Helpline: 0208 312 2244
F: 020 8320 5780
E: info@gbch.org.uk
www.communityhospice.org.uk
Chief Executive: Kate Heaps
To provide specialist palliative care and support, free of charge, to patients and their families living within the boroughs of Greenwich and Bexley in our inpatient unit, in the community, day hospice or outpatient clinic. Counselling and bereavement support are also offered.
Employees: 150
Volunteers: 600
Regional offices: 1
Income: £7,000,000 (2011-12)

Greyhound Rescue West of England (GRWE)

PO Box 4243, Radstock BA3 3ZL
Helpline: 0700 078 5092
E: enquiries@grwe.com
www.grwe.com
Chief Executive: Rachel Grocott
Greyhound Rescue West of England is dedicated to the rescue, rehabilitation and rehoming of abused and abandoned greyhounds and lurchers. The charity receives no financial help from the greyhound racing industry and is completely reliant on donations. From humble beginnings in the west of England, GRWE now operates nationally and last year rehomed over 600 of these special dogs.
Employees: 1
Volunteers: 120

Grooms Shaftesbury

50 Scrutton Street, London EC2A 4XQ
T: 020 7452 2000
F: 020 7452 2001
E: info@livability.org.uk
www.johngrooms.org.uk
In January 2007, John Grooms and the Shaftesbury Society took the historic decision to merge and create a new charity. At our heart is a vision of working with people and communities affected by poverty and disability, helping them to maximise their potential. The new organisation started its work in July 2007.

Groundwork North East

Grosvenor House, 29 Market Place
T: 0191 567 2550 ext 32
E: nichola.hesslewood@groundwork.org.uk
www.communityfoundationsurrey.org.uk

Groundwork UK

Lockside, 5 Scotland Street, Birmingham B1 2RR
T: 0121 236 8565
F: 0121 236 7356
E: info@groundwork.org.uk
www.groundwork.org.uk
Chief Executive: Tony Hawkhead
Groundwork supports communities in need, working with partners to help improve the quality of people's lives, their prospects and potential and the places where they live, work and play. Our vision is of a society of sustainable communities that are vibrant, healthy and safe, that respect the local and global environment and where individuals and enterprise prosper.
Employees: 75

Group B Strep Support

PO Box 203, Haywards Heath, West Sussex RH16 1GF
T: 01444 416176
F: 0870 803 0024
E: info@gbss.org.uk
www.gbss.org.uk
Chief Executive: Jane Plumb MBE
Group B streptococcus (GBS) is the UK's most common life-threatening infection in newborn babies, causing sepsis, meningitis & pneumonia. Yet most GBS infections are preventable by offering antibiotics in labour to women whose babies are at higher-risk. GBSS raises awareness amongst pregnant women and their health professionals how to do this and save tiny lives.
Employees: 4
Regional offices: 0
Income: £160,875 (2012-13)

Grubb Institute

Cloudesley Street, London N1 0HU
E: info@grubb.org.uk
www.grubb.org.uk
Executive Director: Bruce Irvine
The Institute is an applied research foundation working globally to mobilise values, faiths and beliefs as a resource for the transformation, healing and repair of organisations, people and society. The institute's work is informed by a Christian theology that recognises the heritage, culture and traditions of the many diverse faiths and spiritualities present in our society.

Guernsey Arts Commission

Guernsey Arts Commission, Guernsey Information Centre, North Esplanade, St Peter Port, Guernsey GY1 2LQ
T: 01481 709748
E: joanna.littlejohns@cultureleisure.gov.gg
www.arts.gg
Head of Arts Development: Joanna Littlejohns
The Guernsey Arts Commission's aim is to help the arts in Guernsey to grow and develop and to involve more people in the arts; for the arts to be recognised and valued as a vital part of island life.
Employees: 4
Volunteers: 35
Regional offices: n/a

Guidance Council

NIACE, 21 De Montfort Street, Leicester LE1 7GE
E: info@guidancecouncil.com
www.guidancecouncil.com
Promotes and advises on the provision of good-quality career guidance for learning and work, accessible to all individuals throughout their lives.

Guideposts Trust Ltd

Willow Tree House, Two Rivers, Station Lane, Witney, Oxfordshire OX28 4BH
T: 01993 893560
E: gpt@guidepoststrust.org.uk
www.guidepoststrust.org.uk
Guideposts aims to provide services to help all individuals lead independent lives, fulfil their aspirations and maximise their potential. We work with people who have mental health issues, dementia, learning disabilities, physical impairments, and their carers and families, to help them make the best possible choices for quality care. We seek to achieve excellence in our work and

lead the way in researching, delivering and disseminating good practice.
Employees: 100
Volunteers: 100
Regional offices: 7

GuideStar UK

17 Exeter Street, London WC2E 7DU
T: 020 7632 0222
F: 0870 112 3846
www.guidestar.org.uk
GuideStar UK aims to promote the voluntary and community sector, for the benefit of the public, by creating a comprehensive and readily available source of information about the sector's diverse and important work. It offers all charities a free opportunity to explain their work and improves access to information about the sector for a wide range of stakeholders.
Employees: 9

Guild of Aid

10 St Christopher's Place, London W1U 1HZ
T: 020 7935 0641
E: admin@professionalsaid.org.uk
www.guild-of-aid.org.uk
Chief Executive Officer: Finola McNicholl
Aims to help UK citizens aged over 18 who are of good education in need of financial assistance. We offer weekly grants and contributions towards essential household goods. To apply, you must have claimed state benefits and have approached other funds for help.
Employees: 4
Volunteers: 19
Regional offices: 0

Guild of Health Ltd

9 St Georges Road, Folkestone, Kent CT19 4BE
T: 01303 277399
E: glan.izzard@ukgateway.net
www.gohealth.org.uk
Helps people to experience within the fellowship of God's family the freedom of life promised by Jesus Christ.

Guild of Pastoral Psychology

82 Boston Gardens, Brentford, Middlesex TW8 9LP
T: 020 8568 2195
E: administration@ guildofpastoralpsychology.org.uk
www.guildofpastoralpsychology.org.uk
Acts as a meeting ground for all those interested in the relationship between religion and depth psychology, particularly

the work of CG Jung and his followers and communicates the results of recent practice and research to everyone interested professionally or personally.

Guild of St Raphael

St John's Church, 2 Green Lane, Stoneycroft, Liverpool L13 7EA
T: 0151 228 2023
E: straphael@enterprise.net
Teaches and practises the ministry of Christ's healing in the Church of England through the sacraments and prayer in full co-operation with the medical profession.

GuildHE Limited

Woburn House, 20 Tavistock Square, London WC1H 9HB
T: 020 7387 7711
F: 020 7387 7712
E: info@guildhe.ac.uk
www.guildhe.ac.uk
Executive Secretary: Alice Hynes
The objectives of the charity are to promote and improve the efficiency of charitable colleges of higher education in England and Northern Ireland by promoting discussion and consultation, formulating policies and providing representation, information, advice and assistance.
Employees: 5

Guillain Barre Syndrome Support Group

Woodholme House, Heckington Business Park, Station Road, Heckington, Sleaford, Lincolnshire NG34 9JH
T: 01529 469910
Helpline: 0800 374803
F: 01529 469915
E: executive@gbs.org.uk
www.gbs.org.uk
Office Executive: Caroline Morrice
To provide support, information and other assistance to sufferers and their families; to promote research into causes, prevention and treatments; and to advance the education of the public and of the medical professionals.
Employees: 3
Volunteers: 150
Income: £174,590 (2012-13)

Habitat for Humanity Great Britain

46 West Bar Street, Banbury,
Oxfordshire OX16 9RZ
T: 01295 264240
F: 01295 264230
E: supporterservices@
habitatforhumanity.org.uk
www.habitatforhumanity.org.uk
National Director: Rebecca Martin
Housing charity, dedicated to the elimination of poverty housing and homelessness around the world. We work with impoverished people to help them build and renovate their own simple, decent low-cost homes.
Employees: 18
Volunteers: 250
Regional offices: 2

Haemochromatosis Society

Hadley Green Road, Barnet,
Hertfordshire EN5 5PR
T: 020 8449 1363
E: info@haemochromatosis.org.uk
www.haemochromatosis.org.uk
Director: Janet Fernau
Advice and education for sufferers of haemochromatosis.
Volunteers: 12
Regional offices: 3
Income: £22,009 (2010-11)

Haemophilia Society

Petersham House, 57a Hatton Garden,
London EC1N 8JG
T: 020 7380 0600
Helpline: 0800 018 6068
F: 020 7387 8220
E: sue@haemophilia.org.uk
www.haemophilia.org.uk
The Haemophilia Society works to secure the best possible care, treatment and support for people with haemophilia and related or associated bleeding disorders, and their families.
Employees: 9
Volunteers: 350
Regional offices: 18

Hairline International

The Hair Trust, 191 Station Lane,
Lapworth, Solihull, West
Midlands B94 6JG
T: 01564 782270
E: info@hairlineinternational.co.uk
Supports adults and children who have alopecia or other hair loss conditions.

Hambleton and Richmondshire Carers Centre

32 High Street, Northallerton,
Northallerton, North Yorkshire DL7 8EE
T: 01609 780872
F: 01609 788489
E: info@hrcarers.org.uk
www.hrcarers.org.uk
Chief Executive: Andrea Hobbs
Our principal aim is to support carers of all ages in a way that is centred on individual needs and supports their general health and well-being. Provide advice and information to carers and their families, provide emotional support, work in partnership to raise awareness of issues, provide social groups and activities to reduce isolation, signpost and refer to other support agencies, undertake carers assessments, work in partnership and collaborate where appropriate to strengthen local and sub-regional services for carers.
Employees: 7
Volunteers: 10
Regional offices: 0
Income: £200,000 (2012-13)

Hamlet Trust

c/o Mental Health Foundation, 9th Floor,
Sea Containers House, 20 Upper Ground,
London SE1 9QB
T: 020 7803 1160
E: office@hamlet-trust.org.uk
www.hamlet-trust.org.uk
Pursues development, education and research initiatives in mental health in central and Eastern Europe, with special emphasis on the social integration of people with long-term mental health problems in the community.

Hammersmith Management College

E: s.khan@hmclondon.com

Handicap International UK

CAN Mezzanine, 32–36 Loman Street,
London SE1 0EH
T: 0870 774 3737
F: 0870 774 3738
E: hi-uk@hi-uk.org
www.handicap-international.org.uk
We support people in situations of vunerability who, due to a physical, mental or psychological condition, have difficulty in playing their role in society, thus finding themselves in a situation of disability.
Employees: 6
Volunteers: 155

Hannahs (formely Dame Hannah Rogers Trust)

Woodland Road, Ivybridge,
Devon PL21 9HQ
T: 01752 898100
F: 01752 898116
E: charlotte.simonds@discoverhannahs.org
www.damehannah.com
Chief Executive Officer: Bronwen Hewitt
Hannahs offers education, care and life opportunities for children and adults with a range of disabilities. The Trust offers a school, respite centre, children's home, adult transition project and an innovative service for adults. We have two centres – Hannahs at Ivybridge and Hannahs at Seale-Hayne.
Employees: 300
Volunteers: 150
Regional offices: 2

Hansard Society

40–43 Chancery Lane,
London WC2A 1JA
T: 020 7438 1222
F: 020 7438 1229
E: pressoffice@lse.ac.uk
www.hansardsociety.org.uk
Chief Executive: Fiona Booth
The Hansard Society is the UK's leading non-partisan political research and education charity, which exists to strengthen parliamentary democracy and encourage greater public involvement in politics.
Employees: 22
Volunteers: 2

Happy Days Children's Charity

Clody House, 90-100 Collingdon Street,
Luton, Bedfordshire LU1 1RX
T: 01582 755999
F: 01582 755900
E: happydayscharity@yahoo.co.uk
www.happydayscharity.org
Chief Executive: Ryan Sinclair

We fund and organise holidays, days out and theatre trips throughout the UK for disadvantaged young people with special needs. We help young people in special needs schools, in hospitals and in hospices, and we help individual families.
Employees: 10
Volunteers: 1
Income: £919,000 (2012-13)

Harvest Fields Commissioning International

PO Box 740, Hemel Hempstead, Hertfordshire HP1 3RH
T: 07941 502613
E: info@hfci.net
www.hfci.net
Offers leadership training and materials as well as TV, film and media production and media training in over 50 countries worldwide. We also provide humanitarian assistance in developing countries.

Havering Mind

E: reach.us@haveringmind.org.uk

HCPT The Pilgrimage Trust

Oakfield Park, 32 Bilton Road, Rugby, Warwickshire CV22 7HQ
T: 01788 564646
F: 01788 564640
E: hq@hcpt.org.uk
www.hcpt.org.uk
Chief Executive: Phil Sparke
Disabled and disadvantaged children and adults enjoy life-changing pilgrimage holidays to Lourdes in the south of France, supported by volunteers, thanks to HCPT.
Employees: 12
Volunteers: 5000
Income: £4,400,000 (2010-11)

Headliners (formerly known as Children's Express)

Rich Mix, 35–47 Bethnal Green Road, London E1 6LA
T: 020 7749 9360
E: fiona.wyton@headliners.org
www.headliners.org
Director: Fiona Wyton
Aims to inspire children and young people to investigate and challenge the world around them, enhance their personal development and promote their right to be heard as equals. We provide learning through journalism, participation and volunteering programmes for young people aged 8–19 throughout England and Northern Ireland. We support young people to produce stories for publication and broadcast in the mainstream media on issues that concern

them to campaign for change, benefitting them and their communities.
Employees: 25
Volunteers: 8
Regional offices: 4

Headlines, the Craniofacial Support Group

8 Footes Lane, Frampton Cotterell, Bristol BS36 2JQ
T: 01454 850557
E: info@headlines.org.uk
www.headlines.org.uk
Group Administrator: Gil Ruff
Provides help, advice and contact to anyone (including their families) having or dealing with craniosynostosis or craniostenosis and all of the associated conditions and syndromes. Merged with Apert Syndrome Support Group.
Employees: 1
Volunteers: 10

Heads Teachers and Industry Ltd

Herald Court, University of Warwick Science Park, Coventry, Warwickshire CV4 7EZ
T: 02476 410104
F: 02476 415984
E: a.evans@hti.org.uk
www.hti.org.uk
The work of the charity continues to underpin research into educational leadership at the business/education interface.
Employees: 19

Headway – the Brain Injury Association

190 Bagnall Road, Old Basford, Nottingham NG6 8SF
T: 0115 924 0800
F: 0115 958 4446
E: services.director@headway.org.uk
www.headway.org.uk
Our aim is to promote understanding of all aspects of brain injuries and to provide information, support and services to people with brain injuries, their families and carers.
Employees: 35
Volunteers: 7
Regional offices: 112

Headway Devon

E: paul@headwaydevon.org.uk

Healing Foundation

The Royal College of Surgeons, 35–45 Lincoln's Inn Fields, London WC2A 3PE
T: 020 7869 6920
F: 020 7869 6929
E: info@thehealingfoundation.org
www.thehealingfoundation.org
Chief Executive: Brendan Eley
The charity's aims are relieving sickness and protecting and preserving public health by: carrying out and funding research into improving treatments for the benefit of people who suffer from physical, psychological, social or emotional disadvantage as a result of physical disfigurement or functional impairment present at birth or acquired through accident, disease, or illness and preventing accidents that may cause such conditions; disseminating research results and training health workers in appropriate treatments, and informing people about their availability.
Employees: 5
Volunteers: 30

Health Foundation

90 Long Acre, London WC2E 9RA
T: 020 7257 8000
F: 020 7257 8001
E: jacquelyn.bell@health.org.uk
www.health.org.uk
Chief Executive: Stephen Thornton
The Health Foundation is an independent charitable foundation working to improve the quality of healthcare across the UK and beyond. Our endowment enables us to spend more than £20 million annually to develop leaders in healthcare, test new ways of improving the quality of health services and disseminate evidence for changing health policy and practice.
Employees: 25

Health Poverty Action

Ground Floor, 31–33 Bondway, London SW8 1SJ
T: 020 7840 3777
F: 020 7840 3770
E: general@healthpovertyaction.org
www.healthpovertyaction.org
Director: Martin Drewry
Health Poverty Action works to strengthen poor and marginalised people in their struggle for health through development initiatives in 13 countries and campaigning for change.
Employees: 500
Volunteers: 10
Regional offices: 14
Income: £10 (2011-12)

HealthProm

Star House, 104–108 Grafton Road,
London NW5 4BA
T: 020 7284 1620
F: 020 7284 1881
E: general@healthprom.org
www.healthprom.org
Working in partnership to promote health
and social care for women and children in
Eastern Europe and Asia.
Employees: 4
Volunteers: 9
Income: £400,000 (2010-11)

Hearing Concern

95 Gray's Inn Road, London WC1X 8TX
T: 020 7440 9871
F: 020 7440 9872
E: info@hearingconcern.org.uk
www.hearingconcern.org.uk
Hearing Concern is a national charity
dedicated to improving the quality of life for
those who are hard of hearing. We are a
volunteer-led organisation with main
objectives to provide advice, information and
support, to promote commmunication
access and to raise public and professional
awareness of the issues associated with
hearing loss.
Employees: 9
Volunteers: 200
Regional offices: 1

Hearing Dogs for Deaf People

The Grange, Wycombe Road,
Saunderton, Princes Risborough,
Buckinghamshire HP27 9NS
T: 01844 348100
F: 01844 348101
E: info@hearing-dogs.co.uk
www.hearing-dogs.co.uk
Supplies trained dogs to assist the profoundly
deaf by alerting them to specific household
sounds by touch and provide companionship
and independence.
Employees: 99
Volunteers: 500
Regional offices: 60

HEART UK

7 North Road, Maidenhead,
Berkshire SL6 1PE
T: 01628 628638
F: 01628 628698
E: ask@heartuk.org.uk
www.heartuk.org.uk
Provides information and support for
anyone at high risk of premature coronary
heart disease. Promotes the early detection
and preventive counselling of families prone
to premature coronary heart disease and
inherited high cholesterol.
Employees: 8

Heart UK, the Cholesterol Charity

7 North Road, Maidenhead,
Berkshire SL6 1PE
T: 01628 777046
Helpline: 0845 450 5988
E: jp@heartuk.org.uk
www.heartuk.org.uk
Chief Executive: Jules Payne
6 in 10 adults in the UK have raised
cholesterol. 1 in 500 people are born with an
inherited high cholesterol condition,
meaning they have a high risk of a heart
attack, stroke or sudden death in their 20s,
30s and 40s. We provide expert support,
guidance and education to people with high
cholesterol, their families and Health Care
Professionals.
Employees: 6
Volunteers: 5

Helen & Douglas House

E: lbeekar@helenanddouglas.org.uk

Helen Arkell Dyslexia Centre

Frensham, Farnham, Surrey GU10 3BW
T: 01252 792400
E: enquiries@arkellcentre.org.uk
www.arkellcentre.org.uk
The Centre helps people of all ages with
dyslexia and other specific learning
difficulties to fulfil their potential by
optimising their educational opportunities
and quality of life; trains teachers in the
special skills needed; helps schools manage
dyslexics in the classroom; raises public
awareness of how dyslexia can be helped.

Help A Poor Child

Devonshire House, Manor Way,
Borehamwood, Hertfordshire WD6 1QQ
T: 020 8236 2953
F: 020 8731 4322
E: info@hapc.co.uk
www.helpapoorchild.com
A non-profit, voluntary organisation,
founded in 1980, to provide assistance to
children and families struggling in terrible
poverty.

Help Age International

PO Box 32832, London N1 9ZN
T: 020 7278 7778
E: hai@helpage.org
www.helpage.org
Operates a global network of not-for-profit
organisations with a mission to work with
and for disadvantaged older people
worldwide to achieve a lasting improvement
in the quality of their lives.

Help the Aged

207–221 Pentonville Road,
London N1 9UZ
T: 020 7239 1802
F: 020 7843 1559
E: contact@ageuk.org.uk
www.helptheaged.org.uk
Our vision is of a future where older people
are highly valued, have lives that are richer
and voices that are heard.
Employees: 2022
Volunteers: 135000
Regional offices: 4

Help the Hospices

Hospice House, 34–44 Britannia Street,
London WC1X 9JG
T: 020 7520 8200
F: 020 7278 1021
E: info@helpthehospices.org.uk
www.helpthehospices.org.uk
Chief Executive: David Praill
Aims to further hospice care by supporting
independent hospices by being a servant
centre for them and raising awareness of the
hospice movement.
Employees: 60
Volunteers: 5

Helplines Partnership

Business Design Centre, 52 Upper Street,
London N1 0HQ
T: 0300 330 7777
E: mirelle.frost@helplines.org
www.helplines.org
Chief Executive: Theodore Spyrou
Helplines Partnership is the membership
body for organisations that provide helpline
services in the UK and internationally. We
facilitate high quality service delivery to
callers by providing a range of services,
including training (accredited qualifications),
innovative contact solutions, quality
standards, individually tailored support and
information resources through web portals.
We raise the profile of the sector through
representation of our members' interests
and influencing the social policy agenda,
giving providers of helpline services a voice
to build sustainability and promote
excellence, choice and accessibility for
everyone.
Employees: 25
Volunteers: 10
Regional offices: 3

HemiHelp

6 Market Road, London N7 9PW
T: 0845 120 3713
E: info@hemihelp.org.uk
www.hemihelp.org.uk
Provides information and support for children and young people with hemiplegia and increases public awareness of the condition. Facilitates research into hemiplegia and its associated conditions.
Employees: 8

Henry George Foundation of Great Britain Ltd

212 Piccadilly, London W1J 9HG
T: 020 7377 8885
F: 020 8393 3526
E: office@henrygeorgefoundation.org
www.henrygeorgefoundation.org
Raises awareness of social injustice stemming from unjust property ownership and capitalisation of land rent and other resource rents.

Henry Smith Charity

65 Leadenhall Street, London EC3A 2AD
T: 020 7264 4970
E: dc@henrysmithcharity.org.uk
www.henrysmithcharity.org.uk
Director: Nick Acland

Heritage Care

Connaught House, 112–120 High Road, Loughton, Essex IG10 4HJ
T: 020 8502 3933
F: 020 8502 3543
E: stephen.lenton@heritagecare.co.uk
www.heritagecare.co.uk
Chief Executive: Kim Foo
Heritage Care is a registered charity that provides a range of flexible individualised services that support independence and choice for people with learning disabilities, mental health support needs and older people. Our care and support services include supported living, domiciliary services, packages for self-directed support, extra-care schemes, registered care homes, day services and respite/short-break services. We support 1,000 service users each day and employ over 1,800 staff employed across 130 locations.
Employees: 1850
Volunteers: 50
Regional offices: 7
Income: £37,000,000 (2010-11)

Herpes Viruses Association (also called HVA or SPHERE)

41 North Road, London N7 9DP
T: 020 7607 9661
Helpline: 0845 123 2305
E: info@herpes.org.uk
www.herpes.org.uk
Director: Marian Nicholson
Helps and advises people with herpes simplex (cold sores and genital herpes) and herpes zoster, by answering phone calls, emails and letters; offers one-to-one counselling; promotes public awareness of the virus and reduces anxiety; disseminates information to the public and the medical profession; acts as a pressure group for research; undertakes research wherever possible; encourages and promotes self-help groups. Certified by the Information Standard.
Employees: 2
Volunteers: 24
Income: £110,000 (2012-13)

Herpetological Conservation Trust

655A Christchurch Road, Boscombe, Bournemouth, Dorset BH1 4AP
T: 01202 391319
E: enquiries@herpconstrust.org.uk
www.herpconstrust.org.uk
Co-ordinates and implements conservation efforts for threatened amphibians and reptiles, particularly in the UK and Europe and promotes research.

Hextol Foundation

E: chris.milner@hextol.org.uk

HFT the Home Farm Trust

Peter Needham, Merchants House North, Wapping Road, Bristol BS1 4RW
T: 0117 930 2600
E: info@hft.org.uk
www.hft.org.uk
Provides, for people with learning disabilities, residential and other services that develop their potential and sustain their rights.

Hi8us Projects Ltd

Ground Floor, Toepath House, Limehouse Court, London E14 7EQ
T: 020 7538 8070
F: 020 7987 4522
E: jerry@hi8us.co.uk
www.hi8us.co.uk

Hi8us Projects Limited was established in 1994 to produce innovative media with young people in their communities.
Employees: 5
Regional offices: 1

High/Scope UK

Anerley Business Centre, Anerley Road, Anerley, London SE20 8BD
T: 0870 777 7680
F: 0870 777 7682
E: susan.noble@southtyneside.gov.uk
www.high-scope.org.uk
Aims to improve the life chances of children through high-quality care and education using the high/scope approach. Disseminates information on the effectiveness of using the high/scope approach to care and education for young children. Aims to increase the use of the approach within social service, education, voluntary and independent settings.
Employees: 7

Highbury Vale Blackstock Trust

Elizabeth House, 2 Hurlock Street, London N5 1ED
T: 020 7690 1300
E: director@ehlc.co.uk
www.elizabeth-house.org.uk
Centre Director: Centre Director
Community Centre serving the local community by offering Play Services (After School's Club and Playscheme), Youth Work Programmes and meeting facilities to local groups and individuals.
Employees: 9
Volunteers: 2
Regional offices: 0
Income: £243,224 (2012-13)

Hillingdon Autistic Care and Support

E: louise@hacs.org.uk

HiPACT

c/o Choice, York House, Empire Way, Wembley, Middlesex HA9 0PA
T: 020 8900 1221
E: info@hipact.ac.uk
An association of universities that provides education for practical development in developing countries and aims to increase the number of overseas students entering British higher education, especially member universities, as well as to widen backgrounds of higher education entrants in the UK.

Historic Churches Preservation Trust

31 Newbury Street, London EC1A 7HU
T: 020 7600 6090
F: 020 7796 2442
E: info@historicchurches.org.uk
www.historicchurches.org.uk
Provides for the preservation, repair, maintenance, improvement, upkeep, beautification and reconstruction of churches in the UK and of monuments, fittings, fixtures, stained glass, furniture, ornaments etc.
Employees: 5
Volunteers: 3

Historical Association

59a Kennington Park Road,
London SE11 4JH
T: 020 7735 3901
F: 020 7582 4989
E: enquiry@history.org.uk
www.history.org.uk
The Historical Association is the national voice for history. It exists to bring together people of all communities who have an interest in the past. It promotes and supports the study and teaching of history at all levels: teacher, student, amateur and professional.
Employees: 7
Volunteers: 229
Regional offices: 60

HIV/Aids Association of Zambia UK

Suites M13/M17, Premier Business Centre, 47–49 Park Royal Road,
London NW10 7LQ
T: 020 8090 0424
F: 020 8181 4518
E: info@haaz.org.uk
www.haaz.org.uk
Aims to protect and preserve public health by the provision of culturally appropriate HIV/AIDS and STD prevention campaigns to Zambian/African communities in the UK. Addresses the needs of Zambians/Africans directly affected by HIV/AIDS.
Employees: 2
Volunteers: 15

Hollybank Trust

Roe Head, Far Common Road, Mirfield,
West Yorkshire WF14 0DQ
T: 01924 490833
F: 01924 483902
E: s.hughes@hollybanktrust.com
www.hollybanktrust.com
Chief Executive and Principal: Steven Hughes
A charity trust working with children, young people and adults who have profound physical disabilities. We have a commitment for life for those in our care. We have a specialist school with an attached children's home, independence homes and homes for life in the neighbouring communities. We are open 52 weeks a year. Our multidisciplinary staff number 450. Internationally renowned for our work in IT, access technology and social care.
Employees: 450
Volunteers: 45
Regional offices: 1

Home from Hospital Care after Treatment

Prospect Hall, College Walk, Selly Oak, Birmingham, West Midlands B29 6LE
T: 0121 472 4499
E: homefromhospitalcare@tiscali.co.uk
www.home-from-hospital-care.org.uk
Director: Geraldine Amos
Volunteers from our Welcome Home Service offer practical, commonsense support for up to six weeks after discharge from hospital. We will shop, call in for a friendly chat, go to the bank, help with completing benefit forms etc. Our volunteers call in at least once a week. We can also supply lists of cleaners, gardeners, hairdressers, chiropodists etc.
Employees: 7
Volunteers: 60
Regional offices: 1
Income: £90,000 (2010-11)

Home-Start Canterbury and Coastal

E: sari@homestartcanterbury.org

Home-Start Haringey

E: fatmata@home-start-haringey.org

Home-Start South Hams, Plymouth and Tavistock

Age Concern Building, Ilbert Road, Kingsbridge, Ilbert Road, Kingsbridge, Devon TQ7 1DZ
T: 01548 854513
E: andreachandler.homestart@gmail.com
www.homestart-southhams.org.uk
Scheme Manager: Andrea Chandler
We believe every child deserves the best start in life and parents are best placed to provide it but that sometimes, for some families this can be difficult. We offer one-to-one befriending and mentoring support to families with a child under 5, who are experiencing difficulties. We also offer gentle group support to parents at risk of exclusion.
Employees: 5
Volunteers: 100
Regional offices: 1
Income: £160,000 (2012-13)

Home-Start Stoke-on-Trent

E: chris.pointon@homestartstoke.org.uk

Home-Start UK

2 Salisbury Road, Leicester LE1 7QR
T: 0116 233 9955
Helpline: 0800 068 6368
F: 0116 233 0232
E: info@home-start.org.uk
www.home-start.org.uk
Chief Executive: Kay Bews
Home-Start offers support, friendship and practical help to parents with young children, in local communities throughout the UK and with British Forces in Germany and Cyprus. 337 independent schemes managed by and offering support from 20,226 volunteers, supported 34,952 families and 69,672 children during 2007/8.
Employees: 117
Volunteers: 20226
Regional offices: 12

Home-Start Worthing and Adur

E: naomi.elliott@wahomestart.org.uk

Homeless Action in Barnet

E: joe@habcentre.org

Homeless International

Queen's House, 16 Queens Road, Coventry, West Midlands CV1 3EG
T: 024 7663 2802
F: 024 7663 2911
E: info@homeless-international.org
www.homeless-international.org
Chief Executive: Larry English
Aims to relieve poverty, in particular that is caused by homelessness, internationally. We work through lasting relationships with local partners in Asia and Africa, within which there is confidence to create solutions to the challenge of urban poverty. Typically we provide resources, technical assistance and financial services for community-led processes.
Employees: 16
Income: £8,154,297 (2011-12)

Homeless Link

1st Floor, 10–13 Rushworth Street, London SE1 0RB
T: 020 7960 3010
F: 020 7960 3011
E: irmani.darlington@homelesslink.org.uk
www.homeless.org.uk
The Citizenship Foundation is an independent charity that aims to empower individuals to engage in the wider community through education about the law, democracy and society. Founded in 1989, we focus particularly on developing young people's citizenship skills, knowledge and understanding.
Employees: 30
Volunteers: 15

Homeopathy Action Trust

PO Box 9022, Melton Mowbray, Leicestershire LE13 9BZ
T: 0844 800 2840 (also fax)
E: info@homeopathyactiontrust.org
www.homeopathyactiontrust.org
Executive Director: Simon Wilkinson-Blake
The principal activity of the company is the promotion of homeopathy through funding of education and research and the raising of funds to support homeopathic activities.
Employees: 2
Volunteers: 8

HOPE

Rear of 124 Bridge Street, Worksop S80 1HT
T: 01909 531294
F: 01909 530320
E: sandy@hopeservices.org.uk
www.hopeservices.org.uk
Aims to relieve hardship and distress of homeless persons by the provision of friendship, practical assistance, material help and hope.

Hope and Homes for Children

East Clyffe, Salisbury, Wiltshire SP3 4LZ
T: 01722 790111
F: 01722 790024
E: sue.rooke@hopeandhomes.org
www.hopeandhomes.org
Chief Executive: Rick Foulsham
Provides family-based care for orphaned and vulnerable children in Central and Eastern Europe and Africa.
Employees: 45
Volunteers: 7

Hope for Children

Hope House, 14a Queensway, Hemel Hempstead, Hertfordshire HP1 1LR
T: 0870 751 9861
E: hope@hope4c.org
www.hope4c.org
Aims to assist children, in particular those living in developing countries and the UK, who suffer through being handicapped, orphaned, poor and exploited.

Hope UK

25(F) Copperfield Street, London SE1 0EN
T: 020 7928 0848
F: 020 7401 3477
E: m.watson@hopeuk.org
www.hopeuk.org
Chief Executive Officer: Sarah Brighton
Hope UK enables children and young people to make drug-free choices. A network of over 150 volunteer drug educators, trained to Open College Network accreditation standards, provide interactive drug awareness sessions for children and young people and any group with an interest in them. Hope UK also provides accredited two-day courses for family and youth workers.
Employees: 12
Volunteers: 149
Regional offices: 3
Income: £200,972 (2011-12)

HOPE worldwide

360 City Road, London EC1V 2PY
T: 020 7713 7655
F: 020 7812 1236
E: wil.horwood@hopeworldwide.org.uk
www.hopeworldwide.org.uk
Chief Executive: Wil Horwood
Bringing hope to, and changing the lives of, disadvantaged and vulnerable people. In the UK we work in the areas of homelessness and addiction recovery. Overseas, we support a wide range of poverty reduction initiatives through grants and management support. We have a strong volunteerism ethos and develop initiatives that connect volunteers with poverty issues.
Employees: 10
Volunteers: 890
Regional offices: 2
Income: £863,104 (2011-12)

Horder Centre for Arthritis

St John's Road, Crowborough, East Sussex TN6 1XP
T: 01892 665577
E: info@hordercentre.co.uk
www.hordercentre.co.uk
Provides professional help by all available methods for people suffering the pain and disabling effects of all forms of arthritis in order to restore maximum independence and alleviate pain wherever possible.

Horse Rangers Association (Hampton Court) Ltd

E: director@horserangers.com

Horsham Voluntary Action

Lavinia House, Dukes Square, Denne Road, Horsham, West Sussex RH12 1GZ
T: 01403 255277
E: admin@horshamva.org.uk
www.horshamvoluntaryaction.org
Manager: Kelly Davies
Horsham Voluntary Action's mission is 'To promote, develop and support charities and voluntary organisations for the benefit of the community in the Horsham area'. Our aim is to be the major source of support and information for local voluntary organisations, ensuring that the interests of the voluntary sector are taken into account by local government and statutory authorities.
Employees: 5
Volunteers: 11
Regional offices: 0
Income: £96,500 (2012-13)

Hospice Information Service

51–59 Lawrie Park Road, Sydenham, London SE26 6DZ
T: 020 8768 4500
E: info@stchristophers.org.uk
www.stchristophers.org.uk
An information exchange and communication network for the hospice movement; phone and written enquiries welcomed from healthcare professionals and members of the public.

Hospitality Action

62 Britton Street, London EC1M 5UY
T: 020 3004 5500
F: 020 7253 2094
E: help@hospitalityaction.org.uk
www.hospitalityaction.org.uk
Chief Executive: Penny Moore
Hospitality Action helps those who work/have worked within the UK hospitality industry. We ensure all applicants are receiving their full state entitlement when unable to work and can assist where the state

is unable to. In addition to signposting and support we offer one-off grants for essential needs, short-term ongoing support for periods of crisis and a befriending scheme for socially isolated individuals. We also provide educational seminars on drug and alcohol misuse.
Employees: 12
Volunteers: 40

HOST UK

E: spm@hostuk.org

House of Saint Barnabas in Soho

1 Greek Street, Soho Square, Soho, London W1V 6NQ
T: 020 7434 1894
F: 020 7434 1746
E: finance@hosb.org.uk
Provides temporary housing and care to homeless women (18–55 years of age).

Housing Associations' Charitable Trust (HACT)

Octavia House, 50 Banner Street, London EC1Y 8ST
T: 020 7247 7800
F: 020 7247 2212
E: hact@hact.org.uk
www.hact.org.uk
Director: Heather Petch
HACT pioneers housing solutions for people on the margins. We identify emerging need, and then develop, test and promote practical solutions for social inclusion. We work through partnerships and networks, acting as a bridge between housing associations and the wider third sector.
Employees: 9
Volunteers: 1

Housing Justice

South London Mission, 256 Bermondsey Street, London SE1 3UJ
T: 020 3544 8094
E: a.gelder@housingjustice.org.uk
www.housingjustice.org.uk
Chief Executive: Alison Gelder
A national voice for churches and Christians on housing and homelessness. We help churches help homeless people through practical support, training, resources, consultancy and events. We raise awareness about housing and homelessness and campaign for positive change, particularly through the annual Poverty and

Homelessness Action Week (end of January - beginning of February).
Employees: 10
Volunteers: 25
Regional offices: 2
Income: £415,235 (2012-13)

Howard League for Penal Reform

1 Ardleigh Road, London N1 4HS
T: 020 7249 7373
F: 020 7249 7788
E: info@howardleague.org
www.howardleague.org
The Howard League for Penal Reform works for a safe society where fewer people are victims of crime. The Howard League for Penal Reform believes that offenders must make amends for what they have done and change their lives. The Howard League for Penal Reform believes that community sentences make a person take responsibility and live a law-abiding life in the community.
Employees: 13
Volunteers: 300

Hubventures

E: eleri.smith@hubventures.org

Hull Churches Home from Hospital Service

E: administrator@hchfh.org.uk

Human Givens Foundation

Chalvington, East Sussex BN27 3TD
T: 01323 811662
E: info@hgfoundation.com
www.hgfoundation.com
Aims to promote research and public education into the 'givens' of human nature and their application in the treatment and care of those suffering from mental illness.
Employees: 1

Human Relief Foundation

PO Box 194, Bradford, Yorkshire BD7 1YW
T: 01274 392727
E: mohammed@hrf.co.uk
www.hrf.org.uk

Human Scale Education

Unit 8, Fairseat Farm, Chew Stoke, Bristol BS40 8XF
T: 01275 332516
E: info@hse.org.uk
www.hse.org.uk
The charity aims to promote education in small groups, in which effective learning can be encouraged and undertaken with mutual respect. The charity also supports and

campaigns for state funding for small alternative schools and it supports the restructuring of state secondary schools.

Humane Research Trust

Brook House, 29 Bramhall Lane South, Bramhall, Cheshire SK7 2DN
T: 0161 439 8041
E: info@humaneresearch.org.uk
www.humaneresearch.org.uk
The Humane Research Trust encourages and supports new medical research that does not include the use of animals, with the objectives of advancing the diagnosis and treatment of disease in humans. The Trust encourages scientists to develop innovative alternatives to the use of animals and so eliminate the suffering of animals that occurs in medical research and testing. The Trust fulfils an important role in educating the next generation of researchers.
Employees: 4
Volunteers: 50

Humane Slaughter Association

The Old School, Brewhouse Hill, Wheathampstead, St Albans, Hertfordshire AL4 8AN
T: 01582 831919
E: info@hsa.org.uk
www.hsa.org.uk
Promotes humane methods of slaughter.

Humanity at Heart

22–24 Keymer Road, Hassocks, West Sussex BN6 8AN
T: 01273 846135
E: humanity@humanityatheart.org.uk
www.humanityatheart.org.uk
Aims to relieve the suffering and poverty of children in Romania and elsewhere and to effect this by giving aid, support and training where appropriate, either directly or through the agency of other charities.

Huntington's Disease Association

Suite 24, Liverpool Science Park, Innovation Centre 1, 131 Mount Pleasant, Liverpool L3 5TF
T: 0151 331 5444
F: 0151 331 5441
E: info@hda.org.uk
www.hda.org.uk
Chief Executive: Cath Stanley
Provides care, advice, support and education to both families and professionals affected by Huntington's disease.
Employees: 30
Volunteers: 200+
Regional offices: 20

Hyperactive Children's Support Group

71 Whyke Lane, Chichester, West
Sussex PO19 7PD
T: 01243 539966
E: hyperactive@hacsg.org.uk
www.hacsg.org.uk
Founder/Director: Sally Bunday
Provides support, ideas and information to
parents, carers and professionals concerned
for ADHD/hyperactive children. Non-
medication therapies a priority.
Employees: 2
Volunteers: 8
Income: £6,500 (2011-12)

Hypothalamic Hamartoma Uncontrolled Gelastic Seizures UK

ABS House, 35 Chiltern Avenue,
Amersham, Buckinghamshire HP6 5AE
T: 01494 728564
E: hhugsuk@hotmail.com
www.hhugs.com
Aims to relieve persons suffering from
hypothalamic hamartoma.

Hysterectomy Association

West View, West Street, Broadwindsor,
Beaminster, Dorset DT8 3QQ
T: 08432 892142
E: info@hysterectomy-association.org.
uk
www.hysterectomy-association.org.uk
CEO: Linda Parkinson-Hardman
The Hysterectomy Association was created
to provide impartial, timely and appropriate
information, products, books and support to
women who are facing a hysterectomy.
Volunteers: 2
Income: £15,000 (2010-11)

I CAN

8 Wakley Street, London EC1V 7QE
T: 020 7843 2552
Helpline: 020 7843 2544
F: 0845 225 4072
E: info@ican.org.uk
www.ican.org.uk
Chief Executive: Virginia Beardshaw
I CAN is the children's communication
charity. Communication is the essential 21st
century life skill – the foundation on which
children learn, achieve and make friends. I
CAN works to develop speech, language and
communication skills for all children. Any
parent with a question or concern about
their child's communication can contact the I
CAN Help Enquiry Service for a call or email
from a speech and language therapist.
Employees: 235

IA (The Ileostomy and Internal Pouch Support Group)

Peverill House, 1-5 Mill Road,
Ballyclare BT39 9DR
T: 028 9334 4043
Helpline: 0800 018 4724
F: 028 9332 4606
E: info@iasupport.org
www.iasupport.org
National Secretary: Anne Demick
IA is a national support group run by and for
people with ileostomies and internal
pouches, their families and carers. The core
objectives are to help those facing these
operations to return to a normal active
lifestyle as soon as possible after surgery. IA is
totally funded by donations and
subscriptions and most of the 10,000
members have either an ileostomy or an
internal pouch.
Volunteers: 800
Regional offices: 52 member
organisations

ICA:UK

41 Old Birley Street, Unit 14,
Manchester M15 5RF
T: 0161 232 8444
E: martin@ica-uk.org.uk
www.ica-uk.org.uk
Chief Executive: Martin Gilbraith
ICA:UK is concerned with the human factor
in world development – creating a humane
and sustainable future for all, through
partnership and participation. We work
nationally and internationally to enable
individuals, organisations and communities
to work together to bring about positive
change.
Employees: 5
Volunteers: 30
Regional offices: 1
Income: £191,462 (2010-11)

iDE UK

8a Accommodation Road,
London NW11 8ED
T: 020 8905 5597
E: info@ide-uk.org
www.ide-uk.org
Chief Executive: Lewis Temple
International Development Enterprises UK
(iDE UK) helps poor farming families in
Africa and Asia to escape from poverty by
doubling their income. IDE's mission is to
create income and livelihood opportunities
for the rural poor.
Employees: 3
Volunteers: 15
Income: £1.5 (2010-11)

IGD

Grange Lane, Letchmore Heath,
Watford WD25 8GD
T: 01923 851950
F: 01923 852531
E: igd@igd.com
www.igd.com
IGD is a charity that actively helps people to
grow by bringing together intelligence,
opinion and experience from the food and
grocery chain. IGD's principal objectives are:
to promote education and training,
particularly industrial and technical education
and training required for persons working in
the food industry.
Employees: 78
Volunteers: 11

Imkaan

Tindlemanor, 52–54 Featherstone Street,
London EC1Y 8RT
T: 020 7250 3933
E: policy@imkaan.org.uk
www.imkaan.org.uk
Chair: Amrit Wilson

Our mission is to act as a collective voice for the South Asian women's and other refuges, by promoting their needs and views to relevant policy makers and agencies and by providing targeted organisational support.

Immigrant Counselling and Psychotherapy

96 Moray Road, Finsbury Park,
London N4 3LA
T: 020 7272 7906
F: 020 7272 6920
E: info@icap.org.uk
The charity's objective and its principal activity is to provide culturally sensitive counselling for people of Irish origin.
Employees: 4
Volunteers: 15

Immigration Advisory Service

County House, 190 Great Dover Street,
London SE1 4YB
T: 020 7967 1221
E: info@iasservices.org.uk
www.iasuk.org
Provides the best possible free legal advice and representation to immigrants and asylum seekers, without prejudice or discrimination, in which the interests and welfare of the client are paramount.

Impact Foundation

151 Western Road, Haywards Heath,
West Sussex RH16 3LH
T: 01444 457080
F: 01444 457877
E: impact@impact.org.uk
www.impact.org.uk
Promotes activities for the prevention of disablement, and for the cure, mitigation and relief of disabling conditions.
Employees: 6
Volunteers: 8

Impetus Trust

20 Flaxman Terrace, London WC1H 9PN
T: 020 3384 3940
E: claire@impetus.org.uk
www.impetus.org.uk
Chief Executive: Daniela Barone Soares
Impetus Trust is a leader of venture philanthropy in the UK. We bring strategic funding and expertise to charities that turn around the lives of disadvantaged people. We give support to our chosen charities over a defined period of time so that they become more sustainable and robust by the time our partnership ends.
Employees: 28
Volunteers: 150
Income: £5.9 (2011-12)

In Kind Direct

62 Cornhill, London EC3V 3NH
T: 020 7398 5510
F: 020 7398 5544
E: robin@inkinddirect.org
www.inkinddirect.org
Chief Executive: Robin Boles
In Kind Direct, one of The Prince's Charities redistributes new goods donated by 900 of Britain's best-known manufacturers and retailers to voluntary and community organisations working at home and abroad. Since 1997, In Kind Direct has distributed over £130 million in value of goods to 6,500 organisations assisting millions of people in need every year.
Employees: 15
Income: £14,351,146 (2011-12)

INCLUDE

60 Queens Road, Reading RG1 4BS
T: 0118 902 1000
E: ncrawley-lyons@cfbt.com
www.include.org.uk
INCLUDE is committed to the inclusion of all young people into mainstream education, training and employment.

Inclusion London

E: libby.oakley@inclusionlondon.co.uk

Independence Initiative

64–68 Balliol Road, Bootle,
Liverpool L20 7EJ
T: 0151 284 1100
F: 0151 286 0015
E: joewelsh@independenceinitiative.co.uk
www.independenceinitiative.co.uk
The Independence Initiative works with individuals, agencies and the community to facilitate the long-term rehabilitation of people with a history of drug misuse and also provides support for their families. It provides a personal programme, addressing individual needs, overcoming barriers to social inclusion and assisting integration into the community.

Independent Academic Research Studies (IARS)

159 Clapham Road, London SW9 0PU
T: 020 7820 0945
E: t.gavrielides@iars.org.uk
www.iars.org.uk
Director: Dr Theo Gavrielides
IARS is a leading, international think-tank with charitable mission to give everyone a chance to forge a safer, fairer and more inclusive society. We achieve our charitable aims by producing evidence-based solutions to current social problems, sharing best practice and by supporting young people and the community to shape decision-making. IARS is an international expert in criminal justice, restorative justice, human rights and inclusion, citizenship and user-led research.
Employees: 10
Volunteers: 15
Regional offices: 1
Income: £308,739 (2012-13)

Independent Adoption Service

121–123 Camberwell Road,
London SE5 0HB
T: 020 7703 1088
F: 020 7277 1668
E: b.liston@tactcare.org.uk
www.i-a-s.org.uk
Aims to find permanent adoptive families for children of all ages, with special emphasis on working with black families, sibling groups and older children.

Independent Custody Visiting Association

PO Box 1053, Colne, Lancashire BB9 4BL
T: 01282 870325
F: 020 7278 9027
E: info@icva.org.uk

Independent Home Solutions CIC

The Old Crumpet Factory, 16 Brockham Lane, Brockham, Surrey RH3 7EL
T: 01737 845630
F: 01737 841650
E: info@ihscic.org.uk
www.independenthomesolutions.org.uk
Managing director: Alison Goodall
Our experienced team specialises in providing quality and bespoke home adaptations for our disabled or elder clients. Popular alterations are: level access shower rooms, ground floor extensions, garage conversions, ramps, improved access, through floor or stair lifts. We help our clients to retain their independence, safety and dignity. The IHS team oversees every project from conception to completion so that we ensure a successful outcome and peace of mind for our clients.
Employees: 14
Volunteers: 2
Regional offices: 1
Income: £450,000 (2012-13)

Independent Living Alternatives

Trafalgar House, Grenville Place, Mill Hill,
London NW7 3SA
T: 020 8906 9265
F: 020 8959 1910
E: paservices@ilanet.co.uk
www.ilanet.co.uk
Director: Tracey Jannaway
Independent Living Alternatives is a user-controlled disability organisation established in 1989 promoting the right of disabled people to live independently. ILA provides innovative and flexible alternatives to institutional and domiciliary care and has a comprehensive range of personal assistance services.
Employees: 4
Volunteers: 15
Regional offices: 1
Income: £658,370 (2011-12)

Independent Panel for Special Education Advice

6 Carlow Mews, Woodbridge,
Suffolk IP12 1EA
T: 01394 380518 (also fax)
www.ipsea.org.uk
Provides free and independent advice to parents of children with special education needs, second professional opinions on children's learning difficulties, and a representation service for parents wanting to appeal to the Special Educational Needs Tribunal.
Employees: 4
Volunteers: 200

Independent Theatre Council

The Albany, Douglas Way,
London SE8 4AG
T: 020 7403 1727
E: admin@itc-arts.org
www.itc-arts.org
Chief Executive: Charlotte Jones
The Independent Theatre Council represents, supports and develops those producing professional performing arts in the UK. We are over 400 companies and producers, united in the knowledge that together we are stronger. ITC's commitment to represent your interests includes advice on management, financial and legal matters, peer learning, training opportunities and a professional network. ITC is a strong voice.
Employees: 5
Volunteers: 0
Regional offices: 0

India Welfare Society

177 Kensal Road, London W10 5BJ
T: 020 8969 9493
F: 020 8960 2637
E: iwslondon@hotmail.com
www.indiawelfaresociety.org
Attends to the welfare of people in the UK, particularly members of the Indian community who are in need, hardship or distress.
Volunteers: 30

Industrial Careers Foundation

8 Nightingale Place, Buckingham,
Buckinghamshire MK18 1UF
T: 01280 823363
E: geoff@icf.org.uk
www.icf.org.uk
Aims to excite and interest young people aged 15–19 in the satisfaction and complexities of a management career in business.

Industry and Parliament Trust

Suite 101, 3 Whitehall Court,
London SW1A 2EL
T: 020 7839 9400
F: 020 7839 9401
E: admin@ipt.org.uk
www.ipt.org.uk
Chief Executive: Sally Muggeridge
Established in 1977, the Trust is dedicated to fostering mutual understanding between business and parliament for the public benefit. The IPT is independent, non-partisan and non-lobbying. IPT facilitates educational exchange Fellowships for MPs, MEPs, peers and officers of both Houses with a range of companies from different sectors of commerce and industry.
Employees: 10

Infertility Network UK

Charter House, 43 St Leonards Road,
Bexhill on Sea, East Sussex TN40 1JA
T: 0800 008 7464
F: 01424 731858
E: clarelewisjones@infertilitynetworkuk.com
www.infertilitynetworkuk.com
Chief Executive: Clare Lewis-Jones
At I N UK we aim to ease the feelings of isolation on both an emotional and practical level. Members of I N UK tell us frequently that by accessing our services, they are helped in the management of their illness.
Employees: 12
Volunteers: 80
Regional offices: 3
Income: £316,383 (2012-13)

Information Point for Centronuclear and Myotubular Myopathy

12 Bluebell Close, Huntington, Chester,
Cheshire CH3 6RR
T: 01244 316531
E: centronuclear.org@btinternet.com
www.centronuclear.org.uk
Founder: Toni Abram
The Information Point is a website for anyone affected by centronuclear / myotubular myopathy, the aim of which is to reach out to more families globally, to give them information about managing the condition. It is currently the only organisation in Europe/UK that provides comprehensive information and resources for the condition.
Volunteers: 1

Inland Waterways Association

Island House, Moor Road, Chesham,
Buckinghamshire HP5 1WA
T: 01494 783453
E: iwa@waterways.org.uk
www.waterways.org.uk
Chief Executive: Neil Edwards
The goals of the association are the preservation, conservation, restoration and development of the inland waterways of Great Britain.
Employees: 14
Volunteers: 17000

Innovative Vision Organisation (IVO)

Innovative Vision Organisation, 123 High Cross Road, Tottenham,
London N17 9NR
T: 020 8365 0349
Helpline: 07943 317905
F: 020 8365 1477
E: info@ivo.org.uk
www.ivo.org.uk and www.ivouk.org [bc neither web address works]
Executive Director: Daisy Byaruhanga
IVO provides care and support, and advice to African people living with HIV/AIDS; facilitates youth sexual health workshops – we facilitate community discussions around domestic violence; offers volunteering opportunities; is running free online training.
Employees: 2
Volunteers: 25
Regional offices: 1

INQUEST

89–93 Fonthill Road, London N4 3JH
T: 020 7263 1111
F: 020 7561 0799
E: inquest@inquest.org.uk
www.inquest.org.uk
Co-Directors: Deborah Coles and Helen Shaw
INQUEST is the only registered charity in England and Wales that provides a free advice service to bereaved people and their advisors on contentious deaths and their investigation, with a particular focus on deaths in custody. INQUEST gives advice and a free handbook to any bereaved family about inquest procedure. Informed by casework, INQUEST undertakes research and develops policy proposals to campaign for changes to the inquest and investigation process.
Employees: 9
Volunteers: 3
Income: £496,844 (2010-11)

Inspire!

E: david.blagbrough@inspire-ebp.org.uk

Institute for Community and Development Studies

Day Lewis House, 324 Bensham Lane, Thornton Heath, London CR7 7EQ
T: 020 8664 2600
F: 020 8664 2656
E: icdsabcd@aol.com
www.partnershipventure.com
The charity exists primarily to advance education in accordance with Christian beliefs, values and identity, and biblical teachings in particular, by training students wishing to become community development leaders and facilitators working in inner-city areas.
Employees: 15
Volunteers: 80

Institute for Complementary Medicine

Unit 25, Tavern Quay Business Centre, Sweden Gate, London SE16 7TX
T: 020 7231 5855
F: 020 7237 5175
E: info@i-c-m.org.uk
www.i-c-m.org.uk
Director: Frances Fewell
The ICM believes in promoting the standard of best practice and safe practice for all practitioners and therapists who work within complementary medicine. ICM facilitates the British Register of Complementary Practitioners and can supply names of highly qualified practitioners of various kinds of complementary medicine. It also has contact with other support groups.
Employees: 5
Volunteers: 1
Regional offices: 1

Institute for Conservation

3rd Floor, Downstream Building, 1 London Bridge, London SE1 9BG
T: 020 7785 3805
F: 020 7785 3806
E: admin@icon.org.uk
www.ukic.org.uk
Acts as a professional body for conservators of objects, for example, works of art, stonework, metalwork, etc. The Institute educates its members and the public about conservation techniques and developments in the profession.
Employees: 4
Volunteers: 80

Institute for European Environmental Policy London

28 Queen Annes Gate, London SW1H 9AB
T: 020 7799 2244
E: aglynn@ieep.eu
www.ieep.org.uk
Aims to analyse environmental policies in Europe, to increase the awareness of the European dimension of environmental policy and advance European environmental policy making.

Institute for Jewish Policy Research

4th Floor, 7-8 Market Place, London W1W 8AG
T: 020 7436 1553
E: jpr@jpr.org.uk
www.jpr.org.uk
Executive Director: Dr Jonathan Boyd
The Institute for Jewish Policy Research is an independent think-tank that informs and influences policy, opinion and decision-making on social, political and cultural issues affecting Jewish life.
Employees: 6

Institute for Outdoor Learning

Plumpton Old Hall, Plumpton, Penrith, Cumbria CA11 9NP
T: 01768 885800
E: institute@outdoor-learning.org
www.outdoor-learning.org
The aim of the Institute is to advance the education of the public in and through outdoor education.
Employees: 3

Institute for Philanthropy

2 Temple Place, London WC2R 3BD
T: 020 7240 0262
F: 020 7240 8022
E: contact@instituteforphilanthropy.org.uk
www.instituteforphilanthropy.org.uk
The Institute for Philanthropy works to increase effective philanthropy in the UK and internationally. We do this by: providing donor education and building donor networks; serving as a forum for new ideas; developing promising models for promoting philanthropy.
Employees: 15

Institute for War and Peace Reporting

48 Gray's Inn Road, London WC1X 8LT
T: 020 7831 1030
F: 020 7831 1050
E: gerryb@iwpr.net
www.iwpr.net
Aims to advance education and training in public-interest journalism and in the causes, conduct, effects and resolution of international, ethnic and group conflict and civil war for the public benefit. IWPR links local writers for story development, research, writing and training; organises public seminars and workshops; provides communications, networking, collaboration and financial support for local media; and undertakes consultancy and research.
Employees: 19
Volunteers: 5

Institute of Alcohol Studies

Elmgren House, 1 The Quay, St Ives, Cambridgeshire PE27 5AR
T: 01480 466766
E: info@ias.org.uk
www.ias.org.uk
Chairman: Derek Rutherford
Aims to increase knowledge of alcohol and of the social health consequences of its use and abuse and to encourage and support the adoption of effective measures for the management and prevention of alcohol-related problems.

Institute of Business Ethics

24 Greencoat Place, London SW1P 1BE
T: 020 7798 6040
F: 020 7798 6044
E: info@ibe.org.uk
www.ibe.org.uk
Director: Philippa Foster Back

The Institute aims to advance public education and good practice in business ethics.
Employees: 9

Institute of Cancer Research

123 Old Brompton Road,
London SW7 3RP
T: 020 7352 8133
F: 020 7370 5261
E: jonathan.kipling@icr.ac.uk
www.icr.ac.uk
Chief Executive: Peter Rigby
The Institute is one of the world's leading cancer research organisations and is internationally renowned for the quality of its science. Together with the Royal Marsden NHS Foundation Trust it also forms the leading and largest comprehensive cancer centre in Europe. Our integrated work in genetics, molecular biology and drug development is unrivalled in the world and provides the opportunity for Institute scientists to transform the prospects for cancer patients.
Employees: 943

Institute of Fundraising

Park Place, 12 Lawn Lane,
London SW8 1UD
T: 020 7840 1000
F: 020 7840 1001
E: info@institute-of-fundraising.org.uk
www.institute-of-fundraising.org.uk
Chief Executive: Lindsay Boswell
The professional body for UK fundraising. We support fundraisers, through leadership, representation, setting standards and training, and we champion fundraising as a career choice.
Employees: 42
Volunteers: 300
Regional offices: 13

Institute of Group Analysis

1 Daleham Gardens, London NW3 5BY
T: 020 7431 2693
F: 020 7431 7246
E: sue@igalondon.org.uk
www.groupanalysis.org
The IGA was founded in 1971 by Dr SH Foulkes and a group of colleagues to provide clinical training in group analytic psychotherapy. Since then, group analysis has developed a strong presence in many regions of the UK, making the IGA a truly national organisation. Members come from different

social and ethnic backgrounds, reflecting the social environment in which we live.
Employees: 6
Volunteers: 100

Institute of Money Advisers

T: 0113 242 0048
E: office@i-m-a.org.uk

Institute of Psychoanalysis

Byron House, 112a Shirland Road,
London W9 2BT
T: 020 7563 5000
F: 020 7563 5001
E: nick.childs@iopa.org.uk
www.psychoanalysis.org.uk
CEO: Dr J Levett
Founded in 1924, the Institute of Psychoanalysis has trained psychoanalysts, many of whom have become leaders in the mental health field. The Institute welcomes applicants from all types of professional and academic backgrounds, from all over the world. Many students are psychiatrists or medically qualified, some are child or adult psychotherapists, psychologists, social workers or academics, and some come from other backgrounds altogether. The Institute training leads to the title 'psychoanalyst', as recognised by the IPA.
Employees: 18
Regional offices: 1

Institute of Transactional Analysis

Broadway House, 149–151 St Neots Road, Hardwick, Cambridge CB23 7QJ
T: 0845 009 9101
E: admin@ita.org.uk
www.ita.org.uk
Promotes the study and application of transactional analysis in the UK; maintains a register of approved practitioners and monitors standards of application; provides information and support for any individual or organisation that wishes to know more about transactional analysis.

Insulin Dependent Diabetes Trust

PO Box 294, Northampton NN1 4XS
T: 01604 622837
F: 01604 622838
E: enquiries@iddtinternational.org
www.iddtinternational.org
Offers care and support to people with diabetes and their families and ensures that people with diabetes have an informed choice treatment; informs and disseminates information to the general public and health

professionals to create a better understanding of life with diabetes.
Employees: 5
Volunteers: 50

Integrated Spinal Rehabilitation Foundation

Spinal Treatment Centre, Salisbury District Hospital, Odstock Road, Salisbury SP2 8BJ
T: 01722 336262
E: info@inspire-foundation.org.uk
www.inspire-foundation.org.uk
Promotes research into, and the development of, electronic, mechanical and medical aids to assist the mobility and enablement of people suffering spinal cord paralysis and its associated effects.

Inter Faith Network for the United Kingdom

Ground Floor, 2 Grosvenor Gardens,
London SW1W 0DH
T: 020 7730 0410
F: 020 7730 0414
E: ifnet@interfaith.org.uk
www.interfaith.org.uk
Director: Harriet Crabtree
The Inter Faith Network works to promote greater understanding between people of different faiths in the UK. It links in membership national faith community representative bodies; national, regional and local inter faith organisations; and educational and academic bodies.
Employees: 4
Volunteers: 1

Inter-Action Associated Charitable Trusts and Companies

HMS President (1918), Near Blackfriars Bridge, Victoria Embankment,
London EC4Y 0HJ
T: 020 7583 2652
F: 020 7515 4450
E: edbiaction@aol.com
Inter-Action applies entrepreneurial skills to obtain social and community benefits. It sets up model projects, especially in the areas of digital media, social enterprise training and education, which incorporate these aims, and offers training and consultancy to other groups locally and internationally, helping them to adapt model projects to their own communities' needs.
Employees: 3
Volunteers: 5

Interact Worldwide

325 Highgate Studios, 53–79 Highgate
Road, London NW5 1TL
T: 020 7241 8500
F: 020 7267 6788
E: programmes@interactworldwide.org
www.interactworldwide.org
Interact Worldwide is an international charity
with over 30 years' experience and relies on
donations to fund its overseas projects and
programmes. Interact Worldwide works on
issues of sexual and reproductive health and
HIV/AIDS in solidarity with indigenous
partner organisations in Africa, Asia and Latin
America. We take a rights-based approach,
which is a framework that allows poor and
marginalised people to demand as a 'right'
the basic conditions that allow them to live in
dignity.
Employees: 26
Volunteers: 5
Regional offices: 2

Interaction

3 Hoath Farm Cottages, Bekesbourne
Lane, Canterbury, Kent CT3 4AB
T: 01227 455313
E: enquiries@pamhid.com
www.pamhid.com
Senior Trustee: Robert Hayward
InterAction has a vision of a world in which
better mental health policy processes are
created in developing countries and those in
transition, which better involve people with
mental health problems and grass-roots
organisations, with better outcomes for
individuals, households and communities.

Intercontinental Church Society

Unit 11 Ensign Business Centre,
Westwood Way, Westwood Business
Park, Coventry, West Midlands CV4 8JA
T: 024 7646 3940
F: 024 7767 5868
E: enquiries@ics-uk.org
www.ics-uk.org
Mission Director: Rev Richard Bromley
Aims to advance the Christian gospel by
evangelical mission and ministry to English-
speaking people throughout the world.
Employees: 5
Regional offices: 1

Intercountry Adoption Centre

22 Union Street, Barnet,
Hertfordshire EN5 4HZ
T: 020 8449 2562
Helpline: 020 8447 4753
E: pa@icacentre.org.uk
www.icacentre.org.uk
Chief Executive: Gill Haworth
Intercountry Adoption Centre (IAC) is a
registered Voluntary Adoption Agency which
specialises in intercountry adoptions but also
offers a domestic service, including for
adopters who have previously adopted
overseas through IAC and who wish
subsequently to adopt children from the UK.
We provide intercountry adoption
assessments and subscription services
nationally to local authorities and other
voluntary adoption agencies. IAC is unique in
being internationally accredited by some
states of origin as their partner agency.
Volunteers: 0
Regional offices: 1

InterHealth Worldwide

Partnership House, 157 Waterloo Road,
London SE1 8US
T: 020 7902 9000
F: 020 7928 0927
E: info@interhealth.org.uk
www.interhealth.org.uk
InterHealth provides whole-person
healthcare to individuals and organisations
involved in service throughout the world.
InterHealth is motivated by Christian beliefs
and values and by humanitarian ideals to
provide compassionate and professional care
without discrimination.
Employees: 22
Volunteers: 4

Interights

Lancaster House, 33 Islington High Street,
London N1 9LH
T: 020 7278 3230
E: sharrington@interights.org
www.interights.org
Interights works to ensure that human rights
are defended effectively in domestic courts
and before regional and international bodies.
We contribute to the development of a
cumulative and progressive interpretation of
universal human rights and to their effective
use in both international and regional arenas
as well as national courts.
Employees: 25

Interlink Foundation

Fourth Floor Offices, 97 Stamford Hill,
London N16 5DN
T: 020 8802 2469
F: 020 8800 5153
E: admin@interlink-foundation.org.uk
www.interlink-foundation.org.uk
Chief Executive: Chaya Spitz
The Interlink Foundation strengthens and
improves community services by supporting
the work of Orthodox Jewish charities and
community organisations. We provide
specialist advice to community groups,
advocate on their behalf and build bridges
between the Orthodox Jewish community
and public bodies.
Employees: 10
Regional offices: 2
Income: £414,091 (2011-12)

International Action Network on Small Arms

56–64 Leonard Street, London EC2V 4JX
T: 020 7065 0870
F: 020 7065 0871
E: contact@iansa.org
www.iansa.org
The International Action Network on Small
Arms (IANSA) is the global movement
against gun violence – a network of 700 civil
society organisations working in 100
countries to stop the proliferation and
misuse of small arms and light weapons
(SALW). IANSA seeks to make people safer
from gun violence by securing stronger
regulation on guns in society and better
controls on arms exports.
Employees: 4
Volunteers: 4

International Alert

346 Clapham Road, London SW9 9AP
T: 020 7627 6800
F: 020 7627 6900
E: general@international-alert.org
www.international-alert.org
Secretary General: Dan Smith
International Alert is one of the world's
leading peace-building organisations. We
help people find non-violent solutions to
conflict and have nearly 30 years of
experience working in 25 countries around
the world to build lasting peace. We also seek
to influence the policies and ways of working
of governments, international organisations
like the UN and multinational companies, to
reduce conflict risk and increase the
prospects of peace.
Employees: 200
Regional offices: 15

International Alliance of Patients' Organisations

49-51 East Road, London N1 6AH
T: 020 7250 8280
F: 020 7250 8285
E: info@patientsorganizations.org
www.patientsorganizations.org
CEO: Joanna Groves

IAPO is a unique global alliance representing patients of all nationalities across all disease areas and promoting patient-centred healthcare around the world. Our members are patients' organisations working at the international, regional, national and local levels to represent and support patients, their families and carers. A patient is a person with any chronic disease, illness, syndrome, impairment or disability.

International Children's Trust

67A Lincoln Road, Peterborough, Surrey PE1 2SD
T: 01733 576597
F: 01733 571236
E: admin@ictinfo.org.uk
www.childrens-trust.org

The Trust funds, develops and supports partners who are working with severely disadvantaged and 'at risk' children, their families and their communities in low- and middle-income countries. It develops an effective network through the International Children's Trust between its partners whose similarities and differences combine to form a collective experience in the field of international child development for the purpose of learning and giving strength through mutual support.
Employees: 5

International Community Assist

Churchview, 13 Woodland Road, Patney, Devizes, Wiltshire SN10 3RD
T: 01380 840990
E: icauk@btopenworld.com
www.ica-uk.co.uk

Aims to alleviate poverty through provision of general assistance in the developing world.

International Development Partnerships

31-33 Brunel Road, London W3 7XR
T: 020 7286 9756
E: office@idp-uk.org
www.idp-uk.org
Chief Executive: Andrew Chadwick

We provide broad-based humanitarian assistance to rural communities in Ethiopia, particularly: improving access to healthcare; providing clean water and sanitation facilities; rehabilitating schools; improving agricultural production; protecting the environment and preserving Ethiopia's heritage.
Income: £100,000 (2011-12)

International Fund for Animal Welfare

8th Floor, Camelford House, 87–89 Albert Embankment, London SE1 7UD
T: 020 7587 6700
F: 020 7587 6720
E: info@ifaw.org
www.ifaw.org

Promotes the compassionate treatment of animals as sentient beings; to protect them from cruelty; to preserve their natural habitat; to preserve them from extinction.

International Glaucoma Association

Woodcote House, 15 Highpoint Business Village, Henwood, Ashford, Kent TN24 8DN
T: 01233 648164
Helpline: 01233 648170
F: 01233 648179
E: info@iga.org.uk
www.glaucome-association.com
Chief Executive: David Wright

Provides a fellowship for those suffering from the eye disease glaucoma and those concerned in its diagnosis and treatment; presses for increased resources for what is frequently a neglected condition so that there is an improved awareness and better long-term monitoring of the disease. This is necessary because the loss of sight from glaucoma is largely preventable yet it accounts for 13% of the registered blind.
Employees: 14

International Guide Dog Federation

Hillfields, Burghfield Common, Reading RG7 3YG
T: 0118 983 8356
E: enquiries@igdf.org.uk
www.igdf.org.uk

First and foremost, membership of the IGDF enables guide dog organisations around the world to join a community dedicated to serving the visually impaired. That community needs and wants to share its knowledge and the IGDF facilitates that.
Employees: 1

International Institute for Environment and Development

3 Endsleigh Street, London WC1H 0DD
T: 020 7388 2117
F: 020 7388 2826
E: info@iied.org
www.iied.org
Director: Camilla Toulmin

IIED seeks to make the world a fairer and more sustainable place, in alliance with like-minded partners. Acting as a catalyst, broker and facilitator, we seek to add voice to poorer and more vulnerable groups to ensure their interests are heard in decision-making and can bring about progressive change.
Employees: 70

International Institute of Communications

2 Printers Yard, 90a The Broadway, London SW19 1RD
T: 020 8417 0600
F: 020 8417 0800
E: info@iicom.org
www.iicom.org

The Institute's principal activity is the organisation of overseas meetings and conferences, carrying out research and publishing material in the field of worldwide communications.
Employees: 5
Volunteers: 20

International League for the Protection of Horses

Anne Colvin House, Snetterton, Norfolk NR16 2LR
T: 0870 870 1927
F: 0870 904 1927
E: nagtrader08@gmail.com
www.ilph.org

Our aim is a world where horses are used but never abused. Our mission is to protect horses from abuse and alleviate their suffering by rehabilitation, campaigning and educating worldwide.
Employees: 131
Volunteers: 8
Regional offices: 5

International Longevity Centre-UK

22–26 Albert Embankment, Vauxhall, London SE1 7TJ
T: 020 7735 7565
E: louisetasker@ilcuk.org.uk
www.ilcuk.org.uk
Chief Executive: Baroness Sally Greengross

The International Longevity Centre-UK is an independent, non-partisan think-tank dedicated to addressing issues of longevity, ageing and population change. We develop ideas, undertake research and create a forum for debate.
Employees: 8
Regional offices: 1

International Network for the Availability of Scientific Publications

60 St Aldates, Oxford OX1 1ST
T: 01865 249909
F: 01865 251060
E: inasp@inasp.info
www.inasp.info
The charity exists for the benefit of people in resource-poor countries, to promote education, knowledge and learning by enhancing local capabilities to manage and use information and knowledge.
Employees: 16

International Seafarers Welfare & Assistance Network

Cygnet House, 12-14 Sydenham Road, Croydon, Surrey CR0 2EE
T: 0300 012 4279
Helpline: 020 7323 2737
F: 0300 012 4280
E: iswan@iswan.org.uk
www.seafarerswelfare.org
Executive Director: Roger Harris
The objectives of ISWAN are to promote the relief of need, hardship or distress amongst seafarers of all nationalities, races, colours and creeds.
Employees: 13
Regional offices: Surrey
Income: £520,925 (2012-13)

International Seafarers' Assistance Network

8th Floor, Cygnet House, 12–14 Sydenham Road, Croydon, Surrey CR0 2EE
T: 020 8680 2232
F: 020 3251 0221
E: info@seafarerhelp.org
www.seafarerhelp.org
Provides support, information and advice to seafarers around the world, through a network of maritime agencies.
Employees: 3

International Service

2nd Floor, Rougier House, 5 Rougier Street, York YO1 6HZ
T: 01904 647799
F: 01904 652353
E: is@internationalservice.org.uk
www.internationalservice.org.uk
Chief Executive: Jo Baker
An international development agency working in Latin America, Africa and the Middle East. We support in-country partners to develop and deliver sustainable solutions to inequality and poverty. Partners range from a local, grassroots level to government departments. Promoting access to equal rights is at the core of our work.
Employees: 18
Volunteers: 250
Regional offices: 6

International Stress Management Association UK

PO Box 108, PO Box 108, Caldicot, Avon NP26 9AP
T: 01179 697284
E: stress@isma.org.uk
www.isma.org.uk
Chair: Jenny Edwards
ISMA is a registered charity with a multidisciplinary professional membership. It exists to promote sound knowledge and best practice in the prevention and reduction of human stress. It sets professional standards for the benefit of individuals and organisations using the services of its members.
Employees: 1

International Students House

229 Great Portland Street, London W1W 5PN
T: 020 7631 8300
F: 020 7631 8307
E: marketing@ish.org.uk
www.ish.org.uk
Helps students achieve the academic and personal aims that have brought them to the UK; provides the best opportunities for international students to experience the many facets of life in the UK and give them a deeper understanding of British society; gives British students the opportunity for friendship with people from widely differing backgrounds and cultures and by these means makes an effective contribution to better international relations.
Employees: 130

International Tree Foundation

Sandy Lane, Crawley Down, Crawley, West Sussex RH10 4HS
T: 0870 774 4269
F: 01342 718282
E: info@internationaltreefoundation.org
www.internationaltreefoundation.org
The Foundation plants and protects trees and educates about the value of trees.
Employees: 4
Volunteers: 50
Regional offices: 23

International Voluntary Service

Thorn House, 5 Rose Street, Edinburgh, Lothian EH2 2PR
T: 0131 243 2745
F: 0131 243 2747
E: info@ivsgb.org
www.ivsgb.org
Development Director: Helen Wass O'Donnell
IVS GB is a peace organisation that promotes intercultural cooperation and intercultural understanding through voluntary work. Volunteer projects work for sustainable development of local and global communities throughout the world. IVS is open to everyone from 18 to 70 years. We offer short-term projects of two to four weeks, long-term opportunities and we are a sending organisation for EVS (European Voluntary Service).
Employees: 3
Volunteers: 3
Regional offices: 1

International Youth Hostel Federation

2nd Floor, Gate House, Fretherne Road, Welwyn Garden City, Hertfordshire AL8 6RD
T: 01707 324170
F: 01707 323980
E: jpowell@hihostels.com
www.hihostels.com
Chief Executive: Mikael Hansson
Promotes the education of all young people by encouraging in them a greater knowledge, love and care of the countryside, towns and cities in all parts of the world; provides hostel accommodation with no distinction of race, nationality, colour, religion, sex, class or political opinions; and develops a better understanding of other people, both at home and abroad.
Employees: 20

Internet Watch Foundation

Suite 7310, First Floor Building 7300,
Cambridge Research Park,
Waterbeach CB25 9TN
T: 01223 203030
E: bill@iwf.org.uk
www.iwf.org.uk
Chief Executive: Susie Hargreaves
The IWF is the UK reporting hotline for
images of child sexual abuse online, extreme
adult pornography and non-photographic
images of child sexual abuse. Our vision is to
eliminate online child sexual abuse.
Employees: 20
Regional offices: 1
Income: £1,200,907 (2011-12)

INTRAC

PO Box 563, Oxford OX2 6RZ
T: 01865 201851
F: 01865 201852
E: info@intrac.org
www.intrac.org
Provides specially designed management
training, consultancy and research services to
organisations involved in international relief
and development; improves the
organisational effectiveness and programme
performance of northern NGOs and
southern partners.
Employees: 28
Volunteers: 3
Regional offices: 3

Involvement and Participation Association (IPA)

42 Colebrook Row, London N1 8AF
T: 0171 354 8040
F: 020 7354 8041
E: involve@ipa-involve.com
www.ipa-involve.com
Promotes employee information and
consultation processes, and partnership in
the workplace.
Employees: 6

Iranian Association

Palingswick House, 241 King Street,
London W6 9LP
T: 020 8748 6682
F: 020 8563 7549
E: info@iranian-association.org.uk
Aims to assist the development of the Iranian
ethnic community in Britain in terms of
settlement, social welfare, training and
education.
Employees: 13
Volunteers: 35

Irish in Britain

356 Holloway Road, London N7 6PA
T: 020 7697 4081
F: 020 7697 4271
E: shutton@irishsocieties.org
www.irishinbritain.org
CEO: Jennie McShannon
Irish in Britain is the national representative
body for the Irish in Britain. Working
together with over 100 Irish cultural and
community members we endeavour to raise
the profile and contribution of the Irish
community in Britain through research,
policy and parliamentary work, campaigns
and community development support. Our
mission is to achieve a confident, healthy and
empowered Irish community participating
fully in Britain. Follow us on: Twitter: @
irishinbritain Facebook: Irish in Britain
Employees: 11
Regional offices: 3

Irish Traveller Movement in Britain

The Resource Centre, 356 Holloway Road,
London N7 6PA
T: 020 7607 2002
F: 020 7607 2005
E: info@irishtraveller.org.uk
ITM aims to develop the capacity and skills of
members of the socially and economically
disadvantaged community of Irish travellers
in such a way that they are better able to
identify, and help meet, their needs and to
participate more fully in society; and to
promote equality and diversity and racial
harmony for the benefit of the public by
encouraging others to understand the
culture and needs of Irish travellers.
Employees: 1
Volunteers: 11

Isbourne Foundation

Wolseley House, Oriel Road,
Cheltenham GL50 1TH
T: 01242 254321
E: info@isbourne.org
www.isbourne.org
The Foundation helps individuals to develop
their self-awareness in harmony with natural
and spiritual laws.
Employees: 3
Volunteers: 10

Islamic Relief

19 Rea Street South, Digbeth,
Birmingham, West Midlands B5 6LB
T: 0121 605 5555
F: 0121 622 5003
E: saleh.saeed@irworldwide.org
www.islamic-relief.com
Chief Executive Officer: Saleh Saeed
Dedicated to the service of the world's
poorest people through emergency
intervention at the time of disasters and
through long-term development in the fields
of education, health, income generation and
water and sanitation.
Employees: 240
Volunteers: 100
Regional offices: 25

IVAR

26 Russell Square, Bloomsbury,
London WC1B 5DQ
T: 020 7631 6608
F: 020 7631 6688
E: kulwinder@ivar.org.uk
www.ivar.org.uk
Director: Ben Cairns
IVAR's mission is to support the
development and sustainability of charities
and other voluntary, community and not-for-
profit organisations through research,
education and training.
Employees: 3

Iyengar Yoga Institute

223A Randolph Avenue, London W9 1NL
T: 020 7624 3080
F: 020 7372 2726
E: office@iyi.org.uk
www.iyi.org.uk
Aims to advance public education in the
classical teachings of the science of yoga;
promotes and advances the study and
practice of yoga; supports research into the
therapeutic effects of yoga as a means of
improving the mental and physical health of
the community and publishes the results of
such research.

J

J P Morgan Chase

10 Aldermanbury, London EC2V 7RF
T: 020 7325 1308
E: chris.hancock@jpmorgan.com
Funds educational projects, primary and
secondary schools and universities,
community projects (usually relating to the
needs of inner-city children), arts education,
and education for the disadvantaged.
Individuals are not funded directly.

JAT

Berkeley House, 1st Floor, 18–24 High
Street, Edgware HA8 7RP
T: 020 8952 5253
F: 020 8952 8893
E: admin@jat-uk.org
www.jat-uk.org
Director: Janine Clements
JAT provides sexual health and HIV
education for Jewish youth in schools, youth
groups and summer camps. We also run a
programme for parents on how to talk to
their children about sex. We offer financial,
practical and emotional support for Jewish
people with HIV.
Employees: 4
Volunteers: 20

Jennifer Trust for Spinal Muscular
Atrophy

40 Cygnet Court, Timothy's Bridge Road,
Stratford upon Avon,
Warwickshire CV37 9NW
T: 01789 267520
F: 01789 268371
E: office@jtsma.org.uk
www.jtsma.org.uk
We inform, support and empower families
and individuals affected by all forms of SMA
and raise awareness of the condition. We also
fund and support the research community
addressing the causes, treatment and
management of SMA.
Employees: 13
Volunteers: 170

Jewish Association for the
Mentally Ill

Olympia House, Armitage Road,
London NW11 8RQ
T: 020 8458 2223
F: 020 8731 7395
E: info@jamiuk.org
www.jamiuk.org
Provides services and support to people with
severe and enduring mental health problems.
Employees: 8
Volunteers: 37

Jewish Bereavement Counselling
Service

Bet Meir, 44A Albert Road, Hendon,
London NW4 2SJ
T: 020 8385 1874
E: enquiries@jbcs.org.uk
www.jvisit.org.uk/jbcs
Offers emotional help and support to
members of the Jewish community who
have been bereaved, and serves as a resource
and information centre to both the Jewish
and the non-Jewish community within
London and around the UK.

Jewish Council for Racial Equality

PO Box 47864, London NW11 1AB
T: 020 8455 0896
E: admin@jcore.org.uk
www.jcore.org.uk
Encourages the Jewish community to play a
more active role in race relations.

Jewish Lads and Girls Brigade
including Outreach/Kiruv and
Hand-in-Hand Young Volunteers

3 Beechcroft Road, South Woodford,
London E18 1LA
T: 020 8989 8990
F: 020 8530 3327
E: getinvolved@jlgb.org
www.jlgb.org
Aims to train its members in loyalty, honour,
discipline and self-respect so that they may
become a credit to their country and their
community. We are committed to enhancing
the lives of Jewish young people through a
diverse range of experiences and activities
within a friendly and safe environment,
encouraging development within the Jewish
and wider community.
Employees: 10
Volunteers: 250
Regional offices: 1

Jewish Marriage Council

23 Ravenshurst Avenue, Hendon,
London NW4 4EE
T: 020 8572 2691
E: info@jmc-uk.org
www.jmc-uk.org
Chair: Martyn Zeidman
Provides confidential support for all Jewish
people.
Employees: 2
Volunteers: 20
Regional offices: 1

Jewish Women's Aid

PO Box 2670, London N12 9ZE
T: 020 8445 8060
Helpline: 0808 801 0500
F: 020 8445 0305
E: info@jwa.org.uk
www.jwa.org.uk
Executive Director: Emma Bell
Aims to raise awareness of the issues of
domestic abuse against women, within the
Jewish community, and to campaign on their
behalf; provides a refuge for Jewish women
and their children fleeing domestic abuse;
fosters links with organisations in both the
Jewish and the wider community; provides
professional advice services; and researches,
develops and produces resources and
publicity material.
Employees: 15
Volunteers: 150
Regional offices: 1

Jigsaw4U Ltd

40 Mill Green Road, Mitcham,
Surrey CR4 4HY
T: 020 8687 1384
F: 020 8687 9730
E: info@jigsaw4u.org.uk
www.jigsaw4u.org.uk
Director of Operations: Pam Byfield
Jigsaw4u is a child-centred charity supporting
children and young people through grief, loss
and trauma whilst also empowering them to
have a voice in decision-making about their
own lives. The organisation delivers a wide
range of projects including those that work
with sexual exploitation, home school links,
domestic abuse, participation for disabled
young people, pre and post bereavement,
advocacy and going missing.
Employees: 19
Volunteers: 40
Regional offices: 0
Income: £615,641 (2012-13)

John Ellerman Foundation

Aria House, 23 Craven Street,
London WC2N 5NS
T: 020 7930 8566
E: enquiries@ellerman.org.uk
www.ellerman.org.uk
Director: Nicola Pollock
The John Ellerman Foundation was
established in 1971 as a generalist
grantmaking trust. Today the Foundation
uses Sir John's legacy to make grants totaling
around £4.5 million a year, mostly in the UK
in three categories, Arts, Environment and
Welfare.
Employees: 6

John Huntingdon's Charity

E: jill@johnhuntingdon.org.uk

Joint Committee of the Order of St John and British Red Cross Society

5th Floor, 22–26 Albert Embankment,
London SE1 7TJ
E: balwinder@jointcommittee.freeserve.
co.uk
Provides financial assistance in the form of
grants to ex-service war disabled men and
women disabled in the First and Second
World Wars. Help is also available for widows
of war disability pensioners and for sick and
elderly ex-members of the nursing services
of HM Forces and to officers and members
of the Voluntary Aid Detachment of the Red
Cross and St John Ambulance who gave
service to the wounded in the second World
War or earlier.

Joint Council for the Welfare of Immigrants

115 Old Street, London EC1V 9RT
T: 020 7251 8708
F: 020 7251 8707
E: info@jcwi.org.uk
www.jcwi.org.uk
Chief Executive: Habib Rahman
JCWI was established in 1967 to provide
immediate and direct support to immigrants
and to respond to the injustice and
unfairness of UK immigration control. JCWI
exists to campaign for justice in immigration,
nationality and refugee laws and policy.
Employees: 10
Volunteers: 2

Joint Educational Trust

6–8 Fenchurch Buildings,
London EC3M 5HT
T: 020 3217 1100
Helpline: 0560 150 3524
F: 020 3217 1110
E: smulligan@rncf.org.uk
www.jetcharity.org
Aims to assist children who have experienced
recent tragedy or trauma, or are at risk in
some way, where boarding school or
independent day school can provide the
answer. The aim is that children will recover
their education in a safe and secure
environment, and build on their successes in
adult life.
Employees: 2
Volunteers: 20
Regional offices: 1

Joint Epilepsy Council

PO Box 186, Leeds, West
Yorkshire LS20 8WY
T: 01943 87182
E: sharon.jec@btconnect.com
www.jointepilepsycouncil.org.uk
Chief Executive: Sharon Wood
The Joint Epilepsy Council of the UK and
Ireland (JEC) is an umbrella charity providing
the representative voice working for the
benefit of people affected by epilepsy.
Employees: 1
Volunteers: Varies

Joseph Levy Foundation

1 Bell Street, London NW1 5JY
T: 020 7616 1200
F: 020 7616 1206
E: info@jlf.org.uk
www.jlf.org.uk
Director: Sue Nyfield
The Foundation supports general charitable
purposes, giving grants to registered
charities. The trustees believe in an inclusive
society and recognise the needs of all its
citizens. The Foundation works with charities
that enable people to build a better future in
their communities and to improve their
quality of life. The Foundation is currently
closed to unsolicited applications.
Employees: 2
Volunteers: 0
Income: £795,766 (2011-12)

Joseph Rowntree Foundation

The Homestead, 40 Water End, York,
North Yorkshire YO30 6WP
T: 01904 629241
F: 01904 620072
E: sarah.carrette@jrf.org.uk
www.jrf.org.uk
Chief Executive: Julia Unwin
The Joseph Rowntree Foundation's aim is to
search, demonstrate and influence, providing
research, evidence, solutions and ideas that
will help to overcome the causes of poverty
and inequality. Our three main research
themes are Poverty, Place and An Ageing
Society.
Employees: 700

Josephine Butler Educational Trust

4 The Hedges, Penenden Heath,
Maidstone, Kent ME14 2JW
T: 01622 679630
E: jbt@liverpool.anglican.org
The Trust disseminates knowledge and
educates the public about the law as it affects
prostitution of women and children,
international sexual slavery and all forms of
exploitation of prostitution by third parties.

Journalists Charity

Dickens House, 35 Wathen Road,
Dorking, Surrey RH4 1JY
T: 01306 887511
F: 01306 888212
E: enquiries@pressfund.org.uk
www.journalistscharity.org.uk
Director: David Ilott
Helps journalists and their dependants in
times of need. Also provides sheltered
housing and a nursing home.
Employees: 20
Volunteers: 30

Jubilee Sailing Trust

Merlin Quay, Hazel Road, Southampton,
Hampshire SO19 7GB
T: 023 8044 9108
F: 023 8044 9145
E: pressoffice@jst.org.uk
www.jst.org.uk
Chief Executive: Amanda Butcher
The JST was founded in 1977 to give disabled
people the opportunity to discover the thrill
and adventure of offshore tall ship sailing as a
member of a mixed-ability crew. The JST
operates two beautiful purpose designed
and built tall ships, Lord Nelson and
Tenacious and is the only organisation in the
world that can integrate mixed-ability crews

on year-round voyages to northern Europe, the Canaries and the Caribbean.
Employees: 58
Volunteers: 500

Judith Trust

5 Carriage House, 90 Randolph Avenue, London W9 1BG
T: 020 7266 1073
F: 020 7289 5804
E: judith.trust@lineone.net
www.judithtrust.org.uk
Chair: Annette Lawson
The Judith Trust's vision is a world without struggle: a better life for people with both learning disabilities and mental illness needs and their carers. The Trust funds commissioned research and, on the basis of outcomes, advocates for policy change and implementation.
Employees: 1

Julia Margaret Cameron Trust

E: administrator@dimbola.co.uk

Just a Drop

Gateway House, 28 The Quadrant, Richmond, Surrey TW9 1DN
T: 020 8910 7981
F: 020 8334 0555
E: nikki.davis@reedexpo.co.uk
www.justadrop.org
Polluted water is the world's biggest killer of children under five. Just a Drop raises money to build wells, install hand pumps and carry out health and sanitation programmes to give them and their families clean, accessible water.
Employees: 1
Volunteers: 10

JustGiving

1st Floor, 30 Eastbourne Terrace, London W2 6LA
E: press@justgiving.com
www.justgiving.com
CEO: Zarine Kharas
JustGiving has been helping charities and their supporters raise money online since 2001. Whether it's online fundraising, regular giving, text donations, automatic Gift Aid reclaim or detailed reporting – we make sure you have the tools you need all in one place.

JUSTICE

59 Carter Lane, London EC4V 5AQ
T: 020 7329 5100
F: 020 7329 5055
E: lpepler@justice.org.uk
www.justice.org.uk
Director: Roger Smith

JUSTICE is an independent law reform and human rights organisation. Since its formation in 1957, JUSTICE has been at the cutting edge of the debate on legal reform. It is widely respected for the breadth, depth and quality of its analysis. Today, more than ever, JUSTICE is involved in the issues that will shape the future legal landscape.
Employees: 8
Volunteers: 6

Kairos Community Trust

110 Brixton Road, London SW9 6BE
T: 020 7840 0330
F: 020 7582 4211
E: kairos@classmail.co.uk
Helps homeless people to recover from situations causing their marginalisation, providing detox and treatment for substance misuse and suitable accommodation. It fosters their recovery in a community residential setting and alleviates poverty.
Employees: 21
Volunteers: 20

Karuna Trust

72 Holloway Road, London N7 8JG
T: 020 7700 3434
F: 020 7700 3535
E: info@karuna.org
www.karuna.org
Works for the relief of poverty, the advancement of education, cultural conservation and advancement of the Buddhist religion. Continues to expand the funding work begun by Aid for India, both in India and elsewhere and promotes, amongst the poorest people of the world, dignity, initiative and self-reliance.
Employees: 9
Volunteers: 5

Keep Britain Tidy

Elizabeth House, The Pier, Wigan, Greater Manchester WN3 4EX
T: 01942 612621
F: 01942 824778
E: press@keepbritaintidy.org
www.keepbritaintidy.org
Chief Executive: Phil Barton

Keep Britain Tidy is a campaigning environmental charity that encourages everyone to be litter free, to waste less and to live more. It runs a variety of programmes including WasteWatch, Eco-Schools in England, the Blue Flag Award for beaches and the Keep Britain Tidy Network for local authorities and land managers as well as a number of volunteering programmes.
Employees: 100
Volunteers: 75000

Keep Fit Association

Suite 105, Astra House, Arklow Road, London SE14 6EB
T: 01403 266000
F: 020 8692 8383
E: office@emdp.org
www.keepfit.org.uk
Provides the opportunity for people of all ages and aptitudes to develop their individual potential through the medium of movement, dance and exercise by making full use of their physical and intellectual capabilities and social involvement.
Employees: 2
Volunteers: 20
Regional offices: 82

Kent Volunteers

E: caroline.reade@kent.gov.uk

Kenward Trust

Kenward Road, Yalding ME18 6AH
T: 01622 814187
F: 01622 815805
E: audrey.pie@kenwardtrust.org.uk
www.kenwardtrust.org.uk
Chief Executive: Angela Painter
The Kenward Trust is a registered social and healthcare Christian charity that provides drug and alcohol recovery, reintegration and resettlement services in Kent and East Sussex. This includes residential rehabilitation and supported housing for people with drug and alcohol misuse issues, education and prevention initiatives for children and teenagers, supported housing for 16–25 years olds and offender resettlement.
Employees: 52
Volunteers: 29
Income: £1,700,000 (2011-12)

Keratec

Keratec Eyebank, Department of Anatomy, St Georges, University of

London, Cranmer Terrace,
London SW17 0RE
T: 020 8672 2325
F: 020 8682 3026
E: rostron@sgul.ac.uk
www.kerateceyebank.co.uk
Medical Director: Chad Rostron
The charity is committed to developing the treatment of corneal disease. Corneal opacity is a major cause of blindness worldwide, and we are researching new methods of treatment to restore sight in those suffering from conditions such as keratoconus, trachoma and corneal scarring.
Employees: 1
Volunteers: 1

Keratoconus Self-Help and Support Association

PO Box 26251, London W3 9WQ
Helpline: 020 8993 4759
E: anneklepacz@aol.com
www.keratoconus-group.org.uk
The association provides information and support to those with this eye condition. It organises conferences, members meetings, and produces a regular newsletter and other information.
Volunteers: 12
Income: £10,802 (2012-13)

KeyChange Charity

5 St Georges Mews, 43 Westminster Bridge Road, London SE1 7JB
T: 020 7633 0533
E: info@keychange.org.uk
www.keychange.org.uk
Provides residential and nursing care for older people, provision for homeless women, and street outreach to women in the sex industry.

KeyRing

27 Corsham Street, London,
London N1 6DR
T: 020 7324 0750
E: enquiries@keyring.org
www.keyring.org
Chief Executive: Karyn Kirkpatrick
KeyRing supports vulnerable adults to live independently at the heart of their community. KeyRing has been supporting people for over 20 years and over 800 people across England and Wales are unlocking their potential through KeyRing.
Employees: 120
Volunteers: 96
Regional offices: 5

KIDS

49 Mecklenburgh Square,
London WC1N 2NY
T: 020 7520 0420
F: 020 7520 0406
E: kevin.williams@kids.org.uk
www.kids.org.uk
Chief Executive: Kevin Williams
Provides services to disabled children and young people and their families.
Employees: 600
Volunteers: 200
Regional offices: 5
Income: £11,500,000 (2010-11)

Kids Can Achieve

E: pat.lee@kidscanachieve.co.uk

Kidsaid

4 St Giles Terrace,
Northampton NN1 2BN
T: 01604 630332
E: info@kidsaid.org.uk
www.kidsaid.org.uk
Chair of Trustees: Nick Griffin
A Northamptonshire based charity that provides therapy and support to children who have suffered bereavement, abuse, domestic violence, family breakdown, bullying or any form of trauma.
Employees: 2
Regional offices: 1

Kidscape Campaign for Children's Safety

2 Grosvenor Gardens,
London SW1W 0DH
T: 020 7730 3300
F: 020 7730 7081
E: contact@kidscape.org.uk
www.kidscape.org.uk
CEO: Claude Knights
Kidscape is committed to keeping children safe. Launched in 1985, it is the only nationwide charity dedicated exclusively to preventing child sexual abuse and bullying before it happens.
Employees: 22
Volunteers: 1
Regional offices: 1

Kidsout UK

14 Church Square, Leighton Buzzard,
Bedfordshire LU7 1AE
T: 01525 385252
F: 01525 385533
E: kidsout@kidsout.org.uk
www.kidsout.org.uk
CEO: Gordon Moulds CBE
Our mission is to help transform the lives of disadvantaged children and young people in the UK by providing fun opportunities and positive experiences to significantly enhance their wellbeing and outlook for a happier future. Our projects currently support children who have experienced domestic violence, children with disabilities, children with English as an additional language, children struggling academically and those not in education, employment or training.
Employees: 7
Volunteers: 50

King's Fund

11–13 Cavendish Square,
London W1G 0AN
T: 020 7307 2400
F: 020 7307 2801
E: library@kingsfund.org.uk
www.kingsfund.org.uk
The King's Fund is an independent health charity that does work based on evidence of need and a commitment to the values of social justice and public service. It supports the health of the people of London by influencing health policy and stimulating good practice in service provisions. Works across the UK to tackle problems, promote mutual learning and disseminate new ideas.
Employees: 113

King's Medical Research Trust

Weston Education Centre, 10 Cutcombe Road, London SE5 9RJ
T: 020 7848 5866
E: marc.masey@nhs.net
The Trust aims to relieve suffering and cure illness and disease by continuous research into causes, prevention, diagnosis and treatment, and by publishing the results for public good.

Kingham Hill Trust

Oak Hill College, Chase Side, Southgate
T: 020 8449 0467
E: tonys@oakhill.ac.uk
www.oakhill.ac.uk
Bursar: Tony Sims

Kingston Centre for Independent Living

E: robert.reilly@kcil.org.uk

Kingsway International Christian Centre

KICC Prayer City, Buckmore Park,
Maidstone Road, Chatham,
Kent ME5 9QG
T: 020 8525 0000
E: ade_d'almeida@kicc.org.uk
www.kicc.org.uk
CEO: Oladipo Oluyomi
KICC is an independent, interdenominational
and international church. KICC actively
supports the community via a range of
counselling services, skills training and a
supplementary school for GCSE pupils. KICC
also works in partnership with statutory and
voluntary organisations to improve social
conditions.
Employees: 51
Volunteers: 1200

Kingwood Trust

2 Chalfont Court, Chalfont Close, Lower
Earley, Reading RG6 5SY
T: 0118 931 0143
F: 01189 311937
E: info@kingwood.org.uk
www.kingwood.org.uk
Chief Executive: Sue Osborn
Kingwood pioneers best practice that
acknowledges and promotes the potential of
people with autism and Asperger's. We
support adults with a range of skills and
abilities to achieve their full potential.
Employees: 130

Kith and Kids

c/o Haringey Irish Centre, Pretoria Road,
London N17 8DX
T: 020 8801 7432
F: 020 8885 3035
E: projects@kithandkids.org.uk
www.kithandkids.org.uk
Aims to achieve empowerment and social
inclusion with families living with disability.

Klinefelter Organisation

3 Coxwell Road, Faringdon,
Oxfordshire SN7 7EB
T: 01367 241409
www.ksa-uk.co.uk
Provides information and support to, and
facilitates social contact between, adults who
have Klinefelter's syndrome and their
partners; works together to improve
understanding of the syndrome by the
general public and professionals; ensures that
people with Klinefelter's syndrome are
treated with dignity and are not subjected to
discrimination; acts as advocates for those

affected, to promote appropriate medical
and other treatments.

Koestler Trust

168A Du Cane Road, London W12 0TX
T: 020 8740 0333
E: mlewis@koestlertrust.org.uk
www.koestlertrust.org.uk
The charity promotes the creative enterprise
of inmates and former inmates of prisons,
young offender institutions and secure units.
Employees: 6

Krishnamurti Foundation Trust

Brockwood Park, Bramdean,
Hampshire SO24 0CQ
T: 01962 771525
F: 01962 771159
E: kft@brockwood.org.uk
www.kfoundation.org
The Trust works to advance the education of
the public in philosophy, sociology,
psychology and comparative religion and, in
particular, to promote the study of the
teachings in those fields of Jiddu
Krishnamurti.
Employees: 48
Volunteers: 20

Kurdish Cultural Centre

14–16 Stannary Street, London SE11 4AA
T: 020 7735 0918
E: admin@kcclondon.org.uk
www.kcclondon.org
Aims to assist and advise the Kurdish
community in matters relating to education,
health, immigration, integration, legal issues,
housing, social activities and welfare;
supports cultural events, meetings and
seminars; encourages a positive relationship
and wider co-operation between the Kurdish
community and other communities.

Kurdish Human Rights Project

11 Guilford Street, London WC1N 1DH
T: 020 7405 3835
F: 020 7404 9088
E: khrp@khrp.org
www.khrp.org
KHRP is an independent, non-political
human rights organisation and registered
charity dedicated to the promotion and
protection of the human rights of all persons
in the Kurdish regions of Turkey, Iraq, Iran,
Syria and elsewhere.
Employees: 9
Volunteers: 10

L'Arche

10 Briggate, Silsden, 10 Briggate, Silsden,
Keighley, West Yorkshire BD20 9JT
T: 01535 656186
F: 01535 656426
E: info@larche.org.uk
www.larche.org.uk
National Coordinator: John Sargent
We are people with and without learning
disabilities sharing life in communities,
belonging to an international federation. Our
mission is to: nurture communities of faith in
which mutually transforming relationships
can flourish; promote the gifts of people
with learning disabilities enabling them to
take a full part in L'Arche and society; be open
and outward looking and actively engaged
with those around us responding to changing
needs and circumstances.
Employees: 338
Volunteers: 158
Regional offices: 9

La Leche League Great Britain

PO Box 29, West Bridgford, Nottingham,
Nottinghamshire NG2 7NP
T: 0845 456 1855
Helpline: 0845 120 2918
E: hfbutler.lllgb@btinternet.com
www.laleche.org.uk
Chair of Council of Directors: Helen Russ
Provides information and support for
breastfeeding mothers through a national
telephone helpline, email help and a network
of local groups, all run by trained volunteers.
Publishes books and leaflets on
breastfeeding. Promotes the benefits of
breastfeeding and works with health
professionals nationally and locally; trains
mothers with the help of health professionals
through the national peer counsellor
programme.
Employees: 4
Volunteers: 250
Regional offices: 77

Landlife

National Wildflower Centre, Court Hey
Park, Liverpool L16 3NA
T: 0151 737 1819
E: info@landlife.org.uk
www.landlife.org.uk
Aims to protect and promote wildlife,
working with people for nature – working
with nature for people and creating new
habitats for people to enjoy.

Landmine Action

1st Floor, 89 Albert Embankment,
London SE1 7TP
T: 020 7820 0222
F: 020 7820 0057
E: info@landmineaction.org
www.landmineaction.org
Landmine Action is a not-for-profit
organisation committed to good governance
and the development of civil society through
the promotion of international humanitarian
law, the relief of poverty and the
empowerment of communities marginalised
by conflict.
Employees: 7
Volunteers: 2

Landscape Design Trust

Bank Chambers, 1 London Road, Redhill,
Surrey RH1 1LY
T: 01737 779257
E: lorraine@landscape.co.uk
www.landscape.co.uk
Our object is the advancement of awareness
and understanding of the landscape for the
benefit of the environment and the
community.
Employees: 8

Landscape Institute

33 Great Portland Street,
London W1W 8QG
T: 020 7299 4508
E: mail@landscapeinstitute.org
www.landscapeinstitute.org
The Landscape Institute is the Royal
Chartered body for landscape architects,
professionals who inspire people to expect
the best from the natural and built
environments. Parks, streets, regeneration,
waterways and open space – this is the work
of landscape architects. The Institute is a
charitable body working to enhance and
conserve our landscapes whether rural,
urban or coastal.
Employees: 20

Langley House Trust

PO Box 181, Witney,
Oxfordshire OX28 6WD
T: 01993 774075
F: 01993 772425
E: info@langleyhousetrust.org
www.langleyhousetrust.org
The Langley House Trust is a national
Christian charity that provides resettlement
support for ex-offenders (and those at risk of
offending) working towards crime-free
independence and reintegration into society.
The Trust's residential projects along with
move-on accommodation provide a range of
supported accommodation. The Trust works
with those who are hard to place and accepts
both men and women of any or no faith.
Employees: 205
Volunteers: 20
Regional offices: 3

LASA

E: cashcroft@lasa.org.uk

Lattitude Global Volunteering

Lattitude, 44 Queens Road,
Reading RG1 4BB
T: 0118 959 4914
F: 0118 957 6634
E: nadie@lattitude.org.uk
www.lattitude.org.uk
Chief Executive: Belinda Coote
Lattitude Global Volunteering has 35 years'
experience of working with young people.
Every year we place 2,000 UK and overseas
volunteers in 23 different countries. Our
aims: to provide placements that allow
young people to develop their skills and
broaden their education; to promote access
to volunteering opportunities for all young
people, regardless of background; to help
overseas communities by providing
volunteer support whilst empowering our
young people to make a real difference.
Employees: 28
Volunteers: 150

Law Centres Network

64 Great Eastern Street,
London EC2A 3QR
T: 020 7749 9120
F: 020 7749 9190
E: info@lawcentres.org.uk
www.lawcentres.org.uk
Director: Julie Bishop
Established in 1978, the Law Centres
Network (a business name of the Law
Centres Federation) is a charity and a
company limited by guarantee. LCN supports
and promotes Law Centres in England, Wales
and Northern Ireland. Law Centres provide
free legal advice on social welfare law to
disadvantaged people in their communities,

helping them alleviate their poverty and
disadvantage.
Employees: 10
Regional offices: 50

LawWorks

10–13 Lovat Lane, London EC3R 8DN
T: 020 7929 5601
F: 020 7929 5722
E: rg@lawworks.org.uk
www.lawworks.org.uk
Chief Executive: Robert Gill
Brokers and develops pro bono legal services
linking those who need free legal help with
lawyers willing to provide it.
Employees: 14
Volunteers: 2000
Regional offices: 1

LDN Research Trust

PO Box 1083, Buxton, Norwich,
Norfolk NR10 5WY
T: 08444 145295
E: contact@ldnresearchtrust.org
www.ldnresearchtrust.org
Trustee: Linda Elsegood
We aim to raise awareness of LDN for
autoimmune conditions and to raise funds to
help initiate clinical trials for conditions
where LDN could be of benefit.
Volunteers: 30

Leadership Trust Foundation

Weston under Penyard, Ross on Wye,
Herefordshire HR9 7YH
T: 01989 767667
F: 01989 768133
E: enquiries@leadership.co.uk
www.leadership.org.uk
Aims to enhance and develop leadership in
all aspects of society.
Employees: 80
Volunteers: 200

League Against Cruel Sports

New Sparling House, Holloway Hill,
Godalming, Surrey GU7 1QZ
F: 020 7378 7745
E: info@league.uk.com
www.league.uk.com
Campaigns for the abolition of cruel sports
where animals are hurt, at risk of trauma,
injury or death for sport. Seeks change where
abolition is not politically achievable and
provides protection for animals endangered
by cruel sports.
Employees: 25
Volunteers: 50
Regional offices: 30

League of British Muslims

Ilford Muslim Community Centre, Eton Road, Ilford, Essex IG1 2UE
T: 020 8514 0706
F: 020 8599 7052
E: leagueofbm@btconnect.com
The principal objectives of the charity are to advance the religion of Islam and to advance Islamic education amongst Muslims resident in England and Wales.
Employees: 1
Volunteers: 12

League of Jewish Women

6 Bloomsbury Square,
London WC1A 2LP
T: 020 7242 8300
E: office@theljw.org
www.theljw.org
President: Marilyn Brummer
The League of Jewish Women (LJW) is one of the leading voluntary Jewish women's service organisations in the UK. Affiliated to more than 30 other national and international organisations, membership is open to all Jewish men and women. LJW is the UK affiliate of the International Council of Jewish Women. LJW is a voluntary service organisation that provides help wherever it is needed, within both the Jewish and the wider community.
Employees: 2
Volunteers: 2500
Regional offices: 1

League of Mercy

PO Box 68, Lingfield, Surrey RH7 6QQ
T: 020 8660 4496 (also fax)
E: admin@leagueofmercy.co.uk
www.leagueofmercy.co.uk
Works for the advancement of the Christian Faith; the relief of persons who are in need, hardship or distress and the advancement of education on the basis of Christian principles.

League of Remembrance

55 Great Ormond Street,
London WC1N 3HZ
T: 020 7829 7818 (also fax)
E: hayley.dodman@gosh.nhs.uk
Provides companionship, financial assistance and support to dependants and retired members of the armed forces and retired nurses.
Employees: 1
Volunteers: 38

Learning and Skills Network

Regent Arcade House, 19–25 Argyll Street, London W1F 7LS
T: 020 7297 9000
F: 020 7297 9001
E: enquiries@lsneducation.org.uk
www.lsneducation.org.uk
LSN is an independent not-for-profit organisation committed to making a difference to learning and skills.

Learning for Life

2 Rickett Street, London SW6 1RU
T: 020 7385 8765
F: 020 7385 9154
E: info@learningforlifeuk.org
www.learningforlifeuk.org
Director: Ujwala Samant
Learning for Life assists and relieves needy persons and their dependants who are employed or have been employed in the motor, agricultural engineering and cycle and allied trades and industries.
Employees: 3
Volunteers: 30

Learning from Experience Trust

Goldsmiths College, Deptford Town Hall, New Cross Road, London SE14 6AF
T: 020 7919 7739
F: 020 7919 7762
E: su@gold.ac.uk
www.learningexperience.org.uk
Aims to advance education by promoting research into, and developing the concept of, experiential learning and its assessment, and encouraging its recognition and use in education, training, industry, commerce and the public service.
Employees: 5

Learning Plus Uk

1st Floor, Kings Lodge, 194 Kings Road, Reading, Berkshire RG1 4NH
T: 0118 956 8408
E: donna.roberts@learningplusuk.org
www.learningplusuk.org
Office Manager: Donna Roberts
Employees: 6

Learning South West

Bishops Hull House, Bishops Hull, Taunton, Somerset TA1 5EP
T: 01823 335491
F: 01823 323388
E: phil_barker@learning-southwest.org.uk
www.learning-southwest.org.uk
Chief Executive and Company Secretary: Paula Jones
The charity's objectives are to advance education of young persons and adults by: promoting excellence in the delivery of

learning and skills; providing advice, training and the provision of resources to providers of learning and skills; and researching and disseminating good practice.
Employees: 31

Learning Through Landscapes

The Studio, Castle Hill, c/o The Castle, Winchester, Hampshire SO23 8UL
T: 01962 846258
E: enquiries@ltl.org.uk
www.ltl.org.uk
Executive Director: Juno Hollyhock
Learning through Landscapes is the UK charity dedicated to enhancing outdoor learning and play for children. Our vision is that every child benefits from stimulating outdoor learning and play in their education. We aim to enable children to connect with nature, be more active, be more engaged with their learning, develop their social skills and have fun!
Employees: 20
Volunteers: 8
Regional offices: 4

Leeds Church Institute

E: haydn@leedschurchinstitute.org

Legal Action Group

242 Pentonville Road, London N1 9UN
T: 020 7833 2931
F: 020 7837 6094
E: lag@lag.org.uk
www.lag.org.uk
Director: Steve Hynes
LAG is a national, independent charity that aims to promote equal access to justice for all members of society who are socially, economically or otherwise disadvantaged. To this end, it seeks to improve law and practice, the administration of justice and legal services through campaigning as well as publishing legal books, its monthly magazine Legal Action and providing training for solicitors, barristers and legal advisers.
Employees: 9
Volunteers: 2

Legislation Monitoring Service for Charities, Voluntary Organisations and their Advisers

Church House, Great Smith Street, London SW1P 3AZ
T: 020 7222 1265
E: info@lmsconline.org
www.charitylaw.info

LMSC's principal objective is monitoring and disseminating information about legislative and policy developments in the UK and Europe likely to have an impact on charities.

Leicestershire Centre for Integrated Living

E: stephen.cooper@lcil.org.uk

Leo Baeck College

The Sternberg Centre, 80 East End Road, London N3 2SY
T: 020 8349 5600
E: info@lbc.ac.uk
www.lbc.ac.uk
Principal: Rabbi Dr Deborah Kahn-Harris
Established in 1956, LBC trains rabbis and educators for Jewish congregations, communities and schools in the UK, Europe and worldwide with over 250 graduates; promotes the study of Judaism in a spirit of reverence for Jewish tradition; instills the love of learning in the Jewish community by raising the level of knowledge. Resources include Judaica and research library.
Employees: 13
Volunteers: 2

Leo Trust

Boldshaves Oast, Woodchurch, Ashford, Kent TN26 3RA
T: 01233 860039
F: 01233 860060
E: leotrust@btconnect.com
www.leotrust.com
Chief Executive: Joe Graham
The Leo Trust is a residential care home for adults with learning difficulties, which seeks to promote the relief, welfare and preservation of health of the residents and to provide opportunities to develop them into productive members of the community.
Employees: 32
Volunteers: 1

Leonard Cheshire

66 South Lambeth Road, London SW8 1RL
T: 020 3242 0200
F: 020 7802 8250
E: info@lcdisability.org
www.leonard-cheshire.org
Aims to work with disabled people and their carers throughout the UK and the world by providing the environment and services necessary for each individual's physical and mental wellbeing.
Employees: 8000
Volunteers: 6000
Regional offices: 10

Lepra

28 Middleborough, Colchester CO1 1TG
T: 01206 216700
E: lepra@lepra.org.uk
www.lepra.org.uk
Chief Executive: Sarah Nancollas
Lepra is fighting diseases of poverty by working towards our vision of a world in which the poorest and most marginalised people have equitable access to health and an improved quality of life.
Employees: 60
Volunteers: 3
Regional offices: 1
Income: £5,375,000 (2011-12)

Lesbian and Gay Christian Movement

Oxford House, Derbyshire Street, London E2 6HG
T: 020 7739 1249 (also fax)
E: lgcm@lgcm.org.uk
www.lgcm.org.uk
Chief Executive: Rev Sharon Ferguson
We aim to encourage fellowship, friendship and support among individual lesbian and gay Christians and to help the whole church re-examine its understanding of human sexuality and to challenge homophobia.
Employees: 2
Volunteers: 10

Let's Face It Support Network for the Facially Disfigured

72 Victoria Avenue, Westgate-on-Sea, Kent CT8 8BH
T: 01843 833724
E: chrisletsfaceit@aol.com
www.lets-face-it.org.uk
Founder/Chief Executive: Christine Piff
Aims to provide counselling, advice and support to patients with facial disfigurement, however caused, and their families, by meetings, letter writing, telephone contact and hospital visits. This includes head and neck cancer patients.
Employees: 1
Volunteers: 40
Regional offices: 8
Income: £30,000 (2012-13)

Leukaemia Care

1 Birch Court, Blackpole East, Worcestershire WR3 8SG
T: 01905 755977
F: 01905 755166
E: care@leukaemia.org.uk
www.leukaemiacare.org.uk

Provides support, information and assistance to people affected by leukaemia or allied blood disorders.
Employees: 8
Volunteers: 125

Leukaemia Research Fund

43 Great Ormond Street, London WC1N 3JJ
T: 020 7405 0101
E: info@lrf.org.uk
www.lrf.org.uk
Works to defeat the leukaemias and related blood diseases (lymphomas, myeloma, myelodysplasia, myeloproliferative disorders, aplastic anaemia).

Lewy Body Society

Hudson House, 8 Albany Street, Edinburgh EH1 3QB
T: 0131 473 2385
E: info@lewybody.org
www.lewybody.org
CEO: Jacqueline Cannon
The only charity in Europe dedicated to Lewy body disease, which is the second most common cause of age-related dementia. The Society's mission is to support research into and raise awareness of this terrible neurogenerative disease.
Volunteers: 10
Regional offices: 2

Liberal Judaism

The Montagu Centre, 21 Maple Street
E: shelley@liberaljudaism.org
Operations Director: Shelley Shocolinsky-Dwyer

Liberty

21 Tabard Street, London SE1 4LA
T: 020 7403 3888
Helpline: 0845 123 2307
E: webmaster@liberty-human-rights.org.uk
www.liberty-human-rights.org.uk
Liberty is also known as the National Council for Civil Liberties. Founded in 1934, we are a cross-party, non-party membership organisation at the heart of the movement for fundamental rights and freedoms in England and Wales. We promote the values of individual human dignity, equal treatment and fairness as the foundations of a democratic society.

Library Campaign

13 Shrublands Close, Chelmsford CM2 6LR
T: 01273 887321
E: librarycam@aol.com

Supports friends and user groups of pubicly funded libraries to advocate and lobby for library provision support.

LIFE

LIFE House, Newbold Terrace,
Leamington Spa,
Warwickshire CV32 4EA
T: 01926 421587
F: 01926 336497
E: jo@lifecharity.org.uk
www.lifecharity.org.uk
Chief Executive: Martin Foley
LIFE is a charity that offers an innovative approach to supporting women and families throughout pregnancy and beyond, including the provision of supported housing for pregnant women and mothers of young children.
Employees: 140
Volunteers: 380
Regional offices: 60

Life Academy

9 Chesham Road, Guildford,
Surrey GU1 3LS
T: 01483 301170
F: 01483 300981
E: info@life-academy.co.uk
www.life-academy.co.uk
Chief Executive: Stuart Royston
Life Academy is a charity that enables people to learn about managing the changes in their lives through life and retirement planning and financial education. We achieve this through: life and retirement planning courses; financial literacy education; qualifications in life and retirement planning; developing partnerships to reach individuals and creating innovative approaches for learning.
Employees: 5
Income: £374,000 (2010-11)

Life Education Centres

County House, 14 Hatton Garden,
London EC1N 8AT
T: 020 7831 9311
F: 020 7831 9939
E: jeani@lifeeducation.org.uk
www.lifeeducation.org.uk
National Director: Stephen Burgess
Helping children make healthy choices. Life Education??s main work is with primary schools and with parents, delivered through local Trusts, to
ensure that children develop the vital knowledge, skills and attitudes need to make

informed choices about health that will enhance and enrich their lives.
Employees: 7
Volunteers: 400
Regional offices: 40

Life For The World

Micklefield Christian Centre, Buckingham Drive, High Wycombe,
Buckinghamshire HP13 7YB
T: 01494 462008
Helpline: 0845 241 0973
E: wycombe@lftw.org
www.lftw.org
Chief Executive: John Lowton
Provides training, education, advice and consultancy for service providers (drug and alcohol misuse).
Employees: 5
Volunteers: 10
Regional offices: 2
Income: £47,760 (2012-13)

Life Opportunities Trust

Hempstead House, 1 Hempstead Road, Kings Langley, Hertfordshire WD4 8BJ
T: 01923 299770
F: 01923 299771
E: rverlander@lot-uk.org.uk
www.lot-uk.org.uk
Chief Executive: Ralph Verlander
Provides domiciliary and residential services for adults with learning disabilities.
Employees: 165
Volunteers: 14

Lifeline Community Projects

Lifeline House, Neville Road,
Dagenham RM8 3QS
T: 020 8597 2900
F: 020 8597 1990
E: andriasoteriou@lifelineprojects.co.uk
www.lifelineprojects.co.uk
PA to Chief Executive: Andria Soteriou
Employees: 155
Volunteers: 20

Lifeline International

25 Jellicoe Road N17 7BL
T: 020 8365 9815
F: 020 8805 9411
E: dupsy25@hotmail.com
www.lli.org.uk
Chair: Grace Labaran
Works to relieve the poverty and hardship of teenage mothers and their babies in Africa, whether through deprivation of family, skills, education, or otherwise, so that they may participate in a learning environment and/or life skills programme, enabling them to

integrate into their communities and gain employment.
Employees: 10
Volunteers: 3
Regional offices: 5

Lifeline Project Ltd

39–41 Thomas Street,
Manchester M4 1NA
E: fazackerley2@btinternet.com
www.lifeline.org.uk
The charity aims to relieve poverty, sickness and distress among those persons affected by addiction to drugs of any kind, and to educate the public on matters relating to drug misuse.
Employees: 460

Lifeworks Charity Ltd

E: joparsons@lifeworks-uk.org

Lightforce International

Christian Centre, Strudwick Drive,
Oldbrook, Milton Keynes,
Buckinghamshire MK6 2TG
T: 01908 553070
F: 01908 553077
E: grr@lightforce.org.uk
www.lightforce.org.uk
International Director: George Ridley
Aims to advance the Christian religion and to relieve people in any part of the world who are in condition of need, hardship and distress, in particular by deploying human and material resources.
Employees: 235
Volunteers: 15
Regional offices: 4

Lin Berwick Trust

Eastgate House, Upper East Street,
Sudbury, Suffolk CO10 1UB
T: 01787 372343
E: info@thelinberwicktrust.org.uk
Provides relief for physically disabled people, their families and carers, through the provision of holiday accommodation.
Employees: 3
Volunteers: 15

Linacre Centre for Healthcare Ethics

38 Circus Road, London NW8 9SE
T: 020 7806 4088
E: admin@linacre.org
www.linacre.org
Promotes understanding of the Catholic viewpoint on bioethical issues. The Centre's perspective is informed by Catholic moral teaching, but in defending such teaching it

seeks also to appeal to non-religious, philosophical reasoning to enable dialogue with those of no religious faith.

Ling Trust Ltd

13 East Stockwell Street,
Colchester CO1 1SS
T: 01206 769246
F: 01206 767287
www.lingtrust.org.uk
The Trust provides high-quality housing support, housing services and care to people with housing, support and care needs; provides educational and supported employment opportunities to people with disabilities; provides alternative day support to day centres; assists with self-directed support and care initiatives; brokers housing, support and care services for people with disabilities.

LINK Centre for Deafened People

19 Hartfield Road, Eastbourne, East Sussex BN21 2AR
T: 01323 638230
F: 01323 642968
E: enquiries@hearinglink.org
www.linkcentre.org
LINK provides intensive, residential rehabilitation programmes for deafened adults and their partners; a national network of deafened volunteer information officers; a national self-management programme for deafened adults; social support groups; groups for new cochlear implant users; training for professionals; research into the effects of acquired profound deafness.
Employees: 13
Volunteers: 60

Linkage Community Trust

Scremby Grange, Spilsby PE23 5RW
T: 01754 890339
F: 01754 890538
E: info@linkage.org.uk
www.linkage.org.uk
Works to advance the general education and social development of people with disabilities, to develop such skills as are necessary to enable such people to qualify for useful occupation and, where this is not possible, to provide long-term care facilities.

LionHeart

Surveyor Court, Westwood Way,
Coventry, West Midlands CV4 8BF
T: 0845 603 9057
F: 024 7647 4701
E: mcarter@lionheart.org.uk
www.lionheart.org.uk
Chief Executive: Mike Carter
LionHeart provides advice, information, counselling, befriending, financial help by

grant or loan, and help in kind to members of the Royal Institution of Chartered Surveyors (RICS) and their dependants who experience difficulties in their lives, including bereavement, unemployment, ill-health, accident or disability, separation of families or difficulties in retirement.
Employees: 11
Volunteers: 225

Lions Clubs International and British Isles and Ireland

257 Alcester Road South, Kings Heath, Birmingham B14 6DT
T: 0121 441 4544
F: 0121 441 4510
E: secretary@lions.org.uk
www.lionsmd105.org
Council Chairman: Martin Morgan
Lions Clubs International is the world's largest service club organisation. With 1.4 million members in 206 countries who work together through selfless, effective community service to answer the needs that challenge communities around the world.
Employees: 4
Volunteers: 17000
Regional offices: 13

Listening Books

12 Lant Street, London SE1 1QH
T: 020 7407 9417
E: info@listening-books.org.uk
www.listening-books.org.uk
Director: Bill Dee
Listening Books supplies an online and postal audiobook library service to anyone across the UK who struggles to read due to an illness, disability or learning difficulty. Members can choose from thousands of titles across a range of formats (MP3 CDs, internet streaming or downloads).
Employees: 9
Volunteers: 10+
Regional offices: 1

Little Hearts Matter

11 Greenfield Crescent, Edgbaston, Birmingham B15 3AU
T: 0121 455 8982
F: 0121 455 8983
E: info@lhm.org.uk
www.lhm.org.uk
The charity promotes the relief and welfare of persons affected by single ventricle cardiac disease and advances the education of the medical profession and the general public on

the subject of single ventricle cardiac disease and its implications for the family.
Employees: 3
Volunteers: 12

Little Sisters of the Poor

St Peter's Residence, 2A Meadow Road, South Lambeth, London SW8 1QH
T: 020 7735 0788
E: lsplondonstpeter@aol.com
Cares for elderly people of modest means of all denominations or those of none.

Livability

50 Scrutton Street, London EC2A 4XQ
T: 020 7452 2000
F: 020 7452 2001
E: info@livability.org.uk
www.livability.org.uk
Chief Executive: Dave Webber
Livability offers a wide range of innovative services that support and enable disabled people throughout their lives and provides community organisations with the resources, advice and confidence to bring life to local neighbourhoods. Livability was formed in 2007 by the merger of John Grooms and the Shaftesbury Society.
Employees: 2000

Live Music Now!

Mill House, Newsham Bridge, Malton, North Yorkshire YO17 6TZ
T: 01653 668551
E: keisha@macfarlane.org.uk
www.livemusicnow.org
Provides performance opportunities for talented young professional musicians under the age of 27 years and brings the experience of live music back into everyday life.

Living Paintings

Unit 8, Kingsclere Park, Kingsclere, Newbury, Berkshire RG20 4SW
T: 01635 299771 (also fax)
E: camilla@livingpaintings.org
www.livingpaintings.org
Charity Director: Camilla Oldland
Living Paintings helps blind and partially sighted people feel visual images. We make special versions of pictures with raised surfaces that come to life when fingers feel them. Sound recordings direct the fingers, telling the stories of the pictures and describing their features. For children and adults the senses of touch and hearing combine to make up for the missing sense of sight.
Employees: 7
Volunteers: 120

Living Streets

31–33 Bondway, London SW8 1SJ
T: 020 7820 1010
F: 020 7820 8208
E: info@livingstreets.org.uk
www.livingstreets.org.uk
Aims to improve conditions for walking journeys and for safe, convenient and environment friendly ways for people on foot. Represents the interests of walkers (particularly in urban areas) to central and local government and the media.
Employees: 12
Volunteers: 150
Regional offices: 76

Local Investment Fund

Seventh Floor, Ibex House, 42–47 Minories, London EC3N 1DY
T: 020 7680 1028
E: information@lif.org.uk
www.lif.org.uk
LIF is dedicated to providing loan finance to economically viable, community-based voluntary organisations that are run as not-for-profit enterprises. It bridges the gap between grant dependency and mainstream banking finance.

Local Trust

Unit 5, Angel Gate, 320–326 City Road, London EC1V 2PT
T: 020 7812 1598
E: info@localtrust.org.uk
www.localtrust.org.uk
Funding Administrator: Michael Williams
Employees: 11

Localgiving.com Ltd

Localgiving.com, 6th Floor, 233 High Holborn, London WC1V 7DN
T: 0300 111 2340
E: help@localgiving.com
www.localgiving.com
Founder & CEO: Marcelle Speller
Localgiving.com is a non-profit internet platform for small charities and local community groups founded by Marcelle Speller, OBE. We have thousands of charities online and we've helped them to raise millions of pounds since our commercial launch in December 2011. We enable unregistered charities and groups to benefit from Gift Aid and boost donations by 25%.
Employees: 14
Volunteers: 0
Regional offices: 1

Locality

33 Corsham Street, London N1 6DL
T: 0845 458 8336
E: info@locality.org.uk
www.locality.org.uk
Locality is the leading nationwide network of settlements, development trusts, social action centres and community enterprises.

Lodge Trust

The Lodge, Main Street, Market Overton, Oakham Leicestershire LE15 7PL
T: 01572 767234
E: admin@lodgetrust.org.uk
www.lodgetrust.org.uk
Provides individual support for adults with learning disabilities in Christian homes and working environments.

London Funders

314 - 320 Grays Inn Road, London WC1X 8DP
T: 020 7255 4488
E: info@londonfunders.org.uk
www.londonfunders.org.uk
Director: David Warner
London Funders fulfils its mission by providing a unique space where funders can discuss issues affecting London and the work that they do, learn from each other, share experience and knowledge, be briefed on changes in public policy and the implications for London, and, increasingly look at how they can work better together to improve the lives of Londoners.
Employees: 2

London Gypsy and Traveller Unit

E: srowles@lgtu.org.uk

Long-Term Conditions Alliance

202 Hatton Square, 16 Baldwins Gardens, London EC1N 7RJ
T: 020 7813 3637
F: 020 7813 3640
E: thelongtrail@ltca.org.uk
www.ltca.org.uk
Chief Executive: David Pink
Umbrella body of over 100 patient groups and professional organisations working to improve the lives of people with long-term conditions.
Employees: 5

Look National Office

Queen Alexandra College, 49 Court Oak Road, Harborne, Birmingham B17 9TG
T: 0121 428 5038
E: information@look-uk.org
www.look-uk.org
CEO: Aliona Laker
Provides practical help, support and information to families with visually impaired children. Promotes improved services nationally.
Employees: 4
Volunteers: 2

Love Walk

Pier Street, Isle of Dogs, London E14 3HP
T: 020 7515 5901
E: info@mudchute.org
Provides a high standard of care for adults with physical disabilities, encouraging maximum independence and autonomy.

Lubavitch Youth

107–115 Stamford Hill, London N16 5RP
T: 020 8800 0022
F: 020 8809 7324
E: info@lubavitchuk.com
www.lubavitchuk.com
Works to further the needs of the Jewish ethnic minority, in the widest possible context.
Volunteers: 200
Regional offices: 18

Lupus Patients Understanding and Support (LUPUS)

Flat 28, Odette Court, Station Road, Borehamwood, Hertfordshire WD6 1GQ
E: roz@lupus-support.org.uk
www.lupus-support.org.uk
Director: Rosalind Share
A non-profit organisation providing free information and free online psychological support for individuals affected by SLE, lupus variant conditions and the antiphospholipid antibody (Hughes) syndrome. The Lupus Counselling Service is maintained by qualified psychotherapists/counsellors. We offer online psychological support services and research into the unmet needs of individuals affected by lupus. We also offer information and support to carers and families, as well as doctors, nurses and other health professionals.
Employees: 0
Volunteers: 3
Regional offices: 0

LUPUS UK

St James House, Eastern Road, Romford,
Essex RM1 3NH
T: 01708 731251
E: headoffice@lupusuk.org.uk
www.lupusuk.org.uk
Director: Chris Maker
Provides communication between patients;
educates patients, the general public and the
medical profession about the symptoms and
problems of systemic lupus erythematosus;
raises funds and provides practical help and
lupus research.
Employees: 7
Volunteers: 250

Lutheran Council of Great Britain

30 Thanet Street, London WC1H 9QH
T: 020 7554 2900
E: enquiries@lutheran.org.uk
www.lutheran.org.uk
General Secretary: James Laing
Established in 1948, the Lutheran Council is a
communion of churches that have come
together to express their shared Lutheran
heritage and identity through common work
in Britain, enriched by their cultural and
linguistic diversity.
Employees: 20

Lyme Disease Action

Sand, Sidbury, Sidmouth,
Devon EX10 0QN
E: lda@lymediseaseaction.org.uk
www.lymediseaseaction.org.uk
Chairman: Stella Huyshe-Shires
Lyme Disease Action was established for the
relief of persons suffering from Lyme disease,
other borrelioses and associated diseases by
raising awareness of the public at large and
scientific and medical education and
research in topics related to Lyme disease,
other borrelioses and associated diseases.
Volunteers: 8
Income: £17,300 (2012-13)

Lyme Trust

39 London Road, Newcastle,
Staffordshire ST5 1LN
T: 01782 634725
F: 01782 634510
E: thelymetrust@tiscali.co.uk
www.thelymetrust.ik.com
The charity provides accommodation for
people with mild to moderate mental health
difficulties and assists them into a successful
return to life in the community.
Employees: 18
Volunteers: 1

Lymphoedema Support Network

St Luke's Crypt, Sydney Street,
London SW3 6NH
T: 020 7351 0990
Helpline: 020 7351 4480
F: 020 7349 9809
E: adminlsn@lymphoedema.freeserve.
co.uk
www.lymphoedema.org/lsn
Chair: Anita Wallace
Provides information and support to people
with lymphoedema and promotes better
awareness of lymphoedema as a major
health condition to local health authorities,
healthcare professionals and politicians.
Employees: 2
Volunteers: 15

Lymphoma Association

PO Box 386, Aylesbury,
Buckinghamshire HP20 2GA
T: 01296 619400
Helpline: 0808 808 5555
F: 01296 619415
E: j.coldwell@lymphomas.org.uk
www.lymphomas.org.uk
Chief Executive: Sally Penrose
The Lymphoma Association is the only
specialist UK charity that provides accurate
medical information and support to
lymphatic cancer patients, their families,
friends and carers. Support services include a
freephone helpline, a buddy scheme that
puts people in touch with others who have
been through a similar experience of
lymphoma, a network of support groups
throughout the UK, free literature and an
interactive website with a chatroom and
forum.
Employees: 23

Macfarlane Trust

Alliance House, 12 Caxton Street,
London SW1H 0QS
T: 020 7233 0057
F: 020 7233 0839
E: macfarlane@macfarlane.org.uk
Works to meet the needs of those people
with haemophilia who became infected with
HIV through treatment with contaminated
blood products in the UK, and their
dependants; and dependants of those who
have died.
Employees: 5
Volunteers: 10

MacIntyre Care

602 South Seventh Street, Milton
Keynes MK9 2JA
T: 01908 230100
F: 01908 694452
E: bill.mumford@macintyrecharity.org
www.macintyrecharity.org
MacIntyre is a national charity that provides
learning, support and care for more than 700
children and adults with learning disabilities,
at more than 120 MacIntyre services across
the UK.
Employees: 1320
Volunteers: 50

Macmillan Cancer Support

89 Albert Embankment,
London SE1 7UQ
T: 020 7840 4648
F: 020 7840 7841
E: info@macmillan.org.uk
www.macmillan.org.uk
More people are being diagnosed earlier and
living with cancer for longer. Cancer is
becoming a part of more people's daily lives.
Cancer has an impact on every aspect of
your life – from your emotions to your
finances. And as you learn to cope with the
shock and distress of diagnosis and the
changes cancer can bring, you need a range
of support – and so do your family and
friends. That's where Macmillan comes in.
Volunteers: 70000

Macular Disease Society

PO Box 1870, Andover,
Hampshire SP10 9AD
T: 01264 350551
Helpline: 0845 241 2041
F: 01264 350558
E: info@maculardisease.org
www.maculardisease.org
Chief Executive: Helen Jackman
Macular disease is the UK's most common
cause of sight loss. The Macular Disease
Society is the only UK charity supporting
people with macular disease and seeking a
cure. We provide information and support to
anyone affected by macular disease and
professionals working with people with the
condition. We have over 15,000 members
and support many more through our
national network of local support groups and
our telephone helpline, counselling,
advocacy and low vision services.
Employees: 23
Volunteers: 1000

Magdi Yacoub Institute

Heart Science Centre, Harefield,
Middlesex UB9 6JH
T: 01895 828952
F: 01895 828954
E: preay@myi.ac
The Institute aims to improve the
understanding of important clinical cardiac
problems by combining a broad basis of
research at both clinical and fundamental
levels.
Employees: 3

Magistrates' Association

28 Fitzroy Square, London W1T 6DD
T: 020 7383 2672
F: 020 7383 4020
E: secretariat@magistrates-association.
org.uk
www.magistrates-association.org.uk
Promotes the sound administration of the
law.
Employees: 11
Volunteers: 30000

Maharishi Foundation

The Golden Dome, Woodley Park Road,
Skelmersdale, Lancashire WN8 6UQ
T: 01695 557403
E: info@t-m.org.uk
Promotes the full development of the
individual, using scientifically verified
programmes that have been shown to
unfold the full potential of the mind, create
better health, improve social behaviour and
relationships and establish a more peaceful
world.

Maidstone Community Support Centre

E: matt@mcsc.org.uk

Make-A-Wish Foundation UK

329–331 London Road, Camberley,
Surrey GU15 3HQ
T: 01276 24127
F: 01276 683727
E: info@make-a-wish.org.uk
www.make-a-wish.org.uk
Works to grant the wishes of children living
with life-threatening illnesses.
Employees: 48
Volunteers: 750
Regional offices: 16

Making Space

46 Allen Street, Warrington,
Cheshire WA2 7JB
T: 01925 571680
E: business.support@makingspace.co.uk
www.makingspace.co.uk
Senior Administrator: Sarah Thomas
Employees: 512
Volunteers: 116

Mammal Society

2b Inworth Street, London SW11 3EP
T: 020 7350 2200
F: 020 7350 2211
E: enquiries@mammal.org.uk
www.mammal.org.uk
The Society works to protect British
mammals, halt the decline of threatened
species, and advise on all issues affecting
British mammals. We study mammals,
identify the problems they face and promote
conservation and other policies based on
sound science.
Employees: 4
Volunteers: 20
Regional offices: 1

Management Strategies for Africa

Orion House, 104/106 Cranbrook Road,
Ilford, Essex IG1 4LZ
T: 020 8636 9975
F: 020 4636 9994
E: info@msforafrica.org
www.msforafrica.org
Chairman/Chief Executive Officer: Marc
A. Okunnu, Sr.
Management Strategies for Africa (MSA) is a
charitable social enterprise, a not-for-profit
organisation. This means that social service
and the desire to contribute to the
development of Africa are the driving forces
behind the organisation. MSA is concerned
with organisational effectiveness and
performance improvement in relation to
meeting SRH goals, within the context of
health sector-wide approaches.
Employees: 2
Income: £39,311 (2011-12)

Mankind

PO Box 124, Newhaven, East
Sussex BN9 9TQ
T: 01273 510447
E: admin@mankindcounselling.org.uk
www.mankindcounselling.org.uk
CEO: Martyn Sullivan
Mankind offers counselling services to men
over the age of 18 who are suffering the
continuing effects of childhood sexual abuse
and/or adult sexual assault at any time in
their lives. Counselling services are also

offered to partners, family and those affected
by sexual violence towards males.
Employees: 5
Volunteers: 15
Regional offices: 1

Marfan Association UK

Rochester House, 5 Aldershot Road, Fleet,
Hampshire GU51 3NG
T: 01252 810472
F: 01252 810473
E: contactus@marfan-association.org.uk
www.marfan-association.org.uk
Chairman/Support Coordinator: Diane
Rust
Provides updated Marfan information to
patients, their families and the medical
profession; provides means for patients and
relatives to share their experience, to support
one another, and to improve medical care;
supports and fosters research.
Employees: 5
Volunteers: 3
Regional offices: 1

Marie Curie Cancer Care

Camelford House, 87–89 Albert
Embankment, London SE1 7TP
T: 020 7599 7777
F: 020 7599 7788
E: info@mariecurie.org.uk
www.mariecurie.org.uk
Employing more than 2,700 nurses, doctors
and other healthcare professionals, we
provide care to around 25,000 people with
cancer every year, along with support for
their families.
Employees: 3849
Volunteers: 14102

Marie Stopes International

153–157 Cleveland Street,
London W1T 6QW
T: 020 7574 7400
E: services@mariestopes.org.uk
www.mariestopes.org.uk
Provides reproductive healthcare/family
planning services and information, to enable
individuals all over the world to have children
by choice, not chance. MSI's goal is the
prevention of unwanted births.

Marine Conservation Society

Unit 3, Wolf Business Park, Alton Road,
Ross-on-Wye, Herefordshire HR9 5NB
T: 01989 566017
E: info@mcsuk.org
www.mcsuk.org
Chief Executive: Sam Fanshawe

UK charity is dedicated to the protection of the marine environment and its wildlife.

Employees: 50
Regional offices: 1

Marine Society and Sea Cadets

202 Lambeth Road, London SE1 7JW
T: 0117 953 1991
E: southwest-area@sea-cadets.org
www.sea-cadets.org

The Marine Society and Sea Cadets (MSSC), a charity formed in 2004 from a merger of The Marine Society and the Sea Cadet Association, exists to offer seafarers and prospective seafarers a range of services to enhance their wellbeing and lifestyle.

Employees: 200
Volunteers: 9000
Regional offices: 6

Marine Stewardship Council

3rd Floor, Mountbarrow House, 6–20 Elizabeth Street, London SW1W 9RB
T: 020 7811 3300
F: 020 7811 3301
E: info@msc.org
www.msc.org

Conserves marine fish populations and the ocean environment on which they depend, and promotes to the public the benefit of effective management of marine fisheries.

Employees: 12
Volunteers: 1

Mark Hall and Netteswell Community Association

E: moothouseca@moothouse.plus.com

Maroa Christian Counselling International

37 Clothworkers Road, Plumstead, London SE18 2PD
T: 020 8316 7074 (also fax)
Helpline: 07719 229897
E: maroacounselint@aol.com
www.maroa.org.uk
Director: Rebecca Adeosun

Our aim is to enable those we serve to live their lives to the fullest through counselling.

Volunteers: 2
Regional offices: 1

Marriage Care

Bishops Park House, 25-29 Fulham High Street, London SW6 3JH
T: 020 7371 1341
Helpline: 0800 389 3801
E: info@marriagecare.org.uk
www.marriagecare.org.uk
Chief Executive: Mark Molden

Marriage Care is a faith based national charity with over 50 centres across England and Wales. Its key activities are to provide relationship counselling and marriage preparation services. Last year, the charity supported almost 4500 people across just under 100 locations who sought help with relationship issues or relationships education.

Employees: 20
Volunteers: 750
Regional offices: 53

Mary Frances Trust

E: patrickwolter@maryfrancestrust.org.uk

Mary Ward Centre

42 Queen Square, London WC1N 3AQ
T: 020 7269 6061
E: mwenquiries@marywardcentre.ac.uk
www.marywardcentre.ac.uk

Aims to work for the advancement of public education and the promotion of social service for the benefit of the community.

Maternity Action

E: katiewood@maternityaction.org.uk

Mathematics in Education and Industry

E: sue.owen@mei.org.uk

Matthew Trust

PO Box 604, London SW6 3AG
T: 020 7736 5976
E: amt@matthewtrust.org
www.matthewtrust.org

The Matthew Trust is a small registered charity providing last-stop support and care for people aged eight years old and upwards, living in all communities of our society throughout the UK, who have a mental health problem of any kind.

MB Reckitt Trust

1 Croftlands, Westbourne Road, Lancaster, Lancashire LA1 5DB
www.mbreckitttrust.org
Chair: Alyson Peberdy

The aim of the Trust is to promote research and activities that evaluate and develop social

structures, processes and attitudes in order to release energies for change, from the perspective of Christianity and the other principal faith traditions.

ME Association

7 Apollo Office Court, Radclive Road, Gawcott, Buckinghamshire MK18 4DF
T: 01280 818968
Helpline: 0844 576 5326
E: meconnect@meassociation.org.uk
www.meassociation.org.uk
Chairman: Neil Riley

We are a campaigning national charity that provides information and support to an estimated 240,000 people in the UK who have ME/chronic fatigue syndrome, their families and carers. This is provided through a quarterly magazine, literature, education and training. We also run ME Connect, the UK's premier helpline for people with ME/CFS, and fund biomedical research.

Employees: 4
Volunteers: 35
Income: £496,962 (2011-12)

Medact

The Grayston Centre, 28 Charles Square, London N1 6HT
T: 020 7324 4739
E: info@medact.org
www.medact.org
Chair of the Trustees: David McCoy

Medact is an organisation of health professionals undertaking education, research and advocacy on major threats to global health, such as poverty, conflict and environmental change.

Employees: 2
Volunteers: 4

Media Trust

4th Floor, Block A, Centre House, Wood Lane, London W12 7SB
T: 020 7871 5600
F: 020 7871 5601
E: jades@mediatrust.org
www.mediatrust.org
CEO: Caroline Diehl

Media Trust works in partnership with the media industry to build effective voluntary and community sector communications. Its vision is of a society in which the voluntary and community sector is widely visible and celebrated for what it achieves; the public can easily access the voluntary and community sector; and voluntary organisations can access the resources, skills and contacts they need to communicate effectively with target audiences via a wide range of media and communication.

Employees: 70
Volunteers: 20
Regional offices: 1

Mediation Works Milton Keynes

Acorn House, 379 Midsummer
Boulevard, Central Milton Keynes,
Buckinghamshire MK9 3HP
T: 01908 200828
F: 01908 200842
E: mkcms@mkcommediation.org.uk
www.mediationworksmk.org.uk
**The Chairman: Milton Keynes
Community Mediation Service Ltd.**
We operate in and around Milton Keynes, our main aim is to resolve conflict amicably and to open communication between all disputants. Our second aim is to recruit and train volunteers to CROCNAC and Community Legal Service QM standards in Community Mediation and provide support and ongoing training to our mediators.
Employees: 6
Volunteers: 35
Regional offices: 1
Income: £80,000 (2012-13)

MediaWise Trust

University of the West of England, Canon
Kitson, Oldbury Court Road, Bristol,
Avon BS16 2JP
T: 0117 939 9333
F: 0117 902 9916
E: info@mediawise.org.uk
www.mediawise.org.uk
Director: Mike Jempson
Provides information, advice, research and training on media ethics issues.
Employees: 2

Medical Council on Alcohol

5 St Andrews Place, London NW1 4LB
T: 020 7487 4445
F: 020 7935 4479
E: info@medicouncilalcol.demon.co.uk
www.medicouncilalcol.demon.co.uk
Aims to improve medical understanding of alcohol-related problems.
Employees: 5
Volunteers: 55
Regional offices: 33

Medical Engineering Resource Unit

Unit 2 Eclipse Estate, 30 West Hill, Epsom,
Surrey KT19 8JD
T: 01372 725203
F: 01372 743159
E: info@meru.org.uk
www.meru.org.uk
Chief Executive: Jonathan Powell
Provides individual aids and services for disabled children and young adults that are not available commercially. Carries out research and development of devices and equipment that may have a more widespread use for the same disabled group.
Employees: 11
Volunteers: 20

Medical Foundation for HIV & Sexual Health (MEDFASH)

BMA House, Tavistock Square,
London WC1H 9JP
T: 020 7383 6345
E: enquiries@medfash.bma.org.uk
www.medfash.org.uk
Chief Executive: Ruth Lowbury
Promotes excellence in the prevention and management of HIV and other sexually transmitted infections.
Employees: 2

Medical Foundation for the Care of Victims of Torture

111 Isledon Road, Finsbury Park,
London N7 7JW
T: 020 7697 7777
F: 020 7697 7799
E: scarruth@torturecare.org.uk
www.torturecare.org.uk
Chief Executive: Simon Carruth
Provides adult and child survivors of torture and organised violence living in the UK with medical, psychotherapeutic and social care and practical assistance; documents evidence of torture; provides training for health and social care professionals and others who work with torture survivors; educates the public and decision-makers about torture and its consequences; campaigns to improve the law and practice in the UK regarding the treatment of survivors in the asylum system.
Employees: 171
Volunteers: 250
Regional offices: 4

Medical Women's Federation

Entrance B, Tavistock House North,
Tavistock Square, London WC1H 9HX
T: 020 7387 7765
E: admin.mwf@btconnect.com
www.medicalwomensfederation.co.uk

The MWF promotes the personal and professional development of women in medicine and women's health issues.

Medway Youth Trust

Connexions, 205–217 New Road,
Chatham, Kent ME4 4QA
T: 01634 334343
F: 01634 335555
E: john.paton@mytconnexions.org.uk
www.medwayyouthtrust.org
Chief Executive: Graham Clewes
We deliver the Connexions service in Medway to provide information and guidance to young people. Whilst our focus is careers we look to provide a much wider service to include delivery of the Prince's Trust progamme, National Citizenship Service amongst others.
Employees: 49
Volunteers: 9
Regional offices: 1
Income: £1,900,000 (2011-12)

Men's Health Forum

Tavistock House, Tavistock Square,
London WC1H 9HR
T: 020 7388 4449
F: 020 7388 4477
E: office@menshealthforum.org.uk
www.menshealthforum.org.uk
Chief Executive: Peter Baker
The Men's Health Forum works to improve the health of men and men's health services.
Employees: 13

Mencap

123 Golden Lane, London EC1Y 0RT
T: 020 7454 0454
Helpline: 0808 808 1111
F: 020 7696 5548
E: help@mencap.org.uk
www.mencap.org.uk
Mencap is the leading charity working with people with a learning disability in England, Wales and Northern Ireland. We campaign to ensure that people with a learning disability have the best possible opportunities to live as full citizens and aim to influence new legislation. We can support people with a learning disability to get a job, take a college course or find a place of their own to live in.
Employees: 5500
Volunteers: 20000
Regional offices: 15

Menerva Educational Trust

Smiths Wood Studios, 62 Endcliffe Hall Avenue, Sheffield S10 3EL
T: 0114 266 4449
E: shelaghmarston@btinternet.com
The trust aims to advance society's knowledge of women's achievements/potential in all areas of life; to educate and inform society about the opportunities available to women in public life and to highlight the means of preparing girls for leading roles in all areas of responsibility and decision-making.

Meniere's Society

The Rookery, Surrey Hills Business Park, Wotton, Dorking, Surrey RH5 6QT
T: 01306 876883
Helpline: 0845 120 2975
E: info@menieres.org.uk
www.menieres.org.uk
Director: Natasha Harrington-Benton
The Meniere's Society is the only registered charity in the UK dedicated solely to supporting people with vestibular (inner ear) disorders causing dizziness and imbalance. The Meniere's Society is a national organisation offering information and support to those affected by vestibular conditions and those who care for them; as well as health professionals and the general public. Research also funded.
Employees: 2
Volunteers: 12

Meningitis Now

Fern House, Bath Road, Stroud, Gloucestershire GL5 3TJ
T: 01453 768000
Helpline: 0808 801 0388
F: 01453 768001
E: joannec@meningitisnow.org
www.meningitisnow.org
Chief Executive: Sue Davie
Meningitis Now is a charity with almost 30 years' experience. Formed in 2013 by bringing together Meningitis UK and Meningitis Trust, founders of the meningitis movement in the UK. We exist to save lives and rebuild futures by funding research, raising awareness and providing support. Our vision is a future where no one in the UK loses their life to meningitis and everyone affected gets the support they need to rebuild their lives.
Employees: 66
Volunteers: 1460
Income: £3,196,946 (2011-12)

Meningitis Research Foundation

Midland Way, Thornbury, Bristol BS35 2BS
T: 01454 281811
Helpline: 0808 800 3344
E: info@meningitis.org
www.meningitis.org
Chief Executive: Christopher Head
Meningitis Research Foundation is a national registered charity whose vision is a world free from meningitis and septicaemia. The charity funds research to prevent meningitis and septicaemia, and to improve survival rates and outcomes. The Foundation promotes education and awareness to reduce death and disability, and gives support to people affected.
Employees: 50
Volunteers: 30
Regional offices: 4
Income: £1,800,000 (2010-11)

Meningitis UK

25 Cleeve Wood Road, Downend, Bristol BS16 2SF
T: 0117 373 7373
F: 0117 373 7374
E: information@meningitisuk.org
www.meningitisuk.org
Chief Executive: Steve Dayman
Meningitis UK's sole focus is to eradicate meningitis. Meningitis is a terrifying disease, which can kill in less than four hours and tragically is most prevalent in children. We feel that focusing on prevention, as opposed to treatment, is the only way to successfully eradicate the disease and prevent its devastating consequences. We are confident that with enough support we will be able to put a stop to the heartache and devastation it causes.
Employees: 12
Volunteers: 5

Mental Health Foundation

1st Floor, Colechurch House, 1 London Bridge Walk, London SE1 2SX
T: 020 7803 1100
F: 020 7803 1111
E: info@mhf.org.uk
www.mentalhealth.org.uk
CEO: Jenny Edwards CBE
The Foundation provides information, carries out research, campaigns and works to improve services for anyone affected by mental health problems. We aim to help people survive, recover from and prevent mental health problems by learning what makes and keeps people mentally well; communicating our findings widely; turning

our research into practical solutions that make a difference to people's lives.
Employees: 50
Volunteers: 10
Regional offices: 4

Mental Health Matters

Avalon House, St Catherine's Court, Sunderland Enterprise Park, Sunderland, Tyne and Wear SR5 3XJ
T: 0191 510 3399
F: 0191 487 7945
E: ghiscox@mentalhealthmatters.co.uk
www.mentalhealthmatters.com
The principal aim of the charity is to act as a national organisation for all matters concerning mental health and mental illness, and to assist sufferers and carers of sufferers of mental health problems.
Employees: 200

Mental Health Providers Forum

c/o Mental Health Foundation, 9th Floor, Sea Containers House, 20 Upper Ground, London SE1 9QB
T: 020 7803 1107
F: 020 7803 1111
E: i.petit@mhpf.org.uk
www.mhpf.org.uk
Chief Executive: Judy Weleminsky
The Mental Health Providers Forum is a not-for-profit umbrella organisation that brings together voluntary sector service providers to improve services for people with mental health needs. We work to influence national and regional mental health strategies; improve the quality and accessibility of services in the community; and to increase opportunities for voluntary and community sector providers to delivery quality services.
Employees: 6

Mentor Foundation (International)

Unit 1, Elms Lodge Farm, Melton Road, Barrow upon Soar, Loughborough, Leicestershire LE12 8HX
T: 01509 221622
F: 01509 808111
E: mandy@mentorfoundation.org
www.mentorfoundation.org
Executive Director: Jeff Lee
The Mentor Foundation is an international non-government not-for-profit organisation with a focus on the prevention of drug misuse and the promotion of health and wellbeing of young people. Mentor seeks to identify, support and share information on

effective practice that will protect young people from the harm that drugs can cause.
Employees: 5
Volunteers: 1
Regional offices: 1

Mentoring and Befriending Foundation

Suite 1, 4th Floor, Building 3, Universal Square, Devonshire Street North, Ardwick M12 6JH
T: 03300 882877
E: info@mandbf.org
www.mandbf.org
Chief Executive: Steve Matthews
The Mentoring and Befriending Foundation (MBF) aims to increase the effectiveness and quality of mentoring and befriending as methods of enabling individuals to transform their lives and/or reach their full potential. MBF does this by providing training and resources, quality assurance, network membership, consultancy services and contract/project management for organisations and people interested in mentoring and befriending.
Employees: 22

Merchant Navy Welfare Board

30 Palmerston Road, Southampton, Hampshire SO14 1LL
T: 023 8033 7799
F: 023 8063 4444
E: enquiries@mnwb.org.uk
www.mnwb.org.uk
Chief Executive: David Parsons
The Board is the umbrella for those charities involved in the welfare of merchant seafarers, fishermen and their dependants visiting, or residing in, UK and Gibraltar. It manages 17 Port Welfare Committees and provides grants, training and support services for its constituent charities. It also advises and acts as a clearing house for seafarers and their families seeking assistance.
Employees: 6

Merlin

12th Floor, 207 Old Street, London EC1V 9NR
T: 020 7014 1600
F: 020 7014 1601
E: carolyn.miller@merlin.org.uk
www.merlin.org.uk
Chief Executive: Carolyn Miller
Merlin is the UK's leading international health charity. Undaunted and determined, Merlin saves lives. We deliver medical expertise to the toughest places and stay to help build lasting healthcare. Our mission is to end the needless loss of life in the poorest countries caused by a lack of effective healthcare. We help communities set up medical services for the long term including hospitals, clinics, surgeries and training nurses and other health workers.
Employees: 96 UK 168 international
Regional offices: 16 international
Income: £68,910,291 (2011-12)

Merseyside Jewish Community Care

Shifrin House, 433 Smithdown Road, Liverpool, Merseyside L15 3JL
T: 0151 733 2292
F: 0151 734 0212
E: info@mjccshifrin.co.uk
merseysidejewishcommunitycare.co.uk
Chief Executive: Lisa Dolan
MJCC offers caring welfare services to Jewish people facing a crisis or needing longer term support. We provide practical assistance to Jewish parents and children, older people, disabled people, the visually impaired, people coping with mental health problems, families on low income and people who have become isolated from the community. We offer daytime activities, kosher meals services, small crisis grants and links and referrals to other caring agencies.
Employees: 11
Volunteers: 263
Regional offices: 0

Metamorphic Association

67 Ritherdon Road, London SW17 8QE
T: 020 8672 5951
E: office@metamorphicassociation.net
www.metamorphicassociation.org.co.uk
Promotes good health and wellbeing through awareness, understanding and use of the metamorphic technique in the UK and internationally, and to uphold standards in practising and teaching the technique.

Metanoia Institute

13 North Common Road, Ealing, London W5 2QB
T: 020 8579 2505
F: 020 8832 3070
E: kate.fromant@metanoia.ac.uk
www.metanoia.ac.uk
Chief Executive: Sheila Owen-Jones
Metanoia Institute is a higher education institute and professional training establishment, specialising in the training of counsellors, psychotherapists, counselling psychologists, coaches and organisational development consultants. We also have a clinic, staffed by students in fully supervised supervision, offering lower cost counselling and psychotherapy services to the general public.
Employees: 80
Volunteers: 100
Income: £2,500,000 (2012-13)

MHA Care Group

Epworth House, 3 Stuart Street, Derby DE1 2EQ
T: 01332 296200
E: enquiries@mha.org.uk
www.mha.org.uk
Provides a range of accommodation and care services, based on Christian principles, which are open to all older people in need, whatever their beliefs.

Mid Sussex (South) Council for Voluntary Service

E: sue@msscvs.org.uk

Middlesbrough Voluntary Development Agency

St Mary's Centre, 82-90 Corporation Road, Middlesbrough TS1 2RW
T: 01642 249300
F: 01642 249600
E: general@mvdauk.org.uk
www.mvda.info
CEO: Dinah Lane
MVDA exists to support an effective and enterprising voluntary and community sector (VCS) that makes a difference to the lives of Middlesbrough people. It supports, promotes and develops local voluntary and community action by providing information, training and one-to-one support for VCOs; promoting and developing volunteering, through a brokerage service and support for good practice in volunteer management; representing the interests of the VCS and organising meetings and events to enable networking and collaboration.
Employees: 10
Volunteers: 5
Regional offices: 0
Income: £933,527 (2012-13)

Migraine Action Association

Floor 4, 27 East Street, Leicester, Leicestershire LE1 6NB
T: 0116 275 8317
E: info@migraine.org.uk
www.migraine.org.uk
Director: Joanna Hamilton-Colclough
Supports research and investigation into migraine, its causes, diagnosis, prevention

and treatment; disseminates information on progress in research and the latest treatments and offers reassurance, understanding, information and encouragement to migraine sufferers, their families and friends.

Employees: 4
Volunteers: 3
Regional offices: 1
Income: £250,000 (2011-12)

Migrant Helpline

The Rendezvous Building, Freight Service Approach Road, Eastern Docks, Dover, Kent CT16 1JA
T: 01304 203977
F: 01304 203995
E: dover@migranthelpline.org
www.migranthelpline.org.uk
Provides relief for asylum seekers, refugees and migrants who are in distress.
Employees: 205
Volunteers: 28
Regional offices: 8

Migrants Resource Centre

24 Churton Street, London SW1V 2LP
T: 020 7834 2505
F: 020 7931 8187
E: info@migrants.org.uk
The Migrants Resource Centre works with migrants and refugees and in partnership with other agencies to effect social justice and change, enabling migrants and refugees to fully participate in this society.
Employees: 14
Volunteers: 12

Mind

Granta House, 15–19 Broadway, London E15 4BQ
T: 020 8519 2122
F: 020 8522 1725
E: contact@mind.org.uk
www.mind.org.uk
Aims to raise awareness of mental health and to campaign for the rights of everyone experiencing mental distress.
Employees: 116
Volunteers: 20

Mind in Camden

Barnes House, 9-15 Camden Road, London NW1 9LQ
T: 020 791 0822
F: 020 7485 0842
E: rdean@mindincamden.org.uk
www.mindincamden.org.uk
Director: Brian Dawn
Mind in Camden provides high quality support and capacity building services to benefit people who are struggling with

mental distress including: hearing voices, extremes of mood, anxiety, unusual beliefs and post-traumatic reactions. We have a mental health day service; a service to support people who are dependent on benzodiazepines; and projects for young voice hearers, for voice hearers in London prisons and a London-wide Paranoia project.
Employees: 15
Volunteers: 90
Regional offices: 0
Income: £877,432 (2012-13)

Mind in Tower Hamlets and Newham

Open House, 13 Whitethorn Street
T: 020 7510 1081
E: cecilia.morkeh-yamson@mithn.org.uk
www.mithn.org.uk
Finance Manager: Cecilia Morkeh-Yamson Pelligrin

Mind the Gap

Silk Warehouse, Patent Street, Bradford, West Yorkshire BD9 4SA
T: 01274 487390
F: 01274 493973
E: arts@mind-the-gap.org.uk
www.mind-the-gap.org.uk
Mind the Gap believes in quality, equality and inclusion. Our mission is to dismantle the barriers to artistic excellence so that learning disabled and non-disabled artists can perform alongside each other as equals.

Minorities of Europe

Legacy House, 29 Walsgrave Road, Coventry CV2 4HE
T: 024 7622 5764 (also fax)
E: admin@moe-online.com
www.moe-online.com
Aims to develop a range of programmes and projects that meet the needs of young people and disadvantaged groups/ communities in Europe.
Employees: 6
Volunteers: 36

Minority Rights Group International

54 Commercial Street, London E1 6LT
T: 020 7422 4200
E: minority.rights@mrgmail.org
www.minorityrights.org
MRG works to secure the rights of ethnic, religious and linguistic minorities, and indigenous peoples, and acts as an advocate of the rights of minorities. MRG works across groups to build units and raise awareness of minority rights within a clear framework of international standards in a non-partisan way.

Miscarriage Association

c/o Clayton Hospital, Northgate, Wakefield, West Yorkshire WF1 3JS
T: 01924 200795
Helpline: 01924 200799
F: 01924 298834
E: info@miscarriageassociation.org.uk
www.miscarriageassociation.org.uk
National Director: Ruth Bender Atik
Miscarriage can be a very unhappy, frightening and lonely experience. The Miscarriage Association strives to make a positive difference to those it affects. We offer support, provide information, promote good practice amongst health professionals and work to raise public awareness about the facts and feelings of pregnancy loss.
Employees: 5
Volunteers: 100

Missing People

Roebuck House, 284 Upper Richmond Road West, London SW14 7JE
T: 020 8392 4590
Helpline: 116000
F: 020 8878 7752
E: info@missingpeople.org.uk
www.missingpeople.org.uk
Executive Director: Martin Houghton-Brown
We are a lifeline when someone disappears. We are caring and highly trained staff and volunteers working in collaboration with partners across the UK. For those left behind, we provide specialised support to end the heartache and confusion and search for their missing loved one.
Employees: 50
Volunteers: 70
Regional offices: 1

Mission Aviation Fellowship UK

Castle House, Castle Hill Avenue, Folkestone, Kent CT20 2TN
T: 01303 852800
F: 01302 852800
E: alex.finlow@maf-uk.org
www.maf-uk.org
Chief Executive: Ruth Whitaker
Mission Aviation Fellowship is a Christian organisation with the mission to fly light aircraft in developing countries so that people in remote areas can receive the help they need.
Employees: 79
Volunteers: 1000
Regional offices: 2
Income: £11,000,000 (2011-12)

Mission Care

Graham House, 2 Pembroke Road,
Bromley, Kent BR1 2RU
T: 020 8289 7925
E: admin@missioncare.org.uk
www.missioncare.org.uk
Works for the relief of sickness and poverty,
the relief of the aged, handicapped or infirm
and the advancement of the Christian
religion.

Mobility Information Service

20 Burton Close, Dawley, Telford,
Shropshire TF4 2BX
T: 01743 340269
E: info@starthere.org
www.mis.org
Provides an information service by letter,
email and phone, with a 24-hour answering
service. Leaflets are available covering various
aspects of disability.
Volunteers: 10

Mobility Trust

17B Reading Road, Pangbourne, Reading,
Berkshire RG8 7LR
T: 0845 450 0359
F: 0118 984 2544
E: mobility@mobilitytrust.org.uk
www.mobilitytrust.org.uk
Provides powered wheelchairs and scooters
for severely disabled children and adults who
cannot obtain them through statutory
sources or purchase such equipment
themselves. We do not give grants.
Employees: 4

MOC Foundation

341 Lauderdale Tower, Barbican,
London EC2Y 8NA
T: 07973 885784
F: 020 725660
E: info@mocfoundation.org
www.mocfoundation.org
Chair: Jose Carlos Martines
Provides humanitarian aid for the relief of
poverty in less developed regions of the
world.
Volunteers: 9
Income: £35,000 (2011-12)

Money Advice Trust

21 Garlick Hill, London EC4V 2AU
T: 020 7489 7796
Helpline: 0808 808 4000
F: 020 7489 7704
E: info@moneyadvicetrust.org
www.moneyadvicetrust.org
Chief Executive: Joanna Elson
The Money Advice Trust (MAT) is a charity
formed in 1991 to increase the quality and
availability of free, independent money
advice in the UK. MAT's vision: to help

people across the UK to tackle their debts
and manage their money wisely. MAT does
this through direct service provision
(National Debtline, Business Debtline and
My Money Steps) as well as supporting the
advice sector through training (wiseradviser).
Employees: 173
Income: £10,469,402 (2010-11)

Money Management Council

Hollymount, 3 Paget Crescent,
Huddersfield HD2 2BZ
T: 01484 425164
E: info@moneyeducation.co.uk
www.moneyeducation.co.uk
Promotes better understanding, improved
general education and increased self-help in
personal and family money management.

Montessori Education UK Ltd

21 Vineyard Hill, Wimbledon,
London SW19 7JL
T: 020 8946 2283
www.montessorieducationuk.org
Promotes the education of children
according to the Montessori method.

More Music

13-17 Devonshire Road, Morecambe,
Lancashire LA3 1QT
T: 01248 31997
E: sandra.wood@moremusic.org.uk
www.moremusic.org.uk
Artistic Director: Peter Moser
More Music is a community music and
education charity based in the West End of
Morecambe, working throughout
Lancashire, the North West and
internationally. We provide a year round
programme that covers a breadth of music
making activity involving people of all ages
and all backgrounds. We are one of the
longest running and most highly regarded
community music and education
organisations in the UK.

MOSAIC Black and Mixed Parentage Family Group

Community Base, 113 Queens Road,
Brighton BN1 3XG
T: 01273 234017
F: 01273 234018
E: info@mosaicbrighton.org.uk
www.mosaicbrighton.org.uk
Director: Naima Nouidjem
MOSAIC exists to empower black, Asian and
mixed-parentage families to combat racism

and to support the development of positive
cultural and racial identity.
Employees: 4
Volunteers: 30
Regional offices: 1

Mosaic Clubhouse

65 Effra Road, Brixton, London SW2 1BZ
T: 020 7924 9657
E: m.ness@mosaic-clubhouse.org
www.mosaic-clubhouse.org
Chief Executive: Maresa Ness
Employees: 16
Volunteers: 4
Regional offices: 1
Income: £557,704 (2012-13)

Motability

Warwick House, Roydon Road, Harlow,
Essex CM19 5PX
T: 01279 635999
Helpline: 0845 456 4566
F: 01279 632000
E: fundraising@motability.co.uk
www.motability.co.uk
Motability is a national charity, set up on the
initiative of the government in 1977, to assist
disabled people with their mobility needs.
We direct and oversee the Motability
Scheme, which enables disabled people to
obtain a car, powered wheelchair or scooter
simply by using their government-funded
mobility allowances.
Employees: 100

Mothers Apart from their Children

BM Box 6334, London WC1N 3XX
E: enquiries@matchmothers.org
www.matchmothers.org
MATCH offers non-judgemental emotional
support to mothers apart because of their
own short- or long-term mental or physical
ill-health when children are fostered or
adopted, to mothers whose children have
been abducted abroad by their fathers, to
mothers apart as a result of alienation
following high-conflict family breakdown
when children profess not to want to see
their mothers, and to mothers of adult
children apart as a result of family rows.
Volunteers: 10
Income: £5,000 (2010-11)

Mothers Union

Mary Sumner House, 24 Tufton Street,
London SW1P 3RB
T: 020 7222 5533
F: 020 7222 1591
E: mu@themothersunion.org
www.themothersunion.org
The Mothers' Union is an Anglican
organisation that promotes the wellbeing of
families worldwide.
Employees: 47
Volunteers: 36000000
Regional offices: 70

Motivation

Brockley Academy, Brockley Lane,
Backwell, Bristol BS48 4AQ
T: 01275 464012
F: 01275 464019
E: info@motivation.org.uk
www.motivation.org.uk
President: David Constantine
Motivation is an international charity
transforming the lives of disabled people.
Our wheelchairs and training give people
independence, confidence and hope for the
future.
Employees: 38
Volunteers: 4
Regional offices: 1

MS Trust

Spirella Building, Bridge Road,
Letchworth, Hertfordshire SG6 4ET
T: 01462 476700
Helpline: 0800 032 3839
E: info@mstrust.org.uk
www.mstrust.org.uk
Chief Executive: Pam Macfarlane
Works with and on behalf of 100,000 people
with MS in the UK.
Employees: 24

Multiple Births Foundation

Hammersmith House, Level 4, Queen
Charlotte's Hospital, Du Cane Road,
London W12 0HS
T: 020 3313 3519
E: mbf@imperial.nhs.uk
www.multiplebirths.org.uk
Director: Jane Denton
The Multiple Births Foundation offers
professional advice, education and support
to parents and carers of twins, triplets and
more, and to the health professionals who
care for them.

Multiple Sclerosis International Federation

3rd Floor, Skyline House, 200 Union
Street, London SE1 0LX
T: 020 7620 1911
E: info@msif.org
www.msif.org
Works in worldwide partnership with
member MS societies and the international
research community to eliminate multiple
sclerosis and its consequences, and speaks
out globally on behalf of those affected by
multiple sclerosis.

Multiple Sclerosis National Therapy Centres

Bradbury House, 155 Barkers Lane,
Bedford MK41 9RX
T: 01234 325781
E: info@msntc.org.uk
www.ms-selfhelp.org
Supports multiple sclerosis therapy centres
with training, education, information, etc.

Multiple Sclerosis Society of Great Britain and Northern Ireland

MS National Centre, 372 Edgware Road,
London NW2 6ND
T: 020 8438 0739
F: 020 8438 0701
E: info@mssociety.org.uk
www.mssociety.org.uk
Supports people affected by MS; encourages
people affected by MS to attain their full
potential and promotes research into MS.
Employees: 529
Volunteers: 8000
Regional offices: 400

Muntham House School Ltd

E: triciajeffs@muntham.org.uk

Muscular Dystrophy Campaign

61A Great Suffolk Street,
London SE1 0BU
T: 020 7803 4800
Helpline: 0800 652 6352
F: 020 7401 3495
E: info@muscular-dystrophy.org
www.muscular-dystrophy.org
Chief Executive: Robert Meadowcroft
The Muscular Dystrophy Campaign is the
leading UK charity fighting muscle-wasting
conditions. We are dedicated to beating
muscular dystrophy and related
neuromuscular conditions by finding

treatments and cures and to improving the
lives of everyone affected by them.
Employees: 60
Volunteers: 30000
Regional offices: 11

Museums Association

24 Calvin Street, London E1 6NW
T: 020 7426 6910
F: 020 7426 6961
E: info@museumsassociation.org
www.museumsassociation.org
Director: Mark Taylor
Represents museums and art galleries and
their staff; protects and develops
professional standards in museums.
Employees: 26

Music Education Council

54 Elm Road, Hale, Altrincham,
Cheshire WA15 9QP
T: 0161 928 3065
E: ahassan@easynet.co.uk
Promotes and advances music education and
training in the UK.

Muslim Aid

PO Box 3, London E1 1WP
T: 020 7377 4200
F: 020 7377 4201
E: hr@muslimaid.org
www.muslimaid.org
Muslim Aid was established to provide
humanitarian relief aid to the poorest, more
deprived and most vulnerable in society
worldwide. Emergency relief for victims of
disasters like floods, earthquakes, famines as
well as war is an important part of the aid we
provide.
Employees: 10
Volunteers: 10
Regional offices: 5

Myasthenia Gravis Association

The College Business Centre, Uttoxeter
New Road, Derby, Derbyshire DE22 3WQ
T: 01332 290219
Helpline: 0800 919912
F: 01332 293641
E: mg@mga-charity.org
www.mga-charity.org
CEO: Alasdair Nimmo
Funds research into the cause of myasthenia
gravis in order to find a cure; provides a
support network for myasthenics and their
families, increases public and medical

awareness of the problems of myasthenia gravis.
Employees: 16
Volunteers: 30
Regional offices: 57

Myositis Support Group

146 Newtown Road, Woolston,
Southampton SO19 9HR
T: 023 8044 9708
E: irene@myositis.org.uk
www.myositis.org.uk
Promotes the relief of persons suffering from dermatomyositis, polymyositis and inclusion body myositis; promotes research for a cure and better treatment. We also help to relieve the isolation felt when diagnosed with a rare condition and give support and up-to-date information to sufferers and their families.
Employees: 1
Volunteers: 8

Myotonic Dystrophy Support Group

19/21 Main Road, Gedling, Nottingham,
Nottinghamshire NG4 3HQ
T: 0115 987 5869
Helpline: 0115 987 0080
E: mdsg@tesco.net
www.myotonicdystrophysupportgroup.
org
National Coordinator: Margaret Bowler
We support families who have myotonic dystrophy, both congenital and adults. We supply information to the medical practitioners. There is a website and helpline, annual conference and area informal meetings.
Employees: 2
Volunteers: 25
Regional offices: 1
Income: £72,000 (2011-12)

NACRO

169 Clapham Road, London SW9 0PU
T: 020 7840 6418
F: 020 7735 4666
E: sue.kesteven@nacro.org.uk
www.nacro.org.uk
Aims to prevent crime by developing and implementing effective approaches to tackling crime and dealing constructively with offenders.
Employees: 1600
Volunteers: 700

NAGALRO

PO Box 264, Esher, Surrey KT10 0WA
T: 01372 818504
E: nagalro@globalnet.co.uk
www.nagalro.com
NAGALRO is the professional association for children's guardians, children and family reporters and independent social workers. NAGALRO promotes good practice; provides support and advice to individual members; contributes to developments in the Guardian and Family Court service; supports communication between individual guardians and Cafcass; encourages quality standards in independent social work with children and families; makes links with childcare solicitors and other professionals; provides professional insurance cover; produces a quarterly journal; and organises interdisciplinary conferences and training.
Volunteers: 15

Nakuru Environmental and Conservation Trust

5 Kingsend Court, Ruislip HA4 7DB
T: 01895 633650
E: nectecology@yahoo.co.uk
www.nectuk.org
Chair: Nim Njuguna
Promoting global citizenship and sustainable development through undertaking environmental service projects with communities in Kenya's Rift Valley Province. Encouraging young people from Kenya and the UK to work and learn from each other by discovering, celebrating and exploring

similarities and differences between their cultures.

NAPAC

Weston House, 42 Curtain Road,
London EC2A 3NH
T: 020 8313 9460 (also fax)
E: peter@napac.fsnet.co.uk
www.napac.org.uk
Provides relief and support to people who have experienced abuse in childhood and those affected by abuse and advances the education of the public and relevant professional bodies with regard to child abuse.
Employees: 7
Volunteers: 4

Narcolepsy Association UK (UKAN)

PO Box 13842, Penicuik EH26 8WX
T: 0845 450 0394
E: jennie@emms26.fsnet.co.uk
www.narcolepsy.org.uk
An association of people with narcolepsy, their relatives and others interested in improving their lot. Objectives are the benefit, relief and aid of persons suffering from narcolepsy; to promote awareness and provide authoritative information to narcoleptics, to the medical profession and to the public; and to encourage research into the causes and treatment of narcolepsy.
Employees: 1
Volunteers: 12

National Adult School Organisation

Riverton, 370 Humberstone Road,
Leicester LE5 0SA
T: 0116 253 8333
E: gensec@naso.org.uk
www.naso.org.uk
General Secretary: Patricia Dean
NASO is a voluntary organisation, with about 80 groups located throughout England. Anyone interested in spending some of their leisure time in discussing topics of current interest would find a warm welcome. We aim to broaden our horizons through stimulating conversation with people who become our friends.
Employees: 1
Volunteers: 40
Regional offices: 40

National AIDS Trust

New City Cloisters, 196 Old Street,
London EC1V 9FR
T: 020 7814 6767
F: 020 7216 0111
E: info@nat.org.uk
www.nat.org.uk
Chief Executive: Deborah Jack
The National AIDS Trust is the UK's leading
independent policy and campaigning charity
on HIV. We develop policies and campaign to
halt the spread of HIV and improve the
quality of life of people affected by HIV, both
in the UK and internationally.
Employees: 20
Volunteers: 15

National Alliance of Women's Organisations

Suite 405, Davina House, 137–149
Goswell Road, London EC1V 7ET
T: 020 7490 4100
E: info@nawo.org.uk
www.nawo.org.uk
Aims to bring together all women's
organisations in the country working to
eliminate all forms of discrimination against
women.

National Animal Welfare Trust

Tyler's Way, Watford–By–Pass, Watford,
Hertfordshire WD25 8WT
T: 020 8950 0177
F: 020 8420 4454
E: d.warner@nawt.org.uk
www.nawt.org.uk
Chief Executive: David Warner
The National Animal Welfare Trust's primary
purpose is to rescue and re-home domestic
animals and provide a place of sanctuary or
retirement for animals of all types.
Employees: 110
Volunteers: 350

National Ankylosing Spondylitis Society (NASS)

Unit 0.2, 1 Victoria Villas, Richmond,
Surrey TW9 2GW
T: 020 8948 9117
F: 020 8940 7736
E: admin@nass.co.uk
www.nass.co.uk
Director: Debbie Cook
NASS provides advice, support and
information for patients with AS. We support
research in this field, have over 100 branches
in the UK and also campaign for access to

treatments and better services for all AS
patients.
Employees: 5.5
Volunteers: 200
Income: £350,000 (2010-11)

National Association for Able Children in Education

PO Box 242, Arnold's Way,
Oxford OX2 9FR
T: 01865 861879
F: 01865 861880
E: info@nace.co.uk
www.nace.co.uk
NACE is a network of educators passionate
about enabling able pupils to fulfil their
potential within inclusive school
communities. We develop and exchange
strategies for effective practice and further
the professional development of our
members; provide responses on issues
affecting the education of able children and
advice to government agencies; undertake
development projects; provide professional
expertise, advice, training and consultancy
services, conferences, events, publications
and resources.

National Association for Children of Alcoholics

PO Box 64, Fishponds, Bristol,
Avon BS16 2UE
T: 0117 924 8005
E: admin@nacoa.org.uk
www.nacoa.org.uk
NACOA aims to offer information, advice
and support to children of alcohol-
dependent parents; to reach professionals
who deal with these children in their
everyday work; to raise the profile of children
of alcohol-dependent parents in the public
consciousness; and to promote research into
the particular problems faced by those who
grow up with parental alcoholism and the
prevention of alcoholism developing in this
vulnerable group of children.

National Association for Environmental Education (UK)

University of Wolverhampton, Walsall
Campus, Gorway, Walsall, West
Midlands WS1 3BD
T: 01922 631200
E: info@naee.org.uk
www.naee.org.uk
Promotes environmental education in the
UK and elsewhere in schools, colleges and
institutions responsible for teacher

education and all other educational
institutions.
Employees: 1
Volunteers: 1

National Association for Pastoral Care in Education

University of Warwick, Gibbet Hill Road,
Coventry CV4 7AL
T: 024 7652 3810
E: base@napce.org.uk
www.napce.org.uk
NAPCE establishes links between all those
who have an interest in pastoral care and
personal-social education. It has a
membership of 600 individuals and
organisations. NAPCE supports all who have
a professional concern for pastoral care;
promotes the theoretical study of pastoral
care; disseminates good practice; promotes
the education, training and development of
those engaged in pastoral care; and liaises
with other organisations with similar aims.

National Association for Patient Participation

10 Rosegarth Avenue, Aston,
Sheffield S26 2DD
T: 0870 774 3666 (also fax)
E: danny.daniels@napp.org.uk
www.napp.org.uk
NAPP is the umbrella group for patient
participation groups (PPGs) in primary care.
NAPP offers guidance on starting and
maintaining PPGs, and advice to primary care
organisations on PPGs as well as identifying
and disseminating good practice.
Volunteers: 15

National Association for Premenstrual Syndrome

41 Old Road, East Peckham, Tonbridge,
Kent TN12 5AP
T: 0870 777 2178
E: contact@pms.org.uk
www.pms.org.uk
Provides clinically authoritative, independent
advice, information and support to all those
experiencing, and treating, PMS and
menstrual ill health.

National Association for Small Schools

Quarrenden, Upper Red Cross Road,
Goring, Oxfordshire RG8 9BD
T: 01491 873548
E: quarrenden.tay@btinternet.com
www.smallschools.org.uk
Chairman: Bill Goodhand

Provides a voice and a link for those who believe that small schools, in rural and urban areas, have educational and social roles too precious to lose.

National Association for Special Educational Needs

NASEN House, 4–5 Amber Business Village, Amber Close, Amington, Tamworth, Staffordshire B77 4RP
T: 01827 311500
F: 01827 313005
E: welcome@nasen.org.uk
www.nasen.org.uk
NASEN is the leading organisation in the UK that aims to promote the education, training, advancement and development of all those with special and additional support needs. NASEN reaches a huge readership through its journals: British Journal of Special Education, Support for Learning, the new online publication Journal of Research in Special Educational Needs and the magazine Special.
Employees: 14

National Association for the Relief of Paget's Disease

323 Manchester Road, Walkden, Worsley, Manchester M28 3HH
T: 0161 799 4646
F: 0161 799 6511
E: diana.wilkinson@paget.org.uk
www.paget.org.uk
Chair: Roger Francis
Aims to raise awareness of Paget's disease among the public at large and the medical profession; to offer information and support to sufferers and to sponsor research into the causes and treatment of the disease.
Employees: 2
Regional offices: 1

National Association for the Teaching of English

50 Broadfield Road, Sheffield, South Yorkshire S8 0XJ
T: 0114 255 5419
F: 0114 255 5296
E: info@nate.org.uk
www.nate.org.uk
NATE currently has over 3,000 members, affiliated to a network of regional branches. The association has a range of committees and working parties that address current concerns, disseminate knowledge and ideas, promote the work of the association and seek to represent the views of the association to national bodies, local authorities, the

DfES, OFSTED, QCA, examination boards, etc.
Employees: 8
Volunteers: 70

National Association for Voluntary and Community Associations

The Tower, 2 Furnival Square, Sheffield S1 4QL
T: 0114 278 6636
F: 0114 278 7004
E: navca@navca.org.uk
www.navca.org.uk
Chief Executive: Kevin Curley
NAVCA is the national voice of local voluntary and community sector infrastructure in England. Our 360 members work with 170,000 local community groups and voluntary organisations, which provide services, regenerate neighbourhoods, increase volunteering and tackle discrimination, in partnership with local public bodies.
Employees: 40
Volunteers: 8
Regional offices: 398

National Association of Child Contact Centres

Minerva House, Spaniel Row, Nottingham NG1 6EP
T: 0845 450 0280
E: contact@naccc.org.uk
www.naccc.org.uk
Chief Executive: Yvonne Kee
Promotes safe child contact within a national framework of around 350 child contact centres. These are safe, neutral places where children of separated families can spend time with one or both parents and sometimes other family members. NACCC offers a range of support services to its membership and also provides a voice for child contact centres, promoting their role with national and regional decision-makers.
Employees: 7
Volunteers: 12

National Association of Deafened People

Dalton House, 60 Windsor Avenue, London SW19 2RR
T: 0845 055 9663
E: enquiries@nadp.org.uk
www.nadp.org.uk
Chairman: Ross Trotter
NADP supports all those who have suffered hearing loss during their lifetime. We provide our quarterly newsletter Network to provide information and updates on any

developments affecting our members. We campaign and also provide information and advice on employment, telecommunications, equipment and other subjects. NADP has some local groups and other contacts in various parts of the country, which arrange social events and provide support at grassroots level.
Volunteers: 12
Income: £23,507 (2011-12)

National Association of Decorative and Fine Arts Societies

NADFAS House, 8 Guilford Street, London WC1N 1DA
T: 020 7430 0730
F: 020 7242 0686
E: enquiries@nadfas.org.uk
www.nadfas.org.uk
Aims to increase the enjoyment, knowledge and care of the arts, and to stimulate interest in the preservation of our cultural heritage.
Employees: 14
Volunteers: 10000

National Association of Independent Schools and Non Maintained Special Schools

PO Box 705, York YO30 6WW
T: 01904 621243 (also fax)
E: cdorer@nasschools.org.uk
www.nasschools.org.uk
Chief Executive: Claire Dorer
The umbrella organisation for non-maintained special schools and independent schools catering for pupils with special educational needs. Works as the voice of the sector to ensure high-quality education and care for children with special educational needs.
Employees: 2
Income: £275,000 (2010-11)

National Association of Laryngectomy Clubs

Lower Ground Floor, 152 Buckingham Palace Road, London SW1W 9TR
T: 020 7381 9993
E: website@nalc.gov.uk
www.nalc.ik.com
Promotes the welfare and rehabilitation, in any way possible, of laryngectomy patients and their families within the British Isles.

National Association of Local Councils

109 Great Russell Street,
London WC1B 3LD
T: 020 7637 1865
F: 020 7436 7451
E: nalc@nalc.gov.uk
www.nalc.gov.uk
NALC represents the interests of around 8,500 town and parish councils in England. These councils serve electorates ranging from small rural communities to major cities, and are independently elected. Working with our member councils, NALC lobbies national government to advance and protect the interests of these councils and their communities. NALC provides support and advice to our members through a network of county associations and is committed to developing the role of town and parish councils.

National Association of Round Tables of Great Britain and Ireland

Marchesi House, 4 Embassy Drive, Edgbaston, Birmingham B15 1TP
T: 0121 456 4402
F: 0121 456 4185
E: john@roundtable.org.uk
www.roundtable.org.uk
General Secretary: John Handley
A young men's fellowship organisation.
Employees: 6
Regional offices: 670

National Association of Swimming Clubs for the Handicapped

The Willows, Mayles Lane, Wickham, Fareham, Hampshire PO17 5ND
T: 01329 833689
E: r.a.oleary@btinternet.com
www.nasch.org.uk
Chairman: Tracey Kitching
Encourages, promotes and develops swimming among handicapped people, in recognition of the immense value of swimming for both physical and psychological rehabilitation.

National Association of Toy and Leisure Libraries

1A Harmood Street, London NW1 8DN
T: 020 7428 2280
Helpline: 020 7428 2286
F: 020 7428 2281
E: admin@playmatters.co.uk
www.natll.org.uk
Promotes and supports toy and leisure libraries in the UK. Provides training, quality

assurance, publications, information and advice. Toy libraries loan carefully chosen (and sometimes specially adapted) toys and play equipment to families, formal and informal child-carers and professionals. Toy libraries may also offer stay-and-play opportunities. They provide friendship and support for parents and other carers, and through leisure libraries a meeting place for adults with special needs.
Employees: 24
Volunteers: 1
Regional offices: 3

National Association of Women's Clubs

5 Vernon Rise, London WC1X 9EP
T: 020 7837 1434
E: nawc@btconnect.com
www.nawc.org.uk
National Chairman: Maureen Harwood
Provides facilities for social life and opportunities for informal education within the means of all women.
Employees: 3
Regional offices: 120

National Association of Youth Theatres

c/o York Theatre Royal, St. Leonard's Place, York YO24 3LD
T: 07515 651481
E: info@nayt.org.uk
www.nayt.org.uk
Chief Executive: Jill Adamson
NAYT works with over 1,000 groups and individuals to support the development of youth theatre activity through information and support services, advocacy, training, participation and partnerships.
Employees: 1

National Benevolent Fund for the Aged

32 Buckingham Palace Road,
London SW1W 0RE
T: 020 7828 0200
F: 020 7828 0400
E: info@nbfa.org.uk
www.nbfa.org.uk
Interim Executive Director: Andrew Ross
NBFA was founded to improve the quality of life for older people who live on a low income. NBFA does this by providing direct, practical assistance through the provision of

emergency alarms, TENS pain relief machines and free break-aways.
Employees: 4
Volunteers: 10

National Benevolent Institution

Peter Herve House, Eccles Court, Tetbury, Gloucestershire GL8 8EH
T: 01666 505500
Helpline: 01666 505200
F: 01666 503111
E: welfare@nbi.org.uk
www.nbi.org.uk
The NBI was founded in 1812 by Peter Herve to provide a regular payment and one-off grants to people who have reached pension age or are over 50 years of age with a disability.
Employees: 5
Regional offices: 1

National Blind Children's Society

Bradbury House, Market Street, Highbridge, Somerset TA9 3BW
T: 01278 764764
Helpline: 0800 781 1444
F: 01278 764790
E: enquiries@nbcs.org.uk
www.nbcs.org.uk
Chief Executive: Carolyn Fullard
The Society provides services for the families of children and young people with a visual impairment from birth to the completion of full-time education, including: family support, educational advocacy, IT advice, activities and CustomEyes large-print children's books. Subject to criteria grants may be given for computers and communication aids.
Employees: 30
Volunteers: 14
Regional offices: 3
Income: £1,200,000 (2010-11)

National Campaign for the Arts

1 Kingly Street, London W1B 5PA
T: 020 7287 3777
E: nca@artscampaign.org.uk
www.artscampaign.org.uk
Aims to inform the public, brief the media and alert politicians to the need for greater public funding of the arts and campaigns for improvements in arts funding, arts education and access to the arts.

National Cancer Alliance

30 Hill Top Road, Oxford OX4 1PE
T: 01865 793566
E: nationalcanceralliance@btinternet.com
www.teamworkfile.org.uk

Represents the interests and voices the concerns and views of cancer patients and their carers; increases public and professional awareness about cancer services, including diagnosis, treatment and care; encourages all those involved in cancer services to work cooperatively to provide the most effective care; promotes and monitors high-quality national standards for cancer treatment and care.

National Centre for Social Research

35 Northampton Square,
London EC1V 0AX
T: 020 7250 1866
E: info@natcen.ac.uk
www.natcen.ac.uk
Chief Executive: Norman Glass
Our aim is a society better informed through high-quality social research.

National Childbirth Trust

Alexandra House, Oldham Terrace,
London W3 6NH
T: 0870 770 3236
Helpline: 0870 444 8707
F: 0870 770 3237
E: enquiries@national-childbirth-trust.
co.uk
www.nctpregnancyandbabycare.com
Chief Executive: Belinda Phipps
The NCT wants all parents to have an experience of pregnancy, birth and early parenthood that enriches their lives and gives them confidence in being a parent. It provides local support and puts parents in touch for social networking. The NCT also runs antenatal classes and provides information on maternity issues, breastfeeding and postnatal support, including specialist groups for caesareans and miscarriage. It has approximately 300 branches throughout the UK.
Employees: 80
Volunteers: 7000
Regional offices: 300

National Childminding Association

Royal Court, 81 Tweedy Road, Bromley,
Kent BR1 1TG
T: 0845 880 0044
F: 0845 880 0043
E: info@ncma.org.uk
www.ncma.org.uk
NCMA is a charity and professional association. We work with registered childminders, nannies as well as other individuals and organisations, such as local and national government, to ensure families in every community in England and Wales have access to high-quality, home-based childcare, play, learning and family support.

We also aim to ensure that everyone who supports registered childminding has access to the information, training and support they need.
Employees: 382
Regional offices: 7

National Children's Bureau

8 Wakley Street, London EC1V 7QE
T: 020 7843 6000
E: pbell@ncb.org.uk
www.ncb.org.uk
Chief Executive: Dr Hilary Emery
NCB is the leading national charity that supports children, young people and families and those who work with them. Our vision is a society in which children and young people are valued, their rights respected and responsibilities enhanced; our mission, to advance the wellbeing of children and young people across every aspect of their lives.
Income: £11,520,000 (2012-13)

National Children's Centre

Brian Jackson House, New North Parade,
Huddersfield, West Yorkshire HD1 5JP
T: 01484 519988
F: 01484 435150
E: info@nccuk.org.uk
www.nccuk.org.uk
Aims to advance public awareness in subjects connected with the care and upbringing of children in order to promote a better quality of life for the child.
Employees: 30
Volunteers: 10

National Coastwatch Institution (NCI)

1 Walk Terrace, West Street, Polruan by Fowey, Cornwall PL23 1PN
T: 01726 870659 (also fax)
Helpline: 0300 111 1202
E: public.relations@nci.org.uk
www.nci.org.uk
Chairman: Alan Richards
NCI was set up in 1994 to restore a visual watch along the coast after many coastguard stations were closed. Today 50 stations are operational and manned by over 2,000 volunteers at no cost to the public. Our mission is to assist in saving lives at sea and along the UK coastline. NCI is part of the national Search and Rescue organisation and is dependent on public support to cover running costs.
Volunteers: 2000

National Communities Resource Centre

Trafford Hall, Ince Lane, Wimbolds
Trafford, Chester CH2 4JP
T: 01244 300246
E: s.wyatt@traffordhall.com
www.traffordhall.com
Offering training and support to all those living and working in low-income communities around the UK. The centre develops skills, confidence and capacity to tackle problems and reverse poor conditions.

National Community Safety Network

1 Hunters Walk, Canal Street, Chester,
Cheshire CH1 4EB
T: 01244 322314
E: enquiries@community-safety.net
www.community-safety.net
NCSN is the leading practitioner-led organisation supporting those involved in promoting community safety/crime reduction throughout the UK. It has just under 400 organisational members and individual members in the public, private and voluntary sectors, all with a common interest in promoting safer communities. NCSN gives a national voice to practitioners; influences national policy and practice; supports the professional development of practitioners; and promotes joint working in the UK and Europe.
Employees: 3
Volunteers: 1

National Confederation of Parent Teacher Associations

39 Shipbourne Road, Tonbridge,
Kent TN10 3DS
T: 01732 375460
F: 01732 375461
E: dwb@ncpta.org.uk
www.ncpta.org.uk
NCPTA is the only membership organisation for PTAs and other home/school groups in England, Wales and Northern Ireland. Members enjoy high levels of support and advice on a variety of subjects such as fundraising ideas, running a PTA, registering as a charity and holding successful events.
Employees: 20
Volunteers: 130000
Regional offices: 11

National Confidential Enquiry Into Patient Outcome and Death

PO Box 5662, London W1A 5WP
T: 020 7631 3444
F: 020 7631 4443
E: info@ncepod.org.uk
www.ncepod.org.uk
NCEPOD aims to review medical clinical practice and to make recommendations to improve the quality of the delivery of care. We do this by undertaking confidential surveys covering many different aspects of medical care and making recommendations for clinicians and management to implement.
Employees: 32

National Consumer Federation

24 Hurst House, Penton Rise, London, Surrey WC1X 9ED
T: 020 7837 8545
E: secretary@ncf.info
www.ncf.info
Chair: Arnold Pindar
Aims to educate and inform consumers, with reference to the key guiding principles of choice, information, representation, access to goods and services, quality, fairness, safety and redress.
Employees: 1
Volunteers: 25
Income: £1000,020,000 (2012-13)

National Council for Palliative Care

The Fitzpatrick Building, 188–194 York Way, London N7 9AS
T: 020 7697 1520
F: 020 7697 1530
E: enquiries@ncpc.org.uk
www.ncpc.org.uk
Chief Executive: Eve Richardson
NCPC is the umbrella organisation for all those providing, commissioning and using palliative care and hospice services in England, Wales and Northern Ireland. NCPC promotes the extension and improvement of palliative care services for all people with life-threatening and life-limiting conditions. NCPC promotes palliative care in health and social care settings across all sectors to government, national and local policy makers.
Employees: 17

National Council for Voluntary Organisations

Regents Wharf, 8 All Saints Street, London N1 9RL
T: 020 7713 6161
F: 020 7713 6300
E: caroline.grais@ncvo.org.uk
www.ncvo-vol.org.uk
NCVO's vision is of a society in which people are inspired to make a positive difference to their communities. NCVO believes that a vibrant voluntary and community sector deserves a strong voice and the best support. NCVO aims to be that support and voice.
Employees: 130
Volunteers: 1
Regional offices: 1

National Council for Voluntary Youth Services (NCVYS)

Third Floor, Lancaster House, 33 Islington High Street, London N1 9LH
T: 020 7278 1041
F: 020 7833 2491
E: mail@ncvys.org.uk
www.ncvys.org.uk
Chief Executive: Susanne Rauprich
The National Council for Voluntary Youth Services (NCVYS) is a network of over 290 national organisations and regional and local networks. NCVYS is the only national independent body that represents and supports voluntary and community youth organisations in England, helping to build their capacity and deliver quality youth work. Our mission is to ensure the development and recognition of the voluntary youth sector, which involves, empowers and meets the needs of all young people.
Employees: 33
Regional offices: 1
Income: £2,000,000 (2010-11)

National Council of Women of Great Britain

72 Victoria Road, Darlington DL1 5JG
T: 01325 367375
E: info@ncwgb.org
www.ncwgb.org
President: Elsie Leadley
Works for the removal of discrimination against women; encourages the effective participation of women in public life and acts as a coordinating body to which societies with similar aims may affiliate.
Employees: 1

National Day Nurseries Association

National Early Years Enterprise Centre, Longbow Close, Huddersfield, West Yorkshire HD2 1GQ
T: 0870 774 4244
F: 0870 774 4243
E: info@ndna.org.uk
www.ndna.org.uk
NDNA is a national charity dedicated to the support and promotion of high-quality care and education for all children in the early years. It provides a code of practice for provider members and encourages all providers to follow the accreditation scheme, Quality Counts.
Employees: 50
Volunteers: 250
Regional offices: 5

National Deaf Children's Society (NDCS)

15 Dufferin Street, London EC1Y 8UR
T: 020 7490 8656
Helpline: 0808 800 8880
F: 020 7251 5020
E: helpline@ndcs.org.uk
www.ndcs.org.uk
Chief Executive: Susan Daniels
In all our work we aim to: empower deaf children, young people and their families to determine what happens in their lives and shape the services they receive; increase awareness of the support deaf children and young people need to achieve and challenge social attitudes which prevent them achieving; influence and challenge key decision-makers to make deaf children and young people a political priority.
Employees: 140
Volunteers: 240
Regional offices: 5
Income: £18,000,000 (2011-12)

National Development Team for Inclusion

First Floor, 30-32 Westgate Buildings, Bath BA1 1EF
T: 01225 789135
F: 01225 338017
E: mark.collings@ndti.org.uk
www.ndti.org.uk
Chief Executive: Rob Greig
The National Development Team for Inclusion is a not-for-profit organisation concerned with promoting inclusion and equality for people who risk exclusion and who need support to lead a full life. We have a particular interest in issues around age,

disability, mental health and children and young people.
Employees: 20
Volunteers: 10

National Eczema Society

Hill House, Highgate Hill,
London N19 5NA
T: 020 7281 3553
Helpline: 0800 089 1122
F: 020 7281 6395
E: mcox@eczema.org
www.eczema.org
Provides information and support to people with eczema and their carers, including health professionals.
Employees: 8
Volunteers: 20

National Energy Action

St Andrew's House, 90–92 Pilgrim Street, Newcastle upon Tyne NE1 6SG
T: 0191 261 5677
F: 0191 261 6496
E: info@nea.org.uk
www.nea.org.uk
Aims to develop policies and practices to tackle the heating and insulation problems of low-income households through improvements in energy efficiency.
Employees: 60
Volunteers: 30
Regional offices: 8

National Energy Foundation

Davy Avenue, Knowlhill, Milton Keynes MK5 8NG
T: 01908 665555
F: 01908 665577
E: enquiries@nef.org.uk
www.nef.org.uk
CEO: Kerry Mashford
NEF aims to give people, organisations and government the knowledge, support and inspiration they need to understand and improve the use of energy in buildings.
Employees: 25
Volunteers: 3

National Extension College Trust Ltd

Joydon, 33 Adelaide Close, Stanmore, Middlesex HA7 3EN
T: 020 8420 6055
E: info@nec.ac.uk
Provides the learning resources and opportunities to enable individuals to meet their vocational and personal goals.

National Eye Research Centre

Bristol Eye Hospital, Lower Maudlin Street, Bristol BS1 2LX
E: nerc-charity@bris.ac.uk
www.nerc.co.uk
The NERC funds and publishes research into the causes and treatment of eye diseases and disabilities and the prevention of blindness. The major part of the research it supports is carried out by the Unit of Ophthalmology at the University of Bristol, but research is also supported in Yorkshire, where it has a branch known as Yorkshire Eye Research, and in other eye research establishments throughout the UK.

National Family Mediation

4 Barnfield Hill, Exeter, Devon EX1 1SR
T: 0300 400 0636
F: 01392 271945
E: general@nfm.org.uk
www.nfm.org.uk
CEO: Jane Robey
NFM is a network of local not-for-profit family mediation services in England and Wales, which offers help to couples, married or unmarried, who are in the process of separation and divorce. We provide high-quality mediation to everyone who needs it in all communities, helping clients to reach joint decisions about the issues associated with their separation – children, finance and property. Several NFM services also provide specialist services for children. NFM has well-established quality assurance standards.
Employees: 12
Volunteers: 1
Regional offices: 47

National Federation of Shopmobility UK

163 West Street, Fareham PO16 0EF
T: 0844 414 1850
E: info@shopmobilityuk.org
www.shopmobilityuk.org
Executive Director: Richard Ashdown
Provides advice, guidance and support to organisations and individuals considering developing Shopmobility in their locality. Influences policy on mobility and access issues and supports the organisations and individuals campaigning for improvements.
Employees: 2
Volunteers: 5
Regional offices: 1

National Federation of the Blind of the UK

Sir John Wilson House, 215 Kirkgate, Wakefield, West Yorkshire WF1 1JG
T: 020 8452 8336
Helpline: 01924 291313
F: 01924 200244
E: nfbuk@nfbuk.org
www.nfbuk.org
President: Norma Town
The Federation, through its blind and partially sighted membership, seeks to promote a better quality of life for all visually impaired people through local activities at branch level and nationally through campaigning.
Employees: 2
Volunteers: 1
Regional offices: 19

National Federation of Women's Institutes

104 New Kings Road, London SW6 4LY
T: 020 7371 9300
F: 020 7736 4333
E: pr@nfwi.org.uk
www.thewi.org.uk
General Secretary: Jana Osborne
The largest women's voluntary organisation in the UK, with over 212,000 members in over 6,600 WIs in England, Wales and the Islands. We offer women the best opportunity to make an impact in their communities; to influence local, national and world issues affecting the social, economic and environmental life of families and communities; and to learn new and traditional skills.
Regional offices: 70

National Federation of Young Farmers' Clubs

YFC Centre, 10th Street, Stoneleigh Park, Kenilworth, Warwickshire CV8 2LG
T: 024 7685 7200
F: 024 7685 7229
E: james.eckley@nfyfc.org.uk
www.nfyfc.org.uk
Chief Executive: James Eckley
The National Federation of Young Farmers' Clubs (NFYFC) is the head body of 659 Young Farmers' Clubs (YFCs) located throughout England and Wales. The NFYFC is dedicated to providing a framework within which its clubs can provide young people aged 10–26 with a wealth of new experiences and opportunities.
Employees: 70
Volunteers: 5000
Regional offices: 49

National Flood Forum

E: amanda.davies@floodforum.org.uk

National Gardens Scheme

Hatchlands, East Clandon, Guildford,
Surrey GU4 7RT
T: 01483 211535
E: ngs@ngs.org.uk
www.ngs.org.uk
Opens gardens of quality, character and
interest to the public for charity.

National Group on Homeworking

Office 26, 30–38 Dock Street, Leeds,
Yorkshire LS10 1JF
T: 0113 245 4273
F: 0113 246 5616
E: admin@ngh.org.uk
www.homeworking.gn.apc.org
Aims to educate the public and policy makers
on issues concerning homeworking; to
alleviate poverty among homeworkers by
working, campaigning and lobbying to
improve their working terms and conditions.
Employees: 8
Volunteers: 9

National Gulf Veterans and Families Association

Building E Office 8, Chamberlain Business
Centre, Chamberlain Road, Hull,
Humberside HU8 8HL
T: 0845 257 4853
F: 01482 808731
E: info@ngvfa.org.uk
www.ngvfa.org.uk
Chair: Nigel Graveston
Aims to relieve persons who served in the
Gulf conflict and their families, and those
involved in future desert conflicts who are in
conditions of need, hardship, sickness or
distress.
Employees: 6
Volunteers: 30
Income: £154,162 (2012-13)

National Housing Federation

Lion Court, 25 Procter Street WC1V 6NY
T: 020 7067 1010
F: 020 7067 1011
E: info@housing.org.uk
www.housing.org.uk
Chief Executive: David Orr
The National Housing Federation is the voice
of affordable housing in England. We believe
that everyone should have the home they
need at a price they can afford. That's why
we represent the work of housing
associations and campaign for better
housing. Our members provide two and a
half million homes for more than five million

people. Each year they invest in a diverse
range of projects that help create strong,
vibrant communities.
Employees: 135
Regional offices: 3

National Information Forum

33 Highshore Road, London SE15 5AF
T: 020 7708 5943
E: info@nif.org.uk
www.nif.org.uk
Aims to ensure that disabled people,
refugees and asylum seekers and others
severely disadvantaged by lack of
information have all the information they
need, in ways that they can access; to offer
advice to information providers on how to
provide information well.

National Institute of Adult Continuing Education

Renaissance House, 20 Princess Road
West, Leicester LE1 6TP
T: 0116 204 4200
F: 0116 285 4514
E: enquiries@niace.org.uk
www.niace.org.uk
Director: Alan Tuckett
NIACE exists to encourage more and
different adults to engage in learning of all
kinds. We campaign for – and celebrate the
achievements of – adult learners, young and
old, in all their diversity. NIACE is the largest
organisation working to promote the
interests of learners and potential learners in
England and Wales.
Employees: 275

National Institute of Medical Herbalists

Clover House, James Court, South Street,
Exeter, Devon EX1 1EE
T: 01392 426022
F: 01392 498963
E: info@nimh.org.uk
www.nimh.org.uk
President: Desiree Shelley
Promotes the importance of herbal
medicine. Makes people more aware of
herbal medicine and its benefits. Assists with
training to those who wish to pursue as a
career.
Employees: 2

National Justice and Peace Network

NJPN, 39 Eccleston Square,
London SW1V 1BX
T: 020 7901 4864
E: admin@justice-and-peace.org.uk
www.justice-and-peace.org.uk
Chair: Anne Peacey
We are a grassroots body working with
groups and individuals of all faiths and none
who share our aims and values based in the
Christian Gospels. We engage with all who
seek to challenge unjust structures which
perpetuate poverty, violence and
environmental degradation, including
individuals, diocesan and local groups,
national agencies and religious communities,
offering opportunities for action,
information sharing, friendship and mutual
support.
Employees: 1
Volunteers: 10
Regional offices: 0
Income: £90,000 (2012-13)

National Kidney Federation

The Point, Coach Road, Shireoaks,
Worksop, Nottinghamshire S81 8BW
T: 01909 544999
Helpline: 0845 601 0209
F: 01909 481723
E: nkf@kidney.org.uk
www.kidney.org.uk
Chief Executive Officer: Timothy Statham
The National Kidney Federation (NKF) is the
patient's voice and is fighting to achieve
high-quality renal treatment across the UK. It
is the only national kidney charity run by
patients, for patients. It is funded entirely by
donations and sponsorships. The Federation
is able to monitor and compare renal services
across the country because of its unique
structure. It is run by representatives of the
78 separate Kidney Patient Associations
geographically spread across the UK.
Employees: 18

National Literacy Association

87 Grange Road, Ramsgate,
Kent CT11 9QB
T: 01843 239952 (also fax)
Helpline: 07989 715732
E: wendy@nla.org.uk
www.nla.org.uk
The NLA works in partnership with a range
of organisations to promote awareness of
and support children's literacy needs. As well
as campaigning for the needs of the 20% of
children who continue to underachieve, we
do practical work in schools, with children in

public care, with parent groups and in the wider community. We also produce a range of resources that are distributed free of charge to schools, parent groups and others.
Employees: 1
Volunteers: 15

National Literacy Trust

68 South Lambeth Road,
London SW8 1RL
T: 020 7587 1842
F: 020 7931 9986
E: contact@literacytrust.org.uk
www.literacytrust.org.uk
The National Literacy Trust is concerned with raising literacy standards for all age groups throughout the UK. The Trust's purpose is to make an independent strategic contribution to the creation of a society in which all can enjoy the skills, confidence and pleasures of literacy.
Employees: 21

National Music for the Blind

2 High Park Road, Southport,
Merseyside PR9 7QL
T: 01704 228010
E: music4blind@gmail.com
www.music4blind.webs.com
Provides a free fortnightly USB service to all visually handicapped persons in the UK. The USB memory stick contains nostalgic music programmes, plays, documentaries, comedy shows, old radio and much more from the vast library of the charity. 14 days to listen then return using freepost wallets.

National Operatic and Dramatic Association

58–60 Lincoln Road,
Peterborough PE1 2RZ
T: 0870 770 2480
F: 0870 770 2490
E: everyone@noda.org.uk
www.noda.org.uk
Promotes and improves the art of amateur theatre, to cultivate the improvement of public taste in the art.
Employees: 8
Volunteers: 180
Regional offices: 11

National Organisation for the Treatment of Abusers

PO Box 356, Hull HU12 8WR
T: 01482 896990 (also fax)
E: notaoffice@nota.co.uk
www.nota.co.uk
NOTA has a growing multidisciplinary membership comprising practitioners, managers and policy makers from the public,

private and voluntary sectors. NOTA brings a wide variety of perspectives to interventions with sexual aggressors. It is the only professional multidiscplinary organisation in the UK and Ireland dedicated to work with sexual abusers. It is consequently in a unique position to promote and develop work in this area of public protection.
Regional offices: 13

National Osteoporosis Society

Camerton, Bath BA2 0PJ
T: 01761 471771
F: 01761 471104
E: h.kingman@nos.org.uk
www.nos.org.uk
The National Osteoporosis Society (NOS) campaigns to ensure that all people with or at risk of osteoporosis receive appropriate advice and treatment to enable them to avoid fractures and to enjoy a better quality of life. The NOS provides information and support for people with osteoporosis and their carers by promoting education for the public and health professionals, by lobbying government and health organisations and by encouraging fundraising for support services.
Employees: 60
Volunteers: 500

National Patients Support Trust

First Floor, 162 Shepherds Bush Road,
Hammersmith, London W6 7PB
T: 020 7603 9770
E: npstcharity@btconnect.com
www.npst.co.uk
Trustee: Cornelius Oconnor
Provides relief and assistance for patients and former patients of NHS hospital trusts suffering from disease and from other physical and or mental disability or disabilities.
Employees: 6

National Pensioners Convention

Walkden House, 10 Melton Street,
London NW1 2EJ
T: 020 7383 0388
E: admin@npcuk.org
www.npcuk.org
The NPC is Britain's biggest campaigning organisation for older people, representing over 1,000 local, regional and national pensioner groups with a total of 1.5 million members. The NPC promotes the welfare and interests of all pensioners. It lobbies MPs and government on policies affecting older people and stages an annual three-day Pensioners' Parliament in Blackpool, where

over 1,000 representatives discuss issues of concern.
Employees: 4
Regional offices: 18

National Playbus Association

Brunswick Court, Brunswick Square,
Bristol BS2 8PE
T: 01458 850804
E: playbus@playbus.org.uk
www.playbus.org.uk
Promotes the use of playbuses and converted vehicles as mobile community resources, and acts as an umbrella organisation that promotes good practice in mobile community work.

National Portage Association

Kings Court, 17 School Road, Hall Green,
Birmingham, West Midlands B28 8JG
T: 0121 244 1807
F: 0121 244 1801
E: info@portage.org.uk
www.portage.org.uk
Portage is a home-visiting educational service for pre-school children with additional support needs and their families.
Employees: 5

National Reye's Syndrome Foundation of the UK

15 Nicholas Gardens, Woking,
Surrey GU22 8SD
T: 01932 346843
E: gordon.denney@ukgateway.net
www.reyessyndrome.co.uk
Promotes research into the cause, treatment, cure and prevention of Reye's syndrome and Reye-like illnesses; provides support for parents whose children have suffered from these diseases and creates awareness and professional knowledge.

National Rheumatoid Arthritis Society

Unit B4, Westacott Business Centre,
Westacott Way, Littlewick Green,
Maidenhead, Berkshire SL6 3RT
T: 0845 458 3969
Helpline: 0800 298 7650
F: 0845 458 3971
E: enquiries@nras.org.uk
www.nras.org.uk
Chief Executive: Ailsa Bosworth
NRAS provides support, information and advocacy for people with rheumatoid arthritis and juvenile idiopathic arthritis, their

families, friends and carers. We are also a resource for health professionals with an interest in rheumatology and work closely with rheumatology teams across the UK.
Employees: 20

National Skills Academy for Social Care

85 Tottenham Court Road,
London W1T 4TQ
T: 020 7268 3082
E: debbie.sorkin@nsasocialcare.co.uk
www.nsasocialcare.co.uk
Chief Executive: Debbie Sorkin
Employer-led organisation helping people working at all levels in adult social care, as well as people using care and support services, to strengthen their leadership capacity.
Employees: 20
Income: £3,000,000 (2011-12)

National Society for Clean Air and Environmental Protection

44 Grand Parade, Brighton BN2 9QA
T: 01273 878777
E: pmitchell@nsca.org.uk
www.nsca.org.uk
Aims to secure environmental improvement by promoting clean air through the reduction of air pollution, noise and other contaminants, while having regard for other aspects of the environment.

National Society for Epilepsy

Chalfont Centre, Chalfont St Peter,
Gerrards Cross, Buckinghamshire SL9 0RJ
T: 01494 601322
E: margaret.thomas@epilepsynse.org.uk
www.epilepsynse.org.uk
The National Society for Epilepsy's mission is to enhance the quality of life of people affected by epilepsy by promoting research, education and public awareness, and by delivering specialist medical care and support services.

National Society for Phenylketonuria (UK) Ltd

PO Box 26642, London N14 4ZF
T: 020 8364 3010
E: info@nspku.org
www.nspku.org
The NSPKU exists to help and support people with PKU, their families and carers. The NSPKU actively promotes the care and treatment of PKUs and works closely with medical professionals in the UK. It organises conferences and study days throughout the

UK, publishes a wide range of publications (including food lists) for parents, PKUs and medical professionals. The NSPKU also sponsors medical research into PKU.

National Society of Allotments and Leisure Gardeners

O'Dell House, Hunters Road, Corby,
Northamptonshire NN17 5JE
T: 01536 266576
F: 01536 264509
E: geoff@nsalg.demon.co.uk
www.nsalg.org.uk
National Secretary: Geoff Stokes
National representative body for the allotment movement.
Employees: 5

National Trust

Heelis, Kemble Drive, Swindon,
Wiltshire SN2 2NA
T: 01793 817400
F: 01793 817401
E: enquiries@thenationaltrust.org.uk
www.nationaltrust.org.uk
We protect and open to the public over 300 historic houses and gardens, and 49 industrial monuments and mills. We also look after forests, woods, fens, beaches, farmland, downs, moorland, islands, archaeological remains, castles, nature reserves and villages.
Employees: 4000
Volunteers: 40000
Regional offices: 11

National Village Halls Forum

Somerford Court, Somerford Road,
Cirencester, Gloucestershire GL7 1TW
T: 01285 653477
E: acre@acre.org.uk
www.acre.org.uk
Acts as the national representative body for village halls; promotes the exchange of information and ideas about the use, management and development of village halls; raises awareness of the need for public financial support for community building projects; discusses common problems and draw attention to the likely effects of proposed legislation or policy changes for village halls.

National Voices

1st Floor, Bride House, 18-20 Bride Lane,
London EC4Y 8EE
T: 020 3176 0738
E: info@nationalvoices.org.uk
www.nationalvoices.org.uk
Chief Executive: Jeremy Taylor
National Voices is the coalition of health and social care charities working to strengthen

the voice of patients, service users and those who represent them.
Employees: 7

National Women's Register

23 Vulcan House, Vulcan Road North,
Norwich, Norfolk NR6 6AQ
T: 01603 406767
F: 01603 407003
E: office@nwr.org.uk
www.nwr.org.uk
Chair of Trustees: Pamela McKee
NWR is an international organisation of women's discussion groups. Each group aims to provide its members with the opportunity to take part in stimulating discussions on a wide range of topics. Meetings are very informal and held in people's homes, where you will find a warm welcome whatever your age or personal circumstances. Groups organise their own programmes that can include speakers, book groups, day conferences, educational workshops and other social events.
Employees: 5
Volunteers: 24

National Youth Agency

Eastgate House, 19–23 Humberstone Road, Leicester, Leicestershire LE5 3GJ
T: 0116 285 3700
F: 0116 285 3777
E: nya@nya.org.uk
www.nya.org.uk
Acts as a resource centre for youth work policy makers and practitioners in England. Its major concerns include: informal personal and social education, employment, education and training initiatives; community involvement and participation by young people; counselling, information and advice for young people; work with young people at risk or in trouble.
Employees: 75
Volunteers: 100
Regional offices: 1

National Youth Orchestra of Great Britain

32 Old School House, Britannia Road,
Kingswood, Bristol BS15 8DB
T: 0117 960 0477
E: info@nyo.org.uk
www.nyo.org.uk
Works to discover and foster exceptional musical talent in young people and to help provide them with tuition and experience in orchestral musical skills; to give concerts of the highest standard; and to inspire young people to take an interest in music.

National Youthbike

PO Box 27, Horncastle,
Lincolnshire LN9 6XB
T: 01507 524432
E: nationalyouthbike@yahoo.co.uk
www.youthbike.com
Chair: Tony Nightingale
Promotes the education and social
development of young people in the UK in
life skills, engineering, design and
information technology by assisting them in
their preparation for and participation in the
annual National Youthbike weekend event.
Volunteers: 17

Natural Death Centre

In The Hill House, Watley Lane, Twyford,
Winchester SO21 1QX
T: 01962 712690
E: contact@naturaldeath.org.uk
www.naturaldeath.org.uk
Manager: Rosie Inman-Cook
Aim to improve the quality of dying and
funerals. Information for families caring for
the dying at home. Also how to get your
affairs in order. Empowers people organising
inexpensive and or environmentally friendly
funerals, sometimes without funeral
directors. Advice on rights and laws
concerning burials on private land or at
natural burial grounds. List suppliers, who
deal direct with the public. Advice on
keeping costs down. Telephone helpline on
all related topics.
Volunteers: 5
Regional offices: Hants

Nautilus International

1-2 The Shrubberies, George Lane, South
Woodford, London E18 1BD
T: 020 8989 6677
F: 020 8530 1015
E: mjess@nautilusint.org
www.nautilusint.org
General Secretary: Mark Dickinson
The Nautilus Welfare Fund, a charity
administered by Nautilus International,
provides support and assistance for retired
seafarers and their dependants.
Employees: 65
Regional offices: 2

Naz Foundation International

2nd Floor, 5 Harbour Exchange,
London E14 9GE
T: 020 7570 6092
F: 020 7691 7062
E: kim@nfi.net
www.nfi.net
Chief Executive: Shivananda Khan

With a primary focus on males who have sex
with males (MSM), NFI's mission is to
empower socially excluded and
disadvantaged males to secure for
themselves social justice, equity, health and
wellbeing through technical, institutional and
financial support.
Regional offices: 1

Neighbourhood Initiatives Foundation

The Poplars, Lightmoor, Telford,
Shropshire TF4 3QN
T: 0870 770 0339
www.nif.co.uk
Aims to engage residents and other
stakeholders in identifying and realising the
needs of their communities and to help local
people play a full part in planning and being
involved in the regeneration of their own
neighbourhoods.

Nell Bank

Denton Road, Ilkley, West
Yorkshire LS29 0DE
T: 01943 602032
F: 01943 601690
E: nell.bank@bradford.gov.uk
www.nellbank.com
Centre Manager: Bruce Fowler
Educates young people in the principles of
responsible citizenship by providing them
with training and recreation and community
service opportunities. Provides affordable
day and residential outdoor education
experience in stunning and contrasting
environments to 20,000 children and young
people each year. Enables hard-to-reach
groups to access outdoor experience via
nationally significant activities, adapted
accommodation and equipment.
Employees: 9
Volunteers: 100
Regional offices: 0

Network 81

1–7 Woodfield Terrace, Stansted,
Essex CM24 8AJ
T: 0845 077 4056
Helpline: 0845 077 4055
F: 0845 077 4057
E: network81@btconnect.com
www.network81.org
Chair: Eirwen Grenfell-Essam
Network 81 offers help and support to
parents throughout all stages of assessment
and statementing as outlined in the
Education Act 1996 and Code of Practice
2001. Our national helpline offers an
individual service linked to a national

network of local contacts. Network 81
produces a range of literature aimed at
familiarising parents with the assessment and
statementing procedures. We also run
extensive training programmes for parents
and those working with parents.
Employees: 4
Volunteers: 80

Network for Peace

5 Caledonian Road, London N1 9DY
T: 07794 036602
E: mail@networkforpeace.org.uk
www.networkforpeace.org.uk
Coordinator: Claire Poyner
After the demise of the National Peace
Council, one of the oldest peace
organisations in the UK, Network for Peace
was set up with the aim of continuing with
the networking role of the NPC. NfP
provides a regularly updated website, which
includes links to websites of members, news
and an extensive diary of events. This
information is also available as a bi-monthly
newsletter.
Employees: 1

Neuroblastoma Society

Beverley Home, Oxford Road, Frilford,
Abingdon, Oxfordshire OX13 5NU
T: 0186 539 1207
E: publicity@neuroblastoma.org.uk
www.nsoc.co.uk
Provides funds for British medical research
into improving the treatment of the
childhood cancer neuroblastoma with an
eventual cure in mind.

Neurofibromatosis Association

Quayside House, 38 High Street, Kingston
upon Thames, Surrey KT1 1HL
T: 020 8439 1234
F: 020 8439 1200
E: info@nfauk.org
www.nfauk.org
Charity Manager: Mike Mills
The Association works to raise awareness of
neurofibromatosis; provide help, support
and advice to those affected, their families
and the professionals working with them;
provide relevant, up-to-date information and
facilitate research.
Employees: 6
Regional offices: 1

Neurological Alliance

Stroke House, 240 City Road,
London EC1V 2PR
T: 020 7566 1540
F: 020 7735 1555
E: admin@neural.org.uk
www.neural.org.uk
The Neurological Alliance is a collaborative forum of a wide range of neurological charities. The Alliance campaigns for the highest standards of service and care for the 10 million people in the UK with a neurological condition.
Employees: 2
Regional offices: 13

New Bridge Foundation

27A Medway Street SW1P 2BD
T: 020 7976 0779
E: info@newbridgefoundation.org.uk
www.newbridgefoundation.org.uk
New Bridge was founded in 1956 to create links between the offender and the community. It offers a wide range of programmes to help prisoners keep in touch with the outside world and prepare themselves to rejoin it. The keynote service remains the friendship and support given by volunteers to longer-term prisoners, especially those no longer in contact with family and friends.
Employees: 17

New Choices for Youth

E: marcias@ncytrust.org

New Economics Foundation

3 Jonathan Street, Vauxhall,
London SE11 5NH
T: 020 7820 6300
F: 020 7820 6301
E: info@neweconomics.org
www.neweconomics.org
Executive Director: Stewart Wallis
Aims to put people and the environment at the centre of economic thinking. We aim to improve quality of life by promoting innovative solutions that challenge mainstream thinking on economic, environment and social issues. We work in partnership and put people and the planet first.
Employees: 45
Volunteers: 2
Regional offices: 1
Income: £3,300,000 (2011-12)

New Horizon Youth Centre

68 Chalton Street, London NW1 1JR
T: 020 7388 5560
F: 020 7388 5848
E: info@nhyouthcentre.org.uk
www.nhyouthcentre.org.uk
Director: Shelagh O'Connor
New Horizon Youth Centre is a day centre working with young people age 16 to 21 who are vulnerable, homeless or at risk. New Horizon Youth Centre aims to enable young people to gain skills and knowledge to improve their life chances and to help them move from adolescence into adulthood.
Employees: 28
Volunteers: 45
Regional offices: 1
Income: £1,309,659 (2011-12)

New Kadampa Tradition – International Kadampa Buddhist Union

Conishead Priory, Ulverston
T: 01229 588533
E: info@kadampa.org
www.kadampa.org
General Secretary: Stephen Cowing

New Philanthropy Capital

3rd Floor, Downstream Building, 1 London Bridge, London SE1 9BG
T: 020 7785 6300
F: 020 7785 6301
E: jjames@philanthropycapital.org
www.philanthropycapital.org
Chief Executive: Nigel Harris
NPC advises donors on how to make their giving to charities more effective. Our aim is to increase the quantity and quality of resources available to the charitable sector. We do this through a combination of independent research and tailored advice. Our research identifies charities that are achieving excellent results and where funds and resources can be targeted most effectively. Our advice for donors guides them on how to ensure their money has high impact.
Employees: 38
Volunteers: 3

New Politics Network

6 Cynthia Street, London N1 9JF
T: 020 7278 4443
F: 020 7278 4425
The network promotes political engagement and democratic renewal. Our aim is to provide support and advice on increasing involvement and participation in politics.
Employees: 5
Volunteers: 7

New Start Trust

Alderman Downward House, 1st Floor, The Birtles, Civic Centre, Wythenshawe, Lancashire M22 5RF
T: 0161 498 0615
F: 0161 436 5570
E: info@newstarttrust.org
www.newstarttrust.org
Works to relieve poverty, sickness and distress for those people who are dependent on or affected by addiction to drugs.
Employees: 10
Volunteers: 2

Newcastle Action for Parent and Toddler Groups Initiative

Heaton Community Centre, Trewhitt Road, Heaton, Newcastle upon Tyne, Tyne and Wear NE6 5DY
T: 0191 265 6158 (also fax)
E: karen@napi.org.uk
www.napi.org.uk
Project Manager: Karen Williams
To promote the education and development of under school aged children in the City of Newcastle upon Tyne by the provision of advice, information and support services for parent and toddler groups and like groups.
Employees: 13
Volunteers: 0
Regional offices: 0
Income: £248,532 (2012-13)

Newcastle Council for Voluntary Service

Higham House, Higham Place, Newcastle upon Tyne NE1 8AF
T: 0191 232 7445
F: 0191 230 5640
E: sally.young@cvsnewcastle.org.uk
www.cvsnewcastle.org.uk
Chief Executive: Sally Young
Newcastle CVS works to support, develop, promote, connect and represent voluntary and community organisations in Newcastle. Our work helps to make Newcastle a better place by helping to develop a thriving voluntary and community sector. We do this through our three service areas; supporting and developing local organisations to thrive, networking and involving local organisations to engage, representing and influencing on behalf of the voluntary and community sector. Newcastle CVS also runs Ellison Services, a community accountancy organisation providing payroll.
Employees: 32
Volunteers: 70
Regional offices: 1
Income: £998,000 (2012-13)

Newcastle Tenants and Residents Federation

Fawdon Community Centre, Fawdon Park Road, Fawdon, Newcastle upon Tyne, Tyne and Wear NE3 2PL
T: 01912 852724
E: enquiries@newcastletenantsfed.org.uk
www.newcastletenantsfed.org.uk
Newcastle Tenants and Residents Federation is a registered charity representing tenants and residents associations (TARAs) throughout Newcastle upon Tyne. We are also one of the oldest Federation's in the country, having been formed in 1977. Our focus is on working with tenants and residents to relieve deprivation and improve housing conditions and living environments across the city.
Employees: 3
Volunteers: 2
Regional offices: 0

Newlife

Newlife Centre, Hemlock Way, Cannock, Staffordshire WS11 7GF
T: 01543 462777
E: enquiries@info.newlifecharity.co.uk
www.newlifecharity.co.uk
Medical research, awareness and service, relevant to all birth defects.

NHS Confederation

29 Bressenden Place, London SW1E 5DD
T: 020 7074 3282
F: 020 7959 7273
E: info@nhsconfed.org
www.nhsconfed.org
We help our members provide better health and healthcare by: influencing the development and implementation of policy and the wider public debate on the full range of health and health services issues, speaking out independently on behalf of our members; supporting health leaders through information sharing and networking; promoting excellence in employment to improve the working lives of staff and, through them, to provide better care for patients; providing tailored services and products to enable boards to develop their objectives.
Employees: 40

Niemann-Pick Disease Group UK

Suite 2, Vermont House, Concord, Washington, Tyne and Wear NE37 2SQ
T: 0191 415 0693
E: niemann-pick@zetnet.co.uk
www.niemannpick.org.uk
Executive Director: Toni Mathieson

The group aims to make a positive difference to the lives of those affected by Niemann-Pick diseases and their families, through the provision of effective support in the three main areas of care, information and research.
Employees: 4
Volunteers: 12
Income: £228,846 (2010-11)

Nightstop UK Ltd

45A Otley Road, Shipley, West Yorkshire BD18 3PY
T: 01274 533004
F: 01274 532314
www.nightstop-uk.org
Nightstop UK advises and supports Nightstop schemes that offer appropriate, safe accommodation for young people aged 16 to 25. This accommodation is provided in the homes of approved volunteers. By our action we seek to challenge public perception of youth homelessness and endeavour to shape public policy on youth homelessness.
Employees: 7
Volunteers: 12
Regional offices: 44

No Panic

93 Brandsfarm Way, Telford, Shropshire, Shropshire TF3 2JQ
T: 01952 590005
Helpline: 0808 808 0545
F: 01952 270962
E: ceo@nopanic.org.uk
www.nopanic.org.uk
Chief Executive: Colin Hammond
Works for the relief and rehabilitation of people suffering from panic attacks, phobias and obsessive/compulsive disorders.
Employees: 1
Volunteers: 107

Noise Abatement Society

44 Grand Parade, Brighton BN2 9QA
T: 01273 682223
E: nas@noiseabatementsociety.fsnet.co.uk
www.noiseabatementsociety.com
The Noise Abatement Society is a registered charity. Its aims are to eliminate excessive noise in all its forms by campaigning to raise awareness, by lobbying parliament and through education to improve the quality of life for all. It is an active and effective problem-solving organisation with strong contacts in government. The society runs the only telephone noise helpline in the UK.

Nordoff-Robbins Music Therapy

2 Lissenden Gardens, London NW5 1PQ
T: 020 7267 4496
F: 020 7267 4369
E: admin@nordoff-robbins.org.uk
www.nordoff-robbins.org.uk
Provides music therapy treatment for people with special needs and training for music therapists.
Employees: 50
Volunteers: 50

Norfolk Community Law Service Ltd

E: ros@ncls.co.uk

Norm UK

PO Box 71, Stone, Staffordshire ST15 0SF
T: 01785 814044 (also fax)
E: info@norm-uk.org
www.norm-uk.org
Aims to advance the education of the public in all matters relating to circumcision and other forms of surgical alteration of the genitals, including alternative treatments and offering information and advice on such matters.
Employees: 1
Volunteers: 14

North Taunton Partnership

Priorswood Community Centre, 13-14 Priorswood Place, Eastwick Road, Taunton, Somerset TA2 7JW
T: 01823 353643
E: lesley.priorswoodcc@yahoo.co.uk
www.priorswoodcommunitycentre.co.uk
Manager: Lesley Thomas
The Charity's objects are to promote charitable purposes for the benefit of the community of North Taunton and in particular the advancement of education, the promotion of health and the relief of poverty, sickness and distress. These aims are achieved by offering advice surgeries, social groups, exercise classes and activities for young people during the school holidays through our Pride in Priorswood program.
Employees: 4
Volunteers: 32
Regional offices: 1
Income: £85,848 (2012-13)

Northallerton & District Voluntary Service Association

E: secretary@ndvsa.co.uk

Northern Ireland Council for Voluntary Action

61 Duncairn Gardens,
Belfast BT15 2GB
T: 028 9087 7777
F: 028 9087 7799
E: info@nicva.org
www.nicva.org
Chief Executive: Seamus McAleavey
NICVA is an umbrella organisation, seeking to represent the interests of voluntary and community organisations throughout Northern Ireland. In its role as a voluntary sector development agency, NICVA acts as a catalyst to promote innovation and new approaches to the challenge of social need.
Employees: 45
Income: £2,765,162 (2011-12)

Norwich Door To Door

E: n-norwich@btconnect.com

Norwood

Broadway House, 80–82 The Broadway, Stanmore,
Middlesex HA7 4HB
T: 020 8954 4555
F: 020 8420 6800
E: suzanne.nehard@norwood.org.uk
www.norwood.org.uk
Chief Executive: Norma Brier
Norwood is Anglo-Jewry's largest children and family services organisation, supporting children and their families, and adults, in coping with learning disabilities and social disadvantage. Every year we help thousands of children and their families by providing vital, specialised care to the most vulnerable members of our community.
Employees: 1100
Volunteers: 700
Regional offices: 4

Notts Housing Advice

E: admin@nottshousingadvice.org.uk

Nova Wakefield District Limited

11 Upper York Street, Wakefield,
Wakefield, West Yorkshire WF1 3FQ
T: 01924 367418
E: fiona.cooper@nova-wd.org.uk
www.nova-wd.org.uk
CEO: Alison Haskins
Nova Wakefield District is the new support agency for the community and voluntary sector. We work with organisations big and small throughout the district, helping with development, volunteering, funding, contracts, governance and influencing issues pertinent to the sector.
Employees: 13
Volunteers: 13

Novas Scarman Group

68 Parkway, London NW1 7AH
T: 020 7424 3000
E: enquiries@novas.org
www.novas.org
**Co-Group Chief Executive/Founder:
Michael Wake**
Novas changes lives through arts, enterprise and community support, developing opportunities through community support, education, training, employment, art, culture and regeneration. We have a reputation for delivery of quality community-based services and innovative approaches working with people who experience inequality, exclusion and discrimination. Over the last three years Novas has transformed itself from predominantly a provider of hostels to being at the cutting edge of tackling social disadvantage through social enterprise, innovation and positive impact.
Employees: 350

NSPCC

Weston House, 42 Curtain Road,
London EC2A 3NH
T: 020 7825 2500
Helpline: 0808 800 5000
F: 020 7825 2525
E: info@nspcc.org.uk
www.nspcc.org.uk
Chief Executive: Andrew Flanagan
The NSPCC's purpose is to end cruelty to children. Our vision is of a society where all children are loved, valued and able to fulfil their potential. We seek to achieve cultural, social and political change – influencing legislation, policy, practice, attitudes and behaviours and delivering services for the benefit of children and young people.
Employees: 2600
Volunteers: 27 500
Regional offices: 60
Income: £148,600,000 (2010-11)

Nubian Life Resource Centre Ltd

50 Commonwealth Avenue,
London W12 7QR
T: 020 8749 8017
E: info@nubian-life.org.uk
Provides for the relief of elderly African Caribbean people living in the UK.
Employees: 14

Nuffield Trust

59 New Cavendish Street,
London W1G 7LP
T: 020 7631 8450
F: 020 7631 8451
E: info@nuffieldtrust.org.uk
www.nuffieldtrust.org.uk
Chief Operating Officer: Kim Beazor
The Trust's mission is to promote independent analysis and informed debate on UK healthcare policy, with a particular focus on long-term, strategic direction. The core objectives are: to improve the health of the people of the UK, to improve the quality of healthcare and to improve the quality of health policy; to communicate evidence and encourage an exchange around developed or developing knowledge in order to illuminate recognised and emerging issues.
Employees: 5

Number One Community Trust (TW) Ltd

1 Rowan Tree Road, Tunbridge Wells,
Kent TN2 5PX
T: 01892 514544
E: onecommunity@btconnect.com
www.numberonecommunitytrust.org.uk
Chair of Trustees: Adrian Cory
Runs a community centre in a deprived area offering a wide range of services including pre-school, cafe and a variety of clubs/ groups for people of all ages.Aims to promote the physical, mental and spiritual health and wellbeing of local residents; improve the social and economic wellbeing of local residents; support the advancement of education and training; assist those who are seeking employment; and encourage environmental improvements in the neighbourhood.
Employees: 9
Volunteers: 47
Regional offices: 1
Income: £227,308 (2012-13)

Nurture Group Network

18a Victoria Park Square, Bethnal Green,
London E2 9PF
T: 020 3475 8980
E: info@nurturegroups.org
www.nurturegroups.org
Chief Executive: Kevin Kibble
Works to advance the education of children with special educational needs.
Employees: 10
Regional offices: 3
Income: £223,881 (2011-12)

NYAS (National Youth Advocacy Service)

Egerton House, 2 Tower Road,
Birkenhead, Wirral,
Merseyside CH41 1FN
T: 0151 649 8700
Helpline: 0300 330 3131
F: 0151 649 8701
E: main@nyas.net
www.nyas.net
Chief Executive: Christine Renouf
NYAS offers an unusual range of preventive interdisciplinary welfare and legal services, information, consultation, support and representation to children, young people and vulnerable adults in England and Wales. It has a team of in-house lawyers and a sessional workforce of more than 350 children's advocates and caseworkers, who include some of the most experienced welfare professionals in the country.
Employees: 130
Volunteers: 65
Regional offices: 8

Nystagmus Network

25 Pen-y-Lan Terrace, Cardiff, South Glamorgan CF23 9EU
T: 0845 634 2630
Helpline: 02920 454242
E: info@nystagmusnet.org
www.nystagmusnet.org
Chair: Richard Wilson
NN provides support and information to people with nystagmus. We raise awareness of the challenges presented by this incurable eye condition which affects at least 60,000 people in the UK. We also encourage and fund scientific, medical and social research into nystagmus.
Employees: 2
Volunteers: 12
Income: £112,000 (2012-13)

Oakleaf

E: deeptiparmar@oakleaf-enterprise.org

Oasis UK

Oasis Trust, 1 Kennington Road, London SE1 7QP
T: 020 7921 4200
E: enquiries@oasisuk.org
www.oasistrust.org
Oasis demonstrates that Christian faith works by delivering practical solutions to the breadth of people's needs wherever they are encountered. Our work in the UK is focused around hubs. These are areas of activity in which we provide integrated and diverse services in order to benefit the whole person and the whole community.

OBJECT

PO Box 63639, London SW9 1BQ
E: ido@object.org.uk
www.object.org.uk
Object challenges 'Sex Object Culture' – the objectification of women, particularly the normalising of the porn and sex industries – by lads' mags or lap-dancing. We are concerned by the damning messages and attitudes this sends about women's status and value and women and men's sexual identity. We campaign, lobby and provide information.

OCD Action

Suite 506-507, Davina House, 137-149 Goswell Road, London EC1V 7ET
T: 020 7253 5272
Helpline: 0845 390 6232
E: info@ocdaction.org.uk
www.ocdaction.org.uk
Director: Joel Rose
OCD Action is the largest national charity focusing on Obsessive Compulsive Disorder. The charity provides support and information to anybody affected by OCD, works to raise awareness of the disorder amongst the public and healthcare workers, and strives to secure a better deal for people with OCD. Formed by a group of leading professionals and volunteers in 1994, the charity is recognised as a strong voice for people with OCD and a vital source of help.
Employees: 7
Volunteers: 30
Regional offices: 2
Income: £270,000 (2012-13)

Ockenden International

Constitution Hill, Woking, Surrey GU22 7UU
T: 01483 772012
E: oi@ockenden.org.uk
www.ockenden.org.uk

Ockenden works to promote independence and self-reliance amongst refugees, displaced people, returnees and their host communities throughout the world.

Odyssey Trust (UK)

Omnibus Business Centre, 39–41 North Road, London N7 9DP
T: 020 7700 6177
F: 020 7700 6232
E: info@theodyssey.co.uk
www.odysseytrust.org
The Trust provides high-quality treatment and support services that respond to the changing needs of people affected by substance misuse.

Off Centre Hackney

E: martin.williams@offcentre.org.uk

Officers' Association

1st Floor, Mountbarrow House, 6–20 Elizabeth Street, London SW1W 9RB
T: 020 7808 4160
F: 020 7808 4161
E: info@officersassociation.org.uk
www.officersassociation.org.uk
The Officers' Association (OA), founded over 90 years ago, is the only charity dedicated exclusively to supporting officers and ex-officers and their dependants from all three services. It achieves this in two ways: providing employment services for service leavers and ex-serving officers; providing benevolence services in the form of financial and welfare support. The OA offers a resource based on a thorough understanding of the background and needs of commissioned officers and their families.
Employees: 24
Volunteers: 600

Olmec

47–49 Durham Street, London SE11 5JA
T: 0845 880 0110
E: bparker@olmec-ec.org.uk
www.olmec-ec.org.uk
We are a dynamic community investment foundation and work alongside disadvantaged communities to deliver programmes that lead to positive impact. We are driven by principles of self-help, empowerment and social justice and our work ranges from addressing issues of under-representation of minority communities, to breaking down the barriers to employment faced by refugees. We also engage in research and use it as a tool to influence policy and provision.
Employees: 8

One Parent Families

255 Kentish Town Road,
London NW5 2LX
T: 020 7428 5400
F: 020 7482 4851
E: membership@gingerbread.org.uk
www.oneparentfamilies.org.uk
Aims to improve the economic, legal and
social position of one-parent families.
Employees: 27
Volunteers: 4

One Plus One Marriage and Partnership Research

1 Benjamin Street, London EC1M 5QG
T: 020 7553 9530
E: kb@oneplusone.org.uk
www.oneplusone.org.uk
Director: Penny Mansfield
OnePlusOne puts research into practice,
investigating what makes relationships work
- or fall apart - and making the findings
accessible to everyone interested in
strengthening and supporting couple and
family relationships. Our goals are to support
couples and parents to manage relationship
issues earlier and more effectively, and
champion the adoption and implementation
of policies and services that value
relationships and espouse early relationship
support and encourage a culture of
relationship support.
Employees: 20
Volunteers: 8
Income: £1,800,000 (2012-13)

One World Trust

3 Whitehall Court, London SW1A 2EL
T: 020 7766 3470
F: 020 7839 7718
E: gbergh@oneworldtrust.org
www.oneworldtrust.org
The One World Trust promotes education
and research into the changes required
within global organisations in order to
achieve the eradication of poverty, injustice
and war. It conducts research on practical
ways to make global organisations more
responsive to the people they affect, and on
how the rule of law can be applied equally to
all. It educates political leaders and opinion-
formers about the findings of its research.
Employees: 8
Volunteers: 12

Online Centres Foundation

The Workstation, 15 Paternoster Row,
Sheffield, Unknown S1 2BX
T: 0114 227 0035
E: alison.broadley@ukonlinecentres.com
www.ukonlinecentres.com

Onside

E: martine.vantomme@onside-
advocacy.org.uk

Open College Network YHR

OCNYHR, OCN House, Lower
Warrengate, Wakefield, West
Yorkshire WF1 1SA
T: 01924 434600
F: 01924 364213
E: enquiries@ocnyhr.org.uk
www.ocnyhr.org.uk
Chief Executive: John Lawton
OCNYHR is a national Awarding
Organisation committed to providing a high
quality and responsive accreditation service.
Regulated by Ofqual, OCNYHR offers a wide
range of qualifications within the
Qualifications and Credit Framework (QCF).
At OCNYHR, we also provide our
Recognised Centres with bespoke
accreditation through our Customised
Accreditation Service. OCNYHR is also an
Access Validating Agency, licensed by the
Quality Assurance Agency (QAA), to
develop, approve and certificate Access to
Higher Education Diplomas.
Employees: 30
Volunteers: 0
Regional offices: 0
Income: £1,500,000 (2012-13)

Open Doors International Language School

E: croberts@odils.com

Open Spaces Society

25A Bell Street, Henley-on-Thames,
Oxfordshire RG9 2BA
T: 01491 573535
E: hq@oss.org.uk
www.oss.org.uk
General Secretary: Kate Ashbrook
We campaign to create and conserve
common land, village greens, open spaces
and rights of public access, in town and
country, in England and Wales.
Employees: 5
Volunteers: 40

Operation Black Vote

18A Victoria Park Square, London E2 9PB
T: 020 8983 5474
F: 020 7684 3889
E: simon@charter88.org.uk
www.obv.org.uk
Operation Black Vote began in July 1996 as a
collaboration between two organisations:
Charter88 (which campaigns for democratic

reform) and the 1990 Trust, the only national
Black generic policy research and networking
organisation, which uses information
technology as a primary means of
communication.
Employees: 8
Volunteers: 4

Operation Florian

6 Worcester Close, Bracebridge Heath,
Lincoln, Lincolnshire LN4 2TY
T: 01522 569728 (also fax)
E: opflorian@aol.com
www.operationflorian.com
Operation Florian was established as a charity
in 1995. It is a UK Fire Service Humanitarian
Charity working to promote the protection
of life amongst communities in need, world
wide, by the provision of equipment and
training to improve fire fighting and rescue
capabilities.
Employees: 1

Opportunity Links

Trust Court, Vision Park, Histon,
Cambridge CB24 9PW
T: 01223 566522
F: 01223 500281
E: info@openobjects.com
www.opp-links.org.uk
Managing Director: Paul Bogen
Opportunity Links works with the public
sector to develop and manage quality
information that supports families in making
important life choices.
Employees: 62
Volunteers: 4
Regional offices: 2

Optua

Optua House, Hill View Business Park,
Claydon, Ipswich, Suffolk IP6 0AJ
T: 01473 836777
F: 01473 836778
E: enquiries@optua.org.uk
www.optua.org.uk
Chief Executive: Colin Poole
We are a Suffolk-based disability charity
providing a range of services and
opportunities for disabled people including
leisure and sport activities, community
transport, advice and advocacy, community
brain injury services and homecare.
Employees: 230
Volunteers: 300
Regional offices: 2

OPUS

26 Fernhurst Road, London SW6 7JW
T: 020 7736 3844
E: director@opus.org.uk
www.opus.org.uk
Chair: Jeremy Leathers

OPUS is an organisation of people who believe that it is important that we and others develop a deeper understanding of organisational and societal processes and the way in which we relate to them; and that we use such understanding to act with authority and responsibility in our various roles. OPUS exists therefore to promote the development of the reflective citizen.
Volunteers: 350
Regional offices: 24
Income: £89,330 (2012-13)

ORBIS Charitable Trust

4th Floor, Fergusson House, 124–128 City Road, London EC1V 2NJ
T: 020 7608 7260
F: 020 7278 5231
E: info@orbis.org.uk
www.orbis.org.uk
Now celebrating 30 years of sight-saving work, ORBIS is a nonprofit humanitarian organisation dedicated to blindness prevention and treatment in developing countries. According to the World Health Organisation, 39 million people worldwide are blind, yet 28 million don't need to be. With your help, we can bring sight back into their lives.
Employees: 18
Volunteers: 3

Orione Care

13 Lower Teddington Road, Hampton Wick, Kingston upon Thames KT1 4EU
T: 020 8977 5130
E: info@orionecare.org
www.orionecare.org
Orione Care is a working name of The Sons of Divine Providence, a charity that provides housing and care services for older people and people with learning disabilities. The charity has a Roman Catholic ethos but people of all faiths and none are welcome to use its services.
Employees: 112
Income: £3,600,000 (2012-13)

Ormiston Children and Families Trust

Central Office, 333 Felixstowe Road, Ipswich, Suffolk IP3 9BU
T: 01473 724517
F: 01473 705025
E: income.generation@ormiston.org
www.ormiston.org
Chief Executive: Geoffrey Prescott
Our vision is of a society where all children and young people have choices to realise their full potential and to achieve happiness and fulfilment, free from prejudice, isolation and stigma. To achieve this vision, we work to identify the most challenged children and young people and enable them to have choices to realise a happy and fulfilling future.
Employees: 213
Volunteers: 140
Income: £6,254,000 (2010-11)

Orphans In Need

22a Atlas Way, Sheffield S4 7QQ
T: 0800 999 0852
E: info@orphansinneed.org
www.orphansinneed.org
Orphans in Need helps some of the world's most vulnerable and needy people. It is committed to the alleviation of all forms of poverty and deprivation, in all parts of the globe. However, the organisation's primary focus is on orphans and widows; often the weakest members of any society, and the most affected by the scourge of poverty.
Employees: 4
Volunteers: 30
Regional offices: 2

Orphans Relief Fund and Charitable Trust

163-165 Dukes Road, Park Royal, London W3 0SL
T: 020 8205 8272
F: 020 8205 8922
E: orfact@hotmail.com
www.orfact.co.uk
Works for the relief of poverty and advancement of education for orphans, widows, refugees, the impoverished and the vulnerable around the world. This is carried out through education and support services, vocational training and development projects and emergency aid and relief.
Employees: 6
Volunteers: 6

Otherwise Club

1 Croxley Road, London W9 3HH
T: 020 8969 0893
E: info@otherwiseclub.org
www.otherwiseclub.org
Aims to advance the education of children whose families have opted for out-of-school education and who remain responsible for their children's education at all times, without distinction of race, sex, political, religious or other opinions, through the provision of facilities.

Outreach International

The Cambodia Trust, 4C Station Yard, Thame, Oxfordshire OX9 3UH
T: 01844 214844
E: office@cambodiatrust.co.uk
www.cambodiatrust.com

Outreach International is committed to cross-cultural exchange and education. We combine the desire of young people to travel and work overseas with the needs of local communities. We give volunteers a deep understanding of traditional life in Ecuador, Cambodia and the Pacific coast of Mexico, whilst providing benefits to the host communities and children from humble backgrounds.

Outsiders

4S Leroy House, 436 Essex Road, London N1 3QP
T: 01997 421019
F: 020 7460 2247
E: trust@outsiders.org.uk
www.outsiders.org/uk
Provides help for people with physical and social disabilities, especially those who live in emotional isolation.

Ovacome

B5 City Cloisters, 196 Old Street, London EC1V 9FR
T: 020 7299 6654
Helpline: 020 7299 6650
E: ovacome@ovacome.org.uk
www.ovacome.org.uk
Ovacome is a support organisation for all those affected by ovarian cancer. It links sufferers, provides information, runs a support line, and awareness-raising activities.
Employees: 6

Ovarian Cancer Action

8–12 Camden High Street, London NW1 0JH
T: 0300 456 4700
F: 0300 456 4708
E: info@ovarian.org.uk
www.ovarian.org.uk
Chief Executive: Gilda Witte
Ovarian Cancer Action (OCA) is the UK's leading ovarian cancer charity, dedicated to improving survival rates for women with ovarian cancer. It funds innovative research into the disease at the Ovarian Cancer Action Research Centre (OCARC); raises awareness of the symptoms with national awareness campaigns aimed at women and healthcare workers; and gives a voice to those affected by it, acting as an advocate with policy makers, healthcare professionals and scientists.
Employees: 10
Volunteers: 50
Regional offices: 1

Overeaters Anonymous

PO Box 19, Stretford,
Manchester M32 9EB
T: 07000 784985
E: oagbnsb@hotmail.com
www.oagb.org.uk
Welcomes those with the desire to stop eating compulsively, offering identification and acceptance; relieves our compulsion to overeat/undereat, or an obsession with food/dieting by living by spiritual principles based on the 12 steps of Alcoholics Anonymous.

Overseas Development Institute

203 Blackfriars Road, London SE1 8NJ
T: 020 7922 0300
F: 020 7922 0399
E: p.gee@odi.org.uk
www.odi.org.uk
Director: Alison Evans
Our mission is to inspire and inform policy and practice that lead to the reduction of poverty, the alleviation of suffering and the achievement of sustainable livelihoods in developing countries. We do this by locking together high-quality applied research, practical policy advice, and policy-focused dissemination and debate. We work with partners in the public and private sectors, in both developing and developed countries.
Employees: 184
Volunteers: 20
Income: £18,000,000 (2010-11)

Oxfam GB

John Smith Drive, Cowley, Oxford,
Oxfordshire OX4 2JY
T: 0300 200 1300
F: 01865 472600
E: givetime@oxfam.org.uk
www.oxfam.org.uk
CEO Oxfam GB: Mark Goldring
Oxfam is a development, relief, and campaigning organisation that works with others to achieve a just world without poverty.
Employees: 4951
Volunteers: 27000
Regional offices: 8

P3

E: andrew.regan@p3charity.org

PAC

5 Torriano Mews, London NW5 2RZ
T: 020 7284 0555
Helpline: 020 7284 5879
F: 020 7482 2367
E: advice@pac.org.uk
www.pac.org.uk
CEO: Peter Sandiford
PAC provides confidential advice, information and support for anyone affected by adoption or any other form of permanent care, including adoptive parents, adopted adults, birth parents and other birth family members, foster carers where permanence is the plan, special guardians and prospective adopters. Services include: advice line; individual counselling; individual, couple and family consultations; family therapeutic work; support with contact arrangements between adoptive and birth families; support for birth relatives, including fortnightly birth mothers drop-in.
Employees: 25
Volunteers: 4

PACE

34 Hartham Road, London N7 9JL
T: 020 7700 1323
E: info@pacehealth.org.uk
www.pacehealth.org.uk
Chief Executive Officer: Margaret Unwin
Promotes the health and wellbeing of the lesbian, gay, bisexual and transgender community; promotes the empowerment and emotional wellbeing of LGBT users of mental health services; promotes good policies and practice in relation to working with these client groups.
Employees: 23
Volunteers: 22

PACT (Parents and Children together)

7 Southern Court, South Street, Reading,
Berkshire RG1 4QS
T: 0300 456 4800
E: info@pactcharity.org
www.pactcharity.org
Chief Executive: Jan Fishwick
PACT helps hundreds of families every year through adoption and fostering services and community projects. PACT is one of the UK's leading Voluntary Adoption Agencies (VAA) placing children with secure and loving families and supporting them with specialist therapeutic support.
Employees: 70
Volunteers: 50
Regional offices: 3
Income: £4,663,973 (2012-13)

Pain Relief Foundation

Clinical Sciences Centre, University Hospital Aintree, Lower Lane,
Liverpool L9 7AL
T: 0151 529 5820
F: 0151 529 5821
E: secretary@painrelieffoundation.org.uk
www.painrelieffoundation.org.uk
Administrator: D Emsley
Aims to research human chronic pain to find the causes and mechanisms of why chronic pain persists. Also to find new and improved methods of treating all such conditions to ease the suffering of patients. Our ultimate aim is to find cures for all pain. Additionally, we provide ongoing education for health professionals at all levels and disciplines who are dealing with human chronic pain at the point of treatment.
Employees: 6
Regional offices: 1

Painswick Rococo Garden Trust

E: rococogarden@hotmail.co.uk

Paintings in Hospitals

Floor One, Menier Chocolate Factory, 51 Southwark Street, London SE1 1RU
T: 020 7407 3222
F: 020 7403 7721
E: mail@paintingsinhospitals.org.uk
www.paintingsinhospitals.org.uk
Director: Stuart Davie
Aims to relieve sick, infirm and convalescent persons by providing pictures and works of art on loan in order to improve the

environment of hospitals and other healthcare establishments.
Employees: 5
Volunteers: 50
Regional offices: 7

Pan London HIV/AIDS Providers Consortium

347–349 City Road, London EC1V 1LR
T: 020 7713 0444
The Consortium intends to be a collective group for the HIV voluntary sector; to act as a strong lobbying voice; to provide organisational support to HIV voluntary sector organisations; to improve networks; to act as a liaison between the voluntary sector and statutory sector.

Panos Institute

9 White Lion Street, London N1 9PD
T: 020 7278 1111
F: 020 7278 0345
E: info@panos.org.uk
www.panos.org.uk
Executive Director: Mark Wilson
Panos London stimulates informed and inclusive public debate around key development issues in order to foster sustainable development. We are working to promote an enabling media and communication environment worldwide.
Employees: 25
Volunteers: 2

Papworth Trust

Bernard Sunley Centre, Papworth Everard, Cambridge, Cambridgeshire CB23 3RG
T: 01480 357200
Helpline: 0800 952 5000
F: 01480 357201
E: info@papworth.org.uk
www.papworth.org.uk
Chief Executive: Adrian Bagg
Papworth Trust is a leading disability charity. We support over 20,000 people each year through a wide range of services, including accessible homes, personal care, leisure and learning opportunities, and support for people to find and keep jobs.
Employees: 500
Regional offices: 24

Parents for Inclusion

Winchester House, Kennington Park Business Estate, Cranmer Road, London SW9 6EJ
T: 020 7735 7735
Helpline: 0845 652 3145
F: 020 7735 3828
E: info@parentsforinclusion.org
www.parentsforinclusion.org
Parents for Inclusion is a network of parents of disabled children and children with special needs. In our families and as an organisation we have worked together with disabled people to build inclusive communities in ordinary life, where all people are truly welcome. We work closely with disabled adults, to bring their understanding and experience to parents, so that parents can become real allies to their disabled children.
Employees: 9
Volunteers: 5

Parents in Partnership

Cornerstone House, 14 Willis Road, Croydon, Surrey CR2 8DA
T: 020 8684 9082
E: office@pipcroydon.com
pipcroydon.com
Chairman: Jackie Sanders
Employees: 5
Volunteers: 4
Regional offices: 1

PARITY

Constables, Windsor Road, Ascot, Berkshire SL5 7LF
T: 01344 621167 (also fax)
E: postmaster@parity-uk.org
www.parity-uk.org
Chair: John Mays
Fosters and promotes equal treatment of the sexes under the law and by public authority, for example in state pensions, other social security provisions, bus concessions, etc.
Volunteers: 10
Regional offices: 1

Parkinson's Disease Society of the UK

215 Vauxhall Bridge Road, London SW1V 1EJ
T: 020 7931 8080
F: 020 7233 9908
E: enquiries@parkinsons.org.uk
www.parkinsons.org.uk
Helps and supports people with Parkinson's and their relatives; collects and shares information on Parkinson's; and encourages

and provides funds for research into the disease.
Employees: 150
Volunteers: 3500
Regional offices: 14

Parliamentary Advisory Council for Transport Safety

3rd Floor, Clutha House, 10 Storey's Gate, London SW1P 3AY
T: 020 7222 7732
F: 020 7222 7106
E: admin@pacts.org.uk
www.pacts.org.uk
Executive Director: Robert Gifford
To protect human life through the promotion of transport safety for the public benefit; to exercise scrutiny of legislative and policy proposals.
Employees: 3
Volunteers: 5
Income: £181,000 (2010-11)

Parliamentary Human Rights Foundation 2000

PO Box 8198, London W3 6GA
T: 020 8723 0728
Works for the advancement of education for the general public, in particular, students of further and higher education, by the design and development of skills-based courses in human rights education at under- and post-graduate level, primarily within the context of parliamentary government.

Partially Sighted Society

1 Bennetthorpe, Doncaster, South Yorkshire DN2 6AA
T: 0844 477 4966
F: 0844 477 4969
E: info@partsight.org.uk
partsight.org.uk
Executive Director: Anita Plant
Provides help, advice and training in enabling people with a visual impairment to make the best use of their remaining vision. Directly assists partially sighted people in their daily lives; promotes research and development in order to better understand the problems of being partially sighted. In-house design and print facility to produce heavily lined stationery.
Employees: 4
Regional offices: 1

Partners of Prisoners and Families Support Group

Valentine House, 1079 Rochdale Road, Blackley, Manchester M9 8AJ
T: 0161 702 1000
Helpline: 0808 808 2003
F: 0161 850 1988
E: mail@partnersofprisoners.co.uk
www.partnersofprisoners.co.uk
CEO: Diane Curry OBE
Provides information, advice and support to the partners, families and friends of those in prison.

Partnership at Work

301B The Argent Centre, 60 Frederick Street, Birmingham B1 3HS
T: 0121 244 3752
F: 0121 244 9752
E: info@partnershipatwork.org.uk
We aim to work collaboratively with voluntary youth, community and play organisations to improve the quality of working lives for their staff and volunteers. We do this by providing sector-specific information, advice and support on human resource management and employment legislation.
Employees: 4
Volunteers: 3
Regional offices: 1

Patients Association

PO Box 935, Harrow, Middlesex HA1 3YJ
T: 020 8423 9111
Helpline: 0845 608 4455
F: 020 8423 9119
E: mailbox@patients-association.com
www.patients-association.org.uk
The Patients Association is a healthcare charity that for more than 40 years has advocated for greater and equitable access to high-quality, accurate and independent information for patients, and for greater and equitable access to high-quality care and for involvement in decision-making as a right.
Employees: 5
Volunteers: 11

Patients Forum

Riverbank House, 1 Putney Bridge Approach, London SW6 3JD
T: 020 7736 7903
F: 020 7736 7932
E: support@datadial.net
www.thepatientsforum.org.uk
The Patients Forum is a network of national and regional organisations concerned with the healthcare interests of patients and their families and carers. Full membership is open to national and umbrella organisations

representing the interests of users of health services, and their families and carers. Associate (non-voting) membership can be obtained for healthcare service providers, as well as all regulatory bodies.
Employees: 1
Regional offices: 1

Pax Christi

Christian Peace Education Centre, St Joseph's, Watford Way, London NW4 2LH
T: 020 8203 4884
F: 020 8203 5234
E: info@paxchristi.org.uk
www.paxchristi.org.uk
Founded in the Catholic Church, but open to all faiths, Pax Christi is a gospel-based lay-inspired peacemaking movement. It strives to help both the Church and the wider community proclaim peace through the witnesses and actions of its members. The three major objectives of Pax Christi are: reconciliation; the promotion of a culture of peace and non-violence; and providing the means to bring about peace (for example through training and education resources).
Employees: 1
Volunteers: 9

Pay and Employment Rights Service (Yorkshire) Ltd

E: fawzia@pers.org.uk

PayPal Giving Fund

Surrey TW9 1EH
T: 020 8439 2381
E: info@paypalgivingfund.org
www.paypalgivingfund.org.uk
CEO: Nick Aldridge
PayPal Giving Fund UK is a registered charity (No. 1110538) and enables eBay and PayPal users to give to good causes quickly and easily. PayPal Giving Fund certifies charities to participate in the eBay for Charity programme, and collects donations from eBay and PayPal users. It also distributes those donations and Gift Aid to donors' chosen charities, which receive 100% of the funds raised.

PDSA for Pets in Need of Vets

Head Office, Whitechapel Way, Priorslee, Telford TF2 9PQ
T: 01952 290999
F: 01952 291035
E: rydstrom.marilyn@pdsa.org.uk
www.pdsa.org.uk
Director General: Marilyn Rydstrom
PDSA cares for the pets of people in need by providing free veterinary services to their sick

and injured animals and promoting responsible pet ownership.
Employees: 1780
Volunteers: 4850
Regional offices: 6

Peace Brigades International UK Section (PBI UK)

1B Waterlow Road, London N19 5NJ
T: 020 7281 5370
E: admin@peacebrigades.org.uk
www.peacebrigades.org.uk
Director: Susi Bascon
Peace Brigades International provides protective accompaniment to human rights defenders (HRDs) at risk in Colombia, Guatemala, Honduras, Kenya, Mexico and Nepal. The presence of PBI volunteers represents the international community's concerns and deters against threats being carried out. This is backed up by international, political and diplomatic support and dialogue with authorities at all levels. PBI UK also lobbies the UK government, EU and UN bodies for better mechanisms and policies to protect HRDs worldwide.
Employees: 3
Volunteers: 30
Regional offices: 1
Income: £270,000 (2011-12)

Peace Direct

Development House, 56–64 Leonard Street, London EC2A 4JX
T: 0845 456 9714
F: 020 7794 2489
E: robert@peacedirect.org
www.peacedirect.org
Peace Direct's focus is grassroots peace-building in areas of conflict across the world. This is achieved through funding projects, including collaborative projects and one-off grants; persuasion and promotion of the value of non-violent approaches; and learning through peace activities around the world.
Employees: 7

Peace Pledge Union

1 Peace Passage, London N7 0BT
T: 020 7424 9444
F: 020 7482 6390
E: mail@ppu.org.uk
www.ppu.org.uk
The oldest, secular pacifist organisation in the UK, the Union supports research, provides advice and information about the causes and effects of wars and violence, and ways of resolving conflicts peacefully.
Employees: 2
Volunteers: 4

Peacemakers

E: info@peacemakers.org.uk

Peel Institute

Peel Centre, Percy Circus,
London WC1X 9EY
T: 020 7837 6082
F: 0807 278 3855
E: r.hamilton@peelinstitute.org.uk
www.peelinstitute.org.uk
Chief Executive: Rob Hamilton
A community hub in the heart of King's
Cross, providing a wide range of services for
all ages and sections of the local community.
Activities include crèche, child care, youth
services, adult education, advice and
advocacy to sports and older people's
projects, all provided in a fully accessible
purpose built community centre.
Employees: 33
Volunteers: 50
Income: £750,000 (2012-13)

Pelvic Pain Support Network

PO Box 6559, Poole, Dorset BH12 9DP
T: 01202 603447
E: info@pelvicpain.org.uk
www.pelvicpain.org.uk
The Network's volunteers are patients and
carers who have been supporting those with
pelvic pain, their carers and families since the
year 2000. We attend local, national and
international events and represent pelvic
pain patients at many meetings, seminars
and conferences.
Volunteers: 5

Pennell Initiative for Women's Health

207–221 Pentonville Road,
London N1 9UZ
T: 020 7278 1114
E: publishing.enquiries@helptheaged.
org.uk
www.pennellwomenshealth.org
Champions the cause of women's health by
researching and addressing the physical,
emotional, mental and spiritual needs of
women over 45. We seek to improve every
woman's prospect of living well into a
healthy old age by promoting understanding
of health issues.

Pensions Advisory Service

11 Belgrave Road, London SW1V 1RB
T: 020 7630 2272
F: 020 7592 7000
E: barry.wilkins@
pensionsadvisoryservice.org.uk
www.pensionsadvisoryservice.org.uk
Chief Executive: Malcolm McLean

The Pensions Advisory Service, is an
independent non-profit organisation that
provides free information, advice and
guidance on the whole spectrum of pensions
covering state, company, personal and
stakeholder schemes.
Employees: 35
Volunteers: 450

Penwith Community Development Trust

E: diana.higton@pcdt.org.uk

People & Planet

16 -17 Turl Street, Oxford,
Oxfordshire OX1 3DH
T: 01865 264180
E: people@peopleandplanet.org
www.peopleandplanet.org
People & Planet is the largest student
network in Britain campaigning to end world
poverty, defend human rights and protect
the environment. We're a student-led
movement that empowers young people
with the skills, confidence and knowledge
they need to make change happen, at home
and globally.

People in Aid

Development House, 56–64 Leonard
Street, London EC2A 4JX
T: 020 7520 2513
F: 020 7065 0901
E: jonathan@peopleinaid.org
www.peopleinaid.org
Relief of need anywhere arising out of
poverty, war, disaster, sickness, distress, age,
infirmity and disability, by promoting the
effectiveness and efficiency of organisations.
Meeting these needs by improving the
effectiveness with which they deploy paid
and volunteer personnel.
Employees: 3

People of God Trust

1 Carysfort House, 14 West Halkin Street,
London SW1X 8JS
T: 020 7235 2841
F: 07792 952265
E: pogtrust@gmail.com
Honorary Secretary: Simon Bryden-Brook
A lay initiative, promoting the Catholic
religion in accordance with the Second
Vatican Council, largely by making grants to
appropriate organisations.
Volunteers: 2
Regional offices: 1

People's Trust for Endangered Species

15 Cloisters House, 8 Battersea Park
Road, London SW8 4BG
T: 020 7498 4533
F: 020 7498 4459
E: jill@ptes.org
www.ptes.org
Chief Executive: Jill Nelson
PTES protects endangered species
worldwide and advances public awareness of
which species are endangered, rare or
threatened. It gives grants and runs selected
conservation programmes. The prime aims
of PTES activities are to protect endangered
species through conservation strategies that
are informed by scientific research; to
educate the public and promote open
debate between the public, policy makers
and conservation scientists about issues
surrounding endangered species and their
conservation.
Employees: 13
Volunteers: 1000

Permaculture Association (Britain)

London WC1N 3XX
T: 0845 458 1805
E: office@permaculture.org.uk
www.permaculture.org.uk
CEO: Andy Goldring
The Permaculture Association is the national
charity that supports and promotes
permaculture design throughout the UK and
worldwide through education, research and
networking.
Employees: 10
Volunteers: 150

Perthes Association

PO Box 773, Guildford, Surrey GU1 1XN
T: 01483 306637
E: info@perthes.org.uk
www.perthes.org.uk
Perthes disease is a form of osteochondritis.
A potentially crippling disease of the hip,
Perthes disease is a childhood disorder, which
affects the head of the femur. The
association supports children with Perthes
disease and associated conditions through
the purchase of wheelchairs, buggies and
more specialist equipment which are loaned
free to members (parents and carers)
allowing the children to play with their
siblings and friends, and enjoy a better
quality of life.
Employees: 4
Volunteers: 20

Pestalozzi International Village Trust

Ladybird Lane, Sedlescombe, Battle, East Sussex TN33 0UF
T: 01424 870444
F: 01424 870655
E: debbie.martin@pestalozzi.org.uk
www.pestalozzi.org.uk
Chief Executive: Paul Evans

Our unique two-year scholarship programme in the UK enables our 16–19-year-old students to develop their potential, intellectually and morally, applying their abilities using the Pestalozzi principles of educating the head, heart and hands-on. Our personal selection process carefully identifies motivated young people who have demonstrated the desire to help their home communities. From economically disadvantaged backgrounds around the world, they have exceptional ability but limited educational opportunity.

Employees: 20
Volunteers: 6
Regional offices: 1

Pesticide Action Network UK

56–64 Leonard Street, London EC2A 4LT
T: 020 7065 0905
F: 020 7065 0907
E: admin@pan-uk.org
www.pan-uk.org
Director: Linda Craig

(PAN UK) works to eliminate the dangers of toxic pesticides, our exposure to them, and their presence in the environment where we live and work. Nationally and globally, we promote safer alternatives, the production of healthy food, and sustainable farming.

Employees: 15
Volunteers: 3

Peter le Marchant Trust

Canalside Moorings Beeches Road, Loughborough, Leicestershire LE11 2NS
T: 01509 265590
E: lynnsmith@peterlemarchanttrust.co.uk
www.peterlemarchanttrust.co.uk

The Trust provides trips and holidays on special boats for adults and children with disabilities.

Peter Rigby Trust

The London Centre for Children with Cerebral Palsy, 54 Muswell Hill, London N10 3ST
T: 020 8444 7242
F: 020 8444 7241
E: kath@cplondon.org.uk
www.cplondon.org.uk
CEO: Marc Crank

We provide educational services for children with cerebral palsy. We have an independent approved school for children aged 3 to 11 years. We specialise in an approach known as Conductive Education. We also have an early intervention service and outreach support service within mainstream schools.

Employees: 26
Volunteers: 11
Regional offices: 1
Income: £850,000 (2011-12)

PEYTU

2nd Floor, Scrapstore House, 21 Sevier Street, St Werburgh's, Bristol, Avon BS2 9LB
T: 0117 908 0601
F: 0117 908 0622
E: admin@peytu.co.uk
www.peytu.co.uk
Chief Executive Officer: Sandra Meadows

Independent, not-for-profit and approved by Local Authorities. As a registered charity, our aim is to improve outcomes for children and young people by providing training, information, consultancy and support for those working with and/or caring for them. Our work broadly encompasses workforce development and enhancing opportunities for employment, further education and the promotion of social welfare and recreation for all families.

Employees: 6
Volunteers: 0
Regional offices: 1
Income: £369,670 (2012-13)

PFEG (Personal Finance Education Group)

Fifth Floor, 14 Bonhill Street, London EC2A 4BX
T: 020 7330 9470
Helpline: 0300 666 0127
F: 020 7374 6147
E: gary.millner@pfeg.org
www.pfeg.org
Chief Executive: Wendy van den Hende

PFEG is an educational charity and its mission is to make sure that all young people leaving school have the confidence, skills and knowledge in financial matters to take part fully in society. It offers a range of advice and resources and supports UK teachers working with children and young people aged 4 to 19 from all backgrounds.

Employees: 17
Volunteers: 100
Income: £8,257,805 (2010-11)

PHAB

Summit House, Wandle Road, Croydon CR0 1DF
T: 020 8667 9443
F: 020 8681 1399
E: info@phabengland.org.uk
www.phabengland.org.uk

Via a network of clubs, projects, publications and activities, PHAB promotes and encourages people with and without physical disabilities to come together on equal terms, to achieve complete integration within the wider community.

Employees: 30
Volunteers: 15000
Regional offices: 4

Pharmacist Support

5th Floor, 196 Deansgate, Manchester, Greater Manchester M3 3WF
T: 0808 168 2233
F: 0161 441 0319
E: info@pharmacistsupport.org
www.pharmacistsupport.org
Charity Manager: Diane Leicester

Pharmacist Support is an independent charity providing a range of free and confidential services to pharmacists and their families, former pharmacists, pre-registration trainees and pharmacy students. Support includes financial assistance, an information and enquiry service, a stress helpline, debt, benefits and employment advice and addiction support.

Employees: 9
Volunteers: 30
Regional offices: 0
Income: £1,750,000 (2011-12)

Philadelphia Association

4 Marty's Yard, 17 Hampstead High Street, London NW3 1QW
T: 020 7794 2652 (also fax)
E: office@philadelphia-association.co.uk
www.philadelphia-association.co.uk

The Association helps to relieve mental illness of all descriptions; to maintain therapeutic community households; to offer a forum for research, study and training in community therapy and psychotherapy according to the Association's own philosophy; and to publish relevant texts.

Employees: 1

Phoenix Domestic Abuse & Support Services Ltd

E: kateormerod@phoenixsupport.org.uk

Phoenix Futures

3rd Floor, Asra House, 1 Long Lane,
London SE1 4PG
T: 020 7234 9740
F: 020 7234 9770
E: info@phoenix-futures.org.uk
www.phoenix-futures.org.uk
Chief Executive: Karen Biggs

Phoenix Futures is the leading provider of care and rehabilitation services for people with drug and alcohol problems in the UK. Through 37 years' experience of transforming lives, it has developed a diverse portfolio of services across community, prison and residential settings.
Employees: 550
Volunteers: 50
Regional offices: 4

Pilgrim Hearts Trust

24 Yorkshire Place, Warfield, 24 Yorkshire Place, Bracknell RG42 3XE
T: 01344 307030 (also fax)
E: chalmers-brown@ntlworld.com
www.pilgrimhearts.org.uk
Director: Elaine Chalmers-Brown

Pilgrim Hearts is there to assist those on the edge and those who for whatever reason are not able to benefit from all of life's opportunities. It is a Christian organisation devoted to helping marginalised people, and those with disabilities, from all walks of life and backgrounds. We provide assistance to other organisations and community groups both in the voluntary and public sector.
Employees: 5
Income: £10,000 (2010-11)

Pilgrim Trust

Cowley House, 9 Little College Street,
London SW1P 3HS
T: 020 7222 4723
E: georgina@thepilgrimtrust.org.uk
www.thepilgrimtrust.org.uk

Founded in 1930 to address the country's most urgent needs and promote her future wellbeing, the trustees' current priorities are: preservation, including works of art, historic buildings and academic research; places of workshop, including block grants for the preservation of fabric of historic churches; and social welfare projects, with a particular emphasis on supporting people (particularly the young, minority ethnic groups and women with multiple needs) with drug and alcohol dependence problems, and projects in prisons.

Pilotlight

15–17 Lincoln's Inn Fields, Holborn,
London WC2A 3ED
T: 020 7396 7414
F: 020 7396 7467
E: info@pilotlight.org.uk
www.pilotlight.org.uk

Pilotlight helps small charities to build their capacity in order to plan for sustainability, growth and, where appropriate, replication. The membership of senior business people donate their time to supporting the charities through a combination of coaching and consultancy. The Pilotlight process is designed to enable members to make a difference to small charities in just a few hours a month, and educates this influential group about the charitable sector through practical experience.
Employees: 3

Pituitary Foundation

PO Box 1944, Bristol BS99 2UB
T: 0845 450 0376
Helpline: 0845 450 0375
E: helpline@pituitary.org.uk
www.pituitary.org.uk

Aims to assist people with rare pituitary disorders, supporting patients, their families and carers, and building a network of people in different parts of the country, with the aim of mutual support; to act as a source of information, providing leaflets on the disorders, social security benefits, life insurance policies, pensions, employment issues, etc; and to increase public awareness of these disorders.
Employees: 7
Volunteers: 100
Regional offices: 40

Place2Be

13–14 Angel Gate, 326 City Road,
London EC1V 2PT
T: 020 7923 5527
F: 020 7481 1894
E: enquiries@theplace2be.org.uk
www.theplace2be.org.uk

The Place2Be was established in 1994 in response to increasing concern about the extent and depth of emotional and behavioural difficulties displayed in classrooms and playgrounds.
Volunteers: 350

Plan UK

5–6 Underhill Street, London NW1 7HS
T: 020 7482 9777
F: 020 7482 9778
E: mail@plan-international.org.uk
www.plan-uk.org

Plan is a child-centred development agency with no political or religious affiliations, enabling families and communities in the poorest countries to make lasting improvements to the lives of their children.
Employees: 64
Volunteers: 34

Plant Heritage

12 Home Farm, Loseley Park, Guildford,
Surrey GU3 1HS
T: 01483 447540
F: 01483 458933
E: info@plantheritage.org.uk
www.plantheritage.com
Chief Executive Officer: Chief Executive Officer

Plant Heritage (or National Council for the Conservation of Plants and Gardens to give its full name) is the only charity working to conserve cultivated plants through the National Plant Collections scheme and the Threatened Plants Project.
Employees: 8
Volunteers: 500

Play-Train

The Post Office Building, 149–153
Alcester Road, Moseley,
Birmingham B13 8JW
T: 0121 449 6665
E: team@playtrain.org.uk
www.playtrain.org.uk

Play-Train works to develop both the quality and quantity of creative play opportunities for children out of school, by providing a range of training and consultancy services to organisations working with children in non-school settings.

Plunkett Foundation

2–3 The Quadrangle, Banbury Road,
Woodstock, Oxfordshire OX20 1LH
T: 01993 810730
F: 01993 810849
E: info@plunkett.co.uk
www.plunkett.co.uk

The Plunkett Foundation is an educational charity, based near Oxford in the UK, which supports the development of rural group enterprise worldwide. The Foundation draws on 80 years' practical experience of working with partners from the private sector to promote and implement economic self-help solutions to rural problems.
Employees: 16

Police Foundation

1st Floor, Park Place, 12 Lawn Lane,
Vauxhall, London SW8 1UD
T: 020 7582 3744
F: 020 7587 0671
E: sue.roberts@police-foundation.org.uk
www.police-foundation.org.uk
Director: John Graham

The Police Foundation is the country's only independent charity focused on responding to public concerns about policing, informing their understanding of policing issues and challenging the police service and the government to improve policing for the benefit of all citizens. It does so by promoting debate on policing and police reform, providing commentary, knowledge and insight on important issues and contemporary developments and turning new ideas into policy and practice.
Employees: 8
Volunteers: 1
Regional offices: 1
Income: £336,000 (2011-12)

Policy Studies Institute

50 Hanson Street, London W1W 6UP
T: 020 7911 7500
F: 020 7911 7501
E: psi-admin@psi.org.uk
www.psi.org.uk

One of Britain's leading independent research institutes, conducting research to promote economic wellbeing and improve quality of life. PSI undertakes and publishes research studies relevant to social, economic, industrial and environmental policy. In 1998 it merged to become an independent subsidiary of the University of Westminster. PSI takes a politically neutral stance on issues of public policy and its income is derived from funds for individual research projects: funding sources include government, professional agencies, charitable trusts and private companies.
Volunteers: 46

Polycystic Kidney Disease Charity

91 Royal College Street,
London NW1 0SE
T: 020 7387 0543
Helpline: 0300 111 1234
E: tess.harris@pkdcharity.org.uk
www.pkdcharity.org.uk
Chief Executive: Tess Harris

We provide information, advice and support to those affected by polycystic kidney disease (PKD). We aim to fund research into determining the causes of PKD, discovering treatments and a cure, and raise awareness of PKD, providing information about PKD to

patients, the public, the medical community and the media.
Employees: 2
Volunteers: 50
Income: £90,000 (2011-12)

Pontifical Mission Societies

23 Eccleston Square, London SW1V 1NU
T: 020 7821 9755
E: director@missio.org.uk
www.missio.org.uk

The PMS – Association for the Propagation of the Faith (APF), Society of St Peter the Apostle (SPA) and Holy Childhood/Mission Together are the official support organisation for the overseas mission of the Catholic Church. They provide practical and material support to new or poor faith communities, enabling them to become self-sufficient, and flourish in their own right.

Portchester Community Association

E: manager@portchesterca.org.uk

Portman Group Trust

7–10 Chandos Street, London W1G 9DQ
T: 020 7907 3700
F: 020 7907 3710
E: advice@portmangroup.org.uk
www.portmangroup.org.uk

Supported by the UK's leading drinks producers, the Trust is concerned solely with social responsibility issues surrounding alcohol. It endorses the preservation, protection and promotion of public health through the provision of education and research on alcohol-related matters.

Positive Body Image

PO Box 23266, London SE14 5FQ
E: info@positivebodyimage.co.uk

Positive Body Image aims to use a holistic approach to health and fitness to help individuals improve their physical, mental and spiritual wellbeing and, in so doing, help them to improve their self-image and achieve their potential. Positive Body Image was established to help address the health inequalities experienced by ethnic minority women, but its programmes and services are open to all women.

Positive Parenting Publications and Programmes

2A South Street, Gosport,
Hampshire PO12 1ES
T: 023 9252 8787
E: info@parenting.org.uk

The objectives of Positive Parenting Publications and Programmes are the promotion of moral and family welfare and in particular the care and upbringing of children and good parenting skills.
Employees: 11

Positively UK

345 City Road, London EC1V 1LR
T: 020 7713 0444
F: 020 7713 1020
E: aanderson@positivelyuk.org
www.positivelyuk.org
Chief Executive: Allan Anderson

Positively UK is peer-led charity supporting people living with HIV. We provide information, guidance and skills for people to make informed choices around living well with HIV. Recognised as experts in the field of HIV peer support we work collaboratively with the NHS and other health and social care providers. We inform policy and best practice with government and clinical bodies. We support over 1,400 people annually to promote physical, emotional and social wellbeing.
Employees: 17
Volunteers: 46
Income: £542,273 (2011-12)

Potential Plus UK

Suite 1.2, Challenge House, Sherwood Drive, Bletchley, Milton Keynes MK3 6DP
T: 01908 646433
E: amazingchildren@nagcbritain.org.uk
www.potentialplusuk.org
Chief Executive: Denise Yates

Supports gifted children, their parents, families and teachers and disseminates information concerning gifted children.
Employees: 9
Volunteers: 120

Powerhouse

St Luke's Community Centre, 85 Tarling Road, Canning Town, London E16 1HN
T: 020 7366 6336
F: 020 7366 6337
E: info@thepowerhouse.org.uk
www.thepowerhouse.org.uk

Powerhouse is an organisation of women with learning difficulties. It is committed to promoting women's rights through advocacy, campaigning, one-to-one support, training and awareness-raising.

Practical Action

Schumacher Centre For Technology and Development, Bourton on Dunsmore, Rugby, Warwickshire CV23 9QZ
T: 01926 634407
E: practicalaction@practicalaction.org.uk
www.practicalaction.org
Founded in 1966 as the Intermediate Technology Group by Dr EF Schumacher, its mission is to build on the technical skills of poor people in developing countries enabling them to improve the quality of their lives and that of future generations.

Prader-Willi Syndrome Association UK

125A London Road, Derby, Derbyshire DE1 2QQ
T: 01332 365676
F: 01332 360401
E: admin@pwsa.co.uk
www.pwsa.co.uk
Chief Executive Officer: Susan Passmore
Prader-Willi syndrome is a complex genetic disorder, present from birth. The Association exists to contact and support families concerned with the disorder; to inform health professionals, families and the public in general about the disorder; to raise funds and foster research into its causes and alleviation.
Employees: 9
Volunteers: 70
Regional offices: 1

Pre-school Learning Alliance

The Fitzpatrick Building, 188 York Way, London N7 9AD
T: 020 7697 2595
F: 020 3137 2493
E: info@pre-school.org.uk
www.pre-school.org.uk
Chief Executive: Neil Leitch
The Alliance is the largest and most representative early years membership organisation and voluntary sector provider of quality affordable childcare and education in England. We represent the interests of 14,000 member settings and give direct support to them, via information and advice, specialist publication, acclaimed training programmes and campaigns to influence early years policy and practice.
Employees: 2000
Volunteers: 763
Regional offices: 30
Income: £36,732,000 (2012-13)

Primary Ciliary Dyskinesia Family Support Group

15 Shuttleworth Grove, Wavendon Gate, Milton Keynes MK7 7RX
T: 01908 281635
Helpline: 0300 111 0122
E: chair@pcdsupport.org.uk
www.pcdsupport.org.uk
Chairman: Fiona Copeland
The Group provides support to patients with PCD (also known as Kartagener's syndrome and immotile cilia syndrome) and parents of children known to have the syndrome. It brings the disease to the attention of the medical profession and the public and raises funds for research.
Volunteers: 8
Income: £14,000 (2012-13)

Primary Sclerosing Cholangitis Trust

Hollibury House, 47 Part Street, Southport, Merseyside PR8 1HY
T: 01704 514377
E: info@psctrust.com
www.psctrust.com
The Primary Sclerosing Cholangitis (PSC) Trust is dedicated to discovering the cause and cure of PSC, a chronic progressive liver disease, and related conditions.

PRIMHE

c/o Tipton Care Org, Glebefields Health Centre, St Marks Road, Tipton, West Midlands DY4 0SN
T: 0121 530 8021 (also fax)
Helpline: 01215 308021
E: admin@primhe.org.uk
www.primhe.org.uk
Chair of Trustees: Dr Ian Walton
Helping primary healthcare professionals and staff achieve and deliver the best standards of mental healthcare. PRIMHE provides mental health support, services, resources, education and training.
Volunteers: 5
Regional offices: 1

Prince's Trust

Clarence House, London SW1A 1BA
T: 020 7543 1234
E: info@princes-trust.org.uk
www.princes-trust.org.uk
The Prince's Trust is the UK's leading youth charity that helps young people overcome barriers and get their lives working. Through practical support including training, mentoring and financial assistance, it helps 14–30 year olds realise their potential and transform their lives. The Trust focuses its efforts on those who've struggled at school,

been in care, been in trouble with the law or are long-term unemployed.
Employees: 800
Volunteers: 10000
Regional offices: 9

Prison Advice and Care Trust

Park Place, 12 Lawn Lane, London SW8 1UD
T: 020 7735 9535
E: info@prisonadvice.org.uk
www.prisonadvice.org.uk
Director: Andy Keen-Downs
The Trust's mission is to support prisoners and their families to make a fresh start and to minimise the harm that can be caused by imprisonment on offenders, families and communities.
Employees: 83
Volunteers: 300
Regional offices: 1

Prison Chat UK

PO Box 49449, Penge, London SE20 8YG
T: 020 8778 7741
E: prisonchatuk@aol.com
www.prisonchatuk.com
An online community giving support to those who have a loved one inside the British prison system. All members are connected to the prison system in some way and can offer advice and share their experiences, so creating a community for people to go and get support and answers when a loved one has been taken into custody.

Prison Fellowship England and Wales

PO Box 68226, London SW1P 9WR
T: 020 7799 2500
E: info@prisonfellowship.org.uk
www.prisonfellowship.org.uk
Chief Executive: Natalie Cronin
Prison Fellowship aims to show Christ's love to prisoners by coming alongside them, praying and supporting them to change. We offer our services to all who request them, regardless of their beliefs. We do this through our network of volunteer members and have over 1,500 volunteers throughout England and Wales.
Employees: 18
Volunteers: 1600

Prison Reform Trust

The Old Trading House, 15 Northburgh Street, London EC1V 0JR
T: 020 7251 5070
F: 020 7251 5076
E: geoff.dobson@prisonreformtrust.org.uk
www.prisonreformtrust.org.uk
Promotes public understanding of the need for improvements in our prison system; and

encourages public interest in penal policy and practice.

Employees: 13
Volunteers: 3

Prisoners Abroad

89-93 Fonthill Road, London N4 3JH
T: 020 7561 6820
Helpline: 0808 172 0098
F: 020 7561 6821
E: info@prisonersabroad.org.uk
www.prisonersabroad.org.uk
Chief Executive: Pauline Crowe
Provides practical and emotional support to British citizens in prison overseas, their families and friends, and to ex-prisoners returning to the UK.

Employees: 25

Prisoners Advice Service

PO Box 46199, London EC1M 4XA
T: 020 7253 3323
Helpline: 0845 430 8923
F: 020 7253 8067
E: advice@prisonersadvice.org.uk
www.prisonersadvice.org.uk
PAS provides free, expert legal advice and information to prisoners in England and Wales regarding their rights and conditions of imprisonment; it takes up prisoners' complaints about their treatment inside prison by providing free advice and assistance on an individual and confidential basis. The service also produces a quarterly bulletin on new prison case law and policy, entitled Prisoners' Legal Rights Bulletin.

Employees: 6
Volunteers: 15

Prisoners Education Trust

Wandle House, Riverside Drive, Mitcham, Surrey CR4 4BU
T: 020 8648 7760
F: 020 8648 7762
E: info@prisonerseducation.org.uk
www.prisonerseducation.org.uk
Interim Director: Rachel Youngman
The Trust aims to offer prisoners a chance to change through education and promotes the importance of education in the successful resettlement of offenders. It makes grants to enable prisoners to study through distance learning and other courses that will enhance their chances of employment after release. It also runs projects developing support and advice for prisoner learners and enables

prisoner learners to have a voice about education and learning.

Employees: 12
Volunteers: 12
Income: £1,131,114 (2010-11)

Prisoners' Families and Friends Service

20 Trinity Street, London SE1 1DB
T: 020 7403 4091
F: 020 7403 9359
E: info@prisonersfamiliesandfriends.org.uk
www.prisonersfamiliesandfriends.org.uk
The main aims of the Service are to provide the families and friends of anyone sentenced to imprisonment or remanded in custody with advice and information; support and assistance at court; and support and friendship. The advice is free and confidential, and appropriate to the families' and friends' needs.

Employees: 4
Volunteers: 58

Professionals Aid Council

10 St Christopher's Place, London W1U 1HZ
T: 020 7935 0641
E: admin@professionalsaid.org.uk
www.professionalsaid.org.uk
Chief Executive Officer: Finola McNicholl
PAC can give financial aid to university graduates and individuals from professional backgrounds. We also give small educational grants to help students whose funding has broken down after they have started their course. Limited grants may also be available to help families with the cost of children's education.

Employees: 4

Progress Educational Trust

140 Gray's Inn Road, London WC1X 8AX
T: 020 7278 7870
E: admin@progress.org.uk
www.progress.org.uk
Aims to enhance the public understanding of reproduction and genetics; to encourage discussion of their social, legal and ethical implication and to promote the need for further research in these areas of science and medicine.

Progress Employment Support

The Enterprise Centre, 291- 305 Lytham Road, Blackpool, Lancashire FY4 1EW
T: 01253 477287
F: 01253 477276
E: deborah.parker@progressemployment.org
www.progressemployment.org
CEO: Deborah Parker
A values-driven supported employment agency achieving inclusive employment and business success, by supporting disabled people and their employers to benefit from working together.

Employees: 5
Regional offices: 1
Income: £450,000 (2011-12)

Progressio

Units 9 -12, The Stable Yard, Broomgrove Road, London SW9 9TL
T: 020 7733 1195
F: 020 7326 2059
E: enquiries@progressio.org.uk
www.progressio.org.uk
Executive Director: Mark Lister
Progressio is a UK-based charity working internationally to enable people in developing countries to change the situations that keep them poor. We work in 11 countries and have a history of working in fragile, post-conflict states, developing long-term partnerships with local organisations and community groups in Africa, Latin America, the Caribbean, the Middle East and Asia, providing practical support through around 100 development workers, mostly from the south, who share skills, know-how and training.

Employees: 80
Volunteers: 104

Promise Dreams

Promise House, Edwin House, Boundary Industrial Estate, Stafford Road, Wolverhampton, West Midlands WV10 7EL
T: 01902 212451
F: 01902 783625
E: info@promisedreams.co.uk
www.promisedreams.co.uk
Charity Manager: Beverley Bird
Promise Dreams is a national registered charity, dedicated to helping seriously ill and terminally ill children and their families turn a very special wish into reality.

Employees: 5
Regional offices: 1

Prospect Hospice

E: andrewthompson@prospect-hospice.
net

Prospects for People with Learning Disabilities

69 Honey End Lane, Reading,
Berkshire RG30 4EL
T: 0118 950 8781
E: paula@prospects.org.uk
www.prospects.org.uk
CEO: Paul Ashton
Prospects is a Christian organisation
supporting people with learning disabilities
so that they live their lives to the full through:
residential homes and supported living;
overseas partnerships; church-based
ministry; involvement in Christian
conferences.
Employees: 700
Volunteers: 1300
Regional offices: 7
Income: £10,400,000 (2011-12)

Prostate Cancer UK

Fourth Floor, The Counting House, 53
Tooley Street, London SE1 2QN
T: 020 3310 7000
Helpline: 0800 074 8383
F: 020 3310 7107
E: info@prostatecanceruk.org
www.prostatecanceruk.org
Chief Executive: Owen Sharp
Prostate Cancer UK fight to help more men
survive prostate cancer and enjoy a better
quality of life. We support men through; our
helpline staffed by specialist nurses, our work
in the community, and by providing vital
information on all aspects of prostate
disease. We find answers by funding research
into causes, tests and treatments. And we
lead change, raising the profile of the disease
and improving care. We believe that men
deserve better.
Employees: 185
Volunteers: 1263
Regional offices: 6
Income: £30,000,000 (2012-13)

Prostate Research Campaign UK

10 Northfields Prospect, Putney Bridge
Road, London SW18 1PE
T: 020 8877 5840
E: broche@prostateaction.org.uk
www.prostate-research.org.uk
The Campaign funds scientific and medical
research into prostate disorders, whether
benign or malignant, and provision of
information/education of value to patients
and families.

Psoriasis and Psoriatic Arthritis Alliance

PO Box 111, St Albans AL2 3JQ
T: 0870 770 3212
F: 0870 770 3213
E: info@papaa.org
www.papaa.org
Aims to preserve, protect and relieve persons
suffering from psoriatic arthropathy and
associated conditions.

Psoriasis Association

Dick Coles House, 2 Queensbridge,
Northampton,
Northamptonshire NN4 7BF
T: 01604 251620
Helpline: 0845 676 0076
F: 01604 251621
E: mail@psoriasis-association.org.uk
www.psoriasis-association.org.uk
Chief Executive: Helen McAteer
The Association supports people with
psoriasis, raises awareness of the condition
and funds research into the causes,
treatment and care.
Employees: 5
Volunteers: 2

Psychiatric Rehabilitation Association

Bayford Mews, Bayford Street,
London E8 3SF
T: 020 8985 3570
E: ppra528898@aol.com
www.pra-london.co.uk
Promotes the rehabilitation of the mentally
sick on their return home, to employment
and society by preparatory work and aftercare in the community; and promotes
practical measures in research for the
prevention and combating of mental stress
within the community.

Psychosynthesis and Education Trust

92–94 Tooley Street, London SE1 2TH
T: 020 7403 2100
F: 020 7403 5562
E: enquiries@petrust.org.uk
www.psychosynthesis.edu
The Trust's main purpose is to gain
recognition for the central role of soul and
self in psychology, and to renew the soul in
the everyday life of individuals, the family,
groups, organisations and society. Other
activities include promoting the practice of
transpersonal counselling and psychotherapy
by providing a training centre of excellence,
and providing psychosynthesis educational

techniques suitable for schools and adult
education.
Employees: 29
Regional offices: 1

Public Concern at Work

Suite 301, 16 Baldwins Gardens,
London EC1N 7RJ
T: 020 7404 6609
E: whistle@pcaw.co.uk
www.whistleblowing.org.uk
Acting as a leading, independent authority
on public interest whistleblowing, PCaW
aims to improve standards in the public,
private and voluntary sectors and to assert
the accountability of people in the
workplace.

Public Fundraising Regulatory Association

Unit 11, Europoint Centre, 5 - 11
Lavington Street, London SE1 0NZ
T: 020 7401 8452
E: info@pfra.org.uk
www.pfra.org.uk
Chief Executive: Sally de la Bedoyere
The PFRA regulates the use of face-to-face
fundraising by charities and professional
fundraising organisations, principally on the
street and doorstep. We work with local
authorities to agree equitable access to
fundraising sites and monitor their use to
ensure fundraisers abide by the Institute of
Fundraising's codes of practice.
Employees: 9
Regional offices: 1

Public Law Project

150 Caledonian Road, London N1 9RD
T: 020 7843 1260
F: 020 7837 7048
E: admin@publiclawproject.org.uk
www.publiclawproject.org.uk
Aims to improve access to public law
remedies, such as judicial review, for people
whose access is limited because of poverty,
discrimination or other disadvantages.
Employees: 8
Volunteers: 3
Regional offices: 1

PublicMedia Projects CIC

82A Highfield Road, Dartford,
Kent DA1 2JJ
T: 01322 405540
E: vb@publicmedia.co.uk
www.publicmedia.co.uk
Enterprise Director: Vince Braithwaite

PublicMedia Projects is a social enterprise, community interest company which has been set-up to support the introduction of locally-based media services in the UK. Through new internet and radio services etc., PublicMedia Projects aims to support the social and economic regeneration of local communities, and empower people to engage more effectively in civic society. These services will also create a space for the creative industries to produce content which is both entertaining and engaging.

QED – UK

Quest House, 243 Manningham Lane, Bradford BD8 7ER
T: 01274 483267
F: 01274 305689
E: info@qed-uk.org
www.qed-uk.org
Aims to improve the economic, social and education development of minority ethnic groups. Mainly focusing on disadvantaged South Asian communities.
Employees: 15
Volunteers: 20

Quaker Social Action

E: judithmoran@qsa.org.uk

Quality of Life Trust

6 Alexander Court, St Marks Close, Bexhill-on-Sea TN39 4PN
T: 01424 843326
www.qualityoflifetrust.com
Where disabled and partially sighted people can debate the key issues of the day, from which they have so often been excluded. The main focus will be a magazine and forum.
Employees: 2
Volunteers: 6

Queen Alexandra College

Court Oak Road, Harborne, Birmingham B17 9TG
T: 0121 428 5050
F: 0121 428 5048
E: enquiries@qac.ac.uk
www.qac.ac.uk

Queen Alexandra College aims to challenge discrimination and exclusion by providing opportunities for people with visual impairment and other disabilities to learn, live and work independently.
Employees: 115
Volunteers: 10

Queen Elizabeth's Foundation for Disabled People

Leatherhead Court, Woodlands Road, Leatherhead, Surrey KT22 0BN
T: 01372 841100
F: 01372 844072
E: sue.moller@qef.org.uk
www.qef.org.uk
Chief Executive: Jonathan Powell
QEF works with people living with physical and learning disabilities or acquired brain injuries to gain new skills and increase independence. Whether it's learning everyday skills, rebuilding a life affected by brain injury, acquiring the skills to drive a specially adapted car or training for future employment, QEF supports disabled people to achieve goals for life.
Employees: 300
Volunteers: 300

Queen Victoria Seamen's Rest

121–131 East India Dock Road, Poplar, London E14 6DF
T: 020 7987 5466
E: enquiries@qvsr.org.uk
Provides secure and comfortable accommodation; fosters a spirit of community internally and externally; supports, empowers and enables individuals to enhance their quality of life; provides active rehabilitation opportunities; integrates our services into the lives of the local community.

QUIT

211 Old Street, London EC1V 9NR
T: 020 7251 1551
F: 020 7251 1661
E: reception@quit.org.uk
www.quit.org.uk
Helps smokers trying to stop smoking. QUIT provides practical, relevant and professional support to the 12 million smokers in Britain.
Employees: 60
Volunteers: 200

Race on the Agenda

c/o Resource for London, 356 Holloway Road, London N7 6PA
T: 020 7697 4093
E: rota@rota.org.uk
www.rota.org.uk
Chief Executive: Andy Gregg
To be a BAME-led social policy think-tank that focuses on race equality and issues affecting Britain's BAME communities, and creates an environment for the equalities third sector to flourish. To strengthen the voice of BAME communities through increased civic engagement and participation in society and provide representation of issues affecting BAME communities and the sector that was set up to serve them.
Employees: 7
Volunteers: 3
Regional offices: 1

RADAR

12 City Forum, 250 City Road, London EC1V 8AF
T: 020 7250 3222
F: 020 7250 0212
E: radar@radar.org.uk
www.radar.org.uk
Chief Executive: Liz Sayce
RADAR is the UK's leading pan-disability organisation with a membership of disabled people and 400 disability organisations fast-tracking their views to Westminster and Whitehall and working for an inclusive society.
Employees: 20

Raglan Housing Association

Wright House, 12–14 Castle Street, Poole, Dorset BH15 1BQ
T: 01202 678731
Helpline: 0845 070 7772
F: 01202 665091
E: info@raglan.org
www.raglan.org
Chief Executive: Alan Seabright
Raglan's purpose is to meet a variety of housing needs by providing quality, affordable homes, high-standard services and by promoting and encouraging sustainable

communities. Our resident involvement policy offers a wide range of opportunities for volunteers to monitor performance and contribute to our drive for continuing improvement in the homes and services we deliver.

Employees: 400
Volunteers: 150
Regional offices: 6

Railway Children

1st Floor, 1 The Commons, Sandbach, Cheshire CW11 1EG
T: 01270 251571 (also fax)
E: enquiries@railwaychildren.org.uk
www.railwaychildren.org.uk

Railway Children exists to help street children. No child should have to live alone and at risk on the streets, and this belief is reflected in the charity's vision, which is to create a world of safety and opportunity for children who are at risk on the streets.

Employees: 6
Volunteers: 5

Rainbow Centre for Children affected by Life-Threatening Illnesses or Bereavement

27 Lilymead Avenue, Knowle, Bristol BS4 2BY
T: 0117 985 3343
E: contact@rainbowcentre.org.uk
www.rainbowcentre.org.uk
Centre Director: Angela Emms

The Rainbow Centre supports children and their families experiencing cancer and other life-threatening illnesses or bereavement, using counselling and complementary therapies.

Regional offices: 1

Rainbow Trust Children's Charity

6 Cleeve Court, Cleeve Road, Leatherhead, Surrey KT22 7UD
T: 01372 363438
F: 01372 363101
E: david.halliday@rainbowtrust.org.uk
www.rainbowtrust.org.uk
Chief Executive: Heather Wood

Rainbow Trust provides emotional and practical support for families who have a child with a life-threatening or terminal illness. We offer the whole family individually tailored, high-quality support for as long as they need it.

Employees: 80
Volunteers: 50
Regional offices: 8

Rainforest Foundation UK

233A Kentish Town Road, London NW5 2JT
T: 020 7485 0193
F: 020 7485 0315
E: info@rainforestuk.org
www.rainforestfoundationuk.org
Executive Director: Simon Counsell

The Rainforest Foundation UK supports indigenous peoples of the world's rainforests in their efforts to protect the environment and fulfil their rights to life, land and livelihoods. Since 1989, Rainforest Foundation UK has been at the forefront of rainforest protection, saving an area the size of England and Wales.

Employees: 20
Volunteers: 2

Rainy Day Trust

Federation House, 10 Vyse Street, Birmingham B18 6LT
T: 0121 237 1130
F: 0121 237 1133
E: diane@rainydaytrust.org.uk
www.rainydaytrust.org.uk
General Secretary: Diane Stevens

The Rainy Day Trust is a charity that exists solely to help people who have worked in the UK's home improvement and home enhancement industry including DIY/ hardware stores, garden centres, pottery & glass, housewares and all the manufacturers, distributors and wholesalers who supply them. We can assist in variety of ways, however all applicants should have worked for one/more of the above industries for at least five years.

Employees: 2
Volunteers: 5
Income: £125,316 (2011-12)

Raleigh International Trust

3rd Floor, 207 Waterloo Road, London SE1 8XD
T: 020 7183 1270
F: 020 7504 8094
E: stacey.adams@raleigh.org.uk
www.raleighinternational.org
Chief Executive: Stacey Adams

Raleigh international expeditions involve people from all walks of life, ages and nationalities to make a difference to communities and environments. Through a combination of adventure and challenging projects we inspire people reach their full potential as global citizens. Our vision is to awaken a sense of life-purpose and belonging, and unite people as part of a

global community who can work together to rise to the challenges of the world we live in.

Employees: 36
Volunteers: 600
Regional offices: 1 Scotland 3 International

Ramblers' Association

2nd Floor, Camelford House, 87–89 Albert Embankment, London SE1 7TW
T: 020 7339 8571
F: 020 7339 8501
E: ramblers@london.ramblers.org.uk
www.ramblers.org.uk

Promotes walking, protects rights of way, campaigns for access to open country and defends the beauty of the countryside.

Employees: 60
Volunteers: 5000
Regional offices: 3

Rape and Sexual Abuse Support Centre

PO Box 383, Croydon, Surrey CR9 2AW
T: 020 8683 3311
Helpline: 0808 802 9999
F: 020 8683 3366
E: info@rasasc.org.uk
www.rasasc.org.uk
Chief Executive Officer: Yvonne Traynor

A professional and passionate team working in a centre of excellence dedicated to the healing and empowerment of survivors of sexual violence by providing counselling, helpline support, advocacy through the criminal justice system, training and information for other agencies.

Employees: 38
Volunteers: 28

Rapid Effective Assistance for Children with Potentially Terminal Illness

St Luke's House, 270 Sandycombe Road, Richmond Upon Thames, Surrey TW9 3NP
T: 020 8940 2575
F: 020 8940 2050
E: react@reactcharity.org
www.reactcharity.org

Identifies and responds to the needs of children and young people diagnosed as suffering from potentially terminal illnesses.

Employees: 4
Volunteers: 30
Regional offices: 1

Rare Breeds Survival Trust

Stoneleigh Park, Kenilworth,
Warwickshire CV8 2LG
T: 024 7669 6551
F: 024 7669 6706
E: enquiries@rbst.org.uk
www.rbst.org.uk
Managing Director: Rob Havard
The Rare Breeds Survival Trust is the leading
national charity working to conserve and
protect the UK's rare native breeds of farm
animals from extinction. We believe in the
value of the UK's rich and varied livestock
heritage and that this needs to be conserved
as a vital genetic resource for future
generations and the benefit of agriculture.
Employees: 12
Volunteers: 250
Regional offices: 20
Income: £700,000 (2010-11)

Rare Disease UK

Unit 4D, Leroy House, 436 Essex Road,
London N1 3QP
T: 020 7704 3141
E: info@raredisease.org.uk
www.raredisease.org.uk
Chair: Alastair Kent
The national alliance for people with rare
diseases and all who support them.

Rathbone

4th Floor, Churchgate House, 56 Oxford
Street, Manchester M1 6EU
T: 0161 236 5358
F: 0161 238 6356
E: julie.lewis@rathboneuk.org
www.rathbonetraining.co.uk
Chief Executive: Richard Williams
Rathbone is a charity that provides education
and training opportunities to over 14,000
young people annually. Rathbone is
dedicated to working with young people
who have not had their needs met by
mainstream education. Many such young
people require support to access
opportunities that are tailored to their
learning and social needs. Rathbone has four
core areas: alternative school curriculum for
young people aged 14–16, apprenticeships,
pre-vocational activities and youth
engagement.
Employees: 750
Volunteers: 40
Regional offices: 89

Raw Material Music and Media Education

2 Robsart Street SW9 0DJ
T: 020 7737 6103
F: 020 7733 7533
E: tim@raw-material.org
www.raw-material.org
Promotes education and training in the
creative and expressive arts and media.

Raynaud's & Scleroderma Association (RSA)

112 Crewe Road, Alsager,
Cheshire ST7 2JA
T: 01270 872776
E: info@raynauds.org.uk
www.raynauds.org.uk
Chief Executive Officer: Elizabeth Bevins
Raynaud's is a common condition in which
blood is prevented from reaching the
extremities of the body, mainly the fingers
and toes, on exposure to the cold or any
slight change in temperature. Scleroderma is
an uncommon disease of the blood vessels,
the immune system and the connective
tissue. The Association's aims are to promote
better communication between doctors and
patients, to disseminate information and to
raise funds for research and welfare projects.
Employees: 6

RCJ Advice Bureau

Royal Courts of Justice, Strand,
London WC2A 2LL
T: 020 7947 7119
F: 020 7947 7167
E: james.banks@rcjadvice.org.uk
www.rcjadvice.org.uk
Chief Executive: James Banks
Works to provide access to justice to
unrepresented litigants in the Royal Courts of
Justice and the Principal Registry of the
Family Division, through the provision of
legal and other advice services.
Employees: 21
Volunteers: 35

Re-Solv

30A High Street, Stone,
Staffordshire ST15 8AW
T: 01785 817885
F: 01785 813205
E: information@re-solv.org
www.re-solv.org
Director: Stephen Ream
Re-Solv works to contribute to happier,
healthier, safer social environments by
preventing the death, suffering and crime,

which may result as a consequence of solvent
and volatile substance abuse (VSA).
Employees: 5
Volunteers: 14
Regional offices: 1
Income: £241,086 (2011-12)

Re-Start

56 Davids Way, Hainault, Ilford,
Essex IG6 3BQ
T: 020 8501 1096
Helpline: 020 3087 5699
E: restartoffice@gmail.com
www.restartoffice.blogspot.com
CE: Moinul Khalique
Re-Start is a social-work-led voluntary
organisation, working in partnership with Job
Centre Plus We currently run a number of
programmes, mainly of a solution-focused
therapeutic nature, targeting specific groups,
such as claimants of incapacity benefits in
some of the most deprived parts of east and
north east London. Many of the clients
referred to us sometimes lack the motivation
and determination to change their
circumstances.
Employees: 1
Volunteers: -5

REACH

Camelford House, 87–89 Albert
Embankment, London SE1 7TP
T: 020 7582 6543
F: 020 7582 2423
E: mail@reachskills.org.uk
www.reach-online.org.uk
REACH's aims are to recruit and support
people with managerial, professional,
business and technical experience and match
them with part-time voluntary roles
throughout the UK, and to help voluntary
organisations gain access to these potential
volunteers and benefit fully from their
expertise.
Employees: 7
Volunteers: 60
Regional offices: 3

Reach - Association for Children with Upper Limb Deficiency

Pearl Assurance House, Brook Street,
Tavistock, Devon PL19 0BN
T: 0845 130 6225
E: reach@reach.org.uk
www.reach.org.uk
National Coordinator: Jo Dixon
Reach was formed in 1978 by parents of
children who were missing part of their arm
or a hand, in order to lobby for the provision
of a new artificial arm under the NHS. Since

then Reach has grown to become a national organisation providing support and information for children with hand or arm deficiencies, and their parents.

Employees: 2
Volunteers: 25
Regional offices: 14
Income: £150,000 (2011-12)

Reading Matters

Western House, Western Way, Halifax Road, Bradford, West Yorkshire BD6 2SZ
T: 01274 692219
E: rachel@readingmatters.org.uk
www.readingmatters.org.uk
Chief Executive: Rachel Kelly
Reading Matters' specialises in one-to-one support to motivate children and young people to reach their potential by becoming confident and enthusiastic readers. As an effective literacy support charity, we train adults, young people and children across the UK to offer reading support and manage and support a network of trained volunteer Reading Mentors across West and South Yorkshire.

Employees: 5
Volunteers: 90
Regional offices: 1
Income: £131,862 (2012-13)

Reading Mencap

21 Alexandra Road, Reading, Berkshire RG1 5PE
T: 0118 966 2518
E: businessrelations@readingmencap.org.uk
www.readingmencap.org.uk
CEO: Mandi Smith
We provide services from birth and throughout life for carers and children and adults with Learning Disability and Difficulties (LDD) and aim to reduce inequality in statutory services, combat isolation and discrimination, and to bring to local people an experience of having people with LDD as part of their community.

Employees: 22
Volunteers: 30
Regional offices: 0
Income: £120,000 (2012-13)

Real Life Options

A1 Business Park, Knottingley Road, Knottingley, West Yorkshire WF11 0BL
T: 01977 781800
F: 01977 795361
E: dave.rawnsley@reallifeoptions.org
www.reallifeoptions.org
Chief Executive: Brian Hutchinson

We all strive to enjoy our lives, experience excitement, make our own decisions and aim for the stars. Some of us may need support to help us achieve our goals and aspirations; this includes people with learning disabilities, autism or intellectual impairments. That's where Real Life Options excels. Across the UK we support people to make their own choices, to have the same experiences we take for granted and, above all, to enjoy their lives.

Employees: 2000
Volunteers: 2
Regional offices: 15
Income: £38,018,192 (2012-13)

Realife Trust

3 The Courtyard, Windhill, Bishop's Stortford, Hertfordshire CM23 2ND
T: 01279 504735
F: 01279 757658
E: info@realife.org.uk
www.realife.org.uk
Realife was set up to challenge the idea that segregated support services offer the best option to allow people to benefit from their full rights of citizenship – the right to: a real home; a decent education; a wide circle of friends; and a job and training opportunities should apply to everyone regardless of learning difficulty and/or other disability or disadvantage. The Trust aims to provide information, projects and consultancy to support this aim.

Employees: 12
Volunteers: 20

REDAID

Holly House, 220 New London Road, Chelmsford, Essex CM2 9AE
E: info@redaid.org
www.redaid.org
International humanitarian organisation that works by supporting and funding dedicated local charitable organisations and groups in specific parts of the world. Aims to provide both immediate and long-term sustainable support to the disadvantaged and malnourished.

Redbridge Council for Voluntary Service

3rd Floor, Forest House, 16-20 Clements Road, Ilford IG1 1BA
T: 020 8553 1004
F: 020 8911 9128
E: ross@redbridgecvs.net
redbridgecvs.net
Chief Officer: Ross Diamond
Redbridge CVS is the umbrella body for the voluntary sector in the North East London Borough of Redbridge. We provide the

functions of a CVS and a Volunteer Centre and provide a range of support services to local groups. We exist to support a strong, effective and independent voluntary and community sector in Redbridge.

Employees: 23
Volunteers: 18
Regional offices: 1
Income: £1,576,888 (2012-13)

RedR UK

250A Kennington Lane, London SE11 5RD
T: 020 7840 6000
F: 020 7582 8669
E: jo.barrett@redr.org.uk
www.redr.org.uk
CEO: Martin McCann
RedR is a leading international disaster relief charity that trains aid workers and provides skilled professionals to humanitarian programmes worldwide.

Employees: 120
Volunteers: 8
Regional offices: 6
Income: £3,525,133 (2010-11)

Reedham Trust

The Lodge, 23 Old Lodge Lane, Purley, Surrey CR8 4DJ
T: 020 8660 1461
F: 020 8763 1293
E: info@reedham-trust.org.uk
www.reedham-trust.org.uk
The purpose of the Trust is to help orphans or children from single parent families in the UK where the home circumstances are so unsatisfactory that a boarding environment is essential. Our whole emphasis is on boarding need, not educational need.

Employees: 4

Refuge

4th Floor, International House, 1 St Katharine's Way, London E1W 1UN
T: 020 7395 7700
Helpline: 0808 200 0247
F: 020 7395 7721
E: info@refuge.org.uk
www.refuge.org.uk
Refuge is the national charity that provides a wide range of specialist domestic violence services to women and children experiencing domestic violence. On any given day our services support 3000 women and children.

Employees: 175
Volunteers: 12

Refugee Action

11 Belgrave Road, London SW1V 1RB
T: 020 7952 1511
E: lyna@refugee-action.org.uk
www.refugee-action.org
Chief Executive: Dave Garratt
Across England, Refugee Action works to: provide high-quality reception, advice and information to refugees and asylum seekers; promote the development of refugee communities; improve access to employment and mainstream services, and enhance opportunities for refugees and asylum-seekers; raise awareness, influence policy, and campaign for refugee rights; advise and assist asylum seekers and irregular migrants who are considering voluntary return.
Employees: 205
Volunteers: 200
Regional offices: 9
Income: £18,000,000 (2010-11)

Refugee Council

240–250 Ferndale Road,
London SW9 8BB
T: 020 7346 6700
F: 020 7582 9929
E: supporter@refugeecouncil.org.uk
www.refugeecouncil.org.uk
The Refugee Council gives practical advice and promotes refugees' rights in the UK and abroad. Its objective is to ensure that refugees' rights are respected and they have access to safety, dignity, the means to live and the opportunity to reach their full potential.
Employees: 350
Volunteers: 200
Regional offices: 8

Refugee Legal Centre

Nelson House, 153–157 Commercial Road, London E1 2DA
T: 020 7780 3320
E: rlc@refugee-legal-centre.org.uk
www.refugee-legal-centre.org.uk
Provides legal advice and representation (free of charge) to asylum seekers and refugees.

Refugee Therapy Centre

40 St John's Way, London N19 3RR
T: 020 7272 2565
E: aida@refugeetherapycentre.freeserve.co.uk
www.refugeetherapy.org.uk
Provides counselling, psychotherapy and associated treatment to children, adolescents and young refugees and asylum seekers and their families.

Regard

BM Regard, London WC1N 3XX
E: secretary@regard.org.uk
The national organisation of disabled lesbians and gay men. Addresses the absence of information and lack of understanding about the reality of disabled lesbians and gay men working in the disability movement. The only campaigning organisation and service provider to disabled lesbians and gay men, run by disabled lesbians and gay men.

Regional Studies Association

PO Box 2058, Seaford BN25 4QU
T: 01323 899698 (also fax)
E: support@rsc-london.ac.uk
www.regional-studies-assoc.ac.uk
Provides, as an interdisciplinary group, a forum in which to discuss regional issues and to publish the results of related research.
Employees: 3
Volunteers: 12

Registry Trust Limited

E: mhurlston@hurlstons.com

Rehab UK

62A Peach Street, Wokingham, Berkshire RG40 1XH
T: 0118 989 2282
E: headoffice@momentumscotland.org
www.rehabuk.org
Rehab UK provides rehabilitation, assessment, education and vocational services for people with acquired brain injury. The charity also offers case management and specialist cognitive, social and behavioural support services in the community.

Relate Brighton, Hove, Worthing and Districts

E: jo.carden@brightonrelate.org.uk

Relate Central Office

Herbert Gray College, Little Church Street, Rugby, Warwickshire CV21 3AP
T: 01788 563824
F: 01788 563825
E: enquiries@national.relate.org.uk
www.relate.org.uk
Aims to educate the public concerning the benefits of secure couple relationships, marriage and family life in order to improve the emotional, sexual and spiritual wellbeing of individuals that is derived from committed relationships.

Relate Lincolnshire

E: ron.thorn@relate-lincs.org.uk

Relatives and Residents Association

24 The Ivories, 6–18 Northampton Street, London N1 2HY
T: 020 7359 8148
Helpline: 020 7359 8136
F: 020 7226 6603
E: gillian.dalley@relres.org
www.relres.org
Chief Executive: Gillian Dalley
The Association exists for older people needing, or living in, residential care and the families and friends. As well as a listening ear, relatives need to know how to understand the complex regulations about paying for care, or to complain about the quality of care their loved ones are receiving. It offers support and information via its helpline; specific project work; influencing policy and practice; and working with local relatives and residents groups in care homes.
Employees: 5
Volunteers: 6
Regional offices: 20

Release

388 Old Street, London EC1V 9LT
T: 020 7729 5255
Helpline: 0845 450 0215
F: 020 7729 2599
E: ask@release.org.uk
www.release.org.uk
Executive Director: Sebastian Saville
Release is the national centre of expertise on drugs, law and human rights. We provide legal advice to those affected by the UK drugs laws. We also provide a specialist drugs helpline. Advice can be sought via telephone or email.
Employees: 7
Volunteers: 50

REMA

The Unity Centre, St Leonards Road S65 1PD
T: 01709 720744
E: info@rema-online.org.uk
www.rema-online.org.uk
Chief Executive: Azizzum Akhtar
REMA is the infrastructure support organisation for the Black and Minority Ethnic Voluntary and Community Sector of Rotherham. Our Mission is to support the development of voluntary and community action that is effective, sustainable and brings about positive social change for the BME Voluntary, Community and Faith Sector (VCFS) and communities. We provide small group support, capacity building and recruitment advice. We also support voice

and influence activity by hosting networks for the BME communities.
Employees: 5
Volunteers: 5
Regional offices: 0
Income: £80,000 (2012-13)

Remap

D9 Chaucer Business Park, Watery Lane, Kemsing, Kent TN15 6YU
T: 0845 130 0456 (also fax)
E: data@remap.org.uk
www.remap.org.uk
Aims to relieve and rehabilitate people with disabilities by promoting the use of technology to meet their needs; provide or help to provide specialised equipment designed to enhance their integration into the community.
Employees: 4
Volunteers: 1500

Renaisi Limited

21 Garden Walk, London EC2A 3EQ
T: 020 7033 2600
Helpline: 020 7033 2626
F: 020 7033 2631
E: info@renaisi.com
www.renaisi.com
Chief Executive: Kevin Sugrue
Renaisi is a leading, not-for-profit regeneration consultancy based in east London. Our mission is to help create sustainable, attractive and inclusive neighbourhoods, which foster the talent and diversity of local people. Our approach is centred on the belief that every neighbourhood has the potential to excite and inspire. We work with our clients and their communities to unlock the assets and opportunities that each of these neighbourhoods offer, to drive forward successful regeneration and recovery.
Employees: 70

Rescare

Steven Jackson House, 31 Buxton Road, Heaviley, Stockport SK2 6LS
T: 0161 474 3723
Helpline: 0800 032 7330
E: office@rescare.org.uk
www.rescare.org.uk
Works for the relief and welfare of people with a learning disability in all types of residential accommodation. Gives help, support and advice to the families of such disabled people.

Rescue: the British Archaeological Trust

15A Bull Plain, Hertford SG14 1DX
T: 01992 553377
E: rescue@rescue-archaeology.freeserve.co.uk
www.rescue-archaeology.freeserve.co.uk
Aims to preserve and record the archaeological and historic environment. Acts as a fundraising body and publications outlet, and works to increase public awareness of the destruction of our heritage.

Research Society of Process Oriented Psychology UK

c/o Interchange Studios, Hampstead Town Hall Centre, 213 Haverstock Hill, London NW3 4QP
T: 0870 429 5296
E: contact@rspopuk.com
www.rspopuk.com
RS POP UK is the national forum and organising body for process work in the UK. It organises a full and exciting annual programme of workshops, classes, supervision, training and private therapy with teachers and therapists from the British and international process work community.

Resources for Autism

858 Finchley Road, Temple Fortune, London NW11 6AB
T: 020 8458 3259
F: 020 8458 3222
E: liza.dresner@resourcesforautism.org.uk
www.resourcesforautism.org.uk
Director: Liza Dresner
Provides practical services including play and youth clubs, respite schemes, outreach home support, music and art therapy and advice and information to individuals with an autistic spectrum condition and their families.
Employees: 280
Volunteers: 150
Regional offices: 1
Income: £1,500,000 (2012-13)

RESPECT

1st Floor, 1 Downstream Building, 1 London Bridge, London SE1 9BG
T: 020 7022 1801
F: 020 7022 1806
E: info@respect.uk.net
www.respect.uk.net
Respect is the UK membership association for domestic violence perpetrator programmes and associated support services. Its key focus is on increasing the safety of those experiencing domestic violence through promoting effective interventions with perpetrators. An

information and advice phone line is central to RESPECT's activities: this is used both by those carrying out abuse and those who have suffered it, as well as professionals who come into contact with domestic violence situations.
Employees: 3

RESPOND

Respond, 3rd Floor, 24-32 Stephenson Way, London NW1 2HD
T: 020 7383 0700
E: admin@respond.org.uk
www.respond.org.uk
Chief Executive: Noelle Blackman
Respond exists to: lessen the effect of trauma and abuse on people with learning disabilities their families and supporters. We do this through providing psychotherapy for people with learning disabilities; advice and support for staff and families; training for professionals; education for people with learning disabilities; influencing generic services to make their services accessible; influencing learning disability services to consider the psychological impact of living with learning disabilities; undertaking research and disseminating our findings.
Regional offices: 1

Response International (HMD)

Office 11, Interlink House, 73a Maygrove Road, London NW6 2EG
T: 020 7372 6972
E: ri@responseinternational.org.uk
www.responseinternational.org.uk
Chief Executive: Philip Garvin
Emergency and rehabilitation services for victims of conflict: primary health, landmine action, rehabilitation of torture victims and amputees, reconstruction of health infrastructure, provision of prosthetics, training of health professionals.
Employees: 50
Volunteers: 15
Regional offices: 4

Responsible Use of Resources in Agriculture and on the Land

Chester House, 12 Hillberry Road, Alderholt, Fordingbridge SP6 3BQ
T: 01425 652035
Provides sources of information and ideas to help develop a more planned use of the countryside, and the opportunity for people and organisations of different views to debate all aspects of agriculture that are likely to have a long-term effect on the producer.

Restorative Justice Consortium

Albert Buildings, 49 Queen Victoria
Street, London EC4N 4SA
T: 020 7653 1992
F: 020 7653 1993
E: info@restorativejustice.org.uk
www.restorativejustice.org.uk
Chief Executive: Harriet Bailey
The Restorative Justice Consortium is an
independent membership organisation that
provides support in the development and
promotion of restorative justice (RJ) in
England and Wales. We support those
providing RJ services in a variety of settings,
(the CJS, schools, prisons and wider
community). We promote high-quality
practice in the field, consult with
government and provide advice on the
development of RJ legislation and services.
Employees: 3

Restricted Growth Association

PO Box 5137, Yeovil, Somerset BA20 9FF
T: 0300 111 1970
F: 0300 111 2454
E: office@restrictedgrowth.co.uk
www.restrictedgrowth.co.uk
The RGA is a self-help charity dealing with
the medical and social consequences of
restricted growth/dwarfism. It provides a
telephone helpline, dedicated medical and
benefits advisers and regular opportunities
to meet others in a supportive social setting.
The RGA also produces a variety of
information publications about the different
forms of dwarfism and provides members
with a quarterly magazine.

Retirement Trust

Silton Cottage, Chantlers Hill, Paddock
Wood, Tonbridge, Kent TN12 6LX
T: 01892 838474
E: info@theretirementtrust.org.uk
www.theretirementtrust.org.uk
Chair: Roger Parkes
The Trust aims to bring pre-retirement
advice, support and education to a wide
range of employees.
Volunteers: 5

Rett UK

Langham House West, Mill Street,
Luton LU1 2NA
T: 01582 798910
Helpline: 01582 798911
F: 01582 724129
E: info@rettuk.org
www.rettuk.org
Offers support, friendship and practical help
to those families and carers who have a child
or adult with Rett syndrome. Rett UK helps
inform and train professionals in the fields of

research, education, treatment, diagnosis,
care and understanding of the condition.
Employees: 5
Volunteers: 120
Income: £264,300 (2010-11)

Returned Volunteer Action

76 Wentworth Street, London E1 7SA
T: 020 7247 6406
E: retvolact@lineone.net
Returned Volunteer Action is a membership
organisation open to both people who have
been development volunteers or workers,
and to those interested in the field. It
provides information and training materials
for those interested in becoming volunteers.
A resource list is available on request.
Volunteers: 20
Income: £3,500 (2012-13)

Revolving Doors Agency

Units 28–29, The Turnmill, 63
Clerkenwell Road, London EC1M 5NP
T: 020 7253 4038
F: 020 7553 6079
E: admin@revolving-doors.org.uk
www.revolving-doors.co.uk
Revolving Doors agency is the UK's leading
independent charity dedicated to working
with people with mental health problems in
touch with the criminal justice system.
Employees: 30
Volunteers: 1

RICA (Research Institute for Consumer Affairs)

Unit G03, The Wenlock, 50 - 52 Wharf
Road, London N1 7EU
T: 020 7427 2460
F: 020 7427 2468
E: mail@rica.org.uk
www.rica.org.uk
Co-Directors: Caroline Jacobs and Jasper
Holmes
Rica is an independent consumer research
charity with specialist expertise in product
testing, user trials, focus groups and mystery
shopping. Rica provides unbiased consumer
information for older/disabled consumers
eg. motoring guides including on car
adaptations, an online car search, and other
relevant information. The aim of Rica is to
increase awareness among manufacturers,
service providers and policy makers to
improve products and services to meet the
needs of disabled and older consumers.
Employees: 6

Richmond Fellowship

80 Holloway Road, London N7 8JG
T: 020 7697 3300
F: 020 7697 3301
E: communications@
richmondfellowship.org.uk
www.richmondfellowship.org.uk
Provides residential care, counselling and
support, as well as rehabilitation and work
skills, to men and women who are recovering
from emotional disturbance, addiction and
mental health problems. The Fellowship
encourages greater public awareness and
understanding of mental health problems.
Employees: 686
Regional offices: 4

Riding for the Disabled Association

Norfolk House, 1A Tournament Court,
Edgehill Drive, Warwick,
Warwickshire CV34 6LG
T: 0845 658 1082
F: 0845 658 1083
E: info@rda.org.uk
www.rda.org.uk
Chief Executive: Ed Bracher
RDA is a national charity dedicated to
improving the lives of people with disabilities,
through the provision of opportunities for
riding and/or carriage driving. Through 500
member groups we enable people to
improve their health and wellbeing,
delivering a real and lasting therapy that not
only benefits mobility and co-ordination, but
also encourages confidence and self-worth
whilst having fun. Currently 28,000 people
with a wide range of disabilities and of all
ages ride with RDA.
Employees: 17
Volunteers: 18000
Regional offices: 500
Income: £10,000,000 (2010-11)

Right From the Start

Welcome Cottage, Wiveton,
Holt NR25 7TH
T: 01263 740935 (also fax)
E: info@rfts.org.uk
www.rightfromthestart.co.uk
Aims to protect the mental, emotional and
spiritual wellbeing of children in accordance
with the principles and standards of the
United Nations Convention on the Rights of
the Child, through parent education and
support; and to reduce the violence in
society and reverse the present increase in
uncontrolled and destructive behaviour in
children who have been neglected,
mishandled and hurt.

Rights of Women

52 - 54 Featherstone Street,
London EC1Y 8RT
T: 020 7251 6575
Helpline: 020 7251 6577
F: 020 7490 5377
E: info@row.org.uk
www.rightsofwomen.org.uk
Director: Emma Scott
Rights of Women is a women's voluntary
organisation committed to informing,
educating and empowering women
concerning their legal rights. We provide free
legal advice on issues of family law including:
divorce and relationship breakdown, children
and contact issues, domestic violence,
complaints about solicitors.

RNIB National Library Service

Far Cromwell Road, Bredbury,
Stockport SK6 2SG
Helpline: 0845 762 6843
F: 0161 355 2098
E: reader.advice@rnib.org.uk
www.rnib.org.uk/reading
Head of RNIB National Library Service:
Helen Brazier
Provides books and information for blind
and partially sighted children and adults in a
range of accessible formats including audio
(unabridged Daisy CDs), braille, Moon, large
print (16pt type) and giant print (24pt type).
We also provide free access to online
reference information, braille sheet music,
themed book lists and a quarterly reader
magazine.
Employees: 35
Volunteers: 950
Regional offices: 2

RoadPeace

PO Box 2579, London NW10 3PW
T: 020 8838 5102
Helpline: 0845 450 0355
F: 020 8838 5103
E: rplist@roadpeace.org
www.roadpeace.org
Executive Director: Amy Aeron-Thomas
RoadPeace is Britain's national charity for
road traffic victims, set up in 1992.
RoadPeace provides support for people
bereaved and injured in road crashes through
a national helpline, and gives specialist advice
and support. RoadPeace supports road
danger reduction and the promotion of
transport policies, which give greater
consideration to vulnerable road users and
the environment.
Employees: 4
Volunteers: 100

Roald Dahl's Marvellous Children's Charity

81a High Street, Great Missenden,
Buckinghamshire HP16 0AL
T: 01494 890465
E: richardp@roalddahlcharity.org
www.roalddahlcharity.org
Chief Executive: Richard Piper
Making life better for children with severe,
rare and under-supported health conditions.
Employees: 9
Volunteers: 2
Income: £707,000 (2011-12)

Rochas Foundation UK

Suite 275, Queen Anne's Centre, 28
Broadway, St James' Park,
London SW1H 9JX
www.rochasfoundation.org
The Foundation aims to impact on the lives
of the less privileged people in the
community. This it does mainly through
awareness seminars, training programmes,
informative interactive sessions and reaching
out to people wherever they are.
Employees: 2

Room - the National Council for Housing and Planning

41 Botolph Lane, London EC3R 8DL
T: 020 7929 9495
E: room@rtpi.org.uk
www.room.org.uk
Aims to advance education in planning urban
renewal and community regeneration and
promotes improvement of housing and
environmental conditions for the less well
off.

Roots HR CIC

E: admin@rootshr.org.uk

RoSA

RoSA, PO Box 151, Rugby,
Warwickshire CV21 3WR
T: 01788 551150
Helpline: 01788 551151
E: lindalewis.rosa@btconnect.com
www.rosasupport.org
Agency Director: Linda Lewis
We are an independant charity working with
survivors of rape, sexual assault and
childhood sexual abuse and their families.
We offer a completely confidential service
and support women, men, young people
and children. All counsellors and support
workers at RoSA have received
comprehensive specialist training and work
to BACP guidelines. We are the founder

members of The Survivors Trust, a national
umbrella agency.
Employees: 8
Volunteers: 44
Regional offices: 1
Income: £125 (2012-13)

Rotary International in Great Britain and Ireland

Kinwarton Road, Alcester,
Warwickshire B49 6BP
T: 01789 765411
F: 01789 765570
E: secretary@ribi.org
www.ribi.org
There are some 58,000 Rotarians in Great
Britain and Ireland in 1,845 clubs, helping
those in need and working towards world
understanding and peace.
Employees: 18
Volunteers: 60000

Rounders England

Unit 15, Venture 1 Business Park, Long
Acre Close, Holbrook Industrial Estate,
Sheffield, South Yorkshire S20 3FR
T: 0114 248 0357
E: oliver.wilson@roundersengland.co.uk
www.roundersengland.co.uk
Operations Director: Alison Steel
Rounders England is the sport's governing
body in England. Based in Sheffield it
provides a structure for the sport from the
Board, county associations and clubs, right
the way through to individual members and
volunteers.
Employees: 13
Volunteers: 1000+
Regional offices: 1
Income: £757,800 (2012-13)

Rowntree Society

Tanners Yard, Huntington Road,
Huntington, York, North
Yorkshire YO31 1ET
T: 01904 425499
E: burkeman@gn.apc.org
www.rowntreewalks.org
We want people to engage with the work
that Joseph and others in the Rowntree
family did, and with the ideas and beliefs that
underpinned their work – whether in the
field of business and employment, social
welfare, economics, education, philanthropy,
religion or politics. We seek to ensure that
these ideas are understood, researched and
debated – that they help to inform
contemporary debates about the same
issues.
Volunteers: 12

Roy Castle Lung Cancer Foundation

200 London Road, Liverpool L3 9TA
T: 0871 220 5426
F: 0871 220 5427
E: roycastle@liv.ac.uk
www.roycastle.org
The Foundation secures the development of the Roy Castle International Centre for Lung Cancer research and health promotion; promotes and funds clinical laboratory and epidemiological research into the causes, prevention and treatment of lung cancer; provides amenities intended to improve the quality of life of the patients and relieve and alleviate the distress of relatives of the patients.
Employees: 60
Volunteers: 100
Regional offices: 2

Royal Academy of Dance

36 Battersea Square, London SW11 3RA
T: 020 7326 8000
F: 020 7924 3129
E: info@rad.org.uk
www.rad.org.uk
Chief Executive: Luke Rittner
The Royal Academy of Dance is a global organisation with over 13,000 members. With offices in 79 countries and headquarters in London, it is the largest ballet examination and teacher training institution in the world. Its mission is to promote knowledge, understanding and practice of dance internationally. It seeks to accomplish its mission through examining students of ballet, educating and training teachers of dance and promoting the study and performance of dance.
Employees: 180

Royal Agricultural Benevolent Institution

Shaw House, 27 West Way, Botley, Oxford, Oxfordshire OX2 0QH
T: 01865 724931
Helpline: 01865 727888
F: 01865 202025
E: info@rabi.org.uk
www.rabi.org.uk
Chief Executive: Paul Burrows
The national farming charity for England and Wales. Helping those in need in the farming community during times of hardship.
Employees: 114

Royal Air Force Benevolent Fund

67 Portland Place, London W1B 1AR
T: 020 7580 8343
Helpline: 0800 169 2942
F: 020 7636 7005
E: enquiries@rafbf.org.uk
www.rafbf.org
Controller: Robert Wright
The Royal Air Force Benevolent Fund provides assistance to members and former members of the Royal Air Force, and their dependants, who need support as a consequence of poverty, sickness, disability, accident, infirmity or other adversity.
Employees: 120
Volunteers: 30
Regional offices: 2

Royal Air Force Music Charitable Trust

39 Bristow Road, Cranwell Village, Sleaford, Lincolnshire NG34 8FG
T: 07748 945160
E: office@rafmusic.org.uk
www.rafmusic.org.uk
Administrator: Malcolm Goodman
Promoting welfare funding through the performance of live music by Royal Air Force musicians.
Regional offices: 1
Income: £8,000 (2011-12)

Royal Air Forces Association

117.5 Loughborough Road, Leicester LE4 5ND
T: 0116 266 5224
Helpline: 0800 018 2361
F: 0116 266 5012
E: enquiries@rafa.org.uk
www.rafa.org.uk
Secretary General: Jane Easton
The RAF Association is a membership and charitable organisation offering support to all serving and former members of the RAF and their dependants during times of need. Its network of welfare officers provides advice, financial guidance, friendship and, where appropriate, can signpost to other agencies for assistance.
Employees: 179
Volunteers: 400
Regional offices: 9

Royal Alfred Seafarers Society

Head Office, Weston Acres, Woodmasterne Lane, Banstead, Surrey SM7 3HA
T: 01737 353763
F: 020 8401 2592
E: royalalfred@btopenworld.com
Provides long-term care for retired or disabled seafarers and their dependants.
Employees: 86
Volunteers: 2

Royal Association for Deaf people

18 Westside Centre, London Road, Stanway, Colchester, Essex CO3 8PH
T: 0845 688 2525
F: 0845 688 2526
E: info@royaldeaf.org.uk
www.royaldeaf.org.uk
RAD promote the welfare and interests of deaf people. We believe deaf people should receive the same access and opportunities as hearing people. We mainly support deaf people whose first or preferred language is British Sign Language (BSL) but also work with people with all forms of deafness including those who are hard of hearing, deafened or deafblind.
Employees: 100
Volunteers: 50
Regional offices: 3

Royal Blind Society for the UK

RBS House, 59/61 Sea Lane, Rustington, West Sussex BN16 2RQ
T: 01903 857023
F: 01903 859166
E: royalblindsoc@aol.com
www.royalblindsociety.org
Director: Graham Booth
Aims to assist blind and partially sighted people to cope with the additional costs of blindness, and to experience opportunities that they could not otherwise have.
Employees: 48
Volunteers: 25
Regional offices: 1

Royal British Legion

Haig House, 199 Borough High Street, London SE1 1AA
T: 020 7973 7200
F: 020 7973 7399
E: info@britishlegion.org.uk
www.britishlegion.org.uk
The Royal British Legion provides financial, social and emotional support to millions who have served and are currently serving in the Armed Forces, and their dependants. Currently, nearly 10.5 million people are eligible for our support and we receive thousands of calls for help every year.
Employees: 880
Volunteers: 600000
Regional offices: 65

Royal British Legion Industries Ltd

Hall Road, Aylesford, Kent ME20 7NL
T: 01622 795923
F: 01622 718744
E: hedley.druce@rbli.co.uk
www.rbli.co.uk
RBLI provides employment, training and support for people, including those with disabilities, plus care and support for ex-servicemen, women and families.

Royal British Legion Women's Section

48 Pall Mall, London SW1Y 5JY
T: 020 7973 7378
E: women@britishlegion.org.uk
www.britishlegion.org.uk
Promotes the welfare of ex-service women, the wives, widows, children and dependants of those who have served in any of HM Forces who find themselves in difficulties; to augment the activities of the Royal British Legion and to assist them in raising funds.

Royal College of General Practitioners

30 Euston Square, Stephenson Way, London NW1 2FB
T: 020 3188 7400
E: info@rcgp.org.uk
www.rcgp.org.uk
Encouraging, fostering and maintaining the highest possible standards in general medical practice.
Employees: 170
Regional offices: 31

Royal College of Midwives

15 Mansfield Street, London W1G 9NH
T: 020 7312 3535
F: 020 7313 3536
E: info@rcm.org.uk
www.rcm.org.uk
Aims to advance the art and science of midwifery and to maintain high professional standards.
Employees: 70
Volunteers: 2000
Regional offices: 4

Royal College of Nursing

Room 103, 20 Cavendish Square, London W1G 0RN
T: 020 7647 3599
F: 020 7647 3435
E: membership@rcn.org.uk
www.rcn.org.uk
Promotes the science and art of nursing and the better education and training of nurses and their efficiency in the profession of nursing.

Royal College of Obstetricians and Gynaecologists

27 Sussex Place, Regent's Park, London NW1 4RG
T: 020 7772 6200
E: iwylie@rcog.org.uk
www.rcog.org.uk
Chief Executive: Ian Wylie
The professional membership organisation for obstetricians and gynaecologists. We educate and examine doctors in the speciality both in the UK and throughout the world and we support their continuing development. We set standards for women's health and assist developing countries with maternal health education.
Employees: 140
Income: £11,000,000 (2011-12)

Royal College of Paediatrics and Child Health

50 Hallam Street, London W1W 6DE
T: 020 7307 5616
E: enquiries@rcpch.ac.uk
www.rcpch.ac.uk
Promotes and publishes paediatric research; organises scientific meetings; advises government and other professional bodies on problems of child health; oversees the training of doctors specialising in paediatrics and child health; issues guidance on related issues.

Royal Commonwealth Society

Award House, 7-11, St Matthews Street, London SW1P 2JT
T: 020 3727 4300
E: info@thercs.org
www.thercs.org
Director: Michael Lake CBE
The Royal Commonwealth Society is a network of individuals and organisations committed to improving the lives and prospects of Commonwealth citizens worldwide. Promoting an understanding of the values and working of the Commonwealth, the Society engages with its educational, civil society, business and governmental networks to address issues that matter to the citizens of the Commonwealth and the world.
Employees: 8
Volunteers: 2

Royal Corps of Signals Benevolent Fund

Regimental Headquarters, Griffin House, Blandford Camp, Blandford Forum, Dorset DT11 8RH
T: 01258 482081
E: soinc-rhq-regtsec@mod.uk
Regimental Secretary: Colonel Terry Canham
Employees: 5

Royal Fund for Gardeners' Children

PO Box 346, Hitchin, Hertfordshire SG5 9BT
T: 01462 452827 (also fax)
E: rfgc@btinternet.com
www.rfgc.org.uk
Chairman: T Read
The Fund was founded in 1887 to help the orphans of horticulturists by giving them regular allowances or making grants for special purposes. The work of our Fund has since been extended so that all children in need whose parents are employed in horticulture may be considered for assistance.
Employees: 1

Royal Geographical Society

1 Kensington Gore, London SW7 2AR
T: 020 7591 3088
E: enquiries@rgs.org
www.rgs.org
A world-leading society for geographers and geographical learning dedicated to the promotion and development of knowledge together with its application to the challenges facing society and the environment.

Royal Humane Society

Brettenham House, Lancaster Place, London WC2E 7EP
T: 020 7836 8155
E: info@royalhumanesociety.org.uk
www.royalhumanesociety.org.uk
The Royal Humane Society is a charity that assesses acts of bravery in the saving of human life and makes awards. These range from certificates and testimonials to bronze, silver and gold medals.

Royal Institute of British Architects

66 Portland Place, London W1B 1AD
T: 020 7580 5533
E: info@inst.riba.org
www.architecture.com
RIBA is the UK body for architecture and the architectural profession. Providing support for 40,500 members worldwide in the form of training, technical services, publications and events, and set standards for the education of architects, both in the UK and overseas.

Royal Life Saving Society UK

River House, High Street, Broom, Warwickshire B50 4HN
T: 01789 773994
F: 01789 773995
E: lifesavers@rlss.org.uk
www.lifesavers.org.uk
The Society imparts lifesaving skills and techniques to as wide an audience as possible and remain the UK's leading drowning prevention agency as well as the governing body for both lifeguarding and lifesaving.
Employees: 29
Volunteers: 13500
Regional offices: 50

Royal Literary Fund

3 Johnson's Court, Off Fleet Street, London EC4A 3EA
T: 020 7353 7150
F: 020 7353 1350
E: egunnrlf@globalnet.co.uk
www.rlf.org.uk
Provides assistance to established published authors of several books who are in financial difficulties due to personal or professional setbacks.

Royal London Society

16 Manor Road, Bexhill-on-Sea, East Sussex TN40 1SP
T: 01424 218097
E: office@royallondonsociety.org.uk
www.royallondonsociety.org.uk
Royal London Society is one of Britain's oldest charities seeking to assist in the rehabilitation of offenders and the reintegration into the community of those serving custodial sentences or under statutory supervision.

Royal London Society for the Blind

Dorton House, Wilderness Avenue, Seal, Sevenoaks, Kent TN15 0EB
T: 01732 592665
Helpline: 01732 592500
F: 01732 592668
E: enquiries@rlsb.org.uk
www.rlsb.org.uk
Chief Executive: Brian Cooney
The RLSB exists to provide education, training, transition and employment services that enable people who are blind or partially sighted to overcome the discrimination they face and the social exclusion and poverty that many experience.
Employees: 300
Volunteers: 25
Regional offices: 3

Royal Masonic Benevolent Institution

20 Great Queen Street, London WC2B 5BG
T: 020 7596 2400
E: enquiries@rmbi.org.uk
www.rmbi.org.uk
Provides support to freemasons and their dependants, by providing residential or nursing accommodation through our homes situated throughout the country.

Royal Medical Benevolent Fund

24 King's Road, Wimbledon, London SW19 8QN
T: 020 8540 9194
F: 020 8542 0494
E: cbogle@rmbf.org
www.rmbf.org
Chief Executive Officer: Steve Crone
The objectives of the charity are to prevent or relieve poverty and to relieve need arising from youth, age, ill health, disability and bereavement among people who are doctors or who have worked as doctors, and medical students and the dependants of such individuals.
Employees: 13
Volunteers: 300
Income: £1,622,927 (2011-12)

Royal National College for the Blind

College Road, Hereford HR1 1EB
T: 01432 265725
F: 01432 376628
E: peter.okeefe@rncb.ac.uk
www.rncb.ac.uk
Principal: Sheila Tallon
Vision: to enable people who are blind or partially sighted and who may have other disabilities to achieve their full potential and integration in society.
Employees: 220
Volunteers: 12

Royal National Institute of the Blind

105 Judd Street, London WC1H 9NE
T: 020 7388 1266
F: 020 7388 2034
E: helpline@rnib.org.uk
www.rnib.org.uk
RNIB are the UK's leading charity offering information, support and advice to over two million people with sight problems. We fight for equal rights for people with sight problems. We fund pioneering research into preventing and treating eye disease and promote eye health by running public health awareness campaigns.
Employees: 2923
Volunteers: 5000
Regional offices: 5

Royal National Lifeboat Institution

West Quay Road, Poole, Dorset BH15 1HZ
T: 01202 663000
F: 01202 663167
E: info@rnli.org.uk
www.rnli.org.uk
The RNLI aims to save lives by changing attitudes and behaviour among people who use the sea regularly. Its lifeguards patrol more than 70 beaches and assisted more than 10,000 people last year. Its boats rescued more than 8,000 people – an average of 22 per day.
Employees: 1000
Volunteers: 4600
Regional offices: 10

Royal National Mission to Deep Sea Fishermen

Mather House, 4400 Parkway, Solent Business Park, Hampshire PO15 7FJ
T: 020 7487 5101
E: enquiries@rnmdsf.org.uk
www.fishermensmission.org.uk
Supports fishermen and their families throughout the UK and in the Falkland Islands.

Royal Naval Benevolent Society for Officers

70 Porchester Terrace, Bayswater, London W2 3TP
T: 020 7402 5231
E: rnbso@lineone.net
The Society provides financial assistance when in need to officers of the Royal Navy

and Royal Marines, and their respective reserves, both active service and retired, and to their widows, ex-wives and dependants.

Royal Naval Benevolent Trust

Castaway House, 311 Twyford Avenue, Portsmouth PO2 8RN
T: 023 9269 0112
F: 023 9266 0852
E: chrischatfield@rnbt.org.uk
www.rnbt.org.uk
The RNBT exists to give help, in cases of need, to those who are serving or have served as ratings in the Royal Navy or as other ranks in the Royal Marines, and their dependants. The RNBT also manages its own care home in Gillingham, Kent, which offers first-class nursing and personal care in excellent accommodation for former sailors, Royal Marines, their wives and widows.
Employees: 98
Volunteers: 30

Royal Navy and Royal Marine Children's Fund

311 Twyford Avenue, Stamshaw, Portsmouth, Hampshire PO2 8PE
T: 023 9263 9534
F: 023 9267 7574
E: mabrnchildren@btconnect.com
www.rnrmchildrensfund.org.uk
Assists children, under the age of 25, of serving and ex-serving members of RN and RM who are in need, hardship or distress. Assistance may be given in the form of grants to individuals or by paying for goods or services or facilities for those in need.
Employees: 3

Royal Society

6 Carlton House Terrace, London SW1Y 5AG
T: 020 7451 2500
E: info@royalsoc.ac.uk
www.royalsoc.ac.uk
Promotes the natural sciences, including mathematics and all applied sciences such as engineering and medicine. The Society encourages both national and international scientific activities (in a similar way to national academies overseas), adhering to many international, non-governmental scientific organisations and promoting co-operative research and exchanges through agreements with overseas academies.

Royal Society for Public Health

59 Mansell Street, London E1 8AN
T: 020 7265 7300
E: info@rsph.org.uk
www.rsph.org.uk
A leading independent body with the aims of protecting and promoting public health through education, training and development.

Royal Society for the Prevention of Accidents

RoSPA House, 28 Calthorpe Road, Edgbaston, Birmingham, West Midlands B15 1RP
T: 0121 248 2000
F: 0121 248 2001
E: tmullarkey@rospa.com
www.rospa.com
Chief Executive: Tom Mullarkey
The Royal Society for the Prevention of Accidents (RoSPA) is a registered charity with a mission to save lives and reduce injuries. It promotes safety and the prevention of accidents in the home, on the road, at work, at leisure and in schools and colleges. RoSPA's various activities include collecting data, carrying out research, training and providing expert consultancy.
Employees: 130
Regional offices: 3

Royal Society for the Prevention of Cruelty to Animals

Wilberforce Way, Southwater, Horsham, West Sussex RH13 9RS
T: 0300 123 0100
Helpline: 0300 123 4555
F: 0303 123 0100
E: enq@rspca.org.uk
www.rspca.org.uk
Chief Executive: Mark Watts
The RSPCA will, by all lawful means, promote kindness to, prevent cruelty to, and alleviate suffering of animals.
Employees: 1668
Volunteers: 7000
Regional offices: 5

Royal Society for the Protection of Birds

The Lodge, Potton Road, Sandy, Bedfordshire SG19 2DL
T: 01767 680551
F: 01767 691178
E: alan.sharpe@rspb.org.uk
www.rspb.org.uk
Chief Executive: Mike Clarke
The RSPB speaks out for birds and wildlife, tackling the problems that threaten our environment. Our work helps all nature, every buzzing, crawling, slithering, fluttering part of it, and we look after wild places for you to enjoy too. We have a million members who are inspired by nature and give it a voice. Nature is amazing! Help us keep it that way.
Employees: 2151
Volunteers: 15765
Regional offices: 14

Royal Society of Health

38A St George's Drive, London SW1V 4BH
T: 020 7630 0121
F: 020 7976 6847
E: rsph@rsph.org
www.rsph.org
Chief Executive: Richard Parish
Our aim is to promote continuous improvement in human health worldwide, through education, communication and the encouragement of scientific research.
Employees: 25
Volunteers: 1

Royal Society of Medicine

1 Wimpole Street, London W1G 0AE
T: 020 7290 2900
F: 020 7290 2989
E: tansy.allen@rsm.ac.uk
www.rsm.ac.uk
Chief Executive: Ian Balmer
The RSM is an independent, apolitical organisation and one of the largest providers of continuing medical education in the UK. We provide accredited courses, which are vital in allowing healthcare professionals their continuing freedom to practice. Our aims are: to provide a broad range of educational activities for medical and healthcare professionals including students of these disciplines; to promote an exchange of information and ideas on the science, practice and organisation of medicine.
Employees: 192
Volunteers: 500
Income: £169 (2011-12)

Royal Television Society

3 Dorset Rise, London EC4Y 8EN
T: 020 7822 2810
F: 020 7822 2811
E: info@rts.org.uk
www.rts.org.uk
Chief Executive: Theresa Wise
The society's objective and principal activity is the advancement of public education in the science, practice, technology and art of television.
Employees: 12
Volunteers: 600

Royal Theatrical Fund

11 Garrick Street, Covent Garden,
London WC2E 9AR
T: 020 7836 3322
F: 020 7379 8273
E: admin@trtf.com
www.trtf.com
Chair: Paul Gane
The Fund helps those in the entertainment media who cannot work through illness, adversity or infirmity.
Employees: 2

Royal UK Beneficent Association (Rukba)

6 Avonmore Road, London W14 8RL
T: 020 7605 4200
F: 020 7605 4201
E: charity@independentage.org
www.rukba.org.uk
Grants annuities and provides friendship for older people who are impoverished or infirm.
Employees: 218
Volunteers: 1100
Regional offices: 15

RP Fighting Blindness

PO Box 350, Buckingham MK18 1GZ
T: 01280 821334
Helpline: 0845 123 2354
F: 01280 815900
E: info@brps.org.uk
www.brps.org.uk
Chief Executive: David Head
The charity provides counselling, support and encouragement to those suffering with retinitis pigmentosa. It provides information on all matters of interest to sufferers and their families and establishes links with other organisations concerned with visual handicaps and with social services. It also stimulates further research into the condition.
Employees: 9
Volunteers: 110
Regional offices: 21

Rugby Football Foundation

Rugby House, 200 Whitton Road
T: 020 8831 7985
E: foundation@therfu.com
www.rfu.com/rff
RFF Administrator: Fran Thornber

Runnymede Trust

7 Plough Yard, Shoreditch,
London EC2A 3LP
T: 020 7377 9222
F: 020 7377 6622
E: info@runnymedetrust.org
www.runnymedetrust.org
Director: Dr Robert Berkeley
The Runnymede Trust is an independent policy research organisation focusing on equality and justice through the promotion of a successful multi-ethnic society. Founded as a charitable educational trust, Runnymede has a long track record in policy research, working in close collaboration with eminent thinkers and policy makers in the public, private and voluntary sectors.
Employees: 12
Volunteers: 2

Rural Action Yorkshire

E: leah.swain@ruralyorkshire.org.uk

Rural Community Action Nottinghamshire

Newstead Centre, Tilford Road,
Newstead, Nottinghamshire NG15 0BS
T: 01623 727600
E: enquiries@rcan.org.uk
www.rcan.org.uk
Chief Executive: Robert Crowder
Rural Community Action Nottinghamshire (RCAN) is an independent voluntary organisation and registered charity, which exists to promote the social and economic well-being of rural communities. Examples of our work include tackling health issues, solving transport access problems, improving community facilities, and addressing social exclusion by developing initiatives which allows everyone to play a full part in the life of their community.
Employees: 20
Volunteers: 20

Rural Housing Trust

Unit 8, Graphite Square,
London SE11 5EE
T: 020 7793 8114
E: info@ruralhousing.org.uk
www.ruralhousing.org.uk
Provides affordable housing for local people in villages throughout England.

Rural Media Company

Sullivan House, 72–80 Widemarsh Street,
Hereford, Herefordshire HR4 9HG
T: 01432 344039
F: 01432 270539
E: helenj@ruralmedia.co.uk
www.ruralmedia.co.uk
Chief Executive: Nic Millington
The Rural Media Company brings community and informal education, training and advocacy together with professional filmmaking and media industry skills. Working throughout the UK with local, regional and national partners in public, voluntary and independent organisations, to develop short and long term projects, as well as undertaking commissions for video/DVD.
Employees: 17
Volunteers: 10
Regional offices: 1

RYA Sailability

RYA House, Ensign Way, Hamble,
Southampton, Hampshire SO31 4YA
T: 0845 345 0403
F: 023 8060 4286
E: info@ryasailability.org
www.rya.org.uk/sailability
The RYA programme for disability sailing. Committed to development of sailing clubs and organisations throughout the UK to promote, encourage and find people with disabilities to take up sailing in all its forms.
Employees: 3

Ryder-Cheshire Volunteers

E8A Holly Court, Holly Farm Business Park, Honiley, Kenilworth,
Warwickshire CV8 1NP
T: 01926 485446 (also fax)
E: info@rcv.org.uk
www.rcv.org.uk
RCV believes that everyone has the right to enjoy life with interests and activities that are stimulating, rewarding and fun. We give disabled people the opportunity to take up any leisure or learning pursuit, either in partnership with a volunteer or by joining a local club or college.
Employees: 21
Volunteers: 300
Regional offices: 12

SABRE Research UK

PO Box 18653, Hampstead,
London NW3 4UJ
T: 020 7722 9394
E: office@sabre.org.uk
www.sabre.org.uk
Founder/Trustee: Susan Green
An independent charity that represents the interests of patients and research volunteers by raising awareness of the need to apply rigorous research methodology to the way animal research is conducted and evaluated. A more evidence-based approach is essential if the value of animal experiments is to be determined and the safety and efficacy of medical research to be improved. The charity has no links to political parties, animal lobby groups or the pharmaceutical industry.
Volunteers: 4

SAD Association

PO Box 989, Steyning BN44 3HG
E: info@sada.org.uk
www.sada.org.uk
Informs the public and health professions about SAD (seasonal affective disorder) and supports and advises sufferers of the illness.
Volunteers: 7

Safe Partnership

3 East Street, Wareham,
Dorset BH20 4NN
T: 01929 55100
F: 01929 553300
E: malcolm@safepartnership.org
www.safepartnership.org
Chief Executive: Malcolm Macleod
Safe Partnership is the national charity that provides home security and advice to vulnerable victims of crimes eg domestic violence, burglary, robbery, distraction burglary, identity theft and hate crime and to those in fear of such crimes. We also undertake proactive, preventative work with young people, to help them recognise the early signs of relationship abuse to prevent them becoming victims or perpetrators of violence and crime when they grow up.
Employees: 14
Volunteers: 6

SafeHands for Mothers

23 Fitzjohns Avenue, London NW3 5JY
T: 020 7433 0792
E: ndm@safehands.org
www.safehands.org
Founder Director: Nancy Durrell McKenna
Our vision is a world where no woman dies in pregnancy and childbirth. We work to achieve this through the production of films; documentaries that raise awareness of important issues such as FGM, Obstetric Fistula, Child Marriage and HIV/AIDS, and films which educate frontline health workers, women and their communities.
Employees: 2
Volunteers: 2
Income: £353,735 (2012-13)

Safer Places

PO Box 2489, Essex CM18 6NS
T: 0845 074 3216
Helpline: 0845 017 7668
E: allison.mann@saferplaces.co.uk
www.saferplaces.co.uk
Director of Business Services: Allison Mann
Safer Places is an independent domestic abuse charity dedicated to supporting adults and children affected by domestic abuse. We provide a wide range of services to support clients and respond to their individual needs and circumstances, whether it is in our refuge accommodation or in the community. Work in a holistic and empowering way to help enable clients to live independent lives free from domestic abuse. Services are available in East Hertfordshire, Mid and West Essex and Southend.
Employees: 77
Volunteers: 28
Income: £2,700,000 (2011-12)

Saferworld

The Grayston Centre, 28 Charles Square N1 6HT
T: 020 7324 4646
F: 020 7324 4647
E: communications@saferworld.org.uk
www.saferworld.org.uk
Executive Director: Paul Murphy
Saferworld is an independent international organisation working to prevent violent conflict and build safer lives. Our priority is people – we believe everyone should be able to lead peaceful, fulfilling lives, free from insecurity and violent conflict. We work with local people affected by conflict to improve

their safety and sense of security, and conduct wider research and analysis.
Employees: 99
Regional offices: 8
Income: £6.6 (2011-12)

SAGGA

5 Portway Drive, Tutbury, Burton-on-Trent, Staffordshire DE13 9HU
T: 01283 520685
E: treasurer@sagga.org.uk
www.sagga.org.uk
Provides a pool of professional people with experience of the Scout and Guide movement who are ready to assist with projects connected with the movement; takes an independent look at progress and developments within the movement; supports and encourages Scout and Guide clubs in institutions of higher education.

Sahara Communities Abroad (SACOMA)

108 Cranbrook Road, Ilford,
Essex IG1 4LZ
T: 020 8554 9444 (also fax)
E: perez@sacoma.org.uk
www.sacoma.org.uk
Chief Executive: Perez Ochieng
Supports African migrant communities to develop skills for enterprise and work. We provide information, advice and guidance on matters such as housing, welfare, pensions, business start up, training and education. We provide accredited training and business support for SMEs.
Employees: 24
Volunteers: 40

Sailors' Children's Society

Francis Reckitt House, Cottingham Road, Hull HU6 7RJ
T: 01482 342331
E: info@sailors-families.org.uk
www.sailorschildren.org.uk
Chief Officer: Deanne Thomas
A maritime charity caring for the children of deceased and disabled seafarers and those in severe financial hardship. The aim of the Society is to provide not only the basic necessities of life such as clothing but to allow the children to partake in everyday activities. Financial support includes single parent families, and families where one of the parents is too ill, or disabled to work, and the other acts as carer.
Employees: 6

Sailors' Society

350 Shirley Road, Southampton,
Hampshire SO15 3HY
T: 023 8051 5950
F: 023 8051 5951
E: admin@sailors-society.org
www.sailors-society.org
Chief Executive Officer: Robert Adams
The objectives for which the Society is
established are the advancement of the
Christian religion, the advancement of
education and the relief of poverty and
distress among the world's seafarers and
their families.
Employees: 76
Income: £2,127,000 (2010-11)

Sainsbury Centre for Mental Health

134–138 Borough High Street,
London SE1 1LB
T: 020 7827 8300
F: 020 7403 9482
E: susan.spratt@centreformentalhealth.org.uk
www.scmh.org.uk
Chief Executive: Angela Greatley
Research and development in the field of
mental health, with particular reference to
employment of people with mental health
problems and mental healthcare for
offenders.
Employees: 30

Salmon Youth Centre

E: sam.adofo@salmonyouthcentre.org

Salvation Army

Territorial HQ, 101 Newington Causeway,
London SE1 6BN
T: 020 7367 4864
F: 020 7367 4728
E: thq@salvationarmy.org.uk
www.salvationarmy.org.uk
Expresses practical Christianity through social
action regardless of class, creed or sex.
Programmes include homeless and drug
rehabilitation centres, and nearly 16,000
church and community centres. Also
supports the work of the emergency services
by providing refreshments, shelter and
counselling at major incidents.
Employees: 4000
Volunteers: 40000
Regional offices: 18

Samaritans

The Upper Mill, Kingston Road, Ewell,
Surrey KT17 2AF
T: 020 8394 8300
Helpline: 0845 790 9090
F: 020 8394 8301
E: supportercare@samaritans.org
www.samaritans.org
Chief Executive: Dominic Rudd
Available 24 hours a day to provide
confidential emotional support for people
who are experiencing feelings of distress and
despair, including those that may lead to
suicide.
Employees: 75
Volunteers: 15400
Regional offices: 203

SANE

1st Floor, Cityside House, 40 Adler Street,
London E1 1EE
T: 020 7375 1002
Helpline: 0845 767 8000
F: 020 7375 2162
E: info@sane.org.uk
www.sane.org.uk
Chief Executive: Marjorie Wallace
SANE is a national mental health charity that
works to: raise awareness; combat stigma
and increase understanding of mental illness;
initiate research into causes, treatments and
experiences of mental illness; provide
emotional support and information to
anyone affected by mental illness, including
families, friends and carers. One-to-one
support: helpline and email. Peer support:
Support Forum. For more information, visit
the SANE website.
Employees: 30
Volunteers: 120
Regional offices: 1

Sangat Advice Centre

Sancroft Road, Harrow HA3 7NS
T: 020 8427 0659
F: 020 8863 2196
E: info@sangat.org.uk
www.sangat.org.uk
Manager: Kanti Nagda
Sangat Advice Centre provides legal advice
on welfare benefits, housing, immigration,
debt etc. We represent clients at the
immigration and welfare benefits tribunals.
We also provide IT learning facilities and
assist BME carers.
Employees: 4
Volunteers: 6
Income: £90,000 (2010-11)

Savana

The Dudson Centre, Hope Street, Hanley,
Stoke on Trent, Staffordshire ST1 5DD
T: 01782 221005
Helpline: 01782 221000
E: info@savana.org.uk
www.savana.org.uk
Chief Executive Officer: Justine Eardley-Dunn
Savana is a company limited by guarantee
with charitable status providing support
services for those who have experienced or
who are affected by (including relatives and
supporters) any form of sexual violence or
abuse including within domestic abuse,
whether recently or in the past.
Employees: 11
Volunteers: 30
Regional offices: 1

SAVE Britain's Heritage

70 Cowcross Street, London EC1M 6EJ
T: 020 7253 3500
E: save@btinternet.com
www.savebritainsheritage.org
Campaigns for the retention and
rehabilitation of historic buildings and areas.

Save the Children UK

1 St John's Lane, London EC1M 4AR
T: 020 7012 6400
F: 020 7012 6963
E: supporter.care@savethechildren.org.uk
www.savethechildren.org.uk
Aims to relieve the distress and hardship, and
to promote the welfare of children in any
country or countries, place or places with
particular emphasis on disaster relief,
emergency response, campaigns and
programmes.
Employees: 3673
Volunteers: 11000
Regional offices: 567

SBA The Solicitors' Charity

1 Jaggard Way, London SW12 8SG
T: 020 8675 6440
E: sec@sba.org.uk
www.sba.org.uk
Aims to financially assist solicitors and their
dependants in need, who are or have been
on the roll for England and Wales.

SCA Group

Amplevine House, Dukes Road,
Southampton, Hampshire SO14 0ST
T: 023 8036 6663
F: 023 8036 6666
E: rosalind.lucas@scagroup.co.uk
www.scagroup.co.uk
CEO: Maria Mills
The Social Care in Action (SCA) Group is one
of the leading social enterprises in the UK.
Established over 20 years ago, SCA provides
an outstanding range of health and social
care services including care, NHS dentistry,
transport, a health and wellbeing centre, an
award-winning training centre and
consultancy services. Everything SCA does is
focussed on supporting its customers to lead
better lives.
Employees: 596
Volunteers: 100
Regional offices: 4
Income: £6,671,431 (2010-11)

School for Social Entrepreneurs

18 Victoria Park Square, London E2 9PF
T: 020 8981 0300
F: 020 8983 4655
E: office@sse.org.uk
www.sse.org.uk
The School for Social Entrepreneurs exists to
provide training and opportunities to enable
people to use their creative and
entrepreneurial abilities more fully for social
benefit. We also want to recruit more
innovative and capable people into voluntary
and other organisations.
Employees: 14

School Governors' One-Stop Shop

Unit 11, Shepperton House, 83–93
Shepperton Road, London N1 3DF
T: 020 7354 9805
F: 020 7288 9549
E: info@sgoss.org.uk
www.sgoss.org.uk
Chief Executive: Steve Acklam
SGOSS is dedicated to recruiting volunteers
to fill some of the 40,000 school governor
vacancies that exist across England.
Governors do not have to know about
education or be a parent, they simply need
to be over 18 and want to make a difference.
All of SGOSS's services are free to
volunteers, employers, schools and local
authorities.
Employees: 17
Volunteers: 11500
Regional offices: 1

School Journey Association

48 Cavendish Road, London SW12 0DG
T: 020 8642 2490
F: 020 8673 8763
www.sja-online.org
Provides opportunities to a broad range of
pupils to experience the advantages of
educational travel; provides funds to assist
children in need to take part in educational
visits.
Employees: 6
Volunteers: 12

School Library Association

Unit 2, Lotmead Business Village,
Lotmead Farm, Wanborough, Swindon,
Wiltshire SN4 0UY
T: 01793 791787
F: 01793 791786
E: info@sla.org.uk
www.sla.org.uk
Promotes the development of school
libraries as central to the curriculum at
primary and secondary level and acts as a
national voice for school libraries.
Employees: 6
Volunteers: 80

School-Home Support (SHS)

Cityside House, 40 Adler Street,
Whitechapel, London E1 1EE
T: 020 7426 5000
F: 020 7426 5001
E: enquiries@schoolhomesupport.org.uk
www.schoolhomesupport.org.uk
Chief Executive: Jan Tallis
Through the use of highly trained,
independent practitioners based in schools,
SHS works with disadvantaged children and
their families to overcome the barriers that
get in the way of learning. Currently working
in 90 schools in London, as well as offering
training in family support work in London,
Yorkshire and the North East.
Employees: 100
Regional offices: 1

SciDevNet

97–99 Dean Street, London W1D 3TE
T: 020 7291 3690
F: 020 7843 4596
E: info@scidev.net
www.scidev.net
SciDev.Net aims to: promote for the public's
benefit the advancement of education in
science, technology and other matters
connected with the development of society
and in particular to disseminate useful
research findings and provide for a critical
discussion; undertake any other charitable
purpose.
Employees: 5

Scoliosis Association (UK)

4 Ivebury Court, 323–327 Latimer Road,
London W10 6RA
T: 020 8964 5343
Helpline: 020 8964 1166
E: info@sauk.org.uk
www.sauk.org.uk
Chair of Trustees: Dr Stephanie Clark
SAUK is the only national support
organisation for people with scoliosis and
their families. SAUK aims to: provide advice,
support and information to people affected
by scoliosis, and their families; raise
awareness among health professionals and
the general public.
Employees: 5
Volunteers: 4

Scope

PO Box 833, Milton Keynes MK12 5NY
Helpline: 0808 800 3333
F: 01908 321051
E: response@scope.org.uk
www.scope.org.uk
Chief Executive: Richard Hawkes
We're all about changing society for the
better, so that disabled people and their
families can have the same opportunities as
everyone else. We work with disabled people
and their families at every stage of their lives.
We offer practical support from information
services to education and everyday care. We
challenge assumptions about disability, we
influence decision-makers and we show
what can be possible. Visit the Scope website.
Employees: 3375
Regional offices: 4

Scottish Council for Voluntary Organisations

Mansfield Traquair Centre, 15 Mansfield
Place, Edinburgh EH3 6BB
T: 0131 474 8000
Helpline: 0800 169 0022
F: 0131 556 0279
E: enquiries@scvo.org.uk
www.scvo.org.uk
Chief Executive: Martin Sime
Our vision is of a fair and just society in
Scotland, where the role, contribution and
potential of the third sector is valued and
understood. Our mission is to support
people to take voluntary action to help
themselves and others, and to bring about
social change. Strategic priorities: we support
third-sector organisations to do their work;
we promote and support the shared interests
of third sector organisations; we connect

people with ways to get involved with their communities.

Employees: 96
Volunteers: Varies
Regional offices: 3
Income: £14,513,735 (2012-13)

Scout Holiday Homes Trust

Gilwell Park, Chingford, London E4 7QW
T: 020 8433 7290
E: scout.holiday.homes@scouts.org.uk
www.holidayhomestrust.org.uk
Chairman: Roger Hurrion
Provides affordable self-catering holidays for families or groups with a disabled member or with special needs or low income (no scouting connection necessary).
Employees: 2
Volunteers: 20
Regional offices: 1

Scripture Union

207–209 Queensway, Bletchley, Milton Keynes, Buckinghamshire MK2 2EB
T: 01908 856000
F: 01908 856111
E: info@scriptureunion.org.uk
www.scriptureunion.org.uk
National Director: Tim Hastie-Smith
Scripture Union is a Christian mission movement working with churches to make disciples of Jesus Christ among children, young people and families. Activities include running holidays, church-based events and school Christian groups, producing a wide range of publications and supporting those who use its resources through training programmes.
Employees: 76
Volunteers: 3900
Regional offices: 7
Income: £6,736,000 (2011-12)

Sea Watch Foundation

Ewyn y Don, Bull Bay, Amlwch, Anglesey LL68 9SD
T: 01545 561227
F: 01407 832892
E: info@seawatchfoundation.org.uk
www.seawatchfoundation.org.uk
Scientific Director: Dr Peter Evans
The principal objective of the charity is the study, preservation and protection of cetaceans and promoting awareness for the benefit of the public.
Employees: 4
Volunteers: 15
Regional offices: 1
Income: £140,000 (2012-13)

Seafarers UK

(King George's Fund for Sailors), 8 Hatherley Street, London SW1P 2QT
T: 020 7932 0000
F: 020 7932 0095
E: seafarers@seafarers-uk.org
www.seafarers-uk.org
Director General: Commodore Barry Bryant
Seafarers UK (King George's Fund for Sailors) is the UK's leading maritime welfare charity that supports and promotes the many organisations that look after seafarers in need, plus their families and dependants, across the Merchant Navy, Fishing Fleets, Royal Navy and Royal Marines. Grants totalling £2.5 million are paid annually to more than 70 beneficiary charities.
Employees: 22
Volunteers: 100+
Regional offices: 2
Income: £25,000,000 (2011-12)

Seafarers' Advice & Information Line

PO Box 45234, Greenwich, London SE10 9WR
T: 020 8269 0565
Helpline: 0845 7413 3218
F: 020 8269 0794
E: admin@sailine.org.uk
www.sailine.org.uk
Chief Executive: Emma Knight
Provides advice and casework to all active, unemployed or retired Merchant Navy seafarers, fishermen and their families, operated by Greenwich Citizens Advice Bureaux Ltd and funded by the Seamen's Hospital Society.
Employees: 8
Volunteers: 3

SEAP

E: aoife.murphy@seap.org.uk

SeeAbility

Central Office, SeeAbility House, Hook Road, Epsom, Surrey KT19 8SQ
T: 01372 755000
F: 01372 755001
E: d.scott-ralphs@seeability.org
www.seeability.org
Chief Executive: David Scott-Ralphs
SeeAbility works to enrich the lives of people with sight loss and multiple disabilities across the UK.
Employees: 500
Volunteers: 250
Regional offices: 2
Income: £14,000,000 (2011-12)

Selby Trust Ltd

E: selbytrust@aol.com

Self Help Africa

Second Floor Suite, Westgate House, Dickens Court, Off Hills Lane, Shrewsbury, Shropshire SY1 1QU
T: 01743 277170
F: 01952 247158
E: infouk@selfhelpafrica.net
www.selfhelpafrica.org
Self Help Africa works with rural communities in eight African countries to help them improve their farms and their livelihoods. Self Help Africa helps people in rural Africa grow enough food to feed themselves, earn a living and access basic services. Self Help Africa equips people with the skills they need to move out of poverty by training farmers in new techniques and teaching basic business skills.
Employees: 14
Volunteers: 50
Regional offices: 11

Self management uk

32-36 Loman Street, Southwark, London SE1 0EH
T: 0333 344 5840
E: marketing@selfmanagementuk.org
www.selfmanagementuk.org
Chief Executive: Renata Drinkwater
self management uk is a leading charity which supports people with long-term health conditions. We have over 10 years' experience of delivering self-management training, support and education to well over 120,000 patients. Our aims are: To provide self-management support and training for people living with long-term conditions, increasing their wellbeing and confidence. To promote the value of self-management. To develop innovative and cost-effective ways to deliver self-management education.
Employees: 45
Volunteers: 100
Regional offices: 2

Sense

11–13 Clifton Terrace, London N4 3SR
T: 020 7272 7774
F: 020 7272 6012
E: jacqui.penalver@sense.org.uk
www.sense.org.uk
Sense is a national voluntary organisation that works with and campaigns for the needs of children and adults who are deafblind, providing advice, support, information and services for them, their families, carers and the professionals who work with them.
Employees: 1600
Volunteers: 500
Regional offices: 13

Sequal Trust

3 Ploughmans Corner, Wharf Road,
Ellesmere, Shropshire SY12 0EJ
T: 01691 624222 (also fax)
E: info@thesequaltrust.org.uk
www.thesequaltrust.org.uk
Chair: Dorcas Munday
The Sequal Trust is a national charity that
fundraises to provide communication aids
for disabled people with speech, movement
and/or severe learning difficulties.
Employees: 4

Sesame Institute (UK)

27 Blackfriars Road, London SE1 8NY
T: 020 7633 9690
E: info@sesame-institute.org
www.sesame-institute.org
Makes possible a fuller life, through applied
drama and movement, for those with mental
health difficulties, people working with a
physical challenge and others.

Shaftesbury Young People

The Chapel, Royal Victoria Patriotic
Building, John Archer Way,
London SW18 3SX
T: 020 8875 1555
F: 020 8875 1954
E: info@shaftesbury.org.uk
www.shaftesbury.org.uk
Cares for, educate and encourages looked
after children and young people and children
in need.

Shannon Trust

38 Ebury Street, London SW1W 0LU
T: 020 7730 4917
E: sue@shannontrust.org.uk
www.shannontrust.org.uk
CEO: David Ahern
Shannon Trust runs the Toe by Toe Reading
Plan, an award-winning peer mentoring
programme that encourages and supports
prisoners who can read to give one-to-one
tuition to prisoners who struggle to read.
Our aim is, to engage every non-reading
prisoner early in their sentence; to support
prison staff to run the Toe by Toe Reading
Plan in every prison and young offenders'
institution in the UK; to promote the
benefits of peer mentoring in prisons.
Employees: 4
Volunteers: 160

Shape London

Deane House Studios, 27 Greenwood
Place, London NW5 1LB
T: 0845 521 3457
F: 0845 521 3458
E: info@shapearts.org.uk
www.shapearts.org.uk
CEO: Tony Heaton
Our strategy reflects the artistic and political
'journey' of the disability and deaf
communities and seeks to offer them a new
platform to profile their work. Our strategy
invests in disabled and deaf people as equals
and seeks to ensure that they can play an
active role in the cultural life of London and
the UK. In order to achieve these aims, Shape
will work in partnership with other arts
organisations to build their capacity and their
understanding of the creative potential of
disabled and deaf people.
Employees: 18
Volunteers: 350
Regional offices: 4

Shaping Our Lives: National User Network

BM Box 4845, London WC1N 3XX
T: 0845 241 0383
E: information@shapingourlives.org.uk
www.shapingourlives.org.uk
Chair: Peter Beresford
Shaping Our Lives is a national user
controlled independent organisation started
in 1996. We work with a wide variety of
service users including people with physical
and/or sensory impairments, older people,
users/survivors of mental health services,
young people with experience of being
'looked after', people with learning
difficulties and others. Through networking,
research and development we support the
development of user involvement that aims
to deliver better outcomes for service users.
Employees: 2

ShareAction

Ground Floor, 16 Crucifix Lane,
London SE1 3JW
T: 020 7403 7800
E: info@shareaction.org
www.shareaction.org
Chief Executive: Catherine Howarth
ShareAction is a groundbreaking charity that
promotes Responsible Investment by
pension funds and fund managers. Bringing
together leading charities, trade unions, faith
groups and individual investors, our aim is to
catalyse a shift at each level of the investment
chain, so that Responsible Investment
becomes the norm.
Employees: 15
Volunteers: 60
Income: £370,000 (2012-13)

Shared Care Network

63–66 Easton Business Centre, Felix
Road, Easton, Bristol BS5 0HE
T: 0117 941 5361
F: 0117 941 5362
E: shared-care@bristol.ac.uk
www.sharedcarenetwork.org.uk
We are the national organisation
representing family-based short break
schemes for disabled children.
Employees: 15
Regional offices: 9

Shared Lives Plus

G04 The Cotton Exchange, Old Hall
Street, Liverpool, Merseyside L3 9JR
T: 0151 227 3499
F: 0151 236 3590
E: deborah@sharedlivesplus.org.uk
www.sharedlivesplus.org.uk
Chief Executive: Alex Fox
Shared Lives Plus is a UK charity established
to represent the interests of all those
involved in delivering very small,
individualised, community-based services
such as Shared Lives (formerly known as
Adult Placement). Shared Lives Plus
promotes Shared Lives, Homeshare and
other small community micro services as an
important resource to those seeking
individualised services; promotes a legislative
environment that ensures safety and quality
but allows small community services to
flourish.
Employees: 14
Volunteers: 50
Regional offices: 3

Shaw Trust Ltd

Fox Talbot House, Greenways Business
Park, Bellinger Close, Malmesbury Road,
Chippenham, Wiltshire SN15 1BN
T: 01225 716300
Helpline: 01225 779471
F: 01225 716301
E: sheila.tsiaparis@shaw-trust.org.uk
www.shaw-trust.org.uk
Director General: Tim Pape
Runs work programmes to help people with
disabilities find employment and to remain in
their jobs.
Employees: 1200
Volunteers: 200
Regional offices: 5

Shelter

88 Old Street, London EC1V 9HU
T: 020 7505 2000
F: 020 7505 2169
E: info@shelter.org.uk
www.shelter.org.uk
Shelter's vision is that everyone should have a home – somewhere decent, safe, affordable and permanent. Yet one in seven children in Britain are growing up in bad housing, and thousands of homeless households are stuck in temporary accommodation. Shelter helps more than 170,000 people a year fight for their rights, get back on their feet, and find and keep a home.
Employees: 800
Volunteers: 800

ShelterBox Trust

1A Water Ma Trout Industrial Estate, Helston, Cornwall TR13 0LW
T: 01326 569782
E: ageocur@aol.com
www.shelterbox.org
Chief Executive: Alison Wallace
ShelterBox is an international disaster relief charity that provides emergency shelter and life-saving supplies to families around the world who are affected by disasters. Each big, green ShelterBox is tailored to every disaster but typically contains a disaster relief tent for an extended family, blankets, water purification and storage equipment, cooking utensils, a stove, a basic tool kit, a children's activity pack and other vital items.
Employees: 60
Volunteers: 500
Regional offices: 2

SHINE

42 Park Road, Peterborough PE1 2UQ
T: 01733 555988
E: info@shinecharity.org.uk
www.shinecharity.org.uk
Provides services to people with spina bifida and/or hydrocephalus, and their carers, and promotes their interests in order to help them develop their abilities, receive the best possible services and make the most of life.

Shingles Support Society (SSS)

41 North Road, London N7 9DP
T: 020 7607 9661
Helpline: 0845 123 2305
E: info@hva.org.uk
www.shinglessupport.org
Director: Marian Nicholson
We supply information and advice on medical treatment that your GP can prescribe as well as self-help suggestions for post-herpetic neuralgia (PHN), which, particularly in older patients, may follow shingles (herpes zoster). Early treatment gives a greater chance of eliminating PHN. Certified by the Information Standard.
Employees: 2
Volunteers: 7

Shipwrecked Fishermen and Mariners' Royal Benevolent Society

Shipwrecked Mariners' Society, 1 North Pallant, Chichester, West Sussex PO19 1TL
T: 01243 789329
Helpline: 01243 787761
F: 01243 530853
E: general@shipwreckedmariners.org.uk
www.shipwreckedmariners.org.uk
Chief Executive: Malcolm Williams
The Shipwrecked Mariners' Society exists to provide financial help to merchant seafarers, fishermen and their dependants who are in need. We pay an immediate grant to the widow of a serving seafarer who dies, whether at sea or ashore. Regular grants are paid to elderly seafarers and widows whose circumstances justify ongoing support. Special grants are made to meet particular needs in crisis situations.
Employees: 7
Volunteers: 200

Shpresa Programme (Albanian for Hope)

Mansfield House, 30 Avenons Road, Plaistow E13 3HT
T: 020 7511 1586
E: shpresaprogramme@yahoo.co.uk
www.shpresaprogramme.com
Project Director: Luljeta Nuzi
Aims to enable the Albanian-speaking community in UK to settle and fully participate in society and realise their full potential. We want to promote a positive identity and recognition of our community's cultural and linguistic heritage, both among Albanian speakers and wider society so that we can contribute to community cohesion in the UK.
Employees: 5
Volunteers: 31

Sightsavers International

Grosvenor Hall, Bolnore Road, Haywards Heath, West Sussex RH16 4BX
T: 01444 446600
F: 01444 446688
E: charper@sightsavers.org
www.sightsavers.org
Chief Executive: Caroline Harper
Sightsavers is an international charity that is dedicated to combating blindness in developing countries. We work with partners in over 33 countries, in poor and least-served communities, to support activities that prevent and cure blindness, restore sight and provide education and training for the blind and visually impaired.
Employees: 325
Regional offices: 6

Signalong Group

Stratford House, Waterside Court, Neptune Way, Rochester, Kent ME2 4NZ
T: 0845 450 8422
F: 0845 450 8428
E: mkennard@signalong.org.uk
www.signalong.org.uk
Operations Manager: Tracy Goode
Charity specialising in communication resources and training in learning disabilities and autism. Its aims are to improve communication skills, leading to greater independence, fulfilment of potential, reduction in disturbed and challenging behaviour, improved self-esteem and improved relationships.
Employees: 4
Volunteers: 24
Income: £240,837 (2011-12)

Signature

Mersey House, Mandale Business Park, Belmont, Durham DH1 1TH
T: 0191 383 1155
F: 0191 383 7914
E: joanne.lavender@signature.org.uk
www.signature.org.uk
Works towards the improvement of communication with deaf, deafened, hard of hearing and deafblind people in particular by the education, training and examination of students and tutors in the different modes of communication used by such persons.
Employees: 33
Regional offices: 2

SignHealth

5 Baring Road, Beaconsfield,
Buckinghamshire HP9 2NB
T: 01494 687600
E: info@signhealth.org.uk
www.signhealth.org.uk
Chief Executive: Steve Powell
SignHealth is a charity that aims for a world
where the risk of deaf people developing
preventable health problems is removed,
and where equality, respect and fulfillment
are enjoyed by deaf people experiencing
mental health problems. SignHealth is
committed to bringing better healthcare
and equality of service provision to deaf
people in the UK.
Employees: 120
Volunteers: 20
Regional offices: 6
Income: £4,417,208 (2012-13)

Single Parent Action Network

Millpond, Baptist Street,
Bristol BS5 0YW
T: 0117 951 4231
F: 0117 935 5208
E: info@spanuk.org.uk
www.singleparents.org.uk
Director: Sue Cohen
SPAN is a uniquely diverse organisation
supporting single parents to empower
themselves throughout the UK. SPAN aims
to give a voice to one-parent families living
in poverty and isolation, and support the
setting up and development of self-help
groups. SPAN develops partnerships with
organisations and agencies to improve
policies for one-parent families.
Employees: 17
Volunteers: 5

Sir Halley Stewart Trust

22 Earith Road, Willingham, Cambridge,
Cambridgeshire CB24 5LS
T: 01954 260707 (also fax)
E: email@sirhalleystewart.org.uk
www.sirhalleystewart.org.uk
Trust Administrator: Sue West
The trust aims to promote and assist
innovative research activities or pioneering
developments in medical, social and
religious fields. It emphasises prevention
rather than alleviation of human suffering.
Certain priorities apply, please refer to Trust
website for current details.
Employees: 1
Income: £948,000 (2012-13)

SITRA (Services)

3rd Floor, 55 Bondway, London SW8 1SJ
T: 020 7793 4710
F: 020 7793 4715
E: berihum@sitra.org
www.sitra.org.uk
Chief Executive: Vic Rayner
Provides policy, information, training, events
and consultancy services to the housing with
care and support sector. Sitra has some 600
member organisations including supported
housing providers, housing associations and
local authorities. We publish a popular
monthly bulletin.
Employees: 30
Regional offices: 4
Income: £2 (2010-11)

Skill Force

Edwinstowe House, High Street,
Edwinstowe, Mansfield,
Nottinghamshire NG21 9PR
T: 01623 827619
E: enquiries@skillforce.org
www.skillforce.org
The mission of Skill Force is to develop young
people in order to raise standards in wider key
skills, self-esteem and employability.
Employees: 250

Skills for Care Ltd

Albion Court, 5 Albion Place, Leeds, West
Yorkshire LS1 6JL
T: 0113 245 1716
F: 0113 243 6417
E: info@skillsforcare.org.uk
www.skillsforcare.org.uk
Chief Executive: Andrea Rowe
Skills for Care is the not-for-profit organisation
that aims to improve adult social care services
across the whole of England by supporting
employers' workforce development activity.
Our vision is to put employers in the driving
seat on social care workforce issues; to create a
trained and qualified workforce providing
high-quality care; and to provide an expert
voice on the social care workforce.
Employees: 200
Volunteers: 24
Regional offices: 9

Skills for Communities

265 Anlaby Road, Hull,
Humberside HU3 2SE
T: 0870 803 2768
F: 0870 803 2769
E: info@skills4communities.co.uk
www.skills4communities.co.uk
Skills for Communities has the following aims:
develop and provide a range of
multidisciplinary support and education
services within a broad therapeutic framework

for young people and their families; promote
social inclusion, particularly through the
provision of training and employment
opportunities; provision of advice and
counselling to the youth of the community on
pregnancy and teenage problems, and help to
asylum seekers and refugees through training,
advice, information and guidance the
unemployed and local service providers.
Employees: 4
Volunteers: 2
Regional offices: 2

Skillset Sector Skills Council

Focus Point, 21 Caledonian Road N1 9GB
T: 020 7713 9800
E: michellec@skillset.org
www.skillset.org
HR and Office Manager: Michelle Care

Skillshare International

126 New Walk, Leicester LE1 7JA
T: 0116 254 6627
F: 0116 254 2614
E: info@skillshare.org
www.skillshare.org
CEO: Dr Cliff Allum
Skillshare International works for sustainable
development in partnership with people and
communities in Africa and Asia. We do this by
sharing and developing skills through projects
and volunteer placements. Our programmes
focus on sustainable livelihoods, sport for
development, HIV and AIDS, gender justice
and conflict management.
Employees: 38
Volunteers: 260
Regional offices: 7

Small Charities Coalition

Directory of Social Change, 24 Stephenson
Way, London NW1 2DP
T: 020 7391 4812
E: info@smallcharities.org.uk
www.smallcharities.org.uk
Chief Executive: Alex Swallow
Small Charities Coalition is a national charity
supporting the trustees, staff and volunteers
of small charities. It is free to join to receive
information and support. We provide
information, resources, support and advice on
governance and operational matters. Our
services include: one-to-one and group
mentoring services, access to networks,
brokered training, services and products. We
operate a free trustee recruitment portal
called Trustee Finder and contribute to policy
work on behalf of small charities.
Employees: 4
Volunteers: 10
Income: £170,383 (2011-12)

Smile International

E: ruth.doubleday@smileinternational.
org

Smile Support & Care

Eastleigh Community Enterprise Centre,
Unit 3, Barton Park, Eastleigh,
Hampshire SO50 6RR
T: 023 8061 6215
E: stuart.baldwin@smilesupport.org.uk
www.smilesupport.org.uk
Chief Executive: Stuart Baldwin
Smile Support & Care supports children and
young adults with disabilities either in their
own home or in the community. Working in
southern England, we ensure the people we
support can exercise choice over the way
they take short breaks or engage in any other
activity. We are registered with the Care
Quality Commission, and use a certified
quality management system. To find out
more about us, have a look at our website.
Employees: 130
Volunteers: 10
Regional offices: 2
Income: £1,100,000 (2012-13)

Social Care Association

Thornton House, Hook Road, Surbiton,
Surrey KT6 5AN
T: 020 8397 1411
F: 020 8397 1436
E: info@scad.org.uk
www.socialcareassoc.com
Promotes and encourages a high standard of
service for people receiving residential and
day care. Ensures that training and
professional practice is of a high standard,
and promotes a wide knowledge of
developments through national day and
residential conferences, study days and
education programmes. Also publishes
material on social policy and practice.
Employees: 9
Regional offices: 1

Social Care Institute for Excellence

1st Floor, Goldings House, Hayes Lane,
London SE1 2HB
T: 020 7089 6871
F: 020 7089 6841
E: stephen.goulder@scie.org.uk
www.scie.org.uk
Chief Executive: Julie Jones
The Social Care Institute for Excellence
(SCIE) was established by government in
2001 to improve social care services for
adults and children in the UK. We achieve
this by identifying good practice and helping
to embed it in everyday social care provision.
Employees: 65

Social Emotional and Behavioural Difficulties Association

Church House, 1 St Andrew's View,
Penrith, Cumbria CA11 1YF
T: 01768 210510
E: tcole@sebda.org
www.sebda.org
Executive Director: Ted Cole
SEBDA is a long-established charity that
provides accredited specialist training,
information and support to professionals
working with children with social, emotional
and behavioural difficulties. Members
receive free copies of the Association's
research journal and regular, detailed updates
on policy and practice in its popular
newsletter.
Employees: 3
Volunteers: 1300

Social Enterprise Coalition

South Bank House, Black Prince Road,
London SE1 7SJ
T: 020 7793 2323
F: 020 7968 4922
E: info@socialenterprise.org.uk
www.socialenterprise.org.uk
The Social Enterprise Coalition (SEC) is the
UK trade body that brings together all types
of social enterprise to promote the sector
and share knowledge.
Employees: 7

Social Firms UK

Furness House, 53 Brighton Road, Redhill,
Surrey RH1 6PZ
T: 01737 764021
F: 01737 766699
E: cneville@socialfirms.co.uk
www.socialfirms.co.uk
Social Firms UK is the national support
agency that supports and encourages the
development of social firms - companies set
up specifically to create employment for
disadvantaged people.
Employees: 7
Regional offices: 1

Social Market Foundation

11 Tufton Street, London SW1P 3QB
T: 020 7227 4400
E: enquiries@smf.co.uk
www.smf.co.uk
The Social Market Foundation is a leading
UK think-tank, developing innovative ideas
across a broad range of economic and social
policy. It champions policy ideas that marry
markets with social justice and takes a
pro-market rather than free-market
approach. Its work is characterised by the
belief that governments have an important
role to play in correcting market failures and
setting the framework within which markets

can operate in a way that benefits individuals
and society.
Employees: 12

Social Partnership

44 Castle Street, Liverpool L2 7LA
T: 0151 258 1331
F: 0151 709 7779
E: generalenquiries@tsp.org.uk
The Social Partnership (TSP) aims to
reintegrate socially excluded people into the
community both socially and economically
through the provision of education, training
and employment opportunities.
Employees: 45
Volunteers: 3

Social Perspectives Network

c/o SCIE, Goldings House, 2 Hay's Lane,
London SE1 2HB
T: 020 7089 6840
F: 020 7089 6841
E: media@scie.org.uk
www.spn.org.uk
We are a broad-based coalition of service
users/survivors, carers, policy makers,
academics, students, practitioners working to
ensure that social perspectives are put at the
heart of the evolving mental health policy,
practice, research and legislative agendas.
Social perspectives are holistic and look at
the social issues that affect people's mental
health such as experiences of stigma and
discrimination, relationships, employment,
access to housing and quality health and
social care services.
Employees: 1
Volunteers: 25

Social Research Association

24–32 Stephenson Way,
London NW1 6QB
T: 020 7388 2391
E: admin@the-sra.org.uk
www.the-sra.org.uk
Chair of the Board of Trustees: Patten
Smith
We are the professional membership body
for social researchers. Promoting high-quality
standards of social research, we seek to
represent, support, connect and inform our
members and the wider social research
community.
Employees: 2
Volunteers: 10
Regional offices: 3

Social Venture Network UK

Chandos House, 128 Cotham Brow,
Bristol, Avon BS6 6AE
E: info@svnuk.org
www.svneurope.com

A network of socially and environmentally engaged entrepreneurs dedicated to changing the way the world does business. The network creates opportunities for learning, partnerships, and launching new ventures and is associated with SVN United States and SVN Asia.

Volunteers: 3
Regional offices: 1

Society for Co-operative Studies

c/o Richard Bickle, Co-operative UK, Holyoake House, Hanover Street, Manchester M60 0AS
T: 0121 242 5348
E: richardbickle@cooptel.net
www.co-opstudies.org
The Society welcomes into membership, co-operative members, employees, managers, specialist practitioners, academics and others who share an interest in the UK and world Co-operative Movement. It seeks to advance the education of members and the public on all aspects of the Co-operative Movement, co-operative forms of structure and, in particular, to commission, identify, and publish research on the Co-operative Movement and the exchange of information and experience on co-operative study and research.

Society for Complementary Medicine

3 Spanish Place, London W1U 3HX
T: 020 7487 4334
F: 020 7487 4515
E: bob@scmhealth.org
www.scmhealth.com
The charity provides naturopathic treatment for illness. We can provide bursaries to patients ranging from total support including treatments, supplements and medicines down to partial support or no support if it is not needed.
Employees: 3
Volunteers: 2

Society for Endocrinology

22 Apex Court, Woodlands, Bradley Stoke, Bristol, Avon BS32 4JT
T: 01454 642200
F: 01454 642205
E: sally.spencer@endocrinology.org
www.endocrinology.org
Chief Executive: Leon Heward-Mills
The Society for Endocrinology is the major British society representing scientists, clinicians and nurses who work with hormones. It advances education and research in endocrinology, as well as acting as the discipline's voice with an aim of raising its profile.
Employees: 53

Society For General Microbiology

Marlborough House, Basingstoke Road, Spencers Wood, Reading, Berkshire RG7 1AG
T: 0118 988 1800
E: info@sgm.ac.uk
www.sgm.ac.uk
CEO: Dr Simon Festing
Society for General Microbiology (SGM) is a membership organisation for scientists who work in all areas of microbiology. SGM publishes key academic journals in microbiology and virology, organises international scientific conferences and provides an international forum for communication among microbiologists and supports their professional development. SGM promotes the understanding of microbiology to a diverse range of stakeholders, including policy makers, students, teachers, journalists and the wider public through a framework of communication activities and resources.
Employees: 36
Volunteers: 80

Society for Mucopolysaccharide Diseases

MPS House, Repton Place, White Lion Road, Amersham, Buckinghamshire HP7 9LP
T: 0845 389 9901
F: 0845 389 9902
E: mps@mpssociety.co.uk
www.mpssociety.co.uk
Chief Executive: Christine Lavery
Provides support and individual advocacy to those affected by Mucopolysaccharide, Fabry and other lysosomal diseases throughout the UK. Publishes a wide range of information booklets and a quarterly newsletter. Organises conferences, training and funds research into MPS diseases.
Employees: 10
Volunteers: 180
Regional offices: 1

Society for Promoting Christian Knowledge

36 Causton Street, London SW1P 4ST
T: 020 7592 3900
F: 020 7592 3939
E: pphillips@spck.org.uk
www.spck.org.uk
General Secretary: Simon Kingston
Promotes Christian knowledge by: communicating the faith in its rich diversity; helping people to understand it and to

develop their personal faith; equipping Christians for mission and ministry.
Employees: 30

Society for the Assistance of Ladies in Reduced Circumstances

Lancaster House, 25 Hornyold Road, Malvern, Worcestershire WR14 1QQ
T: 0300 365 1886
E: john.sands@salrc.org.uk
www.salrc.org.uk
General Secretary: John Sands
The Society makes grants to women domiciled and habitually resident in the UK who are living alone in their own home (either owned or rented) and in genuine financial need, irrespective of age or social status.
Employees: 4
Income: £887,720 (2011-12)

Society for the Protection of Ancient Buildings

37 Spital Square, London E1 6DY
T: 020 7377 1644
Helpline: 020 7456 0916
F: 020 7247 5296
E: info@spab.org.uk
www.spab.org.uk
Secretary: Philip Venning
Aims to educate public opinion in the conservative repair of historic buildings and to prevent ill-considered and conjectural restoration. Offers advice and courses for homeowners and building professionals. SPAB is a membership organisation. Its respected magazine, Cornerstone, is sent to all members on a quarterly basis. We advise, we educate, we campaign.

Society for the Protection of Animals Abroad

14 John Street, London WC1N 2EB
T: 020 7831 3999
F: 020 7831 5999
E: john@spana.org
www.spana.org
Chief Executive: Jeremy Hulme
With 19 veterinary centres and 21 mobile clinics, SPANA treated over 300,000 animals last year throughout North and West Africa and the Middle East. Our efforts are concentrated on those areas where the need is greatest: wherever animals are mistreated, neglected or struggling to survive without proper care.
Employees: 17
Volunteers: 20

Society for the Protection of Unborn Children

5–6 St Matthew Street, London SW1P 2JT
T: 020 7222 5845
F: 020 7222 0630
E: information@spuc.org.uk
www.spuc.org.uk
Affirms, defends and promotes the existence and value of human life from the moment of conception; reasserts the principle laid down in UN Declaration of the Rights of the Child that the child needs special safeguards and care, including appropriate legal protection, before as well as after birth; defends and promotes welfare of mothers during pregnancy and of their children; examines existing or proposed laws, legislation or regulations relating to abortion, supporting or opposing as appropriate.
Employees: 34
Volunteers: 100
Regional offices: 6

Society of Analytical Psychology

1 Daleham Gardens, Hampstead, London NW3 5BY
T: 020 7435 7696
F: 020 7431 1495
E: chair@thesap.org.uk
www.thesap.org.uk
Chair: Penny Pickles
The Society's main functions are the development of analytical psychology; training of adult analysts and psychotherapists; provision of Jungian analysis to members of the public through the society's Clinic, plus a consultation and referral service; education through public events and the Journal of Analytical Psychology; professional association for Jungian analysts and psychotherapists.
Employees: 17
Volunteers: 100
Income: £316,559 (2012-13)

Society of Antiquaries of London

Burlington House, Piccadilly, London W1J 0BE
T: 020 7479 7080
F: 020 7287 6967
E: admin@sal.org.uk
www.sal.org.uk
General Secretary: John Lewis
The Society of Antiquaries of London's goals are the encouragement, advancement and furtherance of the study and knowledge of the antiquities and history of this and other countries.
Employees: 20
Regional offices: 1

Society of Authors

84 Drayton Gardens, London SW10 9SB
T: 020 7373 6642
F: 020 7373 5768
E: info@societyofauthors.org
www.societyofauthors.org
General Secretary: Mark Le Fanu
The Society is a trade union with 8,500 members. It lobbies for the profession and gives individual advice and help to members on business issues (eg. contracts, copyright, publishers, agents, etc). Members receive a quarterly journal, The Author.
Employees: 14

Society of Biology

Charles Darwin House, 12 Roger Street, London WC1N 2JU
T: 020 7685 2550
E: info@societyofbiology.org
www.societyofbiology.org
Chief Executive: Dr Mark Downs
Aims to advance the science and practice of biology and education in biology and to coordinate and encourage the study of biology and its application.
Employees: 30
Volunteers: 200
Regional offices: 0
Income: £2,600,000 (2012-13)

Society of Homeopaths

11 Brookfield, Duncan Close, Moulton Park, Northampton, Northamptonshire NN1 6WL
T: 01604 621400
F: 01604 622622
E: sandra_waller@homeopathy-soh.org
www.homeopathy-soh.org
Established in 1978, it is the largest organisation representing professional homeopaths in Europe, with over 1,500 members on its register. Members practice in accordance with the society's Code of Ethics and Practice and carry full public liability and indemnity insurance.
Employees: 20
Volunteers: 20
Regional offices: 1

Soil Association

Bristol House, 40–56 Victoria Street, Bristol BS1 6BY
T: 0117 914 2454
F: 0117 925 2504
E: development@soilassociation.org
www.soilassociation.org
Aims to educate the general public about organic agriculture, gardening and food, and their benefits for both human health and the environment; promotes the production and consumption of organically grown food;

lobbies the authorities for an agricultural policy that is based on ecological and sustainable principles.
Employees: 150
Volunteers: 10
Regional offices: 2

Solicitors Pro Bono Group

10–13 Lovat Lane, London EC3R 8DN
T: 020 7929 5601
F: 020 7929 5722
E: solicitors@probonogroup.org.uk
www.probonogroup.org.uk
The SPBG is an independent charity formed to support, promote and encourage a commitment to pro bono across the solicitors' profession. It seeks to bridge the gap between existing pro bono efforts while working with members to create a more coordinated response to legal need.

Solihull Carers Centre

E: sueshahmiri@solihullcarers.org

SOLVE IT

Satra Innovation Park, Rockingham Road, Kettering, Northamptonshire NN16 9JH
T: 01536 414690
E: manager.solveit@gmail.com
www.solveitonline.co.uk
Business Manager: Deborah Clarke
SOLVE IT provides a free service to young people, parents, carers and those adults affected by volatile substance abuse (VSA), promoting a general awareness to the dangers of these substances, working towards the prevention of related deaths, illness, accidents and social exclusion. It provides education, early intervention, a confidential support and counselling service for those affected by such abuse, including families, training and support for professionals.
Employees: 5
Volunteers: 8
Regional offices: 1

SOS Children's Villages UK

St Andrew's House, 59 St Andrew's Street, Cambridge, Cambridgeshire CB2 3BZ
T: 01223 365589
F: 01223 322613
E: info@sos-uk.org.uk
www.soschildrensvillages.org.uk
Provides loving care and a secure future for homeless, orphaned and abandoned children throughout the world.
Employees: 9
Volunteers: 2

Sound and Music

3rd Floor, Somerset House,
London WC2R 1LA
T: 020 7759 1800
E: info@soundandmusic.org
www.soundandmusic.org
Chief Executive: Susanna Eastburn
Sound and Music's vision is to create a world where new music and sound prospers, transforming lives, challenging expectations and celebrating the work of its creators.
Employees: 10
Regional offices: 1

South Lancashire Learning Disability Training Consortium

E: ceo@slldtc.co.uk

Southampton and Winchester Visitors Group

SWVG, PO Box 1615, Southampton,
Hampshire SO17 3WF
T: 07503 176350
E: info@swvg-refugees.org.uk
www.swvg-refugees.org.uk
Chair: Anne Leeming
SWVG is a group of volunteers who befriend and support asylum seekers and refugees in the Southampton area. We offer financial assistance to those who are homeless and destitute. Through our legal justice project we have access to advice from a leading immigration solicitor. We try to give asylum seekers a voice by reaching out to churches, schools and community groups and we campaign for a fairer asylum system.
Employees: 2
Volunteers: 60
Regional offices: 0
Income: £93,395 (2012-13)

Southampton University Students' Union

Highfield
T: 023 8059 5215
E: j.a.booth@soton.ac.uk
Chief Executive/Chair: Jaki Booth

Southbank Mosaics CIC

E: david@southbankmosaics.com

Southend Association of Voluntary Services

E: asemmence@savs-southend.co.uk

Sova

Head Office, Unit 201, Lincoln House, 1-3 Brixton road, London SW9 6DE
T: 020 7793 0404
F: 020 7793 5858
E: mail@sova.org.uk
www.sova.org.uk
Chief Operating Officer: Sophie Wilson
Sova works in England and Wales with the National Offender Management Service, the Prison Service, probation areas, JobCentre Plus, Social Services and other organisations to strengthen communities by involving local volunteers in promoting social inclusion and reducing crime. Paid staff and volunteers utilise skills to encourage the positive development of a wide client group including offenders, prisoners, young people on youth offending orders, those at risk of offending and asylum seekers.
Employees: 150
Volunteers: 1000

Spadework Ltd

Teston Road, Offham, West Malling,
Kent ME19 5NA
T: 01732 870002
F: 01732 842827
E: spadework1@btconnect.com
www.spadework.net
Provides training opportunities for adults with learning and/or physical disabilities to prepare them for an independent life within the community.
Employees: 13
Volunteers: 20
Regional offices: 2

Spare Tyre Theatre Company

E: lucy@sparetyre.org

Speakability (Action for Dysphasic Adults)

240 City Road, London EC1V 2PR
T: 020 7261 9572
Helpline: 0808 808 9572
E: melanie@speakability.org.uk
www.speakability.org.uk
Chief Executive: Melanie Derbyshire
Speakability is a national charity supporting and empowering people with Aphasia (whatever the cause) and their carers, by offering a free helpline and information service, training resources for carers and a UK-wide network of Aphasia Self-Help Groups. As the voice of people with Aphasia, Speakabilty also campaigns for greater understanding of this communication disability and better service provision.
Employees: 5
Volunteers: 100+

Special Kids In the UK

PO Box 617, Addlestone KT15 9AP
T: 01932 356416
E: information@specialkidsintheuk.org
www.specialkidsintheuk.org
Special Kids in the UK is a charity for families who have a child of any age with additional needs. The charity aims to bring families together, offering friendship and support.

Spinal Injuries Association

SIA House, 2 Trueman Place, Milton Keynes MK6 2HH
T: 0845 678 6633
Helpline: 0800 980 0501
E: sia@spinal.co.uk
www.spinal.co.uk
Executive Director: Paul Smith
SIA is a national, user-led organisation for people with spinal cord injuries and their families. Our purpose is to promote the integration and full participation in society of our members, by encouraging them to become fulfilled and in control of their lives.
Employees: 40
Volunteers: 100
Income: £2,164,274 (2010-11)

Spitalfields City Farm

Buxton street, London E1 5AR
T: 020 7247 8762
F: 020 7247 5452
E: mhairi@spitalfieldscityfarm.org
www.spitalfieldscityfarm.org
Director: Mhairi Weir
Spitalfields City Farm is a community space that inspires and that everyone can enjoy. We challenge people to respect themselves, each other, their environment and animals. We strive to be sustainable and lead by example. We aim to give people the opportunity to become active members of their community and encourage their participation in the development of the farm, and to explore and promote the benefits of healthy and sustainable lifestyles.
Employees: 16
Volunteers: 350
Regional offices: 0
Income: £350,000 (2011-12)

Sport and Recreation Alliance

4th Floor, Burwood House, 14–16 Caxton House, London SW1H 0QT
T: 020 7976 3900
F: 020 7976 3901
E: info@sportandrecreation.org.uk
www.sportandrecreation.org.uk
Chief Executive: Tim Lamb

Sport and Recreation Alliance is the trade association for governing and representative bodies of sport and recreation. It exists to protect, promote and provide for its members – bodies like the FA, the LTA, Ramblers and the Exercise Movement and Dance Partnership. In total the Alliance boasts around 300 members and provides a variety of services and campaigns on a wide range of issues affecting the sector.
Employees: 20

Sports Leaders UK

Clyde House, 10 Milburn Avenue, Oldbrook, Milton Keynes MK6 2WA
T: 01908 689194
F: 01908 393744
E: info@sportsleaders.org
www.sportsleaders.org
The new name for the British Sports Trust, Sports Leaders UK believes in inspiring people and communities through leadership qualifications in sport. Sports Leaders UK believes that everyone has the potential to make a meaningful contribution to their local community, but not everyone has the opportunity or the motivation. Our Sports Leader Awards help people learn essential skills such as working with and organising others, as well as motivational, communication and teamwork skills.
Employees: 32
Volunteers: 1

Spurgeon's Child Care

74 Wellingborough Road, Rushden, Northamptonshire NN10 9TY
T: 01933 417405
E: info@spurgeons.org
www.spurgeons.org
From giving children in care in the UK a voice in their own future, to supporting AIDS orphans in Africa, Spurgeon's exists to create opportunities for vulnerable children and young people to find hope and transformation now and fulfilment in their future. We have over 100 projects in the UK and internationally, each seeking to respond to the needs identified in a local community.

ssafa

Queen Elizabeth House, 4 St Dunstans Hill, London EC3R 8AD
T: 020 7403 8783
F: 020 7403 8815
E: terry.c@ssafa.org.uk
www.ssafa.org.uk
We provide support for the serving men and women in today's Armed Forces and for those who have served, even if it was only for a single day. We also care for the needs of their families and dependants. Last year

alone, our professional staff and trained volunteers gave assistance to more than 50,000 people. We helped to make a real difference to many lives.
Employees: 680
Volunteers: 7000
Regional offices: 100

St Albans Mencap

E: macpheemartyn@aol.com

St Andrew's Healthcare

St Andrew's Hospital, Billing Road, Northampton, Northamptonshire NN1 5DG
T: 01604 616000
E: treading@standrew.co.uk
www.stah.org
Chief Executive and Medical Director: Philip Sugarman
St Andrew's Healthcare, a not-for-profit charity, aims to be the UK's leading independent provider of specialist mental healthcare, complementing and working in partnership with the NHS.
Employees: 2500
Volunteers: 110

St Francis Leprosy Guild

73 St Charles Square, London W10 6EJ
T: 020 8969 1345
E: enquiries@stfrancisleprosy.org
www.stfrancisleprosy.org
President: Mrs Gwen Sankey
St Francis Leprosy Guild supports those caring for leprosy patients in Asia, Africa and South America. Although leprosy can now be cured by multi-drug therapy, many new cases are still being discovered and thousands of cured patients have disabilities and need care and support. Each year the Guild sends grants to eighty hospitals, clinics and centres in 25 countries. Its 'elective' programme helps medical students in the UK to work with leprosy patients abroad.
Employees: 1
Volunteers: 6
Regional offices: 0
Income: £155,000 (2012-13)

St John Ambulance

27 St John's Lane, London EC1M 4BU
T: 020 7324 4000
F: 020 7324 4001
E: chief-executive@nhq.sja.org.uk
www.sja.org.uk
Everyone who needs it should receive first aid from those around them. No one should suffer for the lack of trained first aiders. Our mission is: to provide an effective and efficient charitable first aid service to local communities; to provide training and products to satisfy first aid and related health

and safety needs for all of society; and to encourage personal development for people of all ages, through training and by membership of our organisation.
Volunteers: 44000
Regional offices: 45

St John of God Care Services

Saint Bede's House, Morton Park Way, Darlington, County Durham DL1 4XZ
T: 01325 373701
F: 01325 373707
E: enquiries@sjog.org.uk
The Order's services in England, Scotland and Wales support people with special needs, including those with physical/learning disabilities, mental health problems and Alzheimer's disease. It provides supported housing and domiciliary care services, as well as residential community-based homes, leisure, educational and occupational services and nursing homes.
Employees: 700
Volunteers: 40
Regional offices: 6

St Joseph's Hospice Association

Jospice, Ince Road, Thornton, Liverpool L23 4UE
T: 0151 924 3812
E: enquiries@jospice.org.uk
Maintains hospices to care for the incurably sick and destitute, both in Britain and the third world (Central and South America, India and Pakistan).

St Loye's Foundation

Beaufort House, 51 New North Road, Exeter EX4 4EP
T: 01392 255428
F: 01392 420889
E: info@stloyes.ac.uk
www.stloyes.org.uk
CEO: Christopher Knee
St Loye's Foundation is a national charity and service provider, based in Exeter, Devon for over 75 years. We also have satellite offices in Warrington, Cardiff and North Devon. We specialise in helping people with health, disability and social issues by providing a range of services, including employment training, care and support and learning and skills. Across all these services individuals are given the support and practical knowledge they need to access employment.
Employees: 120
Volunteers: 6
Regional offices: 6

St Peters House Project

1-3 The Pavement, Grovehill Road,
Redhill, Surrey RH1 6TW
T: 01737 773917
Helpline: 01737 763000
E: stephanie@stpetershouse.org.uk
www.stpetershouse.org.uk
Project Director: Stephanie Phillips
Employees: 7
Volunteers: 3
Regional offices: 0
Income: £124,000 (2012-13)

St Vincent de Paul Society (England and Wales)

5th Floor, 291–299 Borough High Street,
London SE1 1JG
T: 020 7407 4644
F: 020 7407 4634
E: info@svp.org.uk
www.svp.org.uk
Chief Executive: Elizabeth Palmer
The St Vincent de Paul Society is an international Christian voluntary organisation dedicated to tackling poverty and disadvantage by providing direct practical assistance to anyone in need. Active in England and Wales since 1844, today it continues to address social and material need in all its many forms.
Employees: 130
Volunteers: 10000
Regional offices: 1100

Staffordshire Council of Voluntary Youth Services

42a, Eastgate Street, Stafford,
Staffordshire ST16 2LY
T: 01785 240378
E: phil@staffscvys.org.uk
www.staffscvys.org.uk
Staffordshire Council of Voluntary Youth: Phil Pusey
Staffordshire Council of Voluntary Youth Services will ensure that Staffordshire County will be internally and externally recognised as having a dynamic voluntary youth sector made up of strong, sustainable, local organisations run by capable people committed to meaningful engagement and effective partnership working, providing safe environments for thousands of children and young people to maximise their personal potential through personal & social development.
Employees: 8
Volunteers: 6000
Income: £325,000 (2012-13)

STAGETEXT

1st Floor, 54 Commercial Street,
London E1 6LT
T: 020 7377 0540
F: 020 7247 5622
E: enquiries@stagetext.org
www.stagetext.org
Chief Executive: Tabitha Allum
STAGETEXT provides and promotes the use of captioning and live speech-to-text transcription (subtitling) in cultural and entertainment venues to enable deaf, deafened and hard of hearing people to access the arts.
Employees: 7
Income: £543,000 (2012-13)

STAR (Student Action for Refugees)

356 Holloway Road N7 6PA
T: 020 7697 4130
E: staradmin@star-network.org.uk
www.star-network.org.uk
Chief Executive: Emma Williams
STAR is the national charity of students welcoming refugees to the UK. Our 12,000 student activists run groups at over 30 universities. They volunteer at local refugee projects, educate fellow students about asylum in the UK, campaign for refugee protection and fundraise for STAR.
Employees: 7
Volunteers: 45

STARS - Syncope Trust And Reflex anoxic Seizures

PO Box 175, Stratford upon Avon,
Warwickshire CV37 8YD
T: 01789 450564
F: 01789 450682
E: info@stars.org.uk
www.stars.org.uk
STARS aims to ensure that anyone presenting with unexplained loss of consciousness receives the correct diagnosis, the appropriate treatment, informed support and sign posting to the appropriate medical professional. STARS offers information and advice to help manage symptoms and regain quality of life. This is achieved through our 24 hour helpline, DoH approved resources, and patients day offering advice and support to patients, carers and medical professionals.
Employees: 1
Volunteers: 3
Regional offices: 1

Stars Organisation Supporting Cerebral Palsy

Marlings, Camden Park, Tunbridge Wells,
Kent TN2 4TN
T: 01892 539283
E: info@stars.org.uk
www.starsorg.co.uk
Aims to raise money and profile for children and adults with cerebral palsy, their families and carers.

Staying First

Mulliner House, Flanders Road W4 1NN
T: 020 8996 8893
E: lorna.revell@sbhg.co.uk
Director: Graham Raine
To provide advice, practical assistance and help to people living in West London to enable them to live in comfort and security in their own homes. Housing advice (private tenants and owner occupiers only), small repairs and home improvement agency for residents in Kensington and Chelsea. Small repairs for residents in Westminster. Furniture recycling and reuse in West London. Debt and welfare benefits advice provided to a number of registered social housing providers.
Employees: 42
Volunteers: 15
Regional offices: 1
Income: £2,500,000 (2011-12)

Stephen Lawrence Charitable Trust

2nd Floor, Downstream Building, 1
London Bridge, London SE1 9BG
T: 020 8100 2800
E: information@stephenlawrence.org.uk
www.stephenlawrence.org.uk
As an educational charity, our mission is to promote diversity in architecture and associated professions, improve the educational achievements of black and ethnic-minority students, and help young people find pathways out of poverty into sustainable, rewarding careers in architecture, building construction and other fields associated with urban design and regeneration.
Employees: 4
Volunteers: 20

Steps Charity Worldwide

Wright House, Crouchley Lane, Lymm,
Cheshire WA13 0AS
T: 01925 750271
F: 01925 750270
E: info@steps-charity.org.uk
www.steps-charity.org.uk
Chief Executive Officer: Tim McLachlan

We provide quality support, information and a voice for families and people with lower limb conditions (hip dysplasia/clubfoot/lower limb deficiency). In order to do this we are committed to furthering research, innovation, services and best practice through a partnership approach.
Employees: 4
Volunteers: 3

Stickler Syndrome Support Group

PO Box 3351, Littlehampton BN16 9GB
T: 01903 785771
E: info@stickler.org.uk
www.stickler.org.uk
Founder and Honorary President: Wendy Hughes
The Stickler Syndrome Support Group provides support for sufferers and their families, plus medical and other professionals with an interest in the syndrome. This support is provided through publications, telephone, website, conferences and family days.
Employees: 0
Volunteers: 8
Regional offices: 0
Income: £31,000 (2011-12)

Stillbirth and Neonatal Death Society

28 Portland Place, London W1B 1LY
T: 020 7436 7940
F: 020 7436 3715
E: support@uk-sands.org
www.uk-sands.org
Director: Neal Long
SANDS provides support for anyone who has been affected by the death of a baby via: our helpline; an online support forum; a network of support groups located throughout the UK; an array of publications and support literature as well as an informative website. We also promote research to help reduce the loss of babies' lives.
Employees: 19
Regional offices: 95 groups

Stonewall

The Tower Building, 11 York Road, London SE1 7NX
T: 020 7593 1850
Helpline: 0800 050 2020
F: 020 7593 1877
E: info@stonewall.org.uk
www.stonewall.org.uk
Chief Executive Officer: Ben Summerskill
Campaigns to achieve legal and social justice for: lesbians, gay men and bisexuals; challenges discrimination and prejudice;

promotes new research and has an information service offering information about LGB rights.
Employees: 70
Volunteers: 200
Regional offices: 3
Income: £4,016,778 (2011-12)

Stonewall Housing

Unit 2A, Leroy House, 436 Essex Road, London N1 3QP
T: 020 7359 6242
Helpline: 020 7359 5767
F: 020 7359 9419
E: bob@stonewallhousing.org
www.stonewallhousing.org
Chief Executive: Bob Green
Stonewall Housing provides housing, advice, care and support to lesbian, gay, bisexual and transgender people so they feel safe and secure and are able to achieve their full potential.
Employees: 16
Volunteers: 2
Income: £683,180 (2011-12)

Stonham

Malt House, 281 Field End Road, Eastcote, Middlesex HA4 9XQ
T: 020 8868 9000
F: 020 8868 9292
E: robert.weatherall@homegroup.org.uk
www.stonham.org.uk
Executive Director: Paul Rydquist
Stonham is England's largest provider of housing and support for socially excluded and vulnerable adults. We run 545 projects across the country and work with over 15,000 people each year, in a mix of residential services and in floating support services (where we support people living in their own homes).
Employees: 2500
Regional offices: 3

Stop Abuse for Everyone

PO Box 121, Exeter EX4 2XN
T: 01392 456092
Helpline: 0800 328 3070
E: chris.collier@btinternet.com
www.safe-services.org.uk
CEO: Doreen Baker
Stop Abuse For Everyone (SAFE) works with all those affected by and experiencing all forms of domestic violence and abuse (DVA) in Exeter, East and Mid Devon. It provides a refuge for women, children and young people with a help/crisis line, outreach services providing support in the community to those who are still experiencing or have

experienced DVA, iIndependent domestic violence advisors who offer support through MARAC, court and other processes.
Employees: 30
Volunteers: 10
Regional offices: 1
Income: £566,263 (2012-13)

Strategic Planning Society

Buxton House, 7 Highbury Hill, London N5 1SU
T: 0845 056 3663
E: membership@sps.org.uk
www.sps.org.uk
Campaigns to develop an understanding of the need for long-range planning in both the private and public sectors of the economy. Aims to enhance the skills of long-range planners and to exchange and extend the information available to long-range planners.

Street Child Africa

Brabant House, Portsmouth Road, Thames Ditton, Surrey KT7 0EY
T: 020 8972 9820
F: 020 8972 9821
E: info@streetchildafrica.org.uk
www.streetchildafrica.org.uk
Director: Anthony Morton-King
Street Child Africa's mission is to champion the rights of African street children and other children at risk. We work in Senegal, Ghana, Uganda, the DRC, Zambia and Mozambique, directly with African partners. Through our partners we support children with education, skills training and a chance to return to their families and communities.
Employees: 10
Volunteers: 7
Regional offices: 1
Income: £640,000 (2012-13)

Streetscene

StreetScene Addiction Recovery, (Registered office), 55 Cobham Road, Ferndown, Dorset BH21 7RB
T: 01202 540337
Helpline: 01202 551254
F: 01202 765946
E: tessa@streetscene.org.uk
www.streetscene.org.uk
CEO: Tessa Corner
Provider of care for people with problems of addiction to drugs / alcohol including; residential treatment, supported after care, day care, re-integration, simple detox. 54 beds of rehab in 3 different locations, 54 beds of support in 6 different locations.

Based in Dorset and Hampshire. Abstinence based philosophy.
Employees: 52
Volunteers: 15
Regional offices: 0

Stroke Association

Stroke Association House, 240 City Road, London EC1V 2PR
T: 020 7566 0300
Helpline: 0303 303 3100
F: 020 7490 2686
E: jbarrick@stroke.org.uk
www.stroke.org.uk
Chief Executive: Jon Barrick
We are the Stroke Association. We believe in life after stroke. We believe that stroke can and should be prevented and we believe that everyone has the right to make the best recovery they can from stroke. We believe in the power of research to develop new treatments and ways of preventing stroke. And ultimately, we believe that together we can change the world for people affected by stroke.
Employees: 619
Volunteers: 5388
Regional offices: 12
Income: £31,100,000 (2012-13)

Student Christian Movement

Unit 504F, The Big Peg, 120 Vyse Street, The Jewellery Quarter, Birmingham B18 6NE
T: 0121 200 3355
E: scm@movement.org.uk
www.movement.org.uk
SCM is a movement seeking to bring together students of all backgrounds to explore the Christian faith in an open-minded and non-judgmental environment. SCM seeks to promote a vision of Christianity that is inclusive, aware, radical and challenging.

Sturge Weber Foundation (UK)

348 Pinhoe Road, Exeter EX4 8AF
T: 01392 464675
E: support@sturgeweber.org.uk
www.sturgeweber.org.uk
Chair: Jenny Denham
Sturge Weber syndrome is a rare neurological disorder, the symptoms of which usually occur in the child's first year of life. The Foundation aims to help and support parents; to raise public and

professional awareness and to raise funds in order to do so.
Volunteers: 6
Income: £20,000 (2011-12)

Sue Ryder

First Floor, 16 Upper Woburn Place, London WC1H 0AF
T: 0845 050 1953
F: 020 7400 0441
E: info@sueryder.org
www.sueryder.org
Sue Ryder Care's mission is care that liberates lives. We inspire, support and care for people with long-term neurological conditions and palliative care needs in our care centres, hospices, their own homes and in the community.
Employees: 2500

Support After Murder and Manslaughter

L&D Tally Ho!, Pershore Road, Edgbaston, Birmingham B5 7RN
T: 0121 471 1200
Helpline: 0845 872 3440
F: 0121 471 1201
E: samm.national@gmail.com
www.samm.org.uk
National Coordinator: Heather Meyer
Offers understanding and support to families and friends bereaved through murder and manslaughter; raises public awareness about the effects of murder and manslaughter; takes up issues of concern arising from the affects of murder and manslaughter; and promotes and supports research into the effects of murder and manslaughter on society. All volunteers, trustees etc. have themselves been bereaved by murder.
Employees: 4
Volunteers: 55
Income: £140,000 (2012-13)

Support After Murder and Manslaughter Abroad

SISEC Ltd, 21 Holborn Viaduct, London EC1A 2DY
T: 020 8886 5878
Helpline: 0845 123 2384
E: lianne@sammabroad.org
www.sammabroad.org
We provide emotional support, information and practical support. We also work to improve the support families receive in the UK after a murder abroad. We seek to provide feedback to the many government agencies involved after a murder abroad, so that they may improve the services they offer

and reduce the distress they cause to bereaved families.
Employees: 0
Volunteers: 7
Regional offices: 0

Supporters Direct

3rd Floor, Victoria House, Bloomsbury Square, London WC1B 4SE
T: 020 7273 1596
F: 020 7273 1605
E: info@supporters-direct.coop
www.supporters-direct.org
Chief Executive: David Lampitt
Supporters Direct helps form and support supporters' trusts, which are not-for-profit, volunteer-run groups of supporters of particular sports clubs who wish to take a stake in the ownership and management of their clubs and reorientate those clubs towards their communities using social enterprise business models.
Employees: 11
Volunteers: 11
Regional offices: 2

SupportLine

PO Box 2860, Romford, Essex RM7 1JA
T: 01708 765222
Helpline: 01708 765200
E: info@supportline.org.uk
www.supportline.org.uk
Chair: Peter Barrell
Provides emotional support and information by telephone helpline, email and post. Service for children young people and adults primarily aimed at those who are vulnerable, at risk, isolated and victims of any form of abuse. We help people develop healthy positive coping strategies, increase their confidence and self-esteem and develop an inner feeling of strength.
Employees: 1
Volunteers: 10
Income: £26,000 (2011-12)

Surf Life Saving Great Britain

19 Southernhay West, Exeter, Devon EX1 1PJ
T: 01392 218007
F: 01392 217808
E: mail@slsgb.org.uk
www.surflifesaving.org.uk
CEO: Esther Pearson
Aims to provide a safe and enjoyable environment on British beaches, promoting

and controlling the work of lifesaving, resuscitation and first aid.
Employees: 8
Volunteers: 100
Regional offices: 1

Surrey Nurturing Links

E: jharris@surreynurturinglinks.org.uk

Survival International

6 Charterhouse Buildings, Goswell Road, London EC1M 7ET
T: 020 7687 8700
F: 020 7687 8701
E: info@survivalinternational.org
www.survival-international.org
Survival International is a worldwide organisation that stands for the right of tribal peoples to defend their lands, protect their lives and determine their own futures.

Survivors of Bereavement by Suicide

The Flamsteed Centre, Albert Street, Ilkeston, Derbyshire DE7 5GU
T: 0115 944 1117
Helpline: 0844 561 6855
E: sobs.admin@care4free.net
www.uk-sobs.org.uk
Chair of the Trustees: Angela Samata
We exist to meet the needs and break the isolation of those bereaved by the suicide of a close relative or friend. Many of those helping have, themselves, been bereaved by suicide. Our aim is to provide a safe, confidential, environment, in which bereaved people can share their experiences and feelings, thus giving and gaining support from each other.
Employees: 2
Volunteers: 150
Regional offices: 47

Survivors Trust

Unit 2, Eastlands Court Business Centre, St Peters Road, Rugby, Warwickshire CV21 3RP
T: 01788 550554
F: 01788 551150
E: info@thesurvivorstrust.org
www.thesurvivorstrust.org
The Survivors Trust is a national umbrella agency for 126 specialist voluntary sector agencies providing a range of counselling, therapeutic and support services working with women, men and children who are victims/survivors of rape, sexual violence and childhood sexual abuse.
Employees: 2

Sustain: the Alliance for Better Food and Farming

94 White Lion Street, London N1 9PF
T: 020 7837 1228
E: sustain@sustainweb.org
www.sustainweb.org
Advocates food and agriculture policies and practices that enhance the health and welfare of people and animals, improves the working and living environment, and promotes equity and enriches society and culture.

Sustrans Limited

National Cycle Network Centre, 2 Cathedral Square, College Green, Bristol BS1 5DD
T: 0117 926 8893
F: 0117 929 4173
E: info@sustrans.org.uk
www.sustrans.org.uk
Sustrans, the sustainable transport charity, works on practical projects to encourage people to walk, cycle and use public transport to reduce motor traffic and its adverse effects.
Employees: 122
Volunteers: 1200
Regional offices: 10

Sutton Trust

9th Floor, Millbank Tower, 21–24 Millbank, London SW1P 4QP
T: 020 7802 1660
F: 020 7802 1661
E: info@suttontrust.com
www.suttontrust.com
The main objective of the trust is to support innovative projects that provide educational opportunities for young people from non-privileged backgrounds. Projects range from early years (0-3 year olds), through primary and secondary schooling, to further and higher education, including research projects, with an emphasis on innovative start-up projects that have the scope to benefit large numbers in the future. The trust does not fund individuals or capital projects.
Employees: 6

Suzy Lamplugh Trust

218 Strand, London WC2R 1AT
T: 020 7091 0014
F: 020 7091 0015
E: info@suzylamplugh.org
www.suzylamplugh.org
As the leading authority on personal safety, the Trust works to reduce violence and aggression in society and helps everyone – men, women and children – to gain the

knowledge and confidence they need to lead safer lives.
Employees: 18
Volunteers: 3

Swan Advice Network

E: swan.management@btconnect.com

Syndromes Without a Name

6 Acorn Close, Great Wyrley, Walsall WS6 6HP
T: 01922 701234 (also fax)
E: swan@geneticalliance.org.uk
www.undiagnosed.org.uk
Chair/Founder: Elisabeth Swingwood
Supports families who have a child with an undiagnosed condition. Provides information and support in a variety of ways and campaigns for equal rights and recognition.

TAEN - The Age and Employment Network

Headland House, 308 - 312 Gray's Inn Road, London WC1X 8DP
T: 020 7837 4762
E: info@taen.org.uk
www.taen.org.uk
Chief Executive: Chris Ball
TAEN - The Age and Employment Network works to remove age barriers to employment opportunities, and for an effective job market that works better for people in mid and later life, employers and the economy. TAEN is not an employment agency but can direct individuals looking for work, who want to change direction, develop their careers or undertake training, to relevant organisations and a number of useful resources.

Take a Break Warwickshire

E: kim@tabw.org.uk

Talking Newspaper Association of the UK

10 Browning Road, Heathfield, East
Sussex TN21 8DB
T: 01435 866102
E: info@tnauk.org.uk
www.tnauk.org.uk
Chief Executive: John Kerby
National Talking Newspapers and Magazines
provides magazines and newspapers in audio
and full (electronic) text for people unable to
read normal print, mainly due to visual
impairment, with the aim of giving them the
same choice of magazines and newspapers
as sighted people. Part of RNIB Group.
Employees: 30
Volunteers: 200

Tall Ships Youth Trust

2A The Hard, Portsmouth PO1 3PT
T: 023 9283 2055
F: 023 9281 5769
E: info@tallships.org
www.tallships.org
The personal development of young people
aged 16–25 through the crewing of Tall
Ships. The mission is delivered through two
magnificent 60-metre square-rigged sail
training vessels, Stavros S Niarchos and
Prince William, and by promoting sail
training around the world.
Employees: 10
Volunteers: 1500
Regional offices: 50

Tamil Refugee Training and Education Centre

221 Forest Road, London E17 6HE
T: 020 8527 4471
F: 020 8527 4479
E: admin@trtec.org
Supported by the European Social Fund, the
Centre was established in 1991 to meet the
training and employment needs of Sri
Lankan Tamil refugees, particularly in regard
to IT skills.
Employees: 7
Volunteers: 4

Target Tuberculosis

82 Queens Road, Brighton, East
Sussex BN1 3XE
T: 01273 827070
F: 01273 821059
E: info@targettb.org.uk
www.targettuberculosis.org.uk
Tackles tuberculosis as a disease as well as the
social and economic issues around it. Forms
partnerships with local organisations mainly
in the Indian subcontinent and sub-Saharan
Africa. Aims to bring TB treatment close to

the patient and improve the quality of life for
patients and families.
Employees: 3
Volunteers: 6

TASHA Foundation

Alexandra House, 241 High Street,
Brentford, Middlesex TW8 0NE
T: 020 8560 4583 (also fax)
E: enquiries@tasha-foundation.org.uk
www.tasha-foundation.org.uk
Provides one-to-one counselling for those
experiencing problems with drug use,
suffering from anxiety and stress. Supports
individuals experiencing mental health
problems.
Employees: 14
Volunteers: 15
Regional offices: 4

TaxAid UK

Room 304, Linton House, 164–180 Union
Street, Southwark, London SE1 0LH
T: 020 7803 4950
Helpline: 0345 120 3779
F: 020 7803 4955
E: admin@taxaid.org.uk
www.taxaid.org.uk
Director: Rosina Pullman
TaxAid runs a free, confidential helpline,
helping people on low incomes with their tax
affairs. It offers face-to-face appointments in
London, Birmingham, Manchester,
Newcastle, Plymouth and Shropshire. It also
runs training programmes for voluntary
sector.
Employees: 11
Volunteers: 40

TBPI Group

1 Malvern Rise, Hadfield, Glossop,
Derbyshire SK13 1QW
E: kwf1961@talktalk.net
www.tbpi-group.org
Supplies information and support to adults
coping with a trauma brachial plexus injury
and helps them achieve a better
understanding of the impact these injuries
may have on the individual, and their family.

Teacher Support Network

40A Drayton Park, London N5 1EW
T: 020 7697 2750
Helpline: 0800 056 2561
F: 020 7554 5239
E: enquiries@teachersupport.info
www.teachersupport.info
Chief Executive: Julian Stanley
We believe that all teachers should have
access to the practical and emotional
support they need to improve their personal
wellbeing and effectiveness. If, as a society,

we are to achieve the best possible education
for our young people, then supporting
teachers is a must. Teacher Support Network
is the largest provider of support services to
UK schoolteachers. We provide counselling,
coaching and advice free of charge.
Employees: 25
Volunteers: 327
Regional offices: 3

Tearfund

100 Church Road, Teddington,
Middlesex TW11 8QE
T: 0845 355 8355
F: 020 8943 3594
E: enquiries@tearfund.org
www.tearfund.org
Aims to relieve poverty, suffering and
distress, prevent disease and ill health among
the people of the world and to promote
Christian education and evangelism.
Employees: 300
Volunteers: 3300
Regional offices: 13

Teenage Cancer Trust

3rd Floor, 93 Newman Street,
London W1T 3EZ
T: 020 7612 0370
F: 020 7612 0371
E: hello@teenagecancertrust.org
www.teenagecancertrust.org
Chief Executive: Siobhan Dunn
Teenage Cancer Trust is the only UK charity
dedicated to improving the quality of life and
chances of survival for young people with
cancer aged 13 to 24. The charity funds and
builds specialist units in NHS hospitals and
provides dedicated staff, bringing young
people together so they can be treated by
teenage cancer experts in the best place for
them. Teenage Cancer Trust relies on
donations to fund its work.
Employees: 105
Regional offices: 0

Telephones for the Blind Fund

7 Huntersfield Close, Reigate,
Surrey RH2 0DX
T: 01737 248032
E: info@tftb.org.uk
www.tftb.org.uk
Provides financial support for installation and
rental for a BT line for the benefit of the
blind. Applicants must be registered blind or
partially sighted, living alone and on low
income. Applications must be made through
registered support workers. Free mobile
phones may also be given on application and
with the same criteria.
Volunteers: 5
Income: £46,515 (2011-12)

Television Trust for the Environment

46 Bloomsbury Street,
London WC1B 3QJ
T: 020 7147 7420
E: tve@tve.org.uk
www.tve.org
Promotes global public awareness of sustainable development through television and the other audio-visual media. TVE aims to provide videos on the environment and development of NGOs in low and middle income countries free of charge, and to raise funding for film-makers in the developing world to make these programmes.

Template Foundation

The Centre, 1 Bath Place, Barnet,
Hertfordshire EN5 5XE
T: 020 8441 2567
E: info@thecentrelondon.org
The Foundation's objectives are to advance the education of the public through the promotion and further study of human behavioural sciences, philosophy, history, the art of human expression and living derived from the Template and Emin archives, including arts such as theatre, dance and music.
Employees: 5
Volunteers: 200

Terrence Higgins Trust

314–320 Gray's Inn Road,
London WC1X 8DP
T: 020 7812 1600
Helpline: 0845 122 1200
F: 020 7812 1696
E: info@tht.org.uk
www.tht.org.uk
Chief Executive: Sir Nick Partridge
HIV and sexual health charity.
Employees: 350
Volunteers: 1000
Regional offices: 17

Textile Institute International

1st Floor, St James's Buildings, Oxford Street, Manchester M1 6FQ
T: 0161 237 1188
E: tiihq@textileint.org.uk
www.textileinstitute.org
Promotes professionalism in all areas associated with the textile industries worldwide.

Thames Reach

E: ashley.nur@thamesreach.org.uk

The Adolescent and Children's Trust (TACT)

303 Hither Green Lane, Hither Green,
London SE13 6TJ
T: 020 8695 8142
F: 020 8695 8141
E: enquiries@tactcare.org.uk
www.tactcare.org.uk
Chief Executive: Kevin Williams
TACT is the UK's largest charity provider of fostering and adoption services. Our core work involves providing high-quality and well-supported fostering or adoptive families for children and young people in the care of local authorities. We are dedicated to providing creative, effective and outcome-focused services. We also campaign and fundraise on behalf of children and young people in care, carers and adoptive families.
Employees: 152
Volunteers: 2
Regional offices: 9

The BB Group

Rochester House, 4 Belvedere Road,
London SE19 2AT
T: 020 8771 3377
F: 020 8771 8550
E: sadie.westwood@thebbgroup.org
thebbgroup.org
CEO: Emma-Jane Cross
The BB Group is an international charity based in the UK. We build communities through socially mediated support connecting people in need with those who can help. Our 2 lead services are MindFull, a national charity that helps young people to improve and sustain positive mental health, emotional resilience and wellbeing; and BeatBullying, an international bullying prevention charity working and campaigning to make bullying unacceptable.
Employees: 50
Volunteers: 15000
Regional offices: 0
Income: £2,500,000 (2011-12)

The Brooke

The Brooke, 5th Floor Friars Bridge Court,
41-45 Blackfriars Road SE1 8NZ
T: 020 3012 3456
F: 020 3012 0156
E: info@thebrooke.org
www.thebrooke.org
The Brooke is an international animal welfare organisation dedicated to improving the lives of working horses, donkeys and mules in the poorest parts of the world. We provide veterinary treatment and community programmes across Africa, Asia and Latin America. The Brooke's goal is to increase the number of working animals we help to two million a year by 2016.
Employees: 100
Volunteers: 30

The Cambridge Centre

E: paula.myers@cambridgecentre.org

The Clinic for Boundaries Studies

49 - 51 East Road, London N1 6AH
T: 020 3468 4194
E: jcoe@professionalboundaries.org.uk
www.professionalboundaries.org.uk
Managing Director: Jonathan Coe
The clinic provides specialist support services for the public alongside training and professional development services for practitioners. It is also involved in research and development around professional boundaries and conduct.
Employees: 12

The Cry-sis Helpline

BM Cry-sis, London WC1N 3XX
Helpline: 0845 122 8669
E: info@cry-sis.org.uk
www.cry-sis.org.uk
From its modest beginnings, Cry-sis has developed to become a well-respected and national charity. It offers support to families with excessively crying, sleepless and demanding babies. To achieve this, Cry-sis runs a national telephone helpline that is available to callers every day of the year between 9.00am and 10.00pm.
Employees: 1
Volunteers: 30

The Dante Leigh Foundation

84 St Gothard Road, West Norwood,
London SE27 9QP
T: 07904 694089
E: mail@dlf-disabilitysupport.org.uk
www.dlf-disabilitysupport.org.uk
Co-Founder: Jean Leigh
Our main aims are to research into the needs and requirements of disabled people, especially young adults with learning difficulties and to work with other organisations to have these 'needs' met whilst raising disability awareness as an everyday issue.
Volunteers: 10
Income: £152 (2010-11)

The Drinkaware Trust

Samuel House, 6 St Albans Street,
London SW1Y 4SQ
T: 020 7766 9900
F: 020 7504 8217
E: llam@drinkaware.co.uk
www.drinkaware.co.uk
Chief Executive: Elaine Hindal
Drinkaware aims to change the UK's drinking habits for the better. We promote responsible drinking and find innovative ways to challenge the national drinking culture to help reduce alcohol misuse and minimise alcohol-related harm.
Regional offices: 1

The Duke of Edinburgh's Award

Gulliver House, Madeira Walk, Windsor,
Berkshire SL4 1EU
T: 01753 727400
F: 01753 810666
E: info@dofe.org
www.dofe.org
Chief Executive: Peter Westgarth
Our mission is to inspire, guide and support young people in their self-development and recognise their achievements. Anyone aged 14–24 can undertake a DofE programme, setting themselves personal challenges in up to five areas – volunteering, physical, skills, expedition and residential. Once successfully completed and assessed they lead to a bronze, silver or gold Duke of Edinburgh's Award.
Employees: 112
Volunteers: 50000
Regional offices: 11

The Ear Foundation

Marjorie Sherman House, 83 Sherwin
Road, Lenton, Nottingham,
Nottinghamshire NG7 2FB
T: 0115 942 1985
F: 0115 924 9054
E: info@earfoundation.org.uk
www.earfoundation.org.uk
Chief Executive: Sue Archbold
Our vision is that all deaf children, young people and adults have the opportunity to hear, communicate and develop spoken language using the latest technological interventions. The Ear Foundation – bridging the gap between clinic-based services, where today's exciting hearing technologies, such as cochlear implants are fitted, and home, school and work where they are used in daily life. Our services include our family programme, education programme, child, user and family-centred research, information forum, assessment and rehabilitation.
Employees: 16
Volunteers: 80
Regional offices: 1

The Eikon Charity

The Eikon Charity, on Fullbrook School site, Selsdon Road, New Haw, Addlestone, Surrey KT15 3HP
T: 01932 347434
E: info@eikon.org.uk
www.eikon.org.uk
CEO: Chris Hickford
The Eikon Charity aims to help socially and economically disadvantaged young people achieve their full potential, and has been working in local Surrey communities for almost two decades, delivering a variety of support programmes for vulnerable young people who are at risk of falling in to crisis: developing an addiction, becoming homeless, being excluded from school etc. We strongly believe in early intervention - helping young people overcome issues before they become significant problems.
Employees: 14
Volunteers: 50
Income: £410,838 (2012-13)

The Electrical Safety Council

Unit 331-3 Great Guildford Business Square, 30 Great Guildford Street, London SE1 0HS
T: 020 3463 5100
E: enquiries@esc.org.uk
www.esc.org.uk
Director General: Philip Buckle
The Electrical Safety Council (ESC) is a UK charity committed to reducing deaths and injuries caused by electrical accidents in the home. We work closely with industry, government, media and consumer organisations to raise awareness of the dangers of electricity.
Employees: 20
Volunteers: 0
Regional offices: 1

The ELLA Foundation

17 Peters Lodge, 2 Stonegrove, Edgware,
Middlesex HA8 7TY
T: 020 8958 5090
E: brian@ella-foundation.org
www.ella-foundation.org
CEO: Brian Chernett
Promoting efficency and effectiveness of charities for the public benefit by providing education, learning, leadership training, mentoring and coaching to the leaders of charities and social enterprises.
Employees: 2
Volunteers: 9
Regional offices: 2
Income: £80,000 (2012-13)

The Federation

505 Barking Road, Plaistow,
London E13 8PS
T: 020 8692 2525
F: 020 8469 4103
E: info@thefederation.org.uk
www.thefederation.org.uk
The Federation is a national membership organisation and registered charity, representing the needs of diverse communities and professionals from the drug, alcohol, criminal justice, mental health and related sectors. We offer a particular expertise in issues pertaining to black and minority Ethnic (BME) communities and professionals.
Employees: 4

The Forum for Health and Wellbeing

Office 2/3, St Mark's Community Centre,
218 Tollgate Road, Beckton,
London E6 5YA
T: 020 7474 3176
E: enquiries@bemccf.org.uk
www.bemccf.org.uk
Director: Sahdia Warraich
The Forum aims to develop and improve services that effectively meet the health and social care needs of black and ethnic minority communities. It develops a strong, collective and informed voice for black and ethnic minority groups, service users and carers. The Forum aims to build the infrastructure of the black and ethnic minority voluntary, community and faith sector to deliver their own health and social care services through providing tailored capacity building and development support, and access to funding.
Employees: 11

The Giving Machine

E: joanne@me2club.org.uk

The Grace Eyre Foundation

E: mburgess@grace-eyre.org

The Grandparents' Association

Moot House, The Stow, Harlow,
Essex CM20 3AG
T: 01279 428040 (also fax)
Helpline: 0845 434 9585
E: lynn.chesterman@grandparents-association.org.uk
www.grandparents-association.org.uk
Chief Executive: Lynn Chesterman
The Grandparents' Association is the only national membership organisation dealing with all grandparent issues, such as bringing up your grandchildren full-time (kinship care), denied contact and childcare, in public and private law. We provide information and

support by way of our helpline, welfare benefits advice service, support groups and various publications and leaflets.
Employees: 13
Volunteers: 114
Regional offices: 2
Income: £327,031 (2012-13)

The Grange

E: karen.pinchbeck@grangecentre.org.uk

The Greensand Trust

E: alexe.rose@greensandtrust.org

The Harland Trust

66 High Street, Weston Favell,
Northampton,
Northamptonshire NN3 3JX
T: 01604 406995
E: alan.harland@ntlworld.com

The Haven

Effie Road, London SW6 1TB
T: 020 7384 0000
F: 020 7384 0001
E: info@thehaven.org.uk
www.thehaven.org.uk
Chief Executive: Pam Healy
Being diagnosed with breast cancer and undergoing treatment affects a patient both physically and emotionally. The Haven offers a free programme of care to support patients and their families during this time. Staffed by a specialist team, Havens are welcoming places providing support, information and complementary therapies before, during and after medical treatment. Working alongside healthcare professionals, Havens promote integrated breast cancer care where conventional and complementary medicine work together.
Employees: 30
Volunteers: 75
Regional offices: 3

The Haven Wolverhampton

E: hcss@havenrefuge.org.uk

The Heritage Alliance

Clutha House, 10 Storeys Gate,
Westminster, London SW1P 3AY
T: 020 7233 0500
E: sam.bradley@theheritagealliance.org.uk
www.theheritagealliance.org.uk
Chief Executive: Kate Pugh
The Heritage Alliance is the largest coalition of heritage interests in England. Established in 2002 by key voluntary sector bodies, it

brings together nearly 90 major national and regional non-government organisations concerned with heritage. Between them, Alliance members represent nearly five million people across Britain. The Alliance provides a forum for members to formulate and promote policy on core issues, make their voices heard collectively and share information and networks.
Employees: 2.4
Volunteers: 6

The Leprosy Mission

Goldhay Way, Orton Goldhay,
Peterborough, Cambridgeshire PE2 5GZ
T: 01733 370505
F: 01733 404880
E: post@tlmew.org.uk
www.leprosymission.org.uk
National Director: Peter Walker
Our vision is a world without leprosy. Our goal is to eradicate the causes and consequences of the disease. This means more than just detecting and curing the leprosy bacillus. It means addressing the underlying cause as well as working to prevent disability and restore dignity and wholeness to people's lives.
Employees: 40

The Lesbian and Gay Foundation

Number 5, Richmond Street,
Manchester M1 3HF
T: 0845 330 3030
F: 0161 235 8036
E: info@lgf.org.uk
www.lgf.org.uk
Chief Executive: Paul Martin
The Lesbian and Gay Foundation is a community-based charity, working to end homophobia and empower people across the north west of England and beyond. In 2013/14 we provided advice, information, support and services to over 40,000 people. The Lesbian and Gay Foundation provides direct services and resources for more LGB people than any other charity of its kind in the UK.
Employees: 49
Volunteers: 200
Regional offices: 1

The Lindsay Leg Club Foundation

The Lindsay Leg Club Foundation, PO Box 689, Ipswich IP1 9BN
T: 01473 749565
E: lynn@legclubfoundation.com
www.legclub.org
President: Ellie Lindsay

The aims of the Lindsay Leg Cub Foundation are twofold: To support the network of Leg Clubs operating around the UK, Europe, Australia and Tasmania, and to communicate the benefits of the Leg Club model to stakeholders. The model features the treatment of patients suffering from or at risk of leg ulceration within a social model of care. Stakeholders include patients, healthcare providers, clinicians, healthcare media.
Employees: 0
Income: £100,000 (2011-12)

The Log Cabin

E: vivien.dymock@logcabin.org.uk

The Makaton Charity

Westmead House, Farnborough,
Hampshire GU14 7LP
T: 01276 606760
Helpline: 01276 606777
F: 01276 36725
E: info@makaton.org
www.makaton.org
Chief Executive Officer: Lysa Schwartz
Makaton uses signs, symbols and speech to help people communicate. Today over 100,000 children and adults, use Makaton symbols and signs, either as their main method of communication or as a way to support speech. The Makaton Charity is responsible for developing and sharing Makaton so that everyone who needs to use Makaton can. We support families and professionals, provide training, resources, information and work with others to influence change for people with communication difficulties.
Employees: 17

The Mare and Foal Sanctuary

Honeysuckle Farm, Haccombe with Coombe, Newton Abbot,
Devon TQ12 4SA
T: 01626 355969
E: office@mareandfoal.org
www.mareandfoal.org
Rescues, provides care for and prevents cruelty and suffering among horses and ponies that are in need of attention because of sickness, maltreatment, ill usage or other causes and provides temporary or permanent homes for such horses and ponies.
Employees: 31
Volunteers: 25

The Marine Society and Sea Cadets

202 Lambeth Road, London SE1 7JW
T: 020 7654 7000
F: 020 7928 8914
E: info@ms-sc.org
www.ms-sc.org
Chief Executive: Martin Coles
To be the leading maritime charity for youth development and lifelong learning. Our vision for Sea Cadets is to give young people the best possible head start in life through nautical adventure and fun, and for the Marine Society to be the first in learning and personal development for seafarers.
Employees: 180
Volunteers: 9000
Regional offices: 6

The Matthew Project

Nedeham House, 22 St Stephens Road, Norwich NR1 3QU
T: 01603 626123
F: 01603 630411
E: rachael.graham@matthewproject.org
www.matthewproject.org
Chief Executive Officer: Rosalie Weetman
The Matthew Project works across Norfolk and Suffolk with young people and adults supporting people with drug and alcohol related issues, providing innovative education about the risks of drugs and alcohol, empowering people to make more informed choices.
Employees: 120
Volunteers: 20
Regional offices: 1
Income: £2,181,562 (2012-13)

The MedicAlert Foundation

MedicAlert House, 327–329 Witan Court, Upper Fourth Street, Milton Keynes MK9 1EH
Helpline: 0800 581420
F: 01908 951071
E: info@medicalert.org.uk
www.medicalert.org.uk
CEO: Mark Rawden
MedicAlert provides vital details in an emergency, because every moment matters. We support members with a wide range of medical conditions and allergies, which we help to describe on custom made medical ID jewellery. MedicAlert keeps secure, detailed medical records for our members. This information can be accessed in an emergency, 24/7 from anywhere in the world, using our emergency telephone

number and we are able to converse in over 100 languages.
Employees: 42
Volunteers: 460

The Migraine Trust

52–53 Russell Square, London WC1B 4HP
T: 020 7631 6970
Helpline: 020 7631 6975
F: 020 7436 2886
E: info@migrainetrust.org
www.migrainetrust.org
Chief Executive: Wendy Thomas
The Migraine Trust is the health and medical research charity for migraine in the UK. We seek to educate health professionals, raise awareness of migraine as a serious public health issue and empower, inform and support those affected by migraine by providing them with evidence based information. The Migraine Trust funds and promotes research into migraine in order to better understand it, improve diagnosis and treatment and ultimately to find a cure.
Employees: 8.8
Income: £526,006 (2010-11)

The National Autistic Society

393–395 City Road, London EC1V 1NG
T: 020 7833 2299
Helpline: 0808 800 4104
F: 020 7833 9666
E: nas@nas.org.uk
www.autism.org.uk
Chief Executive: Mark Lever
The National Autistic Society (NAS) is the UK's leading charity for people affected by autism. The NAS provides information, advice, training and support for individuals and their families; information and training for health, education and other professionals working with people with autism and their families; residential, supported living, outreach and day services for adults; specialist schools and education outreach services for children and young people; employment training and support and social programmes for adults with autism.
Employees: 2782
Volunteers: 1000
Regional offices: 12

The Nationwide Foundation

Nationwide House, Pipers Way, Swindon, Wiltshire SN38 2SN
Helpline: 01793 655113
F: 01793 652409
E: enquiries@nationwidefoundation.org.uk
www.nationwidefoundation.org.uk
Chief Executive: Lisa Suchet
The Nationwide Foundation makes grants to registered charities in the UK. The Foundation's three-year strategy, beginning in 2013 focuses on addressing the housing needs of vulnerable people.
Employees: 3

The NFSH Charitable Trust Ltd

21 York Road, Northampton, Northamptonshire NN1 5QG
T: 01604 603247
F: 01604 603534
E: office@thehealingtrust.org.uk
www.thehealingtrust.org.uk
Chair: Alan Knott
Operating as The Healing Trust we promote public health by delivering spiritual healing, which benefits mind, body and emotions. Healer members are subject to national standards of two years' (minimum) training; they follow a professional code of conduct and have continuous professional development opportunities. The Healing Trust offers a referral service for individuals to find a reputable healer, and operates a network of regional centres that offer healing on a low-cost or donation-only basis.
Employees: 5
Volunteers: 4000
Regional offices: 65

The Not Forgotten Association

4th Floor, 2 Grosvenor Gardens, London SW1W 0DH
T: 020 7730 2400
E: admin@nfassociation.org
www.nfassociation.org
Chief Executive: Piers Storie-Pugh
A tri-service charity which provides entertainment and recreation for the serving wounded, injured or sick and for ex-service men and women with disabilities. This is achieved through a unique programme of concerts, outings, holidays, events and the provision of televisions and/or TV Licences. Our aim is to provide comradeship, hope and something to which ex-service men and women can look forward.
Employees: 6

The Orpheus Centre

E: jessicabolton@orpheus.org.uk

The Printing Charity

First Floor, Underwood House, 235 Three
Bridges Road, Crawley, West
Sussex RH10 1LS
T: 01293 542820
F: 01293 542826
E: info@theprintingcharity.org.uk
www.theprintingcharity.org.uk
Chief Executive: Stephen Gilbert
The Printing Charity helps individuals and
their families, helps people of all ages, and
wants to help more people. Whatever a
person's job is, or was, for three years in an
organisation that produces a printed output;
printing, publishing, operating presses,
driving, cleaning, advertising, photography,
graphic arts, making ink, recycling paper, the
charity is there to help through regular
financial assistance, one-off grants and its
two sheltered homes for retired printers.

The Queen's Nursing Institute

1A Henrietta Place, London W1G 0LZ
T: 020 7549 1400
E: matthew.bradby@qni.org.uk
www.qni.org.uk
Chief Executive: Crystal Oldman
The Queen's Nursing Institute is the charity
dedicated to patient care in the home and in
the community. We work with the public,
nurses and decision-makers to make sure
that high-quality nursing is available for
everyone, where and when they need it.
Employees: 10
Income: £650,000 (2012-13)

The Radio Amateurs' Emergency Network

Hunters Moon, Station Road, Newton Le
Willows, Bedale, North
Yorkshire DL8 1SX
T: 0303 040 1080
E: secretary@raynet-uk.net
www.raynet-uk.net
Chairman: C Clark
The Radio Amateurs' Emergency Network,
known as RAYNET, provides
communications to government, emergency
and voluntary organisations in times of
emergency or community support.
Volunteers: 1500
Regional offices: 14

The Respite Association

102 High Road, Moulton, Near Spalding,
Lincolnshire PE12 6PD
T: 01406 373163
E: preston@respiteassociation.org
www.respiteassociation.org
CEO: Preston Keeling

Aims to relieve the stress on carers by
offering assistance with funding to secure a
short respite break for them. As of 2013 we
have also added an extra service to the above
as we are now offering some Carers free
holiday accommodation on the east coast
for a break without the person they normally
care for to enable a proper break. Details of
both schemes on our website as are
application forms.
Employees: 2
Volunteers: 12
Regional offices: 1
Income: £80,000 (2010-11)

The Rivers Trust

Rain-Charm House, Kyl Cober Parc, Stoke
Climsland, Callington, Cornwall PL17 8PH
T: 01579 372142
E: alan@theriverstrust.org
www.theriverstrust.org
Chief Executive: Arlin Rickard
The Rivers Trust (formerly Association of
Rivers Trusts) is an umbrella environmental
charity representing the rivers trust
movement in England, Wales and Northern
Ireland. It works by supporting its members
in promoting practical and sustainable
solutions to environmental issues across the
UK and Europe.
Employees: 7
Income: £3,175,316 (2011-12)

The Royal Star and Garter Homes

Richmond Hill, Richmond,
Surrey TW10 6RR
T: 020 8439 8000
F: 020 8439 8002
E: generalenquiries@starandgarter.org
www.starandgarter.org
Chief Executive: Mike Barter
The Charity offers residential and nursing
care to physically disabled ex-service men
and women at its Richmond, Surrey, and
Solihull, West Midlands Homes, enabling
them to live as independently as possible,
taking account of their wishes and
capabilities.
Regional offices: 1

The Scout Association

Gilwell Park, Chingford, London E4 7QW
T: 020 8433 7100
F: 020 8433 7108
E: info.centre@scout.org.uk
www.scouts.org.uk
Chief Executive: Matt Hyde
Scouting exists to actively engage and
support young people in their personal

development, empowering them to make a
positive contribution to society.
Employees: 240
Volunteers: 89013

The Seeing Dogs Alliance

116 Potters Lane, Send, Woking,
Surrey GU23 7AL
T: 01483 765556
F: 01483 750846
E: info@seeingdogs.org.uk
www.seeingdogs.org.uk
Furthers the mobility of blind persons
through the use of trained training guide
dogs, known as Seeing Dogs.
Employees: 1
Volunteers: 20

The Sick Children's Trust

80 Ashfield Street, London E1 2BJ
T: 020 7791 2266
F: 020 7709 8358
E: claudette@sickchildrenstrust.org
www.sickchildrenstrust.org
Chief Executive: Claudette Watson
Provides high-quality 'home from home'
accommodation for families whose children
are receiving hospital treatment for serious
illnesses. We exist to support and promote
the child's recovery and further to support
the fabric and wellbeing of the family as a
whole.
Employees: 26
Volunteers: 10
Regional offices: 7

The Sickle Cell Society

54 Station Road, London NW10 4UA
T: 020 8961 7795
F: 020 8961 8346
E: info@sicklecellsociety.org
www.sicklecellsociety.org
Our aim is to enable and assist individuals
with a sickle cell disorder to realise their full
economic and social potential. Objectives are
to provide relief for persons with sickle cell
disorders, the relief of poverty, provision of
recreational activities and improvement of
public information, assisting in research into
the causes, treatment of the condition and
dissemination of such information.
Employees: 6
Volunteers: 20
Regional offices: 2

The SMA Trust

Compton Scorpion, Estate Office,
Shipston on Stour,
Warwickshire CV36 4PJ
T: 01608 663415
E: mandy@smatrust.org
www.smatrust.org
Executive Director: Joanna Mitchell
We are the only Uk charity solely dedicated to funding medical research into Spinal Muscular atrophy (SMA). Our objective is to be active and progressive in the search for a cure and treatments for SMA.
Employees: 3
Volunteers: 6-10
Regional offices: 1
Income: £200,000 (2012-13)

The Social Research Unit

Lower Hood Barn, Totnes, Dartington,
Devon TQ9 6AB
T: 01803 762400
F: 01803 762983
E: jaddy@dartington.org.uk
www.dartington.org.uk
The Social Research Unit at Dartington is an independent charity that seeks to increase the use of evidence of what works in designing and delivering services for children and their families. We are also a strong advocate of prevention and early intervention based approaches.
Employees: 20

The Somerville Foundation

Saracens House, 25 St Margarets Green,
Ipswich, Suffolk IP4 2BN
T: 01473 252007
Helpline: 0800 854759
F: 01473 281823
E: admin@thesf.org.uk
www.thesf.org.uk
National Director: John Richardson
Supports young people and adults born with a heart condition in the UK. Offers support, information and advice to help them stay in control, empowering patients to enable them to take control of their lives and manage their own heart condition. We listen to the patients and respond to their needs, providing them with the support they need and want.
Employees: 6
Volunteers: 20
Regional offices: 1
Income: £250,000 (2011-12)

The Tavistock Centre for Couple Relationships

The Tavistock Centre, 70 Warren Street,
London W1T 5PB
T: 020 7380 1975
F: 020 7388 6162
E: tccr@tccr.org.uk
www.tccr.org.uk
CEO: Susanna Abse
TCCR is the leading provider of highly specialised and affordable couple counselling and psychotherapy. We offer a range of relationship, psychosexual and parenting support services throughout London. Our services include: relationship counseling; couple psychotherapy; wellbeing service; brief counseling; parenting together; psychosexual therapy; divorce and separation unit.
Employees: 42

The Therapy Database

23 Holybourne Avenue, London SW15 4JJ
T: 020 8788 5370
E: admin@therapydatbase.info
www.therapydatabase.info
Trustee Director: Gerard Bonham-Carter
We enable doctors to fulfil their duty to gain their patients' fully informed consent to treatment. We enable patients to fully understand their treatment options. Patients benefit from the powerful placebo effect when they undergo treatments that they believe in. We achieve both goals by enabling patients to access comprehensive and balanced information on Western mainstream treatments and on the alternatives. This fulfils a DOH requirement for valid consent.
Employees: 1
Volunteers: 9

The Vince Hines Foundation

E: cmass@ubol.com

The Vine Day Centre

PO Box 442, 33 Station Road, Aldershot,
Aldershot, Hampshire GU11 9FQ
T: 01252 400196
E: mags.mercer@thevinealdershot.org.uk
www.vinedaycentre.org.uk
Chief Executive Officer: Mags Mercer
The Vine Day Centre has been established in the community of Aldershot, North East Hampshire since 1987, supporting vulnerable and homeless adults since inception and registered as a charity in February 2003. Our primary aim is to reduce social isolation, to facilitate and enable change, and to improve the quality of life for homeless and vulnerable men and women aged 25 years and over.
Employees: 5
Volunteers: 25
Regional offices: 1
Income: £81,257 (2012-13)

Theatres Trust

22 Charing Cross Road,
London WC2H 0QL
T: 020 7836 8591
E: info@theatrestrust.org.uk
www.theatrestrust.org.uk
Director: Mhora Samuel
The Theatres Trust is the national advisory public body for theatres, protecting theatres for everyone. We operate nationally in England, Wales, Scotland and Northern Ireland providing an authoritative and knowledgeable source of expert advice and information on theatres, promoting the value of theatre buildings and championing their future.
Employees: 9
Volunteers: 2

Thera Trust

The West House, Alpha Court,
Swingbridge Road, Grantham,
Lincolnshire NG31 7XT
T: 01476 562777
F: 01476 565677
E: sarah.frost@thera.co.uk
www.thera.co.uk
Thera Trust offers those with a learning disability support and is thereby helping them to get the most out of life.
Employees: 650

Think Global

CAN Mezzanine, 32 - 36 Loman Street,
London SE1 0EH
T: 020 7922 7930
F: 020 7922 7929
E: info@think-global.org.uk
www.think-global.org.uk
Chief Executive: Tom Franklin
Think Global promotes education for a just and sustainable world. We have a network of 200 member organisations that share this commitment and we work with them to change UK education for the better. Our mission is to promote education that puts learning in a global context, fostering critical and creative thinking; self-awareness and open-mindedness towards difference; understanding of global issues and power relationships; and optimism and action for a better world.
Employees: 10

Third Age Trust (National Office U3A)

The Old Municipal Buildings, 19 East Street, Bromley, Kent BR1 1QE
T: 020 8466 6139
E: national.office@u3a.org.uk
www.u3a.org.uk
Chairman: Barbara Lewis
The Third Age Trust is the national representative body for the Universities of the Third Age in the UK. U3As are democratic, self-funded, self-managed, later life learning organisations providing daytime education activities for people no longer in full-time employment.
Employees: 10

This Way Up Youth Project

The Bethany Centre, 155a Kineton Green Road, Olton, Solihull B92 7EG
Helpline: 0121 439 9181
E: ann@twup.org.uk
www.twup.org.uk
CEO: Pete English
Our team works in local Solihull schools supporting young people affected by loss through family breakdown or bereavement. We offer help to those trying to come to terms with this difficult life changing event through our Lost & Found Course. We also train Christian youth and community workers across the country to deliver our course so that more young people can be helped to turn their lives the right way up.
Employees: 6
Volunteers: 5
Regional offices: 1
Income: £76,000 (2011-12)

Thomas Pocklington Trust

5 Castle Row, Horticultural Place, London W4 4JQ
T: 020 8995 0880
F: 020 8987 9965
E: info@pocklington-trust.org.uk
www.pocklington-trust.org.uk
Provides quality housing care and support services for adult people with sight loss. Sponsors social and public health research in the field of visual impairment.
Employees: 19
Volunteers: 116
Regional offices: 10

Thorne House Services for Autism Limited

Exchange Brewery, 2 Bridge Sreet, Sheffield, Yorkshire S3 8NS
T: 0114 384 0284
F: 01405 815209
E: amy.thorndike@autismplus.co.uk
www.autismplus.org
Thorne Services for Autism was established in 1986 and works with 26 local authorities supporting over 180 children and adults on the autistic spectrum. It is currently piloting a new children's service in Sheffield. The charity provides a wide range of projects including residential care, day and community services, educational units and supported living opportunities.

Thrive

The Geoffrey Udall Centre, Beech Hill Road, Beech Hill, Reading, Berkshire RG7 2AT
T: 0118 988 5688
F: 0118 988 5677
E: info@thrive.org.uk
www.thrive.org.uk
Chief Executive: Kathryn Rossiter
Thrive is a national charity whose with the mission to research, educate and promote the use and advantages of gardening for people with a disability. Thrive is the only national charity of its kind working to bring change to the lives of disabled people through gardening. This is done by offering practical advice and inspiration, supporting hundreds of health and education professionals around the country, carrying out research, and running our gardening programmes.
Employees: 60
Volunteers: 170
Regional offices: 2

Through the Roof

PO Box 353, Epsom, Surrey KT18 5WS
T: 01372 749955
E: info@throughtheroof.org
www.throughtheroof.org
CEO: Tim Wood
Mission: transforming lives through disabled people. Our work: providing life-changing opportunities and equipping churches, communities and individuals. Our vision: a world where people live interdependently, mutually giving and receiving as God intended.

Tibet Relief Fund

Unit 9, 139 Fonthill Road, London N4 3HF
T: 020 7272 1414
F: 020 7272 1410
E: info@tibetrelieffund.co.uk
www.tibetrelieffund.co.uk
Chief Executive: Philippa Carrick
Tibet Relief Fund was set up to respond to the needs of Tibetan refugees, following the Chinese invasion of Tibet in 1950. Today, we provide vital support to Tibetans in exile in India and Nepal and inside Tibet, including emergency aid to newly arrived refugees and education, healthcare and income-generating projects for the long-term. Tibet Relief Fund also runs a sponsorship programme to support children, university students, elderly people, monks and nuns.
Employees: 6
Volunteers: 3

Time Banking UK

The Exchange, Brick Row, Stroud, Gloucestershire GL5 1DF
T: 01453 750952
E: info@timebanks.co.uk
www.timebanking.org
Chief Executive: Sarah Bird
We provide information, practical support, inspiration and training to anyone wanting to use time banking as a tool to build community and encourage active citizenship.
Employees: 3
Regional offices: 1
Income: £179,399 (2012-13)

Time For God

Community House, 46 -50 East Parade, Harrogate, North Yorkshire HG1 5RR
T: 01423 536248
F: 05602 053964
E: office@timeforgod.org
www.timeforgod.org
Director: Paul Webster
TFG is a faith based organisation providing gap year opportunities for all ages. It is supported by all the major Christian denominations in the UK. With over 40 years experience, our projects are based in areas of social need.
Employees: 6
Volunteers: 100
Regional offices: 1

TimeBank

2nd Floor, Downstream Building, 1
London Bridge, London SE1 9BG
T: 020 7785 6362
F: 0845 456 1669
E: info@timebank.org.uk
www.timebank.org.uk
Chief Executive: Moira Swinbank
TimeBank tackles social issues by finding
ways for people to give their time that inspire
them and match their lives. We don't just tell
people volunteering is a good idea, we make
sure it really is. We find ways for people to
give their time doing things that they want to
do, that suit how they live and that address
the needs of the world we live in.

Tiny Tickers

E: jon@tinytickers.org

TOC H

PO Box 15824, Birmingham, West
Midlands B13 3JU
T: 0121 443 3552
E: info@toch.org.uk
www.toch.org.uk
Chair of Trustees: Terry Drummond
Striving to eliminate social exclusion, Toc H is
a charity committed to building a fairer
society. Toc H provides alternative education,
self-development and mentoring
programmes for young people, in
partnership with schools, local authorities
and youth agencies. The charity also offers
community centres.
Volunteers: 300

Together for Short Lives

4th Floor, Bridge House, 48–52 Baldwin
Street, Bristol, Avon BS1 1QB
T: 0117 989 7820
Helpline: 0845 108 2201
E: info@togetherforshortlives.org.uk
www.togetherforshortlives.org.uk
Chief Executive: Barbara Gelb
We estimate that there are 23,500 children
and young people across the UK unlikely to
reach adulthood. Together for Short Lives is
the only charity working across the UK
representing all these children and their
families as well as the organisations and
people that support them. We want to help
ensure that all of these children and their
families get the best possible care and
support whenever and wherever they need
it.
Employees: 30
Volunteers: 2

Together Trust

Together Trust Centre, Schools Hill,
Cheadle, Cheshire SK8 1JE
T: 0161 283 4848
F: 0161 283 4747
E: enquiries@togethertrust.org.uk
www.togethertrust.org.uk
Chief Executive: Mark Lee
We provide a range of social care, special
education, community support and
consultancy services in the North West of
England and surrounding areas. In addition
to local authority funded places, Together
Trust services can be purchased by families,
carers, and service users over the age of 18 or
their brokers via a direct payment, individual
budget, individual service fund or personal/
private funds.
Employees: 770
Volunteers: 50
Income: £21,000,000 (2012-13)

Together Working for Wellbeing

12 Old Street, London EC1V 9BE
T: 020 7780 7300
F: 020 7780 7301
E: contactus@together-uk.org
www.together-uk.org
MACA is a leading national charity providing
high-quality services in the community and
hospitals and prisons for people with mental-
health needs and their carers.
Employees: 800
Regional offices: 3

Tommy's

Nicholas House, 3 Laurence Pountney
Hill, London EC4R 0BB
T: 020 7398 3400
Helpline: 0800 014 7800
F: 020 7398 3479
E: mailbox@tommys.org
www.tommys.org
Chief Executive: Jane Brewin
Tommy's is dedicated to funding research
into the cause and prevention of miscarriage,
stillbirth and premature birth, as well as
promoting pregnancy health through a
national information programme.
Employees: 22
Volunteers: 1

Tomorrow's People Trust

1st Floor, Minster House, York Road,
Eastbourne, East Sussex BN21 4ST
T: 01323 418143
E: alevitt@tomorrows-people.co.uk
www.tomorrows-people.org.uk
Chief Executive: Debbie Scott

Tomorrow's People is a national
employment charity helping long-term
unemployed people out of welfare
dependency and into jobs and self-
sufficiency. Advisers work with individuals
directly in their communities helping them
to overcome their barriers to work, and
develop the confidence, motivation and skills
they need to move forward in their lives.
Since 1984 we have helped more than
440,000 people on their journey back to
work.
Employees: 135
Regional offices: 15
Income: £9.6 (2010-11)

Tools for Self Reliance

Netley Marsh Workshops, Ringwood
Road, Netley Marsh, Southampton,
Hampshire SO40 7GY
T: 02380 860697
E: communications@tfsr.org
www.tfsr.org
Chief Executive: Sarah Ingleby
Tools for Self Reliance supports community
development projects managed by African
NGOs in Ghana, Malawi, Sierra Leone,
Tanzania, Uganda and Zambia. We provide
tools and skills training to help artisans and
craft workers develop sustainable, productive
businesses. We raise funds to pay for
technical and business training and support.
Tools for Self Reliance volunteers collect and
refurbish high-quality hand tools and sewing
machines that skilled village trades-people
need to earn a living.
Employees: 10
Volunteers: 600
Income: £553,537 (2010-11)

Torch Trust for the Blind

Torch House, Torch Way, Northampton
Road, Market Harborough,
Leicestershire LE16 9HL
T: 01858 438260
F: 01858 438275
E: volunteers@torchtrust.org
www.torchtrust.org
Chief Executive: Gordon Temple
The principal aim of the Torch Trust is to
meet the spiritual needs of blind and partially
sighted people through producing Christian
literature in accessible media and promoting
Christian fellowship across the UK and
around the world.
Employees: 40
Volunteers: 81

Torridge Community Transport Association

E: john.conniss@torridge-cta.org.uk

Tourette Syndrome (UK) Association

Kings Court, 91 - 93 High Street,
Camberley, Surrey GU15 3RN
T: 01276 482903
Helpline: 0300 777 8427
E: admin@tourettes-action.org.uk
www.tourettes-action.org.uk
Chief Executive: Suzanne Dobson
A registered charity dedicated to providing support and information and promoting medical research on behalf of all those affected by TS. Services for members include a newsletter, networking, events and a binder full of helpful information.
Employees: 6
Volunteers: 4

Tourism for All UK

7A Pixel Mill, 44 Appleby Road, Kendal, Cumbria LA9 6ES
T: 0845 124 9971
E: info@tourismforall.org.uk
www.tourismforall.org.uk
Chief Executive: Ray Veal
Tourism for All UK is an independent charity supporting leisure and tourism opportunities for all, operating an information service to older and disabled people, and working with the industry and government to raise the standards of welcome to all guests.
Employees: 1
Volunteers: 2
Regional offices: 1

Tower Hamlets CVS

E: khadiru.mahdi@thcvs.org.uk

Town and Country Planning Association

17 Carlton House Terrace,
London SW1Y 5AS
T: 020 7930 8903
F: 020 7930 3280
E: tcpa@tcpa.org.uk
www.tcpa.org.uk
Provides an informed and independent voice on national, regional and environmental planning policies and legislation, and to campaign for more local initiatives and decentralisation of decision-making.
Employees: 7
Volunteers: 40

Townswomen's Guilds

Tomlinson House, 329 Tyburn Road,
Birmingham B24 8HJ
T: 0121 326 0400
F: 0121 326 1976
E: tghq@townswomen.org.uk
www.townswomen.org.uk
National Chair: Pauline Meyers
Aims to advance the social awareness of all women, irrespective of race, creed or political affiliation.

Toynbee Hall

28 Commercial Street, London E1 6LS
T: 020 7247 6943
F: 020 7377 5964
E: alexandra.wilkinson@toynbeehall.org.uk
www.toynbeehall.org.uk
Chief Executive: Graham Fisher
Toynbee Hall is a community organisation that pioneers ways to reduce poverty and disadvantage. Based in East London, we provide free legal, debt, and general support service advice; as well as elderly and youth programmes. We have been a catalyst for social reform in the UK for almost 130 years, and continue to bring together communities, organisations and policy makers to create new ways to help those who find themselves in poverty today.
Employees: 75
Volunteers: 100+
Regional offices: 0
Income: £6,000,000 (2012-13)

TPAS England

Suite 4B, Trafford Plaza, 73 Seymour Grove, Manchester, Greater Manchester M16 0LD
T: 0161 868 3500
F: 0161 877 6256
E: info@tpas.org.uk
www.tpas.org.uk
Acting Chief Executive: Jenny Topham
TPAS exists to promote resident and community empowerment. We are a membership organisation of housing associations, local authorities and tenants groups. We provide training, conferences, advice and consultancy services.
Employees: 15
Volunteers: 50

Tracheo-Oesophageal Fistula Support Group

St George's Centre, 91 Victoria Road,
Netherfield, Nottingham NG4 2NN
T: 0115 961 3092
F: 0115 961 3097
E: info@tofs.org.uk
www.tofs.org.uk
Supports the families and carers of children born unable to swallow because of oesophagael atresia, tracheo-oesophageal atresia, tracheo-oesophageal fistula and associated conditions.
Employees: 3
Volunteers: 45

Trafford Carers Centre

E: kelly.hunter@traffordcarerscentre.org.uk

Training for Life

37 Houndsditch, London EC3A 7DB
T: 020 7444 4190
E: info@trainingforlife.org
www.trainingforlife.org
Established in 1994, Training for Life was set up to help the most disadvantaged members of our society who are at risk of social and economic marginalisation. Training For Life is about employability and empowerment. It is about breaking dependency by empowering people to act independently. It is about helping individuals to realise their potential and unleash creativity. Ultimately, it is about energising people who do not see opportunities for themselves.

Training Opportunities

Hanover House, 61–64 Dudley Road,
Wolverhampton, West
Midlands WV2 3BY
T: 01902 877920
E: topps@totalise.co.uk
www.topps.org.uk
Provides information, support and training to women returning to the workplace and young people and women who wish to set up a small business or social enterprise.

Transaid

137 Euston Road, London NW1 2AA
T: 020 7387 8136
F: 020 7387 2669
E: info@transaid.org
www.transaid.org
Chief Executive: Gary Forster
Transaid is an international NGO working through the application of best practice in transport and logistics to alleviate poverty, facilitating access to basic services such as

healthcare, and encouraging economic growth and development.

Employees: 6
Volunteers: 10
Regional offices: 3

Transform Africa

GQ Leroy House, 436 Essex Road, London N1 3QP
T: 020 7354 5455
F: 020 7354 5499
E: charles@transformafrica.org
www.transformafrica.org
Chief Executive Officer: Charles Kazibwe
Transform Africa aims to strengthen and empower African organisations and their communities to more effectively tackle poverty and its causes. We offer training services and work in partnership with local organisations to support local communities.
Employees: 3
Income: £508,333 (2010-11)

Transparency International (UK)

32–36 Loman Street, London SE1 0EH
T: 020 7922 7906
F: 020 7785 6355
E: info@transparency.org.uk
www.transparency.org.uk
We are the UK national chapter of the global anti-corruption non-governmental organisation, Transparency International (TI). TI, which is co-ordinated by an international secretariat in Berlin, is a coalition of more than 90 autonomous national chapters who are committed to fighting corruption using transparency as a major tool. TI is dedicated to combating corruption at the national and international levels through constructive partnerships with governments, the private sector, civil society and international organisations.
Volunteers: 20
Regional offices: 1

Transplant Sport UK

Basepoint Business Centre, Winnall Valley Road, Winchester, Hampshire SO23 0LD
T: 0115 837 0878
E: office@transplantsport.org.uk
www.transplantsport.org.uk
CEO: Kevin Kibble
We are a registered charity whose main aim is to raise awareness of the need for organ donation in the UK and worldwide. Through organising sports and social events for transplant recipients Transplant Sport UK shows the benefits of organ donation and

prove that you can lead a normal and active life again after transplantation.
Employees: 3
Volunteers: 100
Regional offices: 1

Transport Trust

202 Lambeth Road, London SE1 7JY
T: 020 7928 6464
E: hq@thetransporttrust.org.uk
www.thetransporttrust.org.uk
Promotes and encourages the permanent preservation, for the benefit of the nation, of transport items of historical or technical interest and books, drawings, films, photographs and recordings of all forms of transport by rail, air and water.

Travelling Light Theatre Company

E: general.manager@travellinglighttheatre.org.uk

Tree Council

71 Newcomen Street, London SE1 1YT
T: 020 7407 9992
F: 020 7407 9908
E: info@treecouncil.org.uk
www.treecouncil.org.uk
Director General: Pauline Buchanan Black
Promotes for the public benefit, the improvement and development of the environment through the planting, care, nurture and cultivation of trees in town and country.
Employees: 5
Volunteers: 8000

Trees for Cities

Prince Consort Lodge, Kennington Park, Kennington Park Place, London SE11 4AS
T: 020 7587 1320
F: 020 7793 9042
E: sharon@treesforcities.org
www.treesforcities.org
Chief Executive: Sharon Johnson
Advances the education of the public in the appreciation of trees and their amenity value; promotes the protection and planting of trees particularly in inner-city areas.
Employees: 24
Volunteers: 50

Treloar Trust

Holybourne, Alton, Hampshire GU34 4GL
T: 01420 547400
E: info@treloar.org.uk
www.treloar.org.uk
CEO: Tony Reid

The Treloar Trust exists to provide education, independence training and care for physically disabled young people from all over the UK. It aims to provide support and opportunities and to develop individual students' confidence and abilities in all aspects of their lives.

Trigeminal Neuralgia Association

PO Box 234, Oxted, Surrey RH8 8BE
Helpline: 01883 370214
E: naomitna@gmail.com
www.tna.org.uk
CEO: Naomi Gilbert
We exist to reach those affected by trigeminal neuralgia (TN) (sufferers, carers, healthcare professionals and the wider public); to provide evidence-based information, support and encouragement: with opportunities for people to express their feelings and concerns with those who understand their situation, and encouragement to actively self-manage their TN and to add to the body of knowledge about TN by increasing the level of knowledge about TN and TNA UK amongst healthcare professionals, policy-makers and others.
Employees: 1
Volunteers: 20
Regional offices: Select State or Province
Income: £63,000 (2012-13)

Tropical Health and Education Trust

5th Floor, 1 Wimpole Street, London W1G 0AE
T: 020 7290 3892
F: 020 7290 3890
E: sharon@thet.org
www.thet.org.uk
Chief Executive: Andrew Purkis
THET is committed to improving access to and the quality of health services in developing countries. We believe that the most effective way of doing this is to work in partnership with those delivering and running healthcare, helping to strengthen and extend existing services.
Employees: 12
Volunteers: 4

Trust

E: fundraising@trust-london.com

Trust for the Study of Adolescence Ltd

23 New Road, Brighton, East
Sussex BN1 1WZ
T: 01273 693311
F: 01273 679907
E: info@youngpeopleinfocus.org.uk
www.tsa.uk.com
TSA's primary commitment is to improving the lives of young people. We believe that there is a lack of knowledge and understanding about adolescence and young adulthood. The Trust closes this gap by: undertaking applied research; providing training and conferences for professionals; carrying out practice-development projects; producing and marketing publications; influencing policy makers, service providers and public opinion.
Employees: 29

Trust for Urban Ecology

T: 020 8293 1904
E: information@tcv.org.uk
www.urbanecology.org.uk
Supports the conservation of the natural elements of the urban landscape; promotes the use of urban nature areas for the health, enjoyment and education of all sections of the community; and provides information, advice and expertise on the design, creation and management of urban greenspaces.

Tuberous Sclerosis Association

PO Box 8001, Derby DE1 0YA
T: 01332 290734 (also fax)
E: development-support@tuberous-sclerosis.org
www.tuberous-sclerosis.org
Chief Executive: Jayne Spink
Offers support to people with tuberous sclerosis complex and their families or carers. Promoting education, publicity and information to increase awareness and understanding. There are specialist advisers to advise on any problems relating to TSC.
Employees: 11 P/T

Turning Point

Standon House, 21 Mansell Street,
London E1 8AA
T: 020 7481 7600
F: 020 7480 6288
E: info@turning-point.co.uk
www.turning-point.co.uk
Turning Point is the UK's leading social care organisation. We provide services for people with complex needs, including those affected by drug and alcohol misuse, mental health problems and those with a learning disability. We provide services in 200 locations and worked with around 130,000 people last year.
Employees: 1800
Regional offices: 200

Tutu Foundation UK

E: aankrah@tutufoundationuk.org

Twin Ltd

3rd Floor, 1 Curtain Road,
London EC2A 3LT
T: 020 7375 1221
E: info@twin.org.uk
www.twin.org.uk
Uses trade positively to redress the imbalance between north and south, to build better livelihoods for the poorest and weakest in the trading chain and to provoke development and longer term shifts in the political and economic environment.

Twins and Multiple Births Association

2 The Willows, Gardner Road, Guildford,
Surrey GU1 4PG
T: 01483 304442
F: 0870 770 3303
E: enquiries@tamba.org.uk
www.tamba.org.uk
Tamba exists to enable the families of twins, triplets and more to meet the challenge of their unique experience.
Employees: 12
Volunteers: 100

UCCF

5 Blue Boar Street, Oxford OX1 4EE
T: 01865 253678
F: 0116 255 5672
E: helpdesk@uccf.org.uk
www.uccf.org.uk
IT Manager: David Holland
Employees: 106
Volunteers: 50

UK Acquired Brain Injury Forum

c/o Royal Hospital for Neuro Disability,
West Hill, Putney, London SW15 3SW
T: 020 8788 2898
F: 020 8780 4569
E: info@rhn.org.uk
www.ukabif.org.uk
The UK Acquired Brain Injury Forum (UKABIF) is a not-for-profit coalition of organisations and individuals that seeks to promote understanding of all aspects of acquired brain injury and to provide information and expert input to policy makers, service providers and the general public to promote the interests of brain injured people and their families.
Employees: 1

UK Council for International Student Affairs

9–17 St Albans Place, London N1 0NX
T: 020 7288 4330
Helpline: 020 7107 9922
F: 020 7288 4360
E: membership@ukcisa.org.uk
www.ukcisa.org.uk
Chief Executive: Dominic Scott
The UK Council for International Student Affairs (UKCISA) is the UK's national advisory body serving the interests of international students and those who work with them. It aims to encourage best practice, professional development and the highest quality of institutional support for international students throughout the education sector, increase support for international education and raise awareness of its values and benefits, and promote opportunities for greater student mobility.
Employees: 17

UK Council for Psychotherapy

2nd Floor, Edward House, 2 Wakley
Street EC1V 7LT
T: 020 7014 9955
F: 020 7014 9977
E: info@ukcp.org.uk
www.psychotherapy.org.uk
UKCP is recognised as the leading professional body for the education, training and accreditation of psychotherapists and psychotherapeutic counsellors. We represent member organisations and over 7,000 individual therapists – working privately or in public health organisations – offering a wide variety of psychotherapeutic approaches or modalities. We hold a national register of practitioners and exist to uphold the highest standards in psychotherapy.
Employees: 20

UK Council on Deafness

Westwood Park, London Road, Little
Horkesley, Colchester C06 4BS
T: 01206 274075
F: 01206 274077
E: c.long@deafcouncil.org.uk
www.deafcouncil.org.uk

The national infrastructure organisation for
voluntary sector organisations working with
deaf people. Our mission is to create an
environment in which voluntary sector
organisations working with deaf people can
flourish. We aim to support members in their
work with deaf people and to encourage
cooperation between members in
promoting and representing the diverse
interests of deaf people.
Employees: 3

UK Health Forum

Fleetbank House, 2-6 Salisbury Square,
London EC4Y 8JX
T: 020 7832 6920
F: 020 7832 6921
E: dan.french@ukhealthforum.org.uk
www.ukhealthforum.org.uk
Chief Executive: Paul Lincoln

Aims to preserve and protect the health of
the public and to advance public education
about all matters concerning avoidable
chronic disease and its prevention.
Employees: 20

UK Neighbourhood Watch Trust

1st Floor, 52 London Road, Oadby,
Leicester LE2 5DH
T: 0116 271 0052
E: uknwt@neighbourhoodwatch.net
www.neighbourhoodwatch.net
Chair: Roy Rudham

The UKNWT supports and promotes the
Neighbourhood Watch movement by
providing an effective and informative
two-way communications channel through
its website. The Trust promotes best practice
throughout the Neighbourhood Watch
movement; encourages the exchange of
views and ideas through a range of online
forums; broadens the appeal of
Neighbourhood Watch through an editorial
approach on the website that reflects the
concerns and interests of all sections of
society, ethnic groupings and age ranges.

UK Overseas Territories Conservation Forum

Icknield Court, Back Street, Wendover,
Buckinghamshire HP22 6EB
T: 01733 569325
F: 020 8020 7217
E: cwensink@ukotcf.org
www.ukotcf.org
Honorary Executive Director: Dr Mike
Pienkowski

UKOTCF exists to protect and promote the
diverse and increasingly threatened plant and
animal species and natural habitats of UK's
Overseas Territories (UKOTs) and Crown
Dependencies. It aims to do this by providing
assistance in the form of expertise,
information and liaison between non-
governmental organisations and
governments, both in the UK and in the
Territories themselves. UKOTCF has over 25
years experience working with partners in
the UKOTs on various projects.
Employees: 1
Volunteers: 14
Regional offices: 0
Income: £264,803 (2012-13)

UK Public Health Association

2nd Floor, 28 Portland Place,
London W1B 1DE
T: 0870 010 1932
F: 020 7061 3393
E: info@ukpha.org.uk
www.ukpha.org.uk

Promotes and defends public health in the
UK; brings together local and national
statutory and non-governmental
organisations, professional associations,
trade unions, voluntary and community
groups and individuals; promotes the
development of healthy public policy at all
levels of government, including the
European Union, in order to ensure that the
health needs of the UK become a permanent
feature of national policy and spending
decisions.
Employees: 7
Volunteers: 20

UK Skills

1 Victoria Street, London SW1H 0ET
T: 0800 612 0742
F: 020 7543 7489
E: enquiries@worldskillsuk.org
www.ukskills.org.uk

UK Skills is a charity that promotes excellence
in vocational skills and training through
competitions and major awards. UK Skills
recognises that investing in high-quality
training and vocational education lead to a

well-equipped workforce that is the key to
the success of the UK economy.
Employees: 10

UK Thalassaemia Society

19 The Broadway, Southgate Circus,
London N14 6PH
T: 020 8882 0011
F: 020 8882 8618
E: office@ukts.org
www.ukts.org

Campaigns on behalf of people suffering
from thalassaemia; promotes and
coordinates research; educates people on
the problems of thalassaemia; offers
counselling to sufferers and carriers.
Employees: 2

UK Youth

Avon Tyrrell, Bransgore,
Hampshire BH23 8EE
T: 01425 672347
F: 01425 673883
E: info@ukyouth.org
www.ukyouth.org

UK Youth exists to develop and promote
innovative non-formal education
programmes for and with young people –
working with them to develop their
potential.
Employees: 59
Volunteers: 40000

Unique - Rare Chromosome Disorder Support Group

G1, The Stables, Station Rd West, Oxted,
Surrey RH8 9EE
T: 01883 723306
Helpline: 01883 723356
E: craig@rarechromo.org
www.rarechromo.org
Chief Executive Officer: Beverly Searle

Unique provides specialist information and
support to anyone born, often sick &
disabled, with a rare chromosome disorder
and their families. Our aim is to alleviate
feelings of isolation by linking families whose
children have similar clinical and/or practical
problems caused by rare chromosome
disorders. Unique provides family support
services to more than 4,000 UK families.
Employees: 7
Volunteers: 160
Income: £304,109 (2011-12)

United Kingdom Homecare Association

Group House, 2nd Floor, 52 Sutton Court Road, Sutton, Surrey SM1 4SL
T: 020 8288 1551
F: 020 8288 1550
E: enquiries@ukhca.co.uk
www.ukhca.co.uk
The professional association of home care providers from the independent, voluntary, not-for-profit and statutory sectors. UKHCA helps organisations that provide social care, which may include nursing services, to people in their own homes, promoting high standards of care and providing representation with national and regional policy makers and regulators. The association represents over 1,500 members across the UK.
Employees: 10
Volunteers: 14

United Kingdom Sports Association for People with Learning Disability

1st Floor, 12 City Forum, 250 City Road, London EC1V 2PU
T: 020 7490 3057
F: 020 7251 8861
E: info@uksportsassociation.org
www.uksportsassociation.org
Chief Executive: Tracey McCillen
The UK Sports Association (UKSA) promotes, facilitates and supports talented sports people with learning disability in the UK to train, compete and excel in national and international sport. UKSA leads eligibility and classification, is recognised by UK Sport, is a member of the British Paralympic Association and is the official GB member of the International Sports Federation for Para Athletes with Intellectual Disability (INAS), a member of the International Paralympic Committee.
Employees: 1
Volunteers: 30

United Kingdom's Disabled People's Council

Litchurch Plaza, Litchurch Lane, Derby DE24 8AA
T: 01332 295551
F: 01332 295580
E: info@ukdpc.net
www.bcodp.org.uk
Aims to relieve the disability of people with physical, mental or sensory impairments and to further their independence and full participation in the community.
Employees: 10
Volunteers: 50
Regional offices: 1

United Nations Association

3 Whitehall Court, London SW1A 2EL
T: 020 7930 2931
F: 020 7930 5893
E: richardson@una.org.uk
www.una-uk.org
Campaigns for fuller implementation of the UN Charter in British policy decisions. It aims to educate government and as wide a cross-section of the British public as possible in understanding the principles and purposes of the UN. Particular interests include: UN and conflict; international security and disarmament; human rights; refugee issues; economic and social, sustainable development; environmental protection, culture of peace.
Employees: 20
Regional offices: 130

United Response

Vantage House, 1 Weir Road, Wimbledon Park, London SW19 8UX
T: 020 8246 5200
F: 020 8780 9538
E: su.sayer@unitedresponse.org.uk
www.unitedresponse.org.uk
Chief Executive: Su Sayer
United Response is a national charity that works with people with learning disabilities, mental health needs and physical disabilities in over 200 localities across England and Wales. Our mission is to enable people to take control of their lives and our vision is of a society where people with disabilities or mental health needs are equal participants and have access to the same rights and opportunities as everyone else.
Employees: 2900
Volunteers: 300
Regional offices: 4

United Trusts

PO Box 14, 8 Nelson Road, Edge Hill, Liverpool L69 7AA
T: 0151 709 8252
F: 0151 708 5621
E: information@unitedtrusts.org.uk
www.unitedtrusts.org.uk
Fundraising to support the relief of poverty, the advancement of education and such other purposes beneficial to the community. United Trust endorses the Workplace Charity Fund.
Employees: 4
Volunteers: 20

Universities Federation for Animal Welfare

The Old School, Brewhouse Hill, Wheathampstead, Hertfordshire AL4 8AN
T: 01582 831818
F: 01582 831414
E: ufaw@ufaw.org.uk
www.ufaw.org.uk
Promotes humane behaviour towards animals by enlisting the energies of members of the universities and professional people. Obtains and disseminates accurate information relating to the welfare of animals.
Employees: 8

Universities UK

Woburn House, 20 Tavistock Square, London WC1H 9HQ
T: 020 7419 4111
Helpline: 020 7419 5523
F: 020 7388 8649
E: info@universitiesuk.ac.uk
www.universitiesuk.ac.uk
Chief Executive: Nicola Dandridge
Universities UK is the major representative body and membership organisation for the higher education sector. Its members are the executive heads of UK universities. Within it are the England and Northern Ireland Council, Universities Scotland and Higher Education Wales. Our mission is to be the essential voice and best support for a vibrant, successful and diverse university sector, to influence and create policy for HE, and to provide an environment where the sector can flourish.
Employees: 81
Regional offices: 2

University Association for Contemporary European Studies

School of Public Policy, University College London, 29–30 Tavistock Square, London WC1H 9QU
T: 020 7679 4975
F: 020 7679 4973
E: admin@uaces.org
www.uaces.org
The academic association for contemporary European Studies.
Employees: 3

UNLOCK – the National Association of Reformed Offenders

35A High Street, Snodland,
Kent ME6 5AG
T: 01634 247350
F: 01634 247351
E: enquiries@unlock.org.uk
www.unlock.org.uk
Executive Director: Chris Bath
Our vision is of a society in which reformed offenders are able to fulfil their positive potential through equal opportunities, rights and responsibilities. Driven by the needs of reformed offenders, UNLOCK works to reduce crime by helping them overcome the social exclusion and discrimination that prevents them from successfully reintegrating into society. UNLOCK empowers reformed offenders to break down barriers to reintegration by offering practical advice, support, information, knowledge and skills.
Employees: 4
Volunteers: 10

UnLtd - the Foundation for Social Entrepreneurs

123 Whitecross Street, Islington,
London EC1Y 8JJ
T: 020 7566 1100
F: 020 7566 1101
E: pa@unltd.org.uk
www.unltd.org.uk
Chief Executive: Cliff Prior
UnLtd is a charity that supports social entrepreneurs - people with vision, drive, commitment and passion, who want to change the world for the better. We do this by providing a complete package of funding and support, to help these individuals make their ideas a reality.
Employees: 93
Volunteers: 2
Regional offices: 3
Income: £10,000,000 (2012-13)

Upkeep

2 The Courtyard, 48 New North Road,
Exeter BX4 4EP
T: 020 7256 7646
E: info@upkeep.org.uk
www.upkeep.org.uk
Director: Sarah Bentley
Upkeep promotes good practice in building care. We deliver short courses on building repair, maintenance and improvement. We believe that good maintenance of existing buildings is key to a sustainable future. Upkeep also runs the Charities Facilities Management Group, the network for people who look after buildings and facilities issues in the voluntary sector. The CFM Group was set up in 2000 and has 250 member-charities nationwide.
Employees: 1
Volunteers: 2
Regional offices: 1

Urban Forum

33 Corsham Street, London N1 6DR
T: 020 7253 4816
F: 020 7253 4817
E: info@urbanforum.org.uk
www.urbanforum.org.uk
Urban Forum is an umbrella body for community and voluntary groups with interests in urban and regional policy, especially regeneration.
Employees: 5
Volunteers: 15

Urostomy Association

4 Demontfort Way, Uttoxeter,
Staffordshire ST14 8XY
T: 01889 563191
E: secretary.ua@classmail.co.uk
www.urostomyassocation.org.uk
National Secretary: Hazel Pixley
Charity set up in 1971 to provide support for people having a urinary diversion (e.g. urostomy, mitrofanoff, neo-bladder, reconstruction). 16 local branches; magazine published three times a year; leaflets and other publications available.
Employees: 2
Volunteers: 100
Income: £130,000 (2011-12)

Us in a Bus

Queens House, Philanthropic Road,
Redhill RH1 4DZ
T: 01737 764774
E: info@usinabus.org.uk
www.usinabus.org.uk
Chief Executive: Janet Gurney
Us in a Bus has a two-fold focus: we enable people with learning disabilities and complex needs to build bridges with others through interaction, play and self-expression; we support and train those working with or caring for people with learning disabilities. By widening their understanding of the communication needs of those they are caring for, and building their skills in intensive interaction techniques we can help them develop the relationships they already have.
Employees: 14
Volunteers: 2
Regional offices: 1

Variety

E: stuart.rogers@variety.org.uk

Vegetarian Society UK Ltd

Parkdale, Dunham Road, Altrincham,
Cheshire WA14 4QG
T: 0161 925 2000
F: 0161 926 9182
E: info@vegsoc.org
www.vegsoc.org
Head of Finance: Antony Byatt
The Vegetarian Society encourages, supports and persuades people to become and remain vegetarian. At the core of our work lies our recognition that all beings – people and animals – should be safe and well cared for. We work to reduce suffering and help create a more compassionate society.
Employees: 28
Volunteers: 150
Regional offices: 1
Income: £1,189,000 (2010-11)

Victa Children Ltd

Silverstone House, 46 Newport Road,
Woolstone, Milton Keynes,
Buckinghamshire MK15 0AA
T: 01908 240831
F: 01908 668868
E: admin@victa.org.uk
www.victa.org.uk
Chief Executive: Tracie Tappenden
VICTA supports blind and partially sighted children, young people and their families by providing: Family support, Grants, Annual family weekend, Family days, International Youth trips for 18+, Youth weekends for 18+, Youth weekends for 14 - 17 year olds, Multi European camps for 16+. For more

information please visit our website www.victa.org.uk

Employees: 5
Volunteers: 40
Regional offices: 1

Victim Support

Octavia House, 50 Banner Street,
London EC1Y 8ST
T: 020 7336 1730
E: contact@victimsupport.org.uk
www.victimsupport.org.uk
Chief Executive: Javed Khan
Victim Support is the independent national charity for people affected by crime. Staff and volunteers offer free and confidential information and support for victims of any crime, whether or not it has been reported and regardless of when it happened. The organisation operates via a network of affiliated local charities, the Witness Service and the Victim Supportline.
Employees: 1000
Volunteers: 11000
Regional offices: 90

Viewpoint

E: leslie@hertsviewpoint.co.uk

Village Aid

Suite 1, Fearnehough House, Riverside Business Park, Buxton Road, Bakewell, Derbyshire DE45 1GJ
T: 01629 814434
F: 01629 812272
E: keith@villageaid.org
www.villageaid.org
We work with the most marginalised rural communities in West Africa, establishing partnerships with African communities and local organisations to enhance sustainable development and find solutions using African resources and experience. In the UK we aim to raise awareness of development issues and present positive images of African people and their abilities.
Employees: 3
Volunteers: 3
Income: £276,016 (2011-12)

VISION 2020 (UK) Ltd

PO Box 70172, London WC1A 9HH
T: 07837 692026
E: m.broom@vision2020uk.org.uk
www.vision2020uk.org.uk
Interim Chief Operating Officer: Anita Lightstone

Umbrella organisation designed to promote the partnership working between organisations in the visual impairment sector.
Employees: 3
Volunteers: 0
Regional offices: 0
Income: £100,000 (2011-12)

Vision Aid Overseas

12 The Bell Centre, Newton Road, Manor Royal, Crawley, West Sussex RH10 2FZ
T: 01293 535016
F: 01293 535026
E: info@visionaidoverseas.org
www.vao.org.uk
Director: Dr Natalie Briggs
Vision Aid Overseas is a charity dedicated to people in the developing world whose lives are blighted by poor eyesight.
Employees: 7
Volunteers: 1200

Vision Homes Association

Trigate, 210 - 222 Hagley Road West, Oldbury B68 0NP
T: 0121 434 4644
F: 0121 434 5655
E: caroline@visionhomes.org
www.visionhomes.org.uk
Chief Executive: Ewa Stefanowska
Pursues ways of improving facilities and services for adults who have vision impairments and/or additional disabilities. Promotes the provision of residential accommodation and home support throughout the UK.
Employees: 110
Volunteers: 2
Regional offices: 1

Visionary - linking local sight loss charities

5/14 Western Harbour View, Leith, Edinburgh, Leith, Edinburgh EH6 6PF
T: 020 8417 0942
E: visionary@visionary.org.uk
www.visionary.org.uk
Chief Executive: Angela Tinker
Visionary supports local independent charities that support blind and partially sighted people across the UK. Our core aims: To connect: bringing the network of local societies together and learning from best practices. To influence: consulting members on issues that affect them, representing them on the national stage. To develop: offering direct support to members, providing advice, learning opportunities, guidance and funding to facilitate the

development of new local societies and services from existing local societies.
Employees: 2
Volunteers: 12

Vista

Viata House, 1a Salisbury Road, Leicester, Leicestershire LE1 7QR
T: 0116 249 0909
Helpline: 0116 249 8839
E: info@vistablind.org.uk
www.vistablind.org.uk
Chief Executive: Paul Bott
Vista is the leading provider of services to blind and partially sighted people in Leicester, Leicestershire and Rutland. Vista run 4 residential care homes, providing care to older people and to adults with learning disability and sight loss. They also run community services including social groups, rehabilitation and deaf/blind services.
Employees: 250
Volunteers: 100
Regional offices: 2
Income: £5,700,000 (2012-13)

Vita Nova

E: simonbull@vitanova.co.uk

Vitalise

12 City Forum, 250 City Road, London EC1V 8AF
T: 0845 345 1972
F: 0845 345 1978
E: info@vitalise.org.uk
www.vitalise.org.uk
Aims to enable visually impaired and disabled people to exercise choice, and to provide vital breaks for carers and inspirational oppurtunities for volunteers.
Employees: 290
Volunteers: 6000

Vitiligo Society

24 Greencoat Place, London SW1P 1RD
T: 020 7840 0855
Helpline: 0800 018 2631
E: ken125@vitiligosociety.org.uk
www.vitiligosociety.org.uk
Promotes a positive approach to living with vitiligo. Offers support and understanding to people with vitiligo, and their families, and advice on how to cope with the condition. Funds research to establish the causes of vitiligo and finding safe and effective treatments.
Employees: 2
Volunteers: 2

Voice Care Network UK

25 The Square, Kenilworth,
Warwickshire CV8 1EF
T: 01926 864000 (also fax)
E: info@voicecare.org.uk
www.voicecare.org.uk
Chair: Jeremy Stoke
VCN provides information and practical help
for people to keep their voices healthy, to
avoid voice loss, to communicate skillfully
and with confidence through its professional
members who are: teachers and coaches of
speaking voice; speech and language
therapists experienced in clinical treatment
for voice disorders.
Employees: 1
Volunteers: 230

Voluntary Action Calderdale

Resource Centre, Hall Street, Halifax,
West Yorkshire HX1 5AY
T: 01422 348777
E: info@cvac.org.uk
www.cvac.org.uk
Chief Officer: Soo Nevison
We are established as a local infrastructure
organisation supporting the VCS in
Calderdale. We also run small projects that
support the local communities in our
Borough with an aim to improve life chances
for anyone living in Calderdale.
Employees: 12
Volunteers: 45
Regional offices: 0
Income: £750,000 (2012-13)

Voluntary Action History Society

WC1H 0AL
E: georginabrewis@yahoo.co.uk
www.vahs.org.uk
Chair: Dr Peter Grant
The Voluntary Action History Society
(VAHS) aims to advance the historical
understanding and analysis of voluntary
action. VAHS is a network of postgraduate
students, academics and voluntary sector
practitioners. Activities include a seminar
series at the Institute of Historical Research;
conferences and workshops; New
Researchers group for postgraduates and
early-career scholars; and an edited blog.
Volunteers: 15
Income: £1,000 (2011-12)

Voluntary Action Islington

200a Pentonville Road, London N1 9JP
T: 020 7832 5800
F: 020 7832 5835
E: mike.sherriff@vai.org.uk
www.vai.org.uk
Chief Executive: Mike Sherriff

Voluntary Action Islington provides services
to community groups in Islington, including
the accredited Volunteer Centre for the
borough. We have a resource centre with
training and meeting rooms and an online
learning resource - www.
voluntaryactionacademy.org.uk available for
use by organisations across the UK.
Employees: 8
Volunteers: 15
Regional offices: 0
Income: £638,967 (2012-13)

Voluntary Action South West Surrey

39 Castle Street, Guildford GU1 3UQ
T: 01483 504626
E: c.dunnett@vasws.org.uk
www.voluntaryactionsws.org.uk
Chief Officer: Carol Dunnett
We provide information, advice and support
for voluntary and community organisations
in the Boroughs of Guildford and Waverley.
We run a volunteer brokerage service both
online and through our Volunteer Centres.
We have a supported volunteer programme
and a project that supports older people to
volunteer.
Employees: 10
Volunteers: 20
Regional offices: 1
Income: £150,000 (2012-13)

Voluntary Arts Network

Network Office, 121 Cathedral Road,
Cardiff CF11 9PH
T: 029 2039 5395
E: info@voluntaryarts.org
www.voluntaryarts.org
Chief Executive: Robin Simpson
Voluntary Arts Network promotes
participation in the arts and crafts across the
UK and Republic of Ireland. We recognise
that they are a key part of our culture and are
vital to our health, and to our social and
economic development. Over half the UK
adult population already takes part in arts
and crafts activity for self-improvement,
social networking and leisure. Activities
include folk, dance, drama, literature, music,
visual arts, crafts, applied arts and festivals.
Employees: 18
Regional offices: 5

Voluntary Norfolk

St Clements House, 2-16 Colegate,
Norwich, Norfolk NR3 1BQ
T: 01603 614474
E: admin@voluntarynorfolk.org.uk
www.voluntarynorfolk.org.uk
CEO: Brian Horner
Voluntary Norfolk supports volunteers and
voluntary organisations, operating four
Volunteer Centres and a network of
Community Volunteer Co-ordinators,
recruiting, training and deploying many
hundreds of volunteers each year. We deliver
projects including training, worklessness and
neighbourhood development programmes.
Via our social enterprise, Charity BackRoom,
we offer a wide range of individually-tailored
back-office services including HR and
employment law, DBS checks and payroll,
helping charities to free up time and money
for frontline delivery.
Employees: 50
Regional offices: 14
Income: £1,500,000 (2012-13)

Voluntary Sector Training

45 Stortford Road, Great Dunmow,
Essex CM6 1DQ
T: 01371 876747
E: maddy@voluntarysectortraining.org.
uk
www.voluntarysectortraining.org.uk
Director: Linda Riley
We are an independent charity providing
affordable, relevant and accessible training
for Essex's charities and community groups.
We want to support the development of a
strong, effective and diverse voluntary and
community sector in the county.
Employees: 5
Volunteers: 3
Regional offices: 1
Income: £120,000 (2012-13)

Voluntary Services Lewisham

E: evelyn@vslonline.org.uk

Volunteer Centre Greenwich

E: annie@volunteersgreenwich.co.uk

Volunteer Reading Help

Charity House, 14–15 Perseverance
Works, 38 Kingsland Road,
London E2 8DD
T: 020 7729 4087
F: 020 7729 7643
E: info@beanstalkcharity.org.uk
www.vrh.org.uk
Chief Executive: Paul Newman

Volunteer Reading Help is the country's largest literacy charity. Since 1973 VRH volunteers have been going into primary schools across England to spend half an hour twice a week with each child reading, talking and playing games. The aim of the sessions is to boost the literacy skills, self-confidence and self-esteem of the children. Thousands of futures are transformed by our volunteers.
Employees: 79
Volunteers: 1500
Regional offices: 17

Volunteers for Rural India

12 Eastleigh Avenue, Harrow, Middlesex HA2 0UF
T: 020 8864 4740
Helpline: 07786 570377
E: enquiries@vri-online.org.uk
www.vri-online.org.uk
Chair: Shobhana Snow
VRI aims to relieve poverty in India, by undertaking voluntary work, raising funds to assist village development schemes and educating the public in the UK about Indian culture and traditions, and other aspects of Indian life.
Volunteers: 18
Regional offices: 1
Income: £10,000 (2012-13)

VOSCUR

Royal Oak House, Royal Oak Avenue, Bristol BS1 4GB
T: 0117 909 9949
E: info@voscur.org
www.voscur.org
Chief Executive: Wendy Stephenson
Voscur's purpose is to benefit the public by supporting and developing a thriving, effective and influential voluntary, community and social enterprise sector in Bristol - in particular by building the capacity of voluntary groups to pursue or contribute to any charitable purpose, and promote, organise and facilitate co-operation and partnership working between third sector, statutory and other relevant bodies to achieve a thriving voluntary sector.
Employees: 18
Volunteers: 16
Regional offices: 0
Income: £610,051 (2012-13)

VSO

317 Putney Bridge Road, London SW15 2PN
T: 020 8780 7200
F: 020 8780 7300
E: david.son@vso.org.uk
www.vso.org.uk
VSO is an international development agency working through international volunteering. VSO's purpose is to build reciprocal local and global partnerships that bring people together to share skills, creativity and learning to build a fairer world.
Employees: 700
Volunteers: 1450
Regional offices: 5

Wainwright Trust

Plowmans, Crazies Hill, Reading, Berkshire RG10 8LU
T: 01189 402632
E: secretary@wainwrighttrust.org.uk
www.wainwrighttrust.org.uk
Chair: Susanne Lawrence
The Trust seeks to promote diversity and improve equality of opportunity and fairness of treatment in the workplace, and to combat all forms of discrimination in the workplace, whether arising from gender, race, colour, nationality, ethnic or national origins, religion or belief, sexual orientation, disability of family or other status. It does this by spreading knowledge of good practice.

Wales Council for Voluntary Action

Baltic House, Mount Stuart Square, Cardiff Bay, Cardiff CF10 5FH
T: 0800 288 8329
F: 029 2043 1701
E: help@wcva.org.uk
www.wcva.org.uk
Chief Executive: Graham Benfield
Supports working relationships between the voluntary sector, and government and public bodies; supports and promotes the work of voluntary and community groups at national and local level; supports and promotes volunteering and the interest of volunteers; promotes community cohesion and inclusion and builds social capital; develops

and supports new initiatives; enhances resources available to the voluntary sector; and improves its performance and effectiveness.
Employees: 107
Volunteers: 1
Regional offices: 3
Income: £43,300,000 (2011-12)

Walsall Society for the Blind

Hawley House, 11 Hatherton Road, Walsall, West Midlands WS1 1XS
T: 01922 627683
E: areed@wsftb.co.uk
www.walsallblind.org
C.E.O: Amanda Reed
Our mission is to provide information, support and friendship to those affected by sight loss within the Borough of Walsall.
Employees: 17
Volunteers: 60
Regional offices: 1

Walsingham

Walsingham House, 1331-1337 High Road, Whetstone, London N20 9HR
T: 020 8343 5600
F: 020 8446 9156
E: enquiries@walsingham.com
www.walsingham.com
We support people with disabilities to have a full life by tailoring our support to meet their individual needs.

Walter Segal Self Build Trust

15 High Street, Belford, Northumberland NE70 7NG
T: 01668 219247
E: info@segalselfbuild.co.uk
www.segalselfbuild.co.uk
Enables and empowers people on low incomes to build their own homes and community buildings. Promotes sustainable design and long-term use. Encourages the participation of all groups without pre-existing building skills.

War on Want

44–48 Shepherdess Walk, London N1 7JP
T: 020 7324 5040
F: 020 7324 5041
E: drudkin@waronwant.org
www.waronwant.org
Executive Director: John Hilary
War on Want fights poverty in developing countries in partnership and solidarity with people affected by globalisation. We campaign for human rights and against the

root causes of global poverty, inequality and injustice.
Employees: 19
Volunteers: 5

War Widows Association of Great Britain and Northern Ireland

C/O 199 Borough High Street,
London SE1 1AA
T: 0845 241 2189
E: info@warwidows.org.uk
www.warwidows.org.uk
The association seeks to improve the conditions of war widows in Great Britain. This is done by regular meetings with Ministers and pension authorities. We hold regular national and local events, publish a regular newsletter and ensure that widows are represented at significant national events of remembrance.

Waste Watch

56–64 Leonard Street, London EC2A 4LT
T: 020 7089 2100
F: 020 7403 4802
E: info@wastewatch.org.uk
www.wastewatch.org.uk
Aims to be the leading cross-sectoral national organisation that educates, informs and raises awareness on waste reduction, re-use and recycling.
Employees: 28
Volunteers: 2
Regional offices: 1

Water for Africa

12 The Midway, Newcastle-under-Lyme, Staffordshire ST5 1QG
T: 01782 593289
E: info@waterforafrica.org.uk
www.waterforafrica.org.uk
We believe that water, sanitation and health are basic human rights and the key to emerging long-term from poverty. We have set up and successfully run a UK-led organisation over the last four years managed by local professionals. Its service has provided a fast, professional, targeted service directly to benefit the people of Africa who need it most at the fraction of the cost of the cost of traditional methods.
Volunteers: 3

WaterAid

Second floor, 47–49 Durham Street,
London SE11 5JD
T: 0845 600 0433
F: 020 7793 4545
E: wateraid@wateraid.org
www.wateraid.org
Chief Executive: Barbara Frost

WaterAid is a leading independent organisation that enables the world's poorest people to gain access to safe water, sanitation and hygiene education. We work in Africa, Asia and the Pacific region and campaign globally with our partners to realise our vision of a world where everyone has access to these basic human rights.
Employees: 518
Volunteers: 600
Regional offices: 20

Way Foundation (Widowed And Young)

Suite 35, St Loyes House, 20 St Loyes Street, Bedford, Bedfordshire MK40 1ZL
T: 0870 011 3450
E: info@wayfoundation.org.uk
www.wayfoundation.org.uk
Chair: Rachel Green

The Way Foundation helps men and women widowed when aged 50 or under to rebuild their lives, whether or not they have children. We offer support and friendship through a national network of groups, message board and chatroom, newsletter, book loan service and weekend trips for members.
Volunteers: 50

WDC, Whale and Dolphin Conservation

Brookfield House, 38 St Paul Street, Chippenham, Wiltshire SN15 1LY
T: 01249 449500
E: info@whales.org
www.whales.org
Raises public awareness of all the threats facing whales, dolphins and porpoises. The society funds, throughout the world, research and conservation methods concerning whales, dolphins and porpoises and their habitats, and campaigns for their protection from all threats.

Web of Hope

Windlesham Arboretum, Windlesham, Surrey GU20 6BX
T: 0845 521 3493
E: info@thewebofhope.com
www.thewebofhope.com
The Web of Hope will help you on the road to sustainable living, whether as an individual, as part of a local community or a business. We want to enthuse, encourage and inspire you to take the first steps.
Employees: 3
Volunteers: 2

Weight Concern

1-19 Torrington Place,
London WC1E 7HB
T: 020 7679 1853
F: 020 7679 8354
E: enquiries@weightconcern.org.uk
www.weightconcern.org.uk
Executive Director: Dr Laura McGowan

Weight Concern exists to tackle the issue of obesity in the UK. Our vision is to support and empower people to live a healthy lifestyle, and our mission is to increase the understanding of both health professionals and the public about the causes, consequences and treatments of overweight and obesity. We aim to provide clear, evidence-based information on obesity and weight-management to provide a 'voice' for those who have first-hand experience of being overweight.
Employees: 4
Volunteers: 3
Income: £99,125 (2011-12)

Wellbeing of Women

27 Sussex Place, London NW1 4SP
T: 020 7772 6400
F: 020 7724 7725
E: hello@wellbeingofwomen.org.uk
www.wellbeingofwomen.org.uk
Director: Liz Campbell

Wellbeing of Women is a charity dedicated to improving the health of women and babies, to make a difference to everybody's lives today and tomorrow. We provide information, to raise awareness of health issues to keep women and babies well today. We fund medical research and training grants, which have and will continue to develop better treatments and outcomes for tomorrow.
Employees: 10

WellChild

16 Royal Crescent, Cheltenham, Gloucestershire GL50 3DA
T: 01242 530007
E: info@wellchild.org.uk
www.wellchild.org.uk
Chief Executive: Colin Dyer

WellChild is the national charity for sick children. We provide essential practical and emotional support for seriously ill children, young people and those who care for them across the UK to ensure they receive the best possible quality of care.

Wellcome Trust

Gibbs Building, 215 Euston Road,
London NW1 2BE
T: 020 7611 7210
F: 020 7611 8800
E: s.wallcraft@wellcome.ac.uk
www.wellcome.ac.uk
Aims to protect, preserve and advance all or
any aspects of the health and welfare of
humankind and to advance and promote
knowledge and education by engaging in,
encouraging and supporting research into
any of the biosciences.
Employees: 500

Wells for India

The Winchester Centre, 68 St George's
Street, Winchester,
Hampshire SO23 8AH
T: 01962 848043
F: 01962 848029
E: office@wellsforindia.org
www.wellsforindia.org
Wells for India is a small charity that works
with partners – non government
organisations (NGO) in India, who have
direct contact with village committees and
the people of the desert. Our focus is on
water – the provision of sufficient clean
water for drinking, cooking, washing, the
animals and for crops.
Employees: 2
Volunteers: 27

Welwitschia Welfare Centre

Imperial House, 64 Willoughby Lane,
Tottenham, London N17 0SP
T: 020 8808 1255
F: 020 8885 3471
E: info@wwcuk.org
www.wwcuk.org
Chief Executive: Pedro Lunguela
The WWC is a voluntary community charity
organisation. It was set up to help Angolan
community and other Portuguese-speaking
migrants, refugees access the mainstream
services, not to suffer in silence through lack
of knowledge of their rights and
entitlements in their host country. It also
combats poverty and helps the community
integrate into British society. WWC services
are now also offered to other minority ethnic
groups.
Employees: 2
Volunteers: 8
Income: £33,504 (2011-12)

WESC Foundation

E: kgaulton@wescfoundation.ac.uk

West Harton Churches Action Station Ltd

Boldon Lane, South Shields, Tyne &
Wear NE34 0AS
T: 01914 558122
E: ceo@actionstation.org.uk
actionstation.org.uk
Manager: Dave Kippax
To reduce social isolation, increase job
readiness of the community, increase the
overall health of the community and
promote individuals working together for
the benefit of the local community. To
provide a one stop shop.
Employees: 6
Volunteers: 43
Income: £200,000 (2012-13)

West Indian Standing Conference

5 Westminster Bridge Road,
London SE1 7XW
T: 020 7928 7861
F: 020 7928 0343
E: wiscorg@tiscali.co.uk
Aims to be a representative body for West
Indians in Britain and to research into, report
upon, and make representations as
appropriate concerning the conditions of
that community. It establishes and co-
ordinates projects to monitor, assist and
inform statutory and voluntary agencies of
the needs of the West Indian community.
Employees: 6
Volunteers: 3

Western Lodge

E: info@westernlodge.org.uk

Westminster Drug Project

7th Floor, Kingsway House, 103 Kingsway,
Holborn, London WC2B 6QX
T: 020 7421 3100
F: 020 7421 3199
E: communications@wdp-drugs.org.uk
www.wdp-drugs.org.uk
Chief Executive Officer: Stuart Campbell
WDP is a vibrant and innovative charity
committed to helping all those who are
affected by drug and alcohol use. We believe
that with the right support, people can make
long-lasting change in their lives to improve
health, wellbeing and social integration. We
provide drug and alcohol services across
London and the south east of England. We
work with individuals, families and
communities to help people recover from
drug dependency and to reduce crime.
Employees: 360
Volunteers: 100
Regional offices: 24

Weston Park Hospital Development Fund Ltd

E: karen.holmes@cancersupportcentre.
co.uk

WheelPower

Stoke Mandeville Stadium, Guttmann
Road, Stoke Mandeville,
Buckinghamshire,
Buckinghamshire HP21 9PP
T: 01296 395995
F: 01296 424171
E: nigel.roberts@wheelpower.org.uk
www.wheelpower.org.uk
Chief Executive: Martin McElhatton
WheelPower: British Wheelchair Sport
provides, promotes and develops
opportunities for men, women and children
with disabilities to participate in recreational
and competitive wheelchair sport from grass
roots to international level throughout the
UK.
Employees: 10
Volunteers: 250
Regional offices: 1
Income: £1,600,000 (2012-13)

Whitehall and Industry Group

80 Petty France, London SW1H 9EX
T: 020 7222 1166
F: 020 7222 1167
E: charitynext@wig.co.uk
www.wig.co.uk
Chief Executive: Mark Gibson
The Whitehall and Industry Group is an
independent, not-for-profit and non-
lobbying membership organisation.
Established in 1984, we have a charitable
purpose to build understanding and
cooperation between the public, private and
voluntary sectors for the greater public good;
a nation better governed, business better
managed and society better served.
Employees: 23
Income: £1,500,000 (2011-12)

Whizz-Kidz

Elliot House, 10–12 Allington Street,
London SW1E 5EH
T: 020 7233 6600
E: info@whizz-kidz.org.uk
www.whizz-kidz.org.uk
Whizz-Kidz improves the quality of life of
young disabled people under 18 in the UK
through the provision of customised mobility
equipment such as powered and manual
wheelchairs and tricycles. The charity
provides help and advice to children and
their families and raises awareness of

mobility-related issues through national campaigning.

Who Cares? Trust

Kemp House, 152–160 City Road,
London EC1V 2NP
T: 020 7251 3117
F: 020 7251 3123
E: karen.hearn@thewhocarestrust.org.uk
www.thewhocarestrust.org.uk
Aims to improve the delivery of public care and the day-to-day life experience of children and young people in public care through promoting and acting on their views.
Employees: 27
Volunteers: 1

Wigan and Leigh CVS

E: sshaw@cvswl.org

Wildfowl and Wetlands Trust

Slimbridge, Gloucestershire GL2 7BT
T: 01453 891900
F: 01453 890827
E: kath.brice@wwt.org.uk
www.wwt.org.uk
Chief Executive: Martin Spray
The Wildfowl and Wetlands Trust (WWT) is the largest international wetland conservation charity in the UK. Its mission is to promote, protect and develop wetlands and their wildlife. WWT operates nine visitor centres in the UK aimed at bringing people closer to wetland wildlife.
Employees: 420
Volunteers: 520
Regional offices: 9

Wildlife Aid

Randalls Farm House, Randalls Road,
Leatherhead, Surrey KT22 0AL
T: 01372 377332
Helpline: 0906 180 0132
F: 01372 375183
E: becky@wildlifeaid.org.uk
www.wildlifeaid.com
Managing Trustee: Simon Cowell
Wildlife Aid is a registered charity dedicated to the rescue, care and rehabilitation of sick, injured and orphaned British wildlife. Based in Leatherhead, Surrey, since its opening over 25 years ago the centre has grown to be one of the largest wildlife rehabilitation hospitals in the country, dealing with more than 20,000 incidents each year.
Employees: 3
Volunteers: 300
Regional offices: 1

Wildlife and Countryside Link

89 Albert Embankment, London SE1 7TP
T: 020 7820 8600
F: 020 7820 8620
E: enquiry@wcl.org.uk
www.wcl.org.uk
Wildlife and Countryside Link brings together environmental voluntary organisations in the UK united by their common interest in the conservation and enjoyment of the natural and historic environment. Our aim is to maximise the efficiency and effectiveness of the voluntary sector through collaboration. Through Link, groups of people from different organisations get together to exchange information, develop and promote policies, and work to effect change.
Employees: 5
Volunteers: 3

Wildlife Trusts

The Kiln, Waterside, Mather Road,
Newark, Nottinghamshire NG24 1WT
T: 01636 677711
F: 0870 036 0101
E: enquiry@wildlifetrusts.org
www.wildlifetrusts.org
Aims to protect wildlife for the future, and to educate the public in the understanding and appreciation of nature and the need for its conservation.
Employees: 1300
Volunteers: 24000
Regional offices: 47

William Sutton Trust

William Sutton Housing Association,
Sutton Court, Tring,
Hertfordshire HP23 5BB
T: 01442 891100
E: customerservice@affinitysutton.com
www.affinitysutton.com
A registered charity and a housing association registered with The Housing Corporation, which provides affordable housing and associated community support for people in housing need in 44 local authority areas throughout England, including London.

Williams Syndrome Foundation Ltd

161 High Street, Tonbridge,
Kent TN9 1BX
T: 01732 365152
E: enquiries@williams-syndrome.org.uk
www.williams-syndrome.org.uk
CEO: Elizabeth Hurst
Assists research and exchanges information on William's syndrome, a rare disorder caused by an abnormality in chromosomes.

Puts parents in touch through the Parents Association. Stimulates interest, particularly among the medical profession, in the condition.

Wincanton Community Venture

E: sueplace@balsamcentre.org.uk

Windle Trust International

37A Oxford Road, Cowley,
Oxford OX4 2EN
T: 01865 712900
E: cathryn@windle.org.uk
www.windle.org.uk
Windle Trust International provides access to education and training for those affected by conflict in Africa. We equip talented young Africans to meet the challenges of development in their own countries. The Trust's activities include sponsoring study in schools, universities and colleges in Africa and in the UK, and intensive English programmes to enable refugees and other caught up in Africa's conflicts to access training, employment and community leadership roles.

Windsor Leadership Trust

Adair House, Madeira Walk, Windsor,
Berkshire SL4 1EU
T: 01753 830202
F: 01753 842775
E: office@windsorleadershiptrust.org.uk
www.windsorleadershiptrust.org.uk
Chief Executive: Dr James McCalman
For 15 years, the Windsor Leadership Trust has been bringing together top leaders from every sector to reflect on how they can use their influence, decisions and actions to benefit their organisations, and wider society. Through our programmes we enable leaders to explore for themselves the responsibilities of leadership. The different programme levels reflect the increasingly complex challenges leaders face as their roles become more strategic and their leadership responsibilities grow.
Employees: 10

Winston's Wish

Westmoreland House, 80–86 Bath Road,
Cheltenham, Gloucestershire GL53 7JT
T: 01242 515157
Helpline: 0845 203 0405
F: 01242 546187
E: info@winstonswish.org.uk
www.winstonswish.org.uk
Chief Executive: Debbie Kirkham
Winston's Wish helps children rebuild their lives after the death of a parent or sibling,

enabling them to face the future with hope. We offer practical support and guidance to families, professionals and anyone concerned about a grieving child. We want children to avoid the problems that can occur in later life if they are unable to express their grief.

Wireless for the Bedridden

159A High Street, Hornchurch, Essex RM11 3YB
T: 01708 621101
F: 01708 620816
www.w4b.org.uk
Provides radio and television facilities to needy housebound disabled and the elderly poor who cannot afford these.

WISH – a voice for women's mental health

77 East Road, London N1 6AH
T: 020 7017 2828
E: info@womenatwish.org.uk
Director: Joyce Kallevik
Wish provides long-term, gender sensitive support and services to women with mental health needs through the criminal justice and psychiatric system. Wish also provides community support in the greater London area.
Employees: 15
Volunteers: 25
Regional offices: 2

Wishing Well

4 Laurel Avenue, Fleetwood, Lancashire FY7 7PT
T: 01253 773546
E: wishingwellappeal@yahoo.co.uk
www.wishingwellcharity.org.uk
Lead Trustee: Jason O'Flaherty
Wishing Well is a small international development charity. We work with children and families, promote volunteering and support community development initiatives. Wishing Well is currently working in Romania and in the UK. Our projects include: providing educational support to young Roma children; advocacy; work with children with HIV and special needs; delivering a schools' NGO community development training programme and promoting volunteering, including coordinating National Volunteering Week.
Employees: 2
Volunteers: 20
Regional offices: 1

Woking Association of Voluntary Service

E: sylvie@wavs.org.uk

Wolverhampton Domestic Violence Forum

E: admin@wdvf.org.uk

WOMANKIND Worldwide

2nd Floor, Development House, 56–64 Leonard Street, London EC2A 4LT
T: 020 7549 0360
F: 020 7549 0361
E: info@womankind.org.uk
www.womankind.org.uk
Chief Executive: Jackie Ballard
WOMANKIND's mission, which we carry out in collaboration with partner organisations throughout the world, is to achieve lasting improvement in the economic, social and political position of women around the world. Our vision is the creation of a world – just, equitable and peaceful – in which women are equal partners with men in determining the values, direction and governance of their societies at every level for the benefit of all.
Employees: 24
Volunteers: 12

Women and Girls' Network

PO Box 13095, London W14 0FE
T: 020 7610 4678
E: info@wgn.org.uk
www.wgn.org.uk
Offers counselling to women and girls who have experienced any form of violence, whether physical, sexual or emotional.

Women and Manual Trades

Tindlemanor, 52–54 Featherstone Street, London EC1Y 8RT
T: 020 7251 9192
F: 020 7251 9193
E: info@wamt.org
www.wamt.org
Provides services to women who are training and working in the manual trades and allied industries.
Employees: 6

Women's Aid Federation of England

PO Box 391, Bristol BS99 7WS
T: 0117 944 4411
Helpline: 0808 200 0247
F: 0117 924 1703
E: info@womensaid.org.uk
www.womensaid.org.uk
Provides advice, information and signposts temporary refuge for women and their children who are threatened by mental,

emotional or physical violence, harassment or sexual abuse.
Employees: 25
Volunteers: 40

Women's Engineering Society (WES)

Michael Faraday House, Six Hills Way, Stevenage, Hertfordshire SG1 2AY
T: 01438 765506
E: info@wes.org.uk
www.wes.org.uk
The Women's Engineering Society aims to: support members of WES and women in general to achieve their potential as engineers, scientists and technologists; encourage the study and application of engineering; help engineering companies to promote gender diversity and equality in the workplace; lobby Government, organisations and policy makers to strive for equality, both in the workplace and in the promotion of engineering as a career.
Employees: 1
Volunteers: 100+
Regional offices: 1

Women's Environmental Network

PO Box 30626, London E2 7EY
T: 020 7481 9004
F: 020 7481 9144
E: info@wen.org.uk
www.wen.org.uk
Campaigns on environmental and health issues from a woman's perspective, and informs and empowers women and men who care about the environment.
Employees: 11
Volunteers: 2
Regional offices: 100

Women's Farm and Garden Association

175 Gloucester Street, Cirencester, Gloucestershire GL7 2DP
T: 01285 658339
E: admin@wfga.org.uk
www.wfga.org.uk
Creates interest in and promotes the study and practice of agriculture and horticulture among women throughout the UK. Trains returners through the Women Returners to Amenity Gardening Scheme (WRAGS). Offers a programme of specialist workshops, tours and visits to its membership. Offers grants to the membership through the

Christine Ladley Fund for education and work-related funding.

Employees: 15

Women's Health Advice Centre

1 Council Road, Ashington, Ashington, Northumberland NE63 8RZ
T: 01670 853977
E: cathhale@whac.uk.com
www.whac-online.co.uk
Manager: Cath Hale
Incorporated charity aiming to provide people (14+) in Northumberland with quality counselling, personal development, education and information on issues contributing to their general health and well being. Specialising in domestic and sexual abuse, bereavement, mental health, relationship problems, self esteem and suicide.

Employees: 6
Volunteers: 25
Regional offices: 1
Income: £150,000 (2012-13)

Women's Resource Centre

Ground Floor East, 33–41 Dallington Street, London EC1V 0BB
T: 020 7324 3030
F: 020 7324 3050
E: info@wrc.org.uk
www.wrc.org.uk
Chief Executive: Vivienne Hayes
The Women's Resource Centre is a charity that supports women's organisations to be more effective and sustainable. We provide training, information, resources and one-to-one support on a range of organisational development issues. We also lobby decision-makers on behalf of the women's not-for-profit sector for improved representation and funding. Our members work in a wide range of fields delivering services to and campaigning on behalf of some of the most marginalised communities of women.

Employees: 18

Women's Royal Naval Service Benevolent Trust

311 Twyford Avenue, Stamshaw, Portsmouth, Hampshire PO2 8RN
T: 023 9265 5301
F: 023 9267 9040
E: generalsecretary@wrnsbt.org.uk
www.wrnsbt.org.uk
General Secretary: S Ayton
The primary aim of the Trust is to provide relief in cases of necessity or distress amongst its members and their dependants. The Trust

is also empowered, in suitable cases, to make grants for the education of dependants.

Employees: 2
Volunteers: 20

Women's Sports Foundation

3rd Floor, Victoria House, Bloomsbury Square, London WC1B 4SE
T: 020 8697 5370 (also fax)
www.wsf.org.uk
Promotes the interests of all women in and through sport and aims to gain equal opportunities and options for women.

Employees: 5

Women's Technology and Education Centre

Blackburne House Centre For Women, Blackburne Place, Liverpool L8 7PE
T: 0151 709 4356
E: bh.wtec@blackburnehouse.co.uk
Promotes education and training for women; establishes and promotes equal opportunities in education and training. Encourages women into non-traditional jobs.

Women's Therapy Centre

10 Manor Gardens, London N7 6JS
T: 020 7263 7860
Helpline: 020 7263 6200
F: 020 7272 4222
E: enquiries@womenstherapycentre.co.uk
www.womenstherapycentre.co.uk
We offer both group and individual psychoanalytic psychotherapy for women. Therapy is offered on a sliding scale according to financial means. Please see website for up-to-date information on making an appointment.

Employees: 10
Volunteers: 10
Regional offices: 1

Woodcraft Folk

13 Ritherdon Road, London SW17 8QE
T: 020 7703 4173
F: 020 8767 2457
E: info@woodcraft.org.uk
www.woodcraft.org.uk
Unites children, young people and all who are young in spirit. Directs the energy and enthusiasm of youth towards the transformation of society, educating members in the principles of universal tolerance, equality and friendship.

Volunteers: 3500
Regional offices: 500

Wooden Spoon Society

115–117 Fleet Road, Fleet, Hampshire GU51 3PD
T: 01252 773720
F: 01276 502134
E: idoorbar@woodenspoon.com
www.woodenspoon.com
Enhances the quality and prospect of life for children and young persons in the UK and Ireland who are disadvantaged, either physically, mentally or socially.

Employees: 23
Volunteers: 400
Regional offices: 1
Income: £4,228,524 (2011-12)

Woodgreen The Animal Charity

King's Bush Farm, London Road, Godmanchester, Cambridgeshire PE29 2NH
T: 0844 248 8181
F: 01480 832815
E: paula.loveday-smith@woodgreen.org.uk
woodgreen.org.uk
Chief Executive: Paula Loveday-Smith
Animal welfare and rehoming charity.

Employees: 270
Regional offices: 3

Woodland Trust

Kempton Way, Grantham, Lincolnshire NG31 6LL
T: 01476 581111
F: 01476 590808
E: hilaryallison@woodlandtrust.org.uk
www.woodlandtrust.org.uk
The Trust is the UK's leading charity dedicated to protecting, restoring and expanding our native woods. Our long-term aims are to enable the creation of more new native woods, to protect native woods, trees and their wildlife for the future, and to restore our native woodland heritage.

Employees: 320
Volunteers: 1000+
Regional offices: 4
Income: £31,878 (2011-12)

Worcester Volunteer Centre

33, The Tything, Worcester, Worcestershire WR1 1JL
T: 01905 24741
F: 01907 23688
E: sally@wvc.org.uk
www.worcestervolunteercentre.org.uk
Chief Officer: Sally Ellison

Local Infrastructure organisation and volunteer recruitment centre. Aim to promote volunteering, community action & deliver community services through volunteers.

Employees: 15
Volunteers: 110
Income: £300,000 (2012-13)

Work Foundation

21 Palmer Street, London SW1Y 0AD
T: 020 7976 3500
E: partnership@theworkfoundation.com
www.theworkfoundation.com
The Work Foundation aims to improve productivity and performance of all British organisations by enriching the quality and integrity of working life. Our unique understanding of the importance and developing human capital enables us to work with our clients to bring about in-depth sustainable change, through our distinctive brand of research, consultancy, advocacy, leadership and coaching programmes.

Workaid

E: publicity@workaid.org

Workbase Training

Finchley House Business Centre, 707 High Road, London N12 0BT
T: 020 8343 1334
F: 020 8492 0405
E: info@workbase.org.uk
Workbase is a national, non-profit-making incorporated organisation. Its ethos, methodology and management board are based on partnerships between Trade Unions and employers. It is dedicated to improving and promoting opportunities for promoting literacy and numeracy as part of workforce development, and encouraging quality in the voluntary sector.

Employees: 6

Workers' Educational Association

4 Loop Sreet, London EC2A 4XW
T: 020 7426 3450
F: 020 7426 3451
E: london@wea.org.uk
www.wea.org.uk
General Secretary: Ruth Spellman
The WEA creates and delivers around 14,000 courses for adults each year in response to local need across England and Scotland, often in partnership with community groups and local charities. We believe that education is lifelong and should continue beyond school, college and university in order to help

people develop their full human potential in society.

Employees: 3500
Volunteers: 4000
Regional offices: 10

Working Families

1–3 Berry Street, London EC1V 0AA
T: 020 7253 7243
Helpline: 0300 012 0312
F: 020 7253 6253
E: office@workingfamilies.org.uk
www.workingfamilies.org.uk
Supports and acts as a voice for working parents and carers, especially those who are disadvantaged; promotes workplace cultures that support work–life balance and flexible working for all working people; works collaboratively with employers, policy makers, opinion formers and working people as a pragmatic force for change.

Employees: 12
Volunteers: 10

Working with Words

Carlton Centre, Carlton Road, Sidcup, Kent DA14 6AH
T: 020 8302 4619
E: words@mcch.org.uk
www.mcch.org.uk/workingwithwords/index.aspx
Design and Contracts Manager: Colin Thomas
There are 1.2 million people with learning disabilities and 1.7 million adults with low literacy in the UK. Working with Words can help you reach this audience. We produce accessible information and easy read documents, making it easy to understand for people with learning disabilities and low literacy. All of our documents are created using Government and European guidelines and are proof read by our target audience.

World Association of Girl Guides and Girl Scouts

World Bureau, Olave Centre, 12C Lyndhurst Road, London NW3 5PQ
T: 020 7794 1181
F: 020 7431 3764
E: wagggs@wagggsworld.org
www.wagggsworld.org
Provides a dynamic, flexible, values-based educational programme that is relevant to girls' needs. Strives for excellence by providing opportunities to enable girls to make informed decisions. The largest voluntary organisation for girls and young women in the world, WAGGGS bases its work on spiritual values and has a commitment to peace and world citizenship.

Employees: 51
Volunteers: 1000000
Regional offices: 1

World Development Movement

66 Offley Road, London SW9 0LS
T: 020 7820 4900
F: 020 7820 4949
E: wdm@wdm.org.uk
www.wdm.org.uk
Director: Nick Dearden
World Development Movement (WDM) tackles the underlying causes of poverty. We lobby decision-makers to change the policies that keep people poor. We research and promote positive alternatives. We work alongside people in the developing world who are standing up to injustice.

Employees: 30
Volunteers: 5
Regional offices: 1

World Emergency Relief

20 York Buildings, London WC2N 6JU
T: 0870 429 2129
F: 020 7839 8202
E: hannah@wer-uk.org
www.wer-uk.org
Delivers practical, emotional, spiritual and economic aid to children and disaster victims in developing countries.

Employees: 7
Volunteers: 3

World Society for the Protection of Animals

5th Floor, 222 Gray's Inn Road, London WC1X 8HB
T: 020 7587 5000
F: 020 7587 5057
E: wspa@wspa.org.uk
www.wspa.org.uk
For 25 years, WSPA has aimed to promote the concept of animal welfare in regions of the world where there are few, if any, measures to protect animals. Politically, we have campaigned to convince governments and key decision-makers to change practices and introduce new laws to protect or improve the welfare of animals.

Employees: 50
Volunteers: 4
Regional offices: 10

World Vision UK

World Vision House, Opal Drive, Fox Milne, Milton Keynes MK15 0ZR
T: 01908 841000
F: 01908 841001
E: info@worldvision.org.uk
www.worldvision.org.uk
Chief Executive Officer: Justin Byworth
World Vision is a Christian relief, development and advocacy organisation dedicated to working with children, families

and communities to overcome poverty and injustice.

Worshipful Company of Information Technologists

39A Bartholomew Close,
London EC1A 7JN
T: 020 7600 1992
F: 020 7600 1991
E: caroline@wcit.org.uk
www.wcit.org.uk
Getting the maximum benefit from IT is now a prerequisite, not just for commercial organisations but also for the charity sector. We work with a wide range of not-for-profit organisations with the aim of helping them to gain the maximum benefit from their IT. Our members give their time and expertise to provide pro bono IT advice (usually at a strategic level).
Employees: 4
Volunteers: 200

Worster-Drought Syndrome Support Group

10 St Vincent Chase, Braintree,
Essex CM7 9UJ
Helpline: 01376 348948
E: j.leech@btopenworld.com
www.wdssg.org.uk
Chair: Jacqueline Leech
Helps support those with WDS, a rare form of cerebral palsy, and their families.
Volunteers: 6

Worthing Women's Aid

E: katie@ww-aid.org.uk

WPF Therapy

23 Magdalen Street, London SE1 2EN
T: 020 7378 2000
F: 020 7378 2010
E: counselling@wpf.org.uk
www.wpf.org.uk
Chief Executive: Joan Baxter
WPF Therapy works to broaden access to good psychological therapies. It provides therapy to a high standard tailored for each individual as well as training for counsellors and psychotherapists with a wide range of accredited training programmes. The organisation's clinical services and training cover ongoing psychodynamic counselling, psychodynamic psychotherapy, time-limited psychodynamic counselling, group analytic psychotherapy and CBT (cognitive behavioural therapy).
Employees: 150
Volunteers: 100
Regional offices: 27

WRVS

Garden House, Milton Hill, Steventon,
Abingdon, Oxfordshire OX13 6AD
T: 01235 442900
Helpline: 0845 600 5885
F: 01235 861166
E: enquiries@wrvs.org.uk
www.wrvs.org.uk
Chief Executive: Lynne Berry
Works independently and in partnership with government departments, local authorities and the private sector in carrying out welfare and emergency work through a nationwide network based on local authority areas in England, Scotland and Wales. WRVS is the largest active voluntary organisation in the UK.
Employees: 1600
Volunteers: 65000

WWV

7 North Street Workshops, Stoke Sub Hamdon, Somerset TA14 6QR
T: 01935 825588
F: 01935 825775
E: wwv@wwv.org.uk
www.wwv.org.uk
Director: Mike Silvey
Encourages and enables many more people to become volunteers by providing the UK's most comprehensive information on volunteering opportunities throughout the UK and worldwide. WWV also motivates sixth formers, young people at risk, students with disabilities, ex-offenders and injured service people to volunteer, helping them on a one-to-one basis to find the right voluntary placement for them.
Employees: 23
Volunteers: 9

Wycombe Women's Aid Ltd

PO Box 1477, High Wycombe,
Buckinghamshire HP11 9HP
T: 01494 461367
F: 01494 452622
E: wwal@btconnect.com
www.wycombewomensaid.org.uk
Director: Lisbeth Harvey
Wycombe Women's Aid provides support to women and children experiencing the effects of domestic violence by offering safe, temporary and emergency accommodation as well as practical and emotional support within the Refuge and through outreach in the local community of Wycombe, South Bucks and Chiltern Districts of Bucks. This is achieved using an equal opportunities

approach incorporated in a women-centred philosophy.
Employees: 13
Volunteers: 2
Regional offices: 0
Income: £473,970 (2012-13)

Y Care International

Kemp House, 152–160 City Road,
London EC1V 2NP
T: 020 7549 3150
F: 020 7549 3151
E: enq@ycareinternational.org
www.ycareinternational.org
YCI works with vulnerable and disadvantaged young people in developing countries, focusing on street and working children, girls and young women, young refugees and displaced and young people with disabilities.
Employees: 15
Volunteers: 2

YHA (England and Wales) Ltd

Trevelyan House, Dimple Road, Matlock,
Derbyshire DE4 3YH
T: 01629 592654
F: 01629 592702
E: customerservices@yha.org.uk
www.yha.org.uk
YHA operates a network of more than 200 youth hostels across England and Wales. Our accommodation is open to all and everyone can experience a warm welcome, comfortable accommodation, good food and affordable prices. We also have more than 230,000 members, who receive many additional benefits, most notably an exemption from paying a non-member supplement each time they stay with YHA.
Employees: 1150
Volunteers: 5250
Regional offices: 80

YMCA England

29–35 Farringdon Road,
London EC1M 3JF
T: 0845 873 6633
E: enquiries@england.ymca.org.uk
www.ymca.org.uk

The YMCA is a leading Christian charity committed to supporting all young people, particularly in times of need. YMCA England supports and represents the work of over 140 YMCAs providing professional and relevant services that make a difference to the lives of young people in over 250 communities.
Employees: 884
Volunteers: 250
Regional offices: 7

YMCA Indian Student Hostel

41 Fitzroy Square, London, W1T 6AQ W1T 6AQ
T: 020 7387 0411
F: 020 7383 4735
E: gs@indianymca.org
www.indianymca.org
General Secretary/CEO: Thomas Abraham
YMCA stands for worldwide fellowship based on the equal value of all persons, respect and freedom for all, tolerance and understanding between people of different opinions and concern of the needs. YMCA Indian Student Hostel is a project of the National Council of YMCAs of India (NCYI), for the mental, spiritual and physical wellbeing of the youth in accordance with the YMCA worldwide. It provides a home for the youth and helps new arrivals.
Employees: 30
Volunteers: 9

Yorkshire Cat Rescue

The Farm, Lower Pierce Close, Cross Roads, Keighley, West Yorkshire BD22 9AQ
T: 01535 647184
E: mail@yorkshirecatrescue.org
www.yorkshirecatrescue.org
Founder and Chief Executive Officer: Sara Atkinson
A half way home for unwanted and stray cats and kittens in Yorkshire. All cats are neutered, microchipped, vaccinated, treated for worms and fleas. Volunteers needed for cat care, fundraising, admin.
Employees: 6
Volunteers: 40
Regional offices: 1
Income: £204,489 (2011-12)

Yorkshire Coast Enterprise Ltd

E: jennifer.crowther@yce.org.uk

Young Christian Workers

St Joseph's, Off St Joseph's Grove, Hendon, London NW4 4TY
T: 020 8203 6290 (also fax)
E: info@ycwimpact.com
www.ycwimpact.com
National President: Phil Callaghan
The Young Christian Workers (YCW) is an organisation for 16-30 year olds (YCW) and Impact 13-17 years; it is for young people and run by young people. Our purpose is to help all young people live life to the full and realise their potential. The mission of the YCW is lived out among young people in the working world, paid or unpaid work, or those studying. YCW encourage them to grow in confidence and responsibility.
Employees: 1
Volunteers: 50
Income: £113,879 (2012-13)

Young Enterprise

Peterley House, Peterley Road, Cowley, Oxford OX4 2TZ
T: 01865 776845
E: info@young-enterprise.org.uk
www.young-enterprise.org.uk
With direct practical experience, the organisation introduces young people to the world of commerce and industry. It gives school and college students the opportunity to acquire a basic understanding of the world of work and wealth creation.

Young Epilepsy

St Piers Lane, Lingfield, Surrey RH7 6PW
T: 01342 832243
Helpline: 01342 831342
F: 01342 834639
E: info@youngepilepsy.org.uk
www.youngepilepsy.org.uk
Interim Chief Executive: Lisa Farmer
The National Centre for Young People with Epilepsy is the UK's major provider of specialist services for under 25s with epilepsy and other neurological conditions. As well as St Piers School and Further Education College, there is a health centre, a range of epilepsy diagnostic and assessment services, a Childhood Epilepsy Information Service and helpline open Monday to Friday 9am to 1pm and a SureStart centre for all local families.
Employees: 750
Volunteers: 50
Regional offices: 1

Young Explorers Trust

Stretton Cottage, Wellow Road, Ollerton, Newark, Nottinghamshire NG22 9AX
T: 01623 861027
E: ted@theyet.org
www.theyet.org
Chairman of Trustees: Graham Derrick
YET is a registered charity promoting safe and responsible expeditions. It aims to give young people the opportunity to take part in exploration, discovery and challenging adventure to help foster the qualities of service, self-sufficiency and leadership. By giving advice to youth expeditions it aims to help schools, youth organisations and peer groups to run their own expeditions in a safe and responsible manner. It can also give grant aid to individuals and expeditions.
Volunteers: 20
Income: £5,000 (2011-12)

Young Lancashire

10 Fishergate Hill, Preston, Lancashire PR1 8JB
T: 01772 556127
F: 01772 251334
E: grahamw@younglancashire.org.uk
www.younglancashire.org.uk
CEO: Graham Whalley
Young Lancashire is a local infrastructure organisation which offers support to all front line voluntary children, young people and family based organisations to achieve the highest standards of practice and effectiveness in their work by building their capacity to deliver quality services. Our mission is to support children, young people and family based organisations to achieve the highest standards of practice and effectiveness in their work by building their capacity to deliver quality services.
Employees: 3
Volunteers: 12
Income: £250,000 (2012-13)

Young Lives

1st floor, 11 Bridge Street, St Ives, Cambridgeshire PE27 5EH
T: 01480 444333
E: lynn@young-lives.org.uk
www.young-lives.org.uk
Chief Executive: Lynn Hogarth
Employees: 32

Young People Matter

E: m.dawes@youngpeoplematter.org

Young People's Support Foundation

E: k.roberts@ypsf.co.uk

Young People's Trust for the Environment and Nature Conservation

43 South Street, South Petherton, Somerset TA13 5AE
T: 01935 385962
E: peter.littlewood@ypte.org.uk
www.yptenc.org.uk
Encourages young people's understanding of the environment and the need for sustainability.

YoungMinds

Suite 11, Baden Place, Crosby Row, London SE1 1YW
T: 020 7089 5050
Helpline: 0808 802 5544
E: ymenquiries@youngminds.org.uk
www.youngminds.org.uk
Chief Executive: Sarah Brennan
YoungMinds is the UK's leading charity committed to improving the emotional wellbeing and mental health of children and young people. Driven by their experiences we campaign, research and influence policy and practice.
Employees: 35
Volunteers: 15

Youth Access

1–2 Taylors Yard, 67 Alderbrook Road, London SW12 8AD
T: 020 8772 9900
E: admin@youthaccess.org.uk
www.youthaccess.org.uk
Director: Barbara Rayment
Youth Access is the national membership organisation for young people's information, advice, counselling and support services (YIACS). It promotes and encourages the growth of young people's counselling and advisory services; promotes good practice in these services; provides a forum for individuals and agencies; and promotes public recognition of the importance of these services.
Employees: 5

Youth Action Network

Crest House, 7 Highfield Road, Edgbaston, Birmingham B15 3ED
T: 020 7278 1041
F: 0121 455 9697
E: yokeu@ncvys.org.uk
www.youthactionnetwork.org.uk
Chief Executive: Davina Goodchild
Youth Action Network is the national organisation with unique experience and expertise in the Youth Action approach to volunteering.

Our main aims are to develop and support all things Youth Action, so that it is known about and practised more widely.

Our vision is for all young people to have the opportunity to participate in Youth Action volunteering and develop their own solutions to community needs.
Employees: 10
Volunteers: 10

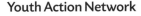

Youth at Risk

The Old Warehouse, 31 Upper King Street, Royston, Hertfordshire SG8 9AZ
T: 01763 241120
F: 01763 244735
E: sue@youthatrisk.org.uk
www.youthatrisk.org.uk
Chief Executive Officer: Sue Handly
Our mission is to enable society's most disadvantaged, difficult and damaged young people to transform their lives and build a future beyond their present expectations; the main activity is to advance the social education of young people at risk either from physical, mental or sexual abuse, drug or other substance abuse, criminal activity, poverty, homelessness, unemployment or illiteracy.
Employees: 11
Volunteers: 800

Youth Sport Trust

SportPark, Loughborough University, 3 Oakwood Drive, Loughborough, Leicestershire LE11 3QF
T: 01509 226600
E: info@youthsporttrust.org
www.youthsporttrust.org
Our charity is passionate about helping all young people to achieve their potential by delivering high-quality physical education and sport.
Regional offices: 1

YouthNet

1st Floor, 50 Featherstone Street, London EC1Y 8RT
T: 020 7250 5700
F: 020 7250 3695
E: media@youthnet.org
www.youthnet.org
Chief Executive: Emma Thomas
YouthNet helps young people make choices today for a brighter tomorrow, by providing impartial information and support about anything and everything for 16 to 25 year olds, whenever and wherever they need it; inspiring them to get involved. YouthNet do this primarily through their three websites: TheSite.org, do-it.org and Lifetracks.com
Employees: 50
Regional offices: 1

Youthscape

3A Upper George Street, Luton, Bedfordshire LU1 2QX
T: 01582 877220
E: chris.curtis@youthscape.co.uk
CEO: Chris Curtis

YWCA England and Wales

New Barkley House, 234 Botley Road, Oxford OX2 0HP
T: 01865 304209
F: 01865 204805
E: info@platform51.org
www.ywca-gb.org.uk
YWCA is the leading charity working with the most disadvantaged young women in England and Wales. Young women face unique problems in today's society. They are largely unheard and lack influence. We want a future where they can overcome prejudice and take charge of their own lives. We run services to support them and campaign with them to combat the discrimination they face.
Employees: 250
Regional offices: 19

Zoological Society of London

Regent's Park, London NW1 4RY
T: 020 7449 6253
F: 020 7586 5743
E: ian.meyrick@zsl.org
www.zsl.org
Director General: Ralph Armond
By conducting scientific research, we promote zoology and the conservation of biological diversity, the welfare of animals and care and breeding of endangered species. We foster public interest and participation in conservation worldwide.
Employees: 725
Volunteers: 300
Regional offices: 1

Zurich Community Trust (UK) Limited

PO Box 1288, Swindon,
Wiltshire SN1 1FL
T: 01793 511227
F: 01793 506982
E: kate.hodges@zct.org.uk
www.zct.org.uk
Head of Zurich Community Trust: Pam Webb
The umbrella for all Zurich's community involvement in the UK and supports the most disadvantaged people. A registered charity in its own right, Zurich Community Trust gives time, money and skills donated by Zurich and its employees in the UK. The Zurich Community Trust has a long history of pioneering grant-making to support less popular issues, and works in genuine partnership with charities and supports around 600 local, national and overseas charities each year.
Employees: 18
Volunteers: 2600
Income: £2,833,000 (2012-13)

INDEX

THE VOLUNTARY AGENCIES DIRECTORY

2014

Spadework Ltd
Tamil Refugee Training and Education Centre
Third Age Trust (National Office U3A)
Training for Life
Training Opportunities
UK Skills
Women and Manual Trades
Women's Technology and Education Centre
Workbase Training
Workers' Educational Association

ADVISORY SERVICES

**see also ADVOCACY SERVICES;
ALBANIAN COMMUNITY GROUPS,
ANGOLAN COMMUNITY GROUPS;
BENGALI COMMUNITY GROUPS;
CHINESE COMMUNITY GROUPS;
CONGOLESE COMMUNITY GROUPS;
ETHIOPIAN COMMUNITY GROUPS;
FINANCIAL ADVICE SERVICES;
IMMIGRATION ADVICE & SUPPORT
GROUPS; IRANIAN COMMUNITY
GROUPS; LEGAL ADVISORY & SUPPORT
SERVICES; PHILIPPINE COMMUNITY
GROUPS; TRAVELLER GROUPS; WEST
INDIAN COMMUNITY GROUPS**

Advice Services Alliance
Advice UK
Cass Centre for Charity Effectiveness
Christians Abroad
Citizens Advice
Cult Information Centre
Direct Help & Advice (DHA)
Enterprising Futures
Family Lives
Federation of Private Residents
    Associations Ltd
Gharweg Advice Training and Careers Centre
INQUEST
LASA
National Information Forum
Olmec
Partnership at Work
Prisoners Advice Service
Rochas Foundation UK
Royal Society for the Prevention of Accidents
Sahara Communities Abroad (SACOMA)
SWAN Advice Network
Way Foundation

DISABILITIES
Action on Disability and Development
Asian Peoples Disability Alliance Ltd
CHANGE
DIAL UK
Disability Alliance
Disability Awareness in Action
Disability Law Service
Disabled Living Foundation
RICABILITY Incorporating RICA (Research
    Institute for Consumer Affairs)

ADVOCACY SERVICES

**see also ADVISORY SERVICES; LEGAL
ADVISORY & SUPPORT SERVICES;**

PEACE CAMPAIGNS; POLITICAL ENGAGEMENT
Action for Advocacy
Action for Social Integration
Advocacy Resource Exchange
Campaign for Freedom of Information
Citizens Income Trust
Conscience the Peace Tax Campaign
Consumers' Association
Direct Help & Advice (DHA)
Fraud Advisory Panel
Henry George Foundation of Great
    Britain Ltd
Joint Council for the Welfare of Immigrants
Library Campaign
Minority Rights Group International
National Council for Voluntary Organisations
National Youth Advocacy Service
Onside
SEAP
Transparency International (UK)
United Nations Association
Vegetarian Society UK Ltd

MEDICAL
Action Against Medical Accidents
Bladder and Bowel Foundation
Medact

AFRICAN & AFRO-CARIBBEAN COMMUNITY SUPPORT GROUPS

1990 Trust
Action for Social Integration
Africa Development Network
African and Caribbean Voices Association
African Community Development
    Foundation
African Community Partnership
Angolan Civic Communities Alliance
Black Training and Enterprise Group
Community Action Project
Community of Congolese Refugees in
    Great Britain
Dudley Caribbean and Friends Association
Ethiopian Community in Britain
Ethiopian Community Centre in the UK
Nubian Life Resource Centre Ltd
Sahara Communities Abroad (SACOMA)
Welwitschia Welfare Centre
West Indian Standing Conference

HEALTH
African Caribbean Leukaemia Trust
African HIV Policy Network
African Medical and Research Foundation UK
Black and Ethnic Minority Diabetes
    Association
Black Health Agency
Ethiopian Health Support Association
Forum for Health and Wellbeing, The
HIV/Aids Association of Zambia UK
Innovative Vision Organisation

AIDS & HIV

African Community Involvement
    Association
African HIV Policy Network
AVERT
Body and Soul
British HIV Association
Cara Trust
Children of Africa
CRUSAID
Ernest Foundation
Food Chain (UK) Ltd
HIV/Aids Association of Zambia UK
Innovative Vision Organisation
JAT (formerly Jewish AIDS Trust)
Macfarlane Trust
Medical Foundation for HIV and Sexual
    Health (MEDFASH)
National AIDS Trust
Pan London HIV/AIDS Providers Consortium
Positively UK
St Peters House Project
Terrence Higgins Trust

ALBANIAN COMMUNITY GROUPS

Albanian Youth Action
Shpresa Programme (Albanian for Hope)

ALCOHOL AWARENESS & SUPPORT GROUPS

Addaction
ADFAM
Al-Anon Family Groups UK and Eire
Alcohol Concern
Alcohol Education and Research Council
Alcoholics Anonymous
ARP
British National Temperance League
Campaign Against Drinking and Driving
Drinkaware Trust
Drug and Alcohol Action Programme
Hope UK
Institute of Alcohol Studies
Kenward Trust
Life For The World
The Matthew Project
Medical Council on Alcohol
Phoenix Futures
Portman Group Trust

ALLERGIES

Action Against Allergy
Allergy UK
Anaphylaxis Campaign
The Medic Alert Foundation

ALTERNATIVE MEDICINE

See COMPLEMENTARY MEDICINE

ANGOLAN COMMUNITY GROUPS

Angolan Civic Communities Alliance
Welwitschia Welfare Centre

ANIMALS

See also BIRD PROTECTION; CAT WELFARE; DOG WELFARE & SERVICES FOR THE DISABLED; HORSE WELFARE; MARINE LIFE & WATERWAYS; WILDLIFE CONSERVATION
Animal Rescue Charity
Blue Cross
Booktrust
Born Free Foundation
British Union for the Abolition of Vivisection
Animal Welfare Foundation
Buglife – the Invertebrate Conservation Trust
Catholic Concern for Animals
Community Hygiene Concern
Compassion in World Farming
Donkey Sanctuary
Environmental Investigation Agency Trust
Farm Animal Welfare Network
Herpetological Conservation Trust
Humane Slaughter Association
International Fund for Animal Welfare
League Against Cruel Sports
Mammal Society
National Animal Welfare Trust
PDSA for Pets in Need of Vets
People's Trust for Endangered Species
Rare Breeds Survival Trust
Royal Society for the Prevention of Cruelty to Animals
Society for the Protection of Animals Abroad
The Brooke
Universities Federation for Animal Welfare
Woodgreen The Animal Charity
World Society for the Protection of Animals

ANXIETY DISORDERS

See STRESS & ANXIETY DISORDERS

ARMED FORCES WELFARE AND SUPPORT SERVICES

See also EX-SERVICEMEN & WOMEN SUPPORT SERVICES
ABF, The Soldiers' Charity
RAF Association
Royal Air Forces Association
Royal Air Force Benevolent Fund
Royal Air Force Music Charitable Trust
Royal British Legion
Royal British Legion Industries Ltd
Royal Naval Benevolent Society for Officers
Royal Naval Benevolent Trust
Soldiers, Sailors, Airmen and Families Association (SSAFA)
Women's Royal Naval Service Benevolent Trust

ARTHRITIC CONDITIONS

Arthritic Association
Arthritis and Musculoskeletal Alliance
Arthritis Care
Arthritis Research Campaign
Horder Centre for Arthritis
National Ankylosing Spondylitis Society (NASS)
National Rheumatoid Arthritis Society

ARTISTS & PERFORMERS SUPPORT GROUPS

Equity Trust Fund
Federation of British Artists
Royal Literary Fund
Royal Theatrical Fund
Society of Authors

ARTS & CULTURE

See also ARTISTS & PERFORMERS SUPPORTGROUPS; ARTS EDUCATION; DANCE; MUSEUMS; MUSIC; THEATRES; ADDICTION SUPPORT SERVICES
Arts and Business
Arts Council England
Artswork
Audi Design Foundation
British Council
British Federation of Film Societies – Cinema for All
British and International Federation of Festivals
Collage Arts
Comic Relief
Common Ground
CreativePeople
Free Form Arts Trust
Guernsey Arts Commission
National Association of Decorative and Fine Arts Societies
National Campaign for the Arts
National Operatic and Dramatic Association
Paintings in Hospitals
Royal Television Society
Southbank Mosaics CIC
Template Foundation
Voluntary Arts Network

COMMUNITY GROUPS

Doncaster Community Arts
Finn-Guild
Kurdish Cultural Centre

FOR DISABILITIES & SPECIAL NEEDS

Action Space Mobile Ltd
Conquest Art – Enriching the Lives of Physically Disabled People
ContoC Christmas Concerts
Disabled Photographers' Society
EPIC Arts
Full Body and the Voice
Living Paintings
Mind the Gap

REHABILITATION OF OFFENDERS

Clean Break

ADDICTION RECOVERY

Vita Nova

ARTS EDUCATION

Associated Board of the Royal Schools of Music
Council for Dance Education and Training
Full Body and the Voice
Music Education Council
Raw Material Music and Media Education
Royal Academy of Dance

ASIAN COMMUNITY SUPPORT GROUPS

1990 Trust
Adhar Project
Alternative for India Development
Asha Projects
Asia House
Asian Family Counselling Service
Black Health Agency
Chinese in Britain Forum
Chinese Information and Advice Centre
Consortium of Bengali Associations
Council of British Pakistanis
Forum for Health and Wellbeing, The
Imkaan
India Welfare Society
Indian Volunteers for Community Service
QED-UK

ASYLUM SEEKERS

See REFUGEE & ASYLUM SEEKERS SUPPORT GROUPS

AUTISM

Autism Independent UK
Autism Plus
Autism Research Ltd – The International Autistic Research Organisation
Education and Services for People with Autism Ltd
Hillingdon Autistic Care and Support
Resources for Autism
The National Autistic Society
Thorne House Services for Autism Limited

AUTOIMMUNE DISORDERS

Behcet's Syndrome Society
British Society for Immunology
Coeliac UK
Guillain Barre Syndrome Support Group

BEHAVIOURAL DIFFICULTIES – SUPPORT FOR PARENTS & CARERS

See also FAMILY SUPPORT

Caspari Foundation for Educational Therapy and Therapeutic Teaching
Centre for Fun and Families
Friends Therapeutic Community Trust
Home Start
Home-Start Canterbury and Coastal
Home-Start Haringey
Home-Start International
Home-Start South Hams, Plymouth and Tavistock
Home-Start Stoke-on-Trent
Home-Start Worthing and Adur
Place2Be
Right From the Start
Social Emotional and Behavioural Difficulties Association
The Respite Association

BEHAVIOURAL TRAINING

Alternatives to Violence Project, Britain

BELIEF SYSTEMS

See also BUDDHIST FAITH; CHRISTIAN FAITH GROUPS; HUMANISM; JEWISH FAITH; MUSLIM FAITH
Alliance of Healing Associations
Faith Based Regeneration Network UK
Guild of Pastoral Psychology
Inter Faith Network for the United Kingdom
Isbourne Foundation
Krishnamurti Foundation Trust
Maharishi Foundation

BENEVOLENT SOCIETIES

Actors Benevolent Fund
Architects Benevolent Society
Cavell Nurses' Trust
Furnishing Trades Benevolent Association
Journalists Charity
LionHeart
National Benevolent Fund for the Aged
National Benevolent Institution
Rainy Day Trust
Royal Agricultural Benevolent Institution
Royal Air Force Benevolent Fund
Royal Fund for Gardeners' Children
Royal Literary Fund
Royal Medical Benevolent Fund
Royal Naval Benevolent Society for Officers
Royal Naval Benevolent Trust
Royal Navy and Royal Marine Children's Fund
Royal Theatrical Fund
Royal UK Beneficent Association (Rukba)
Sailors' Families' Society
Shipwrecked Fishermen and Mariners' Royal Benevolent Society
Society for the Assistance of Ladies in Reduced Circumstances
SBA The Solicitors' Charity
Women's Royal Naval Service Benevolent Trust

BENGALI COMMUNITY GROUPS

Consortium of Bengali Associations

BEREAVEMENT SUPPORT GROUPS

Aftermath Support
Child Bereavement UK
Child Death Helpline
Compassionate Friends
Cruse Bereavement Care
Jewish Bereavement Counselling Service
Jigsaw 4ULtd
Rainbow Centre for Children affected by Life-Threatening Illnesses or Bereavement
Support after Murder and Manslaughter
Support after Murder & Manslaughter Abroad
Survivors of Bereavement by Suicide
Winston's Wish

BIPOLAR DISORDERS

Bipolar UK

BIRD PROTECTION

British Ornithologists' Union
British Trust for Ornithology
Royal Society for the Protection of Birds

BISEXUAL SUPPORT GROUPS

See GAY/LESBIAN/BISEXUAL/TRANSGENDER SUPPORT GROUPS

BLINDNESS & SIGHT IMPAIRMENT

Action for Blind People
Association of Blind and Partially Sighted Teachers and Students
Association of Blind Piano Tuners
Blind Veterans UK
British Blind Sport
British Retinitis Pigmentosa Society
British Wireless for the Blind Fund
Eyeless Trust for Young People and Children Born Without Eyes
International Glaucoma Association
Keratoconus Self-Help and Support Association
Look National Office
Macular Disease Society
National Federation of the Blind of the UK
National Music for the Blind
Nystagmus Network
Partially Sighted Society
Quality of Life Trust
Queen Alexandra College
Royal Blind Society for the UK
Royal London Society for the Blind
Royal National College for the Blind
Royal National Institute of the Blind
RP Fighting Blindness
SeeAbility
Victa Children Ltd
Vision 2020 (UK) Ltd
Vista
Vitalise

Walsall Society for the Blind
WESC Foundation

OVERSEAS AID
Blindaid Africa
ORBIS Charitable Trust
Sight Savers International
Vision Aid Overseas

RESOURCES FOR
CALIBRE Audio Library
International Guide Dog Federation
Listening Books
Living Paintings
RNIB National Library Service
Seeing Dogs Alliance, The
Telephones for the Blind Fund
Thomas Pocklington Trust
Torch Trust for the Blind
Vision Homes Association

BLOOD DISORDERS

Haemophilia Society
Macfarlane Trust
UK Thalassaemia Society

BUDDHIST FAITH

Friends of the Western Buddhist Order
Golden Buddha Centre
Karuna Trust
New Kadampa Tradition – International Kadampa Buddhist Union

BUILDINGS & OPEN SPACE PROVISION

See also ACCOMMODATION & HOUSING
CAN
CRASH
Ethical Property Foundation
Learning Through Landscapes
Open Spaces Society
Room – the National Council for Housing and Planning
Upkeep
Walter Segal Self Build Trust

BUSINESS & ENTERPRISE DEVELOPMENT

Arts and Business
Association of Community Based Business Advice
Black Training and Enterprise Group
Business in the Community
CAN
Co-operatives UK
Enterprising Futures
Ethical Trading Initiative
Industry and Parliament Trust
Institute of Business Ethics
Novas-Ouvertures Group Ltd
School for Social Entrepreneurs
Social Enterprise Coalition
Social Firms UK

Social Market Foundation
Social Partnership
Social Venture Network UK
Society for Co-operative Studies
Strategic Planning Society
Supporters Direct
Training Opportunities
Twin Ltd
UnLtd - the Foundation for Social
  Entrepreneurs
Web of Hope
Yorkshire Coast Enterprise Ltd

BUSINESS & INDUSTRY TRAINING

Association for Project Management
Association of Charity Independent
  Examiners
British Psychological Society
CASE Kent
Enterprising Futures
IGD
Institute for War and Peace Reporting
Inter-Action Associated Charitable Trusts
  and Companies
IVAR
Learning South West
Mathematics in Education and Industry
Royal Institute of British Architects
School for Social Entrepreneurs
Skillset Sector Skills Council
Social Emotional and Behavioural Difficulties
  Association
Stephen Lawrence Charitable Trust
Voluntary Sector Training
Women's Engineering Society (WES)

CANCER RESEARCH & SUPPORT GROUPS

African Caribbean Leukaemia Trust
Angel Foundation
Bowel Cancer UK
Breakthrough Breast Cancer
Breast Cancer Campaign
Breast Cancer Care
Breast Cancer Haven
Breast Cancer Research Trust
British Association for Cancer Research
British Colostomy Association
British Dental Health Foundation
British Voice Association
Cancer Care Society
Cancer Laryngectomee Trust
Cancer Research UK
CancerBACKUP
Cancerkin
Childhood Eye Cancer Trust
CLIC Sargent
Dimbleby Cancer Care
Elimination of Leukaemia Fund
Free Access Cancer Therapy Database
Gorlin Syndrome Group
Institute of Cancer Research
Leukaemia Care

Lymphoma Association
Macmillan Cancer Support
Marie Curie Cancer Care
National Cancer Alliance
Neuroblastoma Society
Ovacome
Ovarian Cancer Action
Prostate Cancer Charity
Roy Castle Lung Cancer Foundation
The Haven
Teenage Cancer Trust
Weston Park Hospital Development Fund Ltd

CARDIAC CONDITIONS & RESEARCH

British Cardiac Patients Association
British Cardiovascular Society
British Heart Foundation
Cardiomyopathy Association
Children's Heart Federation
Circulation Foundation
Coronary Artery Disease Research Association
Coronary Prevention Group
Heart UK, The Cholesterol Charity
Little Hearts Matter
Magdi Yacoub Institute
The Somerville Foundation

CAREERS GUIDANCE & ADVICE

Careers Research and Advisory Centre Ltd
Guidance Council
Industrial Careers Foundation
Medway Youth Trust

CARERS

Carers Association Southern Staffordshire
Carers Centre (LeicesterShire & Rutland)
Carers Network
Carers Trust
Carers UK
Carers' Support - Canterbury,
  Dover & Thanet
Carer Support Wiltshire
Crossroads Care Cheshire West Wirral
  and Shropshire
Enfield Carers Centre
Hambleton and Richmondshire Carers Centre
Solihull Carers Centre
The Respite Association
Trafford Carers Centre

CAT WELFARE

Cats Protection
Feline Advisory Bureau
Yorkshire Cat Rescue

CEREBAL PALSY

Scope
Stars Organisation Supporting Cerebral Palsy
Worster-Drought Syndrome Support Group

CHILD PROTECTION

Ann Craft Trust
ChildLine
Churches Child Protection Advisory Service
ECPAT UK
Kidscape Campaign for Children's Safety
NAPAC
NSPCC
Rape and Sexual Abuse Support Centre
Youth at Risk

CHILDBIRTH SUPPORT SERVICES

See also POST-NATAL SUPPORT GROUPS;
PREGNANCY; STILLBIRTH & NEONATAL
DEATH
Association of Radical Midwives
Birth Companions
Group B Strep Support
Royal College of Midwives

MULTIPLE BIRTHS
Multiple Births Foundation
Twins and Multiple Births Association

CHILDCARE PROVISION

4Children
Caldecott Foundation
Christian Family Concern
Children England
Children's Hope Foundation
National Childminding Association
National Day Nurseries Association
Young Lancashire

CHILDREN & YOUNG PEOPLE

See also BEHAVIOURAL DIFFICULTIES-
SUPPORT FOR PARENTS & CARERS;
CHILD PROTECTION; CHILDCARE
PROVISION, CHILDREN'S ACTIVITY
SCHEMES & CLUBS; COUNSELLING &
PSYCHOTHERAPY SERVICES; EXCHANGE
AND OVERSEAS PROGRAMMES;
FURTHER & HIGHER EDUCATION;
HELPLINES; INFANT & CHILDREN
HEALTH SUPPORT GROUPS; INFANT,
PRIMARY & SECONDARY SCHOOL
EDUCATION; INFANT DEATH;
OUTDOOR EDUCATION & RESIDENTIAL
COURSES; PRE-SCHOOL EDUCATION
4Children
Action for Children
Albert Kennedy Trust
Andy Cole Children's Foundation
Attlee Foundation
Barnardo's
British Youth Council
Bromley Y
Buttle UK
Cabrini Children's Society
Centre for Youth and Community
  Development
Child Accident Prevention Trust
Child Migrants Trust

Child Poverty Action Group
Children and Families Across Borders
(Formerly ISS UK)
Children's Family Trust
Children's Society
City Year London
Coram Family
Coram Voice
Council for Awards in Children's Care
and Education
CXK Limited
Dorset Youth Association
Each One. Teach One
End Child Poverty
Friendship Works
Independent Academic Research Studies
(IARS)
Inspire!
Learning Plus UK
Learning South West
Life Education Centres
Missing People
National Association of Child Contact Centres
National Children's Centre
National Youth Advocacy Service
National Youth Agency
NCB
New Choices for Youth
Potential Plus UK
Peacemakers
Prince's Trust
Roald Dahl's Marvellous Children's Charity
Skill: National Bureau for Students with
Disabilities
Skill Force
The Eikon Charity
Variety
Young Enterprise
Young Lives
Young People's Support Foundation
Youthscape

ACCOMMODATION & HOUSING
Break
BYHP
Centrepoint
Foyer Federation
KeyChange Charity
Nightstop UK Ltd
Reedham Trust
Together for Short Lives

ADVICE & INFORMATION SERVICES
Children's Legal Centre
Counselling and Support for Young People
Kidsaid
National Association of Children's
Information Services
Off Centre Hackney
Youth Access
YouthNet

ALCOHOL & DRUG EDUCATION
Hope UK
Kenward Trust
National Association for Children of Alcoholics
The Matthew Project

ARTS & MUSIC
Action Space Mobile Ltd
Artswork
Creative Youth Network
Live Music Now!
National Association of Youth Theatres
National Youth Orchestra of Great Britain

BEREAVEMENT SUPPORT
Child Bereavement UK
Child Death Helpline
Cruse Bereavement Care
Jigsaw 4 U Ltd
This Way Up Youth Project
Winston's Wish

CARE SERVICES
NAGALRO
Shaftesbury Young People
Spurgeon's Child Care
TACT
Who Cares? Trust

COMMUNITY GROUPS
Albanian Youth Action
Centre for Youth and Community
Development

DISABILITIES
3H Fund
Bexley Snap
BIBIC
CALIBRE Audio Library
Care Co-ordination Network UK
Children's Trust
Dame Hannah Rogers School
Deaf Education through Listening and Talking
Deaf Ex-Mainstreamers Group
Down's Syndrome Educational Trust
Dreamflight
Elizabeth Foundation
Eyeless Trust for Young People and Children
Born Without Eyes
Fledglings Family Services
KIDS
Kids Can Achieve
Lifeworks Charity Ltd
Medical Engineering Resource Unit
National Blind Children's Society
National Deaf Children's Society (NDCS)
Newlife
Parents for Inclusion
Parents in Partnership
Reach- Association for Children with Hand
or Arm Deficiency
The Log Cabin
Treloar Trust
Victa Children Ltd
Whizz-Kidz

GRANTS
Attlee Foundation
BBC Children in Need Appeal
Buttle UK
Children's Country Holidays Fund
Dream Makers National Charity

Dreamflight
Dreams Come True Charity
Help a Poor Child
Make-A-Wish Foundation UK
Prince's Trust
Promise Dreams
Royal Fund for Gardeners' Children
Royal Navy and Royal Marine Children's Fund
Sailors' Families' Society
School Journey Association

OVERSEAS AID
AbleChildAfrica
Blindaid Africa
Children of Africa
Coalition to Stop the Use of Child Soldiers
EveryChild
Gesar Foundation
Global Care
Hope and Homes for Children
Hope for Children
Humanity at Heart
International Children's Trust
Minorities of Europe
Orphans In Need
Orphans Relief Fund and Charitable Trust
Plan UK
Railway Children
Save the Children UK
SOS Children's Villages UK
Street Child Africa
Wishing Well

PERSONAL DEVELOPMENT
Chance UK
Changemakers
Children and Young People's
Diversity Role Models
Empowerment Project
Endeavour Training Ltd
Explore
Headliners (formerly known as Children's
Express)
Inspire!
Nell Bank
The BB Group
TOC H
Woodcraft Folk
Wooden Spoon Society

RESEARCH
Anna Freud Centre
Caspari Foundation for Educational Therapy
and Therapeutic Teaching
ChildNet International
The Social Research Unit
Trust for the Study of Adolescence Ltd

SPEECH & COMMUNICATION SUPPORT
AFASIC
I CAN

SPORT & RECREATION
Children's Links
Construction Industry Trust for Youth
Fair Play for Children Association/
Charitable Trust

Get Hooked on Fishing Charitable Trust
Happy Days Children's Charity
Horse Rangers Association
(Hampton Court) Ltd
International Youth Hostel Federation
Kidsout UK
Play-Train
Youth Sport Trust

CHILDREN'S ACTIVITY SCHEMES & CLUBS

See also OUTDOOR EDUCATION & RESIDENTIAL COURSES

3 Villages Youth Project
Adventure Service Challenge Scheme
Air Cadets
Amal Trust
Ambition
Army Cadet Force Association
Be Your Best Foundation
Boys' Brigade
Camberwell After School Project
CCI
Central Organisation Maritime Pastimes
and Sport Services
Church Lads and Church Girls Brigade
Duke of Edinburgh's Award
Farms for City Children
Girlguiding UK
Girls' Brigade
Girls' Venture Corps Air Cadets
Grail
Hi8us Projects Ltd
HOST UK
Jewish Lads and Girls Brigade including
Outreach/Kiruv and Hand-in-Hand
Young Volunteers
National Council for Voluntary Youth Services
National Federation of Young Farmers' Clubs
National Youthbike
Salmon Youth Centre
Scout Association
Sea Cadets
Tall Ships Youth Trust
World Association of Girl Guides and
Girl Scouts
Young Christian Workers
Young Explorers Trust
Young People Matter

CHILDREN'S HEALTH

See INFANT & CHILDREN'S HEALTH SUPPORT GROUPS

CHINESE COMMUNITY GROUPS

Chinese in Britain Forum
Chinese Information and Advice Centre

CHRISTIAN FAITH GROUPS

A Rocha UK
Aid to the Church in Need (UK)
Apostleship of the Sea
Arthur Rank Centre

Association of Interchurch Families
Bible Society
BMS World Mission
British and International Sailors' Society
Brothers of Charity Services
CARITAS – Social Action
Catholic Association for Racial Justice
Catholic Clothing Guild
Catholic Concern for Animals
Catholic Truth Society
Catholic Women's League
Chapter 1
Christian Aid
Christian Camping International
Christian Education
Christian Family Concern
Church Action on Poverty
Church Army
Church Housing Trust
Church Pastoral Aid Society
College of St Barnabas
Canterbury Diocesan Board of Finance
Evangelical Alliance
Field Lane Foundation
Friends Therapeutic Community Trust
General Assembly of Unitarian and Free
Christian Churches
Gideons International in the British Isles
Grail
Greater World Christian Spiritualist
Association
Grubb Institute
Guild of Health Ltd
Guild of St Raphael
Institute for Community and
Development Studies
Kenward Trust
KeyChange Charity
Kingham Hill Trust
Kingsway International Christian Centre
Langley House Trust
League of Mercy
Leeds Church Institute
Lesbian and Gay Christian Movement
Linacre Centre for Healthcare Ethics
Lodge Trust
Lutheran Council of Great Britain
Maroa Christian Counselling International
MB Reckitt Trust
MHA Care Group
Mission Care
Mothers Union
Oasis UK
Pax Christi
People of God Trust
Pilgrim Hearts Trust
Prison Fellowship England and Wales
Prospects for People with Learning Disabilities
Queen Victoria Seamen's Rest
Salvation Army
Scripture Union
Society for Promoting Christian Knowledge
Time For God
Torch Trust for the Blind
UCCF

CHILDREN & YOUNG PEOPLE

Bethany Children's Trust
Boys' Brigade
Centre for Youth and Community
Development
Friendship Works
GFS Platform for Young Women
Girls' Brigade
Ormiston Children and Families Trust
Student Christian Movement
YMCA England
Young Christian Workers

OVERSEAS AID

African Pastors' Fellowship
BMS World Mission
Catholic Agency for Overseas Development
Christians Abroad
Global Care
Global Connections
HCPT the Pilgrimage Trust
Intercontinental Church Society
InterHealth Worldwide
Learning Plus UK
Lightforce International
Mission Aviation Fellowship UK
Pontifical Mission Societies
Roald Dahl's Marvellous Children's Charity
Tearfund
Youthscape

CHROMOSOMAL DISORDERS

Fragile X Society
Klinefelter Organisation
Unique - Rare Chromosome Disorder
Support Group
Williams Syndrome Foundation Ltd

CHRONIC FATIGUE SYNDROME

See ME

CIRCULATORY DISORDERS

Raynaud's and Scleroderma Association

CIRCUMCISION

Norm UK

CITIZENSHIP

Anne Frank Trust UK
Beacon Fellowship Charitable Trust
British Future
Changemakers
Citizen Organising Foundation
Citizenship Foundation
Common Purpose
Nell Bank
Operation Black Vote OPUS
Royal Humane Society
Royal Life Saving Society UK

COMMUNICATIONS & MEDIA HANDLING

Community Media Association
Community Network
Institute for War and Peace Reporting
Inter-Action Associated Charitable Trusts and Companies
International Institute of Communications
Media Trust
Media Wise Trust
PublicMedia
Radio Amateurs' Emergency Network
Raw Material Music and Media Education
Royal Television Society
Royal Theatrical Fund
Rural Media Company
Telephone Helplines Association
Television Trust for the Environment
U.K-PublicMedia cic

COMMUNITY DEVELOPMENT & RESOURCES

See also UMBRELLA & RESOURCE BODIES; VOLUNTARY ACTION AND VOLUNTEER CENTRES

Access Community Trust
Alington House Community Association
Andover Neighbourcare
ARVAC Association for Research in the Voluntary and Community Sector
Be Your Best Foundation
Bracknell Forest Voluntary Action
Care Bond
Centre for Volunteering and Community Leadership
Chara Trust
Churches Community Work Alliance
Citizen Organising Foundation
Civic Trust
Commonwork Land Trust
Community Action Project
Community Action Network
Community Action Wyre Forest
Community Development Agency Limited
Community Development Finance Association
Community Development Foundation
Community First
Community Foundation Network
Community Links
Community Links Bromley
Community Matters
Develop Enhancing Community Support
Empowering West Berkshire
Faith Based Regeneration Network UK
Federation for Community Development Learning
Gosport Voluntary Action
Groundwork UK
Highbury Vale Blackstock Trust
Horsham Voluntary Action
Hubventures
Institute for Community and Development Studies
John Huntingdon's Charity

Maidstone Community Support Centre
Mark Hall and Netteswell Community Association
Middlesbrough Voluntary Development Agency
National Association for Voluntary and Community Associations
National Communities Resource Centre
National Community Safety Network
National Village Halls Forum
Neighbourhood Initiatives Foundation
North Taunton Partnership
Number One Community Trust (TW) Ltd
Peel Institute
Portchester Community Association
Quaker Social Action
Renaisi Limited
Selby Trust Ltd
The Cambridge Centre
The Vince Hines Foundation
Toynbee Hall
TPAS England
Urban Forum
Voluntary Action Calderdale
Voluntary Action Islington
Voluntary Action South West Surrey
Voluntary Services Lewisham
West Harton Churches Action Station Ltd
Wigan and Leigh CVS

COMPLEMENTARY MEDICINE

Association of Reflexologists
British Acupuncture Council
British Homeopathic Association
British Medical Acupuncture Society
General Council and Register of Naturopaths
Get Well UK
Homeopathy Action Trust
Institute for Complementary Medicine
National Institute of Medical Herbalists
Society for Complementary Medicine
Society of Homeopaths

COMPUTERS & THE INTERNET

AbilityNet
British Computer Society
ChildNet International
Citizens Online
Computers for Charities
Deafax
DoBe.org
FunderFinder
GreenNet Educational Trust
Online Centres Foundation

CONGENITAL DISORDERS

Arthrogryposis Group (TAG)
HemiHelp

CONGOLESE COMMUNITY GROUPS

Community of Congolese Refugees in Great Britain

CONSERVATION GROUPS

See also HERITAGE & HISTORY GROUPS

BTCV trading as The Conservation Volunteers
Churches Conservation Trust
Conservation Foundation
CSV Cathedral Camps
Fountain Society
Friends of Friendless Churches
The Greensand Trust
Historic Churches Preservation Trust
Institute for Conservation
Pilgrim Trust
Plant Heritage
UK Overseas Territories Conservation Forum

CONTINENCE (INCONTINENCE) ADVICE & SUPPORT

Association for Continence Advice
Bladder and Bowel Foundation
ERIC – Education and Resources for Improving Childhood Continence

COUNSELLING & PSYCHOTHERAPY SERVICES

See also CHILDREN AND YOUNG PEOPLE; PSYCHOLOGY

Albany Trust
Arbours Association Limited
Asian Family Counselling Service
British Association for Counselling and Psychotherapy
British Association of Psychotherapists
Bromley Y
Counselling
Counselling and Support For Young People
Crisis Counselling for Alleged Shoplifters
Immigrant Counselling and Psychotherapy
Institute of Group Analysis
Institute of Psychoanalysis
Institute of Transactional Analysis
Kidsaid
Maroa Christian Counselling International
Metanoia Institute
Off Centre Hackney
Psychosynthesis and Education Trust
Refugee Therapy Centre
Research Society of Process Orientated Psychology UK
Samaritans
TASHA Foundation
UK Council for Psychotherapy
wpf Counselling and Psychotherapy
Youth Access

CRIME & JUSTICE

Centre for Crime and Justice Studies
Circles UK
Clinks
Crime Concern Trust
Crime Reduction Initiatives
Crimestoppers Trust
Fellowship of Reconciliation
Howard League for Penal Reform

Hextol Foundation
Skill: National Bureau for Students
    with Disabilities
St Loye's Foundation
The Orpheus Centre

EMPLOYMENT & PROGRESSION SERVICES
Action on Disability and Work UK
Association of Disabled Professionals
Employment Opportunities for People
    with Disabilities
Lifeline Community Projects
Papworth Trust
Progress Recruitment Shaw Trust Ltd
Spadework Ltd
TAEN - The Age and Employment Network

OVERSEAS AID RECREATION
Albrighton Trust Ltd
Conquest Art – Enriching the Lives
    of Physically Disabled People
Disabled Photographers' Society
Disaway Trust
Drake Music Project
EPIC Arts
EXTEND Exercise Training Ltd
Gardening for Disabled Trust
Jubilee Sailing Trust
Lin Berwick Trust
Love Walk
Mind the Gap
Peter le Marchant Trust
Ryder-Cheshire Volunteers
Scout Holiday Homes Trust
Thrive
Tourism for All UK

REHABILITATION SERVICES
ASPIRE

RESOURCES FOR
AbilityNet
British Society of Disability and Oral Health
CALIBRE Audio Library
Clothing Solutions for Disabled People
Dog AID (assistance in Disability)
Dogs for the Disabled
Independent Home Solutions CIC
International Guide Dog Federation
Listening Books
National Music for the Blind
Remap
Seeing Dogs Alliance, The
Sequal Trust
Talking Newspaper Association of the UK

RESPITE CARE & SHORT BREAKS
3H Fund
Adventist Special Needs Association (ASNA)
HCPT the Pilgrimage Trust
Shared Care Network
Take a Break Warwickshire

SPORT
Disability Snowsport UK
Disability Sport England

English Federation of Disability Sport
National Association of Swimming Clubs for
    the Handicapped
Riding for the Disabled Association
Rounders England
RYA Sailability
United Kingdom Sports Association for
    People with Learning Disabilities
WheelPower

DIVORCE & SEPARATION
College of Sexual and Relationship Therapists
    (COSRT)
National Association of Child Contact Centres

DOG WELFARE & SERVICES FOR THE DISABLED
Dog AID (assistance in Disability)
Dogs for the Disabled
Dogs Trust
Greyhound Rescue West of England (GRWE)
International Guide Dog Federation
Seeing Dogs Alliance, The

DOMESTIC VIOLENCE
See ABUSE & VIOLENCE – VICTIMS' &
SURVIVORS' SUPPORT SERVICES

DRUG AWARENESS & SUPPORT GROUPS
Action Against Tranquilliser Addiction
Addaction
Adverse Psychiatric Reactions Information
    Link (APRIL)
ADFAM
ARP
Cranstoun
Drug and Alcohol Action Programme
Drugscope
Foundation66
Hope UK
Inside Out TrustKenward Trust
Life For The World
Lifeline Project Ltd
The Matthew Project
Mentor Foundation (International)
New Start Trust
Phoenix Futures
Re-Solv
Release
SOLVE IT
Streetscene
Westminster Drug Project

DYSLEXIA SUPPORT
Adult Dyslexia Organisation
British Dyslexia Association
Dyslexia Action
Helen Arkell Dyslexia Centre

EATING DISORDERS
beat
Foundations UK
Overeaters Anonymous

EDUCATION
See also ADULT EDUCATION; ARTS
EDUCATION; EDUCATION & TRAINING
SERVICES FOR OVERSEAS RELIEF;
ENVIRONMENTAL EDUCATION;
FURTHER & HIGHER EDUCATION;
HOME SCHOOLING; INFANT, JUNIOR &
SENIOR EDUCATION; LITERACY &
NUMERACY; OUTDOOR EDUCATION &
RESIDENTIAL COURSES; PRE-SCHOOL
EDUCATION; SPECIAL EDUCATIONAL
NEEDS; TEACHING STANDARDS &
SUPPORT
Academy of Youth
ASDAN
Association for Language Learning
British Association for Early Childhood
    Education
British Council
Caldecott Foundation
Campaign for Learning
CapeUK
Centre for Youth and Community
    Development
Christian Education
Council for Awards in Children's Care and
    Education
DEA
Down's Syndrome Educational Trust
Foundation for Conductive Education
High/Scope UK
Human Scale Education
INCLUDE
Joint Educational Trust
Learning from Experience Trust
Learning plus UK
National Association for Able Children
    in Education
National Association for Gifted Children
Open Doors International Language School
Pestalozzi International Village Trust
Rathbone
Treloar Trust
UK Youth

EDUCATION & TRAINING SERVICES FOR OVERSEAS RELIEF
CAMFED International
Corona Worldwide
Education Action International
Filipino International Emergency Services
    Training
International Network for the Availability of
    Scientific Publications
INTRAC
Skillshare International
Think Global
Tools for Self Reliance
Windle Trust International

EMERGENCY SERVICES

Dorset and Somerset Air Ambulance
East Anglian Air Ambulance

EMPLOYMENT & JOB SEARCH SUPPORT SERVICES

Apex-Works
Black Training and Enterprise Group
Employment Opportunities for People
  with Disabilities
Enham
First Step Trust
Involvement and Participation Association
  (IPA)
Medway Youth Trust
Pay and Employment Rights Service
  (Yorkshire) Ltd
Public Concern at Work
Royal London Society for the Blind
Social Firms UK
Social Partnership
TAEN - The Age and Employment Network
Tomorrow's People Trust
Wainwright Trust
Workaid
Work Foundation
Workbase Training
WRN (Women Returners' Network) in
  Association with the Grow Trust

END OF LIFE ISSUES

Dignity in Dying
Help the Hospices
Hospice Information Service
Prospect Hospice

ENDOCRINE DISORDERS

Association for Multiple Endocrine Neoplasia
  Disorder

ENERGY CONSERVATION

Centre for Sustainable Energy
Energy Conservation and Solar Centre
National Energy Action
National Energy Foundation

ENVIRONMENTAL EDUCATION

10:10
Fieldfare Trust Ltd
Nakuru Environmental and Conservation
  Trust
National Association for Environmental
  Education (UK)

ENVIRONMENTAL SUPPORT GROUPS

**See also CONSERVATION; ENERGY
CONSERVATION; ENVIRONMENTAL
EDUCATION; GARDENS & GARDENING;
MARINE LIFE & WATERWAYS; TREE
PRESERVATION**

10:10
Association of Natural Burial Grounds
Aviation Environment Federation
BirdLife International
Black Environment Network
British Cave Research Association
British Ecological Society
British Naturalists' Association
British Waterways
Centre for Accessible Environments
Common Ground
Don't Dump That Ltd
Earthwatch (Europe)
Environment Council
Environmental Awareness Trust
Environmental Law Foundation
Envision
Eye on the Wild
Friends of the Earth
Galapagos Conservation Trust
Game Conservancy Trust
Global Action Plan
Global Witness Limited
Green Alliance
Greenpeace UK
Groundwork North East
ICA:UK
Institute for European Environmental Policy
  London
International Tree Foundation
Keep Britain Tidy
Landlife
Landscape Design Trust
Landscape Institute
Living Streets
National Flood Forum
Nakuru Environmental and Conservation
  Trust
New Economics Foundation
Panos Institute
People and Planet
Rainforest Foundation UK
Royal Geographical Society
Television Trust for the Environment
Trust for Urban Ecology
Wildfowl and Wetlands Trust
Women's Environmental Network
Young People's Trust for the Environment
  and Nature Conservation

ENVIRONMENTAL HEALTH & POLLUTION

Chartered Institute of Environmental Health
Keep Britain Tidy
National Society for Clean Air and
  Environmental Protection
Noise Abatement Society

ENZYME DEFICIENCY DISORDERS

Gauchers Association Ltd

EPILEPSY

David Lewis Centre

Epilepsy Action
Epilepsy Research UK
Fable Charity
National Centre for Young People with
  Epilepsy
National Society for Epilepsy

EQUAL OPPORTUNITIES & DIVERSITY

**See also AFRICAN & AFRO-CARIBBEAN
SUPPORT GROUPS; OLDER PEOPLE;
WOMEN**

Action for Social Integration
British Future
Catholic Association for Racial Justice
Diversity Hub
Inclusion London
Jewish Council for Racial Equality
Lifeworks Charity Ltd
MOSAIC Black and Mixed Parentage
  Family Group
Overseas Development Institute
Parity
Runnymede Trust
Wainwright Trust

ETHIOPIAN COMMUNITY GROUPS

Ethiopian Community Centre in the UK
Ethiopian Community in Britain

EX-SERVICEMEN & WOMEN SUPPORT SERVICES

ABF The Soldiers' Charity
Blind Veterans UK
British Limbless Ex-Service Men's Association
Douglas Haig Memorial Homes
  (Haig Homes)
Ex-Services Mental Welfare Society
  (COMBAT STRESS)
Fire Fighters Charity
Joint Committee of the Order of St John and
  British Red Cross Society
League of Remembrance
National Gulf Veterans and Families
  Association
Not Forgotten Association
Officers' Association
Royal British Legion Women's Section
Royal Corps of Signals Benevolent Fund
Royal Star and Garter Homes

EXCHANGE & OVERSEAS PROGRAMMES

AIESEC (UK) Ltd
Commonwealth Youth Exchange Council
Concordia (Youth Service Volunteers) Ltd
Gap Activity Projects (GAP) Ltd
International Youth Hostel Federation
Nakuru Environmental and Conservation
  Trust
Outreach International

Raleigh International
School Journey Association

FACIAL DISFIGUREMENT

Changing Faces
Headlines, the Craniofacial Support Group
Let's Face it Support Network for the Facially
  Disfigured

FAMILY SUPPORT

**See also GRANDPARENTS; PARENTING;
BEHAVIOURAL DIFFICULTIES – SUPPORT
FOR PARENTS & CARERS**
Asian Family Counselling Service
Aylesham Neighbourhood Project
Association for Family Therapy
Catholic Children's Society
Contact a Family
Direct Help & Advice (DHA)
Family Action
Family Action In Our Region (FAIR)
Family and Childcare Trust
Family Education Trust (Family and
  Youth Concern)
Family Holiday Association
Family Links
Family Lives
Family Matters Institute
Family Rights Group
Furzedown Family Centre
Gingerbread
Home Start
Home-Start Canterbury and Coastal
Home-Start Haringey
Home-Start International
Home-Start South Hams, Plymouth
  and Tavistock
Home-Start Stoke-on-Trent
Home-Start Worthing and Adur
Kith and Kids
MOSAIC Black and Mixed Parentage
  Family Group
Mothers Union
National Association of Children's
  Information Services
One Parent Families
Opportunity Links
Parents for Inclusion
Relatives and Residents Association
Single Parent Action Network
Surrey Nurturing Links
Working Families

(DEALING WITH) ADDICTIONS
ADFAM
Al-Anon Family Groups UK and Eire

(DEALING WITH) BEHAVIOURAL
PROBLEMS
Centre for Fun and Families

FORCES FAMILIES
ABF, The Soldiers' Charity
Army Families Federation

National Gulf Veterans and Families
  Association
Royal British Legion
Royal British Legion International
Royal British Legion Women's Section
Royal Corps of Signals Benevolent Fund
Soldiers, Sailors, Airmen and Families
  Association (SSAFA)
War Widows Association of Great Britain
  and Northern Ireland

HEALTH
Duchenne Family Support Group
Fledglings Family Services
Look National Office
Primary Ciliary Dyskinesia Family Support
  Group

PRISONER SUPPORT
Action for Prisoners' Families
Partners of Prisoners and Families Support
  Group
Prison Advice and Care Trust
Prison Chat UK
Prisoners Abroad
Prisoners' Families and Friends Service

FINANCIAL ADVICE SERVICES

ABF, The Soldiers' Charity
Big Society Capital
Chartered Institute of Taxation
Community Accountancy Self-Help
Elizabeth Finn Care
Money Advice Trust
Money Management Council
Pensions Advisory Service
ShareAction
TaxAid UK

FOSTERING

See ADOPTION & FOSTERING SERVICES

FURTHER & HIGHER
EDUCATION

AGCAS
Air League
British Accreditation Council for Independent
Further and Higher
Business and Education London South
ContinYou
East London Advanced Technology Training
Education
Education and Services for People with
  Autism Ltd
Fellowship of Postgraduate Medicine
Fellowship of the School of Economic Science
GuildHE Limited
Hammersmith Management College
HiPACT
International Students House
Open College Network YHR
Parliamentary Human Rights Foundation
  2000
PFEG (Personal Finance Education Group)

Royal Society of Medicine
Sutton Trust
UK Council for International Student Affairs
Universities UK
University Association for Contemporary
  European Studies
UCCF

GAMBLING SUPPORT GROUPS

GamCare

GARDENS & GARDENING

Association of Gardens Trusts
Garden History Society
Garden Organic
Gardening for Disabled Trust
Good Gardeners' Association
National Council for the Conservation of
  Plants and Gardens
National Gardens Scheme
National Society of Allotments and Leisure
  Gardeners
Painswick Rococo Garden Trust
Thrive
Women's Farm and Garden Association

GASTRO-INTESTINAL
DISORDERS

CORE
National Association for Colitis and Crohn's
  Disease

GAY / LESBIAN /BISEXUAL/
TRANSGENDER SUPPORT
GROUPS

Albert Kennedy Trust
Broken Rainbow LGBT Domestic Violence
  Service UK
Consortium
Consortium of Lesbian, Gay and Bisexual
  Voluntary and Community Organisations
Lesbian and Gay Christian Movement
Lesbian and Gay Foundation
Naz Foundation International
PACE
Positively UK
Regard
Stonewall
Stonewall Housing

GENETIC DISORDERS

Cornelia de Lange Syndrome Foundation
DebRA Ehlers-Danlos Support Group
Genetic Disorders UK
Genetic Interest Group
Haemochromatosis Society
Marfan Association UK
National Society for Phenylketonuria (UK) Ltd
Neurofibromatosis Association
Prader-Willi Syndrome Association (UK)
Primary Ciliary Dyskinesia Family Support
  Group

MULTIPLE SCLEROSIS; MUSCULAR DISORDERS; NEURODEVELOPMENTAL DISORDERS; NEUROLOGICAL DISORDERS; NUTRITION; OBESITY; ORGAN DONATION & REGISTERS; PAIN MANAGEMENT; PALLIATIVE CARE; PATIENT CARE & ENVIRONMENT; PHOBIAS & PANIC ATTACKS; PREGNANCY; REPRODUCTIVE & SEXUAL HEALTH CARE; SPINAL CARE; STILLBIRTH & NEONATAL DEATH; STRESS & ANXIETY DISORDERS; STROKE
ADHD Solutions cic
AFIYA Trust
African Community Involvement Association
African Medical and Research Foundation UK
Alliance of Healing Associations
Aquaterra Leisure
Black Health Agency
British Medical Acupuncture Society
Cicely Northcote Trust
Community Health Involvement and Empowerment Foundation
DIPEx Charity
Ethiopian Health Support Association
Forum for Health and Wellbeing, The
Healing Foundation
Health Foundation
Medical Foundation for the Care of Victims of Torture
Medical Women's Foundation
Men's Health Forum
Metamorphic Association
NFSH Charitable Trust Limited
NHS Confederation
PACE
Pituitary Foundation
Royal College of General Practitioners
Royal College of Nursing
Royal Society for Public Health
Royal Society of Health
Self management uk
St John Ambulance
UK Public Health Association

ADVOCACY
Action Against Medical Accidents
Bladder and Bowel Foundation
Medact

ANGELMAN SYNDROME
Angelman Syndrome Support Group
ASSERT

ASTHMA
Asthma UK

BLOOD PRESSURE
Blood Pressure Association

CONGENITAL DIAPHRAGMATIC HERNIA
Freshwinds

CARE FOR LIFELIMITING ILLNESSES
CDH UK
Rainy Day Trust

CYSTIC FIBROSIS
Cystic Fibrosis Trust

DEPRESSION
Depression Alliance
Fellowship of Depressives Anonymous

DOWN'S SYNDROME
Down's Heart Group
Down's Syndrome Association
Down's Syndrome Educational Trust

DRUGS & REACTIONS
Information Link

GLYCOGEN STORAGE
Association for Glycogen Storage Diseases (UK)

HEADACHE & MIGRAINE
World Headache Alliance

HERPES
Herpes Viruses Association

HOLISITIC MEDICINE
British Holistic Medical Association

HUNTINGON'S DISEASE
Huntingdon's Disease Association

HYGIENE
Community Hygiene Concern

INFERTIILTY
Infertility Network UK

LARYNGECTOMY
Cancer Laryngectomee Trust
National Association of Laryngectomy Clubs

LEG ULCERATION
The Lindsay Leg Club Foundation

LEPROSY
Leprosy Mission
St Francis Leprosy Guild

LUNG DISORDERS
British Lung Foundation

LUPUS
Lupus Patients Understanding and Support (LUPUS)
LUPUS UK
LYME DISEASE
Lyme Disease Action

MENINGITIS
Meningitis Research Foundation
Meningitis Now
Meningitis UK

MIGRAINE
Migraine Action Association
The Migraine Trust

MUCOPOLYSACCHARIDE DISEASES
Society for Mucopolysaccharide Diseases

NARCOLEPSY
Narcolepsy Association UK (UKAN)

OEDEMAS
British Lymphology Society
Lymphoedema Support Network

OSTEOARTHRITIS
The Paget's Association

OSTEOPOROSIS
National Osteoporosis Society

OVERSEAS AID
African Medical and Research Foundation UK
Asian Foundation for Help
Blindaid Africa
Health Unlimited
Healthlink Worldwide
HealthProm
InterHealth Worldwide
Tropical Health and Education Trust
Y Care International
PARKINSON'S DISEASE
Parkinson's Disease Society of the UK

POLIO
British Polio Fellowship

PROSTATE DISORDERS
Prostate Research Campaign UK

RARE DISORDERS
Rare Disease UK

RESOURCES
IA (The Ileostomy and Internal Pouch Support Group)

RESTRICTED GROWTH DISORDERS
Restricted Growth Association

REYE'S SYNDROME
National Reye's Syndrome Foundation of the UK

SEASONAL AFFECTIVE DISORDER (SAD)
SAD Association

SEIZURES
Syncope Trust and Reflex Anoxic Seizures

SHINGLES
Shingles Support Society

SICKLE CELL
Sickle Cell Society

SPINA BIFIDA & HYDROCEPHALUS
SHINE

THYROID DISORDERS
British Thyroid Foundation

TOURETTE SYNDROME
Tourette Syndrome (UK) Association

TRACHEO-OESOPHAGEAL SUPPORT
Tracheo-Oesophageal Fistula Support Group

TUBERCULOSIS
Target Tuberculosis

UNNAMED SYNDROMES
Syndromes Without a Name

URINARY SYSTEM
Urostomy Association

VOMITING
Cyclical Vomiting Syndrome Association UK

HEALTH PROFESSIONALS, ORGANISATIONS FOR

AMSPAR
Association for Perioperative Practice
Association for the Study of Obesity
British Association for Immediate Care
British Homeopathic Association
British Institute of Radiology
British Medical Acupuncture Society
British Psychological Society
British School of Osteopathy
Cavell Nurses' Trust
Centre for the Advancement of Interprofessional Education
Chiropractic Patients' Association
Foundation of Nursing Studies (FoNS)
Metanoia Institute
PRIMHE
Psychosynthesis and Education Trust
Research Society of Process Orientated Psychology UK
Royal College of Midwives
Royal Medical Benevolent Fund
Social Emotional and Behavioural Difficulties Association
Society for Endocrinology
Society for General Microbiology
Society of Homeopaths
The Queen's Nursing Institute

HEALTHCARE & MEDICAL TRAINING

AMSPAR
Association for Perioperative Practice
British Acupuncture Council
British Association for Counselling and Psychotherapy
British Association for Immediate Care
British Association of Dermatologists
British Medical Acupuncture Society
Animal Welfare Foundation
College of Sexual and Relationship Therapists (COSRT)
Fellowship of Postgraduate Medicine
Foundation of Nursing Studies (FoNS)
Metanoia Institute

Response International
Royal College of Midwives
Royal College of Nursing
Royal College of Paediatrics and Child Health
Royal Society of Medicine

HEARING IMPAIRMENTS
See DEAFNESS & HEARING IMPAIRMENTS

HEART DISEASE

See CARDIAC CONDITIONS
HELPLINES
ChildLine
Get Connected Helpline
Helplines Partnership
Message Home Helpline
SupportLine
The Cry-sis Helpline

HERITAGE & HISTORY GROUPS

See also CONSERVATION GROUPS
Ancient Monuments Society
Antiquarian Horological Society
Architectural Heritage Fund
Arts Council England
British Archaelogical Association
British Association for Local History
British Association of Friends of Museums
Churches Conservation Trust
Council for British Archaelogy
CSV Cathedral Camps
Evacuees Reunion Association
Heritage Link
Historic Churches Preservation Trust
Historical Association
National Association of Decorative and Fine Arts Societies
National Trust
Pilgrim Trust
Rescue: the British Archaeological Trust
SAVE Britain's Heritage
Society for the Protection of Ancient Buildings
Society of Antiquaries of London
The Heritage Alliance
Theatres Trust
Transport Trust

HIGHER EDUCATION

See FURTHER & HIGHER EDUCATION

HISTORY

See HERITAGE & HISTORY GROUPS

HOME SCHOOLING

Education Otherwise
Otherwise Club

HOMELESSNESS SUPPORT

Access Community Trust
Alone in London
Big Issue Foundation

Centrepoint
Chapter 1
Church Housing Trust
CRASH
Crisis
Direct Help & Advice (DHA)
Emmaus UK
Foyer Federation
Habitat for Humanity Great Britain
Homeless International
Homeless Link
HOPE
House of Saint Barnabas in Soho
Kairos Community Trust
New Horizon Youth Centre
Nightstop UK Ltd
P3
Salvation Army
Shelter
The Vine Day Centre
Western Lodge

HORSE WELFARE

British Horse Society
International League for the Protection of Horses
Mare and Foal Sanctuary

HOSPICES

See also LIFE-LIMITING ILLNESS SUPPORT
Barnsley Hospice
Claire House – Hospice for Children
Greenwich & Bexley Community Hospice
Help the Hospices
Hospice Information Service
St Joseph's Hospice Association

HUMAN & PERSONAL RIGHTS

Advice on Individual Rights in Europe
Airey Neave Trust
Amnesty International Secretariat
Amnesty International United Kingdom
Anti-Slavery International
Article 19
British Institute of Human Rights
Equality Forum
Fair Trials International
Global Witness Limited
Independent Academic Research Studies (IARS)
Interrights
JUSTICE
Kurdish Human Rights Project
Liberty
Minority Rights Group International
Parliamentary Human Rights Foundation 2000
People and Planet

HUMAN RESOURCES

See STAFF & VOLUNTEERS

HUMANISM

Association for Humanistic Psychology
British Humanist Association
Conway Hall Ethical Society

HYPERACTIVITY DISORDERS

ADD Information Services
Hyperactive Children's Support Group

IMMIGRATION ADVICE & SUPPORT GROUPS

AVID (Association of Visitors to Immigration
    Detainees)
Child Migrants Trust
Immigrant Counselling and Psychotherapy
Immigration Advisory Service
Joint Council for the Welfare of Immigrants
Migrant Helpline
Migrants Resource Centre

IMMUNE SYSTEM DEFICIENCIES

British Society for Immunology
Chronic Granulomatous Disorder

INCONTINENCE

See CONTINENCE (INCONTINENCE) ADVICE & SUPPORT

INFANT & CHILDREN HEALTH SUPPORT GROUPS

ACT (The Association for Children's Palliative
    Care)
Action for Sick Children
ADD Information Services
Angelman Syndrome Support Group
Association for Child and Adolescent Mental
    Health
Association of Young People with ME
Ataxia-Telangiectasia Society
BLISS
Bobath Centre for Children with Cerebral
    Palsy
Brook
CDH UK
Changing Faces
Cherubs UK
Child Brain Injury Trust
Child Growth Foundation
Childhood Eye Cancer Trust
Children's Burns Trust
Children's Heart Federation
Children's Trust
CLIC Sargent
Crohn's in Childhood Research Association
CRY-SIS Helpline
Diabetes Foundation
Different Strokes
Down's Heart Group
Down's Syndrome Association
Ear Foundation
Edward's Trust

ERIC – Education and Resources for
    Improving Childhood Continence
Great Ormond Street Hospital Children's
    Charity
HemiHelp
Hyperactive Children's Support Group
Information Point for Centronuclear and
    Myotubular Myopathy
Maternal and Childhealth Advocacy
    International
Matthew Trust
National Autistic Society National Centre for
    Young People with Epilepsy
Neuroblastoma Society
Perthes Association
Peter Rigby Trust
Rainbow Centre for Children affected by
    Life-Threatening Illnesses or Bereavement
Rainbow Trust Children's Charity
Rapid Effective Assistance for Children with
    Potentially Terminal Illness
Reach – Association for Children with Hand
    or Arm Deficiency
Roald Dahl's Marvellous Children's Charity
Royal College of Paediatrics and Child Health
Sick Children's Trust
Teenage Cancer Trust
The Somerville Foundation
Tiny Tickers
Together for Short Lives
WellChild
YoungMinds

CANCER SUPPORT

Childhood Eye Cancer Trust
CLIC Sargent
Neuroblastoma Society
Teenage Cancer Trust

MENTAL HEALTH

Association for Child and Adolescent
    Mental Health
Matthew Trust
YoungMinds

INFANT, PRIMARY & SECONDARY SCHOOL EDUCATION

See also CHILDREN AND YOUNG PEOPLE; SPECIAL EDUCATIONAL NEEDS

Advisory Centre for Education Ltd (ACE)
Association for Physical Education
Association for Science Education
Association of Governing Bodies of
    Independent Schools
British Centre for Science Education
Commonwealth Education Trust
Dame Hannah Rogers Trust
Deaf Ex-Mainstreamers Group
Each one. Teach one
Heads Teachers and Industry Ltd
Inspire!
Learning Plus UK
Montessori Education UK Ltd
Muntham House School Ltd

National Association for Small Schools
National Association for the Teaching
    of English
National Association of Independent Schools
    and Non Maintained Special Schools
National Confederation of Parent Teacher
    Associations
Newcastle Action for Parent and Toddler
    Groups Initiative
Peacemakers
PFEG (Personal Finance Education Group)
School Governors' One-Stop Shop
School Home Support Service (UK)
School Library Association
SciDevNet
Sutton Trust
Teacher Support Network
The Cry-sis Helpline
Volunteer Reading Help

INFANT DEATH

Foundation for the Study of Infant Deaths
Together for Short Lives

INTERNET

See COMPUTERS AND THE INTERNET

IRANIAN COMMUNITY GROUPS

Iranian Association

JEWISH FAITH

Anglo Jewish Association
Association of Jewish Ex-Servicemen
    and Women
Association of Jewish Refugees in
    Great Britain
Board of Deputies of British Jews
British ORT
Community Security Trust
Council of Christians and Jews
Institute for Jewish Policy Research
Interlink Foundation
Jewish Association for the Mentally Ill
Jewish Bereavement Counselling Service
Jewish Council for Racial Equality
Jewish Lads and Girls Brigade including
    Outreach / Kiruv and Hand-in-Hand Young
    Volunteers Projects
Jewish Marriage Council
Jewish Women's Aid
Liberal Judaism
League of Jewish Women
Leo Baeck College
Lubavitch Youth
Norwood
Merseyside Jewish Community Care

KIDNEY DISORDERS

Africa Resource for Kidney Diseases
British Kidney Patient Association
National Kidney Federation
Polycystic Kidney Disease Charity

LEADERSHIP SKILLS TRAINING

Ashoka (UK) Trust
Diversity Hub
Heads Teachers and Industry Ltd
Institute for Community and Development Studies
Leadership Trust Foundation
Sports Leaders UK
The ELLA Foundation
Windsor Leadership Trust

LEARNING DISABILITIES SUPPORT

See also AUTISM; DYSLEXIA SUPPORT

Ann Craft Trust
ARC
Aurora Health Foundation
British Institute of Learning Disabilities
Brothers of Charity Services
Canterbury Oast Trust
Care Co-ordination Network Cymru
Caring and Sharing Trust
CHANGE
Circles Network
Dante Leigh Foundation
Elfrida Society
Elizabeth Fitzroy Support
Education and Services for People with Autism Ltd
First Step Trust
Full Body and the Voice
Gazelle Personal Development
HFT the Home Farm Trust
Judith Trust
Kingwood Trust
L'Arche
Leo Trust
Life Opportunities Trust
Life Works
Lodge Trust
MacIntyre Care
Mencap
Powerhouse
Prospects for People with Learning Disabilities
Reading Mencap
Real Life Options
Realife Trust
Rescare
RESPOND
Sequal Trust
Shaping Our Lives - National User Network
Signalong Group
Spadework Ltd
St Albans Mencap
The Grace Eyre Foundation
Thera Trust
United Kingdom Sports Association for People with Learning Disability
United Response
Us in a Bus
Walsingham
Working with Words

CHILDREN'S SUPPORT SERVICES

BIBIC

Children's Trust
Norwood

LEGAL ADVISORY & SUPPORT SERVICES

Action Against Medical Accidents
Bar Pro Bono Unit
CANS Legal Information
Children's Legal Centre
Coram Children's Legal Centre
Disability Law Service
Environmental Law Foundation
Fair Trials International
International Action Network on Small Arms
International Alert
LASA
Law Centres Network
LawWorks
Legal Action Group
Norfolk Community Law Service Ltd
Public Law Project
RCJ Advice Bureau
Refugee Legal Centre
Release
Rights of Women
Sangat Advice Centre
Solicitors Pro Bono Group

LESBIAN SUPPORT GROUPS

See GAY/LESBIAN/BISEXUAL/ TRANSGENDER SUPPORT GROUPS

LIFE-LIMITING ILLNESS SUPPORT

Edward's Trust
Rainbow Trust Children's Charity
Rainbow Centre for Children affected by Life-Threatening Illnesses or Bereavement
Rapid Effective Assistance for Children with Potentially Terminal Illness

LITERACY & NUMERACY

Basic Skills Agency
Caxton Trust (working name Catch Up)
National Literacy Association
National Literacy Trust
Reading Matters
Workbase Training
Working with Words

LIVER DISORDERS

British Liver Trust
Primary Sclerosing Cholangitis Trust

MARINE LIFE & WATERWAYS

Advisory Committee on the Protection of the Sea
Association of River Trusts
British Waterways
CIWEM
Inland Waterways Association
Marine Conservation Society
Marine Stewardship Council

Sea Watch Foundation
WDC, Whale and Dolphin Conservation

MARRIAGE & RELATIONSHIP COUNSELLING

Explore
Family Links
Family Matters Institute
Jewish Marriage Council
Marriage Care
National Family Mediation
One Plus One Marriage and Partnership Research
Relate Brighton, Hove, Worthing and Districts
Relate Central Office
Relate Lincolnshire
The Tavistock Centre for Couple Relationships

ME (MYALGIC ENCEPHALOMYELITIS) (CHRONIC FATIGUE SYNDROME)

25% ME Group – Support for Severe ME Sufferers
Action for ME
Association of Young People with ME
ME Association

MEDIA

See COMMUNICATIONS AND MEDIA HANDLING

MEDIATION SERVICES

Centre for Effective Dispute Resolution
Mediation Works Milton Keynes

MEDICAL RESEARCH

Action Medical Research
Alcohol Education and Research Council
Arthritis Research Campaign
Association of Medical Research Charities
Association of Research Ethics Committees
Autism Research Ltd – The International Autistic Research Organisation
Blond McIndoe Research Foundation
Brain and Spine Foundation
Brain Research Trust
Breakthrough Breast Cancer
Breast Cancer Campaign
Breast Cancer Research Trust
British Association for Cancer Research
British Cardiovascular Society
CADASIL Research and Support Trust
Cancer Research UK
Coronary Artery Disease Research Association
Crohn's in Childhood Research Association
Diving Diseases Research Centre
Dr Hadwen Trust for Humane Research
Epilepsy Research UK
Foundation for Women's Health Research and Development
Fund for the Replacement of Animals in Medical Experiments

NUTRITION
Food Commission

OBESITY
British Obesity Surgery Patient Association Trust
Weight Concern

OLDER PEOPLE ADVISORY & SUPPORT GROUPS
Action on Elder Abuse
Age Concern Central Lancashire
Age Concern Eastbourne
Age Concern Hassocks and District
Age Concern Havering
Age UK
Age UK Portsmouth
Age UK Runnymede and Spelthorne
Assist UK
Beth Johnson Foundation
Centre for Policy on Ageing
Contact the Elderly Counsel and Care
Crowthorne Old Age To Teen Society (COATS)
Friends of the Elderly
Guideposts Trust Limited
Help Age International
Help the Aged
International Longevity Centre – UK
Little Sisters of the Poor
National Pensioners Convention
Nubian Life Resource Centre Ltd
RICABILITY Incorporating RICA (Research Institute for Consumer Affairs)
Shingles Support Society

EDUCATION & TRAINING
Third Age Trust (National Office U3A)

GRANTS & LOANS
AFTAID – Aid for the Aged in Distress
National Benevolent Fund for the Aged
National Benevolent Institution
Royal UK Beneficent Association (Rukba)

HOUSING & CARE PROVISION
Abbeyfield Society
AgeCare
Almshouse Association
Anchor Trust
Brendoncare Foundation
Care and Repair England Ltd
Elderly Accommodation Counsel
KeyChange Charity
MHA Care Group
Relatives and Residents Association
Sons of Divine Providence

HEALTH CARE
2CARE
British Geriatrics Society
Shingles Support Society

RECREATION
Albrighton Trust Ltd

EPIC Arts
EXTEND Exercise Training Ltd

RETIREMENT
Civil Service Retirement Fellowship
Retirement Trust

ORGAN DONATION & REGISTERS
Anthony Nolan Trust
British Organ Donor Society
Transplant Sport UK

OUTDOOR EDUCATION & RESIDENTIAL COURSES
See also CHILDREN'S ACTIVITY SCHEMES & CLUBS
Active Training and Education Trust
Adventure Unlimited
Institute for Outdoor Learning

OVERSEAS AID & DEVELOPMENT
Action Against Hunger UK
Action to Regenerate Community Trust
ActionAid
African Pastors' Fellowship
Alternative for India Development
Andy Cole Children's Foundation
Asian Foundation for Help
Association of Dance Therapists
ATD Fourth World UK Ltd
Bangla-Aid UK
Book Aid International
British Overseas NGOs for Development
British Red Cross Society
Build Africa
Catholic Agency for Overseas Development
Christians Abroad
Coalition to Stop the Use of Child Soldiers
CORD
Environment Africa Trust
Eritrean Relief Association (UK)
FARM – Africa
Generation for Change and Development
Gordon Barclay Vietnam Fund
Hamlet Trust
Harvest Help
Help Age International
HOPE Worldwide
Human Relief Foundation
IDE-UK
International Community Assist
International Development Partnerships
International Service
Islamic Relief Worldwide
Landmine Action
Management Strategies for Africa
Minorities of Europe
Mission Aviation Fellowship UK
Mission Care
MOC Foundation
Muslim Aid

One World Action
Oxfam
Overseas Development Institute
People in Aid
Pontifical Mission Societies
Progressio
Rainforest Foundation UK
REDAID
Refugee Action
Refugee Council
Self Help Africa
Survival International
Tearfund
Tibet Relief Fund
Transaid
Transform Africa
Village Aid
World Development Movement
World Emergency Relief
World Vision UK

CHILDREN & YOUNG PEOPLE
AbleChildAfrica
Blindaid Africa
Children of Africa
Coalition to Stop the Use of Child Soldiers
EveryChild
Gesar Foundation
Global Care
Home-Start International
Hope and Homes for Children
Hope for Children
Humanity at Heart
International Children's Trust
Merlin
Minorities of Europe
Orphans in Need
Orphans Relief Fund and Charitable Trust
Plan UK
Railway Children
Save the Children UK
SOS Children's Villages UK
Street Child Africa
Wishing Well
Y Care International

EDUCATION & TRAINING
Ashoka (UK) Trust
CAMFED International
Children of Africa
Corona Worldwide
Filipino International Emergency Services Training
Harvest Fields Commissioning International
HiPACT
International Network for the Availability of Scientific Publications
Practical Action
Skillshare International
Tools for Self Reliance
Windle Trust International

EQUIPMENT
Operation Florian

HEALTH
African Medical and Research Foundation UK

SOVA
UNLOCK - the National Association of
  Reformed Offenders

PROFESSIONAL BODIES' INFORMATION SERVICES

Bank Workers Charity
Charity Retail Association
Chartered Institute of Library and
  Information Professionals
Equity Trust Fund
Hospitality Action
LionHeart
National Association of Local Councils
Pharmacist Support
Registry Trust Limited
Royal Society of Medicine
Society of Authors
Textile Institute International
The Printing Charity

PSYCHOLOGY

See also COUNSELLING &
PSYCHOTHERAPY
Association for Humanistic Psychology
Society of Analytical Psychology

RECYCLING & WASTE MANAGEMENT

Composting Association
Don't Dump That Ltd
Furniture Re-use Network
International Institute for Environment
  and Development
Keep Britain Tidy
Waste Watch

REFUGEE & ASYLUM SEEKERS SUPPORT GROUPS

Action for Social Integration
Association of Visitors to Immigration
  Detainees
Asylum Aid
Boaz Trust
Community of Congolese Refugees in
  Great Britain
Ethiopian Community Centre in the UK
Ethiopian Community in Britain
Ethiopian Health Support Association
Gateway Community Action
Imkaan
Ockenden International
Olmec
Refugee Action
Refugee Council
Refugee Legal Centre
Refugee Therapy Centre
Sangat Advice Centre
Southampton and Winchester Visitors Group
STAR (Student Action for Refugees)
Tamil Refugee Training and Education Centre
Tibet Relief Fund

REHABILITATION

ADDICTIONS
Action on Addiction
Independence Initiative
Kairos Community Trust
Phoenix Futures
Salvation Army

PHYSICAL
ASPIRE
Back-Up (transforming lives after spinal
  cord injury)
Brainwave Centre Ltd
Headway Devon
LINK Centre for Deafened People
Psychiatric Rehabilitation Association
Rehab UK
St Loye's Foundation

REPRODUCTIVE & SEXUAL HEALTH CARE

Brook
College of Sexual and Relationship
  Therapists (COSRT)
Education for Choice
FPA
Interact Worldwide
JAT (formerly Jewish AIDS Trust)
Marie Stopes International
Medical Foundation for AIDS and
  Sexual Health (MEDFASH)
Naz Foundation International
Progress Educational Trust
Safehands for Mothers Charitable Trust
Terrence Higgins Trust

RESEARCH SUPPORT & POLICY DEVELOPMENT

See also MEDICAL RESEARCH:
PROFESSIONAL BODIES' INFORMATION
SERVICES
Arthur McDougall Fund
Audi Design Foundation
British Future
Careers Research and Advisory Centre Ltd
Cass Centre for Charity Effectiveness
Centre for Crime and Justice Studies
Centre for Effective Dispute Resolution
Centris
Charity Retail Association
Conway Hall Ethical Society
Evidence For Development
Historical Association
Inclusion London
Institute for Jewish Policy Research
Institute of Biology
National Centre for Social Research
New Economics Foundation
Police Foundation
Policy Studies Institute
Regional Studies Association
Rowntree Society
Royal Commonwealth Society
SABRE Research UK

Saferworld
Strategic Planning Society
The Clinic for Boundaries Studies

CITIZENSHIP
Operation Black Vote
OPUS

COMMUNITY DEVELOPMENT
ARVAC Association for Research in
  the Voluntary and Community Sector
Lifeline Community Projects

EDUCATION
Federal Trust for Education and Research
National Foundation for Educational
  Research in England and Wales
Royal Society

ENVIRONMENT
British Cave Research Association
British Ecological Society
Royal Geographical Society
Town and Country Planning Association

HERITAGE
British Archaeological Association
British Association for Local History
Society of Antiquaries of London

SOCIAL POLICY & CHANGE
British Future
Centris
Joseph Rowntree Foundation
Rowntree Society
Social Care Institute for Excellence
Social Research Association

RESIDENTIAL & CARE HOMES

British Home and Hospital for Incurables
Elizabeth Finn Care
Journalists Charity
Mission Care

EX-SERVICEMEN/WOMEN
Douglas Haig Memorial Homes
  (Haig Homes)
Royal Star and Garter Homes

FOR PEOPLE WITH DISABILITIES, LEARNING DISABILITIES & MENTAL HEALTH PROBLEMS
Aurora Charity
Canterbury Oast Trust
Carr-Gomm
Chaseley Trust
Community Housing and Therapy
Disabilities Trust
Education and Services for People with
  Autism Ltd
Foley House Trust
Hollybank Trust
Independent Living Alternatives
Leo Trust
Leonard Cheshire
Life Opportunities Trust

Orione Care
Real Life Options
Richmond Fellowship
Sons of Divine Providence
St John of God Care Services
Thomas Pocklington Trust
Thorne House Services for Autism Limited

RESPITE CARE

3H Fund
Adventist Special Needs Association (ASNA)
Break
Learning Through Landscapes
Rainbow Trust Children's Charity
Vitalise

RHEUMATISM

British Sjogren's Syndrome
British Society for Rheumatology

RURAL & FARMING COMMUNITIES

Action for Market Towns
Action with Communities in Rural England
Arthur Rank Centre
Associated Country Women of the World
Campaign to Protect Rural England
Camphill Village Trust Ltd
Composting Association
Countryside Restoration Trust
Countrywide Holidays Association
Farm Crisis Network
Farms for City Children
Federation of City Farms and Community
    Gardens
National Federation of Young Farmers' Clubs
Penwith Community Development Trust
Permaculture Association (Britain)
Pesticide Action Network UK
Plunkett Foundation
Ramblers' Association
Responsible Use of Resources in Agriculture
    and on the Land
Royal Agricultural Benevolent Institution
Rural Action Yorkshire
Rural Community Action Nottinghamshire
Rural Housing Trust
Rural Stress Helpline
Soil Association
Sustain: the Alliance for Better Food
    and Farming
Spitalfields City Farm
Television Trust for the Environment
Wildlife and Countryside Link
Wincanton Community Venture
Women's Farm and Garden Association

SEAFARERS & MARITIME WORKERS

Apostleship of the Sea
Federation of Merchant Mariners
International Committee on Seafarers Welfare
International Seafarers' Assistance Network

Merchant Navy Welfare Board
National Coastwatch Institute
Nautilus UK
Queen Victoria Seamen's Rest
Royal Alfred Seafarers Society
Royal National Lifeboat Institution
Royal National Mission to Deep Sea
    Fishermen
Sailors' Families' Society
Sea Cadets
Seafarers' Benefits Advice Line
Seafarers UK
Shipwrecked Fishermen and Mariners' Royal
    Benevolent Society
The Marine Society and Sea Cadets

SEXUAL ABUSE

See ABUSE & VIOLENCE - VICTIMS' &
SURVIVORS' SUPPORT SERVICES

SIGHT IMPAIRMENT

See BLINDNESS & SIGHT IMPAIRMENT

SMOKING 'STOP SMOKING' SUPPORT GROUPS

Action on Smoking and Health
QUIT

SOCIAL CARE & WELFARE

ATTEND
Avocet Trust
Break
British Association of Social Workers
British Sociological Association
CARITAS – Social Action
Catholic Clothing Guild
Clothing Solutions for Disabled People
Coal Industry Social Welfare Organisation
Community Integrated Care
Community of Reconciliation and Fellowship
Community Resilience
Council of Voluntary Welfare Work
Disaster Action
Disasters Emergency Committee
Field Lane Foundation
Food Chain (UK) Ltd
Foundation for Public Service Interpreting
Heritage Care
Home from Hospital Care after Treatment
In Kind Direct
International Social Service (UK)
Lifeline Community Projects
Mary Ward Centre
National Skills Academy for Social Care
NAGALRO
Rowntree Society
SCA Group
Skills for Care Ltd
Smile Support & Care
Social Care Association
Social Care Institute for Excellence
Stonham
Turning Point

Tutu Foundation UK
United Kingdom Homecare Association

CHILDREN & YOUNG PEOPLE

Child Migrant Trust
National Association of Toy and Leisure
    Libraries
National Council for Voluntary Youth Services
National Playbus Association

FAMILY SUPPORT

Family Action
Family Rights Group
Home Start
Home-Start International

RESEARCH

Cicely Northcote Trust
Joseph Rowntree Foundation
Social Research Association

SPECIAL EDUCATIONAL NEEDS

See also CHILDREN AND YOUNG
PEOPLE; INFANT, PRIMARY AND
SECONDARY EDUCATION
Action Space Mobile Ltd
Adventist Special Needs Association (ASNA)
Adventure Service Challenge Scheme
Centre for Studies on Inclusive Education
Choices 4 All
Dyslexia Action
Dyspraxia Foundation
Happy Days Children's Charity
Independent Panel for Special Education
    Advice
Kidsout UK
Muntham House School Ltd
National Association for Special Educational
    Needs
National Association of Independent Schools
    and Non Maintained Special Schools
Network 81
Nurture Group Network
Parents for Inclusion
Scout Holiday Homes Trust
Special Kids In the UK
South Lancashire Learning Disability Training
    Consortium
Together Trust

SPEECH & COMMUNICATION SUPPORT

AFASIC
British Stammering Association
British Voice Association
CONNECT – the Communication Disability
    Network
European League of Stuttering Associations
I CAN
Speakability (Action for Dysphasic Adults)
Voice Care Network UK

SPINAL CARE

See also NEUROLOGICAL DISORDERS
BackCare
Integrated Spinal Rehabilitation Foundation
Jennifer Trust for Spinal Muscular Atrophy
Scoliosis Association (UK)
Spinal Injuries Association
Steps Charity Worldwide
The SMA Trust

SPORT & RECREATION

Achieve Lifestyle
Association for Physical Education
CTC – UK's National Cycling Organisation
EXTEND Exercise Training Ltd
Fair Play for Children Association / Charitable Trust
Federation Of English Karate Organisations (international)
FIA Foundation for the Automobile and Society
Fields In Trust
Football Foundation
Fulham Football Club Foundation
Get Hooked on Fishing Charitable Trust
Iyengar Yoga Institute
Keep Fit Association
League Against Cruel Sports
Play-Train
Ramblers' Association
Rugby Football Foundation
Sea Cadets
Sport and Recreation Alliance
Sports Leaders UK
Supporters Direct
Surf Life Saving Association of Great Britain
Transplant Sport UK
Youth Sport Trust

DISABILITIES

Action on Disability and Development
Action Space Mobile Ltd
Albrighton Trust Ltd
Amal Trust
Back-Up (Transforming lives after spinal cord injury)
British Blind Sport
Conquest Art – Enriching the Lives of Physically Disabled People
Disability Snowsport UK
Disability Sport England
Disabled Photographers' Society
Disaway Trust
Drake Music Project
English Federation of Disability Sport
EPIC Arts
EXTEND Exercise Training Ltd
Gardening for the Disabled
Jubilee Sailing Trust
Lin Berwick Trust
Love Walk
National Association of Swimming Clubs for the Handicapped
Peter le Marchant Trust
Riding for the Disabled Association

RYA Sailability
Ryder – Cheshire Volunteers
Scout Holiday Homes Trust
Tourism for All UK
United Kingdom Sports Association for People with Learning Disability
WheelPower

STAFF & VOLUNTEERS

Charities HR Network
CSV
HOPE Worldwide
Indian Volunteers for Community Service
REACH
RedR Register of Engineers for Disaster Relief
Returned Volunteer Action
Roots HR CIC
SAGGA
School Governors' One-Stop Shop
TimeBank
Time Banking UK
Time for God
Volunteers for Rural India
Volunteer Reading Help
VSO
WorldWide Volunteering
WRVS
Youth Action Network
Young Lives

STILLBIRTH & NEONATAL DEATH

Miscarriage Association
Stillbirth and Neonatal Death Society
Tommy's, the Baby Charity

STRESS & ANXIETY DISORDERS

Anxiety Care UK
International Stress Management Association UK

STROKE

ARNI Institute
CADASIL Research and Support Trust
Different Strokes
HemiHelp
Stroke Association

STUDENTS

Southampton University Students' Union
UCCF

SUBSTANCE ABUSE

See ADDICTION SUPPORT SERVICES; ALCOHOL AWARENESS & SUPPORT GROUPS; DRUG AWARENESS & SUPPORT GROUPS

TEACHING STANDARDS & SUPPORT

Association for Language Learning

Association for the Teaching of the Social Sciences
Association of Blind and Partially Sighted Teachers and Students
CfBT Education Trust
Commonwealth Education Trust
National Association for Pastoral Care in Education

TECHNOLOGY

See also COMPUTERS & THE INTERNET
Association for Learning Technology
Charity IT Leaders (CITL)
Freeplay Foundation
Millipedia
Online Centres Foundation
Practical Action
Radio Amateurs' Emergency Network
Remap
Royal Television Society
Sequal Trust
Sonic Arts Network
STAGETEXT
Talking Newspaper Association of the UK
Wireless for the Bedridden
Women's Technology and Education Centre
Worshipful Company of Information Technologists
YouthNet

THEATRES

Independent Theatre Council
National Association of Youth Theatres
Spare Tyre Theatre Company
STAGETEXT
Travelling Light Theatre Company
Theatres Trust

THERAPY SERVICES AND CENTRES

Association of Dance Therapists (International)
Association of Therapeutic Communities
British False Memory Society
Community Housing and Therapy
Refugee Therapy Centre

EDUCATIONAL & SPECIAL NEEDS

Caldecott Foundation
Caspari Foundation for Educational Therapy and Therapeutic Teaching
Foundation66
Nordoff-Robbins Music Therapy
RESPOND

MEDICAL & HEALTH BENEFITS

Bobath Centre for Children with Cerebral Palsy
British Association and College of Occupational Therapists
Free Access Cancer Therapy Database
Freshwinds
Gaia House
Iyengar Yoga Institute

Multiple Sclerosis National Therapy Centres
Rainbow Centre for Children affected by
Life-Threatening Illnesses or Bereavement

WOMEN
Women's Therapy Centre

TOWN PLANNING
Town and Country Planning Association

TRAINING
See ADULT EDUCATION & TRAINING;
BEHAVIOURAL TRAINING; BUSINESS &
INDUSTRY TRAINING; HEALTHCARE &
MEDICAL TRAINING; LEADERSHIP
SKILLS TRAINING

TRANSGENDER SUPPORT
GROUPS
See GAY/LESBIAN/BISEXUAL/
TRANSGENDER SUPPORT GROUPS

TRANSPORT
Aftermath Support
Arun Co-ordinated Community Transport
Campaign Against Drinking and Driving
Campaign for Better Transport Charitable
Trust
Car Accident Victims Organisation
Carplus
Chartered Institution of Highways and
Transportation
Community Transport
Community Transport Association
Ealing Community Transport
FIA Foundation for the Automobile and
Society
Institution of Highways and Transportation
Parliamentary Advisory Council for Transport
Safety
RoadPeace
Royal Society for the Prevention of Accidents
Sustrans Limited
Torridge Community Transport Association
Transport Trust

TRAVELLER GROUPS
Advisory Council for the Education of
Romany and Other Travellers
Irish Traveller Movement in Britain
London Gypsy and Traveller Unit

TREE PRESERVATION
Tree Council
Trees for Cities
Woodland Trust

UMBRELLA & RESOURCE BODIES
See also COMMUNITY DEVELOPMENT
& RESOURCES, VOLUNTARY ACTION
Association of British Credit

Association of Charitable Organisations
Association of Chief Executives of
Voluntary Organisations
AVID (Association of Visitors to
Immigration Detainees)
Bracknell Forest Voluntary Action
Braintree District Voluntary Support Agency
British Spiritualist Federation
Castle Point Association of Voluntary
Services (CAVS)
Centre for Effective Dispute Resolution
Central Council of Physical Recreation
Charities HR Network
Charity Administration, Resourcing and
Accountability
Charity Finance Group
Churches Together in Britain and Ireland
Confederation of Indian Organisations (UK)
Co-operatives UK
Cumbria CVS
Development Trusts Association
Enfield Voluntary Action (EVA)
Federation of Irish Societies
Gateshead Voluntary Organisations Council
Gosport Voluntary Action
Greater London Volunteering
Greater Manchester Centre for Voluntary
Organisation
Institute of Money Advisers
Joint Epilepsy Council
Locality
Magistrates' Association
Mid Sussex (South) Council for Voluntary
Service
National Council for Palliative Care
National Council for Voluntary Organisations
National Development Team for Inclusion
Newcastle Council for Voluntary Service
Northallerton & District Voluntary Service
Association
Nova Wakefield District Limited
Northern Ireland Council for Voluntary Action
Redbridge Council for Voluntary Service
REMA
Scottish Council for Voluntary Organisations
Small Charities Coalition
Southend Association of Voluntary Services
Sport and Recreation Alliance
Sustain: the Alliance for Better Food and
Farming
Telephone Helplines Association
Textile Institute International
The Electrical Safety Council
Tower Hamlets CVS
Voluntary Action History Society
Voluntary Norfolk
VOSCUR
Wales Council for Voluntary Action
Woking Association of Voluntary Service
Worcester Volunteer Centre
World Society for the Protection of Animals
WorldWide Volunteering

ADVICE & INFORMATION
Advice Services Alliance
Advice UK
Citizens Advice

Consortium of Bengali Associations
Direct Help & Advice (DHA)
Enterprising Futures
Evelyn 190 Centre
Helplines Partnership
SWAN Advice Network

ARTS & CULTURE
British Federation of Film Societies
British & International Federation of Festivals
Federation of British Artists
National Association of Decorative and Fine
Arts Societies

CHILDREN & YOUNG PEOPLE
Ambition
British Youth Council
Care Co-ordination Network Cymru
Churches Child Protection Advisory Service
Consortium of Voluntary Adoption Agencies
Direct Help & Advice (DHA)
National Association of Child Contact Centres
National Association of Toy and Leisure
Libraries
National Association of Youth Theatres
National Childminding Association
National Council for Voluntary Youth Services
National Day Nurseries Association
National Playbus Association
Staffordshire Council of Voluntary Youth
Services
Young Lives

COMMNUITY DEVELOPMENT
Action for Market Towns
Action with Communities in Rural England
(ACRE)
Civic Trust
Community Matters
Consortium of Lesbian, Gay, Bisexual and
Transgender Voluntary and Community
Organisations
Federation of City Farms and Community
Gardens
National Association for Voluntary and
Community Associations
Shared Lives Plus

DISABILITIES
ARC
Care Co-ordination Network UK
National Association of Swimming Clubs for
the Handicapped
UK Council on Deafness
United Kingdom Sports Association for
People with Learning Disability
United Kingdom's Disabled People's Council

EDUCATION
British Council
National Association of Independent Schools
and Non Maintained Special Schools
National Confederation of Parent Teacher
Associations
Universities UK
University Association for Contemporary
European Studies

ENVIRONMENT
The Rivers Trust
Town and Country Planning Association

HEALTHCARE
Association of Children's Hospices
Alliance of Healing Associations
College of Sexual and Relationship Therapists (COSRT)
Help the Hospices
National Patients Support Trust
UK Neighbourhood Watch Trust
UK Public Health Association
United Kingdom Homecare Association
Visionary

HERITAGE & HISTORY
British Association for Local History
The Heritage Alliance

OVERSEAS AID & DEVELOPMENT
British Overseas NGOs for Development
Overseas Development Institute

PERSONAL DEVELOPMENT
Mentoring and Befriending Foundation

RESEARCH ORGANISATIONS
Association of Medical Research Charities
British Association for the Advancement of Science
British Organ Donor Society
European Association for the Treatment of Addiction

SEAFARERS & MARITIME WORKERS
Federation of Merchants Mariners
British Marine Federation

SOCIAL CARE
British Association of Social Workers
Social Care Association

WOMEN'S GROUPS
National Alliance of Women's Organisations
National Association of Women's Clubs
National Council of Women of Great Britain
National Federation of Women's Institutes
Townswomen's Guilds
Women's Aid Federation of England
Women's Resource Centre
World Association of Girl Guides and Girl Scouts

VISUAL IMPAIRMENT
See BLINDNESS & SIGHT IMPAIRMENT

VOLUNTARY ACTION AND VOLUNTEER CENTRES
See also COMMUNITY DEVELOPMENT & RESOURCES; UMBRELLA AND RESOURCE BODIES
Bracknell Forest Voluntary Action
Cumbria CVS
Enfield Voluntary Action (EVA)

Gateshead Voluntary Organisations Council
Gosport Voluntary Action
Greater London Volunteering
Horsham Voluntary Action
Kent Volunteers
Redbridge Council for Voluntary Service
Northallerton & District Voluntary Service Association
Tower Hamlets CVS
Voluntary Action Calderdale
Voluntary Action Islington
Voluntary Action South West Surrey
Voluntary Norfolk
Voluntary Services Lewisham
Volunteer Centre Greenwich
Wigan and Leigh CVS
Worcester Volunteer Centre

WEST INDIAN COMMUNITY GROUPS
West Indian Standing Conference

WILDLIFE CONSERVATION
See also MARINE LIFE & WATERWAYS
Born Free Foundation
Care for the Wild International
Durrell Wildlife Conservation Trust
Game Conservancy Trust
Wildfowl and Wetlands Trust
Wildlife Aid
Wildlife and Countryside Link
Wildlife Trusts
World Society for the Protection of Animals
Zoological Society of London

WOMEN'S SUPPORT GROUPS
Asha Projects
Association of Breastfeeding Mothers
Breaking Free – Primarily Supporting Women Survivors of Child Sexual Abuse
Bristol Crisis Service for Women
Catholic Women's League
Clean Break
English Province of Our Lady Charity
Eva Women's Aid
FATIMA Women's Network
Fawcett Society
Female Prisoners Welfare Project and Hibiscus
GFS Platform for Young Women
Jewish Women's Aid
Mothers Apart from their Children
Mothers Union
National Alliance of Women's Organisations
National Association of Women's Clubs
National Council of Women of Great Britain
National Federation of Women's Institutes
National Women's Register
OBJECT
Positive Body Image
Positively UK
Powerhouse
Rape and Sexual Abuse Support Centre
Refuge
Rights of Women

Society for the Assistance of Ladies in Reduced Circumstances
Townswomen's Guilds
Trust
War Widows Association of Great Britain and Northern Ireland
WOMANKIND Worldwide
Women and Girls' Network
Women and Manual Trades
Women's Environmental Network
Women's Health Advice Centre
Women's Farm and Garden Association
Women's Resource Centre
Women's Royal Naval Service Benevolent Trust
Women's Sports Foundation
Women's Therapy Centre
Worthing Women's Aid
WRVS
YWCA England and Wales

ACCOMMODATION
Chapter 1
Christian Family Concern
Eaves Housing for Women Limited
House of Saint Barnabas in Soho
LIFE
Women's Aid Federation of England

EDUCATION
CAMFED International
Creative and Supportive Trust
Josephine Butler Educational Trust
Menerva Educational Trust
Training Opportunities
Women's Technology and Education Centre

HEALTH
Association for Post-Natal Illness
Birth Companions
Daisy Network
Disability Pregnancy and Parenthood International
Endometriosis SHE Trust (UK)
Endometriosis UK
FAS Aware UK
Foundation for Women's Health Research and Development
LIFE
Medical Women's Federation
Pennell Initiative for Women's Health
Positive Body Image
Positively UK
WISH- a voice for women's mental health